THE ADVENTURE MEGAPACK

THE MEGAPACK SERIES

The Adventure Megapack
The Cowboy Megapack
The Craig Kennedy Scientific Detective Megapack
The Cthulhu Mythos Megapack
The Father Brown
The Ghost Story Megapack
The Horror Megapack
The Macabre Megapack
The Martian Megapack
The Military Megapack
The Mummy Megapack
The Mystery Megapack
The Science Fiction Megapack
The Second Science Fiction Megapack
The Third Science Fiction Megapack
The Fourth Science Fiction Megapack
The Fifth Science Fiction Megapack
The Penny Parker Megapack
The Tom Corbett, Space Cadet Megapack
The Tom Swift Megapack
The Vampire Megapack
The Western Megapack
The Wizard of Oz Megapack

AUTHOR MEGAPACKS

The Andre Norton Megapack
The B.M. Bower Megapack
The Murray Leinster Megapack
The Second Murray Leinster Megapack
The Andre Norton Megapack
The Rafael Sabatini Megapack

THE ADVENTURE MEGAPACK

25 Classic Adventure Stories from the Pulps

Selected by

JOHN GREGORY BETANCOURT

WILDSIDE PRESS

Contents

SON OF THE WHITE WOLF

Robert E. Howard

CHAPTER I
THE BATTLE STANDARD

The commander of the Turkish outpost of El Ashrat was awakened before dawn by the stamp of horses and jingle of accoutrements. He sat up and shouted for his orderly. There was no response, so he rose, hurriedly jerked on his garments, and strode out of the mud hut that served as his headquarters. What he saw rendered him momentarily speechless.

His command was mounted, in full marching formation, drawn up near the railroad that it was their duty to guard. The plain to the left of the track where the tents of the troopers had stood now lay bare. The tents had been loaded on the baggage camels which stood fully packed and ready to move out. The commandant glared wildly, doubting his own senses, until his eyes rested on a flag borne by a trooper. The waving pennant did not display the familiar crescent. The commandant turned pale.

"What does this mean?" he shouted, striding forward. His lieutenant, Osman, glanced at him inscrutably. Osman was a tall man, hard and supple as steel, with a dark keen face.

"Mutiny, *effendi*," he replied calmly. "We are sick of this war we fight for the Germans. We are sick of Djemal Pasha and those other fools of the Council of Unity and Progress, and, incidentally, of you. So we are going to the hills to build a tribe of our own."

"Madness!" gasped the officer, tugging at his revolver. Even as he drew it, Osman shot him through the head.

The lieutenant sheathed the smoking pistol and turned to the troopers. The ranks were his to a man, won to his wild ambition under the very nose of the officer who now lay there with his brains oozing.

"Listen!" he commanded.

In the tense silence they all heard the low, deep reverberation in the west.

"British guns!" said Osman. "Battering the Turkish Empire to bits! The New Turks have failed. What Asia needs is not a new party, but a new race! There are thousands of fighting men between the Syrian coast and the Persian highlands, ready to be roused by a new word, a new prophet! The East is moving in her sleep. Ours is the duty is to awaken her!

"You have all sworn to follow me into the hills. Let us return to the ways of our pagan ancestors who worshipped the White Wolf on the steppes of High Asia before they bowed to the creed of Mohammed!

"We have reached the end of the Islamic Age. We abjure Allah as a superstition fostered by an epileptic Meccan camel driver. Our people have copied Arab ways too long. But we hundred men are *Turks*! We have burned the Koran. We bow not toward Mecca, nor swear by their false Prophet. And now follow me as we planned— to establish ourselves in a strong position in the hills and to seize Arab women for our wives."

"Our sons will be half-Arab," someone protested.

"A man is the son of his father," retorted Osman. "We Turks have always looted the *harims* of the world for our women, but our sons are always Turks.

"Come! We have arms, horses, supplies. If we linger we shall be crushed with the rest of the army between the British on the coast and the Arabs the Englishman Lawrence is bringing up from the south. On to El Awad! The sword for the men—captivity for the women!"

His voice cracked like a whip as he snapped the orders that set the lines in motion. In perfect order they moved off through the lightening dawn toward the range of saw-edged hills in the distance. Behind them the air still vibrated with the distant rumble of the British artillery. Over them waved a banner that bore the head of a white wolf—the battle-standard of most ancient Turan.

CHAPTER II
MASSACRE

When *Fräulein* Olga von Bruckmann, known as a famous German secret agent, arrived at the tiny Arab hill-village of El Awad, it was in a drizzling rain, that made the dusk a blinding curtain over the muddy town.

With her companion, an Arab named Ahmed, she rode into the muddy street, and the villagers crept from their hovels to stare in awe at the first white woman most of them had ever seen.

A few words from Ahmed and the *shaykh* salaamed and showed her to the best mud hut in the village. The horses were led away to feed and shelter, and Ahmed paused long enough to whisper to his companion:

"El Awad is friendly to the Turks. Have no fear. I shall be near, in any event."

"Try and get fresh horses," she urged. "I must push on as soon as possible."

"The *shaykh* swears there isn't a horse in the village in fit condition to be ridden. He may be lying. But at any rate our own horses will be rested enough to go on by dawn. Even with fresh horses it would be useless to try to go any farther tonight. We'd lose our way among the hills, and in this region there's always the risk of running into Lawrence's Bedouin raiders."

Olga knew that Ahmed knew she carried important secret documents from Baghdad to Damascus, and she knew from experience that she could trust his loyalty. Removing only her dripping cloak and riding boots, she stretched herself on the dingy blankets that served as a bed. She was worn out from the strain of the journey.

She was the first white woman ever to attempt to ride from Baghdad to Damascus. Only the protection accorded a trusted secret agent by the long arm of the German-Turkish government, and her guide's zeal and craft, had brought her thus far in safety.

She fell asleep, thinking of the long weary miles still to be traveled, and even greater dangers, now that she had come into the region where the Arabs were fighting their Turkish masters. The Turks still held the country, that summer of 1917, but lightning-like raids flashed across the desert, blowing up trains, cutting tracks and butchering the inhabitants of isolated posts. Lawrence was leading the tribes northward, and with him was the mysterious American, El Borak, whose name was one to hush children.

She never knew how long she slept, but she awoke suddenly and sat up, in fright and bewilderment. The rain still beat on the roof, but there mingled with it shrieks of pain or fear, yells and the staccato crackling of rifles. She sprang up, lighted a candle and was just pulling on her boots when the door was hurled open violently.

Ahmed reeled in, his dark face livid, blood oozing through the fingers that clutched his breast.

"The village is attacked!" he cried chokingly. "Men in Turkish uniform! There must be some mistake! They know El Awad is friendly! I tried to tell their officer that we are friends, but he shot me! We must get away, quick!"

A shot cracked in the open door behind him and a jet of fire spurted from the blackness. Ahmed groaned and crumpled. Olga cried out in horror, staring wide-eyed at the figure who stood before her. A tall, wiry man in Turkish uniform blocked the door. He was handsome in a dark, hawk-like way, and he eyed her in a manner that brought the blood to her cheeks.

'Why did you kill that man?" she demanded. "He was a trusted servant of your country."

"I have no country," he answered, moving toward her. Outside the firing was dying away and women's voices were lifted piteously. "I go to build one, as my ancestor Osman did."

"I don't know what you're talking about," she retorted. "But unless you provide me with an escort to the nearest post, I shall report you to your superiors, and—"

He laughed wildly at her. "I have no superiors, you little fool! I am an empire builder, I tell you! I have a hundred armed men at my disposal. I'll build a new race in these hills." His eyes blazed as he spoke.

"You're mad!" she exclaimed.

"Mad? It's you who are mad not to recognize the possibilities as I have! This war is bleeding the life out of Europe. When it's over, no matter who wins, the nations will lie prostrate. Then it will be Asia's turn!

"If Lawrence can build up an Arab army to fight for him, then certainly I, an Ottoman, can build up a kingdom among my own peoples! Thousands of Turkish soldiers have deserted to the British. They and more will desert again to me, when they hear that a Turk is building anew the empire of ancient Turan."

"Do what you like," she answered, believing he had been seized by the madness that often grips men in time of war when the world seems crumbling and any wild dream looks possible. "But at least don't interfere with my mission. If you won't give me an escort, I'll go on alone."

"You'll go with me!" he retorted, looking down at her with hot admiration.

Olga was a handsome girl, tall, slender but supple, with a wealth of unruly golden hair. She was so completely feminine that no disguise would make her look like a man, not even the voluminous robes of an Arab, so she had attempted none. She trusted instead to Ahmed's skill to bring her safely through the desert.

"Do you hear those screams? My men are supplying themselves with wives to bear soldiers for the new empire. Yours shall be the signal honor of being the first to go into Sultan Osman's *seraglio*!"

"You do not dare!" She snatched a pistol from her blouse.

Before she could level it he wrenched it from her with brutal strength.

"Dare!" He laughed at her vain struggles. "What do I not dare? I tell you a new empire is being born tonight! Come with me! There's no time for lovemaking now. Before dawn we must be on the march for Sulaiman's Walls. The star of the White Wolf rises!"

CHAPTER III

THE CALL OF BLOOD

The sun was not long risen over the saw-edged mountains to the east, but already the heat was glazing the cloudless sky to the hue of white-hot steel. Along the dim road that split the immensity of the desert a single shape moved. The shape grew out of the heat-hazes of the south and resolved itself into a man on a camel.

The man was no Arab. His boots and khakis, as well as the rifle-butt jutting from beneath his knee, spoke of the West. But with his dark face and hard frame he did not look out of place, even in that fierce land. He was Francis Xavier Gordon, El Borak, whom men loved, feared or hated, according to their political complexion, from the Golden Horn to the headwaters of the Ganges.

He had ridden most of the night, but his iron frame had not yet approached the fringes of weariness. Another mile, and he sighted a yet dimmer trail straggling down from a range of hills to the east. Something was coming along this trail—a crawling something that left a broad dark smear on the hot flints.

Gordon swung his camel into the trail and a moment later bent over the man who lay there gasping stertorously. It was a young Arab, and the breast of his abba was soaked in blood.

"Yusef!" Gordon drew back the wet abba, glanced at the bared breast, then covered it again. Blood oozed steadily from a blue-rimmed bullet-hole. There was nothing he could do. Already the Arab's eyes were glazing. Gordon stared up the trail, seeing neither horse nor camel anywhere. But the dark smear stained the stones as far as he could see.

"My God, man, how far have you crawled in this condition?"

"An hour—many hours—I do not know!" panted Yusef. "I fainted and fell from the saddle. When I came to I was lying in the trail and my horse was gone. But I knew you would be coming up from the south, so I crawled—crawled! Allah, how hard are thy stones!"

Gordon set a canteen to his lips and Yusef drank noisily, then clutched Gordon's sleeve with clawing fingers.

"El Borak, I am dying and that is no great matter, but there is the matter of vengeance—not for me, *ya sidi*, but for innocent ones. You know I was on furlough to my village, El Awad. I am the only man of El Awad who fights for Arabia. The elders are friendly to the Turks. But last night the Turks burned El Awad! They marched in before midnight and the people welcomed them—while I hid in a shed.

"Then without warning they began slaying! The men of El Awad were unarmed and helpless. I slew one soldier myself. Then they shot me and I dragged myself away—found my horse and rode to tell the tale before I died. Ah, Allah, I have tasted of perdition this night!"

"Did you recognize their officer?" asked Gordon.

"I never saw him before. They called this leader of theirs Osman Pasha. Their flag bore the head of a white wolf. I saw it by the light of the burning huts. My people cried out in vain that they were friends.

"There was a German woman and a man of Hauran who came to El Awad from the east, just at nightfall. I think they were spies. The Turks shot him and took her captive. It was all blood and madness."

"Mad indeed!" muttered Gordon. Yusef lifted himself on an elbow and groped for him, a desperate urgency in his weakening voice.

"El Borak, I fought well for the Emir Feisal, and for Lawrence *effendi*, and for you! I was at Yenbo, and Wejh, and Akaba. Never have I asked a reward! I ask now: justice and vengeance! Grant me this plea: Slay the Turkish dogs who butchered my people!"

Gordon did not hesitate.

"They shall die," he answered.

Yusef smiled fiercely, gasped: "*Allaho akbar*!" then sank back dead.

Within the hour Gordon rode eastward. The vultures had already gathered in the sky with their grisly foreknowledge of death, then flapped sullenly away from the cairn of stones he had piled over the dead man, Yusef.

Gordon's business in the north could wait. One reason for his dominance over the Orientals was the fact that in some ways his nature closely resembled theirs. He not only understood the cry for vengeance, but he sympathized with it. And he always kept his promise.

But he was puzzled. The destruction of a friendly village was not customary, even by the Turks, and certainly they would not ordinarily have mishandled their own spies. If they were deserters they were acting in an unusual manner, for most deserters made their way to Feisal. And what was that wolf's head banner?

Gordon knew that certain fanatics in the New Turks party were trying to erase all signs of Arab culture from their civilization. This was an impossible task, since that civilization itself was based on Arabic culture; but he had heard that in Istambul the radicals even advocated abandoning Islam and reverting to the paganism of their ancestors. But he had never believed the tale.

The sun was sinking over the mountains of Edom when Gordon came to ruined El Awad, in a fold of the bare hills. For hours before he had marked its location by black dots dropping in the blue sky. That they did not rise again told him that the village was deserted except for the dead.

As he rode into the dusty street, several vultures flapped heavily away. The hot sun had dried the mud, curdled the red pools in the dust. He sat in his saddle a while, staring silently.

He was no stranger to the handiwork of the Turk. He had seen much of it in the long fighting up from Jeddah on the Red Sea. But even so, he felt sick. The bodies lay in the street, headless, disemboweled, hewn asunder—bodies of children, old women and men. A red mist floated before his eyes, so that for a moment the landscape seemed to swim in blood. The slayers were gone; but they had left a plain road for him to follow.

What the signs they had left did not show him, he guessed. The slayers had loaded their female captives on baggage camels, and had gone eastward, deeper into the hills. Why they were following that road he could not guess, but he knew where it led—to the long-abandoned Walls of Sulaiman, by way of the Well of Achmet.

Without hesitation he followed. He had not gone many miles before he passed more of their work—a baby, its brains oozing from its broken head. Some kidnapped woman had hidden her child in her robes until it had been wrenched from her and brained on the rocks, before her eyes.

The country became wilder as he went. He did not halt to eat, but munched dried dates from his pouch as he rode. He did not waste time worrying over the recklessness of his action—one lone American dogging the crimson trail of a Turkish raiding party.

He had no plan; his future actions would depend on the circumstances that arose. But he had taken the death-trail and he would not turn back while he lived. He was no more foolhardy than his grandfather who single-handed trailed an Apache war party for days through the Guadalupes and returned to the settlement on the Pecos with scalps hanging from his belt.

The sun had set and dusk was closing in when Gordon topped a ridge and looked down on the plain whereon stands the Well of Achmet with its straggling palm grove. To the right of that cluster stood the tents, horse lines and camel lines of a well-ordered force. To the left stood a hut used by travelers as a *khan*. The door was shut and a sentry stood before it. While he watched, a man came from the tents with a bowl of food which he handed in at the door.

Gordon could not see the occupant, but he believed it was the German girl of whom Yusef had spoken, though why they should imprison one of their own spies was one of the mysteries of this strange affair. He saw their flag, and could make out a splotch of white that must be the wolf's head. He saw, too, the Arab women, thirty-five or forty of them herded into a pen improvised from bales and pack-saddles. They crouched together dumbly, dazed by their misfortunes.

He had hidden his camel below the ridge, on the western slope, and he lay concealed behind a clump of stunted bushes until night had fallen. Then he slipped down the slope, circling wide to avoid the mounted patrol, which rode leisurely about the camp. He lay prone behind a boulder till it had passed, then rose and stole toward the hut. Fires twinkled in the darkness beneath the palms, and he heard the wailing of the captive women.

The sentry before the door of the hut did not see the cat-footed shadow that glided up to the rear wall. As Gordon drew close he heard voices within. They spoke in Turkish.

One window was in the back wall. Strips of wood had been fastened over it, to serve as both pane and bars. Peering between them, Gordon saw a slender girl in a travel-worn riding habit standing before a dark-faced man in a Turkish uniform. There was no insignia to show what his rank had been. The Turk played with a riding whip and his eyes gleamed with cruelty in the light of a candle on a camp table.

"What do I care for the information you bring from Baghdad?" he was demanding. "Neither Turkey nor Germany means anything to me. But it seems you fail to realize your own position. It is mine to command, you to obey! You are my prisoner, my captive, my slave! It's time you learned what that means. And the best teacher I know is the whip!"

He fairly spat the last word at her and she paled.

"You dare not subject me to this indignity!" she whispered weakly.

Gordon knew this man must be Osman Pasha. He drew his heavy automatic from its scabbard under his armpit and aimed at the Turk's breast through the crack in the window. But even as his finger closed on the trigger he changed his mind. There was the sentry at the door, and a hundred other armed men, within hearing, whom the sound of a shot would bring on the run. He grasped the window bars and braced his legs.

"I see I must dispel your illusions," muttered Osman, moving toward the girl who cowered back until the wall stopped her. Her face was white. She had dealt with many dangerous men in her hazardous career, and she was not easily frightened. But she had never met a man like Osman. His face was a terrifying mask of cruelty; the ferocity that gloats over the agony of a weaker thing shone in his eyes.

Suddenly he had her by the hair, dragging her to him, laughing at her scream of pain. Just then Gordon ripped the strips off the window. The snapping of the wood sounded loud as a gunshot and Osman wheeled, drawing his pistol, as Gordon came through the window.

The American lit on his feet, and leveled his automatic, checking Osman's move. The Turk froze, his pistol lifted shoulder high, muzzle pointing at the roof. Outside the sentry called anxiously.

"Answer him!" grated Gordon below his breath. "Tell him everything is all right. And drop that gun!"

The pistol fell to the floor and the girl snatched it up.

"Come here, *Fräulein*!"

She ran to him, but in her haste she crossed the line of fire. In that fleeting moment when her body shielded his, Osman acted. He kicked the table and the candle toppled and went out, and simultaneously he dived for the floor. Gordon's pistol roared deafeningly just as the hut was plunged into darkness. The next instant the door crashed inward and the sentry bulked against the starlight, to crumple as Gordon's gun crashed again and yet again.

With a sweep of his arm, Gordon found the girl and drew her toward the window. He lifted her through as if she had been a child, and climbed through after her. He did not know whether his blind slug had struck Osman or not. The man was crouching silently in the darkness, but there was no time to strike a match and see whether he was living or dead. But as they ran across the shadowy plain, they heard Osman's voice lifted in passion.

By the time they reached the crest of the ridge, the girl was winded. Only Gordon's arm about her waist, half-dragging, half-carrying her, enabled her to make the last few yards of the steep incline. The plain below them was alive with torches and shouting men. Osman was yelling for them to run down the fugitive, and his voice came faintly to them on the ridge.

"Take them alive, curse you! Scatter and find them! It's El Borak!" An instant later he was yelling, with an edge of panic in his voice: "Wait. Come back! Take cover and make ready to repel an attack! He may have a horde of Arabs with him!"

"He thinks first of his own desire, and only later of the safety of his men," muttered Gordon. "I don't think he'll ever get very far. Come on."

He led the way to the camel, helped the girl into the saddle, then leaped up himself. A word, a tap of the camel wand, and the beast ambled silently off down the slope.

"I know Osman caught you at El Awad," said Gordon. "But what's he up to? What's his game?"

"He was a lieutenant stationed at El Ashraf," she answered. "He persuaded his company to mutiny, kill their commander, and desert. He plans to fortify the Walls of Sulaiman, and build a new empire. I thought at first he was mad, but he isn't. He's a devil."

"The Walls of Sulaiman?" Gordon checked his mount and sat for a moment motionless in the starlight.

"Are you game for an all-night ride?" he asked presently.

"Anywhere! As long as it is far away from Osman!" There was a hint of hysteria in her voice.

"I doubt if your escape will change his plans. He'll probably lie about Achmet all night under arms expecting an attack. In the morning he will decide that I was alone, and pull out for the Walls.

"Well, I happen to know that an Arab force is there, waiting for an order from Lawrence to move on to Ageyli. Three hundred Juheina camel-riders, sworn to Feisal. Enough to eat Osman's gang. Lawrence's messenger should reach them some time between dawn and noon. There is a chance we can get there before the Juheina pull out. If we can, we'll turn them on Osman and wipe him out, with his whole pack.

"It won't upset Lawrence's plans for the Juheina to get to Ageyli a day late, and Osman must be destroyed. He's a mad dog running loose."

"His ambition sounds mad," she murmured. "But when he speaks of it, with his eyes blazing, it's easy to believe he might even succeed."

"You forget that crazier things have happened in the desert," he answered, as he swung the camel eastward. "The world is being made over here, as well as in Europe. There's no telling what damage this Osman might do, if left to himself. The Turkish Empire is falling to pieces, and new empires have risen out of the ruins of old ones.

"But if we can get to Sulaiman before the Juheina march, we'll check him. If we find them gone, we'll be in a pickle ourselves. It's a gamble, our lives against his. Are you game?"

"Till the last card falls!" she retorted. His face was a blur in the starlight, but she sensed rather than saw his grim smile of approval.

The camel's hoofs made no sound as they dropped down the slope and circled far wide of the Turkish camp. Like ghosts on a ghost-camel they moved across the plain under the stars. A faint breeze stirred the girl's hair. Not until the fires were dim behind them and they were again climbing a hill-road, did she speak.

"I know you. You're the American they call El Borak, the Swift. You came down from Afghanistan when the war began. You were with King Hussein even before Lawrence came over from Egypt. Do you know who I am?"

"Yes."

"Then what's my status?" she asked. "Have you rescued me or captured me? Am I a prisoner?"

"Let us say companion, for the time being," he suggested. "We're up against a common enemy. No reason why we shouldn't make common cause, is there?"

"None!" she agreed, and leaning her blond head against his hard shoulder, she went soundly to sleep.

A gaunt moon rose, pushing back the horizons, flooding craggy slopes and dusty plains with leprous silver. The vastness of the desert seemed to mock the tiny figures on their tiring camel, as they rode blindly on toward what Fate they could not guess.

CHAPTER IV
WOLVES OF THE DESERT

Olga awoke as dawn was breaking. She was cold and stiff, in spite of the cloak Gordon had wrapped about her, and she was hungry. They were riding through a dry gorge with rock-strewn slopes rising on either hand, and the camel's gait had become a lurching walk. Gordon halted it, slid off without making it kneel, and took its rope.

"It's about done, but the Walls aren't far ahead. Plenty of water there—food, too, if the Juheina are still there. There are dates in that pouch."

If he felt the strain of fatigue he did not show it as he strode along at the camel's head. Olga rubbed her chill hands and wished for sunrise.

"The Well of Harith," Gordon indicated a walled enclosure ahead of them. "The Turks built that wall, years ago, when the Walls of Sulaiman were an army post. Later they abandoned both positions."

The wall, built of rocks and dried mud, was in good shape; and inside the enclosure there was a partly ruined hut. The well was shallow, with a mere trickle of water at the bottom.

"I'd better get off and walk too," Olga suggested.

"These flints would cut your boots and feet to pieces. It's not far now. Then the camel can rest all it needs."

"And if the Juheina aren't there—" She left the sentence unfinished.

He shrugged his shoulders.

"Maybe Osman won't come up before the camel's rested."

"I believe he'll make a forced march," she said, not fearfully, but calmly stating an opinion. "His beasts are good. If he drives them hard, he can get here before midnight. Our camel won't be rested enough to carry us by that time. And we couldn't get away on foot, in this desert."

He laughed, and respecting her courage, did not try to make light of their position.

"Well," he said quietly, "let's hope the Juheina are still there!"

If they were not, she and Gordon were caught in a trap of hostile, waterless desert, fanged with the long guns of predatory tribesmen.

Three miles further east the valley narrowed and the floor pitched upward, dotted by dry shrubs and boulders. Gordon pointed suddenly to a faint ribbon of smoke feathering up into the sky.

"Look! The Juheina are there!"

Olga gave a deep sigh of relief. Only then, did she realize how desperately she had been hoping for some such sign. She felt like shaking a triumphant fist at the rocky waste about her, as if at a sentient enemy, sullen and cheated of its prey.

Another mile and they topped a ridge and saw a large enclosure surrounding a cluster of wells. There were Arabs squatting about their tiny cooking fires. As the travelers came suddenly into view within a few hundred yards of them, the Bedouins sprang up, shouting. Gordon drew his breath suddenly between clenched teeth.

"They are not Juheina! They're Rualla! Allies of the Turks!"

Too late to retreat. A hundred and fifty wild men were on their feet, glaring, rifles cocked.

Gordon did the next best thing and went leisurely toward them. To look at him one would have thought that he had expected to meet these men here, and anticipated nothing but a friendly greeting. Olga tried to imitate his tranquility, but she knew their lives hung on the crook of a trigger finger. These men were supposed to be her allies, but her recent experience made her distrust Orientals. The sight of these hundreds of wolfish faces filled her with sick dread.

They were hesitating, rifles lifted, nervous and uncertain as surprised wolves, then:

"Allah!" howled a tall, scarred warrior. "It is El Borak!"

Olga caught her breath as she saw the man's finger quiver on his rifle-trigger. Only a racial urge to gloat over his victim kept him from shooting the American, then and there.

"El Borak!" The shout was a wave that swept the throng.

Ignoring the clamor, the menacing rifles, Gordon made the camel kneel and lifted Olga off. She tried, with fair success, to conceal her fear of the wild figures that crowded about them, but her flesh crawled at the blood-lust burning redly in each wolfish eye.

Gordon's rifle was in its boot on the saddle, and his pistol was out of sight, under his shirt. He was careful not to reach for the rifle—a move which would have brought a hail of bullets—but having helped the girl down, he turned and faced the crowd casually, his hands empty. Running his glance over the fierce faces, he singled out a tall stately man in the rich garb of a *shaykh*, who was standing somewhat apart.

"You keep poor watch, Mitkhal ibn Ali," said Gordon. "If I had been a raider your men would be lying in their blood by this time."

Before the *shaykh* could answer, the man who had first recognized Gordon thrust himself violently forward, his face convulsed with hate.

"You expected to find friends here, El Borak!" he exulted. "But you come too late! Three hundred Juheina dogs rode north an hour before dawn! We saw them go, and came up after they had gone. Had they known of your coming, perhaps they would have stayed to welcome you!"

"It's not to you I speak, Zangi Khan, you Kurdish dog," retorted Gordon contemptuously, "but to the Rualla—honorable men and fair foes!"

Zangi Khan snarled like a wolf and threw up his rifle, but a lean Bedouin caught his arm.

"Wait!" he growled. "Let El Borak speak. His words are not wind."

A rumble of approval came from the Arabs. Gordon had touched their fierce pride and vanity. That would not save his life, but they were willing to listen to him before they killed him.

"If you listen, he will trick you with cunning words!" shouted the angered Zangi Khan furiously. "Slay him now, before he can do us harm!"

"Is Zangi Khan *shaykh* of the Rualla that he gives his commands while Mitkhal stands silent?" asked Gordon with biting irony.

Mitkhal reacted to his taunt exactly as Gordon knew he would.

"Let El Borak speak!" he ordered. "I command here, Zangi Khan! Do not forget that."

"I do not forget, *ya sidi*," the Kurd assured him, but his eyes burned red at the rebuke. "I but spoke in zeal for your safety."

Mitkhal gave him a slow, searching glance which told Gordon that there was no love lost between the two men. Zangi Khan's reputation as a fighting man meant much to the younger warriors. Mitkhal was more fox than wolf, and he evidently feared the Kurd's influence over his men. As an agent of the Turkish government Zangi's authority was theoretically equal to Mitkhal's. Actually this amounted to little, for Mitkhal's tribesmen took orders from their *shaykh* only. But it put Zangi in a position to use his personal talents to gain an ascendancy—an ascendancy Mitkhal feared would relegate him to a minor position.

"Speak, El Borak," ordered Mitkhal. "But speak swiftly. It may be," he added, "Allah's will that the moments of your life are few."

"Death marches from the west," said Gordon abruptly. "Last night a hundred Turkish deserters butchered the people of El Awad."

"Wallah!" swore a tribesman. "El Awad was friendly to the Turks!"

"A lie!" cried Zangi Khan. "Or if true, the dogs of deserters slew the people to curry favor with Feisal."

"When did men come to Feisal with the blood of children on their hands?" retorted Gordon. "They have foresworn Islam and worship the White Wolf. They carried off the young women and the old women, the men and the children they slew like dogs."

A murmur of anger rose from the Arabs. The Bedouins had a rigid code of warfare, and they did not kill women or children. It was the unwritten law of the desert, old when Abraham came up out of Chaldea.

But Zangi Khan cried out in angry derision, blind to the resentful looks cast at him. He did not understand that particular phase of the Bedouins' code, for his people had no such inhibition. Kurds in war killed women as well as men.

"What are the women of El Awad to us?" he sneered.

"Your heart I know already," answered Gordon with icy contempt. "It is to the Rualla that I speak."

"A trick!" howled the Kurd. "A lie to trick us!"

"It is no lie!" Olga stepped forward boldly. "Zangi Khan, you know that I am an agent of the German government. Osman Pasha, leader of these renegades, burned El Awad last night, as El Borak has said. Osman murdered Ahmed ibn Shalaan, my guide, among others. He is as much our enemy as he is an enemy of the British."

She looked to Mitkhal for help, but the *shaykh* stood apart, like an actor watching a play in which he had not yet received his cue.

"What if it is the truth?" Zangi Khan snarled, muddled by his hate and fear of El Borak's cunning. "What is El Awad to us?"

Gordon caught him up instantly.

"This Kurd asks what is the destruction of a friendly village! Doubtless, naught to him! But what does it mean to you, who have left your herds and families unguarded? If you let this pack of mad dogs range the land, how can you be sure of the safety of your wives and children?"

"What would you have, El Borak?" demanded a gray-bearded raider.

"Trap these Turks and destroy them. I'll show you how."

It was then that Zangi Khan lost his head completely.

"Heed him not!" he screamed. "Within the hour we must ride northward! The Turks will give us ten thousand British pounds for his head!"

Avarice burned briefly in the men's eyes, to be dimmed by the reflection that the reward, offered for El Borak's head, would be claimed by the *shaykh* and Zangi. They made no move and Mitkhal stood aside with an air of watching a contest that did not concern himself.

"Take his head!" screamed Zangi, sensing hostility at last, and thrown into a panic by it.

His demoralization was completed by Gordon's taunting laugh.

"You seem to be the only one who wants my head, Zangi! Perhaps you can take it!"

Zangi howled incoherently, his eyes glaring red, then threw up his rifle, hip-high. Just as the muzzle came up, Gordon's automatic crashed thunderously. He had drawn so swiftly not a man there had followed his motion. Zangi Khan reeled back under the impact of hot lead, toppled sideways and lay still.

In an instant, a hundred cocked rifles covered Gordon. Confused by varying emotions, the men hesitated for the fleeting instant it took Mitkhal to shout:

"Hold! Do not shoot!"

He strode forward with the air of a man ready to take the center of the stage at last, but he could not disguise the gleam of satisfaction in his shrewd eyes.

"No man here is kin to Zangi Khan," he said offhandedly. There is no cause for blood feud. He had eaten the salt, but he attacked our prisoner, whom he thought unarmed."

He held out his hand for the pistol, but Gordon did not surrender it.

"I'm not your prisoner," said he. "I could kill you before your men could lift a finger. But I didn't come here to fight you. I came asking aid to avenge the children and women of my enemies. I risk my life for your families. Are you dogs, to do less?"

The question hung in the air unanswered, but he had struck the right chord in their barbaric bosoms, that were always ready to respond to some wild deed of reckless chivalry. Their eyes glowed and they looked at their *shaykh* expectantly.

Mitkhal was a shrewd politician. The butchery at El Awad meant much less to him than it meant to his younger warriors. He had associated with so-called civilized men long enough to lose much of his primitive integrity. But he always followed the side of public opinion, and was shrewd enough to lead a movement he could not check. Yet, he was not to be stampeded into a hazardous adventure.

"These Turks may be too strong for us," he objected.

"I'll show you how to destroy them with little risk," answered Gordon. "But there must be covenants between us, Mitkhal."

"These Turks must be destroyed," said Mitkhal, and he spoke sincerely there, at least. "But there are too many blood feuds between us, El Borak, for us to let you get out of our hands."

Gordon laughed.

"You can't whip the Turks without my help, and you know it. Ask your young men what they desire!"

"Let El Borak lead us!" shouted a young warrior instantly. A murmur of approval paid tribute to Gordon's widespread reputation as a strategist.

"Very well!" Mitkhal took the tide. "Let there be truce between us—with conditions! Lead us against the Turks. If you win, you and the woman shall go free. If we lose, we take your head!"

Gordon nodded, and the warriors yelled in glee. It was just the sort of a bargain that appealed to their minds, and Gordon knew it was the best he could make.

"Bring bread and salt!" ordered Mitkhal, and a giant black slave moved to do his bidding. "Until the battle is lost or won there is truce between us, and no Rualla shall harm you, unless you spill Rualla blood."

Then he thought of something else and his brow darkened as he thundered:

"Where is the man who watched from the ridge?"

A terrified youth was pushed forward. He was a member of a small tribe tributary to the more important Rualla.

"Oh, *shaykh*," he faltered, "I was hungry and stole away to a fire for meat—"

"Dog!" Mitkhal struck him in the face. "Death is thy portion for failing in thy duty."

"Wait!" Gordon interposed. "Would you question the will of Allah? If the boy had not deserted his post he would have seen us coming up the valley, and your men would have fired on us and killed us. Then you would not have been warned of the Turks, and would have fallen prey to them before discovering they were enemies. Let him go and give thanks to Allah, Who sees all!"

It was the sort of sophistry that appeals to the Arab mind. Even Mitkhal was impressed.

"Who knows the mind of Allah?" he conceded. "Live, Musa, but next time perform the will of Allah with a vigilance and a mind to orders. And now, El Borak, let us discuss battle-plans while food is prepared."

CHAPTER V

TREACHERY

It was not yet noon when Gordon halted the Rualla beside the Well of Harith. Scouts sent westward reported no sign of the Turks, and the Arabs went forward with the plans made before leaving the Walls—plans outlined by Gordon and agreed to by Mitkhal. First the tribesmen began gathering rocks and hurling them into the well.

"The water's still beneath," Gordon remarked to Olga, "but it'll take hours of hard work to clean out the well so that anybody can get to it. The Turks can't do it under our rifles. If we win, we'll clean it out ourselves, so the next travelers won't suffer."

"Why not take refuge in the *sangar* ourselves?" she asked.

"Too much of a trap. That's what we're using it for. We'd have no chance with them in open fight, and if we laid an ambush out in the valley, they'd simply fight their way through us. But when a man's shot at in the open, his first instinct is to make for the nearest cover. So I'm hoping to trick them into going into the *sangar*. Then we'll bottle them up and pick them off at our leisure. Without water they can't hold out long. We shouldn't lose a dozen men, if any."

"It seems strange to see you solicitous about the lives of these Rualla, who are your enemies, after all," she laughed.

"Instinct, maybe. No man fit to lead wants to lose any more of them then he can help. Just now these men are my allies, and it's up to me to protect them as well as I can. I'll admit I'd rather be fighting with the Juheina. Feisal's messenger must have started for the Walls hours before I supposed he would."

"And if the Turks surrender, what then?"

"I'll try to get them to Lawrence—all but Osman Pasha." Gordon's face darkened. "That man hangs if he falls into my hands."

"How will you get them to Lawrence? The Rualla won't take them."

"I haven't the slightest idea. But let's catch our hare before we start broiling him. Osman may whip the daylights out of us."

"It means your head if he does," she warned, with a shudder.

"Well, it's worth ten thousand pounds to the Turks," he laughed, and moved to inspect the partly ruined hut. Olga followed him.

Mitkhal, directing the blocking of the well, glanced sharply at them, then noted that a number of men were between them and the gate, and turned back to his overseeing.

"Hsss, El Borak!" It was a tense whisper, just as Gordon and Olga turned to leave the hut. An instant later they located a tousled head thrust up from behind a heap of rubble. It was the boy Musa, who obviously had slipped into the hut through a crevice in the back wall.

"Watch from the door and warn me if you see anybody coming," Gordon muttered to Olga. "This lad may have something to tell."

"I have, *effendi*!" The boy was trembling with excitement. "I overheard the *shaykh* talking secretly to his black slave, Hassan. I saw them walk away among the palms while you and the woman were eating, at the Walls, and I crept after them, for I feared they meant you mischief—and you saved my life."

"El Borak, listen! Mitkal means to slay you, whether you win this battle for him or not! He was glad you slew the Kurd, and he is glad to have your aid in wiping out these Turks. But he lusts for the gold the other Turks will pay for your head. Yet he dares not break his word and the covenant of the salt openly. So, if we win the battle, Hassan is to shoot you, and swear you fell by a Turkish bullet!"

The boy rushed on with his story:

"Then Mitkhal will say to the people: 'El Borak was our guest and ate our salt. But now he is dead, through no fault of ours, and there is no use wasting the reward. So, we will take off his head and take it to Damascus, and the Turks will give us ten thousand pounds.'"

Gordon smiled grimly at Olga's horror. That was typical Arab logic.

"It didn't occur to Mitkhal that Hassan might miss his first shot and not get a chance to shoot again, I suppose?" he suggested.

"Oh, yes, *effendi*, Mitkhal thinks of everything. If you kill Hassan, Mitkhal will swear you broke the covenant yourself, by spilling the blood of a Rualla, or a Rualla's servant, which is the same thing, and will feel free to order you beheaded."

There was genuine humor in Gordon's laugh.

"Thanks, Musa! If I saved your life, you've paid me back. Better get out now, before somebody sees you talking to us."

"What shall we do?" exclaimed Olga, pale to the lips.

"You're in no danger," he assured her.

She colored angrily.

"I wasn't thinking of that! Do you think I have less gratitude than that Arab boy? That *shaykh* means to murder you, don't you understand? Let's steal camels, and run for it!"

"Run where? If we did, they'd be on our heels in no time, deciding I'd lied to them about everything. Anyway, we wouldn't have a chance. They're watching us too closely. Besides, I wouldn't run if could. I started to wipe out Osman Pasha, and this is the best chance I see to do it. Come on. Let's get out in the *sangar* before Mitkhal gets suspicious."

As soon as the well was blocked the men retired to the hillsides. Their camels were hidden behind the ridges, and the men crouched behind rocks and among the stunted shrubs along the slopes. Olga refused Gordon's offer to send her with an escort back to the Walls, and stayed with him taking up a position behind a rock, Osman's pistol in her belt. They lay flat on the ground and the heat of the sun-baked flints seeped through their garments.

Once she turned her head, and shuddered to see the blank black countenance of Hassan regarding them from some bushes a few yards behind them. The black slave, who knew no law but his master's command, was determined not to let Gordon out of his sight.

She spoke of this in a low whisper to the American.

"Sure," he murmured. "I saw him. But he won't shoot till he knows which way the fight's going, and is sure none of the men are looking."

Olga's flesh crawled in anticipation of more horrors. If they lost the fight the enraged Ruallas would tear Gordon to pieces, supposing he survived the encounter. If they won, his reward would be a treacherous bullet in the back.

The hours dragged slowly by. Not a flutter of cloth, no lifting of an impatient head betrayed the presence of the wild men on the slopes. Olga began to feel her nerves quiver. Doubts and forebodings gnawed maddeningly at her.

"We took position too soon! The men will lose patience. Osman can't get here before midnight. It took us all night to reach the Well."

"Bedouins never lose patience when they smell loot," he answered. "I believe Osman will get here before sundown. We made poor time on a tiring camel for the last few hours of that ride. I believe Osman broke camp before dawn and pushed hard."

Another thought came to torture her.

"Suppose he doesn't come at all? Suppose he has changed his plans and gone somewhere else? The Rualla will believe you lied to them!"

"Look!"

The sun hung low in the west, a fiery, dazzling ball. She blinked, shading her eyes.

Then the head of a marching column grew out of the dancing heat waves: lines of horsemen, grey with dust, files of heavily laden baggage camels, with the captive women riding them. The standard hung loose in the breathless air; but once, when a vagrant gust of wind, hot as the breath of perdition, lifted the folds, the white wolf's head was displayed.

Crushing proof of idolatry and heresy! In their agitation, the Rualla almost betrayed themselves. Even Mitkhal turned pale.

"Allah! Sacrilege! Forgotten of God. Hell shall be thy portion!"

"Easy!" hissed Gordon, feeling the semi-hysteria that ran down the lurking lines. "Wait for my signal. They may halt to water their camels at the Well."

Osman must have driven his people like a fiend all day. The women drooped on the loaded camels; the dust-caked faces of the soldiers were drawn. The horses reeled with weariness. But it was soon evident that they did not intend halting at the Well with their goal, the Walls of Sulaiman, so near. The head of the column was even with the *sangar* when Gordon fired. He was aiming at Osman, but the range was long, the sun glare on the rocks dazzling. The man behind Osman fell, and at the signal the slopes came alive with spurting flame.

The column staggered. Horses and men went down and stunned soldiers gave back a ragged fire that did no harm. They did not even see their assailants save as bits of white cloth bobbing among the boulders.

Perhaps discipline had grown lax during the grind of that merciless march. Perhaps panic seized the tired Turks. At any rate, the column broke and men fled toward the *sangar* without waiting for orders. They would have abandoned the baggage camels had not Osman ridden among them. Cursing and striking with the flat of his saber, he made them drive the beasts in with them.

"I hoped they'd leave the camels and women outside," grunted Gordon. "Maybe they'll drive them out when they find there's no water."

The Turks took their positions in good order, dismounting and ranging along the wall. Some dragged the Arab women off the camels and drove them into the hut. Others improvised a pen for the animals with stakes and ropes between the back of the hut and the wall. Saddles were piled in the gate to complete the barricade.

The Arabs yelled taunts as they poured in a hail of lead, and a few leaped up and danced derisively, waving their rifles. But they stopped that when a Turk drilled one of them cleanly through the head. When the demonstrations ceased, the besiegers offered scanty targets to shoot at.

However, the Turks fired back frugally and with no indication of panic, now that they were under cover and fighting the sort of a fight they understood. They were well protected by the wall from the men directly in front of them, but those facing north could be seen by the men on the south ridge, and vice versa. But the distance was too great for consistently effective shooting at these marks by the Arabs.

"We don't seem to be doing much damage," remarked Olga presently.

"Thirst will win for us," Gordon answered. "All we've got to do is to keep them bottled up. They probably have enough water in their canteens to last through the rest of the day. Certainly no longer. Look, they're going to the well now."

The well stood in the middle of the enclosure, in a comparatively exposed area, as seen from above. Olga saw men approaching it with canteens in their hands, and the Arabs, with sardonic enjoyment, refrained from firing at them. They reached the well, and then the girl saw the change that came over them. It ran through their band like an electric shock. The men along the walls reacted by firing wildly. A furious yelling rose, edged with hysteria, and men began to run madly about the enclosure. Some toppled, hit by shots dropping from the ridges.

"What are they doing?" Olga started to her knees, and was instantly jerked down again by Gordon. The Turks were running into the hut. If she had been watching Gordon she would have sensed the meaning of it, for his dark face grew suddenly grim.

"They're dragging the women out!" she exclaimed. "I see Osman waving his saber. What? Oh, God! They're butchering the women!"

Above the crackle of shots rose terrible shrieks and the sickening *chack* of savagely driven blows. Olga turned sick and hid her face. Osman had realized the trap into which he had been driven, and his reaction was that of a mad dog. Recognizing defeat in the blocked well, facing the ruin of his crazy ambitions by thirst and Bedouin bullets, he was taking this vengeance on the whole Arab race.

On all sides the Arabs rose howling, driven to frenzy by the sight of that slaughter. That these women were of another tribe made no difference. A stern chivalry was the foundation of their society, just as it was among the frontiersmen of early America. There was no sentimentalism about it. It was real and vital as life itself.

The Rualla went berserk when they saw women of their race falling under the swords of the Turks. A wild yell shattered the brazen sky, and recklessly breaking cover, the Arabs pelted down the slopes, howling like fiends. Gordon could not check them, nor could Mitkhal. Their shouts fell on deaf ears. The walls vomited smoke and flame as withering volleys raked the oncoming hordes. Dozens fell, but enough were left to reach the wall and sweep over it in a wave that neither lead nor steel could halt.

And Gordon was among them. When he saw he could not stop the storm he joined it. Mitkhal was not far behind him, cursing his men as he ran. The *shaykh* had no stomach for this kind of fighting, but his leadership was at stake. No man who hung back in this charge would ever be able to command the Rualla again.

Gordon was among the first to reach the wall, leaping over the writhing bodies of half a dozen Arabs. He had not blazed away wildly as he ran like the Bedouins, to reach the wall with an empty gun. He held his fire until the flame spurts from the barrier were almost burning his face, and then emptied his rifle in a point-blank fusillade that left a bloody gap where there had been a line of fierce dark faces an instant before. Before the gap could be closed he had swarmed over and in, and the Rualla poured after him.

As his feet hit the ground a rush of men knocked him against the wall and a blade, thrusting for his life, broke against the rocks. He drove his shortened butt into a snarling face, splintering teeth and bones, and the next instant a surge of his own men over the wall cleared a space about him. He threw away his broken rifle and drew his pistol.

The Turks had been forced back from the wall in a dozen places now, and men were fighting all over the *sangar*. No quarter was asked—none given. The pitiful headless bodies sprawled before the bloodstained hut had turned the Bedouins into hot-eyed demons. The guns were empty now, all but Gordon's automatic. The yells had died down to grunts, punctuated by death-howls. Above these sounds rose the chopping impact of flailing blades, the crunch of fiercely driven rifle butts. So grimly had the Bedouins suffered in that brainless rush, that now they were outnumbered, and the Turks fought with the fury of desperation.

It was Gordon's automatic, perhaps, that tipped the balance. He emptied it without haste and without hesitation, and at that range he could not miss. He was aware of a dark shadow forever behind him, and turned once to see black Hassan following him, smiting methodically right and left with a heavy scimitar already dripping crimson. Even in the fury of strife, Gordon grinned. The literal-minded Soudanese was obeying his instructions to keep at El Borak's heels. As long as the battle hung in doubt, he was Gordon's protector—ready to become his executioner the instant the tide turned in their favor.

"Faithful servant," called Gordon sardonically. "Have care lest these Turks cheat you of my head!"

Hassan grinned, speechless. Suddenly blood burst from his thick lips and he buckled at the knees. Somewhere in that rush down the hill his black body had stopped a bullet. As he struggled on all fours a Turk ran in from the side and brained him with a rifle-butt. Gordon killed the Turk with his last bullet. He felt no grudge against Hassan. The man had been a good soldier, and had obeyed orders given him.

The *sangar* was a shambles. The men on their feet were less than those on the ground, and all were streaming blood. The white wolf standard had been torn from its staff and lay trampled under vengeful feet. Gordon bent, picked up a saber and looked about for Osman. He saw Mitkhal, running toward the horse-pen, and then he yelled a warning, for he saw Osman.

The man broke away from a group of struggling figures and ran for the pen. He tore away the ropes and the horses, frantic from the noise and smell of blood, stampeded into the *sangar*, knocking men down and trampling them. As they thundered past, Osman, with a magnificent display of agility, caught a handful of flying mane and leaped on the back of the racing steed.

Mitkhal ran toward him, yelling furiously, and snapping a pistol at him. The *shaykh*, in the confusion of the fighting, did not seem to be aware that the gun was empty, for he pulled the trigger again and again as he stood in the path of the oncoming rider. Only at the last moment did he realize his peril and leap back. Even so, he would have sprung clear had not his sandal heel caught in a dead man's abba.

Mitkhal stumbled, avoided the lashing hoofs, but not the down-flailing saber in Osman's hand. A wild cry went up from the Rualla as Mitkhal fell, his turban suddenly crimson. The next instant Osman was out of the gate and riding like the wind—straight up the hillside to where he saw the slim figure of the girl to whom he now attributed his overthrow.

Olga had come out from behind the rocks and was standing in stunned horror watching the fight below. Now she awoke suddenly to her own peril at the sight of the madman charging up the slope. She drew the pistol Gordon had taken from him and opened fire. She was not a very good shot. Three bullets missed, the fourth killed the horse, and then the gun jammed. Gordon was running up the slope as the Apaches of his native Southwest run, and behind him streamed a swarm of Rualla. There was not a loaded gun in the whole horde.

Osman took a shocking fall when his horse turned a somersault under him, but rose, bruised and bloody, with Gordon still some distance away. But the Turk had to play hide-and-seek for a few moments among the rocks with his prey before he was able to grasp her hair and twist her screaming to her knees, and then he paused an instant to enjoy her despair and terror. That pause was his undoing.

As he lifted his saber to strike off her head, steel clanged loud on steel. A numbing shock ran through his arm, and his blade was knocked from his hand. His weapon rang on the hot flints. He whirled to face the blazing slits that were El Borak's eyes. The muscles stood out in cords and ridges on Gordon's sun burnt forearm in the intensity of his passion.

"Pick it up, you filthy dog," he said between his teeth.

Osman hesitated, stooped, caught up the saber and slashed at Gordon's legs without straightening. Gordon leaped back, then sprang in again the instant his toes touched the earth. His return was as paraly- zingly quick as the death-leap of a wolf. It caught Osman off balance, his sword extended. Gordon's blade hissed as it cut the air, slicing through flesh, gritting through bone.

The Turk's head toppled from the severed neck and fell at Gordon's feet, the headless body collapsing in a heap. With an excess spasm of hate, Gordon kicked the head savagely down the slope.

"Oh!" Olga turned away and hid her face. But the girl knew that Osman deserved any fate that could have overtaken him. Presently she was aware of Gordon's hand resting lightly on her shoulder and she looked up, ashamed of her weakness. The sun was just dipping below the western ridges. Musa came limping up the slope, bloodstained but radiant.

"The dogs are all dead, *effendi*!" he cried, industriously shaking a plundered watch, in an effort to make it run. "Such of our warriors as still live are faint from strife, and many sorely wounded. There is none to command now but thou."

"Sometimes problems settle themselves," mused Gordon. "But at a ghastly price. If the Rualla hadn't made that rush, which was the death of Hassan and Mitkhal—oh, well, such things are in the hands of Allah, as the Arabs say. A hundred better men than I have died today, but by the decree of some blind Fate, I live."

Gordon looked down on the wounded men. He turned to Musa.

"We must load the wounded on camels," he said, "and take them to the camp at the Walls where there's water and shade. Come."

As they started down the slope, he said to Olga:

"I'll have to stay with them till they're settled at the Walls, then I must start for the coast. Some of the Rualla will be able to ride, though, and you need have no fear of them. They'll escort you to the nearest Turkish outpost."

She looked at him in surprise.

"Then I'm not your prisoner?"

He laughed.

"I think you can help Feisal more by carrying out your original instructions of supplying misleading information to the Turks! I don't blame you for not confiding even in me. You have my deepest admiration, for you're playing the most dangerous game a woman can."

"Oh!" She felt a sudden warm flood of relief and gladness that he should know she was not really an enemy. Musa was well out of earshot. "I might have known you were high enough in Feisal's councils to know that I really am—"

"Gloria Willoughby, the cleverest, most daring secret agent the British government employs," he murmured. The girl impulsively placed her slender fingers in his, and hand in hand they went down the slope together.

EVERY MAN A KING

E. Hoffmann Price

CHAPTER I

"Do you have to go? At this hour?" Olajai turned from her mirror, but did not leave off unfastening the red velvet hood whose twinkling pendants trailed past her cheeks, and to her shoulders. "Couldn't it wait till tomorrow?"

Timur frowned, which made it all the more certain that the King Maker's granddaughter had not married him for his looks. He snatched a shirt of link mail from a hook, and as he worked it down over his broad shoulders, he grumbled, "One of Bikijek's pets, and he's got the king's seal. Either be a good dog, or run out and join your brother at Saghej Well!"

Olajai said, wistfully, as she wiped off the last bit of dead-white makeup, "And I thought it'd be lovely, living in Samarkand."

Olajai was shapely of body, and exquisite of face; the Turki heritage, showing in the peach blow tinge of her cheeks, gave features whose every line was sharp and clean and delicate in its drawing. This was Timur's first and only wife, and thus far, he was glad that there were no others.

Though not quite twenty-seven, he looked older, for mountain blizzards and desert blasts had weathered his flat face. Wind blown sand and storm driven sleet had set the Mongol slant of his eyes in a permanent squint; and for all the blue Zaytuni silk tunic he put on over his shirt of linked mail, and his gold embroidery boots, and plumed pork pie hat, he seemed out of place in a palace.

"I'll get away as soon as I can," he promised, and limped out.

Bow legged, and never built for walking, he was further handicapped by an ankle which had stopped a well-aimed arrow. In the tiled reception room, he said to the waiting official, "Something important going on?"

The square-rigged Kipchak did not answer; he merely tapped the big four-cornered seal. In the court, a sleepy groom held his horse, and Timur's.

They skirted the plaza of splendid Samarkand. The bitter clear moon brought out the blue of tile-fronted palaces, and the golden crests of tall minarets. Samarkand, the jewel of the Jagatai Empire, was now the prize of the Kipchak Horde who had overrun the land: and Timur was weary of serving invaders. But for luck, and a friend at Elias Koja's court, he might be an exile, like Olajai's brother, Mir Hussein. Yet, though his position as administrator of affairs gave plenty of enemies and little satisfaction, it at least enabled him to stand between Bikijek's rapacious clique of nobles, and his own conquered neighbors.

Timur trailed the official, instead of riding boot to boot. There was more than just the matter of rank involved. Then, wary ever since that first strange warning, he noted the stirring in the shadows of the archway to the left. Here the street was narrow; here he and his guide faced a cold, white moon.

A bowstring twanged, the strident note of a horseman's bow. Timur ducked. His sword was half unsheathed when the arrow thumped home, nailing the Kipchak squarely in the throat. The fellow made a choking sound, and lurched from the saddle.

Timur wheeled, chin in, and crouching low, so that there was hardly a vulnerable spot exposed. The Ferghana stallion stretched out in a great bound; hooves struck fire. When things happened too fast for thought, Timur Bek was driven by the instinct to close in, to cut down.

Then a man came out, barefoot, and bearded. "Go home, Timur Bek. There was no other way to warn you."

The face was in shadow, but Timur recognized the voice and the figure. "Good shooting, for a scholar! Why?"

"Allah will enlighten you. Also, the man you were following won't be able to tell anyone you've been enlightened."

"What is this, Kaboul?"

"If all is well with your family, then this is a mistake. And the peace upon you."

Kaboul the Darvish turned into the shadows of the archway. On the ground, Timur saw a horseman's bow, but neither quiver nor arrows.

"One man, one arrow."

And now Kaboul was going back to his cubicle to write a Persian quatrain, or an ode in Turki!

Timur, retracing his course, held his horse to a walk, for in spite of the menace which threatened Olajai he could not risk the sound of galloping. When he finally reached the wicket which gave entrance to the rear court of his house, he hitched himself up and stood in the saddle. Then, catching the crown of the wall, he swung himself to the top, and dropped to the grass inside. His first move was to unbolt the little gate, and lead his horse in, for he dreaded the helplessness of being afoot.

His felt boots made no sound. As he hurried past the servants' quarters and down a hallway, he heard voices, in front: a challenge as of a drowsy porter, then brusque answer, and a scuffle which ended in a groan.

There was time. He hurried back, mounted up, and again felt complete. He nudged the stallion with his boot, and stroked the sleek neck, wheedling the bewildered beast into the tiled passageway.

A woman cried out, more in wrath and indignation than in fright. "Father of pigs! Get out of here or I will have you skinned alive."

"That's her, Olajai Turcan Aga!"

"Come down, *khanoum*; we won't hurt you."

"So you do know that this is Timur's house. You know, and come in?"

They laughed at the threat. "And we know where Timur is."

That was when the lame rider's scowl became a grin. "Come down, Olajai!" he called. "We're leaving town!"

The deep-chested hail made the men at arms whirl about. They had curved swords, they had maces; they wore peaked helmets, and armor of overlapping plates sewed on leather, but they were afoot, and they were surprised.

The stallion snorted. He quivered, then leaped as Timur's legs tightened. The heavy blade licked out, finding the gap between neck-guard and hauberk. As the stroke bit home, Timur traversed, so that the wall covered his left. He swayed in the saddle; a spike-headed "morning star" ripped his tunic, exposing the link mail beneath, and then his blade flickered, slashing the man's forehead.

Blood blinded; that one was out of action.

"Come down; we're riding!" Timur shouted.

Some were scrambling now to get to the front court and their waiting horses; several tried to close in with swords. Blades clanged. Timur hewed down, slicing off plates of armor.

Olajai snatched a tall Chinese vase from the landing and heaved it at the head of the rearmost. While his helmet saved him from a smashed skull, the impact dropped him in his tracks. She dashed down the stairs and plucked the fellow's helmet from his head.

"Put it on!" she cried, crowding up on Timur's left.

"Grab a horse!" he answered, and booted the stallion after the handful who had raced for their mounts.

And when his horse got firm footing on the hard-packed earth, Timur charged with effect.

Olajai followed. She was not dressed for riding, but the ripping of her gown took care of that. And she picked a good mount.

Two of the raiders galloped across the square. Two others fled afoot. Timur snatched the bow whose case hung from the saddle of Olajai's horse. As he strung it, she passed him an arrow.

The hindmost of the footmen pitched on his face.

Timur grinned. "Good bow. Now keep behind me; there'll be the devil to pay at the gate."

* * * *

There was, but it did not last long.

Guardsmen were turning out. The two surviving horsemen had attended to that. But the moon was bright, and Timur's bowstring twanged, once, twice, thrice: the deadly Turki arrows, released at a dead run, cleared a path. Then a whirl of steel, and the fugitives went pelting down one of the lanes which threaded the orchard girdle of Samarkand.

CHAPTER II

THE BEGGAR

Once a bend in the lane furnished momentary cover, Timur pulled up. "Get Eltchi Bahadur and as many others as you can, and ride direct for Saghej Well. I'll keep the Kipchaks off your heels, and I'll meet you later."

Olajai had long since learned to think quickly, and to move while thinking; she waved, reined her horse down a cross lane, and galloped to notify the chief of Timur's fifty picked fighting men who had followed him from his home in Kesh. And since they lived outside the city walls, Olajai's task was safe enough.

Her brother, Mir Hussein, was at Saghej Well with forty odd retainers. They had outraced the Kipchaks to find refuge in the wastelands, and their heads apparently were not considered worth the cost in horseflesh.

Timur dismounted. When he heard the approach of the pursuers, he pretended to be picking a stone from his horse's hoof. In a moment they came into view, and in the full moon, they saw him. Olajai could not be far away. The horsemen reined in. It was over, they thought.

The fugitive, having the advantage of the moon, fired from his own shadow. A man toppled. Timur swung into the saddle, and the Ferghana stallion took off in a falcon swoop.

He twisted, shooting as he rode. And this was not his second choice horse!

They would stick. Speed was not the essence of this chase, since he had neither rations nor water nor a spare mount. As he gained a lead, he reined in a little, holding the distance just beyond arrow range. For all they knew, Olajai was ahead of him, just beyond sight.

Timur now had time to ponder on the reasons behind the raid on his house. Bikijek's resentment at a man who spent too much time blocking the sale of justice, blocking the extortion of doubled taxes, and the making of false returns: that was one fair guess. The other, plain court jealousy. Though the attempt to kidnap Olajai suggested a third answer—a blow at her exiled brother, or a stranglehold on Timur himself.

And as he rode, his memory reached back to that night when he had drunk his guests off their feet; it all came back, that survey at sunrise, of his littered banquet room.

He recalled the drums which had rolled and thundered across the broad median. They blotted out the muezzin's call to prayer.

From a high window he could see the horsetail standards at Biki-jek's door. The puppet king, Elias Koja, old Togluk Khan's son, let Bikijek play with the tokens of royalty, instead of setting to work with a running noose.

It would not, it could not last long, and when it ended, the Golden Horde of the Kipchak would restore order.

Order; herds eaten by Kipchak soldiers, granaries emptied by Kipchak officers, towns and farmsteads burned, and all Timur's broad acres in Kesh devastated with the rest. All because Bikijek, chief lord of the young king's court, had drums beaten five times daily before his palace.

Ten or a dozen local emirs, so busy battling each other that they had not stopped Elias Koja when his father sent him south to be Grand Khan of the Jagatai; that was the trouble. Rugged indi-vidualists, every man a king, and so now they had the Horde on their necks, and now their lands were the proving ground of an apprentice whose father had handed him the entire Jagatai heritage in which to learn the trade of kingship.

Timur had laughed aloud, for wine and fermented mare's milk had made him see the truth with a bitter clarity which his sober and busy days had never permitted. "First I fought Uncle Hadji, after Uncle Hadji and I drove Beyan Selduz out of town. Then they murdered Uncle Hadji, and I got an army to avenge him, and then the army divided into three parts and we had a war to settle the di-viding of the booty. Every man a king. Allah! What we need is one king, and that one home grown. Too bad Mir Hussein's grandfather isn't alive."

He had smiled, in half drunken grimness and regret, thinking of the King Maker and the King Maker's grandson, handsome, hard fighting, Mir Hussein, fickle, crackbrained, unpredictable Hussein who had the loveliest sister in the world.

"Allah curse Bikijek, Allah curse every man who does not curse Bikijek's religion and his father and his grandfather!"

He had spoken aloud. A grave voice had made him turn. There, in the arched doorway stood a ragged man with a snarled beard; the slanting rays kept his face from being any too clear.

"Who asks Allah to curse the religion of another true believer?"

Timur snorted. "I'm talking to myself. Only way to do, if you want to hear sense for a change."

Then his eyes became used to the glare: he saw the grimy khelat, the greasy skullcap, the girdle of frayed rope, the dirty hands which fingered a wooden bowl. Dirty hands, this beggar had, but fine and long, made for good penmanship. And he wore a writing case at his girdle and a scroll carefully wrapped in a clean red silk scarf.

'Well, darvish!' Timur found a gold piece. "Guest of Allah, and a lot more welcome than these Kipchak pigs!"

Only then had his eyes a chance to focus sharply on the seamed face, shrewd, ironic, kindly; somewhat of a dish face, with broad, flat nose, Mongol features and melon head like Timur's own.

And Timur knelt on the littered tiles, catching the beggar's hand, too swiftly for any evasion; he kissed it.

"By the Splendor! I'd heard—I didn't recognize—"

The darvish freed his hand, made a gesture to decline the reverence "Kaboul Shah Aglen, now the Guest of God and the least of the slaves." Timur Bek had risen, to step back, entirely bewildered. Kaboul Shah Aglen, eighth in direct descent from Genghis Khan's son, Jagatai, begging his bread, and for shoes, growing calluses on his feet!

Kaboul smiled, "The darvish robe would fit you, Timur Bek. Last night's friends are this day's enemies. Become intoxicated by the splendor of Allah, and become His Guest, and the peace will be with you."

Outside, just then, horses had begun to squeal and snort; saddle drums rolled, for Bikijek was riding to the mosque. As the lordly sounds died out, Kaboul Aglen went on, "When Togluk Khan comes south to cure the disease which his son ignores, your palace becomes a mirage, and you'll be stealing sheep again. Get out, while you still can leave without killing too many horses.

"Genghis Khan, the master of all mankind, once had to steal a horse to keep from wearing out his boots. In me, the circle closes on itself. I beg my bread, as in the end all the race of Genghis Khan must do."

Timur's face darkened; Karashar Nevian, his ancestor, nine generations back had been Genghis Khan's uncle and advisor. Then he laughed, and it was like trumpets braying before the charge. "See here! You're the heir to the Jagatai throne, you, not Togluk Khan nor Togluk Khan's son. I'll make you Grand Khan in Samarkand!"

The beggar shrugged. "No time; too soon, you'll be riding for your neck. You, not Bikijek."

Timur flipped the golden dinar into the bowl.

The beggar whisked it out. "What is nothing now will be your fortune soon, and the peace upon you!"

And here it was: hard riding pursuit behind him, while his wife raced to round up what fighting men she could find. So he laughed again, from thinking on the words of Kaboul Aglen, and the murderous bowstring a scribe could pluck.

* * * *

Forty-two horsemen, all with spare mounts, waited with Olajai when two days later, Timur's horse stumbled toward the rendezvous, where tents were scattered about a spring which kept the grass green.

Hashim, melon headed and scar-faced, came running to greet him; and he walked back, clinging to Timur's stirrup leather. "We ride again, *tura!*" he said, using the Turki word for "my lord." "It is like the old days again."

Then Timur saw Tagi Bouga Barlas, his distant cousin, hard bitten and grinning; Sayfuddin, the greatest archer of them all, coddling a bow; and roaring Elthci Bahadur whose strength and skill had thus far hacked his way out of all the traps into which he charged. They crowded about, grimy and sweat gleaming; jeweled collars and gold inlaid helmets and embroidered belts grotesque against greasy *khalat*s, and sheepskin jackets.

"*Hai*, Timur Bahadur!"

Quickly they broke camp and rode, for they had rested while Timur led the Kipchak riders a crazy chase in circles. And now, being among friends, Timur dozed in the saddle; and Olajai rode beside him.

CHAPTER III

BATTLE

Five days brought Timur to the Jihun's poplar lined banks; and swimming this river put the Jagatai realm behind them. At the Well of Saghej they found Mir Hussein, with Dilshad Aga, his wife, and some forty horsemen.

The King Maker's grandson was handsome as his sister was lovely; a small, pointed black beard, and high arched brows, and a high bridged, straight nose with nostrils whose flare made one think of a stallion scenting a fight. Until his army had been scattered, he had been King in Kandahar; now he had lost everything but hope.

There was no meat, so they ate cooked millet and buttered tea. Mir Hussein said, "Bismillahi, it could be worse."

Timur grimaced. "We can't eat sand very long. But with a couple good raids, I'll have an army at my back. The men of Kesh were giving me hard looks, you'd think I'd sold them out, just because I took the thankless job of trying to stand between them and those Kipchak hounds! But this fast ride has set a lot of them thinking."

"Inshallah! But I can't show up in Kandahar with a guard of forty men."

Timur chuckled sourly. "No, they've probably got a new king there. That's the trouble, too many kings, instead of one good one. Now, your grandfather—"

Mir Hussein sighed. "May God be well pleased with him! But do you think he could improve things? He used to pull kings out of his saddlebags, but this is different. Still, you'd do pretty well as Grand Khan of the Jagatai."

Dangerous ground. If Timur did raise an army to drive the present puppet out of Samarkand, he'd be quite a hero, but once he took the throne, jealousy would start feud. Mir Hussein was good in battle, and good nowhere else. "You're the grandson of Mir Kazagan," Timur countered. "How's Tekil?"

"Hungry and looking for business. At least seven hundred Turkomans and the like."

"Our hundred will draw his following," Timur argued. "And with that start, we'll begin to make an impression."

So they rode through the march of hell, across the black sands of Kivac. The scrawny oasis looked like a small paradise, for the lips of Timur's men were cracked from thirst.

The citadel loomed up, above the poplars. "I don't like it," Timur said. "No one working in the fields. No one tending the ditches."

Instead of pressing on to the city, they made camp at the fringe of green which marked the beginning of cultivation.

Timur beckoned to Eltchi Bahadur and Tagai Bouga Barlas. "We'll ride in and pay our respects to Tekil."

Hussein cut in, "No! Let me go. He knows I've spent a couple of months at the Well of Saghej, and he made no trouble. Let me talk to him."

Timur's eyes narrowed. "Hmmm ... don't tell him I'm here. Just say you know where I am."

The deep-set Turki eyes sparkled. "So you've been thinking about that mess in Samarkand?"

Where Hussein had been the ill favored one, it now seemed that Timur's head was most in demand.

That night, Timur posted double guards and slept with his boots on. While his fame as a captain would always get him followers, it would also make his head a prize in a land where every man was a king, and allegiances changed overnight.

In the morning he heard trumpets and drums, and saw Mir Hussein's standard, and the riders who came from the gates, the fields and through the groves.

"Break camp, and be ready to mount up!" Timur commanded.

Then he rode out with twenty men to meet Tekil.

Ceremonious greetings: the burly governor fairly fell from his horse to be the first to dismount. A big, red-faced man, a hearty, smiling man. "Welcome, welcome, Timur Bek! Kivak is yours. You and your brother, I bid you welcome."

Tekil had an escort of perhaps two hundred horses. Timur wondered where the others were. He caught old Hashim's narrowed eyes, and made a twist of head and chin. The old fellow gave a gesture of assent; and unobtrusively edged from the clump of horsemen, to head back to camp.

More compliments. Hussein was smooth and smiling and affable. Tomorrow, he and Timur would with pleasure and heartiness attend the governor's banquet. Today, Allah bear witness, things were in an uproar in camp. Horses, badly overtaxed, needed attention. And some of the party was still unaccounted for. Ay, Wallah! Some baggage animals, carrying all the gifts designed for His Excellency, were lagging a day's march behind.

Something was wrong, something was off color; Hussein's fluent patter confirmed Timur's earlier premonitions. He said, cutting in brusquely, "Allied-to-Greatness, we beg permission to turn from the light of your Presence!"

Words and music did not matter. He was in the saddle before Tekil fairly realized that another speaker had addressed him. Tagi Bouga Barlas mounted up; and so did Hussein.

Tekil's face changed. And then came the great bawling voice of Eltchi Bahadur, and the pounding of hooves. "To horse, O Bek! The bastard's got us hemmed in!"

"Swords out!"

And Timur had scarcely shouted his command when an arrow smacked home with a solid thump. Eltchi was shooting, shooting hard, fast, straight. "Get out of my way," he howled, "get out of my way!"

Timur and Mir Hussein were blocking his line of fire. Then the visitors and the host's men went into action, blades out; some lancers maneuvered for working space, while others threw their lances down and snatched maces from their saddle bows.

"To camp!" Timur shouted. "Archers fall out!"

There was no drill by command, as such; it was rather instinctive teamwork, based on many a pitched battle and running fight. Eltchi Bahadur charged headlong at the Tekil's guard. Hacking and hewing, he was swallowed up by milling horsemen and billowing dust.

Meanwhile, as though called by signal, half Timur's escort swooped to right and left, and the bows began to twang. Hard driven shafts laced the flanks of Tekil's tight packed traitors; murderous, close range archery; cunningly driven shafts, some picking men, others nailing horses whose fall would block the movement of other riders.

Stung by the ferocious archery, Tekil's men opened out. Timur and Hussein pressed in, head on, to divide the enemy. And from the rear came the brawling, booming voice of Eltchi Bahadur. He looked as though an avalanche had passed over him, but he was hewing his way back to meet Timur.

Timur's archers fell back, shooting as they withdrew and covering the retreat. Over the roar of battle, he heard the approach of his main detachment, and saw his chance. "This way, you bawling bull!" he shouted to Eltchi, and pointed toward a low hillock.

In a moment, Timur's standard was on the knoll.

Dust ringed the oasis. The rest of Tekil's men were closing in. It was now clear where the governor's force had been. It was all too clear that the riders trailing Timur out of Samarkand had been baiting him, while a courier rode directly to Tekil. Bikijek, he now concluded, had known all the while where Mir Hussein was, and had counted on Timur's joining his brother-in-law: the two were to be settled beyond the border of the Jagatai territory.

Ten to one: Timur took a fresh horse, and looked out and down at the closing circle of steel. He said to his wife, and to Dilshad Aga, "Keep your heads down. There won't be many of us to block the arrows, not for long."

CHAPTER IV

OLAJAI

The one sided battle was reaching its end as the sun slowly dragged down toward the horizon. Olajai, ignoring arrows, went about during lulls, carrying a goatskin jar of brackish water.

"Easier each round," Timur said, and licked the dust from his lips.

She laughed. "They're well whittled down, too!"

Of Tekil's men, scarcely fifty were able to fight: the others were dead, or they had left the field because of wounds. As for Timur, only seven were about his standard.

Charge after charge had been swept back, for in the beginning, Tekil's men had blocked each other, only a few at a time being able to present themselves to the enemy; and closing in on Eltchi Bahadur was a swift way to the mercy of Allah.

Those who first charged up the little knoll had struggled in sandy soil, facing a hail of arrows: and the next wave had been blocked by windrows of fallen horses and men. Finally, exhaustion took the heart from all but the strongest. Skill failed, and so did the will.

"Only seven to one now, my dear! Give Bahadur a drink!"

He turned to his sister-in-law: "I'll get you horse tails, tie them to the standard."

There were plenty of once splendid mounts who had no further use for their tails. Timur hacked, and Dilshad Aga set to work.

Timur waited. The ring of winded, wounded enemies waited. The air had the dead stillness of a well-fired oven, except when hot wind drove scorching sand. Tagi Bouga Barlas and Sayfuddin were now on foot. Eltchi Bahadur grinned, though wearily; blood and sweat and dust made his homely face a devil's mask.

"*Hai*, Bahadur! The sons of pigs would turn tail if someone knocked that Tekil out of action."

Timur snorted. "I've spent all day trying to get at him. I've been cutting meat till my arm's ready to fall off, he always gets someone between me and him."

Hussein came up; debonair, head cocked like the head of a falcon, eyes aglitter. "Why take down our standard, brother?"

"It's coming up in a second." Then Dilshad Aga called, and Timur went to take the staff. Hussein saw the three horse tails. "The standard of Genghis Khan! By Allah, why not? This is our day. God does what he will do, and here we are."

Timur planted the staff, and said to Hashim, "Sound off!"

The one unbroken saddle drum rolled and grumbled in the hot silence; a hot wind made the three horse tails ripple, then fan out. Timur challenged the enemy: "Sons of Bad Mothers! Here is the standard of Genghis Khan, the Master of all Mankind. He rides again!"

Hussein mounted up, wordlessly, and with the smooth swiftness of a panther. Sword out, he raced down the slope. Then came Eltchi Bahadur's great voice; the drum stopped rumbling. Olajai cried out—many men had died, but this was her brother, and a clump of swordsmen had swallowed him up.

The others were at his heels. Tekil's standard, clipped in half, was trampled in the dust. Eltchi Bahadur smashed home with all his weight and steel. And as he raced, Timur plucked his bow. One shot. Just one. A single shaft, threading through the shifting fighters, caught Tekil between the teeth. The impact knocked him from his horse.

Then an arrow caught Timur's mount. The beast crumpled, flinging the rider asprawl. Timur rolled, recovered, and from the bloody sand he snatched a half-pike. Eltchi Bahadur had hewn a path to Tekil. Timur bore down on the pike, driving through armor, driving it through the man, and deep into the earth.

Whoever could run or ride fled to the fortress. Seven wounded victors left the field, to find whatever safety they could, before Tekil's men recovered from the shock, and began to think of vengeance.

They retraced their course. At the desert's fringe, three of the survivors said, "Lord Timur, Allah does what he will do, and with your permission, we go to our homes in Khorassan, while you raise an army."

This also had happened before, so Timur answered, "Go with my blessing."

Then on the night when they were not far from the Jihun, Timur said to Hussein, "There are not enough for any defense, only enough to be conspicuous. Better we separate. You go to Hirmen, and spend the winter with the Mikouzeri tribesmen. I'll go back home to Kesh, incognito, and I'll meet you in Hirmen, later."

So they parted. And when Timur was alone with Olajai, he said, "*Shireen*, you married a prince in Kesh, and now look! Not one rider behind me."

"I'm not worrying. Though I was scared silly, until you had that crazy notion of hoisting three horse tails!"

He eyed her sharply. "You quit worrying then? Mmmm ... it did something to your brother, the crackbrain, he was off before I knew what was happening."

She nodded. "That shocked me, too. Then, suddenly, I knew that Tekil's men would break. For a crazy instant, it was as if

Genghis Khan had come back through all these nine generations, and out of his grave."

"The sun, my dear. It was bad."

She shook her head. "I didn't see anything, I didn't hear anything, I just felt something. As though you had really had the right, that moment, to put up the horse tail standard. And they felt it."

"You're giving Eltchi Bahadur and Hussein not much credit!"

"I notice you took the tails off before we left. I'm not worried. It's working out. What that darvish said. Only he didn't say all. Maybe he didn't know, maybe he couldn't see so far ahead. But I do."

"What's that?" His voice was sharp.

"My grandfather made kings. He unmade them. Always, he put on the throne of Samarkand someone of the direct line of Genghis Khan. And there was peace, the very name made peace. You know, he could have taken the throne himself."

"He could. And Kazagan Khan would have filled any throne."

"But he didn't, he wouldn't. Timur—don't you see what I mean? You have a right to the name, you've proved the right, back there."

They marched, from brackish well to drywell where there was water only by digging. Then the worst of the two horses collapsed. Timur dismounted and said "Take mine."

She gaped. He said gruffly, "Mount up!"

"Why—darling—whatever—you're crazy."

Her incredulity was natural. A man tramping on foot would be too worn out to fight. It was plain sense that he should ride while Olajai walked.

"But—"

"Mount up!" he commanded and she obeyed.

He tramped along holding the stirrup leather.

And that afternoon toward sunset as they halted to rest he looked at his boots. The soles were gone.

"See! The darvish is right! Timur of the race of Genghis Khan is barefooted. This thing had to be. And now that I cannot go any lower I must go higher and the Power is with God!"

She was no longer worried by his seeming madness in walking while a woman rode. "You lied to me, you knew what happened on that knoll, as well as I did!"

They were coming near to a well, or to where one should be. The sun's level rays bent into their backs so that their shadows reached long and dark ahead of them.

Then he saw the horsemen riding into the glare. "How many?" he asked Olajai, very calmly.

"Ten—twelve—fifteen—too many, Timur, and you've been walking."

"Who are they—what are they?"

"Turkomans," she answered. "I was afraid of that." The Governor of Kivac's force had been largely Turkoman.

Olajai said, lightly, "We can't use horse tails again. We haven't enough horses."

She started to slide out of the saddle, so that he could mount up. He said, "Not yet. The glare keeps them from seeing that there are two of us."

When they reached the well, and its thin cover of scrawny trees, he made the horse turn, so that it screened the next move. Olajai slid from the saddle. He took his lariat and secured it to a root which reached from the wall of the well.

"It's dry. The water is in the other hole. Get down and stay down. You're near enough now to get to the river afoot."

Then he mounted up, drew his sword, and rode at them, shouting his challenge. He had no more arrows. The riders had fanned out to envelop the oasis, so as to block the escape of any other travelers who might be there. Every sign pointed to being cut down and robbed of his arms, his horse gear, the jewels of his belt and scabbard; so he shouted, "Timur, the Man of Kesh, Timur, the son of Tragai!"

A man cried an answer. The archers lowered their bows. That one man rode forward and dismounted.

"Timur Bek! Welcome, and the blessing of Allah, and the Peace of Allah upon you! We heard that you had gone this way, and we came to meet you."

So Olajai came from the pit. Timur gave her bracelets to Hadji Mehemmed, the Turkoman raider with whom he had ridden once, some years previous. And Hadji Mehemmed gave them horses, and an escort of ten men. Olajai said, that night, "This proves it—the horse tails are still with you."

CHAPTER V
"SPREAD *THE* GOOD WORD"

At Bokar-Zendin, Timur left Olajai with friends, for being north of the Jihun again, he risked recognition, ambush, betrayal, which he would not have Olajai share. "More than that," he said, "if you went, I'd be recognized just that much sooner."

"Women's chatter? Well, men haven't done too well by you!"

Timur chuckled amiably at that painfully just quip. "*Shireen*, wherever we were guests, and we couldn't always refuse hospitality without making ourselves even more conspicuous, there'd be women looking at you. They'd guess, and much sooner than any men would, looking at us."

"Mmmm ... yes, of course."

Now that the blame had been passed to superior feminine perception, Olajai felt better about it all. So the Lord of Kesh sneaked thief-like across the lands of his ancestors, not even daring to enter his own estate, for this choice territory was packed with Kipchaks.

A lone archer limped through the market place. Timur, being afoot, had the best possible disguise, yet the risk was deadly enough, since men of Bikijek's clique came in from Samarkand every day.

One by one, he cornered retainers who had ridden with his late father, Emir Tragai. These had to look twice before they could believe that this haggard footman was Timur Bek. Each one said. "Lord Timur, we thought that you had quit us. We were glad when we heard that you'd left Samarkand with a troop on your heels. Then we knew that you were with us in heart, and in the end, you would come back and wipe them out."

"What with?"

"We join whatever army you raise."

Close-mouthed, weather-beaten men listened to him and then spread the word. When he left Kesh, Temouka Kutchin rode after him with twenty horsemen ready for the field.

They took the trail for Badakshan. The story of his desperate fight against Tekil of Kivac had spread, and one chieftain after another joined him. There was Bahram Jalair, and a distant cousin, Saddik Barlas; Kazanchi Hassan with a hundred horse came seeking him. Mir Sayfuddin, whom he had not seen since the disaster in the desert, had meanwhile raised seventy picked men. Another kinsman, Koja Barlas, had a like party. Then came Shir Bahrain, and Ulum Kuli with two hundred horse, Mamut Keli with as many footmen.

Timur's disaster and his barefooted march across the desert recruited more men more easily than any success had ever done.

Even the Kipchak Horde helped him: for with Bikijek's nobles now leading raiding parties over all the Jagatai territory, captain after captain fled to join Timur.

When he met Mir Hussein and they reviewed their combined forces, Timur said, "Now that the enemy has taught them that too much freedom is no freedom at all, they've stopped being kings."

Spies came, saying that the Kipchak raids were becoming more severe. Worse yet, Togluc Khan had sent some 20,000 of the Golden Horde to the north, to reinforce his son, Elias Koja.

"We're not ready. What we have is good, by Allah, but not enough. Time is against us," Hussein said.

"Time is the toy of Allah," Timur retorted. "He does with it what pleases Him."

"It pleased Him to have most of us wiped out facing odds of ten to one," Hussein pointed out, realistically.

And these men would follow Timur only as long as they willed, and no longer. Even Genghis Khan, more nearly an absolute lord than any man who had ever ruled men, had ruled only by the will of his captains: Asiatic democracy, masquerading as a despotism.

So Timur's frown deepened, and even more when he heard that Kesh was heavily garrisoned. Worst of all, spies said that Olajai, finally leaving Bokar-Zendan to him and her brother, had been recognized and trapped; she was a captive in Kesh, a hostage for his good behavior.

Timur asked the messenger, "Who else has heard this?"

"No one, *tura*, save yourself and Mir Hussein."

"I'll take your head," Timur solemnly swore, "I'll skin you and stuff your hide with straw if a word of it leaks out in camp. Is that clear?"

"Aywah, tura."

He gave the man a handful of golden *dinars*, and dismissed him.

Then, to Hussein: "I've got to get her out of there."

"I take refuge with Allah! My own sister, but you can risk a good little army against a walled city, just for a woman? Timur, that's not sense. Your men'll think you're crazy, wasting them on a woman."

Timur smiled. "That's something I'm not telling them."

"Allah! But what?"

"Listen."

The drums sounded assembly, and the trumpets brayed. Timur spoke from the saddle: "O Men! Friends of my father and my uncle, a saint came to me in a dream last night. Allah has promised us our city. Even though we had green boughs instead of lances, our faith would make us win.

"The Presence of Genghis Khan came into the desert, and our enemies ran.

"And if we take Kesh, every captain from Badakshan to Kandahar will join us to share in our next glory. When they join, who will stop us?"

He sold them as they stood there. And not even on the march, the hard forced march on Kesh, did a man of them wonder what Timur would do for siege engines.

"They're drunk," Hussein said. "Drunk and not from wine. How did you do it?"

"I don't know. It came to me."

"Well, if we do capture Kesh," Hussein countered, "they'll besiege us, and have you ever seen a Mongol or Turk who was any good, locked up behind walls?"

Timur laughed triumphantly. "*Hai*! Out of your own mouth, brother! The very truth that's going to make Kesh open up in no time. Go and spread the word! Keep them with a dream in their eyes!"

They rode so fast that there was no news of their coming.

Bivouac: and at dawn, far off, rose the gray walls of Kesh, high above the orchards.

"Now get busy," Timur said to his captains. "Cut off green boughs. Divide into four columns." He saw their faces change at this insane suggestion, but he gave them no chance to object. "Let each column mark the time, and do it in this wise—"

They listened, they grinned, their slanted eyes widened, and then they howled and drew their swords to hew limbs from the forest.

Timur with a picked handful emerged from the woods, and raced down into the plain, and toward the fields. He had all the musicians: and all were sounding off brazen trumpets and saddle drums and ear-slashing cymbals. Musicians on horse, musicians on camel back, and a picked troop of lancers: they moved at the pace of a polo game, Kipchak guards came from Kesh to welcome what they believed to be fellow invaders.

"Swords out!"

Though not caught entirely off guard, they might as well have been. They were cut down, and their horses galloped wildly home with empty saddles: and Timur resumed his bold race.

By now the gates of Kesh were closed. When Timur reined in, his archers shadowed him with a curtain of arrows. He demanded, "Surrender at once, and we'll let you march out alive."

A man in heavy Khorassan mail risked his head. Timur's archers ceased firing. The garrison commander came up to the parapet. The man was puzzled: a hundred horse seemed hardly the right force to take a walled town.

"You're crazy!" he raged. "Or drunk. Who are you?"

"Timur Bek, and what are you doing in my town?"

The bold challenge took the commander aback. "I am Daulat Ali, and I hold this in the name of Elias Koja, Khan of Samarkand, Son of Togluk Khan."

"You can become wealthy and famous by taking my head," Timur reminded him "Bikijek wants it badly."

Daulat Ali was no drill ground soldier; Bikijek didn't send that kind out to hold a town. Yet he was worried. There must be a sizable army on the way, and there had been no warning.

Timur went on. "March your garrison out. One hour's delay, and I'll have the head of every fifth man, taken by count, with no regard to rank."

"You can't take a town with that handful!" Daulat Ali retorted.

"Only Allah knows what is in my hand! Trifle a bit longer, and not one of you leaves alive. Quick, man! You're up on the wall. Look around. Do you want a siege, or do you think you'd like to try a sortie?"

On the four horizons, great columns of dust rose. Each was drawing toward Kesh. Citizens were now on the walls, some of Timur's own people. They began to yell, "Allah! Armies from Khorassan! Armies from Kabul!"

Rioting broke out within the town. Timur grinned when he heard the shouting. "I won't have to take your heads, they'll tend to that before I can save you fellows!"

Heaving water jugs and roofing tiles from housetops may annoy soldiers, but such civilian resistance rarely gets far. That was what worried Daulat Ali. Timur must have promised his people four armies, or they'd never be crazy enough to stone Kipchak hard cases.

Timur could now see the dust columns from the ground level. "If you move fast enough you'll have a chance to warn the apprentice king."

Turning the garrison loose, instead of taking them prisoner or cutting them down would give Elias Koja and Bikijek a nasty shock. Only a strong army could afford such a gesture of contempt. And Daulat Ali, already shaken, signaled to his trumpeters; they sounded recall.

The disarmed garrison filed out, and rapidly enough not to see that they had surrendered to dust clouds raised by horsemen dragging green branches.

And when Timur found Olajai, he said, "Home again, *shireen*, but only Allah knows how long we'll stay."

CHAPTER VI
KING-MAKER

By the time his spies had caught up with him, Timur realized that though he would quickly have to abandon Kesh he had at least succeeded in more than a personal enterprise: his daring capture of the city was bringing hundreds of one-time doubters to his standard.

And then Timur learned that Elias Koja's army, strongly reinforced by his father's troops, had moved out of Samarkand. They were going toward the Jihun, to make a clean sweep of the Jagatai lands and possibly to invade Khorassan.

So Timur and his newly won recruits got out of Kesh before Elias Koja's general, Bikijek, could learn that green branches had swept his garrison out of town.

Timur won the bridge with a few hours to spare. Then from the Khorassan side, he saw *touman* after *touman* of Kipchak troops, each 10,000 strong. The apprentice king's father was out for conquest. "Brother." Mir Hussein said, "our army will scatter like dust, once we start running. They'll forget that trick at Kesh."

"Then we won't run."

"We can't face 60,000 Kipchaks, not when Bikijek leads them."

Olajai came from behind the red carpet which, hanging from its long fringes, separated her quarters from the reception room of the pavilion. "Remember the horse tails, Timur!" she cut in.

Hussein turned on his sister. "You little fool, how long will Allah's patience last! Bluffing Bikijek is not quite the same as scaring a blockhead out of Kesh!"

Timur scowled. "I've got an army. One retreat, and they'll go back to their sheep."

"Yes, and just one bout with the Golden Horde, and they'll be minced mutton. You can't keep on recruiting on the strength of glorious defeats like the one at Kivak!"

"The horse tails," Olojai repeated. "The Presence!"

Timur rose. "We can hold the bridge for a day."

So he went to dispose his six thousand against ten times as many.

From sunrise to sunset, troop after troop of Kipchaks charged the bridgehead, taking their toll, but going down before the stubborn defense. Timur and Eltchi Bahadur plied mace and sword; and the sight and sound of them steadied the little army. Yet when the sun sank, they were tired and battered: wearied from the very cutting down of successive waves.

That night, spies swam the Jihun. In speech and dress and face, they matched the enemy; and they could mix freely, grumbling about the stiff resistance, and muttering about Timur's reserves, spread out, well behind the Jihun. And they muttered about the fall of Kesh....

Meanwhile, Timur was moving, He left only five hundred to hold the bridge: which picked men could do, for another day. The others divided, half going upstream, half downstream, well beyond hearing of the enemy, to risk the dangerous fords.

Bikijek could have made a similar attempt, but with his overwhelming force, it seemed far more sensible to hammer for another day, and drive through the troops who held the bridge.

Finally, there was the rumor of Timur's reserves; Bikijek was too good a general to risk being cut up in such fashion. Once he learned—

But Bikijek had no chance to learn.

Timur's losses by drowning were smaller than they could have been, had he and his captains not known every foot of the treacherous fords. Time and again, he went back, each time with a fresh horse, to lead the next detachment over. And on the final trip, he listened to a spy just returned: "Togluk Khan is dead! His son was about to go home when there was news of us."

Timur turned to Hussein, who commanded the final party.

"Allah is with us! There is a fear in Elias Koja. When he should go to Kipchak to receive the allegiance of his father's lords, and take the old man's throne, he stays here. The raid on Kesh has shaken him!"

Timur led his *hazaras* into the hills well behind the Kipchak camp. He spread them far apart. "Make fires," he commanded. "Many fires. As of many bivouacked *toumans*."

That night, he looked down on the fires of Bikijek's six *toumans*. And that night, Bikijek looked backward and upward at fires which suggested a force at least equal to his own: and a force which had slipped up between him, and Samarkand, and the long trail to Kipchak.

At dawn, with all his men carefully under cover in the woods at the foot of the slope, Timur watched Bikijek's scouts patrolling the river. The Kipchaks were worried; they had not resumed the attack on the bridgehead. Fires behind them at night, and now, they found hoof prints at the dangerous fords. As they saw it, Timur, with far more army than anyone had credited him with having, had held the bridge in order to make a night crossing to cut off their retreat, and so drive them into the river.

Bikijek's troops were soon in motion. First, they were going to withdraw; second, they were going to make the best disposition after what they considered a thorough outmaneuvering.

Then came Timur's charge: not from the distant line of the past night's campfires, but from the forest at the foot of the hills. Either too early, or too late, it could not have succeeded, despite the advantage of surprise; but Timur's lightning slash was timed to the second. He caught the Kipchaks when they were neither set for defense, nor fully committed to withdrawal.

Some tried to rush the bridge. Other *hazaras* fled along the bank. Those who tried to reform and fight it out were blocked by disorganized units. And Timur's troops picked the heart of the opposition: Bikijek's *touman*, and the force led by Tokatmur.

Elias Koja's standard went down before the rush. Tokatmur, second in command to Bikijek, fell under the fury of swords which followed the final flight of arrows. And it was like the moves of a chess game long reasoned out in advance: one-two-three, and checkmate.

The apprentice king escaped, and so did Bikijek, one leaving behind him a throne, the other losing an army. And when the trumpets sounded recall from cutting down the fugitives, Timur formed his troops and raced on to Samarkand.

As he rode back through the city from which he and Olajai had so narrowly escaped, the citizens who crowded the streets and packed the housetops, began to shout, "*Sahib Karan!* Lord of the Age!"

He had conquered a city by dust, and he had triumphed over an army by fire: and Olajai said, "When the Jagatai princes meet they'll make you Grand Khan of Samarkand."

She was right. Hussein had said as much; and the Barlas clan, Timur's uncle's kinsmen, were behind him. But as he rode toward the palace vacated forever by Elias Koja, Timur made plans of his own.

That night, serving men dragged monstrous trays into the banquet hall: camels roasted entire, and sheep; and there was horse-flesh, and leather trays heaped with rice and millet. Others set out jars of wine, and jars of fermented mare's milk, and flagons that only a Mongol could drain.

Eltchi Bahadur was there, roaring as on the battlefield; Hussein, sleek and smooth and handsome as a panther; and the Barlas clan, flat-faced, grim and slant-eyed; Turki and Mongol in silken tunic and silken *khalat*. Though Togluk Khan the tyrant had died a natural death, horsemen still raced northward to deny his son any chance of an equally quiet end.

It was complete; complete, except for two things: Timur Bek was not present, and the grand *khan*'s dais at the head of the great hall was empty. Lords and captains, beks and emirs, ranged in rank on either side, with that one high place vacant: election day in Samarkand.

Some laughed. Some muttered. Ali sniffed the savor of roasted meat, and wine ready for the drinking. But Timur, *Sahib Karan*, the Lord of the times, was late.

Then the drums rolled and the long trumpets brayed. Guards marched in, escorting a horse tail standard. In the courtyard soldiers shouted, "*Hai*, Bahadur! *Sahib Karan*, Timur, Grand Khan of Samarkand, Khan of the Jagatai!"

The uproar of the rank and file told the emirs and the beks how they had better vote; and they knew that wholesale desertions would follow an unpopular choice. Most of the Jagatai princes agreed with their men; but some scowled. For Timur to make a point of delaying his entry until all the others had arrived was laying it on too heavily; and for him to have the horse tail standard carried before him was taking too much for granted.

But the shouts from the court gave the lords no choice.

Then they saw who preceded Timur: a bearded man in the ragged robe of a darvish; a man who protested, a man who, though handled with respect, was being hustled into the hall, and toward the vacant high place.

At the foot of the dais, Timur halted with his barefooted companion. He raised his hand and the shouting ceased.

"O Men! In the days of your grandfathers, Kazagan Khan the Turk could have taken the throne of Samarkand but this he did not do; instead, he set up one of the blood of Genghis Khan, the Master of All Mankind, and used all his force to maintain one whom no one would deny or envy!

"Here is the darvish, here is the Guest of Allah, here is Kaboul Shah Aglen, directly descended from Genghis Khan's son Jagatai! Here is one who cares so little for power that he turns his back on thrones, and contemplates the splendor of Allah! Here is one with wisdom, not pride.

"Where we have each been kings, there has been no strength, and from too much freedom, we had an invader on our necks! So let this man be Grand Khan, for there is not one of us too proud to serve him!"

The shouting drowned the protests of the darvish. He could not deny his duty. They put an embroidered *khalat* over his ragged gown; they made him ascend the dais, and each prince in turn bowed nine times before him, as the ancient custom prescribed.

And when the banquet ended, the following noon, Timur Bek went to his own house, where Olajai waited.

"So you gave away a throne? After the Presence that came to you on the hill at Kivak?"

Timur was a little drunk, and he was tired, and he was hoarse from song and shouting. "He is the ninth generation, and all things go in nines with the race of Genghis Khan. Your brother and the others would soon turn against me—yet I can hold them together, serving him. And we won't have too many kings."

She looked up, smiling; her disappointment was gone. "The Presence will return to you, Timur." Then, just in the interests of discipline: "Allah, but you've slopped wine all over yourself, you're an awful looking mess for a King-Maker, you're as bad as my grandfather. You're ready to fall on your face!"

PEARL HUNGER

Albert Richard Wetjen

CHAPTER I

Captain James Travers roused himself with a mighty effort. He sat upright in his bunk sucking at the listless draught of hot air that drifted through the open porthole at his side. The sweat streamed from him in rivulets, his pajamas clinging to the flesh as the bathing suit clings to a swimmer just emerged from the water. Propping himself up with one trembling arm, the captain ran his hand across his forehead, and wiped the salty drops from his eyes. His head was swimming, and the aching at his temples made him almost scream. But driven by a spasm of fierce energy, he struggled upright from the bunk. Once on the carpeted deck, he groped through the darkness. Across the cabin, in the draw of a tiny writing desk, was a blue-steel automatic—and the captain wanted that weapon.

The touch of the cool metal seemed to revive the captain somewhat. He breathed deeply and started for the door.

The dull hum from the jungle that fringed the shores of the great bay came rifting down through the open skylight to the ears of the sick man. He heard, too, snatches of song, the tinkling of lazy guitars and bursts of drunken laughter from the direction of the Plaza of Lorenço Marques, a riot of color and hectic pleasure under the sullen tropic stars. The dockside lay in the shadows of the cranes and the cargo sheds, lit only by a solitary hurricane lamp glimmering from the head of the ship's gangway.

The captain flung back the half-open door and swayed into the saloon. He was forced to lean against the bulkhead as his heart commenced its passionate thumping again, and his eyes burned and throbbed. He could vaguely see the stars through the open skylight overhead, and even the dim tracery of the mizzen rigging outlined against the sky.

There was a blaze of light in the dark saloon as a door was flung violently open and a burly, white-suited man came forth, his head turned over his shoulder. A shining nickel-steel revolver twinkled from his right hand, while his left tucked under his arm a black tin ditty box, The low-brimmed sun-helmet the man wore obscured his face. Then the door slammed shut, and the man was gone, walking with stealthy haste up the companion to the poop deck, and so down the gangway to the wharf, where the shadows swallowed him.

He did not see the captain leaning against a stanchion with his automatic leveled. Nor did he see the fever beat fold upon fold on the sick man till he dropped the gun and sank sobbing to his knees.

The burly white-suited stranger saw nothing and heard nothing as he went away to life and to safety.

It was a long time before the captain got to his feet again. His face was streaming and drawn when he finally staggered to the door of the cabin from which the stranger had come. He opened it and looked inside. What he saw stiffened him for a moment. His slack jaw came up feebly and every fever-racked muscle tensed.

"All right, Billy," he whispered hoarsely. "All right. I'll square...."

Then, without warning, the fever shook him and laid him low. He choked and slipped to the deck, and the world faded from his eyes.

When the second mate of the barque *Wanderer* came aboard after a riotous time ashore, he found his captain unconscious in the open doorway of the mate's cabin. The mate stretched inside with his face kicked to a pulp and a bullet wound in his throat.

* * * *

Melita's Hotel, standing near Mulinu'u Point, about two miles from Apia, was the centre of the intricate intrigues that on occasions swept the Islands to life. Was there a schooner sunk for the sake of the insurance, was there a fine pearl discovered, did someone want someone else's wife or woman? Melita heard of the thing sooner or later, and she heard as well the deep undercurrents that swayed each affair. She knew not only the results achieved, which everyone knew sooner or later, but she also heard the way the results were won, the causes behind and beyond, secret whispered things not for the average islander to understand.

To Melita came the big pearl buyers, the island traders, the schooner captains, and the freelance adventurers whenever they wanted information about some man or woman or matter. And if Melita did not happen to have the information on the tip of her tongue, she had ways and means of soon acquiring it. And for the services she thus rendered she exacted her due, each man paying according to his ability as judged by the shrewd woman.

She was the daughter of an island adventurer, one of those hardy Scotchmen who stormed the savage Pacific in the old days, and tamed it, somewhat, for the younger generation to rule. Her mother had been a Tahitian princess of the blood, and the runaway match between her father and her mother had been ideally happy for both.

The Scotchman had died, as all men died in those days, violently, a spear passing through his throat in a long-forgotten fray on a long-forgotten island. The princess had gone after him into the Shadow with a broken heart soon after. For Melita there was nothing left but the mission school in Apia, where her father's friends accordingly placed her, and then forgot the whole affair.

In her sixteenth year, possessed of all her mother's glorious beauty, the girl had been courted by a notorious French adventurer who had finally induced her to run away with him, which she did, only to be stranded in San Francisco some two years later.

Her history from that time is uncertain. That she saw many people and places is known. She came back to the islands—her native blood made that inevitable—twenty-six, darkly beautiful, and with a refinement that was not to be learned in the home of the average European. Also she brought with her a fierce resentment of mankind that hid itself under a smiling exterior like the leopard's claws hide under the velvet pads.

She had started the hotel, and she had in time become the pivot round which the island life swung. Her fame ran far and wide, and with it the fame of her beauty.

All island roads led to Melita. If one spent long enough at the hotel, one would sooner or later meet everyone worth meeting between America and Australia. The island traders even made it a practice to purposely miss the tide of an evening, and thus be forced to anchor off the Point for a few hours before they could run into Apia. Not that the hotel was a place for the common sailor-man. There were such places in Apia itself. No one less than a ship's first officer was allowed inside. Melita's hotel, like Melita herself, was select.

CHAPTER II
A BRIBE REFUSED

One night an unwelcome guest climbed the pathway of the Point, and stopped at the top to light a cheroot. His fat body was glowing with the unaccustomed exertion of toiling up the slope, and his breath came in short, painful gasps. His height was perhaps five-feet ten; and what with his paunch and his heavy shoulders he looked a formidable man. He was Steinberger, the owner of the brig Atlantis, and one of the biggest pearl buyers and traders in the south.

Off the Point his brig was even then laying and swinging at anchor, while her officers cursed their employer at holding them up on the voyage while he went to visit a woman.

The beefy German waited until he had in some measure recovered his breath, and, mopping his brow with a white silk handkerchief, stepped up on the broad veranda of the hotel, pulled aside the heavy draperies that served as the house front in hot weather, and entered the big, dim-lit room beyond.

In three tall braziers incense was burning, the heavy blue fumes shrouding the room and making one cough when entering from the clean night air. Soft mats, cushions of various hues, divans and colored rugs were scattered everywhere in profusion, nearly all occupied by white duck-suited figures. The dozen or more ships anchored near Steinberger's brig told where they had come from.

Two native girls were plucking gently at some string instruments in a far corner shrouded in shadow, and others were moving softly about carrying trays or pitchers. All were dressed native fashion in girdles, beads, flowers. They wore nothing more.

On a great heap of gaudy cushions, in the centre of the room, reclined Melita. She was dressed in silk of some dark color, and her wonderful shoulders shimmered white beneath the soft glow from the dim lamps overhead. Half a dozen girls, each a beauty, reclined near, though one would rise now and then to execute some languidly given order.

Several men were sitting cross-legged by the pile of cushions, out-doing each other in praises and spinning fantastic yarns of some outlandish adventures for the delight of the laughing half-caste. Other men were lying dreamy-eyed in other parts of the room, sipping drinks or bestowing their attentions on some minor star of the notorious hotel.

The big German picked a careful way across the littered room, and handing his cap to an attendant, he came to a halt before the cushion dais half seen in the red lamp glow. Melita flung some laughing response to one of the men who had caught her hand and kissed it. With nothing but her great eyes showing above her fan she faced the newcomer. The fan was instantly lowered.

"Why, it is Wilhelm," she laughed gaily, and extended her hand to the other. With an attempt at gallantry the German removed his cheroot from his lips and stooped over the slim fingers, but before he could reach them they slipped from his palm. He stood up with a scowl, sneered at the assembled men about, and then looked insolently at the half-caste.

"I want to talk with you," he stated, jamming his cheroot back in his mouth and his hands in his pockets. It was many years since Steinberger had left the Fatherland, and he spoke with no appreciable accent.

Melita looked bored, but she rose just the same. Steinberger was one of the hotel's best customers, and she could hardly afford to offend him. His arrogant manner and insolent contempt for all women jarred on her, and some day she would send him away and bid him come no more; till then.... She shrugged and with a murmur of apology to the other men attending her she led the way to a room at the back end of the house, as exotically furnished as the big front room was. Steinberger closed the door behind him, and Melita sank easily onto a low divan.

* * * *

THE room was small, but a cunning arrangement of mirrors gave it an appearance of vast dimensions. On two sides the walls had been removed, for the sake of coolness, and copper mesh substituted. On the inside of this mesh hung flimsy, cloudy draperies that effectively prevented any one on the outside from seeing in.

Indifferently Melita waited for the German to begin. He pursed his thick lips, drew hard on his cheroot and breathed heavily. The butt glowed like an ember in the scented gloom, and then was obscured by the heavy smoke. The man could see the ravishing face of the half-caste turned to the floor and idly watching her little foot tracing circles on the rich matting.

"This is what, Melita," commenced the German, placing his cheroot in a nearby ash tray and dropping to the divan beside her, one of his fat hands covering hers. "I have come here to take your sister away, marry her if you like. I want her, and I've got to have her. See if you can't persuade her.... By the way, I've a present for you here!"

He dived into a side pocket, and brought forth a flat velvet case. Touching the catch he showed the woman the little rope of black pearls that reposed on their satin bed.

"For me?"

The German nodded and his piggy eyes narrowed a trifle.

"Collected by myself. Took five years to match. Worth a few dollars, eh?" he chuckled; and then taking them from her hand he fastened them round her throat.

She permitted him to kiss her once, and then she pushed him away. She did not care for Steinberger's embraces—for any man's embraces for that matter. Considering the fire she played with she got along very well without being burnt. Her beauty was such as to rather awe men.

"My sister?" she observed, as she patted the pearls into place. "Is she willing to marry you? Would my pleading make any difference?"

"She has a lover amongst her own people," growled the man savagely. "Some flashy young buck working on a plantation near Apia, I fancy. I'll break his neck if I ever catch him. Last time I offered to take her away from this she refused."

"Of course," observed Melita dryly, and reaching over to one side she struck a little gong. Almost instantly a girl appeared from the room they had just left. It was evident to Steinberger that the girl had been stationed outside the closed door. Melita always took precautions. She turned to the waiting man.

"Tia Kua, you say, Wilhelm?"

"Tia Kua," he muttered savagely; and, rising to his feet, picked up the smouldering cheroot from the ash tray and puffed it to life again. Melita gave a message to the waiting girl, who disappeared through some heavy curtains to one side of the room. Melita sank back on the divan, and eyed the flushed face of the man as he paced impatiently up and down.

"You are fond of women, Wilhelm," she murmured, after a while. The man came to an abrupt halt, sensing the contempt in her tone. He scowled and chewed on his cheroot before replying.

"What I want I get. If I take a fancy to a girl I'm not afraid to pay. You know that!"—with a meaning glance at the necklace that hung from her throat. Melita made a little grimace behind her fan, and her laugh was very soft.

"You have not got me, Wilhelm."

The man's eyes narrowed. He even laughed a trifle curtly.

"It is because I do not want you, yet. Some day I may come for you, instead of your sister."

The half-caste's eyes flashed in sudden anger, but she made no reply. The callous certitude of the man disgusted her. But he was one of the hotel's best customers, and it would not do to check him. It was rather amusing, anyway, to hear him wallowing in his own conceit.

The heavy curtains rustled, and a girl stepped into the room, a girl over whom, had she been white, artists would have raved and sculptors sworn away their souls. She was not very tall, but her slender form was perfect, as was every little feature. She was dressed differently than the rest of the hotel girls, in a sort of yellow silk sarong, caught under the left armpit by a large silver brooch. Her tiny feet were bare, flickering to view under the sarong's hem as she walked.

Her hair was strongly scented and adorned with flowers. The only thing to mar her was the faint blue tattooing that ran from the finger tips to the wrists, and from the soft breasts upward to the base of the throat, but barely visible against the golden-brown skin. Tia Kua was a full-blooded native girl, dark, passionate, lithe and young. Soon, in six or seven years, she would begin to wither and fade. But at the moment she was in the full glory of her seventeen years, a treasure of her sex. Though Melita was her half-sister—they both claimed the same mother—the difference between them was greater and deeper than mere lightness of color.

Steinberger went to meet the girl eagerly, his fat hands trembling and outstretched, a leer distorting his somewhat stubby features. Coolly the girl evaded him and approached Melita. For a moment the two women spoke together in the native tongue, Melita questioning and the other replying and shaking her head. Then the half-caste turned to the waiting German.

"No good, Wilhelm. She does not want you even if you marry her in the white man fashion. She is to be married to her lover the week after next, and they are both returning to their own country. Too bad. But you have a dozen prettier girls on your own island. Why bother about Tia Kua?"

The German swore harshly. He had conceived for the native girl, during his frequent visits to the hotel, one of those inexplicable passions that sometimes sweep men to the oblivion of everything else. As Melita said, there were many prettier native girls who would be only too glad of the chance to marry Steinberger. But perhaps that is why he did not want them, and did want the unobtainable. He continued to swear.

"So she refuses, eh? I'll take her, anyway!"

"Don't get angry, Wilhelm. This is apparently one of the things you don't get. Take your beating with good grace," laughed Melita, with a touch of mockery in her tone.

With a snort Steinberger turned to the girl and commenced offering her bribes. The gifts he promised would have turned the head of any girl—would have turned the head of Tia Kua under ordinary circumstances. But just then she was in love with a pair of languorous dark eyes and a broad-shouldered, muscular body that worked on the plantations outside Apia. She shook her head repeatedly. Steinberger ended up by cursing her in German and English and bêche-de-mer, until Melita interfered with a flash of spirit.

"Get out!" she snapped. "If you can't speak decently here, get out! And you'd better stay out. This is not your poop deck!"

With a snarl the German turned to go, but a sudden thought struck him. His eyes sought the black pearls dangling from Melita's throat, and he held out his hand meaningly. Calmly Melita unsnapped the little gold clasp, and placed the trinket in the fat hand waiting to receive it.

"So," she sneered, and her voice cut like a whip, "that was a bribe. You must be mad over Tia Kua. Women will be your death, Wilhelm."

Swearing beneath his breath the German stamped out of the room, and getting his cap made his way down the Point path to the beach, while the assembled schooner captains and mates in the big room nodded to one another and smiled significantly.

CHAPTER III

THE MAN-HUNTER

The next morning Tia Kua was missing from the hotel, and Steinberger's brig was missing from the anchorage. He had come out of Apia the previous day, and was bound for some unknown destination. Not one of the schooner captains could or would say where.

A grinning Samoan delivered a note at the hotel about two hours after dawn. With quick, nervous fingers Melita ripped open the envelope, and drew out the single sheet of paper it contained, a leaf from a notebook. In Steinberger's sprawling hand was written:

"What I want I get! This time your sister; next time you!"

Melita's face went white with passion. There were still four men in the big room who had not yet rejoined their ships, and she read the note to them. They laughed uproariously, until their eyes were wet and their sides ached. That was Steinberger's way, they explained.

Melita eyed them with disgust. Had it been a white woman who had been abducted she knew that the captains would in all probability have hastened into Apia to inform the authorities. But a native woman! A common native woman! Why, such could be picked up off a thousand and one islands all over the Pacific, and the majority of them were only too anxious to become associated with one of the all-powerful white men. Most likely the kidnapped girl had been half willing to go.

The schooner men were a little puzzled, when they came to talk it over, why Steinberger should have gone to the trouble of abducting the girl at all. He must have been crazy over her. Then they shrugged their shoulders, and told each other that it was none of their business, but that it was a good joke anyway.

And they left Melita to her anger, while they went on board their ships to explain to grinning mates and supercargoes Steinberger's latest folly.

Melita was nearly speechless with rage. She paced her room fiercely, her lips white and her eyes glowing. She refused to be calmed for a long time. That Steinberger—fat, greasy Steinberger—had defied her, treated her like a plaything that waited on his purposes, was intolerable. She who swayed the affairs of all the Pacific treated like a common native, her sister abducted to be Steinberger's mistress!

But she could not move hand or foot to checkmate the German. There were admirers of hers, of course, who would at her word attempt to restore her her sister, but there were only two or three actually powerful enough in the islands to attempt it with any hope of success, and none were handy. Melita could only wait and hope that Tia Kua was not being treated too badly.

* * * *

TWO weeks later a strange ship beat up to the anchorage off the Point and hove to. Melita was frankly puzzled as she watched the beautiful streaming lines and the swan-like grace of the anchoring barque. The tide was yet high, and there was plenty of time to make Apia before it fell. The ship, too, was not a regular caller at the hotel. Melita did not remember ever having seen it before. Whoever was coming to see her was coming for that purpose alone, and not making just a casual call.

A boat dropped from the barque's near side and sped across the intervening water to the shore. Presently a man came up the winding pathway. Even Melita, who was used to all sorts of men, caught her breath sharply. For this man was not the usual shipmaster. He was not gray and a little bent, with the flesh of the neck lightly grooved into squares and lines. He did not lag in his step, nor did the long climb seem to affect his breath very much. He was young and tall, and well worth looking on. Unlike the usual island shipmaster, he was dressed in a thin uniform of blue serge, with the gold braid of his rank on the cuffs, and a gold ship badge in the center of his blue peaked cap. The cap itself was perched far back on his head, exposing a thick crop of wavy gold-brown hair, and a face as tanned as that of any kanaka. A pair of laughing blue eyes held Melita's for a moment, and then hardened a little. The man rested one hand on his hip, and with the other removed his cap from his head. He bowed a trifle.

"Is this the house where Melita lives?" he asked pleasantly enough, though there was that in his voice—a suppressed hardness—that showed he was a man used to command.

Melita was curious. The stranger interested her. She had never seen him before, and she thought she had seen every shipmaster in the Pacific. He looked clean, too, which was more than most of the men she knew did. He was more of a man to like the sea and the sun and the stars at night than the perfumed rooms of the hotel, or some easy amour with native girls in their own villages. He glowed with health, and his lips were firm, which showed that drink had not got him under control. Yes, Melita was curious.

"I am Melita," she said. The man raised his head and smiled, replacing his cap. He came forward a pace.

"May I speak with you alone? My name is James Travers— Captain James Travers. I command and own the barque *Wanderer*, laying out there in the roadstead."

Melita waved away her attendant women, more curious than ever, and motioned the stranger to sit in the swing chair on the veranda beside her. The man nodded and came forward, seated himself carelessly and, crossing one leg over the other, held his knee with clasped hands, rocking to and fro the while. He eyed the woman seriously, and with not a little interest. He had heard her spoken of from China to Australia. She was a character.

"I am looking for a man," he commenced abruptly. "His name is, or was, Brietmann, and he is, or was, half owner of the brig Hamburg, registered at Cape Town. Except that he's big built and inclined to be fat I can give no description of him. Two years ago in

Fu Chow the port captain of one of the big lines informed me that a man named Brietmann had been fined the year before for dangerous sailing while anchoring near other ships. From Fu Chow Brietmann took papers for Apia with the intention, it was said, of going on the island trade. I was told you were acquainted with every shipmaster and trader in the Pacific. Can you help me?"

Melita withdrew her eyes with an effort from the man's face, and conned over in her mind a list of the men she knew. She was silent for so long that the man sneered and, reaching in his pocket, drew forth a piece of wash leather. Unwrapping it he held before the woman's gaze a magnificent ruby that sent blood fires dancing and leaping in reflection in her eyes.

"I'll give this to know," he said, thinking she was reckoning what the information would be worth. Melita looked at the ruby, and put out a hesitating hand. Then her eyes grew hard. The sailor, watching keenly, laughed a little, guessing what she was thinking.

"You can take it. No condition attached, except that you give me the information I need. I just want to know where Brietmann hangs out. No one knew in Suva, no one knew in Papeete. Do you know? I shall not say who gave me the information, if that is what's worrying you."

Melita slipped the stone inside her bodice with sudden decision. It was a princely reward.

"I can't think of anything or anyone right now," she said frankly. "I may later on. There are several big, fleshy men who own brigs in the islands.... But come inside and try my tea. I had it shipped from Yokohama.... Unless you'd prefer whisky?"

The sailor hesitated. He looked down the slope to where the barque lay at anchor, rising and falling to the swell. He looked to the sky away to windward.

"Good wind blowing, and I hate to lose any of it," he muttered to himself. "I'm sailing for Calloa light, to pick up a cargo there," he said aloud. "Nitrates for England. I can't waste much time." Then he looked at Melita, and his decision faltered and died. She was beautiful, and even a man who does not care for women cannot but admire beauty.

Besides, she was the famous Melita, and the sailor was more than half curious to probe into her mentality a bit to see how she came to be so. He stood up from the swing chair abruptly, removing his cap.

"I'll take tea," he said, his voice a little more mellow than it had been.

The experienced Melita smiled a little to herself. She could see the sailor was growing interested in her. She was a new type to him. He, who had sailed far and wide, had battled with wind and water and men, was naturally inclined to be carelessly at ease with all women. He had them classified into two great classes—the thoroughly lost and the thoroughly saved—and each class was as bad as the other.

But Melita defied classification. He remembered that men had told him that she had never been any man's since the break-up of her girlhood romance with that early French adventurer. He grew frank as they sat cross-legged in the now deserted big room and drank tea together from tiny fragile cups, with the fumes of the incense wreathing about their heads.

CHAPTER IV
VENGEANCE TRAIL

"I never met a woman quite like you, Melita. Most women who enter this—this sort of thing"—he waved an expressive arm around—"are apt to become coarse. You dress with taste, you talk with an accent that was learned in London, if I am not mistaken, and you have the manners of a wise old society matron. I conclude you have traveled and mixed with good people."

She nodded absently, her eyes on his corded throat, wondering what it would feel like to the touch, warm and throbbing with life, probably rippling as it moved with the muscle-life beneath the clear skin. She had forgotten to be languid and indifferent.

"Then what are you doing here? You can't be broke and unable to get away. If you are, that ruby will put you on your feet."

Melita roused herself with an effort, and tapped him on the lips with her fan. "My friend, you are encroaching on the secret places of the heart. And why should I worry you with my story? It is the usual and the sordid. A young girl, something of a fool, her head turned by flattery, and a man who had no honor. What men have?"

she sighed, and was silent for a while. "Rest assured I have reasons for staying here and playing with the fools who come.… Take care, my friend, it is not good to know Melita too much." She finished with a light laugh and looked at him.

He nodded seriously, and then grinned. "The fruits of vengeance, eh? Well, I'll tell you. I believe I'm immune from heartbreak, and I don't believe I have a soul to wreck."

Again Melita knew a sudden desire to touch the corded throat and run her fingers through the wavy hair. So strong was the impulse she leaned forward a little, and then caught at her lower lip with her teeth. Travers was busy lighting a battered briar pipe, and when he looked up, noticing nothing, the woman had recovered herself. But she was shaken inwardly. She had never met a man who affected her so.

"Perhaps you would like to look around," suggested the woman, "while I write you a list of the brig owners and captains I know of. The name Brietmann is unknown to me, but—"

"It is possible my man has changed his name. He had cause to," put in the sailor grimly.

Melita nodded. "That was what I was thinking. Perhaps one of the brig captains I know may be your man. The name Brietmann sounds German. There are five Germans who own their own ships. But I'll give you a list. You can make further inquiries as to the length of time each has been in the islands. That's something I'm not acquainted with. Pardon me!"

The sailor nodded, while the woman went off to find a pencil and paper. Left alone in the big room, Captain James Travers whistled softly to himself. He grinned as he wandered round, inspecting the braziers, quaintly moulded, and the pictures that hung here and there on the walls.

Presently he came to a sort of sideboard set in a corner farthest from the veranda, which could be seen through the curtains that served as a house front, and were tied back in the day time. The sideboard was a long affair of mahogany, richly inlaid and carved, with drawers below the serving shelf and a large square of beveled looking-glass above. There were whale's teeth, purple with age; shark's backbones, polished and varnished and worked into the form of walking sticks; a small whale's vertebra; pearl shells, and other shells of all sorts and colors; a piece of fossilized wood from far-off Guinea; native spears and other weapons; necklaces of babies' skulls, and many other curios the admirers of Melita had brought from the Shining Paths to swell her collection.

But what drew the sailor's attention, what wiped the grin from his face and the warmth from his eyes, was the sight of a neat, bright nickel-steel revolver placed in a far corner of the shelf, half hidden behind a monstrosity of a devil-devil mask from Fiji.

Slowly the sailor removed his pipe. He did not feel the hot bowl burn his hand. Nor did he hear the swish of skirts as Melita came softly behind him and started as she caught sight of the reflection of his savage face in the glass. His free hand went out and picked up the revolver, and he turned it over and over in his palm. Finally he held it muzzle down and looked at the initials carved on the bottom of the butt. He started violently as Melita touched his arm and swung round.

"What is it?" she asked curiously.

"Who gave you this?" he demanded savagely, his lips drawn back from his teeth. He rammed his pipe in his pocket and caught the woman's shoulder. "Tell me!"

Melita looked at the bright weapon, and then wonderingly at the sailor. "That was given me by Steinberger," she said steadily. "He told me it had a history. I never found out what."

The sailor let go her shoulder with a bitter laugh, and slipped the revolver in his pocket. "History? Yes, it has a history.… Where does Steinberger live? Where can I find him? Who is he in the islands?"

"Steinberger is a big trader and pearl buyer. He owns and commands the brig Atlantis."

"With a Medusa figurehead and scroll work all down the forefoot?" Melita nodded, her eyes wide with dread. "All right, go on."

"… and has a trading station at Funafuti Lagoon in the Ellice Islands."

"That's enough for me," said the sailor with an oath, and he strode toward the veranda, his face flushed with passion. Melita ran after him and caught at his sleeve.

"Sit down for a moment. There's something I want to say." Her voice was cold and commanding. She, too, had a temper.

The sailor halted, looked down at her, hesitated, and then slowly returned to the cushioned dais where the empty tea cups still stood. He dropped moodily down on crossed legs and picked up his cap. He had forgotten it before. Melita sank beside him.

"I presume this Brietmann you spoke of is Steinberger," commenced Melita abruptly, her fan resting on the sailor's arm as though to hold him still. "I don't know what lies between the two of you, but I can guess that Steinberger's been up to some more of his deviltry.... Will you do something for me for the information you've got, in place of this ruby?"

She brought the red stone to light and slipped it into the angry sailor's palm. He looked at it stupidly for a moment, and then back at the woman. He commenced to say something, but changed his mind. He waited.

"Will you?" the woman persisted.

"Depends what it is," the sailor muttered. "What is it? Yes, I'll do it. Do anything out of gratitude for the information."

"Then listen!" And Melita told the other how Steinberger had abducted her sister. Melita could use language that cut like a knife, and the story she told was not pretty hearing the way she put it. The man almost forgot his own trouble. He saw the point at once.

"You want your sister?" Melita nodded, and leaning back she opened her fan and slowly waved it to and fro. Her own cold passion had exhausted her. The sailor looked at her and then held out his hand.

"That's a bargain," he said curtly. "Steinberger will have no use for women after I've seen him. If your sister is alive, you shall have her back. Expect me any time. Good bye!"

He rose to his feet, jammed on his cap, and with a brief handshake was gone, leaping from the veranda in his haste and running down the pathway to where the boat lay waiting to take him aboard his ship. The clank of the anchor cable came up to the hotel through the breeze, and one by one the barque's sails were hoisted. In two hours she was hull down and sailing fast.

Melita dropped to the cushions when the sailor had gone, and she cried—she who had not cried in years. In her heart strange forces were stirring—forces that had lain dormant since her first lover had kissed her over the mission wall in Apia. Then, after a while, she rose and went out on the veranda to watch the barque running from the coast and from sight. Then she cried again and wished she were clean. Who was she to dream of love?

It was not till nightfall, when the lamps were lit and the schooners from all the Pacific began to drop anchor off the Point, that Melita found the ruby Travers had left among the cushions. She wrapped it tight in its washleather bed and snuggled it close to her heart, torn with fears for the safety of the man she had only known for a brief hour.

Not one of the captains guessed what was passing in the mind of the woman who laughed a little too freely, and who seemed to be in such a cynical mood when they jested with her that night.

CHAPTER V
OUTWARD BOUND

Captain James Travers sat in his saloon beneath the poop deck of the *Wanderer*, and smoked in thoughtful silence. Occasionally he would unclasp his hands from behind his head and, removing his pipe, blow a cloud of smoke up at the lamp that swung uneasily in its gimbals directly above his head.

Now that the first hot rage and exultation of his discovery had died, the sailor was very much at his ease, in spite of the uneasy pitch and chop of the deck as the barque lifted herself over the somewhat short swell and snorted into the trough and into the teeth of a brisk wind, for she was now close-hauled.

His coat was flung over the bunk that stood against the after bulkhead, his cap was perched on a large inkwell that stood on the table, and near it his feet rested and were crossed. He was tilted back in a swivel chair, and his eyes were dreamily fixed on a point that certainly was not in the saloon. He had been sitting thus, reflectively, since the soft-footed Jap steward had removed the supper things and retired to the pantry, half hidden by the butt of the mizzen-mast that ran down through the forward portion of the poop deck.

Travers was worried. He could not forget Melita. It was preposterous he should so persistently remember a woman he had seen for scarce an hour. He had sailed to Samoa expressly to meet a half-caste adventuress, whom, so men had told him, had knowledge of every sailor in the Pacific at her finger tips.

Travers was usually distrustful of such women, on his guard against them when with them, and he had disliked the idea of enlisting the half-caste's services. But the chance of picking up Brietmann's trail, three years old from Fu Chow, had been very alluring, and the debt he had to pay for the death of the one-time mate of the *Wanderer* was long overdue.

And because of these things Travers had run across the sea to Melita. And he had found not the coarse-lipped woman he had expected, but a passionate, cultured woman, albeit a bitter one. Toward him she had softened somewhat.

He could think of that without conceit. For he had not tried to make love to her, to name conditions for his gifts. He was feeling strangely softened toward her himself. She must have had a hard life, and the world was, after all, a rotten place for a beautiful woman. They rubbed against more of the dirt than their plain sisters. They drew men, and the worst kind.

Melita was beautiful; there was no doubt of that. And her skin was as fair as any white woman's, for all her native blood. Not a trace of the kanaka in her, except for the big, dark eyes. It was her face Travers had been seeing for so many years, since he had been old enough to dream of romance. Such a face had disturbed his sleep time and again. The ideal woman! Every man has his ideal woman, and the face of Travers' ideal was the face of Melita. Known her for an hour? He had known her for years! He sighed.

He supposed he was in love. And he thought of the daisy-encircled cottage that every sailor thinks of when he thinks of marriage and love. The sea had been a hard mistress, but if she had led him to his woman the service had been fully repaid. He remembered, too, that men had said she had been no man's woman since her return to the islands. Why should not the two of them start again, together? He smiled whimsically, and with sudden decision swung his feet off the table. He was a creature of impulse to a very large extent.

* * * *

"Toby!" he called lazily. The soft-footed Jap steward appeared after a while, and stood before his captain. "Send the mate down here."

Without a word the steward padded away to the poop deck above, and presently the clatter of shoes on the companion that led from the saloon announced the mate's arrival. He was a gray-haired man, very much tattooed about the hands, with a wrinkled parchment-like skin that gave the impression of great age, or a long time spent in the tropics. He was tall and very thin, and the corners of his big mouth drooped in a melancholy fashion under his fringe of moustache.

He had once been the commander of a famous liner, but drink and recklessness had brought him down to take any job that offered among the trading ships of the seven seas. Travers had picked him up in Sydney when he had been broke, and had given him a chance to get on his feet again. He was a wonderful navigator, and knew most seas like a book, wherefore he was a useful man to have aboard.

"Ever heard of Steinberger, Everett?"

The mate thought for a moment, and, removing his cap, scratched his somewhat bald head. He frowned.

"Seems I have. He's a trader or something in these parts, sir."

"Yes, that's so. We're going to visit him. Mark off the course to the Ellice group, Everett; and then make Funafuti Lagoon."

"Yes, sir." The mate turned to go, replacing his cap.

"Oh, Everett!"

"Sir." The mate hesitated with one foot on the companion and turned half around.

"I'm thinking of getting married!"

"Married?"

"Yes. Just thinking, you know."

"Oh, yes, sir.... Is that all, sir?"

"That's all.... Say, Everett, see if there's any book in the chart room with the marriage service in it, will you?"

"Very well, sir." The mate whistled to himself as he went upon the poop and faced the battering wind. He wondered. Travers grinned to himself, swung his feet on to the table again, and went on dreaming.

CHAPTER VI
CAPTURED

Steinberger was at home at Funafuti. The *Wanderer* swept into the great lagoon, and came to anchor about a quarter of a mile from the shore. The Atlantis lay beached some half a mile away, and a crowd of natives were busily engaged in scraping from her hull the foot-long grasses and the clotted barnacles from her scanty keel. Travers looked at the brig through his glasses and swore harshly.

"Medusa figurehead and scroll work all down the forefoot," he muttered. "Breitmann changed her name, but he couldn't change her markings. Swine!"

The mate came from for'ard after letting go the anchor, and crossed the poop to his captain. "Going ashore, sir?"

Travers nodded as he dropped the glasses back into the rack. He felt in his pocket to make sure he was armed. "Lower away the port boat. And, Everett … if anything happens to me, you'll find a letter in my room that'll tell you what to do."

The gray-haired, wise mate looked at his superior sharply. "Perhaps you'd like to take some of the men with you, sir," he suggested. "They like you well enough to stand by you."

Travers shook his head. "This is a private quarrel, Everett. I'd rather not have witnesses."

"Aye, aye, sir." And the mate touched his cap and turned obediently away to see that the boat was lowered.

The beach was a thing to wonder at, a magnificent sweeping curve, nine miles from tip to tip. Among the groves of coco-palms that fringed the sand could be seen the huts of the principal village. A few frigate birds were lazily sailing above the lagoon. Other life, except for those careening the brig, there was none. Funafuti brooded drowsily beneath the hot breath of noon.

Leaving the boat waiting in the shallows, with orders to push on if he did not return within an hour, Travers walked along the path that led to the trader's house set in a grove of jack-fruit trees, that themselves nestled among a denser grove of palms. His face was set and ugly to look upon, and his right hand rested inside his pocket gripping something hard and cold.

He was still dressed in the light blue serge he affected, disliking the white duck most ship's officers wore, and his peaked cap was still set back on his head, exposing the wavy hair.

Clear to the door of the trader's house Travers went, and with a thrust of his foot swung it open and entered, to find himself in a high-ceilinged room, large and square, with native mats on the floor, an iron bed with the usual mosquito drape in one corner, large square holes in the walls in place of windows, and other doors leading to rooms here and there.

A tall, slender girl was busily engaged in cleaning a large bore sporting rifle to one side of a plain deal table, on which lay cloths and various bottles of oil and jars of grease. She looked up startled as Travers entered and placed her finger to her lips.

One of Steinberger's numerous wives, Travers thought, a trifle grimly. She was a beauty in her way, olive-skinned, big-eyed and black-haired, like most of the island women. Travers politely lifted his cap, though the action was not usual with natives. Sympathetically, he noted the black bruises on the slender wrists, and the angry red weal across the bare breast. It was too plain that Steinberger still remembered some things about his Fatherland.

With a murmured greeting the girl rose from her knees, and again placing her finger to her lips glanced across the room, part of which was hidden from Travers by reason of the open door.

Travers closed the door and looked around. Steinberger was hunched up in a long cane chair, dressed only in his pyjamas and snoring gently. A two-days' growth of beard colored his pink, big-pored face, and an empty "square-face" bottle on the table near the oil bottles showed how he spent his time.

His hands were clasped across his swelling stomach, and his double chin rested on his chest. Travers looked at him long and intently, for he had never seen the face before, and he could not tell after all the years whether the heavy shoulders were the same that he had seen in the saloon of the *Wanderer* that night of fever, death and of anger in Lorenço Marques, Delagoa Bay.

Travers savagely kicked the sleeping man's shins, while the native girl moaned with terror. She expected the stranger to be annihilated for his presumption.

With a tremendous start the sleeping man awoke. He sucked in his breath sharply, brushed a fat hand across his eyes, and scrambled to his feet. Travers was an inch shorter than the German, and he seemed completely dwarfed. Steinberger glared.

"Who the blazes are you? Did you kick me?" he demanded wrathfully, half raising his hand. Travers gritted his teeth, and jammed the muzzle of the revolver he had been nursing into the German's paunch.

"Keep your confounded mouth shut and sit down," he grated harshly. "I want to talk with you. My name's Travers—Captain James Travers, brother to William Travers."

Steinberger collapsed back in his chair as though he had been shot. In his agitation he swore in German, and started suddenly to tremble.

"*Gott in himmel!* I ... you ... why, are you ... What do you want?"

Travers lowered his revolver and stepped back a little. He drew up a chair and sat down, his eyes never leaving the German's face. After a moment, during which nothing could be heard save the quick breathing of the men and the low moaning of the native girl, Travers laid down the revolver on the table at his side. Steinberger snarled and turned his head.

"Stop that whining! Gott! Get out of here!" The native girl shrank back against the wall, but did not speak. Steinberger turned to Travers again. His thick lips were working frightfully, and his fat hands gripped and let loose of the chair arms alternately, the cane squeaking as it was so kneaded. Travers laughed—not a pleasant sound to hear.

"I need not ask if you are Steinberger," he commenced. "But the time I want to talk to you about is a time when you went by the name of Brietmann. Remember it?"

The other man controlled himself with an effort, and a crafty gleam appeared in his eyes. The chair arms squeaked under their kneading.

"What are you talking about? Are you mad? Brietmann? Who is he? I am Steinberger, and anyone in the islands will vouch for me."

"So you deny you were once known as Brietmann—Brietmann who had a half share in and sailed the big Hamburg, the ship you now call the Atlantis?"

"Of course I am not Brietmann! I'm Steinberger, as you'll find out when I have you arrested for pulling a gun on me in my own house."

"Then perhaps you will explain this," said, Travers softly, his eyes narrowing to slits. He motioned towards the nickel-steel revolver on the table. "You'll find the initials 'W. T.' on the butt.... No, you needn't try and look. You're not getting your hands on that gun.... 'W. T.,' you understand? You gave that gun to Melita, boasting it had a history. It has. It's going to have a further history. It's going to kill you!"

"Donner und blitzen! You are mad!" In his excitement the man forgot his carefully cultivated English. "Vat for you want to kill me? Vat do I know of your brother?—did you not say he was your brother? I mean—Himmel! ... Why you look so? Dis is a plot— vat you call a trap, eh? Melita send you to get her sister, an' you make up this excuse. Vat do I know of Travers?"

"Sound like an innocent man, don't you, Brietmann? That night you came aboard the *Wanderer*, thinking all hands were ashore except my brother, I was lying sick with fever in the next cabin. You didn't know that, did you? If you had you'd have come and killed me.... You stole my brother's wife, you swine, and then you had to come and try to get the little money Bill was saving for her. You have nerve all right, Brietmann; I'll say that. To come and tell Bill you had ruined his wife and wanted her legacy from her father. You banked on Bill being a cripple, didn't you? ... Lucky for you I wasn't on my feet that night—and you knew you were the stronger man.

"So you mocked him, and then you robbed him, and when he tried to fight for his honor's sake you knocked him down and kicked his face. He would have shot you, but you were too quick. You shot him instead, with his own gun. There it is—on the table, Brietmann. Sure it has a history.... By God, I could kill you with my naked hands!"

Travers had half risen to his feet in his rage, quivering with passion, his hands opening and closing, his lips drawn clear back from his teeth.

The German rose too, quaking, and shivered back. But his voice blustered and pleaded.

"Ged oud of here! You'll hang—you'll hang for it if you kill me. Mein Gott! I call and twenty men run to kill you!"

The native girl crossed the room and laid a restraining hand on the German's arm. Her big eyes were soft and appealing, and she spoke in a gentle tone, not understanding the forces at work within the two men. It was apparent she loved the shaking man; such is the strangeness of women.

Steinberger shook her off with a snarl, and caught her across the mouth with the back of his hand. Like a whipped dog she crept away, a dumb wistfulness in her eyes, her hands covering her bleeding lips.

The incident steadied Travers, and he straightened with a short laugh. He motioned to the German to sit down, and himself resumed his seat.

"I'm not ready to kill you yet, Brietmann," he said. "I want to tell you first how I've trailed you, port to port, sea to sea, for seven years. I found Mary, my brother's wife, deserted in Australia just two years after you'd stolen her. She was nursing your child then; you'd left them to starve. How many women you've wrecked since then I don't know. But I wager the count's long. As to hanging, there isn't a jury in the world that would convict me. You know it, and I know it. You've got to face it, Brietmann, and try and go out like a man. Seven years I've followed you, and the trail ends right here. It started in Africa, and ends in the islands. I think that's all. Say your prayers."

The Germans' hand crept nervously to his throat. He licked his lips and choked a little. The sweat poured from him in streams as the liquor he had gone to sleep with died within him.

"Mein prayers?" he whispered hoarsely, rising slowly to his feet again. He looked monstrous in his loose pyjamas. Travers rose with an air of finality. He stretched out a hand for the revolver, and then the German sprang.

With a cry like a wild beast he came forward, his great hands reaching for a throat hold and his knees driving for the stomach. Without any great haste Travers stepped to one side and sent the huge, flabby body across the room with a smashing right-hand blow. Steinberger crashed against the wall, and shook the hut to its foundations. He slowly picked himself up, bruised all over and panting with the fear of death. He glanced up wildly, and the oaths fell from his lips in a continuous stream.

Then Travers raised his revolver—the revolver that had shot William Travers seven years before—and prepared to do what he had come to do, what he had crossed the world for, without compunction and without haste. He took aim.... A cold muzzle pressed into the nape of his neck, and a harsh voice spoke:

"Easy, sonny, easy. Put 'em up!"

* * * *

Steinberger wiped his bloody lips and laughed as he scrambled to his feet.

"Keep him there, Walters, till I get him tied," he wheezed breathlessly, and lumbered groggily off into a corner, where he cut a fathom or so of line from a coil of halliard standing there. Coming back he securely tied the raging Travers hand and foot. Then, knocking him down, he beat a tattoo on his ribs with his naked foot, and ground his face into the matting of the floor until the skin was off and the blood ran from the nose.

Travers caught a glimpse of the man who had held him up, a sullen-faced, skinny individual with a heavy black beard and watery blue eyes. From his stained white uniform evidently an officer of the Atlantis. He was grinning with amusement as Steinberger tortured his captive.

The German bent and slapped Travers' face. "So, Melita give you the gun, eh? And I suppose she told you about her confounded sister and me?

I'll get that—! I'll break her now.... You, I'll see you later!"

Travers kept his teeth together to prevent him crying out, and the hot rage within him flamed and leaped. He wished he had shot the German and not waited to talk. He scarce gave heed to

Steinberger's words about Melita's sister, for he had well-nigh forgotten her. But the mention of Melita herself, of getting even with her....

Travers squirmed and writhed and tugged at his bonds. Steinberger laughed triumphantly as he straightened up and wiped his forehead with a hand that still trembled.

"I'll bring Melita here, and you'll see us married native fashion. Then I shall get rid of you and your talk of Bill Travers."

Steinberger bundled his prisoner into a back room and locked him in, after a few parting kicks. Then buckling on his holsters, after dressing himself, he went down on the beach, talking energetically with Walters, the black-bearded officer, and planning the next few moves ahead in the game that had suddenly broken upon him.

CHAPTER VII
"I AM TIA KUA"

Travers lay and ached in every limb, and wondered what was to happen next. He cursed himself for being such a fool as not to let Everett and some of the men guard his rear while he talked to Steinberger. He had been confident of his strength, too blind with his own passions to plan coolly, and this was the result. Himself helpless, and Steinberger off to abduct Melita as he had abducted her sister.

He cursed as the sound of shots drifted through the open window. He guessed that Steinberger had found the waiting boat in the shallows. Would he kill every soul aboard the barque? There were no more shots, and for a long while there was silence, broken only by the lisp of the surf and the roar of the wind through the swaying palms. There was nothing left for Travers to do but wait, and waiting is hardest of all.

A murmur of voices came to the prostrate sailor's ears after a while, and then a body of men came up the path from the beach and stamped into the next room. There were two heavy thuds and a groan, as some bulky objects were lowered to the floor. Then the party stamped out again with a few coarse jests, and the sound of crunching steps on the coral sand of the path died away.

Travers strained his ears toward the next room and caught a muttered oath. He sighed with relief. He would have recognized Everett's voice anywhere.

"That you, Everett?" he called softly. There was silence for a moment.

"Yes. Is that you, sir?"

"Aye.... Are you hurt?"

"No, not much to speak of. Was rushed by about a dozen kanakas and handled pretty rough. They laid out the boat's crew, and came aboard in the boat. I cut loose with a gun when I saw what was happening, but they were too quick." The mate cursed bitterly again, and Travers could be heard writhing about the floor.

"I suppose you're bound hand and foot?" said Travers hopelessly.

"Yes, sir." The mate ceased trying to loosen his lashings. "Stevens is here, bound as well. He's had a crack over the head, and is still unconscious."

"What have they done with the crew?"

"Last I saw of them was swimming for the beach. The big fat man ordered them pitched overboard. He seems to have taken charge of the barque. Is that Steinberger?"

"That's the man.... Say, I'm sorry you fellows are being dragged into this mess."

"O. K., sir. It's all in the day's work."

No more was said. Travers and the mate bent every energy to trying to free themselves. After a while the captain gave up and relaxed, breathless and sweating, his wrists bleeding from his struggles. A faint cutting noise caught his ear. After several attempts he jerked to an upright position and listened, his eyes roving round the bare-walled room. Then he caught sight of the thin knife blade moving in and out through the wall that separated the room from one farther back in the house.

After a while a sort of slot had been cut in the soft wood, and then a slim brown hand appeared and wrenched off large splinters, enlarging the slot until it was a considerable hole, large enough to crawl through. A brown body appeared and, after some trouble, squeezed into the room. A native girl crossed to the astonished and wondering Travers.

She placed her finger on her lips and knelt down, so that her mouth was against the man's ear. He felt the tickle as her lips moved.

It was evident from her quivering that she was very much afraid and that she did not know Steinberger had gone. It was also evident she had had dealings with him, for her arms and breasts were bruised, as those of the girl Travers had seen on first entering the trader's house.

"I hear him say Melita send you. I am Tia Kua," she whispered, and then the sailor knew a vast relief. He grinned as much as his shattered face would allow, and nodded at his bonds.

The girl fumbled with the knots in the signal halliard, and in a few minutes Travers was free.

He rose to his feet, stretched his arms above his head, felt himself tenderly all over, and then patted the girl reassuringly on the shoulder. Ignoring her pleas for quiet, he then kicked down the door of the room that confined him, and quickly released Everett.

It was some time before the two of them could restore the unconscious Stevens to life, but eventually they managed it, and prepared to leave. They searched for weapons, and found plenty to their satisfaction. Travers came across a wallet of paper money in a drawer and handed it to Tia Kua, telling her to keep it as some sort of compensation for what she had been subjected to. Then all four of them went out on to the veranda and started down the path to the beach.

They had not gone more than a dozen yards when they met Walters, the black-bearded officer of the Atlantis. He had been left to watch the prisoners, and was not dreaming of attack. Rather he was anticipating a fine time alone with Steinberger's girls and private stock of liquor. He looked up as he heard the sound of men's shoes on the sand, and the cigar he was chewing dropped from his suddenly slack jaw. Then he came to a halt with a start. His hand went to his holster.

"That's the blighter who swiped me with a belaying pin," muttered the second mate thickly, still groggy from the terrible blow he had received. Pushing Travers aside, he fired before the other man had time to draw his gun. He dropped like a sack of flour, limply and as heavily, and lay still. Travers turned him over with his foot and noted the neat hole in the center of the forehead.

"No need to have finished him," he commented indifferently, and went on.

There was no sign of the *Wanderer* in the lagoon. Travers climbed a tall tree and gazed around on the horizon. The barque was running swiftly before a north wind, and only her tops'ls were visible over the sea rim. After a long look Travers came down to the sand and rejoined his officers.

"Steinberger's taken my ship," he said quietly. He looked at Everett, Everett looked at him. Then both men turned and looked at the brig beached for careening half a mile away.

"We could launch her in a couple of hours, sir," suggested the mate.

Travers nodded and tested the strength of the wind with a wet forefinger.

"We'll take her. She can't sail as fast as the Wanderer, but with this wind she won't lag far behind."

Followed still by Tia Kua, the three officers went down the beach to where the Atlantis lay.

CHAPTER VIII
MAN-BATTLE

It was night when the brig dropped anchor, some little distance from Mulinu'u Point, after the long run south. The lights of three or four schooners, a long, rakish-looking barquentine, and a barque that was plainly the *Wanderer*, shimmered through the night haze that hung over the roadstead. Three other ships were beating up from the east, and it was evident that Melita would have a full house before dawn.

From the fires along the beach it was apparent that a sort of dance picnic was being held for the pleasure of the men of the sea and the world. Half a dozen red glows dotted the sand, and the sound of singing drifted on the breeze.

To escape the festivities Travers landed some distance below the hotel and climbed round the back of the long, low building.

Here Tia Kua took charge and led him down a dark, cool passage to the big room in the front of the place.

It was practically deserted, the majority of the men preferring the revelries of the beach, under the stars, to the stifling languor of the inside, though four of the older men were in evidence near Melita's dais idly smoking long cheroots and talking in low tones together. Of the half-caste there was no sign.

Tia Kua slipped across the room to the heavy curtains that screened Melita's quarters. She listened at the door, and then beckoned to Travers. The four men near the dais watched this byplay with growing interest. Many strange things took place in Melita's house.

Parting the curtain, Travers stepped inside and laid his ear against the door, Tia Kua tensely clutching his arm and listening, too. Steinberger's voice was loud and arrogant, and he was evidently repeating some old argument.

"I've got this little knight-errant of yours, m' dear, and I've got your little sister. You want them back, both of them. All right. You come with me and we'll call it quits. I'll even marry you. At the mission, if you will."

"Wilhelm," Melita's voice was pleading and very soft, and Travers thrilled and tingled to his fingertips, "I've never had much happiness, and this man…. He already means so much. I had hoped…. But you would not understand. I am not a bad woman…. You would only tire of me in a few weeks. Why not make a few people happy for a change? I—"

"I've heard all that already! You know my terms. Take them or leave them. Either you come with me, or I keep your sister and finish this Travers. I'd sooner do that, anyway. I don't mind admitting that man is dangerous to me. But if you come I'll let him go and give him back his ship. Hurry and decide. I've let you fool and argue with me for two solid days, and I've got to get back!"

There was a long silence, broken only by Steinberger's heavy breathing. Then Melita whispered:

"I have a little money, Wilhelm. If you—"

"I have money, too. I want you, not money. Come!"

"You will swear to let Travers go, and my sister?"

"H'm, seems you're very fond of this—sailor!"

"I am."

There was a quiet dignity in the tone that quieted the German. It did not sound like the old Melita. Travers set his teeth and kicked open the door.

* * * *

Melita was standing before Steinberger, nervously twisting her fan in her hands. The German was sitting on the divan and rubbing his palms together like a man confident of the outcome of his plans. He collapsed like a wet rag as his astonished gaze fell on Travers standing in the dim red square of the doorway. There was sticking-plaster and the stain of iodine on Travers' face, and Steinberger boasted a huge purple lump on his jaw. Under other circumstances either of the men would have evoked a laugh.

Melita stared for one intense moment, and then collapsed to her knees and sobbed with relief. Tia Kua ran to comfort her.

Steinberger reached for his holster, and the sailor was on him like a flash, knocking the drawn gun from his hand and sending him spinning across the back of the divan.

The German charged like a bull when he had recovered his feet, and the force of his weight carried Travers until he fell with, a crash, the other's two hundred and fifty-odd pounds of fat holding him down.

The fat hands reached for the sailor's throat, but he got his thumbs in the pig-like eyes and, with a curse, Steinberger reeled back half-blinded. It was not pretty fighting.

Travers was up and after his opponent immediately, pounding his ribs and working his face to a mass of purple bruises. He did not go unpunished himself. Steinberger's weight and superior reach aided him. The German picked up a brazier and cut Travers' head open, half stunning him and driving him to his knees. Before he could follow up his advantage the sailor had staggered to his feet and gone into a clinch.

The mirrors on the walls were shivered as the two men swayed all over the room. Finally they crashed into the divan and split apart, bloody and breathless.

They rested for a spell, teeth showing and eyes glittering with passion. The centuries and epochs of upward climbing from the primeval slime and forest had been for naught. The martyrdom of a million reformers was in vain. Here stood two men locked in mortal combat, unaffected by all that had gone before. They were the result of it all.

Travers was the first to recover. With quick, lithe steps he advanced and jabbed at Steinberger's mouth. With a snarl they closed and for a while wrestled again about the room, stumbling over rugs and matting, low tables and cushions.

The German swore continuously, but the sailor fought in silence. Blood flecks were everywhere. Then Steinberger ran his hand behind the sailor and, feeling the automatic reposing in the hip pocket, drew it after some difficulty. Just at that moment Travers broke the German's hold with a mighty effort and, lifting the huge body, pitched it into a corner.

With a broken arm and collar bone Steinberger rocked to his knees and fired blindly. Travers clapped a hand to his hip, realized what had happened, and then cast frantic eyes around for the gun he had knocked from Steinberger's hand in the beginning. He could see it nowhere.

A bullet snickered over his shoulder and tore a hole in the copper mesh of the walls. Another clipped his neck. Dimly he heard Melita scream and then shout something.

He gasped as a numbing, red-hot pang shot through his left arm. He pawed at the air. This was the end. William Travers, his brother, would never be avenged, nor would Mary, the little wife. For one vivid moment the mists cleared from the sailor's eyes and he looked clear-eyed for his death.

Steinberger staggered, panting, to his feet and sobbed with laughter. His sound arm rose and held the automatic steady. Travers closed his eyes and swayed on his feet.… There came a shot, then a fusillade of shots, and faintly Travers heard Steinberger choke.

He opened his eyes and saw the German go down, fighting for breath, his chest a gory ruin where a soft-nosed bullet had mushroomed.

Melita cried out in a faint voice as she watched the blue smoke curling up from the muzzle of the nickel-steel revolver she had snatched up from the floor. It was the revolver she had given to

Travers, the revolver Travers had knocked from the German's hand in the beginning of the fray.

Travers stumbled forward. He was aware of a warm something flowing down his limp left arm, but he took no heed. He halted beside the dead man and looked down. He felt dizzy and very tired.

"That squares things, Brietmann," he muttered thickly. "Billy'll rest easy now. And may … and may God have mercy on your soul."

Then he turned and saw Melita. Her eyes were wide with horror, and with one hand she held her handkerchief to her mouth. She had forgotten to breathe.

Travers swore feebly and crossed to the motionless girl. At his touch on her arm she shuddered and roused herself. The revolver dropped unheeded to the floor and, swaying against the man's shoulder, she commenced to cry.

Travers raised Melita's face and kissed her lips.

"Melita!" he muttered thickly. "Let's start again … together."

Then blackness came and he fainted.

THE BLACK ADDER

Dorothy Quick

Talfa opened the casement window and, leaning out into the night, tried to see the garden below. It was a quiet, moonless night, and she could distinguish nothing. Even the stars were veiled, and a heavy impenetrable blue-blackness covered everything. But a soft wind carried the scent of the jasmines to her nostrils.

She knew the garden so well that she could visualize it mentally, although its beauties were hidden from her eyes. There was the crystal pool and, beyond it, the marble summer house, always cool and inviting. Inside, on the couch of crimson silk, Boud Ali waited. At the thought of him lying there, his slim, muscular body relaxed on the cushions while the black curls of his hair lay loose about his handsome face, Talfa's heart beat faster and her breasts throbbed against the casement sill.

Boud Ali waited for her, and her every nerve cried out for him, longed for the relief that only resting in his arms could give. So near he was, such a few short steps, and she could feel his lips on hers. Heaven! And yet tonight it could not be!

Talfa shook her head, and the two long braids of blue-black hair slipped over the window-ledge, stretching downward into the night. Talfa, like a Fairy Princess of old, had hair that waved softly about her piquant face and then fell rippling downward until it reached her knees. It was very thick and soft, and she wore it in braids to keep it out of her way. Her deep brown eyes peered out into the night as though they were striving to see the lover who waited for her, and her red lips trembled a little with the sorrow that enveloped her because she could not go to him.

Just two short weeks they had known each other. Only fourteen days ago, she had danced before the Rajah and his guests. Among them had been Boud Ali. As she made the obscene movements that were meant to drive men mad, she had seen him and read desire in his black eyes—desire which had lit a flame in her own heart.

When the dance was over and she and the other dancing-girls lay exhausted on the mosaics of the floor, she had heard the Rajah's voice.

"Choose whom you will among the dancing-girls to be your companion for the night—save those who are virgin: they are for me alone."

Talfa had raised her head and, through the clouds of smoke and incense, she had seen Boud Ali start toward her. Willingly would she have stayed and given to him all he asked, she who had never known the touch of man. But it was not to be so; for before he ever reached her side, the chief eunuch had caught her by the wrist and led her and two other girls back to the harem.

There slaves had bathed them with scented waters, dried their hair, and they had sought their couches. Only Talfa could not sleep. The black eyes of Boud Ali had haunted her, and the heat of the night had been oppressive.

She remembered so well that she had drawn a soft silk mantle over her and stolen silently down to the garden. No guards were about. The garden walls were high and the Rajah unafraid of his women betraying him. They knew too well the penalty that would be theirs if they were caught. For his wives perhaps he kept a stricter watch; but of these Talfa knew nothing, she who had been bought for a concubine because of her beauty and her ability to dance.

For a year she had been in the palace and had never seen the Rajah except on the rare occasions when she was called upon to dance, as she had been tonight. But because she was a virgin, she never was allowed to stay for the aftermath of the feast. The Rajah was generous only with those who no longer tempted him. Talfa knew that some time he would send for her, and then—. But that night she had had no room in her thoughts for anyone beyond Boud Ali.

She had gone down the tiny stairway like a ghost, past the sleeping eunuch, out into the cooling night; beyond the crystal pool she had sought the marble summer house. Here some day she would know the embraces of the Rajah when his eyes would rest upon her with desire. But for tonight she would dream of the young stranger.

As she entered the pavilion someone rose from the crimson couch and came toward her with outstretched hands. In the glow of the moonlight she saw Boud Ali, and a crimson flush stained her slender young body under the silken robe.

Boud Ali spoke, and his voice was low and musical. "Truly the priest spoke well who said we know not the power of our own thoughts. Here have I lain for hours, willing that you should come to me, and so the desire of my life has been granted. You are here!"

Talfa took a step nearer to him. "But how did you come? The walls are far too high to climb."

His clear laugh rang through the scented night. "Nor did I climb! Gold brought me here—gold and a greedy slave, who opened a little-known door in that high wall, and has promised to do so yet again—and will, if you are kind."

The girl moved forward. "I saw you in the banquet hall," she began.

He moved toward her until they stood face to face. "Beloved," he said softly, "I, too, saw such beauty as I had never dreamed, and love was born in my heart. Smile at me, sweet one. Smile, and tell me that I ask not in vain."

Talfa looked deep into his eyes, and the corners of her mouth curved deliciously. With a sudden gesture of surrender, she stretched forth her hands.

The next second she was in his arms and her silken mantle lay unheeded on the floor.

Twice since then the marble summer house had sheltered their love. Gold had truly opened the way for Boud Ali, and Talfa thought little of the risk she ran. She merely waited until the women's house was wrapped in slumber before she stole down the tiny stairway. That death would be her portion if she were discovered, faded away before the magic of her lover's kiss. The fact that the death would be a slow, torturous one, not swift and merciful, she never let come into her thoughts. The moment and Boud Ali were sufficient, and she felt that she would gladly pay any price for the joy, of resting in his arms.

But tonight? Tonight her soul was full of terror, not for herself but for him! They had planned to meet, and her heart had been full of eager anticipation. Then only a few short moments ago word had been brought that the Rajah would visit the women's quarters and that the dancing-girls should be ready to amuse him.

* * * *

Talfa on hearing the news, had prayed silently that his choice fall not on her when the dance was done. Then like a swift stab of horror had come the thought the Rajah would retire to the summer house with whomever he chose. That was the reason she had seen slaves working there today. They were cleaning and perfuming the pavilion for his use. And just at that time Boud Ali would be there waiting. Death would be his portion, and she could not save him. There was no way. The slave who let him into the garden was in the men's part of the palace; so even if she knew which slave it was, she had no way of reaching him. And she would not dare disclose her secret to anyone who could send a message. Talfa, herself, could neither read nor write. Only fifteen years old, she had been educated solely to attract and interest the senses.

In sheer panic, she had left the other girls, who were chattering like a group of excited monkeys, and had sought this window overlooking the garden. Out there, not very far away, her lover was waiting. What was it he had said of the power of thought? Gods! If only her thoughts could warn him! But she had no faith in her powers of concentration. By all the Gods, there must be a way! Then out of the night and her own despair, an idea was born.

At their last meeting they had laughingly, joked of "The Black Adder," a bandit who had been terrorizing the whole province of Tawnpore, so called because he struck quickly like the reptile, and his touch meant death; also because he was always robed in black with a silk hood over his face. No one had the slightest idea of his identity.

When Talfa had playfully refused one of his caresses, Boud Ali had cried, "Submit, or I will call on the Black Adder to make you. See reason, oh, light of my life!"

And then much later, after she had explained that she had refused only for the joy of giving in, they had spoken of the Black Adder again, and Boud Ali had told her some of the bandit's less gory exploits. Perhaps he would remember their conversation and under cover of a song about the Black Adder she could warn the man she loved. No one hearing would think aught, for the Black Adder's name was on every one's lips.

Of her own fate, should she be the chosen one, she had no time to think. Breathlessly she ran to fetch her lute, and quickly returned to her place by the window. She had little time. Soon she would be called for the ritual of bathing, perfuming and robing that always took place before the arrival of the Rajah.

She struck the first notes softly. Then the music grew louder, the strain that had been played the night she first saw Boud Ali. She leaned far out the window and threw her clear sweet voice out into the night.

"I, Talfa, sing a song of the Black Adder," she repeated over and over, then swung into her song:

*

> *"The Black Adder came to the palace of the King.*
> *Within were jewels for his welcoming.*
> *Only the dancing-girl knew waiting was death's sting.*
> *The dancing-girl sang, go away, go away—*
> *The King comes merrily to me this day.*
> *Black Adder, Black Adder, do not dare to stay!*
> *Black Adder, Black Adder, creep into your hole,*
> *Another night brings another goal—*
> *Only tonight would you pay the toll!*
> *Black Adder—"*

*

Her voice died away as she saw the chief eunuch standing beside her. He laughed a shrill, thin laugh that frayed the edge of her nerve.

"Little fool, to sit in the window and sing of the Black Adder when you should be staining your eyes with kohl to snare your lord with their beauty!"

Her lute fell forgotten on the floor as one tiny hand pressed against her heart as though to still its wild beating.

"Come, my pretty one," continued the chief eunuch, as he pulled one of her long braids. "By all the Gods, were I a man, you could make me captive by your hair alone!"

Unresisting, she followed him and passively gave herself into the hands of the women. The fatalism of her race had come to her aid. She had done her best. Now all rested upon the knees of the Gods.

* * * *

Later that evening, robed in blue gauze that revealed more than it concealed, with her long hair flowing about her shoulders, she danced with the other girls before the Rajah. Automatically her body moved to the music. Her thoughts were far away, with Boud Ali—hoping.

Suddenly, as the dance brought her near to the couch where the Rajah was lying, she felt the long ends of her hair seized firmly. She stopped writhing and felt herself gently drawn toward the Rajah.

Presently she stood facing him. He held her hair in his firm hands, having pulled it over her shoulder. She felt his eyes pass over her. Somehow she knew fate was upon her and that she would be the chosen one. Trembling, she heard his voice, "Bid the music stop, and send those other girls away." Then she felt his hands upon her, tearing away her robes.

"With hair like that you need no further covering. Come, dance for me, so; and when the dance is over, if you still please me—and fear not but that you will—you shall be honored with my love."

With a slight shudder she shook her hair over her, and of a truth it was more concealing than the blue gauze had been. "A Rajah has no love to give a dancing-girl," she cried, remembering she had only one life to lose.

The Rajah laughed, then his eyes looked into hers. "Perhaps—who knows?—even love! At any rate, tonight you shall be mine. I swear it! Now—dance."

The music started. Automatically Talfa began to move to its rhythm, and then she started to turn and twist in a series of wild convulsions. Another thought had come to her. Perhaps she could so madden and inflame his senses that he would take her here in this room where they were, and Boud Ali would not be discovered in the summer house, if her song had not been heard.

She danced with a furious abandon such as she had never be-lieved herself capable of. If she had drunk of the most potent of aphrodisiacs she could have put no more into her dance.

At last the music came to an end with a loud crash of cymbals, and she fell exhausted at the Rajah's feet.

The Rajah detached the golden robe from his shoulders and threw it over her. Then he came and lifted her into his arms.

"I, myself, will carry you to the pavilion," he cried, his breath coming quickly, his eyes mad with lust.

Two slaves ran before with lighted torches, and the chief eu-nuch followed behind.

In his arms Talfa lay limply. Soon she would know, and she could hardly bear the suspense. One last effort she would make, for her love's sake. "My lord, why do we not stay here?"

The Rajah made no answer, only strode rapidly on.

Yet another effort she put forth. "Will you not send the men away?"

This time she met with success. "Have no fear. Tonight is yours alone, and tomorrow, and tomorrow, oh lovely one!"

Talfa almost laughed aloud. For her there would be no more tomorrows. When he discovered that another man had spoiled the fruit for him, she had no doubt what her fate would be, unless she could so madden him—

They had reached the pavilion door. The Rajah turned to the slaves. "Put the torches in place and then go—all of you—and come not near until the sun shines brightly from the heavens."

When he had been obeyed, he carried her over the threshold. No one was in the marble summer house!

"Praise to the Gods!" whispered Talfa, and the Rajah hearing, misunderstood, and crushed his lips on hers.

Finally he laid her on the crimson couch and drew away the golden robe. The crimson silk brought out the whiteness of her body. She looked like a living statue as she lay before him.

"Gods!" he cried, "but you are beautiful!" and he moved closer toward her.

All thoughts of submission fled from Talfa. Better death than the embraces of this man. Now that Boud Ali was safe, she was no longer afraid.

She struggled frantically. A cruel gleam came into the Rajah's face, as he pressed her close and sought to force her to comply with his desires.

Just when from sheer exhaustion she could fight no more, she felt the Rajah's arms loosen their hold, and wide-eyed beheld two hands dragging him to his feet.

Forgetful of herself, she looked up. "Gods!" she exclaimed. "The Black Adder!" For holding the Rajah's arms tightly behind his back was a man clothed in black from head to toe with a hood over his face that had slits for eyes and mouth.

The Rajah made a desperate struggle to free himself, but he had been caught off guard and was held by hands of iron.

"What do you want?" he cried finally.

Talfa covered herself with the golden robe before the Black Adder spoke. His voice was muffled by the silken hood, but there was strength in it.

"I had sought your life, oh, Rajah of Tawnpore—your life and your jewels. But even an 'Adder' can be merciful!"

"My guards will give you no mercy," threatened the Rajah in a voice from which he tried vainly to hide his fear.

The Black Adder laughed long and hard. "Think you I am named for nothing? Hidden in the bushes, I heard your order and I waited until the guards had surely gone. Not until the sun is high in the heavens will they come. The Rajah has spoken!"

The ruler of Tawnpore bowed his head. When he finally raised it, he spoke shakily, "Your price?"

The black head leaned over close to the Rajah's. Through the silk, Talfa sensed his eyes upon her and drew her robe closer together over her heaving bosoms.

"I have no price," said the Black Adder. "Yet once I will be merciful. Here, you!" he called to the girl, "tear silken strands from those curtains so that I can bind this man!"

Talfa obeyed silently.

"How dare you?" cried the Rajah.

"Better being bound than dead. I will leave you here on yonder couch and your slaves will release you in the morning. Then you can tell them the Black Adder knows how to be kind."

The Rajah said nothing. Talfa brought the strip of silk to the bandit and under his direction helped to tie the Rajah's hands behind his back.

The Black Adder stretched his arms. "I am afraid," he said softly, "I must rob you of your pearls; and the Ruby of Tawnpore, which I have long envied, will now be mine."

Swiftly he stripped the Rajah of his jewels, which in truth were worth a king's ransom. Working fast, he tied the ruler of Tawnpore securely and laid him on the couch. He bound his body fast about with the crimson silk; then he stuffed a gag into the ruler's mouth and made it fast.

As he finished, Talfa tried to steal toward the doorway and freedom, but swifter than the snake for whom he was named, the man caught her wrist. "Not so—you who are the brightest jewel of all, come with me!"

"No, no!" shrieked Talfa, as he lifted her in his arms.

"Will you come quietly?" he snarled. "Or must I silence you, too?"

Talfa made a gesture of assent. "I have no choice," she whispered.

As he carried her out of the marble summer house that had given her such joy and such misery, Talfa reflected that perhaps it was better this way. At least she was free from the Rajah, and Boud Ali was safe. Perhaps when the Black Adder tired of her, he would set her free; or failing that, if she could find a knife—a strange sense of helplessness descended upon her.

She was conscious that the Black Adder carried her through a low doorway, for he stooped slightly. On the other side were men and horses. A man held her while the bandit mounted an animal as black as himself. Then he leaned over and threw a dark cloak over the Rajah's golden one. She was then lifted up into his arms, and she heard him give the order to ride—and the company moved forth into the night.

They stopped only once, at the outer gates of the palace. Here a paper was given the guards, who let them pass at once. Talfa could see nothing, as the Black Adder had thrown part of the cloak over her head, but she could hear the rustle of the paper.

For a long time they rode furiously. Talfa lost track of time. The swift motion of the horse and the strength of the arms that held her were her last conscious recollections, as she sank into the deep sleep that only comes with exhaustion.

* * * *

It was light when she opened her eyes. Through the folds of the cloak she could see the sun's rays. She stirred a little.

"Beloved, I thought you would never open your eyes," a well-known voice vibrated in her ears.

Talfa sank back, thinking she dreamed. The cloak was pulled off. The sudden light after the darkness made her blink.

Presently her eyes became accustomed to the light, and she looked up at her captor.

"Boud Ali!" she cried, and touched his smooth face with her hand to see if he were real.

"My little love," he murmured. Then, bending over without slackening his horse's gait, he kissed her fiercely.

Presently they came back to earth. "But how?" asked Talfa. "Where is the Black Adder?"

Boud Ali's free hand dangled a bit of black silk before her eyes. "Here," he cried gayly. "I heard your song and knew the message you meant to convey. So I sought out the Rajah and bade him farewell. He gave me a pass for myself and men. Then I gave a purse of gold to the slave for a key to the garden gate, ostensibly to bid a last farewell to you. After that I waited for the Rajah to bring you to me."

"Suppose he had chosen another?" breathed Talfa.

Her lover laughed. "He could not have, my beautiful! I had my men ready to overpower the guards, but when I heard them dismissed, I sent my men back to the horses, and waited. The rest you know."

"Where are we going?" Talfa asked; not that it mattered, now that she was in her lover's arms. Not even the fact that he was the Black Adder made any difference to her.

"To my home in the Hills. We are quite safe. The Rajah will never know you are Boud Ali's, and together we will find happiness."

"And wealth," added Talfa, remembering the Rajah's jewels. "Only, I shall be afraid when you are off on your expeditions."

"I shall never leave you, now that you are really mine," he promised.

Her laughter rang out like tinkling silver bells. "Then there is the end of the Black Adder!"

Boud Ali shrugged, "Why?"

"If you go forth no more—"

His own mirth drowned hers, "Oh foolish, one, I but played a part for one night, and borrowed a name to gain my love. If I had taken you, the Rajah would have found us out and death would have been our lot. But for the Black Adder he will not look. For my part, I shall think kindly of the bandit that all so abuse."

"And I shall ever bless his name!" cried Talfa as she raised her lips for her lover's kiss.

A MEAL FOR THE DEVIL

K. Christopher Barr

Yen Sing, his oily black queue slapping his back at every jounce, climbed to the top of the mast. From its height, he surveyed dazedly this harbor of the white man, full of bustle, full of excitement, fringed by the irregular wharves and piers of busy San Francisco. Yen Sing's slanting eyes noted everything—the plying ferry, the host of small boats, the green slime on the base of the wharf, whence rose a queer pungent odor to his sniffing nostrils.

The ship rose and fell gently on the bosom of the water. Yen Sing liked the lulling sensation. He liked the sparkle of the sun on the ocean. He liked the tang of the salt breeze in his mouth and nose, its crisp caresses on his face.

Most of all he liked his position, high above the rest of the crew. He was exalted, a god, surveying the pitiful human world, spread in a panorama at his feet. Yen Sing shivered. He had no gods. He had foresworn his gods, called them vile names, and thumbed his nose at their crafty wiles, shaken his fist at their images, and then fled, quaking, from their wrath. Why not? What had his gods done for him, save to drive him from place to place, showering upon his rebellious head distress and misery, taking from him all that life held of joy and happiness? Small wonder that he had cursed the gods of his fathers, and fled to strange lands to ease his miseries.

But they had sent after him devils, two chief devils and a number of subordinate and subservient devils. Chief among those was Mazpa, the boa constrictor, who undulated gently in his cage and darted his wicked fangs at the yellow, wizened Chinaman every time he passed him by. Yen Sing had no delusions about Mazpa. Whatever the little round bald Englishman, with the gold-rimmed spectacles said of Mazpa and the other creatures of the jungle which were being transported to England for some strange unfathomable purpose, Yen Sing knew better.

* * * *

It was not for nothing that the boa constrictor had been added to the cargo last of all, when Yen Sing himself had already signed his papers to go to foreign lands as a sailor on the jungle-ship. Mazpa was a devil—a fierce, and inplacable devil—sent by Yen Sing's outraged gods to kill their defiant ex-worshiper, and to conduct his blackened soul to its particular hell. Yen Sing had to be very wary of Mazpa. Sometimes he could stand the worry and the terror no longer and had to escape up the mast into the fresh sweet air of the outside world, to think and rest and gather courage to face again those coal-black, hard eyes, the darting fangs, the snapping jaws, the hostile hiss of the arch-devil, Mazpa.

Nor was Mazpa alone in his glory. There were at least a half dozen other serpents on the ship. These, to Yen Sing's tortured brain, were satellites of the big devil, Mazpa. They were his attendants, lesser beings of the same world, lesser emissaries of his own enraged and avenging gods.

There were monkeys on the ship, too—friendly, chattering little beasts, who held out small hairy hands to Yen Sing, and smiled at him mockingly with their bright, canny eyes. He would stand before their cage whenever He could snatch a moment from his work, jabbering at them in language which the other sailors said was either their own or a kindred tongue, laying his yellow cheeks against the bars, giving them his pigtail to play with.

The monkeys he didn't fear, nor the one lion, the two tigers, and the other large beasts of the jungle. He even liked the screaming, disapproving, gaudy tropical birds that flew excitedly from side to side of their barred home when he approached them. But Mazpa and his snakes—there was a different story.

* * * *

One other devil there was on board the ship, in league with Mazpa, perhaps, but certainly sent to the ship for the same purpose—to run down the Chinaman soul and body, and deliver him to the grasp of his pursuing gods. That was the devil with the thin, wailing voice, who lived in a long black reed, and talked to Sally, the red-headed sailor, whenever that blue-eyed, freckled-faced booze-loving son of the sea put his lips to the reed, and whispered to its inmates. Flute, they called this devil, and whenever he heard the sweet, shrill notes, Yen Sing cowered and hid his face in his hands. He would seek the farthermost corner of the ship, and there remain in fierce and brooding terror until the notes were stilled, and the devil had retired. Then and then only, would he return to his work.

Sally, however, Yen Sing admired nightly. He was fond of this husky sailor in his own queer, Oriental way. He often longed to tell Sally that he was not the priest of a god, as he undoubtedly must think himself, but instead the guardian of a devil, relentless, persecuting, vicious, who would turn upon his own votary when once his way was gained, and rend him limb from limb. But he never could make Sally understand, so he finally gave up trying, and wore himself to a shadow longing for the day of release from the daily nightmare of Mazpa's baleful eyes and the Flute's shrill, pursuing voice.

Up in the sky, clinging to the mast, while the boat rocked gently to and fro in the arms of the water, Yen Sing forgot everything except the busy city spread out before his slanting eyes. He watched the smoke-wreathing itself from countless chimneys to spread its dark haze over the horizon; he marveled at the bustle about the waterfront.

The myriad noises of the city came to him as a subdued roar, like the, sound of distant thunder in the hills in summertime. Especially he admired the white shaft of the Customs House tower, rising from the lesser buildings surrounding it like a maiden above her worshipers. Tall and slim and white it stood, serene in the midst of turmoil.

What was that dark streak coiled about its slenderness? Yen Sing shut his eyes in terror, for he seemed to discern a flat head, two yawning jaws, and the steady gleam of narrow, jetty eyes, Mazpa writhed and swayed on the tower's body. With a shudder, Yen Sing turned away.

Now Mazpa had ideas of his own concerning this jungle-ship. He detested his barred and bolted cage; he hated the motion of the ship. Back in his native jungles, the earth had remained steady, motionless. In this jail of his, this narrow, cramping space, in which he was permitted to exist, there were no tall trees, smooth of trunk, or covered with thick green verdure, whence he might rear his mighty head to survey his domain—the jungle. He loathed with a murderous hatred the white men who held him captive. He longed to enfold them within his gigantic coils, and crush their bones and flesh into one mass. Most of all he detested the wrinkled little yellow man who stole on tiptoe past his cage, shrinking from the infuriated glare of his eyes.

* * * *

Today, as a sailor came to his cage to feed him, Mazpa reared his ugly head with a threatening hiss, his fangs darting wickedly from his open jaws, his eyes fiendish. The sailor, overcome with sudden terror, rushed from the cage, leaving it open. Mazpa rolled forth in stately coils, rolled sedately to his freedom—rolled in quest of a tree.

Yen Sing bent his head, and the pigtail flopped over his shoulder and hung down; Yen Sing blinked. Fascinated, trembling, he looked the length of the mast to the deck below.

There, rearing upward, quite at his ease, as though he were scaling a tree in his native jungles, was Mazpa. Everywhere, it appeared, was Mazpa. Yen Sing closed his eyes; opened them. The vision remained. Came the paralyzing realization that the snake was no hallucination, but a reality.

In a cold sweat of terror, Yen Sing understood. The devil of his gods was ready to carry out their will. Who but a god or a devil would have released the heavy bars and bolts of Mazpa's cage?

The huge flat head reared itself up the mast, diamond hard eyes fixed brilliantly on his. Behind the flattened head lay coil on coil of scales, shining in the sunlight, twisted about the smooth mast like a bracelet on a virgin's arm.

Yen Sing opened his lips to call for help. No sounds issued from them. He gagged with terror. A tremendous fascination drew his eyes to those of the serpent.

Slowly, silently, the snake made his persistent, relentless advance, his forked tongue darting from his scarlet fangs. The Chinaman's body shook, then stiffened. He began to regard his enemy with a stare as glassy as its own. His body, his limbs, his vocal organs were completely paralyzed, it seemed. An age of inertia, and then, very slowly but very surely, he began to move down the mast. Inch by inch he edged nearer, inch by inch Mazpa crept up.

Below, on the deck, the crew were searching for Mazpa, searching with a silent speed that proved how unwelcome a guest Mazpa was, unfettered. The sun still shone, and the waters still danced, but there was a chill in the sunshine, and a threat, a mocking, in the dancing. Sally, his red hair rumpled by the fingers of the breeze, remembered that nature was man's age-old enemy. His lips were tight over his uneven teeth. Through his brain seethed strange thoughts. He thought of Mazpa's mighty coils crushing out the life of a man as easily as he could break a soda-water straw; he wondered what had become of the little yellow Chink. Then he coupled the two thoughts and shuddered.

Below was the blue water, above was the blue sky, with white gulls speeding through its color. His eyes followed their flight mechanically as he straightened a moment to wipe the perspiration from his freckled face. The birds disappeared behind the mast. Sally's mouth fell open, his head jerked back; his eyes widened, his face became a mask of horror.

Up the mast undulated the giant snake; down the mast, a man in another world, edged Yen Sing. While one might have counted ten, the sailor stood like a man in a trance, his gaze riveted on the gently swaying mast.

Then he leaped to action. He summoned the rest of the crew. But what could they do? What could any of them do? Powerless to move, they stood, silent, head upturned, watching, watching. Finally Sally, his body shaking, in a sweat, managed to rouse himself somehow from the coma of terror. He shouted.

The little Englishman appeared from below the deck, a gun under one arm. He followed the mesmerized gaze of the sailors upward. Years in the jungle had taught him self-reliance, self-control He brought his gun slowly to his shoulder, aimed it. But he didn't fire.

A shout from Sally halted his finger on the trigger. A whispered conclave, and Sally disappeared below decks; the Englishman, his hand on his gun, took up a position behind the sailors. His face was troubled, but he was alert, eager—for what? Still the serpent rolled his sickening coils up; still Yen Sing, his pigtail jerking on his shoulder as the boat dipped to the waves, crept slowly downward.

Of the turmoil on the deck, Yen Sing knew nothing. His consciousness was limited to one vivid sensation against a background of unfathomable black—two fiery bits of light, now pin-pricks, now balls of menacing flame, dissolving again into the black of nothingness. He had forgotten that Mazpa was a devil, forgotten his loves, his hatreds, his fears. His whole world lay in those two compelling beacons.

Through the blankness, coming from another planet, pierced a sound, a shrill, thin, wailing sound.

This was the second devil, Flute. Mazpa could not do the trick alone, he needed help. For one brief second, Yen Sing was conscious of a darting, brief-lived, poignant triumph. At least he was not succumbing tamely. It took two devils—two chief devils—to master his stubborn soul.

He loathed the whining voice of Flute, who lived in a black reed, but his bosom swelled with pride. If only he could tear his gaze from those points of flame, he might fool them both. But his momentary return to awareness was gone. Impelled by a power he could not resist, he was forced to watch the pin-pricks. Sound faded from his consciousness. The world vanished. He was alone in space with beacons of light, which he must reach. But his legs would not hasten, nor stop moving. He could deviate neither to the left, nor the right.

* * * *

On the deck, one or two of the crew tore their gaze from the significant silhouettes on the mast, and buried their faces in trembling hands. Their strength was gone. They could no longer watch. The face of the little Englishman was wooden in expression. His fingers played nervously over the barrel of his gun. Drops of perspiration rolled unheeded down his cheeks.

Mazpa, scales shining, calmly proceeded on his journey. Once more he was happy—seeking his prey on a smooth, tall tree.

The song of the flute rose in the air, sure, unwavering, gaining strength with every precious moment. It soared above the deck, clear, confident, wheedling. It wailed, sighed, cajoled. Never had

Sally so played before. Never, probably, would he so play again, for now he was playing for the tremendous stake of a human life. Through the black reed he begged and called. The song was seductive—a beautiful woman begging a favor, a lover wooing, persuasive, tender. Mazpa's flat ugly head swayed in time to the music, but his beady eyes remained fixed on the Chinaman, so near him now. The fangs darted against the sky in a fine forked thread of black. The flute sobbed and pleaded. Mazpa's head swayed slowly, lazily. The flute never ceased to beg. Mighty, ceaseless undulations—a shrill soft voice, wheedling, caressing—coils gleaming, flashing as they moved along the shining mast in the light of the sun, deliberately, inch by inch, scaly arch by scaly arch, giant coil by giant coil—still the seductive voice, the wheedling cajolery.

* * * *

A moment pregnant with suspense, teeming with hope, with fear—cessation of motion, climax of sound—awful silence—a moment brief, yet measured by aeons. Again the undulations; the shrill, sweet summons.

Yen Sing, two tiny points light suddenly flashing from his consciousness, pitched into the blankness they had left. The sailors, swiftly galvanized into action by sharp, almost hysterical orders from the fat Englishman, who threw his gun clattering onto the deck to help them, caught the yellow man in a blanket and rolled him onto the deck.

A shudder convulsed the thin frame—and then another. His hands were icy, inert. One of the sailors chafed them roughly, his own none too warm. Yen Sing thought himself dead, the thin sweet voice of Flute piercing loud in his ears. With a shriek he rolled over, his eyes starting from his head. The two devils were conducting his soul to its allotted hell!

* * * *

San Francisco spread a dust-colored haze over the horizon. White-faced sailors were clustered about him. This was the deck of the jungle-ship. And, amazing spectacle! His mouth dropped widely open; perspiration stood in droplets on his forehead.

Red-headed Sally, his face like paste sprinkled with the cinnamon of his freckles, backed slowly out of sight behind the cabin. Between his lips was a long, black reed, from which issued compelling music, and after him, his eyes half-closed, his head swaying in time to the motion of his coils, while the sailors stood rigid with fascinated repulsion, glided Mazpa, a dazed captive.

A glass was pressed against the Chinaman's bloodless lips. He opened them, and swallowed automatically. His throat burned, but the reality of the world begun to return.

Sally appeared on the deck, walking unsteadily.

"You'd orter see him, fellers," he said, swaying up to the still transfixed group. "All curled up for a nice nap, quiet as a lamb." Then, more jerkily, "Give me a drink, quick!"

He would have fallen, had not the little Englishman, who had followed him across the deck, caught his arm.

Yen Sing, kneeling there, his bright, almond-slanted eyes turning from one to the other of the crowd, slowly comprehended. The Flute, then, was a conqueror of devils, and Mazpa's evil struggle for one more soul had failed just as it was ended, because of Flute, who lived in a black reed and spoke with a shrill voice. Here was a god more powerful than those he had foresworn, a white man's God, and it had saved him—*him!*

He clasped Sally's wide-trousered leg.

"Let me worship thy strange god, oh, Sally," he murmured in his native tongue.

JACK GREY, SECOND MATE

William Hope Hodgson

CHAPTER I

She stepped aboard from one of the wooden jetties projecting from the old Longside wharf, where the sailing ships used to lie above Telegraph Hill, San Francisco. She rejected almost disdainfully the great hand extended by the second mate to assist her over the gangway.

The big man flushed somewhat under his tan, but otherwise gave no sign that he was aware of the semi-unconscious slight. She, on her part, moved aft daintily to meet the captain's wife, under whose wing she was to make the passage from Frisco to Baltimore.

At first it seemed as if she were to be the only passenger in the big steel bark; but, about half an hour before sailing, a second appeared on the little jetty, accompanied by several bearers carrying his luggage. These, having dumped their burdens at the outer end of the gangway, were paid and dismissed; after which the passenger, a gross, burly-looking man, apparently between forty and forty-five years of age, made his way aboard.

It was evident that he was no stranger to sea-craft; for without hesitation, he walked aft and down the companionway. In a few minutes he returned to the deck. He glanced ashore to where his luggage remained piled up as he had left it, then went over to where the second mate was standing by the rail across the break of the poop.

"Here, you!" he said brusquely, speaking fair English, but with an unfamiliar accent. "Why don't you get my luggage aboard?"

The second mate turned and glanced down at him from his great height.

"Were you speaking to me?" he asked quietly.

"Certainly I was addressing you, you—"

He stopped and retreated a pace, for there was something in the eyes of the big officer which quieted him.

"If you will go below I'll have your gear brought aboard," the second mate told him.

The tone was polished and courteous, but there was still something in the gray eyes. The passenger glanced uneasily from the eyes to the great, nervous hand lying, gently clenched, upon the rail. Then, without a word, he turned and walked aft.

* * * *

The *Carlyle* had been two days at sea, and was running before a fine breeze of wind. On the poop the second mate was walking up and down, smoking meditatively. Occasionally he would go to the break and pass some order to the boatswain, then resume his steady tramp.

Presently, he heard a step on the companion stairs, and, the moment afterward, saw the lady passenger step out on deck. She was very white, and walked somewhat unsteadily, as if she were giddy.

She was followed by the captain's wife, carrying a rug and a couple of cushions. These the good woman proceeded to arrange on the captain's own deck-chair, after which she steadied the girl to a sitting position and wrapped the rug around her knees and feet.

Abruptly, in one of his periodic journeys, as the second mate passed to windward of the place where they were sitting, the voice of the lady passenger reached him. She was addressing the captain's wife, but was obviously indifferent whether he heard or not.

"I wish that man would take his horrible pipe somewhere else. The smell of it makes me quite sick!"

He was aware that the captain's wife was trying to signal to him behind the girl's back; but he made no sign that he saw. Instead, he continued his return journey to the break of the poop, with a certain grimness about the corners of his mouth.

Here he proceeded to walk athwartships, instead of fore and aft, so that now he came nowhere near to the girl whose insolent fastidiousness had twice irked him. He continued to smoke; for he was of too big a mind to give way to the smallness of being huffed over the lady's want of manners. He had removed from her presence the cause of her annoyance, and, being of a logical disposition, saw no reason for ceasing to obtain the reasonable enjoyment of his pipe.

As he made his way to and fro across the planks, he proceeded to turn the matter over in his own calm way. Evidently she regarded him—if she thought at all about him—as a kind of upper servant; this being so, it was absurd to suppose that there was an intentional rudeness, beyond such as servants are accustomed to receive in their position of living automata. And here, having occasion to go down on to the main deck to trim sail, he forgot the matter.

When he returned to the poop, the girl was sitting alone; the captain's wife having been called below to attend to her husband who had been ill enough to be confined to his bunk for upward of a week.

As he passed across the planks, he cast occasional glances aft. The girl was certainly winsome, and peculiarly attractive, to such a man as he, in her calm unknowing of his near presence. She was sitting back in the chair, leaning tiredly and staring full of thought out across the sea.

A while passed thus, perhaps the half of an hour, and then came the sound of heavy steps coming up from the saloon. The second mate recognized them for those of the male passenger; yet the girl did not seem to notice them. She did not withdraw her gaze from the sea, but continued to stare, seeming lost in quiet thought.

The man's head appeared out of the companionway, then the clumsy grossness of his trunk and fat under-limbs. He moved toward her, stopping within a couple of yards of her chair.

"And how is Miss Eversley?" the second mate heard him ask.

At his voice, the girl started and turned her head swiftly in his direction.

"You!" That was all she said; but the disgust and the undertone of something akin to fear were not lost upon the second officer.

"You thought—" began the man in tones of attempted banter.

"I thought I had seen the last of you—forever!" she cut in.

"But you see you were mistaken. If the sickness of the sea hadn't claimed you for the last two days, you would have discovered earlier that regret for my absence was wasted."

"Regret!"

"My pretty child—"

"Will you go away! Go away! Go away!" She put out her hands weakly with a gesture of repulsion.

"Come, come! We shall have to see much of one another during the next few weeks. Why—"

She was on her feet, swaying giddily. He took a step forward, as if with an unconscious instinct to bar her passage.

"Let me pass!" she said, with a little gasp.

But he, staring at her with hot eyes, seemed not to have heard her. She put up a hand to her throat, as if wanting air.

"Allow me to assist you below."

It was the deep voice of the second mate. His naturally somewhat grave face gave no indication that he was aware of any tensions.

"I will attend to that," said the male passenger insolently.

But the officer seemed to have no knowledge of his existence. Instead, he guided the lady to the companionway, and then down the stairs to the saloon. There he left her in the charge of the captain's wife, telling the latter that the sea air had proved too much for the young lady.

Returning on deck, he found the passenger standing by the opening of the companion. He had it in his heart to deal with the person in a fashion of his own; but the fellow had taken the measure of the big officer and, though full of repressed rage, took good care to invite no trouble.

On his part, the second mate resumed his steady tramp of the deck; but it may be noted that his pipe went out twice, for his thoughts were upon the girl he had helped below. He was pondering the matter of her repulsion for the male passenger. It was evident that they had met elsewhere, probably at the port where the *Carlyle* had picked them up. It was even more evident that the girl had no desire to continue the acquaintance, if it could be named as such.

Upon this, and much more to the same effect, did he meditate. And so, in due time, the first mate came up to his relief.

CHAPTER II

Three days later, the captain died suddenly, leaving his wife helpless with grief at her loss. By this time, Miss Eversley had gathered strength after her bout with seasickness, and now did her best to comfort the poor woman. Yet the desolate wife would not be comforted, but took to her bunk as soon as her husband had passed into the deep, and there stayed, refusing to be companied by any one. This being so, Miss Eversley was, perforce, left greatly to her own devices, and her own company; for that of Mr. Pathan, the other passenger, she avoided in a most determined manner.

This was by no means an easy matter to accomplish, save by staying in her berth; for did she go upon the poop, the man would, in defiance of all her entreaties or commands, pursue her with his hateful attentions. Yet help was to come; for it happened one day that, the poop being empty save for the man at the wheel, with whom, however, Pathan seemed curiously familiar, the fellow took advantage of the opportunity to try to take her hands. He succeeded in grasping her left, making the remark:

"Don't be so skittish, my pretty. What are your hands, when I am to have the whole of you?" And he laughed mockingly.

For answer, she tried to pull away from him, but without success.

"You see, it's no good fighting against me!"

She glanced round, breathlessly, for help and her gaze fell upon the helmsman, a little, hideous dago who, with an evil grin upon his face, was watching them. At that, she went all hot with shame and anger.

"Let go of my hand!"

"I shall not!"

He reached his left out for her right, but she drew it back; and then, as if with the reflex of the movement, clenched it and struck him full in the mouth.

"Beast!" she said with a little savage note in her voice.

The man staggered a moment; for the blow had been shrewdly delivered, and his surprise almost equaled the pain. Then he came back at her with a rush. The man was no better than some bestial creature at the moment. He seized her about the neck and the waist.

"—you!" he snarled. "I'll teach—"

But he never finished. A great knuckled hand came between their faces, splaying itself across his forehead. His sweating visage was wrenched from hers. A rough, blue-sleeved arm comforted his neck mightily, tilting his chin heavenward. His grip weakened upon her, then gave abruptly, and she staggered back dizzily against the mizzen rigging.

There came a sound of something falling. It was a very long distance away. She was conscious of the second mate in the immediate foreground, his back turned to her; and beyond him, her gross-featured antagonist huddled limply upon the deck. For a moment neither moved; then the man upon the deck rose shakily, keeping his eye mateward.

The big officer never stirred, and the passenger began backing to get the skylight between him and the second mate. He reached the weather side and paused nervously. Then, and not till then, the officer turned his back upon him, and, without vouchsafing a glance in the direction of the girl, walked forward toward the break of the poop.

As she made to go below, she heard the little steersman mutter something to the defeated man; and he, now that he was in no instant danger of annihilation, raised his voice to a blusterous growl. But the big man?

CHAPTER III

The fore-hands of the big steel bark *Carlyle* were a new lot who had been signed on in Frisco, in place of the outward-bound crew of Scotch and Welsh sailormen, who had deserted on account of the high pay ruling in Frisco. The present crowd was composed chiefly of "Dutchmen," and in each watch, consisting of eight men and a boy, there were only two Americans, one Englishman and a German. The remainder were dagoes and mixed breeds.

The two Americans were in the first mate's watch, the Englishman and the German being with the second's crowd, and the whole lot of them, white, olive and mixed, were about as hard a "rough-house" crew, scraped up from the waterfront, as one could find, and acceptable only because of the aforementioned high wages and shortage of men.

And, to complete the number of undesirables aboard, there was Mr. Pathan, the half-breed passenger.

Finally, Mr. Dunn, the first mate, was a nervous little man, totally unfitted to handle anything more than an orderly crew of respectable Scandinavians. The result was that already his own watch had been once so out of hand he had been forced to call upon the second officer to help him maintain authority; since when, automatically, as it were, the second mate had taken, though unofficially, the reins of authority into his own hands.

Thus the situation five days after leaving port, on the homeward passage.

A week had passed.

"If you please, sir, I'd like a word with you."

It was the big boatswain who spoke. He had come halfway up the poop ladder, and his request was put in a low voice, yet with an apparently casual air.

"Certainly, Barton! Come up here if you have anything about which you wish to speak."

"It's about the men, sir. There's something up, an' I can't just put me finger on it."

"How do you mean, something up?"

"Well, sir, they're gettin' a bit at a loose end, an' they're gettin' a bit too free-like with their lip if I tells 'em to do anythin'."

"Well, you know, Barton, I cannot help you in that. If you cannot keep them in hand without aid, you'll never do it with."

"'Tisn't exactly that, sir. I can handle a crowd right enough along with any man; savin' it be yourself, sir"—with an acknowledging glance at his officer's gigantic proportions—"but there's somethin' in the wind, as is makin' 'em too ikey. It's only since the cap'n went, an' it's my belief as yon passenger's at the bottom of it!"

"Ah!"

"You noticed somethin' then, sir?" asked the boatswain quickly.

"Tell me what makes you think the passenger may be in anything that is brewing?" said the second mate, ignoring the man's question.

"Well, for one thing, sir, he's too familiar with the men. An' I've seen him go forrard to the fo'cas'le of a night when 'twas dark. Once I went up to the door on the quiet, thinkin' as I'd get to see what it was as he was up to; but the chap on the lookout spotted me an' started talkin'. I reckoned he meant headin' me off; so I asked him to pass me down the end of me clothesline, for a bluff, an' then I made tracks."

"But didn't you get any idea of what the fellow was doing in the fo'cas'le?"

"Well, sir, it seemed to me as he was palaverin' to 'em like a father; but as I was sayin' I hadn't time to get the bearin's of what was goin' forrard. Then there's another matter, sir, as—"

"And you might tell the man, while he's up, to take a look at the chafing gear on the fore swifter," interjected the second mate calmly.

The irrelevancy of this remark seemed to bring the boatswain up all standing, as the saying goes. He glanced up at the officer's face, and in so doing the field of his vision included something else—the very one of whom they were talking. He understood now the reason of the second's apparently causeless remark; for that keen-sensed officer had detected the almost cat-like tread approaching them along the poop-deck, and changed the conversation on the instant.

For a couple of minutes the boatswain and the second mate kept up a talk upon certain technical details of ship work, until Mr. Pathan was out of hearing.

"I reckon as he thought he'd like to know what it was we're talkin' about, sir," remarked the boatswain, eying the broad back of the stout passenger.

"What is this other matter that you want to speak to me about?"

"Well, sir, some of the hands 'as got hold of booze somehow. I keeps smellin' of 'em whenever one of 'em comes near me, and I reckon as he"—jerking his head in the direction of Mr. Pathan—"is the one as is givin' it to 'em."

The second mate swore quietly.

"What's his game, sir? That's what's foozlin' me. I thinks it's time as you looked inter ther matter!"

"If I thought—"

"Yes, sir?" encouraged the boatswain.

But whatever the second mate thought, he did not put it into words. Instead, he asked the boatswain if he were of the opinion that any of the forecastle crowd were to be depended upon.

"Not one of 'em, sir! There isn't one as wouldn't put a knife inter you if he got half a chanst!"

The second nodded, as if the man's summing-up of the crew were in accordance with his own ideas. Then he spoke.

"Well, Barton, I cannot do anything till we know more definitely what is in the wind. You must keep your eyes open and report to me anything that seems likely to help."

Behind them they heard again the pad of Mr. Pathan's deck shoes.

"You had better overhaul the sheaves in those main lower topsail brace blocks," he remarked for the benefit of the listening passenger. "That will do for the present."

"Very good, sir," said the boatswain, and went down the ladder on to the main deck.

CHAPTER IV

It was in the afternoon watch, and Miss Eversley was sitting with a book in her lap, staring thoughtfully out across the sea.

Forward of her, the second mate tramped across the break of the poop. When she had appeared on deck, he had been pacing fore and aft along the poop, but had kept since then to the fore part of the deck.

Of the male passenger there was no sign. Indeed, since the big officer's "handling" of him, he had kept quite away from her, so that at last she was beginning to find her stay aboard not at all unpleasant. Occasionally the girl's glance would stray inboard to the great silent man, smoking and meditating as he paced across the planks.

It was curious (she recognized the fact) how often of late she had found her thoughts dwelling upon him. He was no longer a nonentity—something below the line of her horizon—but a man, and a man in whom she was beginning to be interested. She remembered now—what at the time she had scarcely noticed—her casual ignoring of his proffered aid as she stepped aboard. It had seemed nothing then to her, no more than if she had casually rejected the aid of a footman; but now she could not comprehend how she had done it.

From this her memory led her to that distinctly-to-be-regretted remark about his smoking. She watched him, and realized the more completely as she did so that she would be vitally afraid to do such a thing again; for, all unaware to herself, the manhood of the man was mastering her. Yet, at this time, she had no realization of the fact; nothing beyond that she was interested in him, perhaps somewhat afraid and certainly a little desirous of knowing him.

On the second mate's part, he was thinking of other things than her. The preceding day he had been obliged to step down on the main deck to exert authority, and had succeeded only by laying out a couple of the crew. That the disaffection was due, in part at least, to Mr. Pathan he had very little doubt; but no proof that would justify him in putting the man in irons, as he had determined to do the very moment such was forthcoming. Also, he knew that the captain's death had unsettled them, and that there were vague ideas among them that now they were under no compulsion to obey orders. It was doubtless, along these lines that Pathan was working with them, and the thought made the big officer grit his teeth.

"Look out, Mr. Grey!"

The words came shrill and sudden in the voice of Miss Eversley, and the second officer turned sharply from where he had stopped a moment to lean upon the rail. He saw that she was on her feet, her arm extended toward him, while her gaze flickered between him and aloft. In the same instant, there was a sort of sogging thud behind him.

His stare had followed the girl's, and for an instant he had seen the dark face of one of the crew over the belly of the mizzen topsail; then he had twisted quickly to see the reason of that noise, though already half comprehending the cause. In that portion of the rail over which he had just been leaning was stuck a heavy steel marlinspike, the sharp point thereof appearing below, for it had penetrated right through the thick teak.

For a moment he looked at it, while his face grew quietly grim. Then he turned and walked toward the mizzen rigging. From here he could look up abaft the mast. Thus he saw the man who had dropped the spike making his way rapidly from aloft.

Getting into the lower rigging, the man—who proved to be one of those the second mate had floored the previous day—called out in broken English his regret for the accident; but the officer, knowing how little of an accident there had been about the affair, said nothing. Then, as soon as the creature put foot on the deck, he caught him by the nape of the neck and walked him forward to where the spike stood up in the rail.

Below on the main deck stood several of the crew, watching what would happen, and fully prepared to make trouble if they got the half of a chance. They saw the second officer grasp the embedded spike with one great hand, then with apparent ease bend it from side to side till it broke, leaving in the rail that portion which had penetrated.

Immediately afterward, quite coolly, and calculating the force of the blow, he struck the man with it upon the side of the head, so that he went limp in his grasp; then he laid him down gently on the hencoop and bade a couple of them come up and carry him to his bunk. And this, being thoroughly cowed, as was the second mate's intention, they did without so much as a murmur.

As soon as the men were gone with their burden, he walked aft to where the girl stood.

"Thank you, Miss Eversley," he said simply. "I should have been spitted like a frog if you had not called."

She made no pretense of replying, and he looked at her more particularly. She was extraordinarily pale, and staring at him out of frightened eyes. He noticed also that she held to the edge of the skylight as if for support.

"You are not well?" he said, and made as if to support her.

But she warded him off with a gesture.

"What a brute you are!" she said in a voice that would have been cold had it been less intense.

He looked at her a moment before he replied, as if weighing the use of speech.

"You don't understand," he remarked at last, calmly. "We have a rough crowd to handle, and half measures would be worse than useless. Won't you sit down?" And he indicated the chair behind her.

"It—it was butchery!" she remarked with a sort of cold anger, and ignoring his suggestion.

"Very nearly—if you hadn't called." There had come a suggestion of humor about the corners of his mouth.

"I—"

She groped backward vaguely for the chair, and seemed unconscious that it was his hands which guided her there.

"Now, see here, Miss Eversley. You must really allow me to be the better judge in a matter of this sort. I cannot afford to sign for the long trip, if only for your sake."

"For my sake!" Her voice sounded scornful. "In what way does it concern me?"

The grimness crept back into his face and chased away the scarcely perceptible humor.

"In this way," he replied in a voice as nearly as cold as her own but for a certain almost savage intensity. "I, and I alone, am keeping matters quiet aboard here; for I may as well tell you at once that the first mate does not count for that much"—and he snapped his finger and thumb—"among the crowd we've got in this packet. They're quiet at present only because they're afraid of me."

"What do you mean?" She asked the question with a brave assumption of indifference, to which her frightened eyes gave no support. "How does it matter to me whether your men are quiet or not?"

He looked at her a moment quietly and with something in the expression of his face that would have been contempt had it not been tempered by a deeper emotion.

"Listen!" he said, and she quailed before his masterfulness. "If that spike had done its work just now, you had been better dead than here. Do you think—"

He did not finish but turned from her and walked forward along the deck, leaving her gazing at the nakedness of a hideous possibility.

CHAPTER V

A week passed in quietness, and, though the second mate and the boatswain between them had kept a strict watch upon the male passenger's movements, there had been nothing that could be looked upon with suspicion; for they had no knowledge of the tightly folded notes flipped to the helmsman, and by him conveyed forward, and read for the delectation of the mutinous crowd in the forecastle.

It was extraordinary that Pathan should discontinue so abruptly his nocturnal visits to the men. Possibly he had caught a stray word or two of the boatswain's confabulation with the second mate, and so taken fright. Whatever it was, the fact remained that it was impossible to come upon anything which would justify their putting him out of the way of doing mischief. Even the boatswain's complaints about the men's behavior seemed to be lacking foundation during this time, and altogether the ship appeared to be quieting down nicely.

Though there had seemed of late little need for anticipating trouble, yet the second mate had his doubts but that there was something under this apparent calm, and, having his doubts, took the precaution to carry a companionable weapon in his side pocket.

In the end, events proved that he was right; for, one afternoon on watch, the boatswain, chancing to have physical trouble with one of the men, the rest of the watch closed in upon him in a mob. At that the second mate went down to take a turn, which turn he took to such a tune that he had three of them stretched out before they were well aware that he was among them. They were beginning to give before his onslaught when suddenly he heard Pathan's voice, away aft, singing out:

"Get on to him, lads! Now's your time! Give the bully a taste of his own sort!"

At that the rest of them turned upon him with a rush, leaving the sadly mauled boatswain to himself. And now the second mate showed of what he was made. They were clinging on to him like a lot of weasels—gripping his legs to trip him, grasping at his hands and arms, and climbing on his back. One of these latter having clasped hands under his chin, was doing his utmost to throttle him.

This the second mate foiled by unclasping the fellow's dirty paws and pulling him bodily over his head, bringing him, with a continuation of the movement, crashing down upon those of his attackers immediately in front. At the same instant, the boatswain, being by now somewhat recovered, laid hold upon one of those in the rear and hauled him off. Even as he did so, there came the sound of a pistol shot.

The second mate hove himself round carrying the mass of clinging men with him. He saw Pathan coming along the decks toward them at a run. In his hand was a pistol, with the smoke still rising from it. Upon the deck lay the boatswain. He was kicking and twitching; for it was he whom the passenger had shot.

"You—skunk!" roared the second mate. He caught two of his attackers by the hair of their heads and beat their skulls together so they became immediately senseless.

He saw Pathan halt within a dozen feet of him and aim straight at his head. He had been dead the following instant, but that there happened a diversion.

A white face flashed into the field of his vision, and the next moment Miss Eversley had thrown a handful of some whitish powder into the man's face. The pistol dropped with a thud, and from Pathan there was nothing save a mixture of gasps and shouts, violent sneezing, and coughs that broke off oddly into breathless blasphemy.

The second mate shouted incoherently. Then the girl was upon his assailants, throwing handfuls of the powder into their faces; whereupon they loosed him, as if their strength had gone from them, and fell to much the same antics as had Pathan. Some of the powder rose and assailed the second officer's nostrils, so that he sneezed violently. It was pepper!

He turned to the girl. At her feet lay the tin with which she had wrought his relief. She herself was standing, crying and sneezing along with the rest, and trying to wipe her eyes with a peppery handkerchief.

The second mate's glance noted the pistol dropped by Pathan, and he stepped over, and, picking it up, put it in his pocket. Between him and the group of sneezing, choking men lay the body of the boatswain. A lot of the pepper had been spilt upon his upturned face, yet he moved no whit. He was quite dead.

"What's happened, Mr. Grey?" asked a thin voice at his elbow.

"Rank mutiny!" he replied.

"Whatever shall we do?" returned the voice, the owner of which was the first mate. "Whatever shall we do?"

"Nothing," said the second mate shortly.

He turned from the mate and bellowed to the other watch who were coming aft in a body, having been aroused by the noise.

"Now then, my lads! Up forrard with you! Smartly!" And he pulled out his revolver.

They went backward with a surge as he covered them.

"Back into the fo'cas'le! Don't stir out till I tell you!"

The threatening weapon, backed by the determination of the man, overawed them and they went quickly.

"Close that door!" he roared.

It was closed immediately. Then he turned his attention to those around. Miss Eversley was standing near, her cheeks white, but her eyes and nose very red. It was plain to him that she was all of a tremble and like to fall, so that, without more ado, he took her by the shoulders and led her to a seat upon a spar lashed along by the bulwarks.

"Now, don't faint," he commanded.

"I'm not going to," she said soberly.

He left her hurriedly; for the men, having recovered from the effects of the pepper, were gathered in a clump and eying him doubtfully. To the right, Pathan had got upon his feet. It is just possible that in another moment they would have been upon him, which would have meant the loosing of the other watch, had he not acted with decision.

"Cyrone and Andy," he shouted, facing them squarely, "aft with you, and tell the steward to pass out the irons!"

At the word, Andy started aft to obey. But Cyrone, one of those who had been foremost in the trouble, made no move.

"Cyrone!" said the second mate.

The man had done well to understand the dangerous quiet in his tone; but he did not. Instead, with unbounded insolence, he turned to the fellows surrounding him.

"Who for the irons, hey? They for we! I know! I know!" he shouted excitedly, and broke off into an unintelligible jargon of words.

"Cyrone!"

"For to—you go!" shouted the wretch in reply. It was evident that he was depending on the others to back him up.

The second mate said no word, but raised his pistol. The men about Cyrone scattered to each side. They had seen the second mate's eyes. In that last moment the fellow himself must have come suddenly into knowledge; for he started back, crying out something in an altered tone.

There was a scream from Miss Eversley, which blent with the sudden crack of the weapon; then Cyrone staggered and fell sideways on to the hatch. There was an instant of strange silence, broken by a dullish thud on the deck behind.

"Jardkenoff, go along with Andy for those irons," said the second mate in a level tone.

At his order the whole of them had started forward like frightened animals.

Jardkenoff ran past him, crying "Yi, yi, sir!" in a shaking voice.

While they were gone for the irons, the second mate bade the others lift the bodies of the boatswain and Cyrone on to the hatch. Then he looked round to discover the cause of that thud upon the deck. He saw that Miss Eversley had fallen forward off the spar on to her face, and at that he hastened to lift her. Fortunately, she had escaped injury, at which unconsciously he sighed relief. Then, taking her into his arms, he carried her to the hatch, singing out to one of the men by name to run aft to bring the steward with some brandy.

All this while, Pathan, the passenger, had stood in a dazed fashion beside the main-mast. Now, thinking he perceived a chance to steal aft to the temporary safety of his room, he began to sidle quietly away. It was no use, for the mate's voice pulled him up short before he had gone a dozen feet.

"You will stay where you are, Mr. Pathan!" was all that he said.

When the irons came, the steward accompanied them, carrying a glass full of brandy. This, under the eye of the second mate, he proceeded to administer. At the same time, the officer was superintending the ironing of Pathan. By the time that this was accomplished, Miss Eversley had begun to come to a knowledge of her surroundings, and presently sat up. Before this, however, the second mate had seen to it that Pathan was removed to the lazarette, for he would not have her upset further by sight of the murderer.

As soon as she was strong enough, he gave her his arm and led her aft to her cabin. In the saloon they came upon the captain's wife sitting limply in one of the chairs. At their entrance, she started up, and cried out something in a frightened voice. The poor woman seemed demented and quite incapable of rational speech. It was evident that the scene on deck—which apparently she had witnessed—had, in conjunction with her recent loss, temporarily unsettled her mental balance.

With difficulty they persuaded her to go to her room, after which the second mate returned to the deck, with the intention of trying to put a little heart into the nonentity whom Fate had placed above him in the scale of authority.

That evening, in the second dog-watch, the body of Cyrone was, by his orders, ignominiously dumped over the side without ceremony, and with a piece of rope and holystone attached to his feet.

CHAPTER VI

The following day it was a somewhat cowed lot of men who came aft, at the second mate's bidding, to the funeral of the boatswain. Nor did his opinion of them, expressed tersely after the body had gone down into the darkness, help to reassure them. He told them that, at the first sign of further insubordination, he would shoot them down like the dogs they were; that, in future, there should be no afternoon watch below, and that work should be continued right through the two dog-watches. On learning this, there came a slight murmur, expressive of discontent checked by fear, from the men grouped below the break.

"Silence!" roared the second officer, and whipped out a pistol from his side pocket.

Instantly the murmur ceased; for the men, as was the second's intention, realized that he would stop nowhere to enforce his commands. And there was still vividly in their minds the execution of Cyrone.

As the men went forward, the first mate ventured a weak protest against the second's measures.

"You'll have 'em murdering us, Mr. Grey, if you go on like that! Why don't you speak to 'em nicely?"

The second mate looked down upon his superior. At first his glance denoted impatient contempt; but after the first moment an expression of tolerance spread over his features as he took in the other's almost pathetic weakness of face and figure.

"I believe you read the Bible, Mr. Dunn?"

"I—I—" began the mate, flushing slightly. "Yes—perhaps I do sometimes. Why?"

"Well, you should know how little use swine have for pearls."

"You think, then, Mr. Grey—"

"I'm certain. That scum would take kindness for a sign of weakening on our part, and then—"

He made an expressive gesture.

"I wish to God we were home!" said the mate fervently.

"You cheer up, mister!" replied the big officer. "If you have any trouble with your lot, don't stop to talk—shoot!"

"It's an awful thing to take a life."

"It is a necessary thing sometimes. And, besides, you have only to bang on the deck for me, and I'll be up in a brace of shakes."

And so, after a few more words of encouragement to the frightened man, the second left him in charge, and went below for a sleep.

True to his word, the second mate kept the mutinous crowd of sailormen hard at it from dawn to dusk. Even the first mate, inspired by his example and encouragement, made a brave attempt to follow in his wake. As the second mate put it, "Sweat the flesh off their bones, and they'll be too tired to use their dirty brains." Also, he was the more confident of keeping them in subjection, now that Pathan was safely ironed in the lazarette.

Thus, at last, matters seemed in a fair way to tend to a happy ending of the troubles that had beset them so far. Yet of one person this could not be said; for the mental condition of the captain's wife showed no signs of improvement. Fortunately, she was in no way violent and gave little trouble, her state being that of one suffering from melancholia in one of its quieter forms.

Then one morning it was discovered she was missing. A search was made through the ship, but without success. She was never found. Evidently the poor creature had crept on deck some time during the night and gone overboard.

From this, onward, nothing disturbed the monotony of the voyage for many days. The second mate kept the crew well in hand, in no way abating rigorous treatment of them, so that did he but raise a hand they jumped to do his bidding.

And now of Miss Eversley. Day by day the girl had found her thought centering upon the second mate. The horizon of her mind seemed bounded by him. She caught herself watching his least gesture as he paced the poop in his meditative fashion, or gave some order to the crew. Did the first mate relieve him, so that he could go below for a sleep, the deck seemed strangely empty, the wind chilly, the sea dull and uninteresting. Yet when he relieved the first mate, how different! Then the wind was warm, the sea full of an everlasting beauty, the deck, nay, the very planks of the deck, companionable.

And so she grew into the knowledge that she loved him, even to the extent of looking forward to her future life as a hideous blank, if he were not to share it; while he—silly man! He would break off his walks to sit and chat with her; but of that which she most desired to hear, not a word. Yet, by his eyes, she guessed that he cared; but for some reason—possibly because she was so much alone—he said nothing.

And so, at last, she might have come to aid him in spanning the gulf that remained yet between them; but that fate, in its own terrible way, took a hand.

CHAPTER VII

"Mr. Grey! Mr. Grey! Jack! Jack!"

The second mate woke with a start and leapt up in his bunk.

Miss Eversley was standing in the doorway of his berth.

"Quick! They've killed the first mate! And they're coming down—now! Pathan has been let out, and he's with them!"

Even before she had made an end of speaking, the second mate had reached the floor with a bound. He snatched the revolver from under his pillow, and ran into the saloon.

From the doorway, giving into the companion stairs came the sounds of whispering, and the padding of many bare feet descending. He made a quick step to meet them; but the girl caught his arm.

"Don't, Jack! Don't!" Then, as he still hesitated: "For my sake—remember! Oh! Is there no place?"

She stopped, for the second mate had caught her by the arm and was running her toward the fore part of the saloon. His wits, slightly bewildered by sleep, had flashed instantly to their normal clearness under the stress of her terror. He realized that, for her sake alone, he had no right to throw away his chances of life.

Just as the foremost of the mutineers stepped silently into the dimly lighted saloon, the big officer pushed open the door of the foremost berth on the port side and thrust Miss Eversley in. At the same moment, the man at the other end discovered them and gave a yell to announce the fact.

The following instant he lay dead, and the man behind him shared the same end. This caused a temporary hesitation on the part of the attackers, and in that slight interval the second officer slipped into the berth after the girl, slammed the door, and locked it.

"Stand to one side," he whispered to her.

As she did so, he hurled himself at the forward bulkhead of the berth. One of the boards started, and he attacked it again, the noise he was making drowning that of the mutineers in the saloon.

Crash! The momentum of his effort had made a great breach in the woodwork and taken him clean through into the absolute darkness of the sail-locker beyond.

In a moment he was back. He caught the girl by the wrist and helped her through. Even as he did so there came a loud report in the saloon, and a bullet stripped off a long splinter on the inner side of the door as it came through.

Immediately, the second officer raised his weapon, and fired— once—twice. At the second shot there came a sharp outcry from one of those beyond the door, and then three shots in quick reply. They hurt no one, for the big officer had bounded into the sail-locker. He had dropped his emptied weapon into his side pocket and was helping Miss Eversley over the great masses of stowed sails.

In the half of a minute he whispered to her to stand. An instant he fumbled, and she heard the rattle of a key. Then a square of pale light came in the darkness ahead of her, and she saw that he had opened a trap in the steel bulkhead that ran across the poop.

The following instant she was in darkness; for the huge bulk of her companion completely filled the aperture as he forced himself through. The light came again, and then she saw his head silhouetted against it in the opening.

"Give me your hand," he whispered, and the moment afterward she was standing beside him on the deck, under the break of the poop.

For an instant they stood there, scanning the decks, but every soul, saving the helmsman, had joined in the attack. Through the opening behind them came the sound of blows struck upon the door of the berth which they had just quitted. No time was to be lost; for the moment that the brutes discovered that rent in the woodwork of the berth, they would be after them.

A sudden idea came to the second officer. He shut down the door of the vertical trap and locked it. The men would search the sail-locker for them, now that it was shut and fastened; while, if he had left it open, they would have been on their track immediately.

"Forrard to the half-deck," he muttered, and they ran out into the moonlight.

Now the half-deck was a little, strongly built steel deck-house, situated about amidships. It had one steel door on the after end, and once they were in, and this shut, they would be comparatively safe, at least for the time being.

Abruptly, as they ran, there came a muffled outcry, and they knew that the door to the berth had been broken down. They reached the half-deck, and, while Miss Eversley sprang over the washboard, the officer ran to slip the hood which held the door back. Even as he reached up his hand there came a shout from the poop. They were discovered.

There came a thudding of rapid feet, and he saw the whole remaining crew of the boat tumbling hurriedly down the ladder on to the main deck. At that critical instant he found that the hook was jammed. He riddled at it a moment; but still it refused to come out of its eye.

The running men were halfway to him, howling like wild beasts, and brandishing knives and belaying-pins. In desperation he caught the edge of the door, put one foot against the side of the house, and tugged. An instant of abominable suspense; then the hook gave, parting with a sharp crack. Through the very supremeness of his effort, he staggered back a couple of paces, then, before he could regain the door to shut it, a couple of the men who had outstripped the others, leaped past him and into the half-deck, with a cry of triumph.

He heard Miss Eversley scream; then a third man was upon him. The second mate tried to slam the door in his face, but the fellow jammed himself in between the door and the side of the doorway. At that the big officer caught him by the chin and the back of the head, and plucked him into the half-deck by sheer strength. Then he brought the door to, and slipped the bolt, just as the rest of the men outside hurled themselves against it.

From the girl there came a cry of warning, and, in the same instant, the loud clang of some heavy missile striking the door by his right ear. He whirled round just in time to receive the united charge of the three he had imprisoned with himself in the deck-house.

Fortunately there was a sufficiency of light in the berth; for the lamp had been left burning by the former occupants when they left to join in the attack on the afterguard.

Two of the men had their knives. The third stooped and made a grab for the iron belaying-pin which he had just thrown at the officer. Him the second mate made harmless by a kick in the face; then the other two were upon him.

He snatched at the knife-hand of the man to the right, and got him by the wrist; tried to do the same to the other and missed. The fellow dodged, rushed in and slashed the second mate's shirt open from the armpit to the waist, inflicting a long gash, but the next instant was hurled across the berth by a terrific left-hand blow.

The second mate turned upon the man whose wrist he had captured. His fingers were hurting intolerably, for the fellow was tearing at them with the nails of his loose hand so that they were bleeding in several places. He caught the wretch by the head, jammed the left arm under his chin, and leaned forward with a vast effort. There was a horrid crack, and the man shuddered and collapsed.

There came a little broken gasp of horror from the girl who was crouched up against the corner on the starboard side. The second mate turned upon her.

"Turn your face to the bulkhead, and stop your ears," he commanded.

She shivered and obeyed, trembling and striving to stifle back a tumult of sobbing which had taken her.

The officer stooped and removed the knife from the hand of the dead man. Upon the door behind him there sounded a perfect thunder of blows. Abruptly, as he stood up the glass of the port on the starboard side was shattered, and a hand and arm came into the light.

The second mate dodged below the line of the bunkboard. There was a loud report, and a bullet struck somewhere against the ironwork. He ran close up to the bunk, still keeping out of sight, then rose upright with a sudden movement and grasped the pistol and the hand that held it, leaned forward over the bunk, and struck with his knife a little below the arm. There came a howl of pain from outside and the body fell away from the port, leaving the loaded pistol in the second mate's grasp.

Not a moment did he waste, but slammed to the iron cover over the port and commenced to screw up the fastening. It was stiff, so that he had to take both hands to it, and because of this he placed the revolver down upon the bedding of the bunk.

This came near to causing his death, for, suddenly, as he wrestled with the screw, a hand flashed over his shoulder and grabbed the weapon. Instinctively the second mate dodged and swung up a defending arm. He struck something. There was a sharp explosion close to his head, and then the clatter of the falling weapon.

By this he had got himself about and saw that the two whom he had temporarily disabled were upon him. Before he could defend himself, one of them struck him with the iron belaying-pin across his head. It sent him staggering across the floor.

As he fell, a scream from Miss Eversley pierced to his dull senses, and he got upon his knees, gasping and rocking, yet still full of the implacable determination to fight. For all his grit he would have been dead but for the girl. He had grasped the legs of one of his assailants; but was too dazed and weakened to put forth his usual strength.

The second man raised the heavy pin for another smite, but it never fell. To the second mate, wrestling pointlessly, there sounded a dull thud and a cry. Something fell upon him all of a heap, as it were, and he was brought to the deck upon his side; yet he had not relaxed his somewhat nervous grip upon the man's legs, so that the fellow came down with him.

For perhaps the half of a minute he held on stupidly while the man struggled violently to get away. Then, almost abruptly, nerve and reasoning-power came back to him, and in the same instant a violent pain smote him between the left shoulder and the neck. He got upon his knees, hurling the dead body of the other man from off his shoulders with the movement.

He was now above his opponent, and at once attempted to capture the fellow's knife. In this he was not at first successful, with the result that he sustained a second stab, this time slitting open the front of his shirt, and cutting his breast. At that, growing inconceivably furious, he regarded not the knife, but smote the man with his bare fist between the eyes and again below the ear, and so shrewd and mighty were the blows that the fellow died immediately.

Perceiving that the man was indeed dead, the second mate got himself upon his feet. He was breathing deeply, and his head seemed full of a dull ache.

He took his gaze from the bodies at his feet, and glanced around. Not two yards distant stood Miss Eversley. She had a revolver in her right hand. At that, the second mate understood how he had escaped with his life. Yet he had no thought of thanking her; for the horror in her face warned him not to do anything that might increase her realization of what she had done. Instead, he made two steps to her, and took her in his arms.

With the feel of his arms about her, she dropped the pistol and broke into violent weeping. And he, having some smattering of wisdom, held his peace for a space.

Presently the extreme agitation of the girl passed off, and she sobbed only at intervals. Later still she spoke.

"I shall never be happy again."

And still the second mate preserved the sweet wisdom of silence.

"Never, never, never!" he heard her whispering to herself.

And so, in a while, she calmed down to quiet breathing. For a space they stood thus, and on the decks all about the little house was silence, save for the occasional pad, pad, of a bare foot, as those without moved hither and thither.

CHAPTER VIII

The day had come and passed, and it was again night.

Within the house things could be seen but dimly, for the lamp was turned no more than a quarter up, and of oil they had no supply beyond the quantity within the lamp itself. Fortunately, there was no immediate need to worry about water; for the water breaker, lashed to the port end of the table, was a quarter full, owing to the boatswain's and carpenter's dislike for soap and water.

As for food, an examination of the bread barge in one of the empty lower bunks showed him that there was enough biscuit to keep the two of them crudely fed for some days, provided they were careful. In the food cupboard there was also half a bottle of ship's vinegar, about half a pound of ship salt pork, some sugar in a soup-and-bully tin, and about three pounds of black molasses in a big seven-pound pickle jar; all of these being the usual savings of rations that might be found in the food locker of any other lime-juicer, windjammer in all the seven seas.

He had, aided by the girl, bound up his wounds, which were not sufficiently serious to trouble him with anything more than a constant smarting; and though he had bled a good deal, he was so full of life and vitality that he was scarcely aware of the loss, except that he was abnormally thirsty; which fortunately the water in the breaker enabled him to quench freely. Yet, all the same he held this need somewhat in check, for they must never run short of the precious fluid.

During the day a certain amount of light had driven in between the crevices about the door. Beyond this there had been none, for the ports were all protected by their iron covers. Fortunately, as the second mate had discovered, all of them had been fastened on the preceding night, previous to their making a refuge of the house, all, that is, save the one through which they had been attacked. To this fortunate happening it is probable they owed their lives.

In the corner of the house to the right of the door there was a grim mound. The second mate had spread a couple of blankets over it to hide its full horror from the eyes of the girl; yet, by this very act, he had made it almost more unbearable than if he had left them in all the stark awesomeness of uncovered death.

Out upon the decks was quietness. Indeed, all through the day there had been but one attempt to molest them, and this the second mate had foiled by quietly opening one of the after ports and firing into the thick of the attacking party. In this way he was persuaded that he could have held the house for as long as it pleased him to do so but for the insurmountable obstacle that confronted him in the shape of lack of ammunition. Yet, even as it was, it was plain to him that the repulse he had given them was likely to keep them at a respectable distance—at least for some while. For, out of a crew of sixteen deck-hands, six had already been killed and several wounded.

In the brief time he had been at the port he had gathered something of the methods they had been about to apply to the felling of the door. They had rigged up a spar on a tackle, so as to form a rough sort of battering ram; yet, in the brief attempt that he had permitted them, the machine had proved unsuccessful, for the suspending rope had been too long, and the rolling of the ship had caused the spar to swing across the after end of the house, in the fashion of a clock pendulum, so that at one moment the business end of the ram was opposed to the door, and another to some portion of the end of the house.

In spite of the failure of the attackers, the big officer was well aware that with a more perfect appliance, and no ammunition with which to beat them off, they would not be long in forcing the door. And then …

The second night of the imprisonment had come. The second mate had gone to the door and was listening; but beyond the pad of a bare foot, or hum of hoarse voices, there was nothing to tell of the watchers about the decks.

For her part, the girl was busying herself clearing away the few eatables from which they had been making a meal. This done, she hesitated a moment, then went over to the second mate.

"Let me stay up tonight and watch, Jack. You have not had any sleep, and I have slept most of the day. I could wake you up the moment anything happened."

The big man put a hand on each side of her shoulders and looked down upon her with a grave half-smile.

"Do, Jack! You can trust me," she urged.

"Trust you, little girl," he replied. "Yes, child, with a thousand lives if I had them."

"Then you will let me stay up and watch?"

He shook his head slowly.

"There will be no need tonight, at any rate. They cannot get at us without noise. We may both sleep."

This he said to quiet her entreaties; for he had no intention to allow her to sit alone in the darkness with her thoughts, and that blanket-covered mound, while he slept. More, he wished her to sleep; for he had a project which he hoped to carry out during the hours of darkness.

For a moment she stood looking up at him in the half-light. Then she slipped her hands on to his shoulders.

"Then I will say good night, Jack, for we must save the oil in the lamp."

The second mate stooped and kissed her.

"Good night, Mary," he said gravely.

"Good night," she whispered, kissing him in return.

Then she left him and went behind the blanket which he had rigged up before the bunks on the starboard side.

A space of about two hours passed, during which the second mate lay awake listening. Presently, realizing that the girl was asleep, he got up and quietly opened the door of the house. He listened a minute and found no one about, then swiftly he carried out each of the dead bodies on to the deck and left them there. He returned to the house and locked the door.

All at once, from outside the door, there rose an outcry. At that, he knew that the dead had been discovered. The outcries sank to a subdued murmur; for there had come fear among the men. Yet from thence onward, the door was never left unguarded day or night.

CHAPTER IX

The morning of the fourth day of their imprisonment dawned, and the second mate was awakened by a noise of hammering close against the port on the left side of the door. He jumped from his bunk quietly, and crept softly to the one on his right. He had the revolver in his hand.

Very cautiously he unscrewed the fastening of the iron cover, and glanced out, but could see no one. For a little he listened, and between the blows he caught a murmur of talk some little distance away. Abruptly he recognized Pathan's voice. At that, quickly but silently, he unscrewed the fastening of the glass and opened it. He thrust his head out and looked to the left.

Close to him, and right in front of the door, stood one of the men. He held the muzzle of a clumsy ship's musket, the butt resting on the deck. The second mate remembered having observed this same antique weapon hanging in the steward's pantry. It was evident that they were but poorly supplied with firearms.

Beyond the guard, he made out a couple more of the men fixing a heavy piece of timber across the other port. Evidently they had hit upon this plan of preventing his interfering with their operations. With the two after ports blocked they could do much as they pleased.

Suddenly a sharp exclamation on his right startled the second officer. He glanced round. There was Pathan fumbling with his revolver.

Instantly the second mate snatched his head into the shelter of the house. Almost at the same moment there sounded a thunderous bang, close to the left. He heard Pathan give a scream of pain, breaking off into a blatter of cursing.

At the risk of his life he shoved his head out. Pathan was nursing his right hand, while big tears of pain were running down his cheeks to that strange accompaniment of blasphemy. On the deck, close to his feet, lay the shattered butt of his revolver. The second mate twisted to the left for a brief glance. He saw that the guard was sitting upon the deck, rubbing his right shoulder. He looked woefully scared, while nearby lay the cumbrous weapon with which he had been armed.

What had happened was now clear to the big officer. The man had fired at the protruding head—but a fraction too late—with the result that the bolt, with which the gun had been loaded, had stricken the passenger's revolver, destroying it and wounding his hand.

Even as the solution came to the officer, the guard had reached for his gun and scrambled to his feet. In another moment he would have clubbed the second mate, but that a bullet sent him twitching to the deck.

The second mate turned his pistol upon Pathan. Could he but rid the ship of that fiend, all might yet be well.

Yet, as he pressed the trigger for the second time, his elbow was jogged from within the house. He swore between his teeth and tried another shot, only to be warned by the unsatisfying click of the hammer that his ammunition had come to an end.

He drew away from the port with an angry gesture, and well it was for him that he did so, for one of the two at work upon the port, seeing that the weapon was empty of cartridges, had run at him with a hammer. The blow missed, and the following instant the second mate had slammed the covers and fastened up the port.

He turned and found the girl standing by him.

"Do you know," he said a trifle sternly, "you made me miss Pathan when you touched me. If I had shot that wretch the men would have been glad enough to come to terms."

He was hot with his failure, or he had not spoken so to her. And she, having but touched him because of the fear which had seized her at his rashness in so exposing himself, burst into crying; for she had been sorely overstrained with the rough happenings of late.

At this his anger left him and he made to comfort her, so, for that morning they sat together, she taking little heed of the various sounds about the house which told him that the fiends outside were preparing to batter down the door. They had covered up the second port immediately after his closing of the cover, so that he had no means of knowing how matters were progressing beyond such as his ears, trained in ship-craft, could tell him.

Very slowly the day passed to its close. He knew that the final struggle was at hand; but he did not by any means consider their chances of life beyond hope; for he knew that the crew had been greatly reduced, so that, could he but avoid the fire of the big musket, he might slay Pathan and put the rest to flight. Yet he had no knowledge but that the house might be their prison for a day or two longer; though, beyond that time they could not hope to stay, for of food they had but little, and less water.

The day had been a fine one, as they could tell by the light which came through the crevices around the somewhat loosely fitting door, and when at last the evening came, the girl went to the door to try to get a look at the sunset.

"Come and look, Jack," she said suddenly, after a period of silence.

He turned from the water breaker at which he was busy emptying the last few drops.

"What is it, Mary?"

His voice was perhaps a trifle uneasy, for he had made the discovery that there was left only half a pannikin of water. During the last two days of their imprisonment he had been limiting his allowance; for he would not see her stinted, and now, through some mischance, the spigot, which someone had fixed near the bottom of the little cask, had been loosened, and the small quantity of the imperative liquid which had been theirs was all squandered save for the drainings which he had emptied into the enameled mug.

He came across to where she stood. For the moment he was minded not to tell her, then, remembering because of the fiends outside, that a clear knowledge of their position was her due, he told her not only of this matter but of the likelihood of the crisis being near at hand.

When he had made an end, she reached up one hand to his shoulder, then held out the other for the mug. She drew him down to the crevice through which she had been peering.

"See," she said, "did you ever see such a sunset?" Her voice dropped. "And it may be our last, Jack." She patted his shoulder as she spoke. "You know, boy, I may be only a silly girl, but I know nothing but a miracle can save us."

It was the first time she had spoken out so plainly, and he, having nothing to answer, stared out blindly into the dying glory outside.

In a little, perhaps the half of a minute, she drew him back somewhat and held the little mug up before them.

"We will drink it together, darling," she whispered, and bent her head over and kissed the brim, then handed it to him; but he was not deceived.

"Fair play, little woman. You have drunk nothing."

He passed it back to her, and she, knowing him, sipped a little, then held it up to him and made him drink from her own hands. He was hideously thirsty, but controlled himself to one gulp only; then took the mug from her and set it down upon the table. For the end was not yet, and she might have need of it ere then.

It was almost dark in the berth, for the oil of the lamp was done this long while, the only light they had coming in through the crannies about the door.

For a while the two of them stood together. He was deep in pondering as to when the attack would come. Probably as soon as it was dark; for, of course, they could not be absolutely sure that he had no further supply of cartridges.

She for her part was leaning forward, peering through the narrow opening at the red splendor of the sun's shroud. Once or twice she ran her fingers up and down this crack, as if she would fain enlarge it. Possibly the tips showed outside, for her hands were very slender; yet, however it may have been, it is certain that one of the devils upon the deck was attracted and crept up on tiptoe. Inside, the girl, staring out, saw something come abruptly between her and the sun. The second mate saw it at the same moment, else she had been dead on the instant.

He pushed her from him, out of a line with the crack, and in so doing brought himself almost directly opposite. There came a sudden spurt of flame into the semi-darkness of the house, and a tremendous report close up against the door. The girl gave a little scream which almost drowned her lover's moan of pain, but not quite.

"You are not hurt, dearest?" she cried out loud.

For a moment he did not answer, and in that quick silence she heard a man outside laugh brutally.

The second mate had his hand up to his eyes and was very silent. In the dimness of the place she saw that he was swaying upon his feet.

"Jack," she said in an intense whisper of fear. "Are you hurt?"

She caught his wrist with a gentle hold. Still he did not reply. Beyond the door she heard the murmur of voices, and odd words and fragments of sentences drifted to her uncomprehending brain.

"—for?"

"Fiddlin' at ther door!"

"—bust! The gun's busted!"

"Thank God!" It was the second mate who had spoken, and the girl loosed her hands from his wrists in her astonishment. Then, with a sudden applying of his words to satisfy the desire of her soul—

"You are not hurt, then, dear?"

"A—a little. My eyes—"

"What? Let me see!" But he swung round from her.

"Can you get me some—something for a bandage?" There was a desperate levelness in his tone.

He took two or three uncertain steps across the floor, as if bewildered. She followed him. He took his hands from his face and moved his head from side to side, as if peering about the house. Abruptly, he turned and blundered into her clumsily. She would have fallen, but that he caught and steadied her.

"Jack! Oh, Jack!" she cried, for even in the dimness of the place she had caught a glimpse of where his eyes ought to have been.

"It's all right, little woman," he replied in a voice that was nearly steady. "I—can't see very well while the pain's bad." He had covered his face again with his hands.

She answered nothing. She was tearing one of her undergarments into strips, and trying to quiet her sobs.

CHAPTER X

The night had come. The second mate, the upper portion of his face swathed in wrappings, was seated on the sea-chest below his bunk. The girl was sitting by him, and their right hands were clasped.

The crack along the edge of the door had been stuffed up with a strip of blanket. Upon the edge of the table was stuck a tiny fragment of candle, and by the light of this she was reading slowly the betrothing passage from the Solemnization of Matrimony—that in which the man plights his troth. The second mate was repeating the words after her.

Presently they had made an end, and the girl slipped her hand gently from his; then, taking hold of his in turn, she read in a firm voice that passage in which the woman gives her troth. At the end, she released the second mate's hand and drew a ring from off one of her fingers. This she put gently into his hand. Then having given him her left, he slid the ring on her third finger, repeating the meanwhile, after her, the passage which she whispered to him.

And after that they sat a while, too full of thought for speech.

Presently the candle went out abruptly, and the two were alone in the darkness.

From the deck beyond the door came an occasional mutter of speech, an occasional padding of feet and an occasional creaking of gear, and the two within sat and waited.

Toward midnight the moon rose and limned the outline of the door in pale light. Presently the girl spoke.

"The moon has risen, Jack."

She rose from his side and moved to the door. Perhaps she might be able to see what the crew were busied at. Abruptly, as she stooped forward to peer, something struck the door a tremendous blow, filling the interior of the house with a deafening, hollow boom. She cried out in fear, and even as she cried came the second blow and the crack of a breaking rivet.

She realized that the attack had begun, and groped a moment for the matches. She struck one and examined the door. To the casual glance it was unharmed; but by the light of the third match she made out that a rivet in the bottom hinge was snapped. By this, a dozen blows had been dealt, and yet, from the second mate, seated upon the sea-chest, no sound.

All at once he spoke.

"Come here, Mary."

She came to him quickly, wondering, half-consciously, at the strange harshness of his tone. By the light of the match which she carried, she saw that he had in his hand the revolver.

"It's no good, Jack," she said despairingly, thinking he had a mind that she should use it in their defense. "There are no cartridges!"

"I kept—one," he said with a jerk, and still in that unnatural voice.

He reached out his left hand to her. And at that she comprehended, and comprehending shrank back with a little wail.

"O-o-h! O-o-h! Jack!" she sobbed, with a sudden plumbing of the abyss of mortal terror.

There came a louder crash on the door, and then the second mate's voice.

"Mary!"

She went up to him, quivering.

"Not yet, Jack! Not yet!"

He put his left arm round her.

"Mary!" he said, and the fierce agony which possessed him spoke out in his voice. "Tell me when the door begins to go!"

And she knew that the time of the door's standing was the span of her life.

At each ringing thud of the ram she could feel the place quiver. By now it had become a steady, almost rhythmic *boom, boom, boom,* which, as a rivet gave, blent into a crash. The inside of the steel house was like the inside of a great drum.

And so a minute passed, and another, and still the door stood, while that dread booming beat out the knell of the two within—he grim for very fear of himself, and she shaking because of the thing that was to happen, and still with some room in her soul for his sufferings, yet unable to say anything; for in those last moments he had become her executioner as well as her lover, and there were things she could not say to the two.

Boom! Boom! Boom! Crash!

"Mary?" His voice sounded like the cry of a lost soul, and the love in the woman answered to it. Yet the physical terror of death was upon her.

"The—the door—is—is—stop! It's only the bottom hinge has broken. It isn't down yet!"

Crash! Crash! Crash!

The girl, all of a shiver, turned suddenly and put her arms round his neck.

"Kiss me, Jack!"

Crash! Crash!

He repelled her for a moment, then, drawing her to him, kissed her good-by.

Crash! C-r-a-s-h!

"Don't! Don't! Not yet! It isn't down yet! Give me—give me as long as you—you can!"

For the arm about her shoulders had tightened with a sudden grip. Then abruptly—

"Have you—have you a—a—a knife, Jack?"

He took his arm from about her and brought something from behind, which he held out for her to take.

She saw it faintly by the glimmer of moonlight that came through the shaken door.

"No, no, no!" she cried, and shuddered. "You—you take it! Give me the pistol. I—I can see."

He gave up the revolver to her and shifted the knife to his right hand. Even as he did so, the door crashed in. He felt the girl thrill in the grip of his arm; then her right hand went up, and, an instant later came the click of the hammer, but no report—the cartridge had missed fire. She had aimed at a dark figure beyond the door-way, which she had recognized as Pathan. Yet the cruelty of fate denied her even the consolation of knowing that she died leaving her lover not at the mercy of that creature.

She cried out her dismay, and then again in terror, for the grip of the second mate's arm warned her that the end had indeed come. There came the rush of feet along the deck, and the blaze of a flare. Then Pathan's voice:

"Don't hurt the girl!"

She caught so much of it. Then the touch of her lover's fingers upon her breast made her quiver. She felt his right arm go back for the blow.

"Oh, my God, help me! Help me! Help me!" he heard her whispering desperately, and it shook him badly in that supreme moment. But, for the love he bore her, he meant that there should be no faltering in his stroke. Abruptly, the girl felt him start violently, and he began to quiver from head to feet. He cried out something in a strange voice.

"Oh, my God!" he said in a sort of whispering, husky shout. "I can see! I can see! Oh, my God, I can see! We're going to win! Mary, Mary! we're going to win! I can see! I can see! I can see! I tell you, I can see!"

He loosed her and put both his hands up to his bandages, which had slid down on to his nose, and tore them away in a mad kind of fashion, while the girl stood limp and sick against him, still half-fainting.

"I can see! I can see!" he began to reiterate again.

He seemed to have gone momentarily insane with the enormous revulsion from utter despair to hope. Suddenly he caught the girl madly into his arms, staring down at her through the darkness. He hugged her savagely to him, whispering hoarsely his refrain of:

"I can see! I can see! I tell you I can see!"

He held her a single instant or two like this; then he literally tossed her into one of the upper bunks.

"Don't move!" he whispered, his voice full of the most intense purpose. "I'm going to get square with that brute now. There's a chance for both of us. Here, take the knife in case I don't manage. Just lie still, whatever happens. You must be out of the way. I could tackle a hundred of them now."

He was silent, listening. By the sound of the men's voices, the second mate knew that they had halted some little distance from the doorway. There they hung for a few moments, no man anxious to be the first to face the big officer. For they had no knowledge of his blindness.

Then he caught Pathan's voice urging them on.

"Go on, lads! Go on! There won't be much fight left in him!"

At that, a feeling of dismay filled him. It was evident that Pathan was not going to head the attack, and he might die without ever getting his hands on to him.

From the irresolute men came a shuffle of feet. Then a man's voice rose—

"Trow de flare into ze hoose."

To the second mate the remark suggested a course of action. He threw himself upon a sea-chest, so that his face could be seen from the doorway. He kept perfectly still. If the man threw the flare into the house they would see his damaged face and think him dead. It might be that the coward Pathan would venture to come into the place—*then!*

Thud! Something struck the floor near him.

He kept his eyes shut. He could see no light; but the smell of burning paraffin was plain in his nostrils. He listened intently and seemed to catch the sound of stealthy footsteps. Abruptly, a voice just without the doorway shouted:

"They're both dead! Both of 'em!"

"What?"

It was Pathan's voice. He heard the noise of booted feet approaching at a run. They hesitated one instant on the threshold, then came within, and a surge of barefoot pads followed. The booted feet came to a stand not two yards away.

For an instant there was silence, a bewildered, awestruck silence. Pathan's voice broke it.

"My God!" he said. "My God!"

Immediately afterward he screamed, as the huge, bloodstained form of the big officer hurled itself upon him. There were cries from the men, and a pell-mell rush to escape. Someone fell upon the flare and extinguished it.

There was a shivering silence. It was filled abruptly by the beginning of a sobbing entreaty from Pathan. This shrilled suddenly into a horrid screaming. The men were no longer trying for the doorway, for the second mate had got between it and them. They could see him indistinctly against the moonlight beyond. He was flogging the steel side of the house with something. Beyond the hideous thudding of the blows, the house was silent.

One of the crouched men, tortured to madness, threw a belaying-pin. The next instant the second mate hurled himself among them. He had the battered steel door for a weapon, and the edge of it was as a plowshare amidst soil.

Amid the cries of the men, the side of the house rang out a dull thunder beneath the weight of some blind, misdirected blow.

Most of the men escaped upon their hands and knees, creeping out behind the man who smote and smote. They got to the forecastle upon all fours, too terrified and bewildered even to get to their feet. There, in the darkness, behind closed and barred doors, they sat and sweated, in company of those who had hesitated to enter the house.

Presently the ship was quiet.

The berserker rage eased out of the second mate and he perceived that the house was empty, and the mutiny truly ended. He cast the heavy steel door clanging through the open doorway, out on to the main deck, a dripping testimony of a man's prowess against enormous odds.

He stood a moment, breathing heavily. Then, remembering, he wheeled round in the darkness to where, in the gloom of the upper bunk, the girl lay shivering, with her hands pressed tightly over her ears.

He caught her up in his great arms, with the one word, "Come!" and stepped through the open doorway into the moonlight, the fallen door ringing under his tread. Then, master of his ship, he carried her aft to the cabin.

SAID AFZEL'S ELEPHANT

Harold Lamb

Put cloth of gold upon a fool and a multitude will do reverence to him; clothe a wise man in beggar's garments, and few will honor him. Yet those few will have their reward.—*Turkestan Proverb.*

CHAPTER I

We were three men with two horses and two swords. We were outcasts in the thickets of the foothills of Badakshan, under the peaks of the Roof of the World. We had earned the wrath of the Mogul of India and there were two thousand riders searching for us.

It was the year of the Ox—the year 1608 by the Christian calendar—and Jani Beg, the Uzbek, had taken Badakshan from my lord, Baber Shirzad Mir, sometimes called the Tiger Lord.

Nevertheless, we three were happy. We had taken Shirzad Mir from the hands of Jani Beg, who had marked him for death.

Aye, Shirzad Mir sat in the clean white robes in which he had prepared to die by a twisted bowstring around the neck, and laughed for joy of seeing the sun cast its level darts of light over the peaks and through the trees that gave us shelter. Our hearts—the *Ferang*'s and mine—were lifted up for a moment by the warmth that comes with early morning. We had an ache in our bellies for lack of food; we had not slept for a day and a night. Also, I was stiff with many bruises.

"Tell me," said Shirzad Mir, fingering his full beard, which was half gray, half black, "how you got me out of the prison of Khanjut."

While I watched, lying at the edge of the thicket on my side, the *Ferang*—the Englishman, Sir Ralph Weyand—explained how we had climbed through the water tunnel of Khanjut into the walls, and how we two alone had freed the *Mir* while Jani Beg and his men were tricked into looking the other way by a herd of cattle that we had sent to the gate of Khanjut.

He spoke in his broken *Mogholi*, but Shirzad Mir, who was quick of wit, understood.

"And whence came you?" he asked.

Sir Weyand told how he had been sent to India as a merchant, and had been driven from the court of the Mogul by the wiles of the Portuguese priests. When he had done, Shirzad Mir rose up and touched his hand to earth, then pressed the back of it to his brow. This is something he has seldom done, being a chieftain by birth, and a proud man. Sir Weyand rose also and made salutation after the manner of his country.

I watched from the corner of my eye, for my curiosity was still great concerning the *Ferang*: also, for all he had borne himself like a brave man that night, he was but a merchant and I knew not how far we could trust him. While I lay on the earth and scanned the groups of horsemen that scurried the plain below us, seeking for our tracks, the thought came to me that our fortunes were desperate.

We were alone. The followers of Shirzad Mir were scattered through Badakshan, or slain. The family of my lord was in the hands of Jani Beg—upon whom may the curse of God fall. To the north of Badakshan we would find none but Uzbeks, enemies. To the east was the nest of bleak mountains called by some the Hindu-Kush, by others the Roof of the World. To the West, the desert.

True, to the south, the Shyr Pass led to the fertile plain of Kabul, but up this pass was coming Said Afzel, the son of Jani Beg, with a large caravan. I had heard that Said Afzel was a poor warrior, being a youth more fond of sporting with the women of his harem and with poets, than of handling a sword. Still, he had followers with him, for he was bearing the gifts of the Mogul Jahangir from Agra to Jani Beg.

Something of this must also have been in the mind of Shirzad Mir, who had been lord of Badakshan for twice ten years, during the reign in India of the Mogul Akbar—peace be on his name!

"I am ruler," he smiled sadly, "of naught save two paces of forest land; my dress of honor is a robe of death. For a court I have but two friends."

Shirzad Mir was a broad man with kindly eyes and a full beard. He had strength in his hands to break the ribs of a man, and he could shoot an arrow with wonderful skill. He was hasty of temper, but generous and lacking suspicion. Because of this last, he had lost Badakshan to Jani Beg, the Uzbek.

He knew only a little of writing and music; still, he was a born leader of men, perhaps because there was nothing he ordered them to do that he would not do himself. Wherefore, he had two saber cuts on his head and a spear gash across the ribs.

Thinking to comfort him, I rose up from the place where I was watching and squatted down by them.

"There are many in Badakshan," I said—long ago he had granted me leave to be familiar with him—"who will come to you when they know you are alive."

"Who will tell them, Abdul Dost?" he asked mildly. "We will be hunted through the hills. The most part of the nobles of Badakshan have joined the standard of Jani Beg."

"The men of the hills and the desert's edge are faithful, Shirzad Mir," I said.

They were herdsmen and outlaws for the most part. Our trained soldiers had been slain, all but a few hiding out in the hills.

"Aye," he exclaimed, and his brown eyes brightened. "Still, they are but men. To take up arms against the Uzbeks we need arms—also good horses, supplies and treasure. Have we these?"

* * * *

So we talked together in low tones, thinking that the *Ferang* slept or did not hear. Presently I learned that he understood, for, with many pains, he had taught himself our tongue.

We spoke of the position of Jani Beg. Truly, it was a strong one. He himself held Khanjut, which was the citadel at the end of the Shyr ravine leading into India. Paluwan Chan, leader of his Uzbeks, was at the great town of Balkh with a garrison. Reinforcements were coming through the passes to the north from Turkestan. Outposts were scattered through the plains. Jani Beg was a shrewd commander. Only once did I know him to err badly in his plans. Of that I will tell in due time.

Shirzad Mir, who was brave to the point of folly, said he would go somehow to Agra and appeal for mercy from Jahangir himself. I had been to Kabul and I knew that the intrigues of Jani Beg had made his quarrel seem that of the Mogul and—such is the witchery of evil words—Shirzad Mir seem to be a rebel.

"That may not be," I answered.

Then the *Ferang* lifted his yellow head and spoke in his deep voice.

"I heard at Agra, Shirzad Mir," he said, weighing his words, "that you were a follower of the Mogul Akbar."

"Of Akbar," nodded my lord, "the shadow of God and prince of princes. He was a soldier among many."

"So it has been told me." Sir Weyand rested his chin on his fists and stared up where the blue sky of Badakshan showed through the trees. "When Akbar was in difficulty what plan did he follow?"

"He was a brave man. God put a plan into his head when it was needed. He had the wisdom of books and many advisors."

"And with this wisdom, I have heard he always did one thing when he was pressed by great numbers of enemies."

Shirzad Mir looked thoughtfully at the *Ferang*. It was a strange thing that this merchant, who carried a straight sword and came over the sea in a boat, should know of the great Akbar. Verily, wisdom travels hidden ways.

"Aye," he said, "the Mogul Akbar would say to his men that they should attack—always attack."

"Then," repeated Sir Weyand promptly, "we will attack. It is the best plan."

I threw back my head and laughed. How should the three of us, with but two horses, ride against the army of Jani Beg? How should we draw our reins against Khanjut? We should be slain as a lamp is blown out in the wind. A glance from Shirzad Mir, who frowned, silenced me when I was about to put this thought into speech.

"How?" he asked, still frowning.

Then I remembered that I also had asked this question of the *Ferang* and that his answer had freed Shirzad Mir. I drew closer to listen.

"In my country," said Sir Weyand, "there is a saying that he who attacks is twice armed."

He then told how an *ameer* of Spain, whose empire extended over *Ferangistan* and the lands across the western ocean, had sent a fleet of a thousand ships against England in Sir Weyand's youth; and how the Queen of England had fitted out a much smaller fleet, dispatching it to sail against the invader.

"Had we waited for the Spaniards on land, the issue might have been different," he said. "As it was, few of the Dons escaped with a whole skin. The advantages of those attacking are these: they can chose the ground best suited to them; they can strike when they are ready; also, their numbers appear greater in a charge or onset."

The thought came to me that perhaps the *Ferang*, being a bold man, would not hesitate to turn against us if the chance offered. After all, he had been sent by his king to get money and trade concessions from India, and the small province of Badakshan could mean little to him. What did we know of the King of England—except that he had ships and very fine artillery?

Still, at this time Sir Weyand needed the friendship of Shirzad Mir. And, although he was a merchant—which is a getter of money—he never in the weeks to come, and I watched closely, shunned the dangers we faced. Instead he welcomed a battle, and laughed, when he swung his long sword, as if he were about to go to a feast. It is written that a fight is like a cup of strong wine to some. Sir Weyand was such a man.

"True," nodded Shirzad Mir, who had listened with care, "the great Mogul Akbar once, when his men were wavering, went forward on his elephant to a knoll where all could see him; then he ordered his attendants to shackle the legs of the elephant with an iron chain so that he could not retreat. Whereupon his men rode forward, and the battle was won. Yet we are only three against as many thousands. In what quarter should we attack?"

"Aye," I put in, "where? We are not yet mad."

"We are like to be so from hunger or thirst," replied the *Ferang*, "if we do not better our fortunes. I heard you say we had no place to flee, and so we must attack."

"Khanjut?" smiled Shirzad Mir almost mockingly.

But the *Ferang* was not in jest.

"If we had a few score followers, it would not be a bad plan. But that is for you to decide, Shirzad Mir. You know the country. If I think of a plan, I will tell you."

That was all he had in his mind. I was disappointed. Perhaps I had expected too much of him.

"Meanwhile we must eat," I pointed out, feeling the urge in my stomach. "Iskander Khan will surely give us food, also weapons, if he has any."

I did not add that my horse was at the *aul* of Iskander Khan. Last night I had ridden a wild ass from Khanjut. But I did not want to do so again—until my bruises healed.

"It is well," said Shirzad Mir.

So he mounted one horse and the *Ferang* the other. I trotted before them, to spy out if the way was safe. Iskander Khan was the friend who had aided us with his herd of cattle and his two sons the night before. His *aul* was hidden in the hills not far away. But, as we traveled, we did not think to find what was awaiting us there.

CHAPTER II

About the time of noonday prayers we came to the Kirghiz' *aul*—three dome-shaped tents of willow laths covered with greased felt and hides. Over the opening of the biggest tent were yaks' tails, also an antelope's head. Under this sat Iskander Khan, cross-legged on the ground.

He was a very old man, bent in the back, with the broad forehead and keen eyes of his race and a white beard that fell below his chest. His eyes were very bright and his skin had shriveled overnight. His turban was disarranged as if he had torn it in grief.

He rose unsteadily to his feet when he saw Shirzad Mir. But my lord—because Iskander Khan had rendered him a great service, and because the Kirghiz was the older man—sprang down from his horse and went to meet him. Iskander Khan touched his hand to the earth and to his forehead three times; then Shirzad Mir embraced him.

"We have come for food," I said, looking for Wind-of-the-Hills, but seeing him not.

Iskander Khan lifted his hands in despair and pointed to the empty huts.

"It is my sorrow," he said, "that Shirzad Mir of Badakshan should come to my *aul* and ask meat when I have none to give. There is kumiss in the cask, and this I will bring you."

He did so, filling a bowl with the mare's milk, which is the distilled drink of the Kirghiz. Neither Shirzad Mir nor I liked kumiss. When we saw how disappointed Iskander Khan was at our refusal, we forced ourselves to drink some. As it happened, this was well, because the strong fluid eased the pang in our insides.

Shirzad Mir glanced curiously about the vacant *aul*. In the days when he had known Iskander Khan, the Kirghiz had many sheep and cattle.

Then Iskander Khan told us what had happened. The herd and flock which his sons had driven to the gate of Khanjut had been taken by Jani Beg, who was greatly angered at the trick we had played on him. Also, the two boys and the daughter of Iskander Khan had been taken by the Uzbek horsemen.

One of the youths Jani Beg had impaled on a spear which was then fastened to the gate of Khanjut. The other Kirghiz had been shot in the stomach with a matchlock ball and thrown from the walls of the citadel.

The girl Jani Beg had had flayed alive. Iskander Khan had been too feeble to ride with his sons. News of what happened had been brought him by a Khirghiz sheep-boy who saw. Truly, a heavy sorrow had been laid on the khan for what he had done for Shirzad Mir.

My lord put his hand on the arm of Iskander Khan and spoke softly.

"It is written that what evil-doers store up for themselves they shall taste. You shall have revenge for the death of your sons. By the beard of the prophet, I swear it."

He felt at the peak of his turban for the jewel he had been accustomed to wear there, intending to give it to Iskander Khan as a token. He smiled ruefully when his hand met naught but the cloth. The small turban of white cotton he wore was part of his grave clothes.

"Truly, Iskander Khan," he meditated aloud, "I am a beggared monarch. I have not even a token to give you for this service."

"I am content, Shirzad Mir."

I thought of the riches that the poet son of Jani Beg was carrying to Khanjut from the Mogul Jahangir, while Shirzad Mir had not so much as a spare horse, and I voiced this thought, being embittered by hunger and much soreness. At this the *Ferang* sprang to his feet so swiftly that I thought he had seen some Uzbeks approaching, so I did likewise. He clapped me on the back, rudely.

"Ha, Abdul Dost!" he cried. "That is the word I have been waiting for. So the caravan of Said Afzel is now in the Shyr Pass? Here is our chance. We will attack Said Afzel!"

"Ride against two score, when we are but three?" I laughed at the man. If he was mad, I must see to it that Shirzad Mir did not suffer from his folly. "I was in Kabul three days ago, and Said Afzel was just setting out. Besides his slaves and personal servants he has a bodyguard of some Pathans. They are well armed; the pass is narrow. Also they have many camels. You know not what you say!"

"Peace, Abdul Dost!" called my lord, whose eyes had taken on a strange sparkle. "You have not wit to see farther than your horse's ears. Let the *Ferang* speak!"

"It is better to be mad than calm at this time when caution will gain us nothing, excellency," said Sir Weyand respectfully. "Here is a noble chance. Said Afzel does not yet know you have escaped. He will not be watchful of danger. His caravan may be numerous but it is made up for the most part of women and eunuchs. Moreover, in the narrow ravine they must extend their line of march. We can choose our place of attack—"

"And they will dig our graves there," I said.

Shirzad Mir frowned at me.

"And we will have the advantage of surprise," continued the *Ferang*. "Jani Beg will hardly think to send reinforcements to his son because he knows that Said Afzel is well attended. We will have time to gain the narrow point of the pass just before dark—the best time to strike."

"How can three horsemen ride against camels and an elephant in a ravine?" I asked, for I was not to be silenced.

Shirzad Mir was foolhardy of his life and it was plain to me he liked well the words of Sir Weyand.

"We will not ride against them, Abdul Dost. If you had thought, you would remember that we could stand on the ridge above the caravan trail, where our arrows will command Said Afzel's men."

It was true I had not thought of that, in my concern for Shirzad Mir. It angered me—a *mansabdar* of the army—to be corrected by a foreign merchant, and I was silent for a space. Not so the Tiger Lord.

"*Hai*—that was well said!" he cried. "Such a plan warms my heart. Now if we had the strong sons of Iskander Khan—" he broke off with a glance at the mourning Kirghiz. "What men and slaves are with the caravan?"

"I heard at Kabul," replied the *Ferang*, settling his tall body against the tent, "that Said Afzel was a courtier and a gallant—fond of music, toys, verses and the Indian dancing girls. He is bringing a throng of such with him, also several camel loads of treasure as gift from the Mogul. What do we care for eunuchs and Ethiopian slaves?"

"Said Afzel has at least seven Pathans with him," I reminded him. "They are good fighters."

"Are you an old nurse, Abdul Dost?" cried my master in great anger. "Speak again, and I will set you to tend swine!" He turned to the *Ferang*. "Said Afzel is truly called 'the dreamer,' Sir Weyand. He is the most elegant in dress and can recite verses as well as his boon companion Kasim Kirlas, the professional courtier. It is true that he travels with cumbrous baggage—unlike his father—and is usually stupefied with *bhang* and opium. I would risk much to set hand on his jewels."

"We would risk much," nodded the *Ferang* bluntly, as was his custom; "especially as there is one of the big Indian elephants in the caravan."

"An elephant!" Shirzad Mir clapped his stout hands and laughed. "*Hai*—an elephant. That would be Most Alast from the stables of Jahangir. I heard it said at Khanjut when I was prisoner. Verily, the star of our good fortune is in the ascendant."

I thought the madness that had come upon Sir Weyand had bitten my lord, for he laughed again and fell to talking in low tones to the other. I strained my ears but could not hear. Being angry and perhaps a little jealous, I withdrew slightly to show them I did not care what they said.

Once Shirzad Mir called to Iskander Khan.

"Have you a great cauldron?" he asked.

The Khirghiz pointed to the ashes of the fire, where a pot stood, large enough to boil a sheep whole.

"Will you give it me?"

Iskander Khan made a sign to show that all he had was Shirzad Mir's for the asking. Once more the two talked together, and I saw them glance at me and laugh. Then Iskander Khan lifted up his white head.

"You will need a good horse, Shirzad Mir," he said slowly. "The one you have is a sorry pony. In a thicket yonder I have Abdul Dost's horse, also an Arab stallion that has carried me for five years. I will fetch it for you so that you may mount as is fitting for a king."

The eyes of the Tiger Lord softened.

"Thrice happy is the man who has a faithful friend," he said and with his own hand helped the aged Kirghiz to rise.

Before the two left the tent to go for the horses, he spoke quickly to Sir Weyand.

The *Ferang* rose and stretched his big frame. I did not move, for they had not confided in me. He disappeared into the tent and presently came forth, lugging a basket filled with something heavy. I wanted to see what was in it, but I would not show him that I was curious.

He was singing to himself after his strange fashion. He moved with his hands that which was in the basket and put it in the cauldron. I watched him.

When he had nearly finished there came a dog that was hungry and whined. Seeing the dog, Sir Weyand threw him a piece of the stuff he was handling. The dog wagged his tail and carried off the stuff. I saw him eat it.

This was very strange, so I rose up without seeming to be interested and walked toward Sir Weyand, until I could see into the pot.

"*B'illah!*" I cried, for the stuff was rotting swine's flesh, which it is defilement for a follower of the prophet to touch. It had been used by Iskander Khan to grease the tents. The *Ferang*, who knew this, laughed.

"Tell me, Abdul Dost," he smiled, rising from his labor when the pot was nearly full, "is that dog better than you, or are you better than that dog?"

He was a *caphar*, one without faith. Those words might well have cost him his life.

"If I have faith," I answered him sternly, "I am better than that dog; if I have not faith, he is better than I." I laid a hand on my sword. "If you wish a quarrel—"

"Peace!" cried the voice of Shirzad Mir behind us. "It is time we mounted."

He was leading a fine gray stallion, and Iskander Khan had Wind-of-the-Hills. Likewise, the Kirghiz gave to us two good bows and quivers full of arrows—also he brought his own sword from the tent and girded it on Shirzad Mir. What man could do more than Iskander Khan did for us?

"The blessing of God go with you, Shirzad Mir," he said in parting. "I shall stay at this tent, and perhaps—"

"I will come back," said my lord swiftly. "I will not forget."

We watched the bent form of the old man go into the empty tent; then we set spurs to our mounts. The cauldron Sir Weyand had slung on a long pole, one end of which he carried and I the other. Shirzad Mir rode bridle to bridle with him—I following behind. Still they talked together eagerly, like boys with a new sport. Once Sir Weyand looked back at me and grinned.

"If you are afraid to come, Abdul Dost," he said, "you are free to drop the pole and go."

Before I could think of a fitting answer, he was speaking again with Shirzad Mir. Verily, I was angered. The pole leaped and jumped, and I was forced to watch lest the vile fat should fly out on me. There was no doubt in my mind that lack of food had unsettled my lord's brain.

Why else should we ride at a fast trot through the hot ravines of the hills to the Shyr Pass, where at any moment we might meet a wandering patrol on the watch for us? And why did we carry that accursed pig's flesh?

As for Sir Weyand, my brain was black with anger. I wanted to swing my scimitar against his long sword. Had it not been for the events of that evening, I should have done so.

* * * *

Our horses were steaming when we came out of a poplar thicket on a hill near the caravan track and saw a boy shepherd watching us from his flock. When he recognized Shirzad Mir, the lad put down his bow and dropped to his knees.

"Hazaret salamet!" he cried joyfully, in the dialect of his tribe.

He had thought Shirzad Mir was dead. My lord questioned him swiftly. The boy told him that the caravan of Said Afzel had not yet passed this point. Our good fortune still held, yet I was doubtful of what was to come. Shirzad Mir bent over the boy.

"Speak, little soldier," he laughed, "how would you like to shoot an arrow in the service of your lord?"

The boy's eyes brightened and he fingered his bow, being both pleased and shy with the attention paid him. He was a slight, dark-skinned Kirghiz—the same that had visited Iskander Khan's *aul*—and the words delighted him. Shirzad Mir honored him by taking him up behind on his horse. My belly yearned for the mutton that we might have cooked and eaten, but my master would not linger.

It was mid-afternoon, and the sun was very hot. We were in the pass now, and once we met a runner coming up the ravine. It was a man of Said Afzel, and when he saw us he bounded up into the rocks. But Shirzad Mir fired an arrow swiftly. My lord was an excellent shot. From the body we took the message.

It said that Said Afzel would camp that night at a certain level spot in the pass, for the caravan track was too narrow, besides being on the bank of the turbulent stream Amu Daria, to travel at night. Probably Said Afzel liked better to sit on the cushions of a silk tent than to ride.

"God is good to us," exclaimed Shirzad Mir and pressed forward.

Although I still said nothing, I had a great foreboding. No man has ever called me a coward, but our strength was sapped by hunger—we had no armor or firearms. We were acting on the mad whim of the *Ferang*, and for the first time in his life my master had put aside my advice for another's—that of the merchant who made me carry the pot of swine-flesh.

We passed the open place where Said Afzel had planned to camp. We knew now that the caravan could not be far away, and

Shirzad Mir sent the boy ahead to spy. He ran swiftly, like a young mountain goat.

We came to the very place where I had first met the *Ferang*, and I bent my ears back like a horse, listening for hoofs on the trail behind us, for here we were in a trap. On one side the cliff rose sheer for perhaps four spear lengths. On the left hand the slope, steep and strewn with rocks and thorns, dropped abruptly to the rushing stream which was deep enough to drown a man.

Truly, I thought, the madness of Sir Weyand had brought us to an evil place. If a patrol of Uzbek horsemen should come behind us we would be caught between them and the caravan.

Even a brave man feels a prickling of the flesh when he knows not what is before and behind him. The mad fantasy of the other two had veiled their minds from danger. Shirzad Mir, to make matters worse, set Sir Weyand and me to rolling some stones into the path from the slope. While we were doing this he dismounted and led our three horses by a roundabout path up to the top of the cliff.

Not until we had the stone heap nearly the height of a man and were panting from the toil—my bruises had not yet healed—did he call for us to cease. Then Sir Weyand made me take the pole with him and carry it up the slope to the top of the cliff. If the foul fat had fallen back on me, I should have struck him, but it was my fate that it did not.

Back into a cedar grove we carried the accursed thing. Here Shirzad Mir had kindled a fire from dried cedar branches.

"The trees may hide the smoke," he said. "Quick—our time is little!"

As if possessed of a demon, Sir Weyand worked at the fire, placing the cauldron over the logs so that the fat began to heat. Meanwhile, Shirzad Mir stood at the edge of the cliff to watch for the coming of the boy.

The sun had dropped behind the peaks at our backs. There was no wind. The scent of the cedars was sweet in my nostrils, but Sir Weyand made me labor over the evil-smelling pot. I had none of his wild hope. For, without doubt, Said Afzel, whom we sought, would ride the elephant, and I had once tried to attack one of the beasts in a battle.

The ravine in which the stream muttered was clothed in shadows and it must have been the time of sunset prayers when the boy came running back up the path, looking for us.

Shirzad Mir called to him, and the youth came nimbly up the cliff, clinging somehow to the sheer rock, until my lord reached him a hand. Then he bowed his head to Shirzad Mir's feet.

"The caravan comes, Lord of Badakshan!" he cried eloquently.

"How many and in what order?" asked Shirzad Mir swiftly.

"Some horsemen, riding slowly, are in front. Then a group of slaves with burdens on foot. Following them some armed riders. Then a black elephant with a glittering *howdah*."

"God is with us!" cried Shirzad Mir. He turned to me merrily. "Ho—Abdul Dost of the dark brow! What think you of an elephant in the ravine of Shyr?"

We had seen none of the beasts in Badakshan before, but something of Shirzad Mir's purpose flashed on me, and I felt the heart-leap of the hunter when he sees game approach his hiding place. Sir Weyand stirred the fat, which was now boiling and bubbling odorously.

Above the place where we had piled the stones so they would look as if they had fallen down the slope, my lord sent the boy with his arrows. He, himself, took his bow and crawled forward to where he could see him down the pass.

At a sign from Sir Weyand, I helped him lift the cauldron from the fire by its stick. We carried it to the edge of the ravine.

"Go with your master," said Sir Weyand to me under his breath, "and take your bow. I will manage the rest of my task alone."

Nothing loath, I obeyed. Crouching beside Shirzad Mir, I could see the caravan coming up the pass, in the quiet of the evening. The bearers and camelmen were pushing ahead with loud cries, for the camping-place was just around a turn.

* * * *

It was a brave sight. The Pathans, as the boy had said, were in the lead—l* * * *ean men, riding easily and fully armed. Next came the Ethiopians, with their heavy burdens. They, of course, were unarmed. I counted seven Pathans.

Then appeared Most Alast, the elephant of the Mogul. He had two red stripes down his forehead, and silver bells at his neck. I could see the white heron's plume of Said Afzel in the *howdah* behind the *mahout*. Slowly, slowly, they came forward.

"It could not be better, Abdul Dost," cried my master joyfully.

I took heart from this. For, though his eyes were shining, he was laughing to himself, which was a good sign. He was not mad. I had begun to see his plan.

Last came the long-haired camels, bearing the women, the baskets which probably contained the treasure, and the eunuch guards of the harem. A few slaves in gorgeous tunics walked with the dirty camelmen.

A lone Pathan brought up the rear. I felt Shirzad Mir's hand on my arm.

"Shoot your arrows among the camelmen, Abdul Dost," he said. "I will take care of the leading riders—I and the boy. When I shout, raise our battle-cry and shout as if you were many men."

I nodded to show that I understood. I strung my bow and waited, lying on my belly. It was just as if Shirzad Mir and I were stalking antelope. Yet never had we stalked such game as this.

The sun had left the pass, but there was still light when the Pathans passed under us and arrived at the heap of stones. After talking together, three of them dismounted and began to clear away the stones, dropping them down the slope into the stream to free the path for the elephant.

We four were silent on the cliff, though I could hear Sir Weyand working at the fire. The swaying *howdah* of Most Alast came nearer—so near I could see the jewels set in the turban of Said Afzel, who was laughing with a fat man on the cushion by him—Kasim Kirlas, I thought. I could have almost reached down and touched their heads.

Then Shirzad Mir bellowed his battle-cry.

"Hai—Shirzad el kadr—hai!"

He leaped to his feet and began to speed arrows down at the riders.

"Hai—Shirzad el kadr!" I echoed, twanging a shaft among the camels.

It must have reached its mark, for one of the beasts yelled with pain. I heard the shrill shout of the boy and the startled cries of the slaves below us.

Then Sir Weyand came to my side.

"St. George for England!" he cried. I asked him later what it was, and he told me.

As he shouted, he pushed the cauldron over on its side. The boiling fat fell on the broad rump of Most Alast.

An elephant has a thick hide, but he is sensitive and nervous as a woman—and the boiling grease was very hot. Most Alast lifted up his trunk and bellowed his pain. Then he charged forward. The *howdah*, with Said Afzel and Kasim Kirlas, slipped its girths as Most Alast shook himself—the fat had missed the *howdah*, to my sorrow—and the two went to earth.

Then Most Alast dashed among the riders. Several horses leaped over the slope in their fright. Finding himself against the stones, the elephant turned in the narrow path and charged back against the camels, which gave way before him. Some stumbled into the brush of the slope. Others pressed against the cliff wall. *B'illah*, there was much confusion!

The camels, being frightened and hurt, began to yell also, and the horses too. The black slaves had leaped to shelter and stood watching, their eyeballs showing white. The camelmen sought safety where they could.

Shirzad Mir had reckoned well what havoc an angered elephant would make along that narrow path.

I was a middling shot with a bow, but my lord was a marksman among many. His shafts sought out the Pathans, who had no time to use their matchlocks before they had to leap out of the way of Most Alast. Yet he killed none. Before long, I knew why.

"Hai—Shirzad el kadr—hai!" cried my lord for the last time, and ordered me to seek the horses.

While the boy plied his arrows from the cliff, we two, with the *Ferang*, rode rapidly down until our horses stood at the slope above the pile of stones. Here Shirzad Mir called upon the Pathans to throw down their arms.

A Pathan is a good fighter when and if it suits him. These men were less afraid of us than of Most Alast, who was trumpeting back and forth along the path, heedless of the efforts of his *mahout*. They saw that we were armed and ready. They did not know how many more of us there were.

Three of the Pathans were hurt by the arrows of Shirzad Mir. Two others had fallen among the rocks and thorns of the slope below. The other two were afoot and watching the elephant.

All who could do so put down their muskets and swords and said that they had had enough of the affair. Shirzad Mir would not move until he had seen the two who were in the thorn thicket climb out, cursing, but little the worse for their fall, and join the others. Then we left Sir Weyand, who had picked up a brace of their discarded pistols, to watch the group, and went forward with me at his side.

"Find Said Afzel," he ordered me.

I saw the Uzbek prince leaning turbanless against a rock, feeling of himself tenderly. It is no light thing to fall from the *howdah* of an elephant. Kasim Kirlas, the professional courtier, was stretched on the ground at his feet—but this was no salaam; the man was stunned.

Shirzad Mir caught the dazed prince by the shoulder and bade him sternly walk before his horse. My lord had drawn his sword, and this he kept near the bare neck of Said Afzel.

"Where is the elephant?" he asked me.

I pointed to the stream below and Shirzad Mir laughed aloud. He ever appreciated a good jest. Most Alast had smelled water, and had somehow got himself down the slope to the stream unhurt. He was drawing water up in his trunk and squirting it over his sore back—*mahout* and all. Later Most Alast lay down in the mud. It was many hours before we could get him to leave it.

Shirzad Mir pushed through the bewildered bearers swiftly. Half of the camelmen had fled. One or two of the eunuchs drew their scimitars when my lord came near the camels on which were the women, but when they saw the plight of Said Afzel, with my lord's sword at his ear, they threw down their weapons.

It was a sorry gathering that we grouped against the cliff wall. Eunuchs and slaves are masters of brave words, but I have yet to see the ones who will face danger to their bodies without shrinking.

I cast about and discovered that the Pathan who had formed the rear guard had fled.

Shirzad Mir was now master of the field. He called to the boy on the cliff—our foes thought that many more were there—to shoot down the first man of the caravan who moved from his place.

Then he ordered me to ride my horse slowly back and forth among the remaining camels, the women and their attendants, and see that none escaped.

It was now growing dark, so of my own will I set four of the camelmen to building a great fire at the lower end of the caravan and another by the heap of stones. So it happened that when it grew dark we had our prisoners securely between the two fires and could see all that passed.

Shirzad Mir had gone straight to the Pathans and talked with them a long time. Presently he came to me and said:

"They will join my party, being men who sell their swords: For this reason I did not slay them. They were near enough for good shooting. I have cared for those who were hurt. The others are cooking food. In the morning we will give them a sword apiece—perhaps."

With the other attendants we did not speak. They were men of low breeding and jumped to obey our orders. Shirzad Mir kept Said Afzel ever at his side, in case of treachery.

One at a time we ate of the food for which we yearned. The boy joined us proudly, and Shirzad Mir set him to collecting the few weapons of the eunuchs. Of these he made a pile and sat on it, feeling greatly the honor we did him.

Shirzad Mir talked with Said Afzel through the night. There was no chance for me to sleep, but I think Sir Weyand slept a little during his watch over the Pathans. Before dawn I had spoken with the *mahout* of Most Alast and given him a handful of gold from the treasure bags. He—one master being as good as another—consented to serve us.

At dawn I had finished my task. The loads were all recovered and placed on the camels and the slaves' backs. All had eaten. The women were put back on their camels, and the eunuchs herded in front.

At first break of light in the sky we set out, my lord and Said Afzel mounted on the elephant, who was now quiet, the injured in litters borne by the slaves, the Pathans on their own horses, and the sheep boy on another.

We struck away from the Shyr Pass into the hills. Then, for the first time in two days and nights, I slept a little in the saddle, being weary, but only a little.

CHAPTER III

Said I not our star was in the ascendant, so that for a space we were given strength to trick our enemies? Later, evil fortune came upon us again, but not then.

Three courses were open to my lord. He could slay Said Afzel, to strike terror into the Uzbeks; he could exchange the prince and the women for his own family, and perhaps a strip of Badakshan; or he could ransom our prisoners for gold with which to pay an army. I urged the first plan, Sir Weyand the second, and the Pathans, who had now cast their fortunes with us, the third.

Our danger was great, for when news of what had happened in the pass reached Khanjut by way of some escaped bearers, the whole army of Jani Beg was sent to hunt us down. As yet we had no followers other than the four uninjured Pathans and the sheep boy, whom Shirzad Mir appointed head of the camelmen and gave a sword, to his great satisfaction. The bearers, the slaves and the camel drivers were useless to us and would have been glad to fall again into the hands of Jani Beg, who would not drive them through the by-paths of the hills, as we did.

* * * *

It is written in the annals of India, the curious thing that my master did in this difficulty.

"We will keep the prisoners and the treasure," he said, "and we will regain the foothills of Badakshan from Jani Beg; also we will gather together a small army.

And this thing we did, by the will of God. How was it done? We held a *durbar*—that is, a crowning ceremony. The people of Badakshan had been told my lord was dead. The *durbar* showed them he was not.

Verily, not before or since has such a *durbar* been held in Hindustan or Badakshan or Turkestan. We traveled with the caravan through the villages of the hills. At each village Shirzad Mir would dismount from Most Alast and spend money—from the bags of Said Afzel—for a feast.

Wine he bought freely, and food, and scattered silver among the people. So that all might see, he held his *durbar*. Said Afzel, the opium-eating prince, he forced to do homage in public to him; fat Kasim Kirlas, the professional courtier, Shirzad Mir made pay him extravagant compliments; el ghias, the buffoon of the caravan, performed his tricks; the musicians of Said Afzel sang—at the sword points of the Pathans—and the dancing girls danced. It was a great feast. Shirzad Mir, looking the proud king he was by birth, sat on cushions under a cloth-of-gold tent which we found in the baggage, and watched idly, saying nothing.

Sir Weyand cleaned his soiled garments and sat at the right hand of Shirzad Mir, as the ambassador from England. Only I did not attend, for at every feast I was out in the lookout places, with certain men of the hills who rallied to our standard, keeping watch. The men of Jani Beg pressed us close. We moved each day, marching in the night to a new village. I kept a good watch and at each new place more of our men came in to see and hear, for rumors of what had happened spread through the hills. Shirzad Mir gave to them gold and weapons from the store we had taken.

In the plain of Badakshan we could not have avoided being overtaken by the cavalry of the Uzbeks. But in the hills they were at a loss—and the people aided us. It was a mad scheme, yet its very madness protected us.

He himself put on the jewels he took from Said Afzel, and—sitting placidly on Most Alast, the black elephant, with the two crimson stripes of the Mogul on his nose—he looked the king he was. The hearts of his old soldiers, who thronged to us from the hills, were uplifted at this sight.

Always Shirzad Mir directed me to travel in a circle, through Anderab, Ghori and Bamian, back to where we had started, at the Shyr Pass. In spite of danger he did this, and we all wondered, until one day we came to the desolate *aul* of Iskander Khan, as Shirzad Mir had planned.

When the old Kirghiz chieftain came forth and lifted up his hands at the sight, Shirzad Mir in his gorgeous robes dismounted from Most Alast and embraced Iskander Khan, while we all watched.

Then my lord pointed to the caravans, to the camels, the treasure and the women.

"Choose," said he to Iskander Khan; "it is all yours for the asking."

But Iskander Khan would not, saying that he was unworthy of such honor. Whereupon Shirzad Mir called for us all to see. He loaded the horse Iskander Khan had given him in his need—the fine Arab stallion—with pots of gold and gems, and put the bridle in the Kirghiz' hand himself.

He put a robe of ceremony on Iskander Khan and girded on him the sword from his own waist.

"This man," he said loudly, "shall be always at my left hand until he dies. Those who do homage to me shall bow to him also."

In this manner did Shirzad Mir pay his debt to Iskander Khan. He was a good man. A man among ten thousand. Aye, among ten times ten thousand.

ADVENTURE'S HEART

Albert Dorrington

CHAPTER I

A VISITOR IN THE DARK

The schooner labored and sagged in the fresh cyclones of wind and brine that blew through and over her. At dawn on the ninth day after her departure from Honolulu, the Pocahontas struck coral in a blinding smother of surf and wind. Mace was hurled into a maelstrom of wreckage and smothering water, and the sensation reminded him of a knock-out he had once received in the early days of his career as a boxer. Above him was the subdued murmur of incoherent voices, while within him was a feeling of intense lassitude, broken only by a faint desire to rise and stand erect.

He rose to the surface with faculties numbed, but with a fighter's knowledge of his desperate chances within the surf-hammered channels of coral. He fought and floated, kicked and dived when the green-headed slopes of water threatened to amputate him on the razor-backed shoals. An old ring veteran had once told him that brains will beat death itself, and the man who at one time had killed an opponent in a boxing contest learned in a flash how not to fight wind and sea on a dead lee shore.

And when his tiring limbs recognized this fact, the sea helped him and the tornado that had blown the schooner to her undoing blew him onto a narrow belt of reef where the tamanu shrubs held true to his drowning grasp. Another green-crested wall of surf hurled him high and dry, where he lay in the hot sun until the fainting blood about his heart resumed its life-giving pressure.

He slept for thirteen hours without a move. When he awoke it was to find that another day had begun with the sun standing like the torn rim of a volcano in the east.

Slowly Mace collected his jaded senses and began an investigation. The tornado had cast him upon a deserted atoll fringed with skeleton puroa trees and wind-shriveled palms. In the center of the atoll was the remnant of a forgotten banana plantation, with here and there a group of upright stakes showing where some native huts once had stood. Everywhere there were signs of recent habitation. The ashes of cooking fires were blown among the rocks and crevices.

Searching the ground closely Mace came upon Scraps of clothing that did not belong to the dresses of South Sea islanders. There were rags of half-scorched cloth that had come from the looms of American factories. In a declivity adjoining some upright stakes, he came upon a charred watch guard that must have belonged to a seafaring man or white trader.

The mental suggestion following the discovery of the relics left Mace in a state of horror and bewilderment. A further search merely confirmed the suspicion that the atoll had recently been the scene of a horrible orgy. Near midday hunger drove him into the deserted plantation searching among the stunted bushes for food. Bananas and papaws were there in abundance; the ground was littered with fiber-covered coconuts, delicious and thirst quenching after his long fast.

Pieces of wreckage drifted in from the outer reefs where the schooner had broken up in the mountainous surf. But the sight of the useless deck hamper scattering about the low beach brought small comfort to Mace as he wandered and crawled along the saucer-shaped edge of the atoll.

Although not faced with immediate starvation he viewed with dismay the loneliness of his surroundings. He dared not count on a ship approaching within hailing distance. Night came with a wisp of moon and the large tropic stars that seemed to lean from the violet dome of mid-heaven. The storm had subsided, leaving no trace of its pitiless wrath on the windless horizon.

Mace found cover inside a jungle of fronds and tamanu leaves on the sheltered side of the atoll. The water had ruined his watch, but he guessed it was late by the sudden nip in the air. Yet he found sleep difficult even on his bed of fragrant ferns.

The stillness was unbroken save for the slow, measured boom of distant breakers. The crying of a tern under the shelf of reef near by added pang on pang to his overwrought nerves. Unable to settle his mind to sleep, Mace crept from his lair of ferns and peered across the coral barriers that seemed to stretch to the horizon.

A faint, splashing sound reached him as if a paddle had struck water near by. Straining forward he listened and again caught the soft swirl and rippling motion as of something afloat. It came nearer, became more audible as the minutes passed. Mace slipped forward in the direction of the sound, scarce daring to breathe.

A native canoe shot into the narrow channel a dozen yards from where he crouched. In the faint moonlight he discerned the solitary figure of an old man paddling close in. Without hesitation Mace approached and saluted with an affectation of geniality.

"Hello, friend! Do you live here, or is it just a place where you come home to sleep?"

The ancient figure in the canoe turned sharply in Mace's direction, the paddle staying in mid-air as if sound of the human voice had petrified his movements. Slowly, very slowly, his glance took in Mace's outline, the supple, Herculean young figure that could have lifted him, canoe and all, from the water.

"Taeo, papalagi! It is well I speak your tongue. I once was cook on a steamer that traded from Sydney to Samoa. At first I thought you were a spirit come to mock me. Oho, there are many spirits here after the burnings and the great storm."

The canoe touched the beach, but the old man made no effort to get out. He sat with his paddle across his huddled knees, while the bones of his face seemed to protrude. Some metal ornaments pierced his ear lobes; a necklace of shark's teeth encircled his wizen throat. He was the oldest man Mace had ever seen, a mummified human, moving and speaking with ineffable weariness and languor. Yet he was human at least, with a brain and heart among the infinite solitudes of sea and sky. Mace stared down at him with a feeling of pity and welcome.

"I'll help you out," he volunteered, placing a hand on the bow of the canoe. "Skipping from a boat is no joy at your time in life, eh?"

"You do not explain," the old man returned without moving. "How did you come here?"

Mace laughed easily. "I got blown in by the big wind yesterday. Our schooner broke up out there. Not a soul came out of it but me!" he added, a sudden tremor in his voice.

The old man nodded and again favored the white man with a covert glance. "Only the broken ships reach here," he said. "I have not seen a ship in eight years; not one!"

"White men have been here," Mace asserted. "And somebody did the cremating pretty thoroughly."

The old man shrugged wearily. "All white people die who come here. It is the law!"

"Why?" Mace demanded hotly.

"Because they destroy happiness—our lives, children, women. They bring disease, they carry plagues that sweep our islands from end to end. There is also the gin and rum. We are a clean race here, stranger. We kill white men so that we may live."

"Seems to me," Mace protested sharply, "that our doctors and missioners have been busy cleaning up your hotbeds of disease since Noah made his first trip. The white man is all right when you don't eat him."

Something like a low chuckle escaped the old man as he crouched over his paddle. "Come, sit near me," he invited. "Let us talk. Big men are always my friends."

Mace squatted on the beach, his curiosity aroused by the old man's manner.

"My name," the visitor went on, "is Sagon. The people in the islands near by call me their spirit-man and doctor."

"Are they very near—these islands?" Mace questioned eagerly.

Sagon indicated a low reef wall in the far south where the Pacific breakers hurled with the sound of gun blasts on the still night air. "Beyond those reefs our people dwell, papalagi! I alone know of your schooner going to pieces on the cruel coral last night. I kept the secret to myself. A spirit whispered that some of the white sailors had reached this island."

"What do you want to do, Sagon?"

"Come with me to my people. Like a brave man you must take your chance with them. If you stay here you will go mad, or"—he paused and nursed his paddle thoughtfully—"some of the chief's men will spy you out. Oho, you will then be destroyed without a hearing. Will you come with me?"

"Sure!"

"Then sit in this boat and paddle by direction. It is a long way; my arms have grown stiff."

Mace clambered into the canoe, glad of an opportunity to escape the dreadful monotony of his sea-girt prison. Far better to die with the voices of men around him than to succumb to madness or plague, alone in the awful wastes of mid-Pacific.

CHAPTER II
A MEANS TO AN END

Day was breaking over the high coral hummocks when the canoe shot into a narrow channel that opened into a dish-shaped lagoon. Myriads of sooty-winged terns and man-o'-war hawks hovered above the dense Pandanus palms that fringed the inner beach. High up on the shelving banks forests of candlenut trees swayed and whispered in the rising southeastern trade winds. The sun flashed its crystal rays over forest and lagoon, where the sponge beds and parrot-billed fish flashed under every dip of the paddle.

A village of palm-thatched huts became visible as the canoe touched the beach. The blue smoke of many cooking fires lay over the forest. Voices of women and men reached Mace, voices filled with laughter and homely badinage, together with the shrill babel of children clamoring for their early meal.

"Say, it sounds good!" Mace declared, stepping from the canoe and assisting the old man to land. "I've got no animus against a town like this, doctor."

Sagon stepped slowly to the beach, his small, black, shriveled figure contrasting strangely with the white man's abundant proportions. "There is peace now," he murmured; "but the storm will beat around the council house in a little while. Palotta will provoke it."

"Is Palotta a woman?"

"She rules here!" Sagon snapped under his breath. "Her father was a brigadier of gendarmery at Nukahiva, over there in the Marquesas. Her mother was a rich Italian and became a queen in these islands. She bought lands from the chiefs and owned twenty trading steamers. Palotta's mother is dead. She now rules here with her brother Avian. But the chiefs are troublesome, as you will see, stranger."

"A woman ruler!" Mace commented and was silent.

Sagon hobbled slowly toward the village, pausing for breath and to enlighten Mace further concerning the female ruler of the islands. "Palotta looks after her little kingdom better than most rulers. She has taught her people the value of many things she learned in the school at Apia. She laughs at my medicine and scorns my charms and herbs. There is no love between us, and some day—" He paused and muttered a string of words in the vernacular that were lost on the white man.

"But this darned hate of her own kind?" Mace broke in at last. "Put me wise, Sagon, that I may help myself."

Sagon shrugged. "A month ago a party of white men landed on the island where I found you. They had come to raid our pearl hatcheries and steal our women for the coffee plantations of Fiji. That was their intention. It was well proved by letters in their keeping. To steal our women and our pearls, to give nothing in return but gunshots, is no bargain to us. There were seven whites in all, and"—the old man made a gesture as he concluded—"you saw the heaps of ashes. So—that was Palotta's justice. Thou shalt not steal. That is good mission-house talk, stranger."

They had reached the village where the news of Sagon's arrival with a white man struck like a fireball. Native women, in their headdress of shells and coral beads, deserted their cooking fires to stare in wonder at the tall stranger striding beside the bent and decrepit doctor. Many of the headmen and warriors assembled at the sudden beating of a war drum, and stood with clubs and spears in hand outside the square, palm-log building in the center of the village.

Hoarse insults were flung at Mace from the more youthful members of the tribe, followed by an aggressive closing of their ranks as he drew nearer. Sagon snarled a word that fell like a lash among them.

"Dogs of the swine yard, can you not see that the papalagi walks with me? His life is my life until the queen decides. Out of our way! Leap, dogs! Begone!"

The skeleton arms of the old doctor made signs that caused the headmen to cover their eyes as though from the unseen shafts of his magic. "Follow me, stranger," he commanded Mace as he hobbled slowly into the log-built council house.

It was almost dark inside. The walls were hung with spears and weapons of the tribe, with here and there a war god of painted wood or stone. A curiously carved throne of sandalwood stood at the far end of the chamber, its highly polished sides glinting with innumerable pearls inset. Above the throne gleamed a naked skull. Mace drew a deep breath and waited.

Outside the council house the shouts of the crowd fulfilled all Mace's longings to hear the voices of his fellow men. The voices became hysterical in their demands for the life of the white stranger. Spearheads and clubs hammered the log walls outside. Why was Sagon protecting the pale devil? they demanded.

The old doctor rolled some betel nut in a moist banana leaf and chewed abstractedly, casting from time to time a glance in Mace's direction.

"Palotta will come with her brother Avian," he intimated at last.

Mace made no reply. He could not escape a thought that rose in him that Sagon was in some way using him as a means to an end. What wizard impulse had impelled the old medicine fraud to seek him on the atoll? he asked himself.

A sudden silence fell on the hostile crowd outside. A squad of headmen filed quickly into the chamber, long-limbed warriors with the blue-and-red tattoo marks of their tribe on their naked bodies. Each headman carried a short, broad-bladed stabbing spear. Without haste or confusion they ranged about the empty throne and glared at Mace standing beside Sagon.

The old doctor chewed betel with supreme indifference. It was as if fifty well-fed geese had waddled into the council house. "These people," he said to Mace, "have no more brains than oysters. All day they eat and brag about their deeds. Listen! She is here!"

CHAPTER III
THE VERDICT OF THE QUEEN

A low murmur passed over the assembly. A drumbeat sounded a slow tattoo; it came nearer until the crowd outside fell back in awe, and the cry "The queen comes!" struck sharp on the ears of the white man.

She came on foot and not in a litter of many-colored silks and veils. A youth of twenty towered beside her; his skin was the color of wild honey; his boyish face was alive with the ardor of life and the fierce joy of ruling a wayward people.

Palotta walked easily into the council chamber. For a fraction of time her glance rested on the tall, white man, and then with an air of business she settled on her throne.

Mace suppressed a cry of surprise. She was barely eighteen. He had expected to see a woman of thirty. His heart thumped like a stone within him. The beauty of her face and form was like a thrust from a jeweled weapon. It was incredible! He had pictured a female judge with the face of a vixen, and he was confronted by a type of loveliness that would have shamed half the film queens of Broadway.

Her skin was fairer than her brother's. It was a golden tan that carried the faint flush of dark roses in her soft cheeks. She was staring fixedly at Sagon as if expecting him to speak.

He did, and for the benefit of the chiefs delivered himself in the vernacular: "I found the stranger on the island where the seven scamps were burned. His schooner was wrecked where Trau Kau lifts her fangs above the tide, O queen. Of all the crew he alone reached the shore. He says that the wind blew him out of his course. He had no wish to violate or trespass on our lands.

"He has told me his own story on our way here, in my little boat. In his own country he is a professional warrior, a fist-man. But he will not talk of his prowess as our warriors do. It is hard, therefore, O queen, to believe him a man of great deeds, such as thy noble brother and the great men here assembled."

Then Sagon subsided into a morose silence. Palotta transfixed Mace with her dark, searching eyes. He met her glance with the composure of one undaunted by fate. In her face there was no sign of hate or condemnation. It was the face of a child thinking hard and swiftly, without reference to the glowering eyes and sullen whispers of the chiefs around her. It was some time before she spoke; then each headman leaned nearer as she addressed Sagon.

"It is hard to believe that white men come here for nothing," she said. "How often do we hear the story of shipwreck and accident? These islands are far removed from the track of ships. They come, these strangers, and they persist in coming. In the north and west they have swept over our islands and submerged our people. They brought the coughing plague, that scourged us last year. Our numbers have fallen grievously. These islands have become our graveyards. We must protect and enforce our laws."

A mutter of approval greeted her. Silence fell again as she continued:

"It is hard to pass judgment, but this stranger must go the way of others. There can be no evasion of our law."

A savage shout welcomed her verdict. The circle of spearmen beamed gratefully upon her. Sagon scratched and combed his thin hair with a talon-like forefinger as one who had listened to a tiresome harangue.

"It is well, O queen," he said. "The white people are our enemies. This stranger deserves death," he added with a scowl in Mace's direction. "Yet there are times when it is foolish to kill without proof of guilt. There are the stranger's warships," he suggested meekly.

"And me, too," Mace declared without heat as he divined something of the argument.

His eyes lighted on a heavy battle-ax hanging from the wall within easy reach. The thought of death did not occur to him. His supreme faith in his own lightning initiative and strength gave a positive joy to the situation. He could not entertain the idea that these slow-footed headmen were capable of finishing him in a mix-up. His health was too raw and buoyant; each limb of his young body refused to believe that human lions could bring him down. His faith in his own invincibility had won him a hundred fights and the sea had trained and tempered him until his flexed muscles leaped.

"Let there be more wisdom in the queen's second thoughts," Sagon droned warningly.

"Sagon is right, my sister. This stranger is not proved guilty." It was Avian who spoke, his right hand resting against the throne. "Although we do not fear the warships, we must do justice. Did the stranger come to steal?" he challenged.

There was no answer from the group of sullen-lipped headmen. The soft noise of Sagon's chewing merely added to the tenseness of the moment.

Palotta regarded her brother in cold-eyed amazement. Twice she was about to speak, but restrained herself as one in dread of bringing the wrath of the headmen upon him.

Avian came to his own rescue, his boyish face illumined by the overwhelming impetus of his thoughts. "We judge men and destroy them!" he almost shouted. "This man we cannot judge, neither can we allow him to go free to carry the news of our rich lands to the rovers and thieves who lie in distant rivers ready to pounce on us with their accursed ships. We cannot allow this man to go!"

"What then?" came from a score of throats.

Avian folded his long, muscle-packed arms, while the chest above the narrow hips expanded to the fullness of a gladiator. Mace marked him in that moment, the quick, snakelike length of torso, the young neck and shoulders built to smash and kill. And Mace knew what was coming.

"Let the stranger be pardoned," Avian begged, "so that I can deliver his body to the sharks that lie under the Red Reef. Let this fist-man from the great water go with me to the Ru Trau Kau, and my people shall see that I can cast his body to the sharks. Their hunger is great. The reefs are red where they watch and feast."

Sagon's jaws snapped. He looked sharply at Mace while a grin split his toothless mouth. "Wisdom at last," he said, chuckling, "and from the mouth of Avian the Strangler!"

Palotta moved uneasily on her throne. A word of protest was on her lips that was drowned by the shouts of approval that greeted Avian's offer.

"Rash boy!" she gasped under her breath. "Your tongue and your pride will humble us both."

Avian leaned toward her tenderly, his shapely hands touching the gold armlets scarcely visible against the amber sheen of her beautiful skin.

"Your eyes do not meet mine, Palotta," he whispered. "The fear of the milk-fed babe is in your heart when I choose to fight. I cannot forever be a toy warrior. These headmen doubt my strength, and you have kept me in leash too long. I swear, sister mine, that the stranger will go over the Red Reef, and I will return to you a man!"

Palotta averted her eyes; pain had dulled their childlike brilliance. Her lips were tight set. "You have gone mad!" she murmured.

Her probing eyes measured Mace's athletic outlines, took in every curve and slant of his physical make-up. The quality and breed of the man was revealed in a flash. She withdrew her glance with a stifled sound in her throat.

"The stranger will not be thrown from the Red Reef, brother mine! Never, never!"

CHAPTER IV
THE PRICE OF A LIFE

There was no mystery about the Red Reef at Langos Bay. It was of coral formation and stood almost in the center of the bay; square-cut, tablelike in appearance, it resembled a red-stone boxing arena when viewed from the beach.

In the past it had served as an altar of sacrifice. In later years, under a more modern regime, it was used as a stage where the young bloods of Langos were permitted to exhibit their skill in wrestling and mimic games of war. On gala days, under the eyes of Palotta, the budding, warriors tested their strength against each other to the shouts of the assembled villagers watching from the beach.

There were other occasions when murderers and felons were clubbed in full view of the community and their bodies cast to the ravening hordes of sharks that cruised in the vicinity. These monsters of the Pacific were fed regularly from the offal thrown to them by the village scavengers and breeders of pigs.

Outside the council chamber Palotta paused and beckoned Sagon who had followed in her wake, leaving Mace in charge of Avian's bodyguard. Palotta regarded the old man critically, her fingers closing idly on the jeweled haft of a knife in her girdle.

"What evil spirit guided the white man here, Sagon? What devil of chance took your canoe to the atoll last night? Speak; was it chance or more of your schemes for my downfall?"

In her eyes was an unloosed tempest of wrath that was not free from terror for the life of her brother, whose foolish pride and tongue had trapped him into a death duel with the white man.

Sagon blinked at her, and his toothless grin struck new fears into her young brain and heart. "I cannot stop your brother's tongue, Palotta. His vanity and ambition will yet send him to the sharks. You heard all that was spoken. The thing happened."

"As you wished it!" she flung out. "There is always a motive behind your actions. I believe that this white man was brought here to provoke Avian!"

"How—how?" Sagon snapped, his impish eyes dilating in sudden rage. "You speak to me like a child, Palotta—I who have watched over you in war and peace. How could this papalagi have been brought here to provoke your brother? Blame the spirit of the storm, the reefs that open ships and drown the rats and men in them. How could I?"

They walked some distance from the council house, each feeling that the last word had yet to be spoken. In Palotta's mind was the conviction that the old medicine man had managed to maneuver her into a desperate position. It seemed as if Sagon had chosen Mace to kill her brother. Her instincts warned her that Avian would be as a babe in the hands of Mace. She dared not think of Mace killing him, yet only one of them could leave the coral platform alive. One of them must go down the steep slope to the sharks; and no man's hand could stretch out to save either.

Palotta halted near a well-constructed house of tamanu wood and sandal logs that stood apart from the low-roofed huts in the main street of the village. It was surrounded by a low stockade where scarlet hibiscus trailed within the well-kept borders. It might have served as the residence of a rajah, and it had been Palotta's home since the death of her mother, some years before.

"Tell me, Sagon," she said slowly, "what you know of the white man. Is he dangerous? Is he what you said, a professional fist-man, a wrestler of repute in his own land?"

Sagon chewed blandly, standing in the limestone path. "I do not talk much, Palotta, but this papalagi is Fate. The cruel sea threw him upon us. His name is Darrel Mace. He is nicknamed 'The Lightning.' I have looked upon him well, I, who have the gift of seeing through men's skins and into the muscles of their hearts and brains. By their voices I know if they lie to me. This man is Fate!"

"What do you mean, Sagon?" Her face had lost its childish look of wonder; it had grown marble-white under the strokes of the native doctor's tongue. She was now quaking for her brother's life, the boy who had clung to her and who had often risked his foolish young life for her in the past. Sagon knew now that her heart was flinching in his chill grasp.

He combed his lime-washed hair with his talon fingers, his old eyes conning her like a trapped bird.

"Fate, my child, threw Mace here. The man, as I know, is the world's gladiator. The sport papers the traders send us carry his pictures. I go here and there among the traders. I am not a Kanaka of this island group. The sea sent Mace to kill Avian. In the hands of the white man your brother will be as the milk-fattened baby. Avian is too ambitious. His tongue has caught him at last."

Palotta leaned against the stockade to prevent herself from falling. "You must help me, Sagon!" she gasped. "Mace must not kill Avian!"

The old doctor blinked at her in the hot sunlight. "There is no way to prevent, except through your brother's honor," he returned icily. "It has gone too far. The chiefs are in favor of a fight. Many of them think your brother will strangle the papalagi. Such ideas come through eating nuts and papaw," he sneered. "Avian is only a boy; he is soft as a girl, but brave as the Malayan tiger. Yet he is too soft, Palotta."

Palotta drew breath sharply; the stockade and house seemed to reel in the blinding glare of the sun. "It must be stopped!" she flung out. "I will prohibit the fight. It would be murder!"

"The chiefs are preparing them already," Sagon told her. "The canoe to take them to the Red Reef is being got ready. The people expect the fight to take place. Listen!"

A murmur of many voices came from the bay. Men called to each other in joyous anticipation of the coming struggle between the brother of the queen and the accursed papalagi. Children and dogs ran toward the beach, followed by crowds of women. Laborers in the fields dropped tools and donned gala attire.

The holiday cries reached the swooning Palotta as she leaned against the stockade. She could think of Avian only as a wayward boy, who had clung to her in her hours of peril when famine and war threatened extermination. All the wealth of her mother's vast hoard counted for naught if evil befell him. The day could end only with a cup of poison for her if the white man triumphed.

"Sagon, you must help me!"

"Show me, Palotta!"

"Speak to Mace. Promise him safety if he will hold his hand."

The old doctor made a gesture of despair. "There is only one way known to me. The stranger can be bought over."

"How much?"

Sagon clawed his chin and ruminated for a period that ached like eternity to the waiting Palotta. When he looked up his nose seemed as sharp as a wolf's.

"A great matter needs large rewards, Palotta. Give me that pearl necklace of your mother's. I shall offer it to Mace; he will take it as the price of your brother's life. Give me the necklace at once! Mace will be on the Red Reef before I can speak in his ear. Quick, or they will be at each other's throats!"

Palotta blanched and threw up her hands. "Follow me to the house!" she said faintly. "I cannot hand it to you here."

Sagon bent his head and followed in her footsteps in the direction of the house.

CHAPTER V

A SCENE OF CONFUSION

For the time being Mace was a prisoner in the hands of a dozen armed natives. When it became known that he was to meet Avian in fair fight on the Red Reef, their ferocious manner relaxed. They brought him cooked meats and fruit in abundance, after the manner of jailers who bestow favors on prisoners doomed to die.

Mace ate sparingly although his healthy appetite craved for more of the delicacies spread before him. The meal over, they escorted him down a palm-shaded path in the direction of the limestone cliffs that shut in the bay of Langos. Halting on the beach, the leader of the escort indicated the red, table-shaped reef that stood in the center of the bay.

"You go there," he announced with a flourish of his short stabbing spear in Mace's direction. "You get planta fight wi' Av'an. Month ago he fight Malinga, the big, big man from Java."

"How did they fight?" Mace questioned easily, his glance fixed on the smooth slopes of the reef.

The chief of the escort showed his dazzling white teeth for a moment. "They fighta anyhow," he responded. "They get holda one anotha. Malinga no holda queen's brother long. Queen's brother play him to edge of rock, an' over he go to the sharks!"

"No funeral and no flowers, eh?" Mace laughed. "Just hit the blamed water and shook hands with the sharks!"

A big canoe ferried him across the bay to the almost perpendicular slopes of the Red Reef. Some steps had been hewn out of the side. Clambering on top, a distance of fifteen feet, Mace found himself on a perfectly flat, tablelike surface of footworn coral, with slightly more space at his disposal than he had found in twenty-four-foot rings. His curiosity took him to the slope that fronted the bay entrance. Peering down he beheld the shadows of a dozen reef monsters of the hammerhead variety, basking in the hot sun rays that poured down on the still waters.

In spite of his debonair manner, Mace was guilty of a slight shudder as he stared down at the family of man-eating sharks. No craftsman of the ring could escape those jaws once his footwork on the coral table betrayed him. There was no referee to call off their torpedo-like rushes and rending jaws. Mace heaved a big sigh and then cast aside his coat and vest, revealing to his escort the wonderful lines of his arms and torso. They drew aside in amazement.

"There is no such man among us," they cried. "Look, brothers, the skin is like the milkwood tree! There can be no strength in it, yet it is like nothing we have ever seen!"

It was low tide and the high cliffs shut out the cool trade wind. A palpitating heat swam over the island and beach. Mace returned to the edge of the reef and continued to peer down at the gray-throated hammerheads sunning their bladelike fins. At sight of his figure above they stirred sulkily away, their swinish eyes following each movement of his shadow. Glancing back at the beach he saw hundreds of villagers streaming toward the sands, where a large crowd had already assembled, squatting near the water's edge, eating fruit and cooked bananas after the manner of holiday folk.

Another canoe put off from the beach; in it were Avian and Sagon accompanied by several chiefs. The brother of Palotta was first up the steps and with a bound reached the top. After him came Sagon, slowly, painfully, like a tree-climbing crab. Breathing in short gasps, the old doctor shuffled to the spot where Mace was still contemplating the dusky shadows below. He looked up quickly as Sagon touched his arm.

"Listen!" the old man whispered with a back glance in Avian's direction. "You must not harm this boy!"

Mace flung around, his eyes kindling strangely. "What's the scrap about, anyway? And say, old man, who's going down that slope, me or him?" He indicated the gray, gleaming hides of the ocean monsters below.

Sagon made gestures of disapproval. "We must think of the young queen," he warned. "She bears you good will. And there is a way out of this trouble, papalagi. Spare the boy and obey me. Now, while these chiefs are telling Avian how to kill you, look down the slope near the sharks. You will see a crevice in the coral. In the fight you must slip down—your muscles are young—and creep into the crevice. There is a big space inside. Wait for me until dark. The people will think the sharks have eaten you. They cannot see this side of the reef from the beach. You will find some pig's blood in a gourd. Cast it into the water. Sabe?"

Mace allowed his swift glance to traverse the southern slope of the reef. He discerned a narrow cleft in the coral, about a foot from the tide level. He nodded thoughtfully and then turned to the center of the reef to find Avian awaiting him.

Sagon shuffled back to the steps, followed by the chiefs and escort, leaving Mace and Avian alone. A thunderous shout went up from the beach as the two faced each other. Avian was naked except for the silk trunks he wore. His body gleamed like beaten gold in the tropic sun glare; his sleek, black hair was brushed back from his broad brow. From his small, Arablike feet to his shapely throat, he was a moving-picture ideal of a Greek Adonis.

He approached Mace, body bent forward, his hands outspread as one about to enter the water. For a fraction of time Mace was puzzled. Against the brother of Palotta he bore no shadow of malice or anger, and for the first time in his life he stood irresolute before his opponent without any fixed scheme of attack or defense.

Avian, with shining eyes and body, did not keep him long in doubt. With a darting feint at Mace's throat, he doubled to the floor, snatching at the American's ankles, and in a flash Mace was flung backward to the foot-beaten floor of the reef.

Mace broke the fall with his elbows and was on his feet almost before Avian had straightened his body.

"Guess you're some ankle-fighter, kid! A rougher man than me would have kicked your face away!"

Avian laughed in the sudden glory of his achievement and stepped round with pantherlike watchfulness to gain another opening. "I shall get you again," he predicted, "and then you will go over."

Mace's eyes grew narrow, but not with anger. Then, with scarcely a motion of his body, he flung forward and boxed Avian's ears, left and right, with his open hands.

"Sorry to do it, kid," he declared. "I've got to put the wind up you to keep you in order. Sabe?" Then his right shot in under Avian's heart. The blow was timed with the ease of a champion, and scarcely a muscle of Mace's body stirred as he delivered it.

Avian recoiled, his head jerked forward, knees sagging as if a knife had reached his spine. For an instant he rocked to and fro within a few feet of the perilous declivity. Mace called to him in sudden anxiety.

"Don't fall off this rock, or those darned goldfish will get you! I just gave you a medicine ball to keep you from curling round my waist. Don't dive at my feet any more!"

Avian rallied with the young blood spinning through his veins. The swooning mist which followed the heart punch vanished. In another instant he was bunching for a leap at Mace.

Curiously enough Mace forgot his man entirely. He was thinking of Palotta and could almost feel that she was a terrified spectator of the present conflict. She was watching from the beach each movement of the boy before him. Mace sighed to think, as Avian crouched in front of him, that her heart would be filled with joy if the boy gladiator could only succeed in hurling him from the reef.

Avian sprang in with a cry of victory, his lithe arms pinning Mace with the strength of a bull-hide thong. With incredible agility he executed a body twist that he evidently had learned from a Japanese wrestler, and in a moment had the American "half-scissored" and apparently sprawling.

A great shout rent the beach; a forest of spears and clubs waved and quivered along the lines of warriors and chiefs.

"The papalagi is finished! The fist-fighter is already in a strangle hold. Wonderful is the strength of our queen's brother!"

"Now for the slow music!" Mace whispered without an effort to change his position. "Put me over the side, kid," he intimated softly. "No rough stuff, or I might put you over instead. Sabe?"

Locked in a seemingly unbreakable hold, Mace was forced to the edge of the reef. Here their white and brown bodies swayed and oscillated to the fierce rhythm of a war song chanted from the beach.

"Down with him, O Avian! Let the sharks tear his body! Down, down, down!"

Mace stumbled, regained his balance, but only to be thrust over and down the steep slope. Avian drew back, lurching blindly after his exertions, and collapsed limply on the floor of the reef.

Realizing that the white man had gone over the side, a scene of indescribable confusion mingled with screams of triumph and joy was visible on the beach. Black shapes capered wildly to and fro, while a dozen canoes put off to bring the victorious Avian home.

CHAPTER VI
TREASON IN THE AIR

Mace's strong fingers clutched the sides of the reef as he slithered over from the gaze of the war-whooping multitude on the beach. But even the abnormal strength of his hands failed to steady his downward rush. His feet struck the water, and the contact sent a chill spasm to his brain. His fingers fought desperately to find the crevice edge, while his glance went out to the slinking gray shadows of the reef monsters that had been visible only a few minutes before.

His grip closed on the edge of the crevice as his body sank into the water. Just here a triangle of fin skated in his direction, the snout of a giant hammerhead heaved its dripping jaws to the surface, the sawlike fangs flashing in the hot sunlight. Mace drew up his knees as though an ax had sliced the air, and with a frantic heave drew his chest and head through the opening in the reef.

The snout of the hammerhead lunged with terrific impact against the wet slope, while the savage rush and thrashing of water showed that the school of sharks had just missed their man.

Inside the crevice Mace discovered a small, cavelike apartment, dark except for the slit of light that streamed through the narrow opening. The floor was of fine coral sand, inviting to the man who had just completed a dangerous trick at the end of a strenuous rough-and-tumble.

Mace stretched himself on the sand, his glance fixed on the crevice through which gleamed the open waters of the bay. Above the crevice he noted a big, native gourd hanging from a peg in the roof. He recalled instantly Sagon's reference to the pig's blood. Rising, he took it down and poured the contents into the shark-infested depths outside.

The sound of voices above warned him that the chiefs had returned to the reef to compliment Avian on his victory. To and fro they paced, acclaiming in loud tones the skill and deftness of Avian's methods of attack and defense. The voices surged nearer, and Mace knew that they were standing directly above the spot where he had pitched over.

"See where the sharks are even now at their work!" a voice exclaimed.

Mace saw by the furious thrashing and leaping of the excited monsters outside the crevice that the chiefs were watching the sharks' unholy scramble in the blood-wash from the gourd. One by one the voices retreated, and a few minutes later the sound of the canoe paddles told him that the party had returned to the beach with the triumphant Avian.

During the long afternoon Mace was afflicted with a great thirst as he lay with his face to the opening in the reef, not daring to show himself lest some watcher on the cliffs might detect his presence.

The tropic night came swiftly, bringing slants of cool air into his rocky prison. He felt that he was at the mercy of Sagon whose influence over the natives would keep wandering canoemen from the vicinity of the Red Reef. Oaf Palotta he had no doubts. She would not betray him. Treachery, if it came, would emanate from the wily old medicine man.

He dozed fitfully in his thirst torment and awoke at the slightest sound from the starlit bay. Occasionally the phosphorescent streaks and flashes of water reminded him of the eternal presence of the shark-shoal cruising like sentinels of an enemy squadron through every passage in the reef-lined bay. Without a canoe or vessel of some kind, he was in a death trap from which there was no escape.

The wisp of moon edged over the forest and showed him the ocean passage through the frowning cliffs. Then his roused ear caught the soft whir of a propeller churning somewhere across the bay. It came nearer, and Mace squeezed through the crevice and peered out.

A twenty-ton launch was gliding toward the reef; it slowed suddenly and swung in a half circle to where he stood.

"Hi, there!" a voice hailed softly. "Get ready to come aboard!"

The launch rounded the curve gracefully and swung with her open gangway close to the reef opening. Mace needed no second invitation; clutching her fender as she squeezed near the rock, he clambered aboard feeling certain that his fate was now in friendly hands.

The launch carried no lights, but the starshine revealed her snow-white decks and glittering brass rails. A native stepped near him, thrusting a silk coat upon him to hide his naked chest. Mace drew it on with a nod of thanks and turned quickly to the wheelhouse and beheld Sagon standing near Palotta and Avian.

The old doctor addressed him curtly. "Our queen is here to help you, papalagi. This vessel will carry you to Nukahiva in the Marquesas, where you will soon find a bigger ship to carry you home. There is nothing more to say."

"Except that I'm grateful to the queen for her kindness," Mace supplemented, conscious that her dark eyes were devouring him from the shelter of the house.

"Brave men are the children of the gods!" she murmured gently. "I thank you for your chivalry and forbearance."

Avian came forward, his boyish face rent with his sense of humiliation and defeat. There were tear stains under his lowered eyes. "You did not fight me in true fashion!" he burst out passionately. "I was like a stick in your hands. The honorable death I deserved was denied me. The fight was a lie! I cannot look my chiefs in the face, never, never!" he cried bitterly.

Mace's hand rested consolingly on his bent shoulder. "Avian, you had me stretched and guessing in the first clinch. You could have rolled me over to those cannibal fish with your feet. Don't worry about the fight bein' a frame-up. You gripped me so darned hard in the second session that I was almost cryin' out for my mammy. I'll never get over that squeeze. I've been coughing queer ever since."

"He is too young for these life-and-death bouts," Palotta declared, Avian's hand held in her own. "In a year or so he will—"

"Walk away with the world's championship,"

Mace broke in with an air of sincerity that made even the unhappy Avian smile.

The sound of paddle strokes sent the old doctor to the rail, peering across the starlit bay, mumbling incoherently. "They are coming!" he chattered excitedly; "Enos, Ganda, and Oke. They suspect treason. We had better beware!"

A big war canoe shot out of the darkness of the wooded shore and approached the launch with swift, measured strokes.

Avian turned quickly to his sister, "Ganda and the others are against us," he intimated under his breath. "We cannot trust this forest spider, Sagon. He is working for our ruin. The canoe carries a dozen spearmen!" he announced with a shrewd glance across the bay.

CHAPTER VII

NO ROOM FOR ARGUMENT

The war canoe drew alongside and hailed the launch. Ganda, the tallest chief on the island, decked, in his flowing heron plumes and battle shield, stood erect in the high-beaked prow. His voice had a challenge that held no doubt regarding his intentions.

"Where is the queen?" he thundered. "Where is the brother that goes to combat with his heart full of lies? The papalagi he fought is not dead. We have been deceived!"

The big war galley was within a cable's length of the launch. Her prow was lighted by candlenut torches held aloft by half a dozen tattooed warriors. The wind-blown flares illuminated the repulsive, paint-smeared occupants of the galley, the steel-barbed weapons glinting with murderous intent.

Sagon touched Palotta's arm in the darkness; his voice was soft and wheedling. "Let Ganda come aboard," he advised, "with Oke and Enos."

Palotta pushed him aside as she stepped to the rail. "How dare these people come armed to address me?" she challenged. "Speak, Ganda! Am I to cringe before the war irons of these Kanakas?"

"We shall answer the queen's question in the council chamber!" Ganda retorted fiercely. "The queen must reply to her chiefs. We have come to bring you and your brother, the sham warrior. We want the papalagi also, who hid from the fight under the Red Reef. Let him come, too."

Mace had been slaking his thirst from an oak cask near the saloon head, which contained fresh water and a cup for the use of the deck hands. Palotta translated Ganda's message to him in an undertone, while he wiped the delicious water drops from his lips.

"Ganda's some bull chief," he commented. "Maybe he'd like a silver band to play our funeral march."

Palotta flung back her answer to the waiting chief. "I will not return to be judged by your people, Ganda. I ask the freedom that is mine by right and birth."

The old doctor made a sign in the darkness. "You must return, O queen," he chided. "The chiefs will compel you!"

Mace moved forward slightly. "See here, Sagon," he drawled. "Who's who in this palaver—the queen or these banana merchants? I guess if she wants to leave these islands she'll choose her own time and her own way."

Sagon recoiled, his old lips snarling a native imprecation. "You shall not leave these islands, dog with the white skin! You die here where the carrion fish can rend your body. Your breed must not escape!"

Palotta interposed with a gesture. "Remember, Sagon," she declared in an undertone. "I gave you my pearls so that he might go free. You shall not betray him now!"

In reply the old doctor clutched the brass rail with his shaking fingers and called to the waiting chiefs in the war canoe. "Come aboard, my children! The white man is here. We must obey the law."

Mace's right hand gripped his waist softly. In a moment Sagon was lifted from the deck and shaken as a lion shakes a vulture. The bones of the old schemer rattled like sticks in the white man's clasp; his scream of protest was heard by the fierce-eyed crowd in the galley.

Mace put him on his feet, still gripping him by one arm. "Those pearls, Sagon!" he ordered. "Which pocket? Quick!"

The old man squirmed and struggled to get free and, with his disengaged hand, Mace rent the other's garments and in a twist of the fingers had drawn the precious rope of pearls from a pocket of grass silk that was near Sagon's heart. Then he released the man.

With a vicious snarl Sagon made a plunge to regain the prize that had been wrested from him. In doing so he slipped and fell overboard.

A soft, gurgling noise was heard down in the water, followed by a smothered yell of terror as a dozen phosphorescent wedges of fire darted under and over the struggling body. In a moment the water was dark again.

Avian approached Mace. "We must fight or run from this war canoe," he said quickly. "What does our friend say?"

Mace shrugged. "No use having a mess when you can walk away," he answered quietly. "There's no gate money for beating this bunch of tinhorns. Shake up your engines and get clear!"

Palotta nodded appreciation. "Let us go, Avian. We can reach the Marquesas on our oil fuel. The launch is well stored. I have always lived in a state of preparation," she confessed hastily. "And now the hour has struck!"

Ganda and the others seemed to guess Palotta's intention. With savage cries they drove the big war galley beak onto the launch as Avian shouted a word to his helmsman to stand clear.

"Make it a running fight!" Mace spoke near Avian's elbow. "I'll stand in the stern and deal with the black stuff if it climbs over the rail."

The launch maneuvered cleverly to avoid the slamming beak of the heavy galley. With shouts and thunders of paddles and spear butts it plunged onto the launch's stern. Only a few seconds were needed for the oil-driven launch to get clear, but Avian had allowed the galley to come closer than was prudent. Her big-bladed paddles almost raised her from the water, hurling her towering beak to the launch's stern rail.

With incredible skill the warriors in the galley's fore part locked their pronged spearheads to the brass rail of the launch, thereby forcing the launch to tow them in her wake. The locked spears, cunningly interwoven, formed a ladder for the first of their boarding party. It was Ganda, who, with shield held before him, crawled up the ladder of spears to the stern rail.

His shaking head plumes and the red paint on his chest and face produced an uncanny effect in the torchlight. He leaped to the rail like a giant from an inferno, shield and spear swaying in his great hands, the spirit of loot and murder in his eyes. He knew now that the launch held the vast hoard of wealth which Palotta had inherited from her mother—gold dollars and gems from all the islands of the archipelago. One straight blow and his own sons would inherit the queen's far-won treasures.

A hose box stood near the stern rail; Mace skipped to it lightly, bringing his head level with the protruding jaw of Langos'

Herculean chief. In his day Mace had met the worst breed of fighters and saloon-bar bandits. To him circumstances never presented new factors whether the man struck with fist, knife, or bottle. His rejoinder had always been effective. There could be no room for argument when men strove to become his executioners. At other times he was genial and lovable.

Ganda's spear drove at him with the force of a shell splinter. Straight toward his heart it came, the black, sinewy arm bunched like a steel rope behind it. Mace leaned forward, his left and right hands touching shield and spear arms with the lightness of a cat; then his lithe body crouched as shield and spear deviated the matter of a hand's breadth. The barbed weapon went wide, bringing Ganda's profile almost to Mace's shoulder.

Ganda's snakelike length of body, with its roots of muscles quivering, was for a fraction of time, "all mussed up," as the ringmen say. His perfect balance was gone, his whole structure out of joint. Mace's right fist smashed under the chin, and the neck of Ganda cracked like a twisted hinge. The blow seemed to generate to Mace's toes, but the crunch and volt came from the lightning in his brain.

Ganda went down the ladder of spears in a limp and spineless heap, his shield and his charms of brass clattering over the prow of the galley. Mace kicked the spearheads from the rail, and the launch shot away at torpedo speed for the open Pacific.

CHAPTER VIII
NOT EVEN A YEAR

The launch throbbed through seas of palm-dotted atolls that stretched like gems of sapphire along the horizon. There were bird-haunted islands that called to them to stay, islands where the shimmering purple of valleys and streams faded like dream-mists from the eyes of waking children.

Palotta, book in hand, reclined in a deck chair in the cool shade of the sun awning, the heavy pearl necklace which Sagon had surrendered drooping from her ivory throat. Mace and Avian studied a navigator's chart inside the small wheelhouse aft.

"To-night we fetch Nukahiva," Avian declared with a side glance at his companion. "Perhaps you are sorry," he added, studying the chart afresh.

Mace sighed. He had spent five blissful days in a floating haven of peace and tranquillity. And it seemed to him that each beat of the propeller was bringing him nearer the end, to the last night when he must say good-by to the woman who had raised his mental outlook to a finer plane.

Avian regarded him a trifle curiously, for in the last few days he had learned to trust the man who had stood by them in their hour of need. "I shall be sorry to lose you, Darrel Mace," he admitted with boyish awkwardness. "It is a pity that friends must go different ways!"

Mace nodded absently. "You see, Avian, I'm a partner in some coffee lands down in the Manono Archipelago, and I'll have to get busy locating my territory. My partners were drowned on those reefs of yours. So I'll have to pursue the venture alone."

His voice, although low, reached Palotta under the awning. She tossed her book aside and lay back in her chair, her eyes tight shut, listening to the beat of the small but powerful engines below. She was bound for a strange island and people who would know her only by repute.

She had lived nearly all her life at Langos with Avian. As a child she had been almost worshiped by the natives until of late when Sagon and Ganda had stirred the chiefs against her. The coming of Mace had brought things to a climax. All her mother's wealth and her own was in the steel-walled vault adjoining her stateroom. Her lands and house she surrendered to the people she still loved and remembered.

Her great courage had been shaken by the events of the last few days, and the new life she was entering held many shadows and fears for her young mind. The world outside Langos was hard and ruled by tyrants more subtle and ferocious than Ganda or Sagon. Her brother, too, was woefully inexperienced in the ways of white men, although the blood of the white race ran pure in his veins. Palotta was lonely, and, for the first time in her life, afraid.

Mace stepped from the wheelhouse, paused an instant opposite her chair to hitch a flapping guy rope to a stanchion. The bronze of his throat and face, the elastic ease of his young body were revealed in the tropic sun flare. Like a boy, anxious to make good in his reputation for tidiness, he picked up the discarded cushions and shawls near her chair and placed them in a dry corner abaft the skylights.

She opened her eyes suddenly and regarded him with attention, for Palotta was gifted with a quaint sense of humor at times.

"I once sentenced you to death," she declared dreamily. "Now I discover that the death penalty has been overlooked. And neither of us appears jubilant," she added with a sigh.

Mace found himself staring into a tiny, lustrous spot between her half-closed eyelashes. "I'm sorry the trip is over," he said. Then with a forced laugh he added: "It may be years before I catch up with that death penalty."

"But you are sorry the trip is over?"

His reply was a fierce intake of breath as he bent over the rail. "I came near drowning on a reef once," he admitted slowly. "It was just a holiday from my job compared to some things."

"Some things!" Palotta laughed mirthlessly. "You poor boy! There are truly many worse fates than drowning!"

Mace felt like a quitter in love as he walked away to the wheelhouse, the fires of his confusion blazing on his cheeks and brow. Her voice sounded faintly behind him, blurred by the mad poundings of his heart. Avian had gone below.

"Mr. Mace! Please come here!"

He halted at the wheelhouse, swung around dutifully and returned to the chair. She was studying the jeweled pendant that hung from the pearls on her breast.

"I am sorry you are unhappy," she began in childlike tones. "Tell me how I can repay you for your devotion and courage. I feel that my life and the life of my brother are still in your keeping."

Mace knelt beside her chair, even though the eyes of the native steersman were staring through the window of the wheelhouse. "I go my way alone tomorrow," he declared huskily. "I will forget today and yesterday. But you must tell me that it is well that I should go, and that I must not love even the memory of you. Say it now, and I'll just disappear, for your peace of mind and my own."

For the first time Mace saw her lips tremble, and his heart leaped wildly. Her voice sounded like a wind reed in the warm silence. "Your country is far away, Darrel, and I do not want to lose you forever!"

"For a year, Palotta?"

She stared over his shoulder as though afraid of unseen hands and spears. The shadows of lonely islands crossed her eyes, and her soul shrank within her. "No, no; not a year!" she almost gasped. Then, with hands outspread, she smiled again. "I do not want you to go, Darrel. I, too, am very unhappy!"

That night the glittering lights of Nukahiva twinkled across the sky line. Pier lamps winked with fairy faces at the dreaming couple standing hand in hand near the port rail.

ANOTHER PAWN OF FATE

F. St. Mars

*But a desert stretched and stricken, left and right, left
and right,*
Where the piled mirages thicken under white-hot light—
A skull beneath a sand-hill, and a viper coiled inside,
And a red wind out of Libya, roaring, "Run and hide!"
—"Jabson's Amen" (Kipling).

* * * *

If you had killed, and what was worse, barely otherwise made
use of, three colts, a heifer, twenty-one sheep and eleven pigs be-
longing to other people, so that four hundred dollars would not
even begin to cover your debts—if, moreover, you had done to
death two valuable dogs sent to interview you upon the subject,
and spoiled the sleep of not less than two dozen stockmen for an
uncounted number of nights, you might have expected consider-
ation—but you would certainly not get it.

All these things, and more, had the jaguar done, and he was
beginning to reap his harvest. Things became hectic for him, and
by the time he had escaped death by bullet and poison four times,
and worse than death by trap upon nine occasions, he came to the
conclusion that a change of air was for him imperative.

The jaguar was like a large leopard, only with his spots run into
rosettes. He was heftier than any leopard, though, and fiercer by
some few fierces.

The trouble was, where was there a refuge to go to for a hunted
wild hunter upon all those desolate plains and sun-baked stretches?
Where, indeed?

The jaguar left home—the ruined tomb of the king of some
long-forgotten race—in the almost intolerable glare of the full sun
upon his journey. He would much have preferred to "flit" during
the darkest night, but a pillar of dust as yet far away but approaching, warned him of the starting of a big hunt on horseback—for
him.

As the horsemen might be accompanied by dogs, he knew he would be found if he stayed. So he decamped—at a long, loose, padded, swinging trot, that hiked him over the rough ground much faster than it appeared to; and, of course, being a cat, a supercat, he hugged what cover he could get.

This time, however, the stockmen were in earnest, and did not stop to think on the brink of a drink when the sun got hot enough to frizzle all things save the little lizards upon the rock-slabs. They kept right on going. So did the jaguar; but with the grim, slow realization that he was a sprinter, but no stayer, and that his ever growing thirst was worse than death.

Thus it came about that by noonday he could not very well ignore the drumming of a bronco's hoofs not far to his right rear, and another to his left.

He heard also a shout, and threw an ominous snarl over his spotted, tawny shoulder in reply as he broke into a gallop.

He was heading toward the coast. The smell of water, any water, in his nostrils made him do that. Water, said instinct, means forest in that land; and he was a forester by right, or his ancestors had been.

Then came the lasso—the first one.

The jaguar did not see it. He heard it fall short just behind, and make slithery noises like a snake. He set back his ears. His fangs bared.

Then came the second lasso.

The jaguar saw that. He had to jump over it as he flew—fairly flew now, in his last desperate dash to the shelter of some thick but shortish grass.

He gained the grass-patch even as the third lasso hit, and slipped along, his back. Untamable, ferocious beyond compare, a dread that stalked by night, a terror among the Indians, intolerant, implacable, lonely, the jaguar dived to the middle of that slight cover quaking in every limb, a beast beaten and cowed even to inertia. It was the lassos that had done it.

For full ten minutes the jaguar lay there, spent, in the middle of the grass-patch, only his head visible, a picture of fury and hate, while the finest horsemen in the world circled around outside, trying to lasso that furious head—and failing.

The broncos would not enter the grass, and the dogs thought that the reason the horses had was a good one—for a cornered jaguar in thick grass is several kinds of a deadly proposition. And in the end the stockmen set fire to the grass, and waited.

* * * *

The seared stems burned like tinder, the flames racing along before the wind in a crackling, reeking furnace, but the jaguar did not move.

The red, dancing, leaping line fairly flew down upon him, chasing its own choking clouds of smoke, till they both together seemed to envelop him, and that terrible, great, spotted, broad head, still and motionless and grinning, faded, faded gradually out before the amazed onlookers—faded and was swallowed up.

Not when the smoke fumes nearly asphyxiated him; not when the smell of his singeing fur mingled with the rest; not till the sting of the flames, actually licking up his legs, broke the spell, did the jaguar come to life, as it were back, and leap for that life ahead of the fire. By then he was invisible.

If it had been a race before, it was a greater race now. The flames fairly tore along in that dry place, and he could not see a yard on either hand whither he was going. He only knew that the flames were gnashing at his tail, and that instinct shrieked in his ear—

"Make for the sea!"

He made for the sea accordingly, the sea he could not see—nor anything else for the first quarter of a mile, for the matter of that—but knew was there.

The fire was far behind when the great spotted cat got to the shore by way of sandhills, and lay down, panting. It had stopped with the gutting of the grass-patch—but the stockmen were not far behind.

They had spotted the jaguar at last, clear of the smoke, galloping like a great dog far across the blistered plain, and were now drumming down upon him, dogs, horses, and men, in a yelling cloud of dust, that—it seemed—must end with his end.

Now for it!

The sea, in that burning sun, almost blinded him; but the jaguar could see far enough across the waves a low line of dark trees, walking, so it seemed, upon the face of the waters—or was it a mirage dancing tauntingly in the heat flurry? Could the jaguar see a mirage anyway?

The big, flat, spotted, brilliant head turned slowly and gazed steadfastly at the excited crowd sweeping down upon him. For a moment he permitted himself a bare-fanged, twisted-lipped, evil snarl—the jaguar's "blessing"—then waded into the warm, glinting, blinding water and resolutely struck out.

The brute was a fine swimmer. Though he personally had been born and had lived upon the plains all his life, and never crossed anything bigger than a stream, he came of forest ancestors used to dealing with the world's largest rivers.

He forged ahead grandly, head well up, and with the confidence that comes of conscious ability.

A rifle cracked along the old-gold sand, but the sundance on the water dazzled, and the bullet spat—plup—yards short. Another and another spoke, and the bark of the .30-30 Marlin repeaters came to the swimmer's ears plainly as the bullets shot up miniature spouts all around him; but the broad, yellow head kept on, and on, and on, steady, straight, untouched, unflurried.

At last one long shot clipped his right ear. It looked like a biscuit from which a piece has been bitten, but even that did not turn or stop him. A last flurry of reports, a last "covey of death" spattering up the surface, and he was out of range—their range anyway.

"Never mind," said the stockmen to each other. "Guess the sharks'll get him, fellers. You betcha."

But the sharks did not get him. They had heard the firing, or felt the concussion of the bullets in the water, or something, and turned their knife-bladed back-fins the other way.

Slowly but strongly the jaguar came to the mangrove forest. It was a remarkably wet, and a lugubrious, dark, noisome, muddy, and smelly place. In fact, it was not like any ordinary forest at all. Dante might have described it.

It was not tall—the sea winds saw to that. It had no true tree trunks—the sea itself saw to that. It was like a forest of pier-piles; a forest of many-headed hydras with hundreds of legs stuck in the mud. And the sea sucked and gurgled in and out among the legs, otherwise roots. Great freak crabs, blue and freakish crabs, red played grimly in and out among the branches that wound and twisted like a thousand snakes.

* * * *

The jaguar—his claws rasped in the wet hollowness—had hauled himself up the roots, high above high tide among the writhing stems and branches, before he discovered that the mangrove forest was a world unto itself—inhabited by its own living beasts and birds, insects and sea folk, beside the crabs.

Wings flapped above, and great herons removed themselves from his company. Some diving bird thing, all wet and shiny, hit the water with a loud plop as it took the sea.

A head, yellow, flat, broad, black-spotted, big and slit-eared, thrust from a tangle of branches and foliage and made evil remarks to his address in a language that—petrified him. It was his own language, the talk of the jaguar people, their swear words.

And the jaguar changed as he stiffened from heavy jaw to padded heel. He contorted into a calamity, ready set for trouble—a cast statue of ferocity. It is a way cats have. Nine times out of ten it is just thrice perfected bluff.

This was the tenth time.

For one thing, the plains jaguar had grown larger; that was fur on end. For another, he had sprouted some height; that was arched back. For another, he moaned, horribly, quietly, and to himself; but it is not quite clear what that was for.

The head remained, like a head in a picture, framed in gnarled stems.

The jaguar did not. He turned half side-wise—to side-leap at need. He stood like a horse hard held with a bearing rein on, champing at air. Then—he faded out, still sidewise, crab-fashion, a step at a time.

But he had seen what human eyes could not have seen—the flick of a thin ear tickled by a fly, two yards to the left of the head among the foliage. And he had smelled what human nostrils most assuredly could not have smelled on the salt breeze—though the bigger cats bear an acrid taint—the odor of not one jaguar, but two, and the other a lady—dux femina facti.

Upon the plains, where the jaguar had lived all his life, the stock-men had seen to it that lady jaguars were rare creatures. Indeed, this plains jaguar had never seen one till that precise psychological moment. If he had, he might not have wandered afar worrying the herders of cattle. As it was—

The return of the jaguar ten minutes later, and flying—at least, he was not touching anything as he came—from the opposite side to that in which he had faded and gone out, was intended as a surprise, and would have been to humans, but not to the other jaguars. Cats do that sort of thing. It is one of their little specialties.

Surprise is the essence of tactics. Meeting it—the art.

The other male jaguar did not show whether he was surprised or not; probably not. He was not there when the plains jaguar landed where his back had been. He left the branch as the other arrived upon it. Also he exploded like a firework benefit in the process. Perhaps he realized what he had missed, or what had missed him.

But both jaguars were so obsessed with each other that they forgot their surroundings. Cats are likely to do that when they squabble, all the world over. There is no health in it, though.

The plains jaguar's lathy hind-limbs landed upon a crab and a branch; you could hear the claws scrape upon the horny carapace. And he knew nothing about crabs! Then he spun with a startling explosion.

The crab had locked home one pincer to his tail. The jaguar would have acted the same if a baby had touched him from behind with a little finger; his nerves were in that state. He pictured rival male jaguars on every hand. He was all heated up and scorched! But even a jaguar cannot for long chase his own tail on mangrove branches slippery with the green scum of the sea.

A loud and spluttering double splash announced the end of his catherine-wheeling.

The other jaguar, to save himself, had sprung at what seemed to be an inviting wall of foliage he could pull himself up on. It grew, however, like a screen that gave toward the sea.

Thus resulted the picture of one fine male jaguar, very flat-eared, hanging futilely on to some branches of mangrove that swung out and out, and bent down and down, until he realized that there was no sense in hanging on to them any longer. He was already up to his neck in water.

Now, see how Fate lets down those good, scientific, learned ones who dogmatize upon the survival of the fittest.

The water was shallowish at that precise spot. There was mud upon which the mangroves throve in their own peculiar way. As the jaguar turned and struck out for the nearest root-landing his hind legs churned up this mud.

* * * *

There was a flash as of red flame in the depths, a blurry, indistinct outline of something big and long that writhed, and—the jaguar shot upward, pawing wildly, with a blood-curdling roar.

Then he fell back inert, struggled feebly, galvanized to madness again, collapsed and drifted away on the strong tide, swimming feebly, banged his head on a root, spun round, drifted on, hit something else, revolved, and so, in and out among the lugubrious roots, was carried, slowly, surely, drifting from sight.

He did not come back.

He had touched off an electric eel, a nasty, big, brown, compressed thing, with a flaring scarlet throat, from what little could be seen; and it, fearing attack, had given him a shock, perhaps two shocks. A flood must have washed the eel to that unfortunate place.

Meanwhile, the plains jaguar, having shaken off the incubus of the crab, slowly scratched, and scraped, and scrambled his way up the first roots he found that offered a hold.

As he did so his tail came within an inch of the gigantic eel thing, and had that tail touched it, contact would have been effected and the tail would have been as good a conductor as any other part of the body so far as the resulting shock was concerned. But that is Fate.

Above, among the twisted mangrove branches, the jaguar found the eternal feminine, sitting humped and cynically comfortable, as she had sat all along. She turned her yellow, spotted head and regarded him with cruel, inscrutable eyes.

Then she rose, and, stretching deliberately and insolently, yawned in his face.

The other jaguar had been the finer beast, but—well, he was gone, and meanwhile there was this one purring and blandishing in his place. Enough. She patted at that other a furtive, saucy pat, the sort of pat that would have ripped half his cheek off if he had not dodged unconcernedly as only cats can.

Then the two slouched off to fish for turtles, which is perhaps a more exciting way of spending a honeymoon than fishing for compliments.

MYSTERY ON DEAD MAN REEF

George Armin Shaftel

CHAPTER I

"What is your real name, lad?" the trader asked.

"Just what I've told you! John Gregg."

"Oh." DeCourcey chuckled. "I was wondering if that was as phony as the rest of your story."

The young man stiffened. "Look here—"

"Easy, easy! You jump off Lassen's trading schooner and swim ashore here, and tell me you were a stowaway and had been kicked off. I talk to Lassen by radio and he tells me you hired him to bring you to Puna-Puka. So what am I to think?"

Gregg shrugged. He fought back the sudden panic tightening his innards and kept his voice cool as he answered.

"I'm broke. I figured you'd give me a job for a while and pay my passage away from here."

The trader chuckled. A small, plump, gray-haired man, De-Courcey had a kindly way about him.

"So you're broke. Yet you told Lassen to come by here next week to pick you up, and promised him three hundred dollars."

DeCourcey's tone was amused, not accusing. And he spoke on quickly, as if not liking to embarrass young Gregg.

"I told Lassen not to come back here until his next regular trip. That's six months from now. So I guess you're marooned here, lad."

So guess again, John Gregg thought suddenly, staring out to sea, excitement flaring within him.

Gregg and DeCourcey, who was the one trader and white resident of the island, were sitting on a coral boulder out on the reef a couple hundred yards from the Puna-Puka beach. They were fishing for malau, a fat big-eyed red fish of gorgeous flavor. The moon had risen, and the southeasterly trade wind had faded to an amorous sigh.

Along the shore the coconut trees stood stately and mute, gleaming faintly above the white glare of the beach. Behind the palms, a few lights shone in the village beyond the trading station.

Within the reef, the water was smooth. But on the outer edge of the coral barrier, the surf smashed and pounded. Across the reef it swept crabs and lobsters with eyes that shone amazingly in the sun's glare. It followed hollows on the broad expanse of coral— shimmering pools in which spotted sea eels lay coiled.

It was ceaseless as time, that surf, beating up an eerie glow of phosphorescence as it struck, lashing across the barrier with a crackling hiss and choking down them into coral caverns.

Gregg stared out beyond the surf, out to sea. Keener-eyed than the trader, he saw lights out there. A yacht was heading in toward Puna-Puka.

Marooned, was he? Like hell! Tonight, he'd swing into action. Tomorrow, he'd get away....

DeCourcey pulled up a fat red fish.

"Enough," he sighed. "Let's turn in."

Gregg waited an hour, lying on his cot on the screened veranda of the trading station. Then he got up. Walked inside.

Moonlight shone on counters and shelves. With poignant home-sickness, Gregg was drawn to thoughts of home. For here were those smells of a country general store—of kerosene, of leather goods and dungarees, of tobacco and candy. At the back of the store was DeCourcey's desk, and iron safe. Between them was his shortwave radio set.

* * * *

Gregg got busy. His lean, rangy figure bent over DeCourcey's roll-top desk, he searched through ledgers and bills of lading and files of correspondence.

In a pigeonhole, he found photographs. And a medal. On the back of this Croix de Guerre medal he found what he sought: the engraved name, Philip DeCourcey Leroux.

Which meant that DeCourcey was Leroux!

"Don't move."

Gregg whirled, and recoiled, blinded by the smack of a flash-light beam into his lean face. He heard a gun being cocked.

"I could shoot you as a thief," DeCourcey said. "I'd be absolutely justified."

Unflinchingly Gregg faced him. He was a serious young fellow, Gregg—a high-tempered youngster who turned defiant and reckless when threatened. His lips tightened with panic, but his gray eyes blazed in anger.

"I'm no thief, Leroux!"

"Please keep on calling me DeCourcey."

"I came here to find you. To take you back to Honolulu!"

The trader swore, his pale forehead knitting in surprise.

"But why?"

"You were the only witness to the DeGroot robbery. You can identify the thief."

"Yes, that's so," the trader admitted.

Gregg's voice was taut. "Am I the man?" he demanded.

"No. He wasn't a tall, good-looking youngster like you. He was burly, putting on lard, and gray at the temples."

"Just the same, the crime's finally been fastened on me!" Gregg said, and the angry resentment of long months of brooding worry was in his voice. "Look, DeCourcey. If you'd come back and testify, you could save me from going to the penitentiary for fifteen to twenty years!"

DeCourcey sighed, his pallid face regretful.

"Sorry, my boy. But I'm fifty-six, and my heart's going back on me. It's a long way to Honolulu—and I've no assurance of getting back here. You haven't the cash to insure that."

"I'll borrow it!" Gregg exclaimed.

"A man suspected of the DeGroot robbery borrow money?"

"I'll get a job and—"

"Maybe." DeCourcey shrugged. "Chances are I'd be stranded in Honolulu, with my little business here going to ruin. No, I won't go."

"But, man alive, you're sentencing me to the penitentiary!" Gregg pleaded.

"Don't think I've got a brass pump for a heart, lad! I'm damned sorry. Look. Suppose I write out my testimony—"

"They'd say I forged it! You've got to appear in person and be identified beyond question."

DeCourcey sighed again. "Then I suggest, Gregg, that you stay here. Puna-Puka is a paradise. When I die, you'll have my business."

"God'l'mighty, I'm young! I've got my whole life ahead of me!"

"And I'm old, with but a year or two ahead of me. I'm spending them right here," DeCourcey said, and his voice was hard. "Go back to bed."

"Go to hell!" Gregg raged.

And he stalked out of the trading station, strode blindly down the beach.

CHAPTER II

DIRTY WORK

Next morning, that yacht was anchored out in the roadstead off Puna-Puka. The village buzzed with excitement. Arrival of a vessel was a rare event. Every native, from older folk in pareus, naked children, young men in dungarees and slim, comely girls wearing fern leaf girdles, were down at the beach when a boat put off from the yacht and headed through the break in the reef toward the village.

"That party looks like money," DeCourcey murmured to Gregg as the yacht's boat reached the beach.

There were four men and two women in the group coming ashore.

"I'm Henry Scanlon." The leader of the group introduced himself to DeCourcey and Gregg. He was short, thick-set and powerful, this Henry Scanlon. His hair was utterly white and his mustache was white, and his fleshy face was sunburned to a flaming red, out of which keen eyes of a Nordic blue stared with a steely directness.

"We're from Globe Picture Syndicate, and we have permission to land to take pictures. Getting background shots for a South Seas epic, you know. My cameraman, Luke Hawes—"

Hawes was lanky, bald and tough. Obviously he was Scanlon's Man Friday. He stood with both hands in his coat pockets, feet spread apart, just like Scanlon stood. He stared hard and unwinkingly at you, like Scanlon did. He was the director's shadow, if you could think of a stocky man throwing a long, lanky shadow.

Gregg didn't like either of them. The third man, Nigel Rorke, was obviously an actor. His was a professional profile with wavy hair and a petulant mouth and an absorbing interest in his fingernails. The fourth man, Nils Rogg, was the yacht's skipper—a chunky, bronzed man with hair so metallically black it screamed toupé. He shook hands like a decent guy, Gregg thought to himself.

Gregg looked at the two women—and his pulse leaped.

"My wife," Scanlon was saying, "and Susan Lanphier, who doesn't need introduction even here at this tail end of creation. When better stars are found, Susan will still outshine 'em!"

DeCourcey said, "We haven't any movies here, but never before have I regretted missing them as much as I do now, Miss Lanphier."

She grinned at him engagingly; and as Gregg was introduced, she stepped forward and shook hands in a friendly, comradely way. But her hand clung to his; and as she looked at him, suddenly she wasn't smiling. Something very intent and meaningful was in her glance for just a split-wink instant.

She was a tall, shapely girl with reddish brown hair that seemed to burn in the sun, and eyes of so deep a dusky blue they were almost violet, and her skin was tanned to a buoyant golden hue. She wore a play suit, just linen shorts and a sheer waist.

In the landing through the surf, the party had got doused with spray, and Susan Lanphier's blouse clung revealingly to her body. She moved with grace, lithe loveliness in every line of her slim-hipped figure. Gregg stared at her, his pulse thudding in his ears.

Her hand pressed his meaningfully, and she turned away.

"We'll want pictures of the village, DeCourcey," Scanlon was saying as the party started toward the trading station.

* * * *

Gregg stood where he was, staring after them; and to himself he reflected that Scanlon hadn't said, "May we take pictures of your village?" No. Scanlon had announced what he wanted! A bossy, demanding, snooty buzzard!

Gregg stood where he was, letting the party get ahead of him. For Susan Lanphier had pressed something into his hand.

He looked at it guardedly. It was a strip of newspaper, folded over. He unfolded it. On it, in lipstick, had been hastily scrawled—I'm in desperate trouble—No more. As if there hadn't been time for more.

Frowning, Gregg thrust the note into his pocket. What the hell, he had enough troubles of his own!

Susan Lanphier was glancing back at him. For an instant there was pleading in her lovely eyes. The sun shone with a flaming beauty in her hair....

"We're looking," the white-haired director told DeCourcey, "for a scene to be the background for the main sets of our picture. I'll sketch what I want. You can tell me if I'll find it on Puna-Puka."

He scrawled on a sheet of paper. "See? A narrow river valley, with a plateau halfway up one wall. On it maybe there should be ruins of an old stone house. Back of the plateau is a high cliff, with a waterfall. See?"

DeCourcey looked at him in amazement.

"You ever been on Puna-Puka before?"

"You mean, there is such a place on the island?" the cameraman blurted, his deadpan face excited.

"Yes." DeCourcey rubbed his chin thoughtfully. "Come along. I'll show it to you."

Funny, Gregg thought as he followed the party. The little trader seemed flabbergasted at Scanlon's precise description of a place he had never seen.

"This movie crowd looks damned eager to find the spot," Gregg told himself. "As if they've been looking for it so much that it's just too good to be true that they've actually located it! Wonder what they expect to find?"

The trader led the party through the village. The Puna-Pukans stared with smiling curiosity at the whites. They were a friendly, courteous people, as hard-working as they were attractive of appearance. Beyond the village, the young men were busy spreading a fertilizer of green pukatea leaves on the taro beds. And on the trail leading inland, the party met young men carrying loads of coconuts, brown ripe drinking nuts; and others bringing in scores upon scores of squawking birds, young boobies, tied together by the feet like bunches of onions.

"Lord, what beauty!" Director Scanlon kept repeating. "Hawes, get that on film!"

And Hawes, his face as expressive as the butt of a log, set to whirring the compact camera he carried.

DeCourcey led the party to the main river of Puna-Puka, and turned inland along its bank.

It was cool on the trail, for overhead arched ancient trees—banyans and mangos and breadfruit. Giant ferns, and clumps of towering bamboo, crowded the path. Tropical flowers, that looked as though they had been carved right out of flaming sunsets, covered the steep walls of the canyon into which DeCourcey led the way.

* * * *

Mile after mile the party walked. The canyon became a steep-walled gorge. Waterfalls pitched in lacy beauty from the rimrock high overhead, plunging down into wide pools as beautiful as the dreams of sweet repose. And neither snakes nor insects existed here to pester men who passed.

DeCourcey stopped, and pointed ahead.

"There it is, Mr. Scanlon! See, where the river forms a wide, shaded pool? Above there, on the east side, the mountain wall cuts back in a flat space. And at the back of the flat, a waterfall drops from the cliff. Like a bridal veil. Right?"

"Right!" Scanlon snapped, his bushy white brows knitted over his steely eyes as he peered ahead. "Isn't it, Hawes?"

"Sure as hell looks like it," Hawes breathed.

"But are there ruins of an old stone house up there?" Susan Lanphier put in.

"Well," DeCourcey admitted, scratching his chin, "used to be a lot of natives living along the river. Every flat you'll find practic'ly has the stone platform for a house on it."

"Then, look," Susan said, pointing farther upstream, "there's another flat above a river pool—and a waterfall pouring over a cliff behind the flat. Maybe that's the spot?"

Scanlon muttered an oath. And Hawes grunted:

"Damnation, Chief, we don't want to make any mistakes."

Scanlon's face mottled with crimson, as if he had a furious, explosive temper that couldn't brook hindrance.

"We'll come back tomorrow," he rapped, "after we've gone over our specifications again."

The party turned back to the village.

By the time they neared the beach, it was dusk. The people of Puna-Puka were strolling down to the lagoon for their evening bathing. Gregg knew what to expect. Though the scene made his pulse quicken, it didn't make his jaw drop and his eyes pop. But it did for the movie people.

Nude bathing in the evening was an ancient custom of the Puna-Pukans. An active people, untouched by want or hardship or disease, they were a handsome and attractive race. The men were muscular, smiling; and the young women, with their smooth, tawny skins and shining hair and great dark eyes and slender, shapely figures, were breathtakingly lovely.

The whole village, grandparents and tiny toddlers as well as young adults, were on their way to the lagoon, laughing and chattering as they walked.*

"Say!" Scanlon gasped. "Hawes, get that! Don't stand there like your camera was a satchelful of cough medicine. Shoot this! Get it all on film. Talk about Bali and Goona-Goona—Lord, what beauty!"

"Got fast film in here, but dunno if it's fast enough," Hawes murmured, lifting his chunky camera.

"DeCourcey," Scanlon rapped, "would they do some of their dances for us? Ask 'em, man!"

The little trader looked doubtful; and Gregg thought, "He doesn't like to see the natives exploited that way any more than I do. He's a good egg, DeCourcey."

* * * *

The trader talked to an elderly native. A couple of big bonfires were started on the white sand of the beach. And some of the pretty young women started dancing the native dances of love. In silence the movie people watched.

After a while, Susan Lanphier ran out among the dancers.

She started dancing with them, her light skin and vivid red hair in heart-stirring contrast to the tawny, dark-haired beauty of the island girls. In their swaying and supple gestures was a beauty distilled from nature around them—the pliant bending of palm fronds moving in a sea breeze, the rhythm of the surf, the lightness and vivacity of tropic birds and flowers.

They danced with an easy and natural pleasure, the Puna-Puka maidens. In Susan Lanphier's dancing was a difference. In it was schooled artistry. In it was knowledge and sophistication. The girl's good, Gregg reflected. Lord, she's got fire!

Abruptly Susan Lanphier straightened out of her dancing, whirled, flung herself in an arrowing dive into the dark waters of the lagoon, utterly vanishing from sight.

Scanlon yelled, and sprang forward. Hawes flung down his camera, and whipped an automatic from his belt. Flame spurted from its muzzle and the flaring whack! whack! of .38 reports thundered across the beach.

Gregg jumped. His fist smacked to the side of Hawes' head and knocked him sprawling on the sand, and Gregg kicked the .38 from his fist. Hawes scrambled up, fists doubled.

"Lay off, you dumb fool!" Scanlon yelled at him, and Hawes subsided. Together, they ran to the lagoon. Nigel Rorke and Skipper Rogg followed close behind.

"Susan!" Scanlon bellowed, hands cupped to his mouth. "Don't be foolish. Come back here!"

But the girl had vanished. Gregg figured that she must have swum under water, and pulled out into some brush, up the beach a way, hidden by the darkness.

"Mr. Scanlon," DeCourcey snapped, "your cameraman shot at the girl. I think you'd better explain that."

"It's none of your business, Mister. I'm fully responsible. Ask your people to find the girl!"

"I will not, since she seems to be in danger of getting shot," the little trader retorted. "I suggest you take your party back aboard ship."

Scanlon crimsoned. His steely gray eyes glinted as he surveyed DeCourcey.

"Forget it, Chief," Nigel Rorke put in hastily. "The girl can't go nowheres. She'll keep."

Scanlon shrugged, turned, and said mildly, "Hawes, you damn fool, likely you ruined your film, dropping your camera that way."

Hawes muttered something, and whirled back to pick up the camera. It had come open, and he hastily clicked it shut. But not so hastily that Gregg didn't get a look inside.

Gregg stood rooted in staring surprise. For the glimpse he'd got of the inside of that camera filled his brain with startled suspicions.

There was no film in Hawes' camera!

CHAPTER III

A MEETING OF LIPS

The movie people went back aboard their yacht.

"Lend me a flashlight," Gregg said to the trader. "I'll see if I can find the Lanphier girl. She's in trouble."

"I'll go with you, lad."

For two hours they hunted along the beach. Fruitlessly.

"I could send the villagers to hunt her," DeCourcey said, "but maybe she'll be safer if she stays hid. Wonder what it's all about?"

Gregg shrugged. He had enough troubles of his own without taking on somebody else's grief. Only, he would like to take a good swift poke at that fake cameraman, Hawes. Wasn't often he saw a human pan he'd like so much to sink a fist into.

Returning to the trading station, they started inside.

"Funny," DeCourcey said. "Veranda lamp's blown out."

Crossing the porch, the trader walked into the store, flashlight on.

"Who's there?" he called suddenly.

And then the flashlight was dashed to the floor, smashing. Something went cr-a-ack! like the sharp impact of a savage hook to the jaw, and the little trader collapsed onto the matting. Gregg lunged forward, and sprang at a shadowy figure—and crashed headlong over a table shoved at him in the darkness. Instantly he was scrambling erect again. But the shadowy figure had fled out of the door, and off the veranda into the darkness.

Gregg followed. He realized he might get a slug triggered into him from ambush, but a reckless, obstinate anger sent him running wildly toward the beach in the hope of tangling with DeCourcey's attacker.

But he found nobody, and no sign of the prowler. Realizing that the trader might have been hurt badly and in need of attention, Gregg finally turned back to the store.

DeCourcey was sitting up and groaning ruefully as Gregg came in. Gregg hastily lit a lamp, and poured a glass of brandy.

"Thanks," DeCourcey said, taking it. "My jaw ain't broken, but it feels like every tooth in my dental plates had a galloping ache!"

"Look around," Gregg said in his earnest, headlong way. "Anything stolen?"

"Why, yes, there is. My shotgun's gone from the wall pegs. So's the pistol I keep on my desk."

"DeCourcey, look! Your radio set. Smashed!"

The sending and receiving set, next to the trader's safe, looked as if a typhoon had struck it.

DeCourcey breathed a rueful oath of dismay.

"One of your natives did it, maybe?" Gregg asked.

"No. I don't lock doors. Any time this past year, a native wanting to rob me could've done it."

DeCourcey looked out the window at the yacht anchored beyond the reef, and gestured toward it.

"Looks like friend Scanlon is making sure I won't be able to communicate with the authorities at Raratonga."

"And that you'll have no guns to defend yourself with!" Gregg added harshly. "What're they up to, DeCourcey?"

"Don't know. Have another drink, lad?"

* * * *

Unable to sleep, Gregg lay on his cot on the veranda, staring at the ceiling. His thoughts ached around in worry.

"You're brooding like a scared woman," he railed at himself. "Forget it! Go to sleep."

But he couldn't forget it. Over and over he asked himself:

"Suppose Scanlon's party pulled something raw, and a fight started, and DeCourcey was killed. Where would I be then, with

DeCourcey dead? Headed for twenty years in the penitentiary, if I ever returned to Honolulu...."

Gregg started violently. Listening hard, straining to see in the dark, he realized he had dozed off and something had wakened him.

A hand grasped his wrist. He reacted like a striking rattler—grappling with the prowler, hooking an elbow about the man's throat and pulling him flat onto the cot as he groped with his other hand for the man's throat.

Fragrant, silky hair pressed against Gregg's cheek; and his arm was clamped about slim shoulders. It was a girl; her breast was soft against his chest. He released her and sat up violently. Snatching the flashlight from under his pillow, he switched it on.

"Please, don't make a light. You nearly ch-choked me—"

It was Susan Lanphier. She was wet; the thin play suit was molded against her slim, lovely figure and she was shivering with chill.

He wrapped a blanket about her, and demanded, "Where've you been, for Pete's sake!"

"Hiding, up the beach. In the water. Th-thanks," she stammered as Gregg poured her a stiff drink of brandy.

"You mind telling me what a movie actress is doing here in the—'tail end of creation,' your director called it, dodging around—"

"He's not my director, and I'm not a movie actress!"

"—like a fugitive from a reform school," Gregg finished. He hated being interrupted. "But you are a fugitive?"

"Look, Mr. Gregg." She spoke with a fire and firmness to match his own temper. "My brother and I started from Honolulu with a party for a vacation trip. That boat out there is his. It's a small diesel cruiser, and we have four men as crew. Mr. Scanlon and his wife and his so-called cameraman came along as guests.

"But they seized the boat. Captain Rogg and one of the crew were men they had planted on us—and they scared the other two men into joining them. There was a fight, and my brother got hurt. Not badly. They keep Tom locked in a stateroom. They've let me be up and about, but they've warned me that if I didn't do what I was told, they'd kill Tom!"

"So why did you bust off the reservation?" Gregg demanded.

"Because, if they find what they're after here, they'll be sure to kill me and Tom anyhow!" Susan exclaimed.

"What're they after?" Gregg swore at himself, as he asked the question.

Damn it, he mustn't let her involve him in her troubles! As far as he was concerned, Susan might as well be a sourpuss maiden aunt. When his own neck was in a sling, he'd be a sucker to take on her troubles too.

But damn it, he had to admit, she wasn't an old maid. Moonlight streaming through the vines over the veranda shone on Susan's lovely young face. The blanket had slipped back from her shoulders, and the line of her throat was sweet and innocent. Her bosom lifted shakily as she sighed with concern.

"You see, we headed for Puna-Puka because, a long time ago, my family owned property here. It got around Honolulu that we were coming here. That's why Scanlon's outfit wished themselves onto us, I guess. We believed what they told us about taking moving pictures. Especially since it looked like we could make a really nice sum of money from them."

"But they're not here to take pictures!" Gregg protested.

"No. They have a map. Oh, I guess it sounds simply insane—"

"Yeah, but go on and tell it," Gregg said grimly.

"You've heard of the German raider, the cruiser Emden?"

"Yeah, even if I did fight the First World War in the second grade at grammar school."

"Well, besides the Emden, there were several other German battle cruisers raiding the steamship lanes. It seems that one of them realized it never would get back to Germany. The commander had a lot of money, a big part of it in gold, taken off merchant ships.

"According to Mr. Scanlon, this German raider was on its way home from Australian waters. The commander decided to cache the money on some little island that nobody ever visited, where it would be safe until after the war."

"So they buried the coin on Puna-Puka!" Gregg's eyes widened.

"Scanlon says so. And he says that the raider was sunk before it got to Germany, and the money's never been recovered!"

"And Scanlon has come to dig it up," Gregg surmised.

"Yes. He has a map he claims was drawn by one of the officers of the German raider."

"Barnum was wrong," Gregg said disgustedly. "There's two suckers born every minute." He looked sharply at Susan. "Or do you believe the money's here, too?"

"I don't know and I don't care!" she flared. "Good heavens, all I'm interested in is getting my brother away from Scanlon. Won't you help me? Can't you get in touch with the authorities?"

Gregg shook his head. "No."

Susan leaned closer to him. "You probably think I'm just throwing hysterics, but don't you see—if Scanlon finds that money he'll kill Tom, and he'll kill me if he can, to shut our mouths! That's why I'm so—"

Gregg interrupted her harshly.

"Look. If I can get your yacht away from them, will you make a bargain with me? I want to leave Puna-Puka. I want to take—something with me. Will you agree to help me in whatever I want to do?"

"I have to agree," Susan said shortly. "But how can you take the *Leeward* away from Scanlon's men?"

Yeah, how could he? Alone, with no weapons, and no way of radioing for help, how could he do the job?

"You just leave that chore to me!" Gregg said, banging it out all the more emphatically because he was so uncertain.

Susan looked at him a little strangely. "You're a pretty skeptical, determined sort of person, aren't you?" she said. Gregg flushed. "What makes you say that?" he demanded. Her eyes clashed with his, but hers were the first to lower.

"Oh, I don't know," she stammered. "It's just—well, I guess I've always lived a sort of sheltered life. I've never come in contact with men who—"

"Didn't look too clean, or act that way either," Gregg finished for her brutally. "Well, it's about time you learned what makes the wheels go round. Never could stand you pampered society dolls anyway. What good are you? When your type gets in trouble, it has to go whining for help...."

That was as far as he got. Not too many generations back in her ancestry, Susan Lamphier's people had been hard-bitten Yankees who sailed the seas and worked and fought, if need be, for what they got. Susan retained their strength of character in her blood.

More, she had their temper. At Gregg's words she lit into the tall, cynical youngster like a little wildcat. Her small feet kicked at his shins. Her nails scratched at his face. And her elbows pounded angrily at his chest.

Startled, Gregg gave way. Then his gray eyes flashed. He wouldn't take it from a man; he wouldn't take it from a girl, either.

He reached out and slapped Susan in the face, a stinging little blow that left the imprint of his fingers on her soft tanned cheek.

Susan stopped fighting. She looked at Gregg? suddenly very much hurt. And then she began to cry. Not loud and harshly, but in soft little sobs, like a small girl who has been punished for something she didn't do.

Gregg got suddenly very red in the face. He began to feel like a heel.

You dope, he thought, taking your anger out on an innocent girl. You ought to be slugged in the jaw and have the stuffing kicked out of you.

The blanket had slipped from Susan's sobbing shoulders. Gregg picked it up and wrapped it around the girl.

"There, there," he soothed. "I—I guess we must have lost our tempers. I should have known better—"

Susan shook the tears out of her eyes.

"You're—you're just a big bully," she said, her spirit coming back. "You don't care anything about a girl's feelings. You—"

"But I'm not!" Gregg protested heatedly. "You're no lily of the valley yourself!"

He shook her shoulders for emphasis. And suddenly Susan began to smile.

"There you go again," she said. "I suppose you'll be hitting me next."

Gregg glared at her. "Dammit," he swore, "I'm going to teach you a lesson! For once and for all, It's about time somebody taught you a thing or two!"

And he folded her suddenly in his arms, hard. Susan fought him. Gregg laughed recklessly, tilted her firm little chin up to his own. He kissed her then. Kissed her with youthful abandon; then a little less harshly … then tenderly. Her soft young body relaxed slowly against his own, and slowly, slowly her lips responded.…

He thrust her from him then.

"I'm sorry," he said hoarsely. "I should have known better. I—I.…"

He turned abruptly on his heel and stalked off, motioning with his head for the girl to follow him. She did; and there was an amused light in her eyes. And a little tenderness, too.

CHAPTER IV
PAYOFF IN BLOOD

Gregg took Susan to a hut back of the trading station, told her to sleep and keep hidden until he came for her. Then he returned to his cot on the veranda. And racked his brain until dawn, groping for some plan of action that would have one chance in ten at least of working.…

After sunup, a boat put out from the *Leeward*.

Stocky, white-haired Scanlon, Skipper Rogg, the cameraman Hawes, Nigel Rorke and two members of the crew landed on the beach. A seaman rowed the dinghy back to the yacht. Scanlon's party came on to the trading station, and Gregg saw that they carried shovels and crowbars.

The trader noticed the shovels, and frowned.

"Scanlon, you have to have a French permit to dig up relics."

"Oh, we're just going to do a little clearing away of brush and rock on that flat, for picture taking. Come along, and see for yourself."

Gregg's heart skipped a beat. If Scanlon did find that buried coin, he would shut DeCourcey's mouth with a bullet. Frowning, Gregg watched the party head inland along the river.

He waited a full hour. Through binoculars, he studied the *Leeward*, anchored beyond the reef.

"Two men, stretching out on deck. Each with a pistol in his belt. How," he mused, "should I tackle 'em?"

He walked up the beach, around a headland. Then he walked out into the surf. Swimming low in the water, lifting his face out only for gulps of air, he headed for the yacht, on the side opposite to the men lying on deck.

Reaching the *Leeward*'s dinghy, he pulled himself hand over hand up its painter to the yacht rail, and drew himself aboard. Carefully, then, he started forward.

Opening a stateroom door, he looked inside, saw it was empty. He moved to the next stateroom, opened the door—and looked straight into the eyes of a young fellow lying on a bunk, his left arm swathed in bandages.

"Lanphier?" Gregg whispered. "I'm here to help you."

"Susan sent you?" the youngster whispered back eagerly.

"Yeah. Hold still, while I untie those ropes."

Young Lanphier looked like his sister, except that his hair was sandy and his features stronger. He was hog-tied into the bunk.

Gregg asked, "How many people on board?"

"Two seamen. And Mrs. Scanlon, in the cabin behind this."

"When you want something, they told you to sing out for it?"

"Yeah."

"All right, call out," Gregg snapped—and flattened himself against the wall beside the door.

"Hey, Swede!" Lanphier yelled. "Bring me a drink!"

He yelled again, and a third time.

"All right, all right. Pipe down, damn it!"

Lazy footsteps sounded on deck. A tall, husky seaman carrying a tray came to the stateroom door, kicked it open and started inside. Gregg stepped into his way, swinging. Fist met jaw with a hard, sharp cra-ack! The seaman staggered back out the doorway and collapsed to the deck, his tray clattering down beside him. Gregg stooped swiftly to snatch the pistol from the man's belt.

But even as he lunged, he saw a shadow on the deck. And Gregg flung himself forward as he snatched at the fallen sailor's gun. A hot flash of pain seared along his ribs as a .38 roared flat and heavy in the warm air. Then the gun in Gregg's hand kicked as it spurted fire—and the other seaman, beyond Gregg, doubled up, clutching at his chest, the gun falling from his fist as he pitched headlong to the deck.

Gregg jumped up, pistol leveled. But the man was dead.

Startled footsteps rounded the bow. Looking up, Gregg saw Mrs. Scanlon coming—and the woman stopped short, both hands to her face, and screamed. Gregg strode toward her.

"You won't be hurt, Mrs. Scanlon. Go back to your stateroom."

He locked her in there. Returning, he tied up the sailor he had knocked senseless and took the dead man's pistol.

"Any more ammunition on board?" Gregg asked Lanphier as he untied him.

"Yes. In my cabin."

"Look, could you and I run this boat?"

"Why, yes, if necessary," the youngster nodded.

"Fine! I'm going ashore. If I come back at all, it'll be with another man and your sister. Have this tub ready to sail back to Honolulu!"

"How about Scanlon and his outfit?"

"If they come back, I won't!" Gregg said grimly....

Rowing ashore in the dinghy, he realized it would be wisest to send Susan back to the yacht now, where she'd be safe. Beaching the boat, he hurried to the trading station.

"Susan! "he called.

"She not here," DeCourcey's native houseboy told him. "That man Hawes come for picks and flashlights. He see girl, and make her go with him." The Puna-Pukan pointed to the trail inland.

Gregg bit off an oath of utter dismay. This was something he hadn't counted on. It was a staggering, crippling blow. All too clearly he foresaw complications.

"This makes a setup too tough for one man to handle!" he warned himself. "Unless I can catch up with Hawes and the girl!"

Turning on his heel, he headed for the trail inland.

* * * *

The sun beat hot on Gregg's shoulders, until the trail reached the canyon where huge ferns and bamboo arched over the river banks to make cool shade. Gregg started running through dense groves of island ebony, of mango and rosewood trees, and jungle-thick growths of crimson hibiscus and the gardenia-like pua. Startled parakeets screamed as he passed, and darted like winged bomb-bursts into tall hutu trees that luxuriated in gorgeous crimson blooms.

But Gregg didn't sight Hawes and the girl. They had too long a start on him. Doggedly he ran on, laboring for breath as the trail climbed the steepening canyonside. Far below, the river formed deep, shaded pools in which fish jumped.

Ahead of him, finally, Gregg saw the terrace overhanging the river on which Scanlon's men were working. He slackened pace, and approached cautiously. Surprise would have to be a big part of his ammunition. Keeping under cover of the brush, he approached Scanlon's party on the plateau gouged out of the side of the canyon wall.

* * * *

From the cliff above, a waterfall poured down in a shower of silvery spray, and flowed in a broad stream across the flat, to arch down again into the river below. Along the edge of the plateau, Gregg saw with surprise that a line of elm trees was growing— huge, magnificent old giants of the kind he'd often seen in New England towns.

He could see now only the stocky, white-haired figure of Scanlon, Susan and DeCourcey. The other men were inside a tunnel they had dug into the back wall of the terrace. Scanlon held a gun in his hand.

Coming closer, Gregg saw Scanlon peer into that tunnel, heard him yell, "Find anything?"

Hawes came out of the tunnel, carrying an old-fashioned Chinese chest of carved wood and leather.

"Just clothes," he said disgustedly, setting the chest down and flipping the lid back. "Scanlon, there's a house in there! Funniest damn' thing. Furniture and a bed that looks a hundred years old. How do you figure it?"

DeCourcey said, "The natives tell me that there was a stone house built here, but an avalanche came down and covered it up. But that was so long ago that nobody now living on the island ever saw the house."

"That's your story," Scanlon retorted, his fleshy face mottled with anger.

He looked toward the tunnel then, for Skipper Rogg and a sailor came out, lugging an old sea chest with a big lock.

"That looks more like it!" Scanlon said. "Quick, get that thing open!"

Hawes broke the lock off with a pick. The men crowded close to look inside as he lifted the top.

"Uniforms!"

"What the hell is this, a costume shop?"

"Dueling pistols, by God! What's this, Skipper?"

"A sextant—and a damn' old one."

"To hell with this trash!" Scanlon burst out. "Go on back inside, everybody! Look sharp. Don't bring out any more junk, damn you!"

"But there's nothing else in there," Nigel Rorke insisted. "Just furniture and books and rugs and pictures."

"We've gone through the place like a cop friskin' a tramp," Skipper Rogg offered weakly.

"The chart says that money is here!" Scanlon raged.

"Maybe the chart is a fake," DeCourcey said mildly.

Scanlon looked at him, eyes narrowed, for a long, thoughtful moment, and the mottled red of his fleshy face deepened. Abruptly he took a step toward the little trader, reached out and grabbed his shirt front in a big fist.

"DeCourcey, you've already looted this hideaway. Haven't you?"

The mild little trader blinked with surprise.

"Me? Good Lord, no!"

Scanlon smashed his fist into DeCourcey's face, knocked him sprawling to the ground. Reaching down, Scanlon hauled him onto his feet.

"What did you do with it?" he roared.

"With wh-what? I tell you—"

"Gold and silver bullion!" Scanlon rasped. "Is it in your trading station?"

"So help me, Scanlon, I've never—"

Again Scanlon knocked him down. And as the gray-haired trader got up, blood streaming across his jaw, Scanlon ordered:

"Hawes—and you, Rorke—make him talk!"

They grabbed DeCourcey. Stripped off his shoes. Hawes struck a match. Touched the flame to the bare sole of DeCourcey's foot—

And Gregg, watching from the brush, sprang into action. The gun blazed from his hand, and Hawes plunged flat on his face to the ground, a bullet in his brain. Gregg burst out of cover then, charged the surprise-stunned group.

They broke and ran for shelter—all except Scanlon, who jerked the muzzle of his gun toward the fighting youngster. But Susan grabbed Scanlon's arm, and the bullet went wild. He pulled violently away from her; struck her across the temple with the gun barrel, knocking her to the ground.

Gregg triggered a slug at him that slashed his thick arm from wrist to elbow. The gun dropped from Scanlon's grasp, but he snatched at it with his left hand, caught it and darted into the tunnel opening.

DeCourcey had scrambled to his feet. He bent now, picked up the senseless girl, and ran unsteadily to meet Gregg.

Scanlon shot at them from the tunnel. Gregg whipped a slug at him that knocked rock fragments into Scanlon's face, and the man dodged back. His men had taken shelter behind the elms at the far end of the terrace, and now they started shooting.

"Here, I'll take the girl, DeCourcey!" Gregg said.

He thrust one of his two guns into DeCourcey's hands, took Susan in his own arms, and started back down the trail to the beach at a lurching run.

A bullet knifed through leaves over Gregg's head, and another hissed past his ear. Behind Gregg, the trader shot back at Scanlon's men, his gun going wham! wham!

And then Gregg heard DeCourcey gasp, heard the thud of a heavy fall. Gregg halted, look back and saw the trader sprawled face down on the path.

"DeCourcey! You hurt?"

"No, I—"

DeCourcey tried to get up, but his right leg buckled under him and he fell. Blood streamed from his thigh. Gregg looked wildly around. A few paces on down the trail was a pile of boulders that had avalanched from the rimrock.

He ran to the midst of the rock fall and put the senseless girl on the ground. Running back to the trail, he helped DeCourcey to his feet, helped him hop into the shelter of the rock barricade. A bullet creased Gregg's hip as they ran, and another slug scattered rock splinters into the side of his face and ricocheted screaming to one side.

Gregg triggered a shot in answer at the four men coming down the trail, and they scattered into the brush for protection.

* * * *

DeCourcey bent over Susan Lanphier. A stain of crimson showed at the roots of her shining bronze-red hair.

"Lad, you think that fat swine fractured her skull?"

"Don't know. I'd like to fracture his!"

"Look, Gregg. You take the girl on down to the beach. I'll stay and keep shooting to hold these crooks back."

"Like hell I will! You'll get killed. Damn it, you're forgetting I got to take you to Honolulu to swear me out of twenty years in prison!"

"But I'm hurt. We can't all get away, boy."

"Listen—soon as it's dark, we'll sneak off. I got a boat on the beach. We'll row out to the yacht. The girl's brother has got control of it by now. We'll get to hell-and-gone away from Puna-Puka!"

Gregg spoke confidently—but his words ended with a choked oath of consternation, for he saw something that staggered him with dismay.

Scanlon and his three men were climbing down the wall of the canyon, descending to the river.

"They'll swim across the river," Gregg realized. "They'll get past us here, and go on down to the beach. They'll find the dinghy, and row out to the yacht. They'll take over the *Leeward* again—and once they've done that, I'm sunk!"

His serious young face wild with panic, he turned to DeCourcey.

"Come on! We got to beat that gang to the beach!"

"You go, lad. Take the girl—"

"No! Man alive, I've told you I've got to take you to Honolulu. Come on!"

"But the girl needs to be taken care of—"

"She's got to take her chances!" Gregg blurted in desperation. "All I know is I'll rot in prison if I don't get you down to the beach in a hurry. Damn it, come on!"

He reached out, to put an arm about DeCourcey's shoulders so as to support him—and DeCourcey, standing on one leg, struck him across the temple with the side of his pistol.

Gregg staggered, stumbled back over a rock and fell. And De-Courcey hopped across the trail, and started down the steep canyon wall toward Scanlon's party descending to the river. Scanlon saw him. Pointed.

"Get him! Get the little ape!" Scanlon ordered his men.

They started shooting, their pistols lancing fire. DeCourcey doubled over and rolled headlong down the slope. He clutched with his hands in a frantic effort to grab rocks or shrubs to ease his sliding fall. But on down he slid and skidded, in a miniature avalanche of dust and rocks, toward Scanlon's men.

Gregg, jumping to the rim of the trail, looked down and saw Scanlon's killers shooting at the little trader as he came hurtling down the slope almost directly toward them. Gregg saw gouts of dust spurt from the trader's coat, as if bullets had thudded into him like slugs striking a dusty pillow.

"The crazy little fool!" Gregg choked—and launched himself down the slope in a reckless, sliding jump.

DeCourcey slammed to the canyon floor and brought up against a pile of driftwood at the river's edge, sprawled out on his face. Slumped and inert he lay. Their guns ready, Scanlon and his three men lunged toward him.

Aruptly DeCourcey raised up on one elbow. The .38 spat flame from his hand.

Instantly the other men shot back at him, and the canyon rocked to the echoing wham-bang! of gun shots. Nigel Rorke stiffened convulsively and dropped, dead before he hit. Skipper Rogg doubled over and keeled head-first into the river.

Then DeCourcey himself was slumping face down into the dust again, his body jouncing to the smash of bullets into his back.

Scanlon and the remaining sailor laughed harshly. They didn't see Gregg, didn't hear him until he was almost on top of them.

Then Scanlon jerked his head around, saw Gregg, and triggered a bullet that seared along Gregg's throat like the slash of a jagged knife. Gregg hit the bottom of the slope and fell on hands and knees. Scanlon's second bullet whipped over his head.

Gregg shot, pointblank. And Scanlon staggered back from the smash of the slug into his chest. His arms dropped, and he swayed. With a terrific effort, he steadied himself, raised his gun—buckled at the knees, and collapsed.

Gregg's gun had barked again as he whirled toward the sailor, but the bullet missed. The fellow flung up his hands.

"Don't shoot! I quit, I give up!" the man yelled—and flung his own weapon to the ground in surrender....

Gregg bent over DeCourcey. Turned the little trader over on his back. DeCourcey groaned, and opened his eyes.

Thank the Lord he's not dead! Gregg thought. And aloud, he said shakily:

"It's all over, pal. Look, I'll carry you to—"

"No, lad. I'm all shot up," the trader whispered. "Listen. I—you look in my safe. I wrote that—that letter for you. You know. My testimony. About the robbery. The DeGroot theft—you wanted it—"

"Don't worry about that! I'll carry you to the beach. We'll—"

But DeCourcey wasn't hearing, wasn't caring. The little trader was slipping beyond reach of voice or aid.

CHAPTER V
THE LAST ACT

Susan's scalp wound proved minor. Next day, Gregg and Susan and her brother Tom returned to the treasure cache on the flat above the river. With a flashlight, Gregg led the way through the tunnel Scanlon's men had dug into the old stone house which been covered, for so many years, by a fall of rock.

Part of the structure had fallen in, but some of the rooms were intact. And as Gregg looked around, he had the eerie feeling of stepping through a door of time into the distant past. He played the flashlight beam on furniture that was a century old, on bookcases, on pictures on the walls, on rugs and mirrors.

"Susan," young Tom Lanphier blurted excitedly. "This must be the house that Captain Lanphier built on Puna-Puka! Gregg, we have a Yankee ancestor who came into the South Seas in 1813 on a United States man-o'-war under Admiral Porter."

"Susan told me that."

"Captain Lanphier liked it so well that he returned some years later with a wife, and settled down for keeps."

"And you two," Gregg asked, "are his legal heirs?"

"Why, yes—if there's anything to inherit."

Gregg flashed his light beam around again, and in his voice was an edge of excitement as he said:

"This place has been hermetically sealed for about three generations, I guess. This Captain Lanphier—was he a cultured man who liked books and pictures and had the money to satisfy his whims?"

"Yes, he was," Susan said, with a sudden catch of expectancy in her voice, for she was quick of intuition.

Gregg turned his flashlight on a table.

"Look at that. Isn't it a beauty? And at least a hundred years old! I don't know the great furniture makers, but these pieces were likely brought from New England—where they had come from England! Chippendale? I bet it is. I bet every one of these pieces is worth a house and lot!

"And look on the wall. Those are engravings by Hogarth. And that portrait over the mantel, of a British naval officer—Come here. So help me, it's a Joshua Reynolds! And look at the books."

"He likely got books off every sailing vessel that put in at Puna-Puka," Tom said, his voice hollow with awe.

"Look at these!" Gregg blurted. "Copies of Chaucer and Beaumont and Fletcher and Goldsmith that were likely old before Captain Lanphier got them.

"And here—a first edition of *Confessions of An Opium-Eater*, and of Dr. Samuel Johnson's *Rasselas*. And, as I live and breathe, a first of Keats' *Lamia*!"

Gregg looked at Susan and her brother, his eyes shining.

"You realize that this house has been a sort of vault, keeping these things safe for you for over a century?"

"They're really valuable?" Susan breathed.

"When Captain Lanphier got 'em, most of them were valuable, but they weren't heirlooms, they weren't museum pieces. But now they are! I'm telling you, you've got a fortune here!" Gregg laughed shakily. "That rat Scanlon came here to find gold, didn't find any—and walked out on a fortune right under his nose! These things are worth a damn' sight more than a satchelful of pirate coin!"

Susan slipped her arm through his. "John, we'll take these things to Honolulu and sell them. Whatever they bring, you'll share equally with us."

Gregg pulled away, his lean face tightening.

"Forget it. I'm not going to Honolulu."

"You're not—You mean, you're staying here?" Susan asked, dismayed. "On the island?"

"You got it," he said harshly. "I'm staying right here."

* * * *

Late that afternoon, the villagers buried DeCourcey on a rise near the beach.

Afterward, Gregg and Susan and her brother went to the trading station. Depressed, Gregg puttered around. This trading station was going to be his and he might as well get used to it.

Tom Lanphier walked out after a bit. Susan sat in a chair and watched Gregg. In the morning, the *Leeward* was sailing away, and leave-taking now was hard.

The lamplight shone with golden sparkles in her bronze-red hair. Gregg was conscious of it, and was conscious of the way she looked at him, concern in her blue eyes. But he made himself turn his back on her. No use storing up any more heartache for himself than he had to.

Looking in the safe, he saw a letter there with his name on it. He remembered, then. DeCourcey had written out his testimony in regard to the DeGroot murder.

"Damned little good it'll do me," Gregg muttered to himself. Only by DeCourcey's appearing in Honolulu in person, being identified and sworn in, could his word that Gregg was innocent of the DeGroot robbery have stood up. Now DeCourcey was dead.

Idly Gregg opened the envelope and unfolded the letter. He read:

* * * *

Dear Gregg,

I've felt awfully bad about refusing to go to Honolulu to testify in court that you're not the man who robbed De-Groot and to identify the man who did do the thievery. I just couldn't do it. You'll understand why when I tell you that I, myself, am the thief who robbed DeGroot.

I was a watchmaker for the firm, remember. The robbery was an "inside job," and my testimony that a thief broke in and chloroformed me after a struggle was just a cover-up.... I chloroformed myself.

I'm writing this letter now, so that if anything happens to me, you'll have a way of proving your innocence of the theft.

In the "H" Street Branch of the National Trust Bank, in Honolulu, I have a safe deposit box, under my full name of Philip DeCourcey Leroux. The court can order the box opened. The jewels are there. And the bank people know that nobody but myself ever had access to that box.

I think that will clear you once and for all of any suspicion.

DECOURCEY.

* * * *

Thunderstruck with surprise, Gregg read the letter a second time, to make sure—and let out a wild whoop of joy.

Whereupon Susan jumped up, startled. He grabbed her by the elbows, waltzed her around the room, and kissed her resoundingly on the lips.

"J-John!" she gasped. "Why this sudden outburst?"

"I'm free! I'm an honest man and I can prove it! I don't have to hide, I've got my life ahead of me and a future Susan! Can I still go to Honolulu with you and Tom?"

"Well, maybe," she said, laughter in her blue eyes. "Do you think you could kiss me like that again?"

Gregg grinned hugely. "Honey," he said, "you ain't seen nothin' yet!"

HAG GOLD

James Francis Dwyer

This morning, reading the latest official statement concerning the enormous amount of gold that the United States is guarding for the terrified governments of Europe, I thought of Macklin, and his fear lest America might incur certain spiritual dangers through acting as keeper for this vast and ever-increasing mass of bullion. He thought that a large percentage of it carried the anathemas of the centuries.

Sitting in the soft Tunisian sunshine, he explained the difference between virgin gold and the metal which he and other seekers sought in the ruined cities of Africa. He termed the latter "hag gold."

"I know that there is a lot of virgin gold pouring into the United States," he said. "Clean, newfound metal from the goldfields of Australia and South Africa, brought to London and sold; but there's also a hell of a lot of stuff that is old. We call it 'hag gold.' It has been possessed by men for hundreds of years. It has brought about murders, piracies, rebellions, acts of torture, and deviltry of every description. It's accursed. It's blood-splashed and evil. Mostly European and—well, yes, there's some, as I said, found in the dead cities of Africa. Now all that stuff, carrying the curses of centuries, rides off to find a nice, peaceful resting-place in the United States. Sometimes I'm scared of the evil it might bring to my country. Hellish scared.... Hag gold. Well, it's dangerous."

My introduction to Macklin came about in a curious manner. I am really a tramp. Not of the mendicant type that begs food and steals transportation, but a respectable tramp with a wanderlust that I feed by personal thrift and an active typewriter. I travel third- or fourth-class, and I shun grand hotels as I would the plague.

At the end of 1937 I was filled with the desire to visit the oases of southern Tunisia. It was the time of the date harvest at Tozeur. Calculating transportation, lodging and food on the lowest basis, and hoping that I might pare them still lower, I set out. The Guide

Bleu of Algérie et Tunisie, put out by the Librairie Hachette, was in my pocket.

Now, on the way back to Tunis, I was thrilled by a few paragraphs in that guidebook. They told of the ruins of Sbeïtla, the ancient Roman city of Sufetula, which some thirteen hundred years ago was a gay spot.

Things hummed in Sufetula 'way back in the six hundreds! There were theaters, hot baths, stadia, and dancing-parlors; and the betting is that one would have to engage one's table on a night when a theatrical company or a mob of gladiators from Rome had ventured into the African "sticks."

I decided to get off the train and take a snapshot of the ruins, which lie some three-quarters of a mile from the modern Sbeïtla, a small village of a few hundred French and a scattering of natives. There is hardly a building above one story in the village, so that a visitor approaching the ruins is astonished at the contrast between the ancient and the modern. The huge crumbling temples have a dignity and beauty that is breath-taking.

I was alone. There was no one in sight. It was a still, warm day. The silence was intense. In a sort of tiptoeing manner I moved through the temples of Juno, Minerva, and Jupiter, circled the arc de triomphe, erected by the orders of Diocletian, crossed to the thermes; then, a bit fatigued, I sat myself down on an overthrown column to rest. It was then I saw Macklin.

* * * *

There are throughout northern Africa many ancient underground aqueducts that date from the days of Roman occupation. The underground method was made compulsory by sandstorms and the necessity of keeping the precious water away from the murderous rays of the African sun.

These aqueducts were constructed with immense effort. Water was brought from sources thirty and forty miles distant, to desert cities. Today a large percentage of these canals are not in use. The towns they served are deserted, and sand has filtered in through the vents that were placed at regular distances.

Now as I sat on the fallen column, I saw the head of a man appear at one of these vents in the ancient aqueduct that once served

Sufetula. He was about a quarter of a mile away. In the thin sunlight I could see his face clearly. For a few minutes he stared in my direction; then he disappeared, coney-fashion, into the ground.

I waited. There were several manholes in the aqueduct between me and the spot where the fellow had disappeared. I had an idea that his curiosity would prompt him to crawl along the tunnel and make a closer inspection.

My surmise was correct. From the nearest manhole the head appeared again; then a strong voice with a distinct American intonation hailed me.

"You startled me," came the voice. "I thought you were the damned guardian of this joint."

"I'm a simple tourist," I said. "Got off the train to look at the ruins."

The man took a grip on the crumbling cement around the vent, dragged himself up, and walked toward me. He was a lean, well-built fellow with a smiling, clean-shaven face. I took him to be somewhere in the early thirties. He wore corduroy trousers, high boots, and a leather jacket with a zipper fastener. Pushed back from his forehead was a battered casque colonial.

"What do you think of it?" he asked, waving his hand at the ruins.

"It's a little frightening," I answered. "Startled me with its silence and air of absolute desertion."

He smiled and sat himself down. "Sometimes there's a mob around here," he said slowly. "Not tourists. Oh, no. Natives."

"Why?" I asked.

"Well, they buzz around all the old ruins of North Africa," he replied. "Hunting. Like me."

"Game?" I queried.

He laughed. "No. Gold. Hunting hag gold."

Now I heard later that there is another reason for that name "hag gold" outside that which the antiquity of the treasure might have conferred on it. In the souks of Tripoli, Tunis and Algiers, where treasure found in dead cities is sold to dealers, the natives giving a reason for the possession of antique jewelry, lie by saying it belonged to their grandmothers! "C'est l'or de ma vieille grand-'mère," they mutter; and possibly whites, wishing to make the lie humorous, might have called it "hag gold."

But to get back to John Macklin. He was, I discovered, a gold-seeker born. His great-grandfather was one of the original founders of Yerba Buena, the baby town that grew up into San Francisco. This ancestor served on the first Committee of Vigilance when the gold boom started. His son made a fortune and lost it. John's father was a fossicker—a gold-seeker—from the time he could walk till the day when he and his burro were found dead in an arroyo in the San Bernardino mountains.

"He left me his taste for gold, several picks, and a baby donkey," said Macklin. "Couldn't have a better legacy."

Along the top of Africa is a string of dead cities that mark the high tide of the Roman flood. Here the Romans ruled and rioted, then departed, leaving the temples, open-air theaters, thermes, and triumphal arches to decay slowly in the African sunshine: Carthage, Timgad, Tipasa, Lambessa, and five-score others.

Macklin had visited them all. Even the remote and off-the-trail places like Baal Regia—City of the Royal Baal—which at one time was the capital of Numidia and is now the haunt of miserable nomads who camp in its enormous cisterns. He had fossicked in ruined temples, palaces and sand-filled aqueducts for treasure that might have been overlooked in the hurried departure of the long-dead inhabitants. For there is much evidence of swift evacuation in these ruins. Take Timgad, the Roman Thamugas, constructed in the First Century. Timgad had a fine prosperous time for four centuries; then the Berbers swept down from the Aures Mountains and pillaged the city. The Timgadians cried for help to Rome; but Rome was busy with pressing affairs at its own gates. The people fled northward, and Timgad slid into the has-been class....

The green lizards ran up and down the fallen columns of the once gay Sufetula as Macklin talked. His was a colorful tale of wandering. It evoked dreams.

"Have you dropped on anything big?" I asked.

He laughed softly. "Well, yes," he said; then, after a pause, he continued: "I get tips where to search. Of course one doesn't scream one's findings to the stars in North Africa. There are laws concerning treasure-trove. It must be reported at once; and the finder, if he is lucky, will get a percentage that might be half and might not be. If he makes the find in any of these old cities, the chances are that he'd get nothing. They are all under the control of the Direction des Antiquités, and a fossicker has no right to search. When I saw you, I was startled. Thought for a moment you were the watchman.

"But you asked about finds. I've found a few things that I wish I could have kept in their original state. Couldn't, you know. Had to drop them into the pot."

He stretched himself on the warm column and stared upward. After a long silence he spoke. "I doubt if any man alive, outside myself, has handled a double fistful of gold octadrachms with the heads of Ptolemy I and Berenice I. I didn't know at the time that they were so rare, but I kept a rubbing of one, obverse and reverse, and showed it to a big French numismatist. He nearly went crazy when I told him that I had handled some twenty of them."

"And did you drop them all into a crucible?" I cried.

"Sure," he answered. "Couldn't get rid of them otherwise. The dealer wouldn't buy them. I sold the chunk of gold in the Souk des Orfèvres at Tunis. Hell of a pity. Who knows whether that chunk is not in the United States now? I mean part of a gold-brick that Uncle Sam is minding for France."

I gulped at the thought of those coins of Ptolemy the First being dropped one by one into a crucible. It seemed a sacrilege.

"Funny about the natives," went on Macklin. "You know, you must have a heat of a thousand centigrade to melt gold. That's difficult to get in desert places, so they hammer gold coins and bits of jewelry into lumps without heating. They caught a few natives the other day in Algiers. Had a beaten-up hunk of gold that showed part of a necklace of Roman filigrane work that brought yelps of delight from the experts. They've sent it to Paris. Yes, it's dirty business to destroy stuff like that, but if you're an unlicensed chercheur d'or, what are you to do?"

I had no answer. In silence we sat and stared out across the tumbling ruins. Suddenly Macklin startled me with a question.

"Staying in Sbeïtla tonight? If you are, you might see something. It's a feast night with a full moon, and there's going to be a sacrificial search."

I was intrigued. "Why a night search?" I asked.

"Well, Africa breeds a desire to do most things at night," he answered. "Possibly the sun is too damn' watchful. Dances, witch-hunting, sacrifices, smellings-out, and all the hocus-pocus of the continent is carried on at night. Queer. You never see anything out of the way during the daytime, but when the night comes down, all the deviltry of the world starts. If you're staying on, you can have a glimpse of a moonlight search after a sacrifice."

"Of what?" I questioned.

"Black goat or something," he said, laughing. "They sprinkle the blood, and if the blood strikes a spot where gold is buried, it sort of glows like fire. Where are you sleeping? Café de la Gare? I'll call for you about nine."

* * * *

Moons are no bigger in Africa than in the other continents, but one thinks so. African moons have so much desert space to shine on that they look bigger. And whiter. It was under a moon of this kind that John Macklin led me back to the ruins. With him was a Negro from the south, a Buzu. A queer, laughing type—a sort of black Pan who leaped from one fallen stone to another, making grimaces and gestures at his shadow, as black as himself on the barren ground.

We reached a point above the main aqueduct, and there we crouched behind a mass of fallen pillars. Macklin whispered to me. The natives would come from a gorge to the north of the ruins and move down to the arches of the aqueduct.

Presently the Negro touched my arm with a finger and pointed. For a moment I saw only the inky shadow made by the party; their white garments blending with the sky and landscape. The compact mass of moving figures was hardly visible, but the pool of intense black that moved around them as they surged forward was plain to the eye.

They moved silently. Not a sound. A queer hurrying stride, the leaders straining toward the entrance to the aqueduct. There were two score, at least.

Macklin whispered to me. "We mustn't move till they go underground," he said, "They'd bolt if they saw us."

The line had lengthened when the leaders reached the stone arches. Eager were the leaders. They dived into the vault, and the swirling human tail slid in, serpent-like, behind them. The landscape was empty.

Macklin pulled me to my feet. The Buzu was scampering toward the dark opening that had swallowed the searchers. Now from the vault came a sort of nasal chant, thin and piercing. It went out over the deserted landscape, a queer probing stiletto of sound, unnerving and disagreeable.

My courage failed me at the black entrance of the aqueduct. Way back in the thick, century-old darkness were pinpoints of yellow light. The nasal chant was louder now.

"Come on!" cried Macklin. "They'll make the sacrifice soon."

"I'm stopping here," I muttered.

"But you won't see anything!" he protested.

"I'll see enough," I said.

Macklin laughed softly and ran ahead on the tracks of the Buzu. I was left alone at the opening. I was, I must confess, too scared to follow him. The whole business seemed evil. There was something foul, something satanic about the affair; I had seen nothing to make me afraid, but I sensed something diabolic.

Head thrust forward, I saw the lights flare up so that the fallen masses of stone and the arched roof were visible at odd moments. Skinny arms were thrust upward. Tattered garments were tossed to and fro in the torchlight. The nasal, wasplike chant became unbearable.

It ceased at the moment when I turned with the notion of running out; ceased with a frightening suddenness. It was then I heard the sound which I have never been able to classify.

It stays with me. Puzzling, mystifying, disturbing. Cry, scream, screech, bleat? I cannot say. Human or animal? I don't know. But it has made a record of its own upon the complicated cells of my brain. At any moment I can start that disk. I hear it distinctly, and with the resurrected cry comes the memory picture of the uplifted arms, the sputtering torches, the wild scurrying of treasure-hunters who followed the sound.

It was an hour before Macklin returned, the Buzu running on his heels. Together we hurried up the slope and hid behind the fallen columns till the outpouring natives moved back across the sand to disappear in the gorge.

"Nothing doing," said Macklin. "The thing was a failure. The blood didn't glow."

"Whose blood?" I questioned.

"Why, the blood of the black goat."

The Buzu chuckled and started to leap from stone to stone as we made our way back to the village.

Well, whether it was a goat or not that helped out that performance in the aqueduct, I was the "goat," the following day.

Macklin came to the little railway station to say good-by to me. He chatted quietly during the short halt of the train from Tozeur; then, as it was pulling out, he thrust a small package into my hands. "Deliver that at Sousse!" he cried. "Don't fail me! Please!"

I shouted protests. I tried to push the little packet back into his hands. He refused to accept it. The train gathered speed. He stood on the platform making motions to me, imploring motions.

He had tricked me. I dropped back on the seat. Macklin had picked me as a simple fool he could use to transport something he was afraid to send by post!

I guessed, of course, that the packet contained a lump of gold that might be seized as contraband by the authorities. They might pounce on me if they had reason to suspect Macklin and had glimpsed him pushing the packet into my hands! Possibly they had noted the clumsy transfer!

Sweating profusely, I read the address. "Madame Macklin, Rue El Keha-oui, next door to the Caré Maure, El Koubba, Sousse."

Softly I cursed Macklin. I am careful when wandering to observe closely the laws of the country in which I am voyaging. Now, I'd become an accomplice of a man who was breaking the law by searching clandestinely in the Roman ruins, and furthermore, refusing to report to the authorities the treasure that he had found!

I realized then that Macklin had nursed me along so that he might use me as a messenger. He had found out my name, my usual address, the magazines I contributed to, everything that had a bearing on my honesty, and he had taken a chance. Angrily I told myself that he had summed me up as a milksop who, lacking the courage to keep the packet, would, on the contrary, rush hotfoot to deliver it the moment I reached Sousse.

"I hope he breaks his neck!" I growled, as the train rushed north toward Sousse.

The Rue El Kehaoui is not an elegant street. It adjoins the souks, and it is the meeting place of a thousand objectionable odors. I wondered if Madame Macklin had chosen the address so that she might be close to the sly dealers who would purchase anything her husband sent her through the medium of fools like myself. I was still angry with Macklin, but frightfully desirous of getting rid of the packet.

I found El Koubba, made inquiries at the shuttered house next door. I was told that Madame Macklin occupied an apartment in the rear. I went through a dark passage and knocked at the door.

For some reason or other I had, when reading the address on the packet, pictured an American woman. Macklin had not spoken of his wife during the hours I spent with him at Sbeïtla, and I had no knowledge that he was married till the packet was thrust into my hands. Now the lady who opened the door to my knock startled me.

She was tall and slight, with a figure whose suppleness was strangely evident in repose. Her body in its slightest movement showed a serpentlike pliancy. It was a little startling. The face was remarkable too. It was foxlike, framed in close-pressing plaits of blue-black hair. Nose and mouth were well shaped, the latter resembling a red butterfly at rest on the extremely pale skin; but it was the enormous eyes that startled me.

Eyes of a pythoness. Eyes that looked through one, peering at a spiritual shadow, so that they gave to the person they looked at the belief that he was transparent. To me, standing at the door, the feeling that those eyes were regarding something or someone beyond me was so strong that I swung on my heel, expecting to find another person in the passageway. Of course I was nervous with the damn' packet in my pocket.

I muttered an introduction. Said I had met her husband at Sbeïtla, and he had given me a commission. I put the packet into her hand, a slim, graceful hand.

In a husky voice she bade me enter. I obeyed. Now that I had got rid of the packet, curiosity returned to me. This Madame Macklin was something out of the way. Extremely so.

The shutters were closed to keep out the glaring sun; so for a moment my eyes found it difficult to take in the furnishings. I stumbled over the inevitable tambour-cushions upon the floor, clutched the side of a chair and seated myself.

Gradually things took shape. A low divan, native rugs, a few chairs. Then I saw the tanned bull's hide.

It was tacked to the wall, stretched horizontally; and as I gazed at it in wonder, it sort of revealed itself. Quietly, like a slow-born revelation, I realized what it was. Upon the tanned inner side was a map! A fascinating map of North Africa!

The map brought me to my feet. Mouth open, I stared at it. I heard my own croaking demand to look at it closer. She must have made a reply in the affirmative, but I didn't hear it. I couldn't hear it. The power of all my senses had gone to my eyes.

The background of that map was rose-madder. The routes were purple—a glowing Tyrian purple; surely, judging from its intensity, made from the shellfish, pur pura murex, which yielded in ancient days the priceless dye. The cities were tinted green, prophet's green, and the wastes between were made wonderful with drawings of animals no one had ever seen. And it was centuries old. It was Arabic work. Crouched before it, devouring the indications of age, I came to the conclusion that it was drawn in Bagdad sometime in the Fourteenth Century!

That it was not earlier was proved in a way by the broad purple line that marked the route of that great Arab wanderer Ibn Batuta, who had traveled as far as Timbuctoo in 1352-1353. And the manner in which that line had been put in, blotting out several imaginary animals, proved that the news of Batuta's trip had come to the map-maker while he was at work on the magic hide. For the line was his line, purple and finely drawn.

Wow, what a map! There was the Mediterranean under its Arabic name. Bahr er Rûm, the country of the Mamelukes, of the Barbarians, of the Caliphs! The Isle of Djerba, the land of the Lotus-eaters! The pays des Lotophages of Flaubert!

Purple routes to dead cities! Routes beaten by the sandals of Romans, Arabs, Berbers, Moors, Garamantes, Phoenicians and scores of other tribes that had braved the unknown!

The unknown and the dangers. The desert, the thirst, the animals that the imaginative map-maker had tried to show! In those empty places he had cleverly drawn heraldic beasts that brought to my mind Swift's satiric verse:

> Geographers, in Afric's maps,
> With savage pictures filled their gaps,
> And o'er unhabitable downs
> Placed elephants for want of towns.

The husky voice of the woman brought me back from the dreamland into which the hide of the bull had taken me. She was telling me it had been in the possession of her family for countless years.

The father, with the wonder hide as his guide, had explored many ruins, dying finally at Tébessa-Khalia—old Tébessa—from the paludienne fever which he had contracted in the ruins. Later I found that the father was a Frenchman, the mother a Greek.

"The skin of the ox drove my father," she said softly.

"It would drive an army!" I cried. "It is a dream map."

She told me then that the thing had been the means of bringing Macklin and herself together. Someone had told Macklin about the pelt of fantasy. He had begged to see it. He and its owner were drawn together.

Then I knew what Macklin had meant when he said: "I get tips." The woman explained. "Sometimes I stare at the map for hours," she whispered, "and I find that my thoughts are drawn to one particular spot. I tell all this to John, and he visits the place. Often he has found valuable things at those spots which have attracted me. Coins and jewelry."

I was a little beside myself as I stood staring at the Hide of Bagdad. Some wise writer has written that life's best gift is the ability to dream of a better life. That may be so; but to me, at that moment, life's best gift would be the possession of that hide.

I had seen a hundred ancient maps. A thousand. The study of cartography has been a passion. But there was no papyrus in any museum of the world that had the power to stir me like this bull's hide. It had the quality of the magic carpet of Prince Housain. On it one floated over the world.

Reverently I touched it. I peered at the network of finely-drawn lines intersecting each other at right angles. The isbas, and zams that told of the altitude of the Pole Star, of the height of the Calves of the Little Bear and the Barrow of the Great Bear above the horizon. Ah, me! How slowly we have crept toward knowledge!

* * * *

There are times when physical movements are not recorded. I have an impression that the woman pushed me away from the map. I don't know. I think she put my hat into my hand and gently directed me to the door. Hours later when I really came to my proper senses, I found that I had taken a room in the Hôtel du Sahel on the Place Colonel Vincent.

I couldn't leave Sousse. Not without the hide. Would Madame Macklin sell it? Imagination pictured it, a bulky roll beneath my arm. I would, I told myself, carry it with me wherever I went. On days when I was sad and depressed, I would unroll it on the floors of cheap hotel rooms, and sprawling beside it, follow with my finger those lines of Tyrian purple that led to the cities cunningly tinted with prophet's green.

I had dreams of exhibiting it on Fifth Avenue. I shut my eyes and saw it stretched in a large window somewhere close to Forty-second Street, with a milling crowd on the sidewalk "*oh*-ing" and "*ah*-ing" as they got glimpses of it. Forgetting everything as they stared! For there was, I knew, no talisman, charm, or potion that possessed the magic of the hide. Not one.

I counted my scanty funds. I would make the woman an offer. Who could tell? She might part with it.

* * * *

I went the following morning to the Rue El Kehaoui. Excitedly I rapped at the door. More like a pythoness than ever was the woman. She was wrapped in a pagne of orange-colored silk; her blue-black hair was unplaited, falling on her shoulders.

I begged another glance at the map. A little startled, so I thought, she admitted me. With the stiff gait of a sleepwalker I stepped across the room.

Now a shutter was open, and the hide exulted in the light. The beasts that surely were seen in visions by the cartographer became alive. The green-tinted cities beckoned to me, and the routes glowed, so I thought, with the blood from the sandaled feet of warriors who had tramped them....

I heard myself making an offer. A ridiculous offer. The woman received it with a smile. "I couldn't sell it," she murmured.

I doubled the sum. She shook her head. Then, seeing that I was unduly excited, she became slightly confidential, in the manner that women have of ridding themselves of unwelcome male visitors.

At the moment, so she said, she was in one of those staring moods that she had spoken of at my first visit. It would last for hours, perhaps days. It concerned a spot where great treasure might be found. When the location became plain to her, she would telegraph Macklin. Of course she could not be disturbed at the moment with offers for the hide. That was unthinkable. Once again she eased me out of the apartment.

A frightful thing is covetousness. It is the one great and deadly sin because it embodies all the other sins. It is their origin....

I walked around Sousse, seeing nothing but the Hide of Bagdad. I wondered why a pelt had been chosen for the map. Was there a queer magic in the bull's hide before the cartographer commenced his design? Possibly my mind was a little unhinged. Sousse itself, being the ancient Carthaginian town of Hadrumetum, has an atmosphere conducive to mental dislocation.

It might, I thought, have been the pelt of a bull that was not of this world! There are a thousand legends regarding bulls. I recalled them: Zeus as a white bull taking Europa! The Minotaur; the bull-cult of Minos!

Sitting in the shade of the grand mosque of Ksar Er Ribat, I remembered the epic of Gilgamesh and the divine bull who was sent to wage a contest on behalf of the goddess. That bull was slain in Babylon. He must have had a magic hide! And there was the sacred bull of Memphis, the most important of all the sacred animals of Egypt. The Memphis bull had a palace of his own and was buried in state when he died. Perhaps the hide of the original Apis, the black bull of Memphis, or his successor bull, had been stripped and taken to Bagdad!

Who could say? Yes, looking back now on those hot hours in Sousse, I think I was a long way off my mental base. But then I couldn't believe that an artist could make such a map without a magic canvas. And even now, I am not convinced. If it pleases you who read this story to think I am mad, your thoughts are excused by the fact that you did not see that hide.... And you never will.

That evening I thought of ways and means of raising money so that I could make a better offer to the woman. I would borrow small sums from friends; I would pledge my work for a year ahead. Into my mind came a startling thought, possibly thrust forward by an Irish rapparee ancestor. "If she won't sell the hide," whispered the spirit of the long-dead kinsman, "why not steal it? In the days of 'Cairbre of the Cat's Head,' the Dwyers took what they wanted."

* * * *

At eight next morning, I was back in the Rue El Kehaoui. I knocked, and Madame Macklin opened the door. She was in a state of great excitement. The big eyes were filled with fear; her cheeks showed marks of tears; her husky voice was broken with sobs.

Hurriedly she told of her trouble. From the hide, on the day previous, she had received one of her unexplainable "tips." She had telegraphed Macklin immediately, urging him to visit Kasserine, a small village thirty kilometers south of Sbeïtla. Near this village are the ruins of old Cillium, a flourishing spot in the days of Constantine.

"Well?" I said, not understanding the cause of her emotion.

"But now the skin of the ox warns me!" she sobbed. "John is in danger! I must go to him!"

I played a Judas to that woman. I sympathized with her. Near-thief that I was, I offered to guard her apartment while she was away. I would watch over the hide.

"No, no!" she cried. "The skin goes with me!"

Two hundred kilometers southward was Kasserine, on the road by which I had come up to Sousse. But I did not falter. "I will accompany you!" I cried. "If there is anything wrong with Macklin, I might be useful."

She didn't make any objections. She was whispering what I thought were prayers as she rushed her preparations. The fear had her in its clutch.

I helped her to take the hide from the wall. Dear Lord, how I thrilled! I put it on the floor and rolled it carefully, the rapparee ancestor whispering to me as I did so. "Stick it under your arm and run," said he, and the brogue in his voice was thick and harsh. "She's upset, an' she'll never chase you! Devil a chase!"

I combated him. "These are modern days," I said aloud. "That cannot be done."

The woman thought I was speaking to her. "It can! It can!" she cried. "The train is at nine-fifteen. Get a carriage!"

At a wild gallop we drove to the station. I bought two billets, troisième classe, to Kasserine. That, in the state of my finances, showed courage. We clambered aboard, and between us on the cushionless seat rode the bull's hide. The Bull's Hide of Bagdad!

Madame Macklin was silent. Vaguely she answered questions that I put to her. What was the actual danger the hide had hinted at? She couldn't say. But it was a great danger. Even then, as we rode through the dreary country with its great stretches of alfalfa, its dry riverbeds and its stony deserts, the hide, so she asserted, was whispering to her.

Once again I saw the ruins of old Sufetula as we slipped by Sbeïtla. I pondered over my meeting with John Macklin. I was a little afraid of the results of that meeting; yet when I touched the hide with eager groping fingers, the fear left me.

* * * *

In the early afternoon we reached Kasserine. Madame Macklin addressed the small stationmaster, a Corsican, like most of the railway officials in Tunisia. Had he noticed an American descending from the train the day previous?

I thought that a queer look of horror came into the eyes of the chef de gare when he heard the question. He swallowed like a pelican. He looked this way and that; then he clutched the lapel of my coat and dragged me into his little den, leaving Madame Macklin standing on the platform.

His words came spattering like machine-gun fire. I had difficulty in getting their meaning. They tore through the receiving-net of my brain in the manner of sharks ripping through the flimsy mesh of a herring fisherman.

There had been a disaster. *"Un épouvantable désastre, monsieur! Dix personnes mortes! Beaucoup blessés! Les soldats sont sur la place!"*

Stupidly I grasped the meaning of his words. Five kilometers from the gare, on the site of ancient ruins, a huge underground cistern of Roman workmanship had collapsed when a number of treasure-seekers were in the reservoir. Five thousand tons of stone had fallen in on them!

"L'Americain?" I cried. "Monsieur Macklin?"

"Mort!" cried the station-master.

I was stunned by the news. Glancing through the window of the little office, I could see Madame Macklin standing on the platform. How the devil could I break the news to her? As I debated, a captain of infantry, back from the place of the accident, cried out the latest news. *"Pas d'éspoir!"* he cried. *"Vingt morts! Dix-neuf indigènes et l'Américain!"*

Madame Macklin heard. She screamed and stumbled toward a bench. The station-master, the captain and I rushed toward her. Of course she knew that the only American in the neighborhood of Kasserine was John Macklin, chercheur d'or from California....

When Madame Macklin came out of the faint, she insisted on visiting the spot where Macklin had met his death. The polite officer drew me aside and hurriedly put forward objections. The recovery of the bodies was out of the question. A fleet-footed native, who had escaped death by a miracle, had described the situation immediately before the collapse of the cistern. A sacrifice had been made—the officer thought it might have been a human sacrifice; then the tremendous clamor of the gold searchers within the huge underground reservoir had acted like an explosive on the masonry that had held itself upright for fifteen hundred years!

The escapee had seen the huge walls quiver. Slowly they folded inward upon the treasure-seekers blinded by their greed. Then with a frightful crash the immense mass had buried the clawing, screaming mob. Buried them under the thousand blocks of stone chiseled by masons in the days of Constantine!

"It would take an army of workmen a year to reach the bodies," whispered the officer.

I imparted a little of this information to Madame Macklin, but she was obdurate. She wished to see the spot, and so the captain offered to take us in his automobile.

We drove through a dreary countryside with the African night creeping down upon it. For a part of the way we followed the piste to Tebessa; then we swung westward over a flat plain till we came to the fatal spot.

There were a hundred bonfires around the enormous depression that marked the spot where the cistern had collapsed. The walls, as the officer explained, had folded in from all sides; and now, in the center of this depression, there was a four-sided pyramid of piled blocks beneath which rested the dead: Nineteen colored and one white.

A company of native soldiers kept order. They beat back the hundreds of indigènes who had come from far-off places to the scene.

I thought that there was a defiant look about the great stones as they sprawled one upon the other. A menacing look. I think the soldiers and the screaming natives saw it. The blocks put out a threat to those who would meddle with them. Perhaps there was treasure there. Great treasure, which they were guarding.

Gently the officer and I led Madame Macklin back to the automobile. We returned to Kasserine. A few minutes before midnight, a train came through from Tozeur and we boarded it. We reached Sousse seven hours later. I took Madame Macklin to her apartment. I carried the hide from the carriage to her sitting-room. I placed it on the divan and left her. It was not the moment to talk of what was uppermost in my mind.

* * * *

For six successive days I visited that apartment in the Rue El Kehaoui. A super-Judas was I in those days. I played the hypocrite, whispering sympathetic words with my tongue while my eyes were upon the rolled hide.

That woman would not permit me to unroll it after our return from Kasserine. There it lay where I had placed it on the divan, and my eyes lusted for a glimpse of it. At times my groping fingers touched it furtively.

I pawned a few bits of jewelry to pay my board. The future was a little frightening. Again the rapparee ancestor whispered of theft. He thought me a fool because I hesitated.

Nervously I questioned the woman as to what she intended to do. She spoke of her mother's relatives in Greece. They lived at Phaleron, a few miles out of Athens. She thought she would go to them. She showed me letters that were very affectionate.

I touched the hide with my hand, hungrily; then I looked at her. The big eyes were upon my face. They were looking into my brain. They were reading my thoughts.

Those enormous eyes were startled with what they discovered. They knew me as a hypocrite because of my ride with her to Kasserine. A wordy deceiver because of my feigned sympathy for Macklin. They knew me a possible thief, a near-thief. Ay, the spirit of theft showed in my eyes! She pushed me gently to the door.

The following morning I went back to the apartment, and the spirit of that rapparee ancestor walked with me. Boldly he walked. Now and then he whispered in Gaelic, words that I did not understand; but they were fine, strong words. Strong and urgent. When we speak of the devil as a tempter, we mean, of course, our unmoral ancestors who knew nothing of our silly modern codes.

I knocked at the door. There was no answer. I knocked louder. I beat it with my fist. I thought the spirit of my ancestor kicked it, but that couldn't be. It must have been my shoe that crashed against it.

An Arab woman thrust a nervous face out of a door and spoke to me in French. *"Madame est parti,"* she said.

"Où?" I shrieked.

"Pour Tunis," she replied. *"Elle rentre dans le pays de sa mère."*

She had fled me! She had taken the early train for Tunis, where she would take a boat for the Piraeus!

"La peau?" I gasped. *"La peau du taureau?"*

She made a gesture with her hand northward. She laughed gayly. I could have killed her. At least my spectral ancestor could....

There are but three trains a day from Sousse to Tunis. I had a wait of seven hours. It was not till after midnight that I reached Tunis. Too late to make inquiries.

I was at the doors of the Società di Navigazione before the place was open. A sleepy clerk looked over the list of passengers that had departed on the Chalkotheka, a small boat which had sailed the previous evening.

"Oui, oui," he muttered. *"Madame Macklin est parti."*

I staggered out onto the Avenue Jules-Ferry. I was a little deranged. I bumped into pedestrians on the sidewalk and did not apologize when they damned my clumsiness.

* * * *

That evening, news of the Chalko-theka was posted in the bureau of the local news-sheet. The steamer had struck what was supposed to be a derelict some hundred and fifty miles off the coast. The passengers and crew had barely time to leap into the boats before the vessel sank. Every scrap of luggage that they possessed went down with the vessel. The passengers were picked up by an Italian steamer bound for Sicily.

I wrote Madame Macklin in care of her parents at Phaleron. I wished to be certain as to the fate of the hide. Her tardy and ungrammatical reply was, I thought, fearfully ungracious. It ran:

You might makes false words with one mermaidens and get it from her. Or you mights steal it from Mister Neptune. There are your chances. I think you bad mans.

As I said before, if it pleases you who peruse this story to think I am mad, your thoughts are excused by the fact, that you did not see that hide. And you never will. But to me it is visible in my dreams. In my glorious dreams.

MAORI JUSTICE

Bob Du Soe

Kamaka had been the first to sight the strange schooner as it headed in toward the opening in the reef, and he had hastened at once to the bungalow to break the news to old man Stovall. He stood there now on the porch, head and shoulders above the old trader, his dark, oily skin glistening in the morning sunlight.

"See, Mr. Stovall, he lose mainmast. He come long way, eh? No storm now for two, maybe three weeks. What you think?"

"It looks to me like the Wasp—Captain Bowker's outfit," the trader answered. "What do you say, Ugly, ever seen her before?"

Ugly Smith, mate, steward, and sometimes even cook on Stovall's own schooner, the *Lalanai*, screwed his homely face into a puzzled frown and shook his head. "No, sir, can't say as I have. They had better have a care, though, or they'll be loosin' more than their stick."

"Not if it's Bull Bowker. See, he's got her in the channel already."

The disabled schooner rose on an oncoming swell, as Stovall spoke, and slid through the narrow channel like an outrigger in the hands of a native. The plunge of her anchor sent a ripple over the lagoon and then a long-boat that had been towing astern was hauled up amidships and a white man with two blacks climbed down into it.

Bowker had reason enough to be in a nasty mood on that particular morning, for his disreputable old schooner had come to anchor with her hull half-full of water and the main mast but a splintered stump. However, he selected a very poor time to indulge his humor.

Ugly, Kamaka, and two of the natives went down to the beach to meet him, as his long boat crossed the lagoon, and as it grounded in the shallow water they waded out to help drag it in. Why Bowker should have been standing carelessly in the bow the way he was no one knew, but there he stood and as the boat suddenly stopped he went sprawling head first into the water. He was on his feet again in an instant, cursing vilely, and then he caught sight of Kamaka who was roaring with laughter.

Without a word his fist shot out and he caught the big Maori square on the mouth. And then, before the astonished native could strike back, if such a thing had occurred to him, Bowker had him covered with his gun.

"Laugh at me, will you?" he swore. "I'll teach you to respect a white man!"

Ugly had been laughing, too, but in an instant his scrawny frame was tense. "Put up that gun, you white-livered bully!" he growled. "You deserve to be laughed at."

Shooting a black and shooting a white man were two different things or Bowker, in his rage, might have killed them both. He waded out of the water, swearing as he went, the gun still held in his hairy fist.

"Put up that gun!" Ugly repeated, "or by cripes we'll make you eat it!"

Bowker pocketed the gun but he took his time about it and there was a look of contempt on his dark, heavy features. That is, Ugly took it for contempt; Kamaka in his native shrewdness read something deeper.

Kamaka was a full-blooded Maori from back of the reefs. The son of a chief, he had said, and there was no reason to doubt him. What had brought him out to old man Stovall's plantation and trading post, no one knew, but there he was and they were glad to have him. For all his breadth of chest and mighty arms he was the culmination of bland good humor and more than that he was strong as an ox and an excellent seaman.

Compared to the big-eared, pug-nosed Ugly Smith, Kamaka was a giant, and yet he never questioned the smaller man's orders. Had Ugly commanded him to seize the enraged Bowker and relieve him of his gun the Maori would have done so without hesitation, though it cost him his life. They were as different as God could make them, and yet they were the best of friends.

"Why he hit me?" Kamaka demanded, when Bowker had moved on up the beach toward the bungalow. "Damn fool, why he hit me?"

"Because he didn't like your sense of humor," Ugly replied. "Guess he thought we should have cried over him."

"I fix him for that. Him fool—damn fool!"

Ugly was a bit surprised at the Maori's anger, though he certainly did not blame him. "No you won't," he said. "You'll forget it unless he starts something else. If he does you can wring his neck. But you'd better keep an eye on that gun if you ever try it."

"I watch him," Kamaka muttered, and his dark, burning eyes followed the swaggering form of the man who had hit him until he disappeared through the door of the bungalow. It was really not vengeance that had stirred the big native. It was simply that his pride, his feelings had been injured, and now he sensed some impending evil.

* * * *

The incident had cooled in Ugly's mind when he was summoned to the house later in the day. Finding Bowker and his employer seated on the porch, a bottle and two glasses between them, he knew they had been talking business.

"Mr. Bowker wants to beach his schooner here and make some repairs," Stovall explained, "and he wants help. I told him I thought you and Kamaka would be willing to give him a hand. There's no one else here who'd be of much help to him."

Ugly nodded. "You're the boss. What's got to be done to her?"

"She's got an open seam," Bowker spoke up, "and I've got to step a new mast. Stovall tells me he's got a stick that will do until I get to Cooktown."

"What have you got for cargo?"

"Shell, but it don't make any difference about that. I won't have to unload her to do the work."

"You'll never get her beached high enough out of water to get at her hull unless you do. Most of it will have to be moved before you can step the mast, anyway."

"I'll take care of that," Bowker snapped. "You tend to the hull. If I wait to unload her she'll be at the bottom."

Ugly shrugged his shoulders. From what he had seen of the schooner, drifting sluggishly in the lagoon, he guessed the owner was about right. He still failed to see, though, how anything could be done with her as she was.

"Well, it's your wreck," he said. "Put your men in the long boat and tow her in."

"My men couldn't pull the long boat, leave alone that water-logged hulk. They damn near gave out before we got here. Use some of these lazy blacks you're coddling here."

Ugly frowned. He resented the inference, but he knew there would be money in the job for Stovall so he left them to finish the bottle while he rounded up a few of the natives.

"Which way he come this place?" Kamaka inquired, as they headed out for the schooner.

"From the south," Ugly replied. "Says he's headed for Cook-town."

"Funny he come from south," Kamaka grunted.

"Why, what's funny about that?"

"Where he come from—south?"

"How do I know? I didn't ask him."

"I no think he come from south—come maybe east," the Maori muttered, and would say no more.

Bowker came down from the bungalow, as the sweating natives towed the vessel broadside to the beach, and made known his presence by a string of unnecessary oaths and orders. Ugly paid no attention to him until that much of the job was finished and lines had been made fast to the nearby fringe of palms. The next thing was to bury an anchor opposite the two masts and heel the craft over with blocks and tackle. There was only one mast, however, and with the hull weighed down, Ugly knew the task would be impossible.

"Well, that's all I can do with her," he turned to Bowker. "The tide will fall a couple feet and that may show up the leak. If it don't you'll have to break out the cargo whether you want to or not."

"Those hatch covers are not going to move," the trader growled. "Drag out that old spar Stovall was talking about and put somebody to work squarin' off the stump of that mast there on the Wasp."

"Why do that?" Ugly was surprised.

"Why? Because I said so. I'm not going to step it. I'm going to splice it."

Such a thing was possible, but it was unnecessary and very apt to prove unsatisfactory. It suddenly struck Ugly that there was something more to the unloading of that cargo than Bowker's stubbornness. Kamaka had said he had come from the east, and Ugly could not help wondering.

"Shell an' what else?" he asked, staring straight into the small, close-set eyes of the trader. "Rum or feathers?"

Bowker's face grew red beneath his ragged beard, and his short, blunt fingers opened and closed menacingly. "Shell!" he hissed, "and mind your own damn business!"

Ugly shrugged his skinny shoulders, as was his habit on such occasions, and walked away. He knew, however, that he had come mighty near the truth about the cargo.

The stump of a mast was trimmed off during the afternoon, and the new one was hauled on board. Work ceased then, that the hull might be examined as the tide reached low ebb. Ugly and Kamaka circled the vessel several times in a dinghy, Bowker following them in the long boat, but they found no sign of the leak. When the tide began to rise again, Ugly turned to the trader with an amused grin.

"Now what?" he inquired.

Bowker muttered an unintelligible answer and climbed aboard his schooner. He called his crew into the cabin a few minutes later, four nondescript blacks, and when they did not come out again, Ugly dismissed his own gang and went back to the bungalow with Kamaka.

"What he got in that boat?" the Maori asked.

Ugly eyed him sharply. "What do you think?"

"I no know. He say he come Bundaberg way—I think he come Caledonia. He say shell—I think he make 'nother lie, too."

"Well, since you've asked me, I'd say you were about right. It's none of our business, though; you'd better forget about it."

"Maybe not our business—maybe plenty our business."

"What do you mean by that?"

"I no know—little more we see."

* * * *

Night, soft and quiet, settled down over the lagoon after a glorious sunset and the few lights on shore threw their reflections out over the still water. Ugly's home was aboard the *Lalanai* and strolling aft to the schooner's stern he lit a pipe and gazed shoreward to where another light glowed in the cabin of the Wasp. The occasional sound of a voice drifted across to him but there was no other disturbance so he stretched out in a hammock that swung beneath the boom and puffed contentedly. The pipe went out after a few minutes, slipped from his mouth, and he slept.

Had Ugly been of a malicious nature himself he would have thought twice before giving in to the drowsiness that crept over him. He awakened once, as a faint splash stirred the water, but the play of a fish was the only thought that came to him, and he dozed off again.

When next he awoke there was the muzzle of a gun pressed against his ribs and Bowker stood over him.

"Get up!" the man whispered hoarsely, "and if you make a sound I'll drill you through."

Ugly swung out of the hammock and found himself surrounded by Bowker's four natives. He glanced quickly about, wondering what had become of Kamaka, but the big Maori was not in sight.

"Lash him up!" Bowker ordered, "an' damn your hides, don't bungle it!"

Ugly was helpless. In an instant the four men had thrown him to the deck and bound him hand and foot.

"That cursed black, now," the bully ordered, "he's aboard here somewhere! Cut his greasy throat!"

Ugly listened to the slap of bare feet as the natives darted about the vessel, expecting each moment to hear the cries of struggle, but the search was unsuccessful. He had been afraid at first that they had surprised Kamaka, also, but now he knew better. In some way the native had eluded them, and the thought was a comforting one.

"Where is that damn black of yours?" Bowker demanded with a kick at his ribs that made him grunt.

"How do I know?" Ugly answered, and then in hopes of aiding Kamaka he declared that the Maori slept on shore.

"That's a lie. He came out here with you, and nobody has seen him leave."

"Been watching us, have you? Just what is your game, any-way?"

"That's my business. Where's that black?" Bowker repeated his brutal kick.

"I don't know," Ugly retorted. "And I wouldn't tell you if I did."

"You wouldn't, eh? You do a lot of talking for a shrimp of your size. We'll see."

Bowker took a dirty rag from his pocket and tossed it to one of the men. "Gag him," he growled, "then take him up on the fo'c'stle."

Ugly clamped his jaw, determined to resist the gag, but it was no use. The native seized his head, a thumb just below each ear, and began to squeeze. The torture was too great. Ugly's mouth fell open and the rag was crammed into it.

"Forward with him!" Bowker snapped. "Tie him to the anchor chain and slip the anchor. No noise while you're at it, either."

Ugly was seized with horror. He was no coward; he had slipped through the devil's clutches more than once, but on those occasions he had at least had a foothold in the land of living—a fighting chance. He struggled frantically at his bonds but they held fast and the realization that there was nothing he could do all but drove him mad. By sheer strength the four natives lashed him to the anchor chain and let it slip over the side.

He hung there, half out of water, half in, waiting for the few remaining feet of chain to be dropped overboard, a thousand insane thoughts racing through his brain. He saw the long boat drift around the bow; saw a line handed down to it, then heard the heavy chain scraping across the deck. The next moment it let go and down he plunged to the bottom of the lagoon.

Even then Ugly did not cease to struggle. A broken wrist or even a dismembered hand would have been nothing could he have torn it loose. It seemed ages instead of seconds that he fought against breathing. His lungs were on the point of bursting; his brain was a mad jumble of terror. And then something brushed against him and he felt a hand at his back. It seized his arms, and the next moment his hands were free. The chain fell away from him and with all his strength he kicked against the bottom of the lagoon and shot to the surface.

At first Ugly thought of nothing but air for his straining lungs, then he made out the black, woolly head of Kamaka.

"Here, you cut rope on feet," the Maori ordered, and held out a knife that had been gripped in his teeth.

Ugly took the blade and when his feet were free he placed a hand on the big fellow's shoulder that he might rest and regain his senses. "I won't forget that, Kamaka," he said weakly. "Never—"

"Too bad I no come more quick," the native replied. "I think this way more better. That devil have gun and four men with knives. I think more better this way."

"Then you saw it all? You knew what he was doing?"

"Sure, I tell you I watch that devil. I see many things. First I hear noise on beach and go for look see. I say before him got no shell. He got feathers, you savvy? Him bird poacher an' thievin' devil. I see."

"So, that's it. I had a pretty good hunch."

"Yeh, I see him men pile many bags on deck, then he take long boat and come out here very quiet. I know then he mean to steal Mr. Stovall's schooner—maybe kill you for keep still, so I swim back."

"Good Lord, Kamaka, the *Lalanai*! I'd forgotten!"

"No trouble. You can swim now. We catch 'em before he take schooner. First he unload feathers from his own boat."

* * * *

The white hull of the *Lalanai* was just visible over by the shore, and striking out quietly they swam toward her. Bowker was bringing the vessel alongside his own grounded craft when they caught up with it and they saw the natives climb aboard and throw a section of hatch cover across the two bulwarks. Almost immediately they began passing across the bags filled with contraband feathers, the breasts of thousands of slaughtered birds.

"You go for Stovall and some of the men," Ugly spoke in a whisper. "I'll stay here. We'll trap 'em red-handed."

"This not Mr. Stovall's business any more," Kamaka replied. "Before, all right—now my business."

"Don't be a fool! That devil has got a gun!"

"I no afraid gun, my friend, now you all right. You stay here. I look see."

"Nothing doing. I'll have a look see myself. Whatever you do, I'm with you."

Kamaka grunted but he did not argue further. He began working his way around between the two hulls. The natives were outlined against the starlit sky, as they crossed back and forth over the hatch covers, and Bowker could be heard urging them to hurry from somewhere on deck.

Paddling softly back to the *Lalanai*'s bow, the Maori took hold of a bobstay and pulled himself up. Ugly followed him and together they worked their way aft, clinging to the outside of the bulwarks. Opposite the forward shrouds Kamaka reached over and secured a belaying pin from the rail.

"You see him there?" he pointed to Bowker. "When hatch cover fall, you throw. You no hit him, more better you dive back into water."

Ugly's nod was not seen in the dark but the big black seemed to know that his friend had understood. He crept forward then, and Ugly waited for the boards to fall. He had no idea of how Kamaka intended to accomplish the task from his uncertain footing but he knew the strength in those powerful shoulders and he did not doubt that he would succeed.

Minutes passed while the men worked steadily with the bags, then a scream from one of them and an oath from Bowker suddenly broke the stillness of the lagoon. The cry, followed by the splash of water, told Ugly that a native had gone down along with the hatch cover. He knew then that Kamaka had been waiting for just the right moment.

Clutching the pin at the small end, Ugly leaped over the bulwark and crouched down in the shadow. Bowker was in plain view, peering into the water between the two schooners, and Ugly hurled his pin. A grunt and a string of oaths followed, then Kamaka landed on deck and seized the enraged poacher before he could recover his wits.

The suddenness of the attack, added to the blow from the heavy pin, had thrown him off guard. Ugly saw him reach for his gun and dashed forward to snatch it away. Kamaka, however, was quicker. He flung the man against the bulwark, twisted his arm behind him, and held it there until the weapon dropped into the water.

"Kill him! Kill him, you damn blacks!" Bowker yelled to his men, but there was no response. Only one of them was on board the *Lalanai* and he stood paralyzed with fright.

Ugly watched the struggling pair, wondering what the Maori would do, then he saw Bowker's feet slowly leave the deck. His thrashing arms and legs seemed suspended in midair a brief moment, then he disappeared over the side.

"Good work, Kamaka!" Ugly declared, but the Maori paid no attention. He climbed to the bulwarks, poised there a minute peering down, then he dove.

Down there in the dark water between the two hulls there was a brief struggle, then all was quiet. One, two, three minutes Ugly waited, then the black, dripping head of Kamaka appeared above the rail.

"You all right now, my friend?" he inquired. "Yes, I'm all right," Ugly answered quietly. "Other men, they no make trouble?"

"No, they never raised a hand."

"They be good now," the big fellow nodded. "That white devil, he make 'em too bad. Funny 'bout him, he no good that devil. He like drown you all same rat but he no like die himself. He fight like hell."

Ugly did not answer. He knew it was the Maori's idea of justice, and a good turn for a wrong done a friend, but somehow the thought made him shudder.

JAVELIN OF DEATH

Captain A.E. Dingle

"Want any more?"

"No, damn your eyes! You've got me now, but I'll take my time and get you for this!"

The fight had been looming up all the cruise, and it came off at last after a weary day when the *Narwhal* had cut-in three whales. Tired and hungry men gladly allowed a smoking supper of dough-nuts fried in whale oil to grow cold in order to watch that battle of giants; and now that the second mate, Radley, lay in a crumpled heap at the feet of Peters, the harpooner, the crowd moved regret-fully toward the forecastle scuttle, sorry it was so soon over.

The harpooner stepped aside and walked aft, bent upon his own supper. The fight over, he was not the man to nurse the cause of it any further.

He had barely passed the try-works when a boy's shout of warn-ing rang in his ears. He turned swiftly, glimpsed running figures and vaguely saw his late antagonist fumbling at the fife-rail. Then a crushing blow on the head felled him, and he pitched headlong to the deck as an iron belaying-pin clattered against the brick base of the try-pots.

When Peters sat up, his head ringing like a released spiral spring, a mob of men surged around him, and in the middle they bustled and thumped Radley until he faced his victim.

Something of the fear of death clouded the second mate's scowling visage. He looked anxiously toward the poop as if he hoped for help to come from that direction. It was his own watch on deck; the other officers, harpooners, carpenter, and the rest of the afterguard were at supper. The poop was deserted except for the lone figure at the wheel. A growing rumble of anger among the men sent a shiver down his spine. Peters got up stiffly.

"Let him go, fellows," he said, looking hard into the eyes of Radley. "He'll remember what he's done after a bit, and he won't enjoy the smell of himself."

Both excellent whalemen, it was more professional jealousy than anything else that had set Radley and Peters by the ears. Nantucket had bred them both, and they had held high records in the whalingest of whaling communities while sailing in separate ships.

There was, too, a reason for Peters' refusal to exact penance for the second mate's treacherous attempt on him. To complain to the skipper about that unseamanlike end to a sailorly scrap might mean that Radley would be disrated, for the *Narwhal*'s skipper had his own downright ideas on man's dealings with man. He was in the whaling business to make a quick competence, and a warring, simmering crew was a serious obstacle in his way.

There was no doubt that he would punish Radley's action by disrating him, and that must inevitably finish the rivalry that already had the ship divided into hot factions. There would be no chance of Peters losing his place at the head of the *Narwhal*'s expert whalemen; nobody else was anywhere near Radley; no man could hope to overtake the big harpooner's lead.

And that was the great reason which prompted Peters to heap coals of fire on the second mate's head. He would not accept an advantage won by reason of another man's blind anger. He had made no mistake, either, when he said that Radley would not admire himself when he cooled off and remembered what he had done.

* * * *

The harpooner came on deck after supper, lighted his pipe at the galley and took his customary seat on the spare topmast in the port waterways. Here he always sat when neither on watch nor asleep. For one thing it was immediately beneath the davits of his own boat; for another thing it was also the resting place—when rest was possible—of his son, the youngster whose shout had warned him of the belaying-pin too late to dodge.

Here Peters strove daily to make a sailor and a whaleman of the boy, and success was coming. Already the young sapling promised to outgrow the parent tree. Wiry, whalebone and whipcord like his father, young Eph Peters already pulled number two oar in the second mate's boat, and, but for the close rivalry between them and the mate's boat of which his father was harpooner, would have before now had his chance with the "iron."

"Yer head hurt much, dad?" asked Eph, sitting in his accustomed place.

"Don't hurt, son. My head's too blame tough to crack as easy as that. But you hollered too late. Might have missed me if I hadn't turned 'round. Forget it. How fur have ye got with them hitches an' knots?"

"I ain't done no hitches ner no knots this watch. What d'ye think I am? Think I kin fool with pieces o' rattlin' stuff an' whale-line while I'm thinkin' of that Radley dog? Just wait till we're fast to a whale. I'll let a hole through him wi' the spare harpoon!"

"If you do, son, I'll hang you up myself!" said Peters very slowly and very quietly. "You'll do your bit the same as always, and never forget that Mr. Radley's second mate o' this ship, an' officer in charge o' your boat. And you ain't going to forget that Mr. Radley and me's nip an' tuck fer high boat this cruise, an' I ain't going to have it said that my son helped me to beat his own boat by playin' the dog. Git on with your larnin', son, and likely you'll be a harpooner yet afore the cruise's up."

To a sailor composed of bone and red blood, humiliation hurts more than a score of husky physical wallopings, and Mr. Radley was a man of that kind. He took his supper alone, undergoing all the bitterness of self-reproach. It was not in him to immediately realize the true sportsmanship underlying Peters' refusal to make capital out of the flying belaying-pin; rather it seemed to him a deliberate assertion of superiority on the part of an inferior. The idea obsessed him, until long before a wakeful watch below was up he had taken to himself the role of the aggrieved party, and his mood was one of surly, smoldering anger, wholly foreign to him in his normal condition.

Thus, when the skipper saw him in the early morning, for the first time since the combat, and demanded to know the cause of his battered and bruised face, Radley told part of the story only, and that part calculated to arouse sympathy toward himself and official displeasure toward Peters. He led the skipper to believe that the harpooner had led the whole watch, or more particularly Peters' boat crew, in an unprovoked attack upon him.

Fully aware of the intense rivalry between the two men, the skipper was inclined to attribute the whole thing to that cause and to judge any such offense as leniently as possible. But, being human, he could not help being influenced slightly by the first version of the story told to him. The other man's version would have to be strongly stated to overcome first impressions. Besides, Mr. Radley was second officer of the ship; Peters was only a member of the afterguard, ex officio as it were by reason of being a harpooner.

"We'll settle this matter in the forenoon watch, Mr. Radley," the skipper said. "You were saying that young Peters is almost ready to have a chance with the 'iron,' weren't you?"

"He's as fit right now as his father is, sir," returned Radley, his eagerness cropping out in spite of himself.

"Then maybe we'll shift your harpooner into the mate's boat, and give the youngster his chance with you. If this business started as you say it did, it won't do any harm to give Peters a lesson by keeping him on board the ship next time we lower away."

* * * *

In whaler fashion the captain and mates ate breakfast at a first table, the harpooners, carpenter, sailmaker, and cooper coming into a second sitting when the others were through. The ship was under cruising rig, jogging serenely through the placid waters of the northwestern Pacific with three lookouts aloft, the tension of momentary expectation pervading all hands.

The smell of whale was in the air. The fires under the try-pots were never cold for many daylight hours together on the Bonin grounds.

Harpooners overhauled irons and lines, seeing that the harpoons were ready to hand in the crotch on the starboard bow of their boats, assuring themselves that each tub of line was snugly coiled ready for running. Seamen looked to oars, to make quite sure that none had been cracked or sprung in the previous day's service.

Peters worked over a bent and twisted soft iron harpoon head by the forward crane of his boat; young Eph, to his wondering surprise, was given a similar job at his own boat, right across the deck from his father.

From time to time the youngster glanced across as if unable to restrain his impatience to impart his great hope to his parent.

Everything pointed to his getting the chance he had dreamed of, the hurling of his first harpoon at a living target.

The carpenter made the rounds of the boats, handing each harpooner the deadly bomb-lance that is reserved for dire extremity. This horribly efficient weapon, when hurled into the side of the whale, nearly always means the end of the chase; for a charge of explosive is carried in the head, a trigger is set which is tripped by the whale's own skin on entering, and in an instant an eruption takes place inside the leviathan that rarely misses a vital part.

Peters had the old whaleman's dislike for such a weapon. He decidedly preferred to turn his fish fin-out by the orthodox methods, and used the deadly tool under silent protest.

Aft on the short poop the mates were clustered, looking at each other inquiringly, and from each other to the companionway by which the skipper must emerge from the cabin. It was apparent that something was afoot apart from the daily routine, and Radley revealed his knowledge of the business by his nervous aloofness.

Presently the skipper stepped out of the companionway, spoke to his officers, and immediately the mate roared out:

"All hands muster aft! Bear a hand now!" and evinced utter astonishment at his own order.

Blankly the men looked at each other as they trooped aft and clustered in a milling mob at the break of the poop. Young Peters alone grinned, for he was now certain that promotion was afoot, and he blushed boyishly at the thought that he was the most likely candidate, else why had he been told off to do a harpooner's job. Who the unlucky man to be disrated was bothered him but little.

Peters hung on the edge of the crowd, still fingering his harpoon-head, as mystified as his mates at the unheard-of departure from sea custom. Neither punishment, promotion, nor any other matter of ship's business that he knew of called for a muster of all hands at two bells in the forenoon watch on the whaling grounds. There was never time for such things; even at that moment any or all of the three lookouts might set the ship in a frenzy of action by a long-drawn "Blo-oo-ow, ah blo-oo-ow!"

"Men," began the captain, holding up a hand, "an assault has been committed by one officer on another. Those men who saw the trouble from the beginning, stand over to starboard; the rest may carry on with their jobs."

The men who had seen the fight—and they numbered the entire ship's company forward except the helmsman—shuffled uneasily and looked disconcertedly at the officers. Radley's bruised face flushed a shade deeper beneath the tan, and he avoided the men's direct gaze.

Peters started as the words were uttered, and an angry flush suffused his powerful countenance while he sharply scrutinized every man around him. To him, the captain's speech meant that some busybody had carried the tale of the second mate's hot-headed and unmanly act right to the fountain of authority, and he boiled at the thought.

He flashed a glance at young Eph, recalling the youngster's heated talk; but Eph looked as surprised as the rest, though he could not and did not try to hide his pleasurable anticipation of promotion. What puzzled the boy was, who was to be disrated for his benefit? Then, suddenly, through his mind flashed the joyful thought that Radley was to be punished, thanks to the unknown tale-carrier, and one of the harpooners would be moved up into the place of the third mate, who, of course, would fill Radley's vacant berth. The harpooner could scarcely be any other than his father, and he, Eph, would achieve his ambition of filling the old man's shoes to complete the family triumph.

"Now men, shake a leg," repeated the skipper impatiently, for not a man had moved over. "I want the men who manhandled Mr. Radley. If I have to find them out myself, I shall make their punishment something to remember. Step out now."

If the crowd were uneasy before, they were stupefied now. Dumbly, with open mouths, they stared at the harpooner, who in turn stared in titter unbelief in his own ears at the skipper.

Not a man there but had guessed he was expected to bear witness against the second mate; truly, their only scruple would be that Peters did not want the unpleasant business known to the captain at all. But "The men who had manhandled Mr. Radley!" And they were to be punished! That put another complexion on the matter, and a deep growl rumbled around the crowd.

Peters, still dumfounded, fingered his harpoon nervously and started toward the ladder, bound to have his doubts set right.

"Stay down there, Peters!" the skipper said, and extended a flat palm toward the ladder.

The growl threatened to burst into furious remonstrance at the obvious twist the skipper had gotten into his yarn. The two men who had led in hustling Radley after the belaying-pin left his hand stepped aside and began calling off names of those who had so willingly lent a hand. The muttering subsided; a heavy silence hung over the clustered men in the waist. Then, pipe-like and clear, far overhead, from fore and main crow's nest simultaneously rang the electrifying hail—

"A-ahblo-oo-ow!"

"Where away?" The skipper's mind was set on whales now; not all the black eyes and bruised noses in the whaling industry could distract his attention from his legitimate business.

"Lone bull down to th' sou'west!"

"Lower away!" pealed the order, given by the skipper and echoed by the first mate as that important officer sprang to his own boat.

If but one boat were to be lowered, it must be his, of course. Peters swiftly clapped his iron on to the shaft and leaped to the bulwarks in readiness.

"You'll stay aboard this time," the skipper called to the chief mate. "Mr. Radley and the third mate will be enough; you will be third boat, if it's wanted."

For a moment the mate looked aggrieved; then he grinned. If he always had gone out with his own boat, he would have been in the contest for high catch, and on a level with his harpooner; but the skipper sometimes took a notion to chase a whale himself, and on those occasions he replaced the mate.

So, while Peters always went along to hurl the harpoon, only a percentage of the boat's catch fell to the credit of the chief mate. Therefore it was only his pride that suffered a little when he was ordered to stay for possible third boat. Peters saw the order from a different angle. He had refrained from taking advantage of Radley's mean action, from a sportsman's motive; he saw the result now. The second mate had not felt the same scruples.

Peters stood moodily watching the chase from the bulwarks by his boat, cold rage in his heart. The mate walked aft with a philosophical air and took the place of the skipper who was on his way aloft with binoculars to watch and direct the chase.

The boats had sailed on leaving the ship, and as long as the sails were visible it was evidence that they had not yet got fast to the whale. Then first one sail was lowered and rolled up, and in a few minutes the other followed, and Peters' interest in the boats smothered his personal feelings. He glanced aloft to the main crow's nest and saw the skipper intently watching the maneuvers of the boats.

Presently a hail carried down, and the mate sprang to alert attention.

"Lower away!" ordered the skipper. "The third mate's in trouble!"

Peters hesitated while the boat's crew jumped to the tackles.

"In with you!" cried the mate, springing into the stern-sheets of the boat, and the harpooner silently took his place.

"Shove off! Give way!" And the boat was thrust clear while a couple of hands stepped the mast and set the spritsail.

Away she sped, and the breeze that was barely sufficient to move the sluggish old whaleship heeled the boat down to the rail and drove her through the sparkling seas with a boiling spout of spray at her stem.

"What's the trouble, Peters?" sang out the mate, as the first two boats rose into plainer view.

"Fighting whale, sir! Third mate's boat's busted, and Radley looks to have his hands full."

"Better have the bomb-lance handy then. That's the stuff for mean whales!" advised the mate, and edged his boat a bit to windward.

* * * *

The whale sounded just as the harpooner caught a glimpse of his black bulk, and the boat was luffed to stop her way until the place where he reappeared was discernible. Then the tub-oarsman sang out:

"There's the third mate's boat, down to loo'ard, sir. She's awash, and there's some men hanging onto her!"

The helm was shifted, and the boat buzzed down to assist, but the third mate was a real whaleman and could endure several more hours in the water if only the whale that put him there were safely ironed.

"We're all right for a while," he hailed. "Better get fast, or you'll lose him. Radley ain't got him yet!"

"Blo-oo-ow!" shouted Peters, with an arm outflung toward the far side of the second mate's boat.

The blunt snout of an enormous cachalot rose from the water, and in a moment it was plain that Radley had an iron in him, for the boat gradually pulled up closer to the whale.

Then Peters' announcement that it was a fighting whale was amply justified. Without warning, gathering way like a torpedo boat, the whale charged fair at his tormentor and the chief mate's crew held their breath.

Peters fixed his eyes upon a slight, springy figure in the bows of the threatened boat, and his grim face relaxed. Eph bent to his bow oar like a veteran; the onrush of the murderous cachalot left him as cool as even his father and mentor could have wished him to be.

A wild shout of warning pealed out as the boat backed off and let the whale charge by a scant oar's length away. The slackened whale-line fouled the oars. Eph's ash loom was flung high in the air, and the youngster himself was hurled over the side of the steeply heeling boat, a turn of the line about his shoulders.

Stoic that he was, Peters uttered no sound, simply flashing a look of appeal to his officer. Then he straightened up and stared at the scene of disaster with incredulous eyes.

As the writhing line snatched Eph from his thwart, seemingly to certain death, Radley left his hold on the steering oar, seized the boat-knife, and in a flash dived straight into the swirling froth that surged over the boy's disappearing form. The boat, heeling giddily to the strain of the snarled line, suddenly righted; the line hung down slack; then two heads broke water together, and a howl of defiance to the whale burst forth as four pairs of steel-muscled arms hauled Eph and Radley aboard.

The thing had taken little time. The men were back at the oars, as if nothing uncommon had happened, when a shot from the mate's boat warned them that the whale was coming again. It was high time to step in if the mate was to strike a blow, and he set his oars in motion.

"Great Jonah! See that thar' whale!" gasped the bowman, glancing over his shoulder.

Again the furious whale bore down on the second mate's boat, and Radley stood up to take a desperate chance with the lance. But the cachalot has a frontal piece impervious to the sharpest blade. The long lance struck, fell back into the water, and in an instant the great blunt head crashed into the boat, smashing it to loose staves and tossing all hands broadcast.

"Give way! Oh, crack your backs!" urged the mate, and a running string of encouraging oaths then came through the clenched teeth of Peters, himself a cracking, swollen-veined bunch of straining sinew.

Once more the whale turned and charged at the fragments of the boat and burst among the planks and oars and swimming men like a mad bull through a paper fence. A malignant devil had taken charge of him and he sought out men from the wreckage with fiendish cleverness.

Around him the sea rolled and tumbled, great clouds of spray wreathing him as in a mist. But through the mist objects flashed at intervals, and Radley could be seen, farflung in the crash, now swimming frantically to get out of the track of the monster.

Skillfully maneuvering, the mate swept his boat around until the whale presented a fair mark for the harpooner. Then he saw what had been hidden before. On the whale's streaming back, hanging on desperately to the shaft of a planted iron, was young Peters, and his white face shone out like an ivory mask against the gleaming black hide.

"My God, Peters!" groaned the mate as the boat surged near. "You can't plant that bomb-lance without—"

The harpooner looked round swiftly, and his grim face paled. The one comprehensive glance showed him Eph's body, covering the vital area of black skin beneath which beat the whale's mighty heart; showed him, much nearer, the agonized face of Radley, fair in the monster's path. And, while the picture flashed through his brain, he reformed that other picture, of a snarled line, a boat-knife, and a son snatched from death.

With silently moving lips, he stood erect in the bows, never waiting for the customary "Stand up and give it to him!" His knee was braced solidly against the thigh-board in the bows, the long, dynamite-headed bomb-lancer was balanced in a hand as steady as a lighthouse. Intuitively the oars hung poised, ceasing their forward impulse, awaiting the order to back water which would come for lightning obedience in a moment.

"Can you? Oh, can you?" breathed the mate.

The harpooner gave no sign.

The rushing shape of the maddened whale flashed past the stem of the motionless boat. Ten fathoms in front of his wicked snout floundered Radley, breathless and weakened, and a fear of death was on his set face, yet he fought stubbornly in the face of the end.

A hissing intake of the breath was heard as Peters stiffened; then like the javelin of fate his weapon was launched, fair at the vital spot of the whale. The iron sank deep into the massive side, six inches from Eph's body, and the ensuing explosion deadened the groan that burst from the harpooner.

"Starn—oh, starn all!" cried the mate, and the oars bit deep to back the boat out of the stricken whale's flurry. One oar was idle. Peters flung aside the coils of the lance warp, swept the churning waters with a swift scrutiny, and plunged overboard into the turmoil.

"There's Mr. Radley, sir!" shouted the bowman, as the second mate's head emerged from the welter.

A sweep of the steering oar brought the boat round, and the spent and sickened officer was dragged into the boat. Every eye then fastened upon the mate in mute inquiry as he scanned the littered waters about the expiring whale for trace of Peters. There seemed no hope of Eph having escaped, for, with the stroke of the lance, the whale's flurry had started.

"There's Peters! And he's got Eph!" whooped the mate, but he added, beneath his breath, "What's left of Eph, I guess!"

Silently the oars moved again, and the harpooner was taken up, gasping painfully from bursting lungs. But there was a lot left of Eph, and it was but a moment before the harpooner was satisfied of the happy circumstance. Eph spoke to him. A wan smile flashed across Peter's face; then he turned to the gunwale and became deathly sick.

"I threw myself off when I saw that lance coming," explained Eph, when the mate had set a weft as a mark on the dead whale and the boat was pulling away to pick up the third mate and his crew. "Mighty close, 'twas, though. I felt that ol' whale heave up!"

When the whale was fast alongside the *Narwhal*, and the crew went to dinner preparatory to commencing cutting-in, Peters sought out the skipper and made a request.

"Eph got fast to that fish, sir, and it wasn't his fault he didn't kill his first whale. The boy's got the stuff in him, and I want you to give him his chance right along now. Won't you let me change boats with him? I'd like to have him along with the mate until he's toughened a bit."

"You want to change into Mr. Radley's boat, eh?" mused the skipper, peering hard into the harpooner's face. "What's the idea? You don't want to start anything with him again, do you?"

"I never started anything with Mr. Radley, cap'n, and I'm not likely to after this day. I want to settle our differences for all time. We're about nose and nose on the catch now, and if we're both in the same boat we'll finish that way. Won't be any cause to start anything then."

The skipper nodded. He had heard from one of the ship-keepers while the boats were away the truth of the previous day's fight, and he had a suitable discipline in mind for the second mate. He was about to say so, when Radley came up with hand extended to Peters and a shamefaced smile on his face. The harpooner gripped that hand as if he meant what the grip implied, and the skipper turned away with a satisfied smile.

THE SCREAMING SKULL

J. Allan Dunn

Outranging the lighter guns of the   , from the start of the fight the skillfully manoeuvered King's ship had been raking the pirate brigantine with a steady fire from a Long Tom mounted in her bows. For three hours they fought, manoeuvering in the smart breeze in the early evening of a glorious day, the crisp seas blue as indigo, yeasty with spin-drift, the smoke of the guns soaring up in puffs like balloons as they were swiftly served by men naked to the waist, wet with sweat, grimed with powder and splashed with blood.

King's man and pirate alike wore bright kerchiefs bound about their brows, but the buccaneers aboard the *Gauntlet* displayed gaudy silken sashes, velvet breeches and high bucket-topped seaboots of leather, whereas the tars trod the sanded decks bare-footed.

Now less than a cable's length away, now nearer half a mile, tacking and veering, striving for the better position, for a rake of the other's deck, the bright red flashes of fire showed belching from the barking dogs of war as pirate's brigantine or the King's corvette rose to the crest of a rolling wave and swift gunners set tow to touch-hole. White splinters flew from the black sides that rose gleaming, varnished with the brine.

The flush-decked corvette, frigate-rigged, was handled with as much precision as the overmanned brigantine, and Swayne cursed as he saw that her captain meant to take full advantage of his heavier metals and repeatedly managed a range where the buccaneer's shot plumped short into the sea.

But at sunset the corvette came down, leaping before a quartering breeze, flinging the seas away magnificently to leeward, buoyant as a cork, her canvas snowy white, the red flag flaming in challenge to Swayne's sable banner, keen to make a finish. The sun hung in the west in a growing confusion of purple cloud and wheeling rays of crimson vapor, wheeling over a background of troubled gold. The clouds overhead were silver-white as pearl on their eastern sides, amber and amethyst toward the west. The two ships, filled with men who longed to be at the death-grapple, to decide the supremacy of law or piracy, seemed inconsequential as they fled on the lifting surface of a sea purple as the skin of grapes.

Swayne strutted in confidence on his quarterdeck, togged out in all the glory that delighted his heart: vermilion, gold-laced coat with a blue sash of silk across it, a wide belt, velvet breeches thrust into boots of Spanish leather, plumes in his hat above his hair that hung below the wide collar, long mustachios fiercely curled, a scar across a nose that bridged out like a prow to his strong face.

Hardly less brave of attire and demeanor was Hoyle, his lieutenant, though his face scowled the more from its pockpittedness than Swayne's from its scar. Hoyle worked the ship, following Swayne's orders. Skinner, the quartermaster, chosen representative of the crew, a check on the captain to a certain extent, stood beside Swayne, his green eyes, flecked with brown spots, watching the corvette, unblinking to the increasing glory of the sunset behind her.

Long of arm and bowed of leg was Skinner, strong and active as a cat. He wore short breeches of striped canvas and a shirt of black silk that fluttered open at his hairy chest. His legs below the knees were bare to the horny soles of the splay feet. A fo'c'stle man was Skinner, though rating counted little in this sea brotherhood. He had pistols and a cutlass that swung unsheathed against the hard muscles of his calf, its edge keen as a razor, keen as the two long dirks in his belt.

Swayne roared an order and Skinner looked at him in a surprise that blended with delight.

"You'll let 'em board?" he shouted above the rush of the wind in the rigging, the seethe of the sea and the reports of the sternchaser that ceased as the helm was put up and the men rushed to the braces.

"We'll meet 'em half way and let the losers go to hell! But we'll set a hurdle or two for 'em to jump. Nettings there. Pikes and cutlasses!"

By the prevailing laws of the Brethren of the Sea, Swayne had the absolute right of determination in all questions concerning fighting, chasing or being chased. In all other matters whatsoever the captain was governed by a majority. His decisions were subject to a later vote if the majority seemed to consider him in the wrong, but here there was no dissenting voice; the pirates believed themselves unmatched at close quarters. The battering from the corvette had enraged them, the pannikins of rum from the broached cask amidships had inflamed their natural deviltry, and they yelled in unison when they saw Swayne meant to come to grips.

* * * *

Axes and pikes and cutlasses were set handy while they worked frantically to stretch the bulwark nettings. On came the King's ship, her men bunched in three groups, some on the yard-arms, some with grappling irons ready to fling aboard. The dazzle of the sunset was in the eyes of the buccaneers but they were used to such matters and they bellowed a brazen defiance as the two ships closed.

Pikes thrust at men, impaling them; axes swung through soft flesh and splintering bone; pistols were fired point-blank, searing and singeing where the bullets entered. Men poured into the brigantine, swarming the nettings actively as baboons, their sharp steel between their teeth, silent but grim as the outlaws of the sea jabbed and struck at them. Men dropped from the yards; there came clash and grate of steel against steel. The grunt of men hard pressed, the groans of the wounded, oaths, yells sounded while the sunset filled the hollows of the waves with blood that mocked the gore that ran on the slippery decks of the *Gauntlet* as men rolled into the scuppers, clutching at each other's wrists and throats, stabbing, slashing.

In the south a squall gathered, hovering while the fight gained fury. Swayne marked it from the corners of his eyes, his lips set, his nostrils wide for better breath as he lunged and parried with his Spanish blade against the onslaught of the corvette's first lieutenant, an old sea-dog with a wrist of steel and the cunning of a master of fence.

Swayne swiftly calculated the chances of victory or defeat, fearing the latter, even for himself in his present issue. He was wounded in the leg by a bullet from the corvette's foretop and at his best he was no match for this man who changed his style of fence at will, who had learned in the schools of France and Italy and Spain and practised them all in bloody battle.

There was no quarter. Every man pirate of them would be hanged at Gallows' Point, Port Royal, if they were taken alive. It had been a mistake to let the King's men board. Slowly but surely they were driving the buccaneers back. Hoyle was down, cleft from shoulder to the middle of his chest by a gigantic seaman whom Swayne himself had spitted the next instant. Skinner was back to the rail, with three or four comrades, fighting like maddened cats against odds.

Swayne shouted for a rally, tried to lead it, and left an opening that was instantly entered by the point of the imperturbable Englishman. The blade ran through his chest and lungs. Swayne stood for a moment with disbelieving amazement in his eyes as the other withdrew his sword and gave him a little nod. His own hilt was suddenly too heavy for his nerveless grasp; his voice failed him; he coughed and fell with a gush of blood from his lips.

The loss of a commander may make for despair of two kinds, the one generated by loss of hope that scatters courage and stays all effort, the other that produces a furious struggle against impending doom. Skinner broke through the cordon that had hemmed him in, hewing a way for himself with his reeking cutlass, his fierce face aflame, filled with the valor of desperation.

"It's over with 'em, lads, or Port Royal for us all!" his great voice roared.

The rally sent the corvette's boarders back to their own deck, cursed at by their officers for cowards, smarting and stiff with wounds, almost spent with the fury of the onslaught, the pirates in little better shape. In the lull the gunner of the *Gauntlet* appeared with case-boxes he had swiftly manufactured during the boarding flurry. They were filled with powder, small shot, slugs and scraps of lead and iron, a sputtering quickmatch in the mouth of each of them as they were flung by lusty arms wherever men grouped aboard the King's ship.

The grenades exploded with frightful execution, scattering their rending contents far and wide. The officers of the corvette jumped to bring order out of the confusion, and lead another charge with fresh men who had not yet been in hand-to-hand conflict. The pirates seized the brief respite to catch their laboring breaths. Swayne was borne down to his cabin; Hoyle left in his own blood—dead.

Then the squall swept down, ravening, fierce and fast, veiling the sunset, darkening sea and sky with its pall. The ships had lain bow-and-stern; now the *Gauntlet* flung into the wind to meet the corvette as she came down it. But the gale came from another quarter. It flung itself upon both vessels, setting the corvette aback as it stormed over its bows, driving the *Gauntlet* ahead as the pirates cut the grappling ropes, glad to see the chance to avoid the mustering boarders, maddened by the bursting of the grenades.

One last battery from the corvette's guns roared out before they were clear, splintering and shattering their quarter. As they rolled to the great waves that enveloped them, leaping and ravening at them out of the roaring blackness, wallowing and plunging before the squall that at once saved them and threatened momentarily to set them on their beam-ends, the carpenter set up a cry for men to start the pumps. The muzzles of the King's ship had been depressed for that farewell broad-side, the cold shot had gone lunging through between wind and water and, with every plunge into the streaking gulfs, water gushed in.

* * * *

Skinner was a seaman, every ugly, efficient inch of him, in all but navigation. And now they had an open sea ahead, to the best of his belief. He had to save ship, to get in sail, to repair rigging shot sway, to hastily fish the foremast, quarter-chewed by a lucky shot, creaking and threatening to go by the board.

At it he went, shouting his orders in that almost Stygian darkness with night following hard on the heels of the squall, overtaking it, mingling with it. Lanterns swung and flitted here and there. The decks were cleared of raffle. In the lee scuppers lay the dead and dying of their own crew and from the corvette. The latter Skinner ordered thrown overboard without shrift or mercy. Their own dead went into the gulping maw of the sea, the wounded taken below.

Within an hour he had done what could be done, save for the needed continuance of the clanking pumps, the mauling and plugging of the carpenter and his mates. The gale shrieked and the sea rose, the tempest leveling the crests and sending it in vast sheets fore and aft; rain fell in torrents and salt and fresh water mingled in a constant flood upon her decks where the scuppers and torn bulwarks eddied as they strove to discharge the waste.

The bellow of the wind outvoiced all thunder, but jagged blades of lightning showed the sable and mountainous clouds from which they came. Still the brigantine held buoyancy; the rags of canvas still set held her from too violent lurching as she rushed down the watery valleys and climbed the seething hills. The pumps gained on the leak and at last the carpenter sealed the shot holes in the stout skin.

Skinner entered the cuddy cabin, below the quarterdeck. A swinging lamp illumined it, filled with the prodigality of loot, silken hangings, rich carpets, cushions on the transoms, a silver crucifix on one wall next to a canvas in a rich frame, both ravished from a Spanish merchantman. Carven furniture, gold plate on the table held by racks.

Outside, through the great stern window, the sea slavered at the glass. On the starboard lounge lay the form of the captain, covered with a rug.

Skinner, bare-legged, the rest of him soaking wet, spilling puddles on the floor, blood on his arms to the elbows, on his face that was framed in hair almost as red, was a repulsive sight. He caught at a flagon of wine that was tucked between cushions, knocked off its neck and drank, regardless of the jagged glass that cut his mouth. He kept at it until he had finished the bottle and, flushed with the heady stuff, flung it crashing against the side of the cabin.

Two men followed him in, Tremaine, the gunner, wide-faced, like an owl, and Raxon, a member of the crew who was looked up to by many of them because of his facility of tongue and flow of language. Raxon was a hatchet-faced sea lawyer, making up in wits what he lacked in bodily strength and favor. Both of them were sopping, smeared with blood and begrimed with powder. Tremaine's gore was partly his own and partly from the men he had fought. That on Raxon came from the dead he had helped to fling overboard. He grinned at Skinner with yellow teeth and a side jerk of his head toward Swayne.

"Dead?" he asked.

Skinner shrugged his shoulders. Tremaine went over to the lounge.

"Did you get it out of him?" asked Raxon.

Skinner stared at him blankly. Something like contempt for the dullness of the other came into the eyes of Raxon. One-time scrivener's clerk was he, shipped from the Port of London in a press-gang that he almost forced himself upon, fearing hue and cry for a murder he had committed; deserter, renegade, rat of the seas, with all a rat's cunning and, perhaps, a rat's courage when driven into a corner. So far he had kept out of corners.

He looked at both his companions, both indispensable to the plan he had in mind, if it was still feasible. If Swayne still lived. For wealth was now being weighed in the uncertain balance of the life of a desperately wounded man. Skinner should be captain. That he lacked navigation was to be lamented but Raxon did not consider that insurmountable. Tremaine, a giant, master gunner, was a necessary factor—not so much so as Skinner perhaps, but Raxon knew that Tremaine admired him and he meant to use the gunner to help him against the other.

Skinner was dull but Tremaine was stupid, away from his calling of gunner-seaman. It would go hard, thought Raxon, if he couldn't use them both to his own ultimate and sole advantage. But—if Swayne was dead?

"He's nigh gone," announced Tremaine, "but there's still breath in him to this mirror." The gunner held up a looking-glass in a frame of rococo silver-gilt and rubbed his great digit through the mist upon it.

"Give him some wine," said Raxon. "Quick! He's got to talk. Look you, Skinner, of all the six men that landed to bury the loot, Swayne alone breathes. The devil himself was against us to-night. First Hoyle killed, then Swayne mortally wounded. Payson, Davis, Poole and Gibbs, every one of them dead—and thrown overboard."

Skinner's eyes, green as sea water, blazed.

"By God!" he cursed as his intelligence reacted to the meaning of the other. "Then Swayne alone knows the place where the treasure's buried,"

"Hoyle and Swayne were the only ones who ever really knew. The other four could have led us close to it. They've gone. Does he take the wine, Tremaine?"

"Aye. He sighed. His eyes are open, but they see nothing."

"They will. Give him more wine. Smile at him, you fool. Make him think you, we are his friends. Skinner, you must do the talking, since you represent the crew. Easy at first, you see? Easy, or he'll die on us. Look."

He had come to the lounge with Skinner and the three of them hung solicitously over the dying man. Raxon drew aside the laced coat, unfastened the cambric shirt with its tucks and frills all wet and red, and showed the slightly puckered wound where the sword had pierced him. Through it oozed crimson froth at every labored breath that barely lifted the captain's chest.

Raxon cursed softly.

"We need a chirurgeon aboard," he said. "He's got to talk. Skinner, you said there was brandy aft. Get it. The wine's not strong enough."

The effect of the cordial opened the captain's eyes again. This time there was recognition in them, but no especial friendliness. He seemed to recognize the errand upon which they had come, catching him on the edge of the gulf of death, bringing him back for their own purposes. The loot that he and Hoyle had buried had been their own accumulated shares of long looting. The crew had long since spent their shares with gaming and women.

* * * *

The *Gauntlet* had been careened for cleaning in an inlet of the Carolina sea Islands when Governor Rodgers arrived at the Isle of Providence with the king's pardon for all buccaneers surrendering in person before the date set as the limit of grace. Swayne, not arriving, had been proscribed but, following the example of Captain Charles Vane, he made no attempt to surrender.

Vane was now delivered over to the law at Jamaica by the men who took him from the island in the Bay of Honduras where he had been wrecked. There were cruisers out rounding up notorious commanders, and Swayne deemed it prudent, lest he be over-hauled, killed, captured or sunk, to bury his treasure for the benefit of his wife and children. Much of it had been taken under privateering rules, most of it from the Spaniards, and he considered it lawful and hard-earned proceeds. Hoyle, a Carolina man like Swayne, and married to the captain's cousin, followed his example.

A boat's crew of four had rowed them ashore to one of the islands lying between Savannah and Charleston, and between Port Royal and Saint Helena Sound. The chest was carried ashore and set down while Swayne selected a place for the men to dig. Before they had finished, according to the measure he had given them, he and Hoyle, who had stepped away, reappeared and told them that they need dig no more, that the chest was already disposed of. Certain other precautions were taken and the boat returned with the crew somewhat chagrined, dimly perceiving that they had been cleverly prevented from ever divulging the place where the loot was buried. It was a shrewd move and Raxon, for one, appreciated it. It was as effective as if Swayne had followed the procedure of other commanders and killed the diggers on the spot lest they talk too much.

"Cap'en," said Skinner, trying to make his hoarse voice pleasant, to cajole his villainous features into a look of sympathy. "You're goin' fast. We've shook off the bloody corvette an' give 'em a taste of hell when Tremaine, here, fixes the case-boxes. So, Skipper, we've saved the ship."

Swayne looked at him with eyes that fixed themselves on the quartermaster's face questioningly. Raxon jabbed the questioner in the ribs.

"Out with it," he prompted. "He'll not last long. Out with it. Fair means or foul. 'Tis a fortune."

"For all hands," backed up Tremaine.

Raxon darted him a look of scorn.

"For three of us, anyway," he corrected. "Let me at him, Skinner."

Skinner gave way, acknowledging the better brain.

"Skipper," said Raxon, his weasel face close down, "you're bound for heaven or hell. In the first place they say there's gold an' jewels like sand and pebbles of the sea. You can't take yours with ye to either one. Left behind in the sand, 'tis only a mockery of what we all fought for. Look you, tell us where 'tis hid, give us a fair share of it for our trouble, and we'll see the rest conveyed to your wife."

Pleased with his own craft, his face half in shadow, Raxon winked at his comrades, who grinned back.

"We'll swear to that, Skipper, on anything ye like. Hoyle's gone but we'll do the like with him." Swayne's eyes held a light in them that made Raxon's voice grow suddenly hard. It was an uncertain light, like the leaping flame of a candle that is guttering down, but it showed mockery and decision for all its fitfulness.

"You can lie to your mates with your glib tongue, Raxon," he said faintly, "but you can't lie to me. Think you I swallow your cant?"

"You wrong us, Skipper. Believe me, 'twill go better with you if you tell us."

"Only fools threaten dying men. The loot will not be lost. The corvette will report the fight and my mortal wound. When that news gets out, Raxon, you fox, I have friends who know its location and will unearth it for those to whom it belongs."

"They'll never get it," said Raxon fiercely. Then, as Swayne smiled at him, he broke into sudden fury. "Give me your dirk, Skinner," he cried. "Tremaine, draw off his boots an' set the lamp to his feet. I'll give you a foretaste of hell, Swayne, if you don't tell."

"So brave? And jumping to my word when I was whole. You dogs! Think you I would trust you? I'm going, Raxon, where you and these two scoundrels cannot follow—as yet. It is in my mind that you will not be long in coming. I'll see to 't—I'll see to 't—" he wheezed, the red froth bubbling about the slit in his chest— "that ye are well received." And he grinned at them out of a face almost as white as his teeth.

"We know the island," muttered Raxon. "We'll dig it over foot by foot but what we'll find it."

"'Twill be a pleasant task. So, you're willing to work for it? I'll give you a cue to follow, lads, as my last words."

The syllables grew fainter, farther and farther apart. It might be that Swayne spoke against time to avoid torture, knowing how close he was to the end. His eyes still mocked them; his teeth gleamed, for he seemed unable to part them and his words hissed.

"Here's a lead for you, my bullies—and, on the word of a dying man, 'tis a good one—go, find your island, if Skinner there doesn't cast you ashore, then ask the secret of the screaming skull!"

He started to laugh; the mirth grew hideous as it changed into a rattle, then a gurgle, as blood broke through his relaxed jaw.

The three looked at each other with eyes that rolled back to the corpse.

"There was a skull," said Skinner slowly. "The black said so—and he said it screamed. Give me that brandy. A murrain on him!"

They drank deeply but hurriedly and they left the cabin. As the ship tossed, the shadows were flung wildly by the gimballed lamp. They flickered on the still features of the dead man, and Raxon, turning as they went out of the cuddy, could have sworn that Swayne, from the far side of the grave, was laughing at them, silently and mockingly.

* * * *

Skinner was voted captain, taking up his quarters in the great stern cabin, wearing boots and velvets, gold lace and a hat with a red plume in it as visible signs of his advancement. There were few of the rough crew who considered the matter of navigation or doubted that Skinner could take them anywhere. He himself believed that he would have slight difficulty in reaching the coast of the Carolinas and entering on the sea islands. As to finding the island of the treasure, he convinced himself that that was equally easy.

Gibbs, the negro who had been in the boat that took the chest ashore, was not dead. Another black had been mistaken for him in the confusion after the fight. Gibbs was wounded badly and was astounded at the care he received until the three considered him able to get out of his fo'c'sle bunk and come aft for a talk, filled with gratitude.

He was not overly bright, which suited their purpose, since they planned—or rather Raxon planned, and was clever enough to let Skinner think he advanced much of the scheme—to keep the loot for themselves.

To that end Skinner used his influence to get Raxon appointed quartermaster. Tremaine remained gunner with his semi-official rating and his extra share. All of the crew had entry right to the cabin, but it was necessary for the three plotters to meet often and these ranks made their conferences seem a part of the barkentine's routine.

To the crafty scrivener's clerk his quarter-mastership seemed a rare joke. He was supposed to look after the interest of the crew he was determined upon keeping out of all knowledge and share of the rich booty. There was one weak spot. Some of them might remember the treasure, especially when the barkentine again entered the sea island estuaries.

But Skinner had not thought of it, or Tremaine; it had been Raxon's wits that took him to the cabin in time to try to get some clue from the dying skipper. For that, he knew that Tremaine and Skinner both respected him, though Skinner's recognition was underlaid with a temper that Raxon handled carefully. Skinner wanted to be the master and Raxon wanted the precious metals, the gems and jewelry that had gone aboard in the chest. So he pandered to the new skipper, flattered him, moulded him like putty.

The condition of the barkentine gave them excuse for putting in somewhere to refit, and to lay low until the cruisers left those waters. Rum was served freely and the men went to bed drunk and arose "half seas over," swearing that the cruise was the right sort and Skinner a proper commander. Thus Raxon calculated to keep any of them from thinking.

He suggested that, since the *Gauntlet* had entered the maze of sea islands by Saint Helena Sound, it would be a good plan for them to go in this time by Port Royal, lest some memory be jogged and, with it the question of the loot brought up. To this Skinner assented. The liquor he swigged kept his confidence in his own powers well cocked, though he remembered the general similarity of the islands, with occasional broad reaches, with rivers flowing into them at one end and tortuous passages amongst them. There was a rude chart aboard, and they could impress a native Indian pilot and work their way to the island of the skull.

For there was a skull, fastened high to a dead pine, and Gibbs told in the cabin one night how it was placed there.

"Cap'en an' Hoyle go asho' first," he said. "Tell us to bring er-long dat ches'. Mighty heavy dat ches'. We couldn' tote it wiv our hands so we put rope about it an' sling two pole. Den we hoist it to shoulder. We row boat in I'll crick an' bye-by we come to bayou. Big 'gator in dat bayou. Time we go out, gittin' dahk, an' dose bull 'gator dey beller like thundeh.

"Big ridge on dat islan'. Pine on ridge. Liveoak an' moss all erlong dat bayou. Magnolia tree. Cactus an' spike-plant plenty. Plenty brush. Plenty deer erlong dat way. An' snake. White-mouf wateh-snake. Ef he bite you, you finish. Wil' pig erlong dat place. Rabbit an' pa'tridge. Win' blow low an' sad throo dem tree. Hants erlong dat place."

Tremaine started to curse at the negro's tediousness, but Raxon checked him with a look and passed more rum to Gibbs. He wanted to get all the negro knew.

"Pow'ful hahd time totin' dat trunk. Cap'en he lead to top of hill. Look oveh otheh islan, an' den one mo' island out to sea. Den we neahly fall oveh something in bresh. Golly! Dat bad voodoo conjuh fo' dose t'ree men erlong wid me. Dead man in de bresh. Ant take all flesh, long time. Davis an' Poole in front. Dey step in rib, mighty nigh trip dem. Payson back wid me. He stumble too. I see white bone. No touch me.

"Cap'en look an' laugh. He pick up dat skull. He hand to Hoyle. I tell him it mighty bad voodoo. I tell him every one touch dose bone die mighty soon. Why fo' I know? Becuse my mudder con-juh-woman. I see li'l snake glide out erlong dat skull befo' cap'en take it up. Dat spirit of dat man.

"Cap'en tuhn oveh dat skull plenty time an' say something to Hoyle erbout makin' dat hant watch oveh dat chest. 'Nail it to tree,' he say. Den I know they gwine to die. I mighty scared niggeh myse'lf. But I not tech any dat bone. Mighty careful how I walk."

Tremaine was listening now with dropped jaw. The negro told his tale so well with intonation and gesture that they could see the thing happening under their eyes and Raxon alone was untouched with superstition. Gibbs's skin had grayed with the renewed terror of the affair; his eyes projected from their sockets and rolled with flashing whites under the cuddy lamp.

"Ev'ry one tech dose bones die, 'cept me," he said solemnly. "An' me—I come mighty close."

Even Raxon got a touch of something weird and looked toward the stern window, fancying a cold draught had crossed and slightly lifted the hair on his scalp. He shoved the goblet at Gibbs and told him to go on. The negro drained it and his skin regained its glossy plum-blackness.

"We git top of dat ridge," he said. "Mighty glad to set down dat ches! Cap'en he tell us where to dig. We bring mattock an' pick erlong, stuck in ropes. Ax too. Cap'en he take axe an' cut sapling—so long. Tell us to dig dat deep. Den he an' Hoyle go off in woods fo' li'l while."

"Did he take a shovel?" Tremaine leaned forward, shooting out the question eagerly, screwing up his eyes at the others.

"No, suh. Dey take ax erlong. Take fowling piece. Dey 'low to shoot pa'tridge. Take skull. We dig, easy at first through sand. Den come rock. Mighty ha'd work, but we know cap'en he 'sist on dat hole bein' deep erlong dat sapling he cut. We sweat; sun staht to go down. All of us in hole so deep no one can see out. Throw up rocks. Bimeby wateh come in fas' but now de sapling reach to bottom an' we climb out.

"Den cap'en shoot, two time. Bimeby shoot two mo'. Bull 'gator beller back in bayou. Bird fly. Buzzut fly erlong. Dat voodoo bird. Den I heah something go tap-tap—loud, like woodpeckeh on holler tree. I look up an' I see cap'en climb way up dead pine, nail white t'ing to tree. Sun low an' shine red. Shine on dat t'ing. By golly, dat de skull!

"Win' staht to blow. 'Gator beller. Buzzut wheel. Cap'en he come down. Come back wid Hoyle. We 'speck he tell us go git ches' an' put in hole, an' I mighty glad to git troo, git off dat islan'. But he only laugh an' say, 'Nem'mine, boys. Job's all oveh. We fix ches'.' Golly, we dig fo' not'ing at all."

The three exchanged glances.

"How far away was the hole from where you put down the chest," Raxon asked.

"I dunno. Mebbe ten rod, mebbe twenty. Mighty hahd to jedge in all dat bresh."

"You think you can find the place?"

Gibbs did not know, but his life hung on the answer. The same thought was in all their minds; it needed but a look between them to leap and kill the man and silence his tongue for ever, to toss him through the stern window into the wake—once they had pumped him dry.

"I don' want to go on dat place agen," he said.

"Could you find it?"

"I reckon so."

They relaxed. Now they would swear him to secrecy, make him a steward, keep him aft, watch him day and night until they got him ashore—drunk, if needs be. They would sober him up at the point of pistol and dirk and force him to bring them to where they would see the skull—or, if the winds had blown it down, at least point out the tree.

"Win' blow hahd when we tuhn back," Gibbs continued. "Howl an' cry. An' den I hear terrible scream. I look back. It come from dat skull!

"Two buzzut circle low oveh dat tree. An' I say, 'Laig, save de body,' an' I run, wid de cap'en laughin' behin' me. 'Gator beller, snake rustle troo de bresh, but I come to de boat. Bimeby dey all come. We go back to ship. What happen? Hoyle die. Cap'en die. Payson, Poole, Davis, all die. How come, suppose dat not voo-doo?"

"The voodoo's worked out now, Gibbs," said Raxon. "Have some more rum. Captain Skinner's goin' to make you steward. You'll sleep in the cuddy. You'll have it soft, Gibbs, with good things to eat an' drink. But, understand, don't you tell that yarn any more. No sense in getting the crew scared. You keep your tongue quiet an' we'll see you get paid for it."

Gibbs showed his ivory teeth in a broad grin.

"Cap'en," he said. "I'm mighty 'bliged. Yes, suh. An' I keep quiet as a winteh terrapin. Me, I don't like talk 'bout dat t'ing."

They sent him forward for his dunnage and Raxon talked fast.

"The skull's a guide of some sort. They took no mattock. They must have found some sort of cave to hide the chest. We'll find it. We've got to find it!"

He saw Skinner's green eyes watching him covertly and he read them, though he affected not to, translating Skinner's thoughts by his own.

"He thinks what's big for three will be bigger for one, he told himself. He's right. I'll make trouble between him and Tremaine. Let one kill the other. Kill each other, if I've luck."

"What made the skull scream?" asked Tremaine.

"It didn't. It was a bird—owl likely. The black was scared stiff."

"Swayne said it screamed. He expected it to scream."

"Maybe he thinks he'll haunt it. It'll take more than a talking skull to keep me from that loot. Eh, Skinner?"

Skinner grunted and knocked the neck off a fresh bottle of brandy.

* * * *

The *Gauntlet* arrived off the low land of Port Royal Sound in the afternoon, doing little more than drifting over a sea that showed hardly a ripple, rising and falling in deep heaves of round swell, the wind, in cats' paws, ruffling the surface and sending the brigantine ahead with little more than steerageway. Her bottom was fouled with long tropical cruising; only the most imperative repairs had been made since the fight. Her water supply was low and foul, and she was in sore need of refitting, careening and the sailmaker's art.

It was fact that none of the crew had drawn a sober breath for days, and this afternoon they were roaring, singing drunk, the intoxication doubled by the Carolina heat that made the pitch show in little beads along the deck planking.

They were all agreeable to entrance into Broad River, where Skinner promised them carousal with plenty of fish and fruit and game while they repaired ship. But Skinner's low brow was creased with care, and Raxon's weasel features looked pinched and anxious.

The same corvette that they had fought had sighted them that morning and had chased them all that day. Luck had been with them in the favor of the variable winds or the corvette, always the faster and the cleaner-bottomed of the two, would surely have overhauled them, at least have got within range of her superior cannon and pounded them to surrender. Thrice they reopened distance that had been gained and sailed on with a slant of favoring breeze while the corvette hung with slack canvas, gripped by the

Gulf Current that set them to the north and leeward of what wind did blow.

To the men, drinking mock healths to the King's ship, yelling bawdy songs, the *Gauntlet* had outsailed the other, showed a fair pair of heels. Now, with the corvette hull down, her canvas, hung wide and high for every puff of the fickle wind, gleaming like a fragment of pearl against the misty horizon, they considered the chase fairly over and jeered at the enemy.

"They'll see us in through their glass," said Skinner moodily. "They'll either follow us or they'll cruise on and off outside between here and Saint Helena Sound like a cat before two mouse-holes, knowing we've got to come out of one or the other."

"Why?" asked Tremaine. "Couldn't we make our way inland, once we've got the loot?"

"Yemassee Injuns revolted three years back," said Skinner. "They got beaten but they ain't forgotten it. Then there's the Cherokees. It's all salt marsh for God knows how many miles back. Swamps on swamps. The 'skeeters 'ud kill us if the Injuns didn't."

"Or the fevers," put in Raxon. "Carolina ague's worse than the rack. Look you, this ship's consort is like to be at Charles' Town. She may send word. Leave one outside while the other follows us in. Or one come one way, t'other another. 'Tis what I'd do. The odds are too strong to risk against such treasure, to my mind. But—" his gaze traveled craftily from Skinner to Tremaine and back again—"if those drunken fools are of a mind to fight, let's give them their belly's full. Fight they must, for that cruiser is rather bull-dog than cat, to my mind. They'll never quit and, by that token, we must be about the last buccaneer of the old fleet. The game's dead and now is the time to quit.

"What think you of this plan? If yon cruiser does not follow us in too closely—"

"She'll not do that," said Skinner. "We'll creep in on the last of the flood, if this wind holds. They'll have the ebb to stem, and the tides run fast and strong. Let us get in and I'll warrant us being let alone till morning."

"Good."

"We've had luck, so far." Skinner went on. "It may hold. The glass is uncertain. This is the hurricane season. 'Twould not surprise me to see it blow before morning, and we'll find a good lee anchorage in case of it. But your plan, Raxon; what of it?"

"'Twas suggested by a word of yours, Captain," said Raxon with a sly wink at Tremaine, whereby he established with the latter the fact that he flattered Skinner for policy and for peace. "There is a pinnace hangs above the stern window on its davits. A small boat, but large enough for four, together with provisions, and yet leaving room for—let us say—a chest. It has seemed to me not altogether fair that we should glean the booty and leave the crew no share—though they have indeed had and spent their share of it and what we take is but for our pains and trouble to see that the wives and children of Swayne and Hoyle are not left to penury.

"Yet, I say, I have a tender conscience, like the both of you. It irks me to feel that each is not left well treated at the last and I think we have agreed that this is like to be the last of the Brethren of the Coast for a whiles.

"So, why not let us provision this boat? Let us leave with the crew our blessing and the ship for their own uses and devices while we go see the loot. For this a small boat will serve as well, perhaps better. Gibbs can row when the wind is not favorable. And, since these foolish fellows might not appreciate the fairness with which we mean to treat them, it might be as well to depart sometimes in the night, this or the next or when it seems most suitable. Or we might go ashore to seek for fresh water and not be able to find our way back. The point is, we make the crew a gift of the good ship *Gauntlet* and all she holds."

"Sink me!" cried Tremaine, clapping his great hand on his thigh with a report like a pistol. "Sink me, Raxon, if you ain't a fox!"

"Nay, give credit where credit is due. I but work out the details from the ideas that the captain, here, sets in my brain."

Skinner chuckled in high good humor. It struck his fancy to leave the crew to wait the inevitable attack by the King's men, holding the empty sack. That was a rare joke and, since he had been given the credit of it, he laughed the more. The touch about the wives and children also amused him.

"We'll see how all works out," he said. "Here is the chart with the sea islands lying close as eggs in a basket, yet with waterways between that are fairly navigable. We'll work up inside close to

Saint Helena Sound, yet carefully, lest the corvette's consort meet us there. Then we'll take boat at midnight. I would give much to see their faces next morning when they find us gone. As for finding us, had they the spirit, as soon discover a pin in a haystack."

"Where'll we go," asked Tremaine, prac-tically, "after we get the loot?"

"Make up the coast for Charles' Town itself. There will be none to positively identify us with the *Gauntlet*. We need show no more of value than will pay our way, or, should there come necessity, 'tis said the governor doth greatly admire the palm of his hand when 'tis gilded. He gets nothing from the cruisers and he has seen more than one buccaneer. Or we can go on to the settlement at Georgetown, or further still, by inland waters, to Albemarle on the Chowan River, where men from Virginia have established them-selves. We can trade the small boat for a larger to some logwood trader, perchance, either by purchase—or other-wise."

* * * *

As the day waned the breeze grew more and more fitful and at. last failed altogether. Now the corvette had the advantage of a breeze further out and came bowling along until her hull lifted.

Skinner ordered the boats out for towing so that they might cross the bar and get fairly into the river before the tide turned. The men refused.

He argued with them for a few minutes, pointing out the neces-sity of taking advantage of the turn of the tide against their pursu-ers, of the probability that, if they did not take out their boats, the seaward breeze would bring the corvette close enough to send shot plumping aboard.

"It's fight or pull, you dogs!" he told them at last. "Take your choice. You can sit and handle oars, but I'm damned if there's one of ye sober enough, to stand upright or see straight, let alone fight. Row, and to-night we'll rest easy, to-morrow we'll feast. Stay here and the most of ye'll be stewing in hell by midnight—and I'll be the first to send some of ye there to tell the devil the rest are com-ing.

"Cross me, will you?" he shouted in fury. "Into those boats, you scum! Into them and pull yourselves sober."

In an instant he was down among them, his sword, once Swayne's, pricking and fleshing them, with Tremaine at his back swinging a cutlass and Raxon looking down from the rail of the poop. One man protested and Skinner shot him through the mouth.

"I'll brook no mutiny," he thundered. "You make me skipper and I'll make ye skip. Look at the corvette coming up hand over hand, you mongrel fools."

The breeze still with her, the cruiser was coming up fast. As they gazed they saw a small ball of white detach itself from her gleaming side and the boom of a gun came faintly over the water.

"That's not for us," said Skinner. "'Tis a signal to her consort. Now, you swabs, will you row and go clear, or stay and be bilboed and hung?"

The boats were outswung, manned and soon the *Gauntlet* began to move slowly but surely toward the shore. Another gun sounded from the cruiser. It was not likely that they were wasting ammunition on the chase at such a distance. The consort would inevitably heave in sight before long. Doubtless they could see her already from the corvette's masthead.

"We'll beat 'em yet," said Skinner. He snuffed the air, looked high and low, scanned the horizon and then went into the cuddy for a look at his glass.

"There'll be no hurricane to-night," he told Raxon and Tremaine. "But we'll make the bar half an hour before the turn. And then our dogs can tow us up the river and out of sight. To hell with the corvette and her consort, too. We'll spend that money yet, fling it to the lasses an' put a jewel on their fingers for a kiss. Eh, lads? We'll ruffle it yet with the best in New York City or belike in London Town itself. We'll pass for rich merchants and choose us each some wealthy wench to wed when we are tired of light-o'-loves!"

Raxon turned to hide the sneer he could not control at the idea of Skinner posing as a merchant, or wooing a rich man's daughter. He had his own ambitions and on their horizon neither Tremaine nor Skinner showed.

The three had the deck to themselves with all the crew still slaving at the sweeps. Skinner put Gibbs at the wheel and the three took the chance to fully provision the stern pinnace, too small for use in towing. Now it was ready for their use at any time, the stowage covered with canvas long before the sweating and sobered men came aboard. The river had curved; the entrance was out of sight, the corvette lost in purple haze as the sun went down.

Still the wind proved freaky. With twilight, a breeze began to blow from the southwest, the prevailing wind of that latitude, coming down the valleys of the rivers that emptied into the isleted estuary. Skinner sought to take advantage of it and follow up the wide and seemingly deep channel. They could see banks of reeds backed by palmettos. Back of them, chinquapin oak, live oak draped with long streamers of moss and thicket plantations of pines. All was on low ground, much of it tidal.

Through the evening sky moved lines of cranes, great flocks of belated ducks coming in from the night. They saw buzzards wheeling and once, when the barkentine tacked, in the momentary silence before she came about, they heard the Carolina nightingale, the mocking bird, that knows no special hours of song. Fish leaped all about them; porpoises and dolphins rolled and the great rays leaped to fall with a resounding crash. Shut in from the sea, here seemed an inter-island paradise—save for the mosquitoes, hovering in clouds.

It was partly the mosquitoes, partly the terrific force of the ebb, increasing momentarily in power and violence as they advanced that proved their undoing. Skinner sought to find anchorage where the breeze would be the strongest and blow the pests from the ship. They passed two islands between which the tide came eddying and swirling to join the main stream.

There was a leadsman in the chains but the men had started drinking again with their supper when they came abroad from towing, and doubtless the man was incapable. The thing came about suddenly enough yet gently, as the *Gauntlet*, clutched by the tide, nosed on a bar of soft but clinging mud and sand, glided on until suddenly she came up with sails shivering, held fast.

Skinner swore volubly but, beneath his cursing, made up his mind that this was the night for their desertion of the barkentine and the crew. On the falling tide they could not hope to get the *Gauntlet* off, nor was there much chance of getting off by kedging and warping, even on the top of the flood, so deep had she keeled into the stuff that would hold her faster yet before the tide changed.

But he did not announce this. After his first outburst, mainly directed at the man with the lead, he made light of the situation.

"It's only soft bottom. No damage. This is a good place to stay till she floods again. Right in the breeze."

He got two fiddles going, had rum brought up and before two hours the deck was a pandemonium that might almost have been heard outside at sea.

If the corvette had sent in boats then the barkentine would have been an easy conquest. To the tunes of the fiddles men howled ribald ditties and danced clumsily, locked with each other like bears broken into a distillery. Raxon watched all from the poop rail, Tremaine beside him, while Skinner mingled at first with the men, edging them on to the intoxication that would presently turn to maudlin daze and then oblivion.

The eyes of the ex-scrivener's clerk glittered, his nostrils dilated. He seemed almost to quiver with repressed activity, like the weasel he was. His brain was busy with many things. Tremaine, big, stolid, leaned his great forearms on the broad rail. Gibbs hovered in the background, waiting orders to bring fresh mugs of wine for the quarterdeck gentry. Tremaine swigged down some rare Xeres as indifferently as if it had been small beer. Raxon drank more appreciatively, more sparingly. He liked the warmth of the wine, the flavor, the effect that charged his courage. But he wanted to keep his head clear.

"Have you had any words with Skinner?" he asked Tremaine.

"Me? None. What of it?"

"Nothing. Tremaine—" he hesitated a moment—"mark you, you are my friend and with them I play fair to the last drop, the last coin. I may be wrong but Skinner seems to grudge you your share in this loot. He seems to fear that you will give us away by your behaviour after we get clear. Nothing outright, mind you, but little doubts that are close to slurs and put, so I think, to sound me as to whether I agree with him. Skinner will bear watching, Tremaine."

"'Stap me, but if I catch him in treachery I'll wring his neck. I'll tear the windpipe out of him and make him chew on't," growled the giant.

"Go easy, man. I'm not sure. If I am, at any time, I'll tell you. Meantime you and I are with each other. We'll pledge to that. Gibbs!"

His face hidden in his cup Raxon grinned, knowing he had sown the swiftly developing seeds of unrest and mistrust in Tremaine's simple mind.

* * * *

Two hours after midnight they were away. The crew lay about the decks in stupor as Raxon and Skinner came up to the poop and lowered the pinnace without a splash. Then, from the stern window, all four swarmed down the ropes and cast off. Gibbs took the sculls and, pulling athwart the current, rowed them up a creek, though he protested against landing there.

"Too dahk fo' to see," he said, "but plenty 'gator lie on dem bank. Swish you wid tail an' you go into wateh—dat end of you. Bimeby, flood come, dey all go into hole undeh wateh. Betteh wait till flood come erlong, wait till sun come up."

"It's a good idea—curse the mosquitoes!" said Raxon. "Think you. the corvette will be in on the flood, Skinner? If so we might lay low and watch what happens." He chuckled in the darkness as if he were looking forward to witnessing a play.

Skinner could match that mood and did so. Tremaine said nothing. Whatever he might have thought concerning the treachery of their desertion was overbalanced by the glitter of gold and jewels that was ever before his eyes.

They all smoked constantly to protect themselves from insect bites, swigging occasionally at the liquor they had brought along, dozing off until the negro wakened them. Dawn was in the sky; Vs of ducks were aflight with the strings of cranes and herons. The tide was high up in the reeds and still rising fast.

Gibbs's eyes showed bursting; his ears seemed to be pricked forward.

"I hear plenty rowing," he said in an awed whisper.

They all listened. Plain to their accustomed hearing came the click-clack of oars in the pins, sounding across the water, far off. They knew it did not come from the *Gauntlet*, did not threaten themselves. Down along the reeds to the exit of the creek they hauled with their hands. Before they quite reached it the sound had ceased but they saw a little flotilla of four cutters, oars shipped now and lugs set to the light wind. Swiftly the cutters came on the incoming tide, making for the barkentine where the buccaneers snored on in drunken sleep. They could see the level sunlight catch and twinkle on weapons, on accoutrements of the officers.

"There'll be rare fun soon," said Skinner. "We're well out of it."

But there was little spectacular about the thing that happened, save for its ending. The cutters were close to the *Gauntlet* before some buccaneer with a splitting head and swollen tongue sought the water tub and sighted them, striving to arouse his stupefied comrades in time for a futile resistance. Hardly a shot was fired. From the creek mouth they could see the flash of blades and hear a few shouts promptly followed by hurrahs that were undoubtedly the cheers of British seamen. It was all over in a few minutes. Then the corvette appeared, following up her boats on the lifting tide, a signal weft flying. A cutter stroked back to her, received orders and returned.

The pirates were bundled overside into the sterns of the boats, huddled under the pistols of their conquerors, bound for judgment and the penalty of their acts as proscribed men. Had the *Gauntlet* been surrendered at Providence, any irregularities would have been winked at and, though probably any present loot would have been appropriated, past offences would have been assumed to have been committed under privateering custom against the King's enemies. Letters of marque were readily enough obtained from venal commissioners and the surrendering buccaneers were given the benefit of a doubt as to their sincerity in adhering strictly to the articles of their commissions.

But these poor wretches were bound for Execution Point, there to swing as examples of those who had defied the King's leniency. Skinner jeered at them and Raxon grinned silently, his tongue showing between his teeth. Tremaine, gold-blinded, looked on without comment. Only Gibbs muttered something in commiseration of his late comrades till Skinner turned fiercely on him.

"Quiet, you black dog! But for us you'd be with them."

"They got 'em asleep," said Raxon. "They've never missed us. They'd not ask for us by rank, knowing they killed Swayne. It may never come out till the trial that we got away. Look, they've set the ship afire!"

"Too much trouble to get her off for a prize," said Skinner with a shrug, as smoke curled up from both hatches and swiftly increased. "That's the end of her. Let's be getting back into cover."

Raxon began to laugh, silently.

"It is rare," he said when his fit was over. "Yon corvette's captain goes bragging that he has killed Swayne. The news goes to Swayne's relatives—if he told the truth in that matter—and they will presently come down to find the treasure—and find it gone."

"Art so sure of finding it?" asked Tremaine.

"Aye," answered Skinner with a snarl. "If we dig the island over."

They did not dare show themselves in the open for fear their absence might be marked, the question of the loot brought up. For two days they did not dare to light a fire and, at the end of that time, they were lost in the labyrinth of the islands where blind channels led into marshes and baffled them fifty times. Reeds grew high above them in the passages and the rough chart was worse than useless. They saw no Indian pirogues nor sign of natives.

On the third day, their best edibles gone, they caught fish and found oysters, not daring to fire a shot at the game they saw. This time they landed and waded to high land to find wood and broil their catch. The mosquitoes plagued them by day and tormented them by night, despite smudges. The bites festered; fevers came on them with chills that held them gripped with ague and left them weak as children.

Gibbs climbed a tree and announced that he saw the main channel and no signs of the cruiser. So they worked their tedious way to open water and crossed it, veering north and seaward, bearing in mind the negro's description of the two islands he had seen between him and the sea from the island of the screaming skull. Now they began to calculate how soon the dead captain's relatives might come with explicit directions.

They were prepared to fight, to murder for the loot; but suppose they arrived too late? They had been ten days in the maze of marshes and islands that were separated and made true islands only at high tide. In the channels, masked by reeds and palmettos, the currents raced, as often against them as in the direction they wished to go, wasting their time. They grew morose in speculation of it. No longer were they three joined in one enterprise. Skinner seldom talked to them and Raxon ever stirred the poison he had brewed in the mind of Tremiane, with Skinner's attitude to color his suggestion.

The big man glowered at Skinner, becoming obsessed with the idea that the other was plotting how to obtain the loot for himself, though Skinner's main worry was that they had lost too much time. Once he set the blame on Raxon for suggesting the small-boat cruise, but Raxon, fairly sure by now of Tremaine's support, snarled back and reminded him that he, as captain, was responsible for the *Gauntlet* having run aground.

Gibbs watched the three white men with rolling eyes, his blubber lips seldom opened in speech. He was the slave of them all, rowing hour after hour while they lolled in the stern sheets, catching their provender, cooking it, and dreading more and more, as they worked up to where they thought the island lay, that the voodoo of the dead man and the skull would surely be worked upon him for coming back into its province.

* * * *

Two more days passed, spent in coasting islands and looking through Gibbs's eyes for familiar signs, searching the trees for one that bore a white object. Their cocksureness faded; they accused Gibbs of misleading them, of deliberately passing signs he knew, threatening him, shaking with malaria, burning with fever, their bones aching with the back breaking dengue.

It was Raxon who, at dawn one morning, shook the rest—save Gibbs—and pointed out, across a wide stretch of golden water, an island with a ridge running lengthwise. The ridge was set with pines and on one of these, near the center, something caught the early light and flared like a ball of fire, then faded to white as the sun rose and the light slid down from the tree-tops.

They gazed at it with jaws agape and straining eyes. It was the island of the skull!

"Say nothing to the black till we get him ashore," whispered Raxon. "He'll not notice it if we set our course right. If he knew it he might balk."

"Let him," said Skinner. "Let him try to thwart us."

But they took Raxon's advice, distracting Gibbs's attention till they had started when he, with his back to the bows of the pinnace, could see nothing. Yet he sensed something. As they neared the shores and looked for a landing, he suddenly stopped rowing.

"Go on," ordered Skinner, but the negro's face seemed to have fallen in, the broad nostrils seemed pinched, the cheeks hollowed, and the flesh was gray and beaded with sweat.

"It de place," he muttered. "Voodoo brought us here."

"Is that the creek you rowed up with Swayne and Hoyle?" demanded Skinner. Gibbs nodded mutely. "Then go up it."

"No, suh. If I go ashore dat place I die fo' suah. No, suh! I don' go."

Skinner whipped out the pistol he had primed and kept beside him on the stern seat.

"You'll die now, if you don't go on," he said grimly. "Row."

"Buccra," pleaded Gibbs, while the tide set them down, past the creek entrance. "Voodoo on dat place. You all die suppose you go. I not go."

His oars trailed. Skinner raised the pistol. The flint lifted. "Take up those oars, you dog!"

Gibbs looked pleadingly at Raxon and Tremaine, but got no sign of pity. The same thing was in the mind of all of them. They had sighted the skull. They could find the excavation that had never been filled in. He could do little more for them. They had never meant him to share the loot and become a danger to them. He was doomed.

Suddenly the negro sprang up and leaped overside, swimming out into the channel. Skinner sighted deliberately and fired. The bullet struck Gibbs at the base of the skull and he sank instantly.

"Let the 'gators eat him," said Skinner. "Tremaine, will you row."

The giant pulled vigorously and they passed in, landing at what seemed a convenient place. Through cactus and agave, through thickets of palmetto and thorny briars, they fought their panting way each intent, in that mad race, on reaching the ridge and finding the pine, heedless of the others. Once they passed a pool where alligators floated like great logs and, skirting it, Skinner narrowly missed being bitten by a water moccasin. He slashed off its head with the cutlass he carried as a brush cutter.

The fever caught Tremaine and he pulled up, shaking and spent. The others did not heed him until they heard his exultant shout. He had found the hole dug by the four men who had died. It was half full of water.

Now they hunted under the hot sun like dogs on a rich scent, thrashing through the brush, seeking caves in a likely looking ledge of sandstone. Noon came and exhausted, torn, bloody, grimed and soaking wet with their own hot sweat, their tongues hanging out of swollen lips, they still pursued the quest, crawling into smothering holes, prodding others with boughs.

There was no sound from the skull that now and then attracted their glance. Once Skinner shook his fist at it, swearing the thing was set there to mock them. They had brought nothing to eat or drink from the boat and none would go back for it, slaking thirst in a hole dug beside a pool too foul for them to risk without some filtration. By mid-afternoon they were done and they flung themselves down exhausted.

The sun began to sink and a wind rose, moaning through the pines. Alligators began to bellow in the lagoons, mudhens called weirdly and once again the long flights of cranes commenced, with the ducks coming in for the night feeding. The buzzards they had seen all day, whenever they happened to look skyward, were still circling, soaring on extended pinions, effortless, afloat rather than flying, watching for carrion.

Tremaine was close to Raxon, who was sick with disappointment and fatigue, sick with the fever, despondent, realizing that they were practically castaways in these fever-ridden, mosquito infested swamps.

"The black was right," said Tremaine huskily. "This place has a conjure, or a curse, or both, upon it. We're fooled. Skinner made hint to me, if we should find the loot, that there would be more for two than for three. But I checked him and he saw I was not with him. You were right, Raxon, he is a scoundrel."

"Aye—did he not want me to join with him against you? Now he turns to you to help him against me. If either one of us fell for his plans he would murder the survivor in his sleep. 'All for one and that one, Skinner,' is his motto. Much good it will do him. There's nothing to divide."

"It must be hereabouts," said Tremaine doggedly, "but we can't find it after dark and 'twill be that in an hour. Better get back to the boat. I'm famished and my throat aches for a swig of liquor. Come on."

They both spoke to Skinner who grunted and slowly followed them down. Tremaine led, traversing the ridge to avoid much of the worst of the thorny, prickly undergrowth and to strike down some gully to the creek.

* * * *

The twilight purpled, the sun swimming in a mist that turned it to a scarlet disc, then to a crimson, lighting luridly bank after bank of clouds that reached half-way to the zenith. The wind soughed mournfully, coming from the southwest with sudden piping gusts. The air seemed cold.

Tremaine turned into a sandy draw and abruptly halted with an exclamation. Fairly in their path was a chest, metal bound, substantial, big enough to hold the ransom of three kings. With hoarse shouts they all raced toward it, trying the lid, flinging back the hasp before they noticed there was no padlock.

The chest was empty—empty as a broken gourd!

A gust of wind came whistling down the draw, driving grains of sand before it. Suddenly a high-pitched scream sounded, exultant, mocking, devilish. Instinctively they looked around and up. Plainly from the head of the gully where they stood they could see the dead pine. The skull seemed to gaze in their direction, the sunset dying it blood-red from dome to gaping jaws, the eye sockets purple.

Again the scream came and Tremaine wheeled and started to bolt down the draw, plunging through the soft sand like a startled bullock. Skinner stood with his face turned up, snarling half in defiance, half in fear, while Raxon's little eyes glittered in his weasel face like those of a trapped animal.

With that fearful cry the buzzards seemed to wheel lower, the sky to darken. Slowly Tremaine came back as the screams ceased, half ashamed of his panic. The wind was still blustery and all about them the palmettos thrashed as the three stared at the empty chest, the end of their hopes.

"'Tis Swayne's folks! They've beaten us to it," croaked Skinner. "And you to blame or 't, Raxon!"

"You lie!" It needed but small spark to set the tinder of their tempers aglow.

Skinner caught up his cutlass and leaped at Raxon, the blade gleaming red in the rays that streamed into the mouth of the gully, his shadow springing grotesque in front of him. Raxon drew his pistol from his belt and fired it pointblank, but the priming was poor, dampened, perhaps by the sweat that had poured out of him all day. There was only a fizz and a flash in the pan. With a squeak of terror he flung the useless weapon at Skinner, turned and ran, dodging behind Tremaine.

Raxon was no fighter.

Furious, frenzied with disappointment, Skinner cursed at Tremaine for being in his way, and cut at him as he seemed disposed to shield Raxon. The blow sank deep in the giant's defending forearm and the hot blood spurted. With a roar of rage, the gunner caught the cutlass blade, regardless of its edge against his palms, and wrested it away. Then his bleeding hands clutched at Skinner's throat, choking him.

Skinner's own hands sought to tear away the frightful grip that shut off blood and breath. He wheezed as his eyes seemed popping out, his body writhing while he strove to reach Tremaine with kicks that the other did not feel. The strangling appeared for the moment to deprive Skinner of reason; he fought without thought of weapons, striving only to loose the vise about his neck.

Raxon stood apart, watching the struggle. There was barren gain for him now in what he had meant to bring about, but he exulted in Skinner's plight. Tremaine's strength could be used to good advantage in getting away from the place.

Suddenly Skinner fell, limp to all seeming, and Tremaine fell over him to his knees, shaking him as a bulldog might shake its victim. Blood was pouring out of Skinner's mouth and nose; his face was almost black. Yet he had one blow left in him, a last convulsive attempt to best the other. Tremaine's grip may have slackened in the fall. Skinner's groping hands found the hilt of Tremaine's two-edged dirk that slid easily from its sheath. Deep into Tremaine's belly Skinner thrust the keen steel. The gunner toppled forward, fairly on top of his victim. His grasp on Skinner's throat relaxed as the blood gushed from him, but those steel-strong fingers had done their work. The last of Skinner's strength went in that stab.

Raxon watched Tremaine writhing on top of the other until he stretched out, shuddered and lay still. He had retrieved and rep-rimed his pistol and now he carefully sent a bullet crashing through Skinner's forehead.

His face was that of a balked devil as he turned to go down to the boat, leaving the two behind him on the blood-soaked sand. The last of the sun had left the gully. It was swiftly dark. All about him the palmettos rustled and clashed as the wind whooped. Out of the darkness the two buzzards had dropped and lit at the head of the draw.

Raxon struggled on as best he could toward the creek, sure that Tremaine had chosen wisely when he picked the gully and that he had only to follow it down to find the water and then the boat. He looked forward to a great draught of brandy. He was in bad shape and felt the fever coming on as he staggered and stumbled through the brush, tripping, held back by thorns, stumbling into bayoneted agaves.

On the brink of the creek, now at low tide, something rustled and struck at him through the soft leather of his Spanish boots. He felt the blow and then the fangs and, though he saw nothing, he visioned a stumpy serpent gliding away. He knew what it was—a moccasin—perhaps the very snake that had slipped out of the skull.

Swiftly the virus ran through his tired body. He felt sick and weak and sat down on a log. Instantly it moved and, with frightful swiftness, flailed with an armored tail that smote Raxon from his feet, his legs broken. Then the bull alligator clamped his jaws upon his prey and waddled toward the creek, dragging the clawing thing that gibbered until first mud, then water, filled its mouth.

High up on the ridge, as the ripples spread out, the palmettos clashed together, the wind whooped, and, high above it, a scream came from the top of the pine where the skull dimly showed. It startled the gluttonous buzzards for a moment; then they went on tearing, gobbling in the dark.

* * * *

A week later, a turtling sloop from Georgetown came to the island and the brother of Swayne's widow, with a cousin and the younger brother of Hoyle landed. They did not go near the gully, where the buzzards had gathered and glutted themselves on rare food, but passed the excavation and, without looking for the chest, went on to the tree of the skull. There was a fair breeze in the pinetops. The three men rolled up the sleeves of their shirts, two took up axes, while the third glanced aloft.

"I thought you said it screamed when the wind blew?" he asked Swayne's brother-in-law.

"It does, but the wind has to be from the southwest and this has quartered from the usual. Moreover it has to be almost a gale to make the device work. It's simple enough. Swayne wrote that he had borrowed it from the Indians of the Isthmus, who use it on the tree-graves of their chiefs. The skull sets in a fork and they made the whistle of a tube, a funnel and a tongue of thin metal, to rest in the crotch below it.

"Swayne wrote he never meant to bury the chest in the hole he made them dig, lest they blab about it, but he did not think of the tree until he had climbed it with the skull he meant to set there as both guide and warning. You have to mount half-way before you note the opening that tells you it is hollow. They could not see him from the hole where they were busy digging and he had Hoyle send up the contents with rope and a sack he made of his shirt. Swayne hauling and pouring the stuff into the hollow of the tree. Well, let's get at it. It should be but a light task."

The keen blades bit into the dead wood fast and, presently, the pine toppled and fell crashing to the ground, hollow for half its length. The stump was a heaped casket of objects that gleamed and shone and sent off dancing rays of colored light. From the trunk there rolled other precious things, while more remained within. Gold and jewels winked more brightly as the dust settled.

Through it one of the three saw the skull bound from the ground and, after its leap, go rolling down into a nearby gully. Then he started to help gathering up the loot.

SIX SHELLS LEFT

Allan R. Bosworth

When he shipped into the navy that bleak December morning, "Soapy" McDowell wasn't half as anxious to serve his country as he was to leave it. You know the old gag that ninety-nine out of a hundred recruits pull—about enlisting two jumps ahead of the sheriff? Well, it was largely true in the case of Soapy—known professionally as Professor J. Pendleton McDowell, medium.

It wasn't Soapy who made up his mind regarding a naval career. It was Chief Boatswain's Mate Hank Miller. On recruiting duty, strolling down the dimly-lighted street on the way to his boardinghouse, Hank was suddenly attracted by sounds of a near riot in the crumbling old house that sat back behind the chinaberry trees. The structure was dark, and Hank paused at the sagging gate and listened.

"Fake!" someone shouted. "Grab him!"

"Just a moment, please—"

"Police! Police!"

Lights flashed on suddenly, and pandemonium broke loose with a crash of overturned chairs and sudden, profane cries. A woman screamed and a solemn-toned bell rang out, then fell to the floor with a flattened, discordant note.

Hank Miller had been on recruiting duty two months and he chafed for action. He bounded up the walk. There was so much noise within that no one heard him leap upon the porch and throw open the door.

Against the farther wall a tall, pasty-faced man shrank. A dozen men and several women moved toward him menacingly; they laid hands on him and dragged him across the overturned table.

"Hold on a minute!" shouted Hank in a voice such as only boatswain's mates can develop. It boomed out over the sounds of conflict, carrying an authoritative note. The embattled ones turned and the sight of a man in uniform calmed their anger. An ominous quiet fell for a few seconds, then everyone tried to speak at once.

"Pipe down!" ordered the sailor. He indicated the tall man. "What's going on here?"

The tall man bowed. "We were in the midst of a seance," he explained. "We were communicating with a departed spirit—this lady's Uncle Abner, I believe it was. Suddenly someone broke the chain and accused me of faking. They threw over the table and turned on the light. They seized me."

"He was ringing the bell and operating the thingamajig that raps on the table," accused a shrill-voiced woman. "He was doin' it with his toes. Look!"

She indicated Professor McDowell's feet. Hank Miller looked down and saw there was no shoe on the right one. The sock ended about midway to the toes, and somehow, those toes appeared extremely capable and dexterous. They undoubtedly were longer than the average toe is wont to be.

"He's a fake, all right. We're going to turn him over to the police," a man asserted.

Hank saw the pleading in the tall man's eyes.

"Wait a minute, folks," he answered. "Maybe he is a faker, but I don't guess any crime has been committed, and this is no time to be putting able-bodied men in jail for nothing. Let me take him in charge. Clear out of here and I'll make a sailor out of him tomorrow. He'll return your money cheerfully, won't you, doc?"

"Er—not doctor, my dear sir, not doctor," the tall man protested. "Professor, if you please, Professor J. Pendleton McDowell."

"You'll return the money—cheerfully?" insisted Hank.

"Well, not exactly cheerfully," admitted the professor. "But I shall return it. Kindly step forward, folks. Fifty cents each."

The crowd left. McDowell looked at Hank Miller.

"Well?" the Professor asked.

"Well, it's up to you!" the sailor answered. "Somebody's going to report this to the police. There's the jail—and here's the navy. You're within draft age, and the army'll get you in the long run. Why not get in a good outfit?"

"I'll choose the navy!" McDowell said. "Let's go."

He limped across the room to where his other low-cut shoe lay. Much to Hank's amazement, he thrust his foot within it without so much as stooping to hold it or untie its laces.

That was how Soapy McDowell became a sailor back in 1917. Hank Miller shook hands with him and thought he had seen the last of the erstwhile professor. But a relenting providence jerked Hank off recruiting duty a couple of months later and ordered him to sea in command of the armed guard aboard the merchantman *Crescenta*. And when Hank got together his six men at the receiving ship at Brooklyn, there was Soapy—a boot fresh from Newport, with the collar-button mark still on his neck.

Beside Soapy there were Reynolds, Jones, Cardini, Morgan and Riley. The last named was a little Irish gunner's mate who could point a five-inch like nobody's business, but the others were seamen and most of them had only had the experience of the spotting board and a few hours' drill at the guns in the armed guard school. They mustered on the dock, got their bags and hammocks together and took a motor sailer over to the Hoboken pier where the *Crescenta* lay, dirty and rusty, making ready to clear for Liverpool.

"She's a hard-looking packet," Hank swore when he saw their future billet. "Slow, and rough in heavy weather, you can bank on that!"

"Wonder she hasn't stopped a torpedo long ago!" Riley agreed. "The navy's still goin' to hell, when you have to do duty aboard a tub like that!"

They went aboard and met the skipper, a weather-beaten old seadog named Jonathan, who whittled himself a pipeful from a plug of chewing tobacco and wished them luck.

Their quarters, allotted from space that was already at a premium, were smelly and crowded, and the one five-inch gun had been mounted aft in a little place where the deck gear had been cleared away and a special platform constructed.

"One good crack out a this baby and the ship'll fall apart!" Riley complained.

"One good crack at a sub is all we'll need!" boasted Reynolds with all the cocksureness of the recruit. Whereupon Riley set him and a couple of the others busy on the gun's camouflage paint job, and they watched the shoreline fade in the mist as the *Crescenta* warped away and slipped out to sea.

* * * *

It was the following morning that Soapy limped up to where the chief stood on deck and voiced his complaint.

"Chief," he said, "this navy is ruining my feet!"

"What?" asked Hank.

"I said this navy is ruining my feet. I can't get a pair of regulation shoes that fit right. And I don't dare wear these socks—I've discovered the dye fades, and that might infect your feet, you know. The first shoes I had issued me cramped the ends of my toes. Then I got this pair, and they're about two sizes too large. They don't cramp my toes, but they blister my heels. I have to hobble around with them untied and slip my feet out so they'll cool every chance I get. But I simply can't ruin my feet—what'd I do when the war is over?"

Hank suppressed a smile. He liked this big faker who was a little older than the average recruit and who went around always with the same grave expression he must have worn when in the midst of his seances, as he called them, back on the outside.

"You can't do that; that's right!" he agreed. "Why not go barefoot if it isn't too cold for you. Everybody goes barefoot down around Guantanamo when the fleet is south. I'll see if Jonathan has any shoes in his slop chest that might fit better, and when we get to Liverpool, or when we come back to the States, I suggest that you buy a pair of non-regulations. You know you don't have to wear strictly regulation stuff aboard a packet like this!"

"Thanks, chief!" Soapy said as he limped away. "But I really wouldn't dare go barefoot. I might step on a nail or something might fall on my feet!"

* * * *

The *Crescenta* lumbered on her way, deep laden and despairingly slow, creaking and groaning in rough weather, shipping heavy seas and rolling scuppers under. The armed guard kept one of its own number on the bridge as a lookout to watch for periscopes and to act as spotter for the gun crew should one be sighted. After interminable days of sailing, they came to the danger zone—that area on the chart which was bounded in red and reported to be alive with those sharks of the deep—the U-boats.

Here the worst thing that could have befallen the *Crescenta* came, and the armed guard, despite the little catch of fear it must have felt in its collective breasts, gathered around the five-inch and snickered with the derision of the navy man for a merchant vessel. The ancient tramp's engines began to lie down on the job every hour or so!

"What a ship!" roared Hank Miller. "The old *Tuscarora* you hear about in the navy—the one with the sixteen decks and a glass bottom—well, she had nothin' on this packet!"

"Yeh, we're loggin' six knots and liable to stop that any minute," Riley grumbled. "We go six miles, then we wallow along while they patch the engines, then we go another six miles. If we sight a sub it'll be our luck to lose headway and drift around broadside for her to aim a fish at."

"Hell, she wouldn't waste a fish on this!" snorted Hank. "She'd stand off and shell us. And I guess you fellows have heard what the Germans threaten to do to armed guards? Treat 'em like pirates—shoot 'em. You might as well be up in a frontline trench as in the armed guard service!"

"There you go, chief, always bein' a Pollyanna!" Reynolds complained.

* * * *

It happened eighteen days out of Hoboken, when, by all rights, the *Crescenta* should have docked at Liverpool. She was hobbling along like a crippled old lady crossing a muddy street. It was a bright day, with low swells, and the armed guard was at breakfast, with Morgan standing lookout.

Nobody saw a thing. The first warning was in the shape of three rapid shots from somewhere on the port quarter. They sang overhead, missing by many yards, and the crew, captain and armed guard tumbled out on deck with their mouths full of food, ready for battle.

"She's in the sun streak!" Morgan sang out, and it was another full minute before they sighted the conning tower. It was far away, and just as they saw the tiny gray oblong the deck gun popped again and another shell screamed overhead.

"Let her have it!" Hank Miller shouted. The gun crew sprang to their posts. Morgan telephoned his estimate of the range as eight thousand yards, which wasn't far off, and the five-inch tore loose with an explosion that shook the *Crescenta*'s ancient deck plates and jarred Captain Jonathan's bridgework.

A fountain spouted short of the low whaleback. Morgan telephoned the information that the shell had fallen two hundred yards low. Different, this was, to gluing your eyes to the slot at the end of a spotting board and having a shipmate move a bit of white cotton about in representation of the "splash!"

Another shell from the submarine shrieked over them, and Riley, pointing the gun, elevated its muzzle a little and jerked the lanyard.

"Boom!"

It was still short, Morgan told them. More shots from the German, but they all went over. Apparently the sub, confident that she was out of range, closed in about five hundred yards, and here a shot from the *Crescenta*'s gun was seen to strike dangerously near the enemy craft. The sub dropped back to its former position, keeping up a continuous fire, but missing. The *Crescenta*'s gun answered steadily, fast as they could reload and fire her.

* * * *

Jonathan had put his wheel hard over, and for a time the *Crescenta* was almost stern-on to the sub, offering as little target as was possible. But the German was far superior in speed; she cruised swiftly around on the port beam, keeping well out about the eight-thousand-yard mark, and began dropping her shells too close for comfort.

Boom!

The next shell screamed its way over the water, and back came the sound of the impact of metal on metal. It had struck the German a glancing blow well aft of the conning tower. The sub veered off almost instantly, keeping up her fire.

"Atta boy!" yelled Hank. "A few more like that and she'll go down like an elevator!"

Crash!

A shell from the German tore into number one hold. She, too, had found the range at last. Another shell came over promptly on the heels of the first and ripped into the engineers' storeroom. Clouds of smoke began to pour past the gun crew.

"Hey, chief! We're afire!" Reynolds shouted.

"Never mind the fire, just keep loadin' this gun!" Hank ordered. "We got to work fast now!"

A seaman came running aft.

"Captain has set off the smoke pots to spoil their aim!" he announced.

"Hell!" snorted Hank. "He's spoilin' ours too! Tell him to lay off so we can see what we're shootin' at!"

The smoke pots evidently failed of their purpose, for another shell hit the *Crescenta* well aft and low down on the water line. She began to circle, and the cry came from the bridge that the steering gear had been disabled. Around in a wide sweep the merchantman steamed, turning her broad, clumsy side full toward the maneuvering submarine.

A shell screeched overhead, but not without effect. It ripped off the *Crescenta*'s mainmast clean as though an ax had sliced through, and down came the wireless antennae in a tangled heap.

"Now we'll play hell gettin' any help, unless somebody's already picked it up!" Hank murmured. "And now—I thought so!"

A cough and a wheeze from the depths of the engine room. The throb of the machinery ceased; the *Crescenta* slowed and lurched helplessly in the swells, her rudder disabled, her engines still.

"Stand by to abandon ship!" Jonathan bawled.

"We'll take the last boat!" Hank shouted. "Keep firing!"

"You're a damn fool!" yelled the skipper. "She'll shell the boats if you keep on!"

"She would anyway!" Hank retorted. "Furthermore, you're another. Now shove off and let us fight—just leave us one boat!"

The submarine, sensing victory, was pouring a rapid and damaging fire at her helpless victim. One shell pierced number two hold, others fell short or went over as the ship wallowed along and lost headway. The gun crew stood by and placed its shots carefully. At least one more indirect hit was tallied against the U-boat as

Jonathan and his crew lowered three of the lifeboats and rowed away from their vessel.

"We're making ourselves unpopular as hell, boys!" Hank said. "The Krauts have announced that they'll treat all armed guards as pirates and shoot 'em. What do you say—shall we stick until the old tub is actually sinkin'— or shall we take to the boat now?"

"Stick, you louse!" came from the headset of the spotter's phone. Morgan was still at his job on the bridge. And the gun crew chorused its assent.

"But say, chief!" broke in Soapy McDowell, who was passing shells. "There are but six shots left!"

"My God—have we been shootin' that much?" demanded Hank. "That's a lot of shells gone! Six left! Hold that fire a minute!"

The chief frowned, glanced over the almost deserted vessel. Out a couple of hundred yards away from the ship the three boats were pulling to safety. Jonathan's voice bellowed out over the intervening distance, advising the crazy fools aboard to save their necks.

"Strategy—we ought to use strategy!" the chief exclaimed. But how?

The next shell from the Germans answered him in part, at least. It shrieked over the water and smashed the remaining lifeboat to splinters where it hung on its davits. Their means of escape was cut off.

"Well, that's something!" Hank announced. "We can't go now. Leave the gun, gang. Let's go forward and wait a minute to see what the Krauts will do. Probably they'll come alongside and board us. When they do, don't make any move unless I give the word. This may be a decent Heinie, this skipper, and they may treat us like prisoners of war are supposed to be treated. And they may shoot us. War sure is hell!"

The submarine's skipper probably was watching them through his glass, but he took no chances on a new trick of the dreaded "Q-boats." His craft circled warily, keeping well off until he was certain no trick was intended. Then he closed in, still circling, while the seven men aboard the *Crescenta* sweated with uncertainty and waited, standing by the rail.

"He's picking up Jonathan!" Reynolds announced suddenly.

The sub had approached the three boats; it threw one of the small craft a line and took it in tow. The other two stood by a minute, several men transferred from the boat which held the skipper to the other two. Then the U-boat proceeded, towing the lifeboat and heading almost directly for the ship.

The minutes dragged like hours. Up came the submarine, so near now the men on the *Crescenta* could recognize their shipmates in the boat astern. Captain Jonathan was not among them. Apparently he had been placed in one of the other boats, and now this one only held enough seamen to man the oars.

* * * *

The submarine halted a quarter of a mile distant from the *Crescenta*, keeping its gun trained on the crippled ship. Its commander and several of his men stepped into the *Crescenta*'s number three lifeboat and had the American seamen row to the ship.

"Ahoy, on deck!" the officer yelled. "Stand by! We have our gun on you!"

"Tell us something new!" growled Hank Miller.

The sub's skipper and eight German sailors swarmed up the boatswain's ladder dangling from the starboard side. Herr Hauptmann was a Prussian, tall and haughty, and he and several others carried automatics.

"We find we shall need some of your supplies," he remarked pleasantly, smiling at Hank. "You and your men will lead the way to the master's cabin, after which we will have no further use for your services."

He gave his men an order and they searched the Americans for weapons.

"I don't like the way he said that," confided Soapy McDowell to Riley as Hank led the way aft. They entered Jonathan's cabin.

The remains of the skipper's breakfast were still on his table, and there lay his pocketknife and a plug of tobacco where the sub's first shell had interrupted him as he whittled a pipeful. The cabin was spacious for a vessel of the *Crescenta*'s age. There were several chairs about the table, and the German ordered Hank to be seated. Soapy McDowell sank into the chair opposite him with a sort of sigh, Riley took his place at the end of the table and Cardini occupied the remaining chair. The officer said something in German, and one of his men departed.

"As you know, armed guards on merchant ships really constitute violation of international law and should be treated as piracy," the German informed Hank. "I should obey orders and have you shot. But I couldn't think of being so cold-blooded, my friends. I shall merely have you tied and left aboard. Then we will replenish our provisions and take what instruments we can use—incidentally unshipping the gun with which you did such accurate shooting and taking it with us if possible—and then we will stand off and enjoy a bit of target practice."

"You dirty so-and-so!" Hank replied. "If you think you can scare us you're off your nut!"

The captain laughed. He jerked a corner of the oilcloth table cover, and dishes and silverware clattered to the deck. The seaman returned with a coil of stout line and they began tying the Americans. They slipped a loop around Hank's hands after they were bound, and made them fast down between his knees by securing the line to a round of the chair. He was trussed up like a pig ready for market.

This work was over in a minute, and the seven Americans were bound helplessly, Morgan and Jones lying on the deck, the rest sitting upright at the table where they could read the despair in each other's eyes. A couple of Germans were put on guard, Lugers in their hands, and the captain led the rest forth in search of provisions. The doomed men could hear them loading canned goods into the boat; heard them knocking off brass and copper fittings and rummaging for documents and instruments. They heard the captain urging haste, and they prayed for the coming of some vessel which might have picked up those first few flashes of the *Crescenta*'s wireless.

"It looks tough, gang!" was all Hank had a chance to say before one of their guards jammed the Luger almost in the chief boatswain's mate's mouth and ordered silence. Hank could see from the expressions in the eyes of the other men at the table just how tough it was. Only Soapy McDowell's face, still gravely pale and holding a quiet dignity, was inscrutable.

The officer was returning; they heard him just outside the cabin door, chuckling over the success of his raid on the *Crescenta*'s stores. He carried his Luger in one hand, the other arm embraced a couple of cartons of toilet soap as though it were worth its weight in gold. Hank remembered how someone had told him how scarce this common necessity was in Germany, where fats were at a premium.

"Very nice, very!" the captain remarked. He placed his pistol on the table and ripped the cover off one of the cartons to smell its contents. "You never know what good soap means, my friends of Yankee pigs, until the day comes when you are forced to do without it."

Hank's eyes were on the Luger, within his reach on the table top. If he could only wrench a hand free! If there were only some way of getting that gun! They'd die like rats in a little while if something didn't happen. He strained and swore under his breath. The thongs held like steel, biting into his sweating wrists.

Across the table, Soapy McDowell sat, face pale, looking straight into the chief's eyes. His own eyes were burning with an intensity that attracted Hank's gaze and held it spellbound; the former "professor" seemed trying to tell the chief something, something that meant a lot to the men in that little room—rescue, perhaps! Hank's eager mind grasped at the thought; instinctively he knew that Soapy dared not say a word, dared not even move his lips lest he be detected.

Then Hank's taut-stretched nerves nearly snapped and he bit his lips to keep from crying out in alarm. A cold and clammy hand was touching his under the table! Sweat started out on the chief's forehead, and his mouth was sticky and dry. Then he remembered and was reassured by that look in Soapy's eyes.

That was no hand—merely McDowell's dexterous foot, slipped out of those oversize regulation shoes! It drew back for a second, then came up again and Hank Miller felt the cold steel of Captain Jonathan's pocketknife, held between Soapy's toes!

* * * *

The loquacious captain was still praising the virtues of the soap he had found; Hank thought he was going to eat it. He even cast rank and station aside for a moment and allowed the two burly seamen to smell its fragrance, and their little pig eyes glittered.

"We regret that your pop-gun is too heavy to take away, since we really have no time to rig a boom and tackle!" the captain declared. "However, the sights and breech plug, as well as a few brass fittings, will come in very useful. This has been a very profitable ship— considering that it hardly appeared to be worth a shell. For my part, I—"

He never finished that sentence. Hank Miller felt the knife cut through the last thong. His hands wrenched free. He jerked them upward and snatched the Luger off the table and shot one of the German seamen where he stood. He grabbed Herr Hauptmann by the collar and used him as a shield while he turned the Luger on the other seaman.

The sailor let his gun fall, and Hank released the skipper, who staggered back against the bulkhead, his hands upraised, his mouth agape with dismay.

"Now, you lousy Krauts, stand by for a ram!" Hank ordered. "Here, Riley, get those guns!"

He stooped and retrieved the knife, slashing the thongs that held the gunner's mate.

Riley freed the others rapidly. There were six other Germans, still busy ransacking the stores. They must have heard the shot.

"Quick, Riley! You and Morgan and Jones! Take the other two Lugers and slip out on the port side here. Keep behind cover so they can't see you from the sub. Get below and get those other Heinies. And listen—I got a plan! When you've got 'em, slip on their uniforms and report back here. Bring an extra uniform!"

"You bet, chief!"

"Very nice, *Schweinhund*!" the captain snarled. "But if you remember, my crew has a gun trained on you! I have changed my mind about leaving you aboard. Put down your gun and I give you my word of honor you'll be treated like prisoners of war."

"What honor?" sneered Hank. "You're in a hell of a position to be telling me what you'll do and what you won't do. We've got you licked. Listen!"

There was a short, sharp scuffle below decks. Riley and his men had caught the Germans coming out of the storeroom with cases of canned goods burdening them. Five minutes later, the little gunner's mate and the other two sailors reappeared, wearing the jackets and the unbecoming flat hats of the vanquished submarine sailors.

"All right!" Hank told them. "Now get me this bird's uniform. With that gold, I guess I'll rate something!"

He motioned with the Luger.

"Sit down, Krauts. We'll see how *you* like being tied."

* * * *

From the deck of the German submarine, the gun crew and the underofficer watched as their men came on the deck of the *Crescenta* and went aft to the gun, preparing to take its sights and other pieces. *Deutschland uber alles*, but it was a great day for the U-boats! There'd be the telling of this and other victories over many a stein when they got back in the Kiel Canal for a period of rest and overhaul!

It wasn't a suspicious move, that gun muzzle swinging around toward them. Someone was about to hammer off part of the breech mechanism—see, they had swung it open, and they crowded about it so you couldn't tell exactly what they were doing. Maybe Mueller was having his little joke, pointing the enemy's disabled gun at his own ship—Mueller was a droll fellow, anyway.

Nobody on the sub knew how it happened. No one of the sub's gun crew lived to tell, but that gun on the *Crescenta*'s deck suddenly belched flame and smoke. A shell struck the sub's deck gun and demolished it, and the men around it were blown into the water, torn, lifeless things.

"That leaves five shells!" announced Hank Miller as he stood by the *Crescenta*'s gun in Herr Hauptmann's uniform. "Now if she surrenders, hold your fire. If she tries to dive, give her hell!"

The panic-stricken underofficer made the conning tower and chose to dive. The hatch clanged shut, the whaleback went awash and slanted forward.

Boom!

A gaping, jagged hole appeared at the base of the conning tower. Water began to pour in. At such close range, the *Crescenta*'s armed guard couldn't miss.

Boom!

She heeled over, torn and dying. Her stern shot into the air, propeller whirling helplessly, then she went down, leaving great patches of scummy oil blubbering up on a silent sea.

Hank Miller turned toward his gun crew, and they saw the pity that was in his eyes. He regarded them silently for a few seconds.

"Well, now we'll have to stay on this packet till we get help, or take to that other lifeboat with a crowd of Krauts!" he said. "But, for the benefit of you gobs that don't savvy just how this thing happened, let me recite a little verse I learned in the Third Reader."

He faced Soapy McDowell and jokingly began to recite:

"Blessings on thee, little man,
Barefoot boy with cheek of tan—"

GODS OF BASTOL

H.P. Holt

There were four of us sitting in the cabin of the *Tumbril*, filling it with tobacco smoke—four men who had just sworn to cling together like the ivy on the old garden wall. And I fear we were not a very practical quartet, either. There was Thurston, the doctor, who could have charmed flocks of patients toward him in any civilized city, but cities bored him; there was Finny, assistant manager of the late, lamented Company that had just gone up in smoke and left us all stranded; Ingle, the *Tumbril*'s chief engineer; and I had been mate of the *Tumbril*.

Finney's weakness was a delusion that he ought to be growing oranges in Florida. Ingle's acquaintance with bottled goods had retarded his advance on the road to fortune.

That morning, after a rusty old freighter had called at the island and dropped a bag of mail, Ditson, the resident manager of the Company, a very decent sort of a chap, had given us news of the crash. He also gave us the straight tip that there weren't any funds left, that everything had gone, and that the best thing we could do was to look after ourselves as well as we could.

The *Tumbril* belonged to the Company and was used for pottering about. Her skipper got wind of the crash before the old mail-boat left again, so he packed up his traps and cleared out in her to seek pastures new. We four had drifted together on the *Tumbril* by common instinct to weigh up the situation. Ratoa, our island home, and also the home of the Company's affair, was so far from Broadway as the crow flies that that crow would never have arrived there even if it carried a spare pair of wings.

We four were all suffering from temporary financial embarrassment in consequence of the Company having failed to pay any salaries for two consecutive months. And because we had all been inseparable while fortune had seemed to smile on us, we now solemnly swore to sink or swim together. It was heroic, for all we had to swim in was the broad Pacific Ocean, and our plight was thus peculiar. With the last of a bottle of rum distributed among four tumblers, we rose, hoisted our glasses, and drank our pledge. After which, for some unaccountable reason, we felt better.

But that was not all. There was a complication, or rather a series of complications. One of them was the disappearance of Dimmick, the best of pals and the whitest man that ever drew breath. He was the Company's mechanical expert. The only fault we had to find about him was that he had a girl in the background, and that made him seem different from us. There wasn't a maiden on earth who would have shed a single tear if we four had all gone to glory. Dimmick didn't really bore us very much by talking about his girl, but, from what he did say we knew he had it badly. The description he gave of her sounded as if it would have fitted something straight out of heaven, but we discounted that because he was in love with her, and forgave him because, though we didn't say so, we all loved him.

Well, Dimmick's girl was a sea-captain's daughter and a distant relation of Ditson, the Company's resident manager. She used to travel with her father on the *Flying Sylph* a lot, and it was arranged that, as they were in that part of the South Pacific just then, she was to come to the island of Ratoa and stay there as the guest of Mr. and Mrs. Ditson for a while. Naturally, Dimmick exhibited symptoms of hysterical insanity; but a couple of months ago news had come from Fiji that the *Flying Sylph* had been lost with all hands. There was no question about the authenticity of the information. The steamer had been found floating bottom-up, and no trace had been found of anybody on board.

When he heard this, Dimmick walked about dazed for a week, and we thought he was going mad. He would have taken the next boat to Fiji, but there wasn't any boat to Fiji, and it wouldn't have done any good, anyway. He tried to settle down to work, but it was a dismal failure, so the chief told him to take a vacation and fish. Dimmick was an enthusiastic fisherman. At first he refused, but we persuaded him, and so he went off in a ketch with two Kanakas who could have kept the vessel afloat in a typhoon.

They came back without him. That was on the day before the Company's crash. According to the Kanakas' story, Dimmick was in the ketch's small boat, angling for tappi, quite close to the island of Bastol, when he fell overboard and was drowned. If a Kanaka tells you a lie, you generally don't know it, so when you are accustomed to them you assume they tell nothing but lies and you act accordingly. Therefore we had grave doubts whether Dimmick had died in the way the Kanakas said.

And now, on the mail steamer, came the staggering surprise. I won't call her an angel, because you couldn't kiss an angel if she'd let you. And I won't call her a fairy, because after all you know a fairy would make a most unsatisfactory and uncertain wife. She came off the gangway the minute the steamer tied up, with her wonderful eyes just ablaze with happy expectation. She looked all around and seemed a bit disappointed at not finding what she sought. Then Thurston, who has more self-possession than any of us, drifted up alongside of her, and went as white as a sheet when she asked for Tom Dimmick.

"Tom Dimmick!—oh—ah—yes," I heard him stutter. "Tom's not here just now. Are you—er—"

I could see he was anticipating the worst. Somehow I myself felt sure of it.

"I am Nancy Carew," she said.

That was the name of Dimmick's girl. And Dimmick's death had just been reported.

"Of course—of course." said Thurston, bending his helmet all out of shape, "You're going to stay with the Ditsons, aren't you? Pardon me, I'll slip up to their place and see about a conveyance. Would you mind waiting here a moment?"

His face was like a piece of uncooked bread, but he actually worked up a smile. Then he came over to me.

"Here's Dimmick's girl in the flesh, and if any of the follows blurt out the fact that he's dead, it'll probably half kill her," he said in a low voice. "For God's sake, pass the word around, quick, to be careful. Maybe we can break it gently—or—oh, I don't know!"

The color was coming back to his face, but he was a badly worried man. While I slipped along and told the rest of the boys, he shot up to the resident manager's house and put the matter squarely up to little Mrs. Ditson. She was a dear soul and a jewel, but she was no fool and saw the folly of hiding the bad news too long.

"Not a word about it this afternoon," she declared. "We'll let her understand that he has gone fishing. Then somehow tonight I will try to tell her."

* * * *

And so Nancy Carew landed at Ratoa under the impression that the man she loved would be with her next day; but Mrs. Ditson, with a task in hand that nobody else on the island would have cared to tackle, did her part bravely and gently. They both had a good cry, and when we saw Nancy Carew next day—the day of the crash—we voted severally and collectively that she was the pluckiest damsel between Siam and Seattle. She was very pale and seemed to have grown thin since the previous day, but she kept a stiff upper lip, and absolute adoration for her came to us all quite naturally.

The mystery of her appearance after the loss of her father's steamer was explained simply enough. The *Flying Sylph*, which, by the way, was fully insured, struck a mass of floating wreckage, had her plates stove in, and began to founder. The crew took to the boats and were picked up by a vessel which did not touch port for a couple of weeks. Hence the erroneous belief that all had perished.

They landed eventually at Fiji, where the girl's father took a temporary job as shore superintendent for a shipping company, and when Miss Carew learned that a trading steamer was leaving there for Ratoa, she gleefully sought that opportunity of paying us a visit, without knowing we even dreamed that her father's vessel had come to grief.

Meanwhile, we four had found sorrow of our own, though sorrow of a very small order compared with hers, in the demise of the Company. We had just gone through the ceremony with the rum and sprawled in our respective seats once more when Thurston thumped the table with his fist.

"I've got an idea—an idea about Dimmick," he said.

"Well?" Finney invited.

"If he'd been here and alive he would have been the first one among us to suggest that pledge, wouldn't he?"

"But he isn't here," drawled Ingle.

Thurston whipped round to face the ship's engineer.

"Are you sure he's dead?" the doctor asked slowly; and there was a queer silence.

"Why, I dunno," replied Ingle at length. "I've wondered. He probably is dead, but there's no believing these darned natives."

"And I've wondered too," declared Thurston, "especially since … since Miss Carey landed here. It's a damnable, situation for her. There's a mystery about the thing, to my mind."

"Well, what are you going to do about it?" queried Finney, a little more awake than usual.

"First of all," said Thurston, his eyes narrowed thoughtfully, "the Kanakas swore that Dimmick fell out of the small boat and was drowned, but they came back without the small boat. What happened to it? They say it disappeared. That sounds fishy, because the sea must have been fairly calm. Then, Dimmick wasn't a bad swimmer. He could have kept afloat for fifteen minutes at least, unless, of course, he got tangled up, or a shark grabbed him. Also, this happened near the island of Bastol, and we don't know Dimmick never got ashore there. As far as I can make out from the Kanakas, they weren't so far off the island."

"Well?" said Finney, sitting bolt upright.

"I propose," said Thurston calmly, "that we run over to Bastol in the old *Tumbril* and see if we can find any trace of him."

"I'm game," Finney replied.

"Count me in," agreed Ingle. "We've coal a plenty aboard for the trip. As there's no Company left, I don't know who owns this boat now, but that's a small matter."

"What about navigation?" Thurston shot at me.

"That's easy," I replied. "Bastol is about three hundred miles away, to the so'west."

"Then we'll start now," said Thurston decisively; and nobody questioned the point.

* * * *

But it took three hours to get steam up, and after a consultation, we had decided to tell Miss Carew what we were up to—to tell her there was nothing for her to base optimism on, but that we meant to have a look around in the neighborhood of Bastol. To our surprise, Nancy Carew immediately packed a small bag and announced her intention of going with us. She agreed that it was a hopeless sort of task, but said if there remained a single stone worth overturning, she meant to have a hand in the overturning of it. Also, naturally, we took with us the two Kanakas who had gone with Dimmick on his fishing excursion.

The clanking *Tumbril* reached Bastol in thirty-six hours. Up to the time its shores loomed up, not a word had been said to the Kanakas about our destination, but the moment they recognized the island, they began to chatter together in their own lingo. Our plan was to drop anchor near the beach, and when Thurston asked the blacks to point out the spot where Dimmick had been lost, their manner gave us the first clue that something peculiar was in the wind. One of them indicated a place about a mile to the west of Bastol, but, prompted by his companion, he then pointed away out to sea and began to exhibit signs of fear.

"They're lying, and lying badly for Kanakas," declared Thurston. "There's something wrong, you may depend on it. However, I'm going ashore. Meanwhile," he added, reaching for the siren lanyard and hanging on to it, "if Dimmick's alive and on the island, it'll do him good to hear this."

The wail of the siren rose piercingly, fell, rose again and ended in five long ear-splitting shrieks. It was the signal with which the fussy *Tumbril* had always announced, from afar, her return to Ratoa, and it was unmistakable.

Then, for a considerable time, we scanned the coast-line, hoping against hope for some answering signal. Again the siren screamed. There was something gruesome about it all. I noticed that Thurston glanced more than once from the skimmering beach to the two Kanakas.

"I don't pretend to understand the inside of natives' heads any better than the next fellow," he said, "but those two chaps are guilty of something, and the Lord only knows what! If I find they've done Dimmick in, they'll have about five minutes left to live."

* * * *

Nancy Carew would have joined the landing party, but Thurston would not hear of it, being distinctly uncertain what kind of reception the natives might offer. One of us had to stay behind with her, and Ingle, who had recently sprained his knee, was chosen for that purpose.

When the two Kanakas were ordered to man the rowboat, they refused point blank to go any way near Bastol. I took them each by an ear and was prepared to deal with them none too gently, when they howled out that Bastol was full of devil-devils.

"Better leave them alone," Thurston suggested "They'd only be a nuisance."

We each took a revolver and in five minutes reached the sandy beach, where we were not altogether surprised to find the remains of the ketch's boat. It had a jagged hole in the bottom. But what did surprise us was a clearly defined trail of footprints in the sand above high-water mark.

For the footprints were those of a man who wore shoes!

"Dimmick wasn't drowned, evidently," exclaimed Finney. "But why the dickens—"

"Come on you fellows" urged the practical-minded Thurston. "There's a trail here going into the center of the island. Let's see if we can follow it."

Shouting at the top of our lungs every few minutes, we advanced about half a mile on rising ground, the footprints being visible where the surface was soft. Then they disappeared altogether, but there were others. And those others were made by feet that had never wore a shoe!

Though none of us said so at the time, each feared that Dimmick must have fallen into the hands of savages and been murdered, and we felt a common desire to hand out punishment to the natives there. But none appeared until we reached the top of the hill. Suddenly from behind a tree stepped an almost naked black man, and before we had time to realized what he was up to, he hurled a long spear into our midst. It grazed Finney's shoulder and then became embedded in a tree behind him.

Simultaneously our three revolvers cracked, and the black, with a yell, disappeared. But immediately afterward, two other spears shot through the air, and then half a dozen. By a series of miracles we dodged them and, dropping into the long grass, blazed away at the natives, who showed themselves more freely as soon as we got to earth. Several of them were hit, and the rest, either bewildered by the effect of firearms, took to their heels.

We lay still for a minute or two, wondering what might happen next, when a faint voice reached us. It seemed muffled and distant, but we leaped to our feet, knowing it must be Dimmick. Answering with a roar in concert, we moved away to the right, from which direction the sound seemed to have come. I was at Thurston's heels, with Finney close up behind, when the doctor gave a cry of warning and, clutching at a sapling, just managed to avoid blundering headlong down into a yawning chasm. He was still balanced perilously when I reached for his coat and pulled him back to safety. As I did so, we heard Dimmick again. He was at the bottom of the chasm.

"Hello!" he called.

"Where are you?" I bellowed back, going close to the edge, and peering down but unable to see far on account of the foliage.

"Can you hear me?" came from Dimmick.

"Yes. How can we get down there?" I replied. There seemed to be no way of descending the edges, which were apparently almost sheer.

"Don't try," Dimmick called up. "You'll have to make a rope somehow. Plenty of vines growing there. Fasten one end to a rock and lower it. You'll want about sixty or eighty feet."

Already we were slashing away from the trees close by us long vine stems which were strong enough to lift a horse.

"And say," Dimmick added in a cheery voice, "if you happen to have a plate of steak and onions handy, you might drop it down now."

* * * *

It took me the best part of an hour to fashion a cable which I felt sure could be trusted, and when the end was lowered it was just long enough. Dimmick called out that he was beginning to climb, and we waited anxiously until, grunting and panting, he came over the end. We helped him to safety without a word, waiting for him to recover his breath, for it had been a hard fight out of the chasm.

"Did those devils throw you down there?" Finney asked.

"No. The rope I made broke, and so did my neck, nearly, when I fell. Gee, it's good to see you fellows! When I heard the old *Tumbril* squeaking though, I thought there was a chance you might find me. Then I heard shots, so I knew you were around and had met my friends the natives. You shouldn't hurt 'em. They're not a bad bunch, in a way; they don't go in for any of this torturing business, I mean. It's straight-away killing and eating with them. At least that's what I understood, though they don't know any *beche-de-mer* lingo, and I only knew an odd word or two of their dialect. They were saving me up for the full moon feast, I gathered."

"Well, let's get out of this." urged Thurston, "or we'll be at the feast yet. We've got a surprise for you on the *Tumbril*."

Dimmick looked up quickly, a wild hope shining in his eyes; but he checked a question that sprang to his lips, for it seemed so futile. Then he smiled somewhat wearily, thinking there was some joke.

"Let me rest a minute or two." he said. "I've had nothing to eat for days."

"How did you get down there?" asked Thurston.

"Fell down. Didn't I tell you once! The vines broke."

"What on earth were you going into that hole for?"

"I'll tell you," Dimmick said. "The natives here are heathen. By that I mean they make their own gods—carved wooden things that they stick up in their huts and worship. And they think those little wooden gods are perfectly marvelous, until something goes wrong, such as when the man who carved it breaks his leg or if his new wife turns out a failure. Then he just makes a new god and throws the old one down into this hole. They keep the place sacred to the memory of gods for which they have no further use.

"Well, when you started kicking up a row with the *Tumbril*'s whistle, all the natives got together and left me kind of lonely and I broke out of the hut they'd fastened me in; and I made a beeline for the gods' hole—"

As he was speaking, a spear glistened in the sun for a moment in its rapid flight through the air and narrowly missed me. We fired half a dozen shots into the trees.

"See that rock?" said Dimmick, pointing to a jagged peak that appeared above water now the tide was low. "That must be the one

I ran into, tearing the bottom out of the boat. I had to swim from it to the beach, and those darned Kanakas wouldn't come anywhere near. They think it's full of devil-devils. They hung about till next day and then disappeared. I'd have swam off to the ketch, but there were altogether too many sharks around."

We were half-way out to the *Tumbril* by now, and the three of us were bursting to tell Dimmick about somebody who was waiting on board for him, but we intended to save it as a surprise. Dimmick was sitting with his back to the steamer.

"You haven't told us," said Thurston, trying to look as if nothing unusual was going to happen, "what in the name of Pete made you bolt into that hole?"

"Oh. I didn't finish, did I?" he remarked. "These natives take no end of trouble in making their wooden gods, and they finish 'em off with a pair of eyes. I thought maybe if I could get down and dig the eyes out of a few dozen—"

Dimmick dipped into each of his bulging coat pocket, and fetched out two hands full of virgin pearls.

"It was a bit dark down there, and I broke my penknife digging 'em out," he said, "but I think I got all there were. Aren't they beauties? Don't they make your mouth water? I'd never have got away with it, though, but for you fellows, so we'll share the proceeds."

The little boat drew alongside the *Tumbril*, and Dimmick, glancing up, saw leaning over the rail the loveliest specimen of womanhood that ever drew breath in the South Seas.

For half a minute he didn't speak. Pearls worth a fortune trickled through his fingers and dropped into the bottom of the boat. Then a queer sound came from the back of his throat, and we made way for him as he dashed over the side, up the rope ladder onto the *Tumbril*, and into the arms of his girl.

THE MINDOON MANEATER

C.M. Cross

Moung Nay was sitting under the banyan tree in front of the *dak* bungalow of which he was the caretaker, feeling the edge of the *dah* he had been sharpening, and gazing thoughtfully at a series of immense tiger footprints that led out from behind the house past where he sat and away into the jungle across the road. There was not a man in the whole Sitang valley who would not have recognized those tracks, and Moung Nay, who had in spite of his scant eighteen, years, justly earned the reputation of being one of the best *shirkurs* of the district, did not need to be told. They had been made by the Mindoon maneater, the tiger which had terrorized the whole country for fifty miles around during the last six years and driven great number of the farmers from the wilder parts to seek safety in the towns; all, in spite of the thousand-rupee bounty on his skin and a long series of hunts organized to rid the district of the scourge.

Countless had been the escapades of Mindoon since as a young tiger he had first earned his name by forcing the abandonment of the village of Mindoon in a series of uncanny raids, against which no traps, watchfulness, or organized hunts had availed. Men, women, and children had continued to disappear with appalling regularity, until finally the demoralized villagers deserted their rice clearings and fled to the more settled parts of the country.

The only effect of this flight, however, had been to enlarge the field of activity for Mindoon to cover the whole Tavoy district, for he was a brute of no common cunning. Thereafter he never killed twice in succession from the same village. A victim snatched from one settlement almost invariably meant that the next one would be from some place forty or more miles away.

He also developed a predelection for young children, and once he was reported to have entered a house filled with a large sleeping family. He made several peregrinations among them as they lay on the floor, in the course of which he received several kicks from individuals who resented the intrusion of what their semiconscious minds took for one of their big dogs, who were then lying mangled near by in the jungle, and concluded his visit by departing with the plumpest child in the room.

Every possible means had been tried to put an end to his career of slaughter. Spring traps consisting of a poisoned spear so arranged that when the tiger touched a string a bent bamboo would drive it into the brute's body, which were usually so effective, had failed miserably when tried against Mindoon. Poison proved equally useless. Mindoon never returned to an old kill.

Organized hunts had been able to do no more than cause him a little excitement and enable him to add to his fame by further exploits. Every party that went out after him came back with fresh stories of his cunning and daring. On several occasions, he had entered the camp of the hunters and carried off one of their number. Moung Nay himself had been present when the tiger, disregarding the tethered cow, had shaken a servant-boy from the very tree (or rather the small bush) on which an army officer was keeping watch and made off before the startled soldier could fire a shot.

Small wonder then that Moung Nay had been busy putting an extra edge on the great knife in his hand and was now studying the tracks of the tiger—or devil, as he with the majority of the inhabitants of the district firmly believed.

"Uncle, rice is cooked," called a child's voice from the back of the bungalow.

"All right, Sharoo," answered Moung Nay, rising and making his way to the house to help his ten-year-old nephew in the task of getting the huge earthen *chattie* off the fire. In a few minutes, the pair were making inroads upon the heaping plates of rice, such as only two hungry Karens can make.

For a time they were too busy to say anything, but at last little Sharoo stopped cramming the rice into his mouth long enough to ask, "Uncle, when will Deputy Commissioner Sahib let you have that rifle he promised you?"

Moung Nay stopped eating and looked out through the door at the tracks. "He says as soon as he gets a permit from Calcutta, which will be next dry season. I wish I had it now."

Sharoo frowned and was about to say something derogatory about the government forbidding guns to people, but he was prevented by a voice from in front of the house shouting, "Ho, Moung Nay, Moung Nay."

Moung Nay leaped to his feet, wiping his mouth on the back of his hand, as Muthoo, the Hindu mail-runner, appeared in the doorway holding out a blue envelope with the impressive "On His Majesty's Service" printed across the top.

Moung Nay stoically took the letter as if he had always been in the habit of receiving such missives regularly, when as a matter of fact this was the first letter of any description that had ever come to him. He tore it open, but after a futile stare at the enclosed sheet, handed it over to Sharoo to see what three years spent at the mission school at Donebu would enable him to do with it. Sharoo grew an inch taller as he rose to the occasion. He was none too enthusiastic about going back to school, but he felt the dignity of his position as he slowly spelled out the following:

Moung Nay:

You are hereby ordered to close the bungalow, and report at once to me at Donebu to assist in hunting down the Mindoon maneater.

C. E. WHITE.

Deputy Commissioner.

Moung Nay turned to the mail-runner. "What is White Sahib thinking of," he said, "to start after the Mindoon devil at this time when the rains will be here in a day or two at the most. Then it will be like trying to chase an eel in the Papoon Swamp to go after old Mindoon. If I only had a gun, I would have a better chance if I stayed right here. That is, if even a rifle would hurt him. Look at those tracks."

The letter-carrier, after a respectful survey of the tracks, shrugged his shoulders. "Have you not heard?" he asked. "Only three days ago at the water feast at the Donebu Pagoda, the striped devil entered the Pagoda grounds in broad daylight and took the boy who was carrying the high priest's fan. White Sahib is very angry. He says, 'This is too much.' He is going to slay Mindoon this time if he has to get permits from Calcutta and arm the whole province."

Moung Nay nodded slowly.

Muthoo continued, "It is very strange how the old fellow always picks out a plump boy if he can. Better look out, Sharoo, you are getting as fat as Ko Bwe's wife. You may get a ride one of these nights, from which there is no return. He must be hungry tonight, too. He got scared away from Saw Ker's last night by a pot of water which fell down upon him as he was trying to crawl by the shelf it was sitting on into the house. So be careful, fat one, and keep away from the jungle."

Sharoo made no answer, and Muthoo went on: "By the way, White Sahib raised the bounty to two thousand rupees yesterday. Much good that will do against a devil."

"Right," agreed Moung Nay. "It would do no good now even if old Mindoon were flesh and blood. He had better wait till the dry season. All we will get now is that Daingu fever. By the looks of those clouds in the south, the rains are close upon us now. But I suppose I must go or White Sahib will be very angry, and I shall never get that rifle he promised me. Have you had rice yet?"

The mail-runner smiled, pointed to the red and white cast marks on his forehead, and vanished down the mail road, breaking out as he entered the jungle into a high-pitched squealing chant that was calculated to induce even Mindoon to leave that part of the country at once.

* * * *

Under ordinary conditions, Moung Nay would never have thought of starting until the next day, but the unusual event of the letter showed White Sahib was in a hurry, and White Sahib was a man to be obeyed. Moreover, Sharoo's school began the day after next in Donebu, and he could take him along and make sure he arrived safely.

Moung Nay and Sharoo therefore lost no time in tying a few necessaries up in a bundle and locking up the bungalow. Nevertheless, it was well past noon before the pair finally set off along a jungle-path which, though untraveled recently on account of old Mindoon, would mean a saving of several miles over the cart-road and would enable them to reach Donebu before night.

For several miles, the path wound along through closely packed clumps of bamboo, the glassy leaves of which formed a most effective sun-shield, but at the same time cut off all view of the heavens. Late in the afternoon, the path entered the more open growth of big mangoes and scrubby trees that characterized the lowlands of the Sittang Valley. Here, for the first time in several hours, the two caught a glimpse of the sky and saw immediately that Moung Nay's prediction of the coming of the rains was to be speedily realized. Already masses of clouds, driven by the first of the monsoons, was pouring up over the mountain ranges to the south. Donebu was only a matter of three miles away now, and Moung Nay quickened his pace to such an extent that little Sharoo's short legs were kept on the run most of the time. Presently there came a flash of lightning, followed by a growl of thunder, and then, with a roar, a squall came driving over the jungle, sending the grub-eaten limbs of mango trees crashing to the ground and following them with a storm of mangoes.

Everything pointed to a miserable, wet night spent in a dripping tree, for it was manifestly impossible to proceed much farther in the gathering darkness and deluge of rain, which experience had taught them was not far off. Suddenly Moung Nay started to run, shouting back: "Come on, Sharoo; we'll see if we can find Ba Tin's old house."

Sharoo's legs did their best, and he was close behind his uncle when, a moment later, they rushed out from the jungle into an abandoned rice-clearing. The owner's thatched house was still standing on its frail bamboo posts. With a glad cry, the two Karens rushed forward, climbed the rickety ladder, and pushed through the doorway into the black interior. The rain held off for a minute or two, but then came down in a torrent that blotted out the sight of the jungle, less than seventy-five yards away, with a white wall of drops and threatened to flay the flimsy thatch roof from the house.

Moung Nay and Sharoo, however, were too accustomed to rain and too thankful for a roof over their heads to spend any time worrying about the weather, especially when there was a good supply of boiled rice in their bundle. Night shut down before they had finished eating, and, without more ado, they stretched out on the floor, and were soon sound asleep.

* * * *

The rain proved to be only a passing storm, and three hours after the two Karens had fallen asleep, the tropical moon was pouring a flood of light down on the old hut in the rice-clearing. A barking deer tripped out of the jungle and nibbled its way daintily across the field, and then back again, finally settling down beneath a lone bush midway between the house and the place where the path vanished into the black jungle to chew its cud and listen to the frogs singing their welcome to the rains.

The hours slipped by, and morning was close at hand, when suddenly the deer sprang to its feet. For a moment it paused, staring with quivering nostrils along the path to where it entered the dark jungle. Then it dashed madly away across the field, and vanished into the jungle on the opposite side.

Presently a shadow drifted out from the jungle under the blazing moon. It was the Mindoon maneater. For a second he hesitated, staring and sniffing in the direction of the house. Then the great, striped sides began to ripple in the moonlight as the great brute slouched cautiously along the path to the foot of the ladder. There he stopped for several minutes, sniffing up at the house and gathering himself. Then he sprang lightly to the platform; slipped through the door; seized Sharoo, and before the boy could do more than scream, had borne him crashing through the thatch wall.

Moung Nay was on his feet in an instant. There before him gaped the hole in the wall, and there across the field was trotting the tiger with Sharoo's limp body swung across his back. Moung Nay did not stop to think. With a shout he sprang through the hole down to the ground, and rushed after old Mindoon clutching his big *dah*. The man-eater was already halfway to the jungle and did not deign to do more than quicken his pace. His long series of escapes had made him contemptuous of any mere man.

Moung Nay raced after him. Once the tiger reached the jungle, pursuit would be useless, as the crafty old desperado well knew. Moung Nay strained every nerve, and his sturdy legs brought him up even with the haunches of the brute, but he did not dare even then, though in a paroxysm of anxiety to save Sharoo, to risk a stroke which would do no more than enrage the tiger and might kill the boy.

Moung Nay was gaining steadily, but the blackness of the shade of the mangoes was all but reached. Five yards more and the tiger would have vanished with his prey. The straining Karen realized it was now or never. Every last bit of reserve strength went into a crucial spurt, and, fixing his eyes on the swelling arch of Mindoon s neck, he threw himself forward as a varsity sprinter throws himself at the tape that means victory or defeat, and struck with all his might at the roots of the jaunty white ruff. He felt the tip of the *dah* bite into the tiger's flesh, tripped, and fell prostrate in the mud and darkness under the first of the mangoes.

Mindoon snarled, half turned, and struck viciously at the body on the ground, ripping Moung Nay's left arm open from shoulder to wrist. Then, without relaxing his grip on Sharoo, was swallowed up in the jungle.

Moung Nay staggered to his feet. The fall and the blow had shaken him. For a full minute he stood with the blood dripping from his arm, staring at the blackness which had engulfed Sharoo. Slowly the realization of what he had done broke in on his mind.

He, with only a *dah*, had dared to chase old Mindoon, the devil of the jungles, and was still alive. A panic seized him; the boy was forgotten, and Moung Nay skulked back to the hut with terrified backward glances. He scrambled up the rickety ladder, but the darkness of the doorway appalled him, and he cowed down in a corner of the platform, clutching the *dah* nervously, and staring at the edge of the jungle.

As the minutes slipped by without incident, his terror passed, and a full comprehension of Sharoo's fate dawned upon him. Few men have ever seen a Karen weep, but as Moung Nay squatted there and thought of the part the little fellow had played in his life, the hunts they had had together, the tears trickled down his cheeks. The ache of his wound finally forced him to bind it up as well as he could with some strips torn from his *lunghi*, but he sat on.

Time passed. The sun rushed up over the Pegu hills and poured its heat down on the drenched earth, but still Moung Nay crouched there, gripping his *dah* and weeping silently.

The sun was some hours into the sky before he finally got up, convulsively clutching the monster knife. He paused for a minute, looking along the trail of tracks to where they disappeared, apparently, in the direction of an enormous padouk-tree. Then he slipped down the ladder and stole as quietly as be could along the trail. He was grimly determined to save what he could of the boy's body, even at the risk of his own life. At least he now knew that old Mindoon was not a devil, or, if he were, he was not invulnerable to a *dah* stroke. But it was no small thing to follow any wounded tiger into the jungle and take away its prey. Moung Nay longed ardently for a rifle in place of his *dah*, or, at least, the full use of both his arms. Still he pressed on slowly, very slowly, ever ready to meet the anticipated coughing roar and charge, while before him in his mind's eye was the image of the torn and half-devoured boy urging him on.

The trail was plain; blood was everywhere. The stems of the elephant-grass on either side of the path Mindoon had broken for himself was smeared with it. Pools of it were thickening on the ground. Moung Nay advanced still more cautiously. In vain, for in spite of his care a log on which he was standing crumbled beneath him, and he pitched through the elephant-grass down into a hollow beneath the tree. The ground was smeared with half-clotted blood. With a shriek of terror Moung Nay slid, in spite of all his efforts, across it, and brought up with a bump against the crouching body of Mindoon. Half-clotted blood from the deep *dah* gash in the neck showed where the jugular vein had been severed.

At Moung Nay's cry a small figure huddled up against the tree-trunk stirred and sat up, trying in a dazed way, at the same time, to feel of a badly bitten arm and a great bump where his forehead had evidently struck a beam as the man-eater had borne him through the wall.

* * * *

It was a long four miles before the two Karens finally reached the first inhabited house on the outskirts of Donebu and sank down on its steps. Any white man would have fainted from the strain of the night's events, and even Moung Nay could only give a very fragmentary account of what had happened when Deputy Commissioner White, who had been swearing all the morning at the dilatoriness of natives in general and Moung Nay in particular, came rattling furiously up to the house in his dog-cart in response to the message brought him by a Kachin about dead devils and bloody men.

He ended by sending the Karens to the hospital in the dog-cart, and going on foot himself to investigate and, if possible, save the skin. He was too late. The news had spread like the waters of the lower Sitang when there is a cloudburst in the hills. Every man, woman, or child who could toddle or totter, or could inveigle any one else into carrying them, were already gathered there in an ecstatic mob about the carcass, venting on it the years of accumulated terror and spite with every conceivable weapon, from the *dah*s of the withered old bamboo-cutters to the fly brush wielded by the doctors syce, and the oiled-silk sunshade in the hands of the haughty Thugyi's wife; and in torrents of abuse poured forth in all of the nineteen languages of Donebu.

Confident in the prestige of his white skin, however, he plunged into the mob in an effort to drive them off; but after his *topi* had been crushed down about his neck by the frenzied hand of his own big *totec*, who ordinarily cringed at his slightest look, and he had seen a group of yellow-robed poongyees, whose cardinal articles of faith are freedom from all emotion, abhorrence of all women, and doing no harm to anything, wildly embrace women of the town and fight their way into the center of the riot and wildly belabor the body with their staffs, he withdrew to a safe distance and watched the surging mass of people as it hacked, trampled, and ground the remains of the tiger into mashed and distorted remnants.

Utter weariness alone finally forced a lull and brought enough of the police-men in the mob to their senses to enable White, with their help, to drive the reluctant mob off and bear the remains back to Donebu, followed by a still jabberingly jubilant procession.

All this happened years ago. Now Moung Nay is chief man of the largest town in the Tavoy district. On special occasions, particularly when Sharoo comes from his position in Rangoon on the commissioner's staff to spend his vacation with Moung Nay, he will unlock his iron-bound teak-box and take out of their wrapping a *dah* and an immense tiger's tooth, the only unbroken thing left in old Mindoon's body by the mob. Then the two men gaze at them for some minutes, while Sharoo's hand steals up to two great dents in his biceps, and Moung Nay fingers silently the scars on his left arm, and both of them think of the race with old Mindoon and death that Moung Nay ran that night out in the Tavoy jungle, and the victory that meant life itself for Sharoo, and for Moung Nay the best rifle money could buy in London and the only perpetual gun permit in all Burma.

THE SPIRIT OF FRANCE

S. B. H. Hurst

"Mergui is a dirty and most immoral town."

Father Murphy, the stout, kindly missionary paused dramatically. "But hitherto we have been spared this—a white girl dancing for Mohammedans and Chinamen! You must do something, Bailey!"

The youthful English magistrate, who, with ten Sikh policemen and one white clerk, was administrator of the affairs of the little town and the district adjoining it on the Tenasserim strip of the coast of Burma, looked through the window of his office at the mud of low tide in the harbor. A puff of wind brought the reek of it. He sniffed, then answered testily:

"You know as well as I do, Padre, that I can do nothing. Until the girl commits a crime I cannot have her arrested. English law does not infringe on the rights of people to live where they wish. If she wants to live among the colored population, that's her business. Let her dance! I have received no complaints about her. If you are worried about her morals, well—that's in your department, not mine!"

The priest sighed.

"Yes," he answered. "But the girl won't listen to me. She politely avoids discussion. Admits being a Catholic, too! Orphan. Daughter of some Frenchman who died up Indo-China way. I don't know how she drifted down here."

"Well, I can't help you, Murphy. I detest having a white woman of her occupation in the town—liable to stir up any sort of trouble. But you can find 'em all over Burma. We must bear our burdens, Padre. Good morning!"

The priest left the magistrate's office. The heat weighed heavily upon his huge figure. He felt, both physically and spiritually, depressed. This pretty child— for she was little more—who politely refused to worry about her soul's welfare! Father Murphy clenched his fists.

"If I have to use force," he said firmly, "I'll do it! I will break the law if need be—the law that protects vice from the assaults of decency! I will break through that ring of Mohammedan and Chinese brutes who leer at her dancing. I may have to hit a few ugly faces, for which Bailey could have me arrested; but I will—for the good of that young woman's soul. It's my duty, and by the living God I'll do it! I'm Irish, and before I got so fat I could use my hands for other things than blessing people!"

He was spared this necessity. His walk had brought him to the tiny church he himself had designed and helped to build. In its quiet he would compose himself. He took off his large solar hat and wiped his streaming forehead. Then he dropped the hat in joyful astonishment. For the girl he had thought apostate was kneeling there, praying!

"Oh, Father, I thank Thee!" he murmured.

The girl looked up and saw him. She was vaguely disturbed. The priest, that massive man of intuitions, felt that she had timed her visit to the church to correspond with his absence. No doubt there were other visits.

"Daughter," he said, "I do not understand this!"

She smiled, mischievously.

"My Father, there is, ah, so veree mouch that ees hard to ounderstand!"

His voice became hard.

"I do not understand why you have refused to talk with me. I do not understand why you have come here when you knew I was away. And ... I have known other women like you. But the others did not avoid the priest. Instead, they sought absolution!"

She shrugged her shoulders. The flash of her smile was of pearls. Her eyes were violet lakes in which dwelt mystery and delight.

"Perhaps they needed it!" she answered.

For a moment the priest was so angry at her pert reply that he could not answer her. She went on. But she no longer smiled, and the lids covered her provocative eyes.

"But I, what am so small, joost come 'ere because, maybe, God ees 'ere! Onnyways, if He is anywhere in Mergui, He will be 'ere! And you know, Father, that there is times when every woman feel lonelee for God. So I do not come when you are here. Becos' I do not want to talk about my sins. Eet would take too much time. And the time I come 'ere is the time I 'ave give to God!"

Her eyes met his defiantly.

Murphy mastered his anger.

"Do you realize that God sees you when you are not in His church—when you are dancing and—and living with those horrible heathen men?"

She raised her small head proudly.

"I do not 'live' with any man!" Her eyes blazed, her little hands clenched. "For what you 'ave said, but that you are a priest, I would strike you! I live with no man! I 'ave never lived with any man! And I have never even kissed any man but my father—what is died!"

The flash left her eyes. Her head drooped. She sank down upon the wooden bench and sobbed.

Father Murphy was deeply distressed. He could not believe her, but ...

"My child! My poor child!" He laid a hand gently upon her shoulder. "But you must realize how your dancing for such creatures seems!"

"To dance is all I know," she sobbed. "I 'ave tried to dance for the white men, but they do not want me. They want women who will kees after dancing—who will kees and love for money. I must live! Mohamet Ali and his nasty bearded men 'ave never tried to kees me. Mohamet looks cruel, but he treats me square! And the Chinamen are afraid of him. The men for whom I dance know that if they try to kees me they will 'ave a long knife in their ribs. Mohamet is 'eathen, you say. Yes. But I would razzer dance for heem than for white men who do not want dancing as mouch as they want something else!"

"Some other way of making a living may be found," began the baffled priest.

She interrupted fiercely. "To scrub floors, eh! I 'ave a right to live my own life. I love to dance!"

"I know you are French, of course, and you said you were an orphan; but you have not told me your name," the priest conciliated.

She answered with proud mischievousness:

"When I was leetle girl, my father called me 'Leetle Spirit of France,' because eet is the spirit of France to dance and sing—and to fight! So now I call my name, 'Spirit of France!' But you will say I am conceit—is it not?"

And she laughed and bowed and went out into the glaring morning.

Murphy sighed. A bit of human thistledown!

* * * *

The Mergui day dragged its festering way through the hours. Night came over the place with the stars peering dubiously through a velvet pall, with the bats and huge moths winging like evil souls visiting friends still incarnate, with phallic music throbbing feverishly. Sikh policemen stalked here and there, daintily contemptuous of the filth of it all.

In a small, low-lit courtyard danced the Spirit of France. Avid eyes glowed at her beauty, wondering how long Mohamet Ali would continue to bestow upon her his quite unusual protection. There were no Burmese there; only Mohammedan traders, adventurers from Northern India, with their co-religionists of Mergui.

The music throbbed and the girl whirled to it, abandoned to a sheer ecstasy of physical rhythm, borne upon the swell of the poetry of herself.

But this night the mood of her audience was different. Its sensuous absorption of her was sporadic. Piqued, she danced the more enticingly. The shadows of the place were gathered and twisted and festooned about her, but her audience was far from paying her its customary attention. Mohamet Ali and his nearest friends paid no attention at all. In vain she danced closer to him. If he looked at her at all it was an abstracted look that did not see her. Matters of great moment seemingly engaged him. He talked in undertones to his friends. They smoked and drank their coffee, but the sensuality of their faces was sublimated to a fierce interest in the affair of their conversation.

The Spirit of France danced on, puzzled, irritated, vastly curious. About what thing were they talking? Their hairy faces were grouped together. They had even laid aside their pipes.... The Spirit of France changed the rhythm of her dancing. She moved like a leaf before vagrant puffs of wind ... slowly. Pausing, and bending, and moving again. In sleepy cadence she danced before Mohamet Ali and his lieutenants....

Fragments of words came to her straining ears. But she could not linger there. Burning with curiosity, she dared not wait for more. She whirled into allegro again, and the music caught her mood and ran with her.

But again and again she floated like a lazy leaf before Mohamet Ali, and the fragments of their words wove themselves into a baffling tapestry—a picture blurred, and without outline, yet vividly colored with significance. Significance of what?

They were laughing now, those bearded men from the North. Grimacing, rather, much as tigers grimace. The Spirit of France shivered. But she fought the fear in her gallant heart and killed it before it could grow to terror. And she danced on.

But what were they planning? It did not seem to concern herself; they had hardly glanced at her for an hour. The Mohammedans of lesser parts had been beckoned into conference. The girl felt a premonition of death touch her soul heavily. Neither was it a new thing they planned. She felt intuitively that these fierce men were discussing something done before that was to be done again. Their minds were running in old, well-loved grooves.

Mohamet Ali was looking at her! The Spirit of France danced the more merrily. He beckoned her towards him.

"Little sparrow," he said, "dance no more this night. Go and sleep."

"And I will dance for you tomorrow night?"

The heavy lids of the man flickered. The eyes of his companions became blank—a blankness that seemed overdone.

"Yes, you will dance for me again," said Mohamet gravely, "because you are under my protection. Sleep now. I will send for you when I want you. Here is your money."

* * * *

He was dismissed. And she was racked with a problem. There had been something terrible about those men. Never before had they been like that. But Mohamet had not been lying—he really meant she should dance for him again. But what were they planning? Pirates, robbers, fierce men of the North. What did they plan? The few words she had gleaned made darkness—darkness fraught with something terrible. It was three hours past midnight.

As she began to undress she heard footsteps along the narrow street. There were two men. One spoke to the other as they passed her window. His voice was like the hiss of a snake.

"Let them cry for help! We have cut their talking wire!"

"And the girl?" muttered the other.

"Nay, Mohamet Ali says that he himself will slay the man that so much as touches a hair of her head!"

They passed on. But the Spirit of France knew! Crouched on her bed, shivering, hardly breathing, she knew.

The disconnected words. The cruel grimaces. Religious fanaticism, like burning oil, was to be poured upon the Christians. Four white men and ten loyal Sikhs in Mergui—and the telegraph wire to Rangoon had been cut!

But she would not be harmed. She had no doubts about that. Her safety was assured. Mohamet would rather die than break his word. And the man who touched her would surely die. Mohamet and his men had treated her decently. To do so was a queer freak in their cruel natures. But they had done so, and would continue to do so. And the white people—had reviled her. They had tried to make a prostitute of her. And the fat priest—

She writhed on her bed at the memory of it—at the memory of all her treatment at the hands of the Christians. She fought the problem. If she stayed in her room she was safe. If she warned the unsuspecting white men her doom was certain. It would be better, far better to kill herself than to fall into Mohamet's clutches again. If she warned the white men! ... And what would the white men do for her if she did warn them? Continue to revile her, to offer cheap pay for her lovely body? She smothered a bitter laugh. For there would be no white men left to revile her, and she would be worse than dead. What chance had four Englishmen, with their ten fighting Sikhs, against five hundred Mohammedans, every one believing that Paradise waited the man who died fighting against an unbeliever?

She walked up and down the floor. This was agony. It was horrible to think of those men being killed! But she was safe! And if she warned the Christians her fate would be more horrible than theirs! But—she might die!

The Spirit of France. Her little pet name of childhood. And the brave things her father had told her about the spirit of France—about the gallantry of that distant homeland she had never seen! The history of a nation seemed to be watching her....

How would France face such a problem? ... How would the glorious national spirit of France respond to such a situation? ...

She was walking stealthily to the door, cursing herself. Valuable time was wasted while she dwelt upon her own safety.

"I am a disgrace," she muttered.

She crouched in the dark doorway. More men were coming along the street. She held her breath, her soul damning these men for detaining her from her duty. They passed, and her light feet were flying as they had never flown before. Like a leaf still, but now like a leaf before a hurricane, the Spirit of France was running through the streets of Mergui.

* * * *

Scandalized, Father Murphy woke to her tearing away his mosquito curtains, to her fierce shaking of his arm.

"What! What are you doing here? Go away. George!"

He called for his servant—converted, and baptized with that familiar name.

The Spirit of France sneered. But she continued to pull fiercely at the furious priest.

"Your servant!" she laughed shrilly. "He weel 'ave run away—with all your other made-Christians!"

She pulled at the priest, swearing like a cat. And, somehow, she told her story.

"But such a thing cannot happen in Burma anymore!" the priest exclaimed.

"Come! Come and see, foolish man!" she stormed. "They 'ave cut the telegram!"

"Go away while I put on some clothes!"

"There is not time!"

"Wait outside! I will not run through the streets in pajamas to save my life!"

She waited, feverishly biting her fingernails. Then, the hour before the dawn saw a heavily panting Father Murphy doing his utmost to run with the Spirit of France through the streets of Mergui towards the fairly stout jail and the magistrate's office.

"Hurree! Hurree!"

"The doctor!" panted the priest. "We must wake Doctor Pelham!"

They roused the doctor, a calm and cynical person.

"I'm safe," he drawled. "I'm an infidel, and these chaps, you say, are out to kill the Christians!"

"Don't jest at this terrible moment," said Murphy severely.

"Not jestin'. How many times have you called me an infidel, Murphy? But I'm accustomed to being woke up at ghastly hours to go on unpleasant business. I'll go with you."

"Hurree!" cried the girl. "I 'ear 'em!"

"So do I," replied the doctor. "But there is time to get my bag. Somebody will need surgical aid—most of us, probably."

They reached the jail. In the yard were all the Sikhs. They had just wakened the magistrate, reporting "some sort of disturbance." The Spirit of France shrilled out the truth. The magistrate was skeptical. He could not know that this was the beginning of the riots of 1897.

"Telegraph Rangoon immediately," the magistrate told his white assistant.

The Spirit of France laughed wildly. Then she sat down weakly.

"Wire's down, sir!" reported the operator.

"Now you know I tell truth," the Spirit of France cried indignantly. "They are going to keel every Christian in Mergui. I 'ear them when I dance, but am not sure till they pass my window after cutting the telegram wire."

"So," said the young magistrate cheerfully. "Then we'll have to fight it out alone. Have to anyway, because it would be days before Rangoon could get help to us. But I would like to let the boss know who did this thing." He turned to the Spirit of France, and bowed. "I—I'm much obliged to you for what you have done. And now you had better go."

"Go!" She jumped to her feet. "M'sieu, many times 'ave I fired a gun. I fight joust so well as onybody!"

"Don't doubt it," responded the magistrate. "It isn't that. The point is that if you leave us now Mohamet Ali will not hurt you. He will just regard you as a frightened woman—liable to do anything. Run along, now. Cry, and say the noise has terrified you! Don't suppose Mohamet knows you roused Father Murphy and the doctor; so, goodbye—and thank you!"

He held out his hand.

"I stay 'ere and fight for you!" she answered firmly.

"Do you realize," he said gently, "that there is little chance of any of us seeing the sunset—that we'll do well to last until noon? Do you know that if you stay here and help us Mohamet will give orders to his men to take you alive? Do you realize what horrible things will be done to you then?"

She laughed.

"Do you realize that my father was a Frenchman? He call me for pet name 'Little Spirit of France!' Do you realize Spirit of France—what eet mean? Give me a gun, please!"

The magistrate beckoned to Sergeant Ruttan Singh.

"Give the mem sahib a gun, Sergeant."

Then he turned to the Spirit of France. His voice shook somewhat. Trying to honor her, he spoke in such awful French that she was hard put to it not to laugh. But his words more than excused his accent.

He turned to the still heavily breathing priest.

"Padre, have you any scruples about pulling the trigger when the sight's on another human being?"

"Not a one—in this case!" responded Father Murphy cheerfully and with perfect conviction.

"Good! We will divide. You will take three Sikhs and defend the northwest corner."

"I was Irish before I was a priest. Give me a rifle!" answered Murphy.

"They are coming!" whispered the Spirit of France.

"We will be ready," replied the magistrate quietly. "Take the southeast corner, will you, Doctor? It's liable to be hot there while it lasts, but you're a first-class shot."

"Very good, General," drawled the doctor. "But won't my friends laugh when they hear of this! Old Pelham, the infidel, killed in a religious war!"

The magistrate grinned.

"All right, then. I will command at the northeast, and Mason and Ruttan Singh shall have the southwest corner. Now we are ready. Good thing we have lots of ammunition. Here they come! Steady now! Don't waste a shot! If they get over the wall, shoot; and keep on shooting as long as any of 'em are in the yard! And if a head shows let it have it!" He walked across the room and whispered to the doctor, "If I go first, Pelham, and you see that we're done in, and the girl is still alive— keep a bullet for her."

The doctor nodded.

"And I'll tell Ruttan Singh to tell his men to do the same," the magistrate added.

* * * *

As it grew light the raging hundreds beyond the circling wall began firing their first broadside—of verbal filth, that hymn of hate which has sounded down the years, that way of honoring God peculiar to religious enthusiasts. Some scattered shots were fired which did no damage, and Mohamet Ali could be heard shouting to his followers.

"We have days of time, oh men of the True God! Haste not! Let the infidels shudder a while as death stares them in the eye. Let them die slowly!"

A mocking voice answered him.

"That hellcat pet of thine was seen warning the fat mullah of the infidels, oh Mohamet Ali!"

"So, the woman, eh! A snake in my bosom!" Mohamet foamed down his beard, but realizing the probable effect on his followers, controlled himself "So it was written, then, that she should furnish amusement for the Faithful! See that she is not killed! Catch the cat alive and unhurt. She asked me if she should dance for me again! She shall! But it will be such a dance as she has never dreamed of!"

He followed with unprintable threats. He gesticulated and raved about the fun to follow the killing of the white men. But he showed a little too much of himself. The doctor took a snap shot at him, and Mohamet Ali lost the greater part of one of his ears.

"Damn rotten miss," muttered that sarcastic medico. "Must have lost my temper at hearing such an awful creature call me an infidel. Can't shoot straight when my trigger hand itches to punch a chap's nose."

"Magistrate Sahib." Ruttan Singh saluted. "It is sunrise and the flag has not been hoisted. Will the sahib give the order?"

"Rutah Singh, you know it is certain death to venture out of here into the yard?"

The big Sikh grinned.

"Death is at our elbows, sahib!"

"Yes, and there's something about the old rag that makes it more enjoyable to fight when it's flying; but we can't afford to lose a man. Sorry, Ruttan Singh, but we must fight this fight with the flag lying on the table yonder."

"Very good, sahib," replied Ruttan Singh regretfully, saluting and returning to his post.

The sun rose, and the besieging horde became suddenly quiet. It turned as one man towards Mecca, and said its morning prayer.

"Can't we rush 'em?" muttered the priest to the magistrate.

"No! It's tempting, but we've got to hold the fort! Never can tell what may turn up, you know; but if we rushed out on those praying people we'd all be killed in short order!"

"Religion is a fearful and wonderful thing!" remarked the doctor.

"I wish they'd hurry," whispered Mason.

"So do we all," answered the doctor. "But let's not show it."

The praying ended.

"Ready, everybody!" shouted the magistrate.

Forgetting, of course, Mohamet Ali's cautious suggestion that they let the Christians die slowly, and stimulated to paradisiacal ardor by their prayers, the followers of the prophet leaped shrieking at the wall, and went over it like a brown wave.

* * * *

Then for some minutes there was very warm work. Rapid firing did not stem the wave. It broke it, but those unhit dashed with a truly terrible bravery at the bars of the jail windows. Shrieks, groans and monstrous blasphemies made a frightful din as they charged. The defenders were for the most part grimly silent. Only the doctor muttered encouragingly.

"A little lower, young lady. These birds are flying low."

But the Spirit of France never heard him. Her mind was set on the fearful hairy faces against whom her soul raged, while a mockery of memory wondered why she had danced for them. She fought joyously. In her blood a long line of heroes surged. As she dashed the sweat from her eyes she saw with surprise that the yard was filled with dead men.

Such a stout defense was too much, even for such fanatics. The canny Mohamet saw that he was not getting value for his dead. He called his men.

"Lot of wounded out there," remarked the doctor casually. "But I have two minor casualties to attend to in here. Ruttan Singh has a bullet in his shoulder, although he won't admit it; and one of his men is hit. Ah! Hullo, General; close shave that!"

A bullet had grazed the magistrate's forehead, and he was bleeding freely.

"You attend to the men! Give me ze plaster for ees head!"

And the Spirit of France began deftly to bind the magistrate's wound.

"It may be inhuman," said the young man, "but those chaps out there will have to attend to their own wounded, Doctor. Do you think I should let them carry them off under a flag of truce?"

The doctor gave him a searching look. The magistrate's wound had shaken him badly.

"Take a big drink and don't be an ass," advised the doctor. "Good work, young lady. Now, before the charming enemy tries another charge, please help me bandage this fine sergeant of Sikhs."

But Mohamet Ali had thought of a better and more entertaining plan of campaign than charging across that death-strewn yard. And the one redeeming feature of a Mergui morning, the brief breeze from the sea, would aid the new plan. Mohamet disclosed his new and brilliant plan to his lieutenants behind the wall. It was hailed with shrieks of approbation, delighted yells. It gratified the lust for cruelty of a mob maddened by primitive emotion. Hence there was a pause in the conflict.

"What now?" said the doctor. "Are the brutes saying their prayers again?"

"Not at this hour!" answered the priest.

"Well, I don't pretend to be an authority," retorted the doctor. "But I wish we could see over the jail wall! They are up to some deviltry! And they could bring up a dozen batteries along the side of the hill while we couldn't see them doing it!"

"There is no artillery they can get," said the distressed magistrate.

"That's right—there isn't," soothed the doctor.

The wait was nerve-racking—the wait and the impossibility of seeing what the enemy was doing. But the doctor had more than his suspicions. The yells of delight could mean only one thing. Yes, that would be it. A whiff of sea breeze confirmed his deduction.

"But I won't tell the others," he muttered grimly. "Bad enough when it comes, without having 'em suffer the dread of waiting for it."

The enemy had become silent. Then there was some chuckling borne on the breeze. It was followed by a great yell. The breeze became pungent.

"They are trying to smoke us out!" shouted the priest gamely.

"Yes," drawled the doctor. "Better tie wet towels over our faces!"

He turned away. He was very pale now. Should he tell his friends? What a mercy they didn't realize. But a short-lived mercy. Better let them know—they were brave men. He beckoned the priest and the magistrate.

"May as well tell you," he whispered. "They are rounding up cases of oil from the Chinese stores. They will pour the oil over the wall, and the fires will do the rest! The delay is caused by the Chinks. They don't want to supply oil for which they know they won't be paid— and they don't want to be mixed up in their affair. The Mohamet Ali gang can run up country, having no property here to leave when our people get here—but the Chinks have stores they don't want to lose!"

He whispered this very gently:

"Hadn't we better shoot the girl and then rush out on them and end it?" said the magistrate now, with full hold on himself, as calm as the doctor.

"But … who will … shoot her?" whispered the priest. No one answered.

"Oh, hell, let's stick it out!" said the doctor. "The oil isn't here yet!"

* * * *

The wounded Ruttan Singh reeled to the magistrate. He saluted stiffly.

"Sahib, there is a steamer coming into the harbor!"

"Thank you, Sergeant!" the magistrate answered. "Don't tell anyone! It's probably one of those native owned coast boats, Mohammedan crew. There is one due here today. And while they perhaps would not help the enemy, they certainly won't help us. They couldn't, anyhow. When they see the row, they will run out of the harbor without discharging the cargo!"

The smoke became worse. The defenders peered through it as best they could, guns ready, but the Mohammedans kept their heads behind the wall.

Coughing, the doctor turned to the window.

"Hullo!" he muttered. "That isn't a native coast boat. Damn the smoke—I can't see!"

He wiped his eyes carefully, and looked again. The breeze blew more strongly. The doctor clenched his fists.

"No," he said, and his voice sounded far away to him, and like an excited girl's. "No." His voice rose so that all heard him. "No! It's a small cruiser—flying the American flag!"

The magistrate gasped. He clapped his hands excitedly.

"Of course!" he shouted. "I forgot. The Florida, going to Rangoon for the governor's big tomashe! I had word she would call here. But—she's two days ahead of time! Hurrah! We're saved!"

"No chance," snapped the doctor. "Look! The oil!"

"But the Americans will help us!" the magistrate screamed.

"How's her captain to know we need help? Until it's too late? He'll find our ashes when he comes ashore! They are starting the oil! The captain will see the fire and hear the fuss, but how will he know what's going on? Unless he knows what's happening— It isn't his business to land on British territory to put out fires!"

"Oh, God," groaned the priest, "is there no way we can let that American captain know we need help?"

"Of course there is!"

* * * *

It was the Spirit of France who shouted. It was the Spirit of France who seized the flag lying on the table and dashed for the jail door. Understanding, the men tried to stop her—to do the work themselves. But she eluded them.

She dashed out into the yard—a Joan of Arc, undaunted among the flames and smoke. Mohamet Ali saw her.

"Don't shoot!" he screamed to his men. "Does she come to me for mercy? Don't shoot her—my mercy waits!"

The girl turned and dashed for the flagpole. Swiftly ran the Spirit of France. Her nimble fingers were at the flag halyards. The smoke beat about her. The red flame of the oil creeping across the yard struck at her like tongues of snakes. But—a long moment—and she was hoisting the flag! Half mast and Union down—a signal of distress everywhere! And Mohamet understood. Of the volley that broke around the girl he fired the first shot.

She was hit. She was hit again. But she managed to stagger into the doctor's arms, and he lifted her into the jail.

"Tear it down! Down with that signal!" screamed Mohamet Ali.

But his men could not obey! The flaming oil made a barrier of safety for the flag which even their fanaticism could not pass. And the flag stiffened in the morning breeze, and sent its message seaward.

The yelling besiegers redoubled their efforts. They were shooting the Chinese who wouldn't give them oil. Was there time? Surely, the American captain would understand! But was there time? If Mohamet Ali could get more oil quickly—

A shell from the American cruiser shrieked over the jail. A messenger!

A messenger of comfort and hope to tell the defenders their signal had been seen—for of course a bombardment of the enemy would have been dangerous to the defenders of the jail.

"American bugles coming up the hill!"

"The girl?" asked the magistrate. "Is she dead?"

"No," said the doctor gruffly. "No. Badly wounded, but we'll pull her through!"

The Spirit of France opened her eyes.

"You won't die," said the doctor gently.

She smiled.

"The Spirit of France will never die!" she answered.

THE BOX OF THE IVORY DRAGON

James L. Aton

CHAPTER I

Shanghai … February … Clammy morning … The great city where East meets West shivered in damp and foggy cold. Sikh policemen muffled in greatcoats hummed manfully as they breasted the frosty air. White men of affairs whirled along to work in closed cars; lesser white men damned fate in rickshaws. Chattering coolies in quilted winter coats lurched along the Bund in vain search of warmth.

The strip of garden between Bund and harbor that in summer had sheltered the choice loafers of Asia was now abandoned to the cold—and to Kelley.

Quite unmindful was Kelley of the air's wintry sting. He had no greatcoat and no gloves; yet he lolled on a bench, facing the chill from the harbor, and did not shiver. Part of his inner warmth came from an overdose of hootch; more of it came from the marrow of the man, grown mighty on winter seas.

From the misty harbor came a raucous medley of fog-horns. The lone man on the bench ignored them expertly; he was otherwise busy. Deep from his pants pocket he had pulled the handful of small coins that made up his available cash assets, and was looking them over—appraisingly, yet not cheerlessly.

"Heck!" he meditated. "Guess I'll have to hunt for a job!"

He was a big man, was Kelley—too big for speed. There was a military erectness to his shoulders; a hint of the stevedore in his huge hands, the roll of the sea in his legs, the devil-may-care glint of the soldier of fortune in his steel-blue eyes. With more fire than wisdom he had adventured to the ends of the earth—and had now no more than a jingle of small change to show for all that he had fought and dared.

Of the coins in his palm, many were pocket pieces, rich with associations, but poor in purchasing power. The pennies were from dirty Singapore ... the eight-sided annas from red-and-yellow Bombay ... the copper sens from the toy streets of Tokyo ... the smart yellow franc from a wine-shop in Marseilles ... the quarter from singing New Orleans. The few Shanghai dimes and coppers that topped the heap were reminders of the five hundred dollars that he had squandered in four glorious days on shore.

The thought came that he might walk up Broadway to a native money-changer and swap his assortment of alien coins for a Shanghai big dollar; but—

"Nix!" he muttered. "I won't do it— I'll hunt for a job."

From his coat-pocket he took the paper he had picked up that morning off the street, and began awkwardly to seek the column that told of help wanted. He was no reader; it would have been more in keeping with his genius to have prowled along the water-front, seeking a berth on an outbound steamer. But he had been on salt water steadily for a long year; he had it in mind now to stay on shore and see somewhat of this land of China.

The want ads, when he found them, were few in number, as becomes a land where the man-supply exceeds the demand: "Number one office coolie, able to speak French, English and Mandarin" ... "Experienced compradore by established house in Tientsin" ... "Chinese student will exchange letters with American man for mutual self-improvement—" ... "Russian Countess travelling to France wishes companion who will act also as nurse-maid" ... "Missionary family will employ trained amah—call mornings only" ...

"Nothing for me," reflected Kelley. Already his huge hands were crumpling the paper when a line in the lower right-hand corner caught his eye:

American with military training for special service. Apply at once, top floor, 600 N.

Szechuen Road.

Kelley started. Across the wide sweep of the traffic-congested Bund he dodged his way, and stopped in front of a stately Sikh policeman who held the head of a narrow cross-street.

"Hey, Bud, where's this location?" The American put his finger on the ad.

The bearded Sikh read the name, then pointed—a vague gesture indicating some far-off indefinite spot in the teeming city back from the harbor. Kelley went his way along the narrow cross-street, keeping his eye out for some fellow white man from whom he might seek more explicit direction.

In the middle of the third square back from the Bund, he first saw the Lank Man with the Brown Beard, bargaining with a Chinese peddler who had spread his wares of polished brass out on the narrow walk.

"It's worth five dollars." The Lank Man held a brass bowl in his hand. "I'll give you that—no more."

"No can do," the peddler was saying. "Eight dollars best price. I tell you true."

Kelley forgot his objective for a moment and stopped to stare.

Indeed, the Lank Man with the Brown Beard would have won many stares on any street in any city. Some would have gaped at his abnormally lank tallness, some at the outsprouting luxuriance of his whiskers, some at the light summer suit and topcoat that flapped about his leanness in the moisture-laden winter wind. Whether in New York or London, in Shanghai or Winnipeg, he would have stood forth, unreal, foreign, alien, one apart from the conventionalities of this world. American he was, but, rarest of all Americans, an artist— glorious rebel against the ways of the majorities.

"I cannot afford eight dollars," began Brown Beard. "I—" he glanced up and saw Kelley gaping. "How do you like it?" He held out the brass bowl. "The tracing, I admit, is crude—but the shape! Manf only a Chinaman could dream of a curve like that."

Kelley became aware that Brown Beard was speaking certainly to him.

"I don't know nothing about that junk," he admitted. "It all looks alike to me."

"Each of us has his separate dream." Brown Beard looked keenly at Kelley. "There are some things, I fancy, in which you could see beauty." He handed the bowl back to the watchful peddler, then with a deft motion drew something from his inner coat-pocket "There, what do you make of this?"

Kelly looked curiously at the dagger which Brown Beard placed in his hand.

"That's Jap stuff!" he exclaimed eagerly|. "Samurai, or whatever you call it. That's a real one—you don't see many like it They held 'em like this—" He illustrated "Doggone hard things to dodge."

He continued to hold the dagger, studying it with approval.

"That's a dandy!" he said, avidly. "That's a real curio. I'd rather own that than some of them old ones I saw in the Tower of London."

Brown Beard's eyes were fixed thoughtfully on Kelley.

"I thought you'd see beauty in that," he said as he put the dagger carefully back in his pocket. "Now you can understand how I see beauty in yon brass bowl."

"No, I can't," disputed Kelley. "A bowl ain't no use; a dagger is—anyway, it has been. Just think—maybe kings have been killed with that there weapon."

"Maybe they have." Brown Beard was still eyeing Kelley; the intentness of his gaze was well-nigh disconcerting … Kelley's mind swung back to his errand.

"Maybe you can tell me where this street is." He drew the paper from his pocket and pointed to the ad. "I won't try to pronounce it."

"Ha!" There was meaning in Brown Beard's ejaculation as his eye caught the ad. "Six hundred North Szechuen!"

"Is that some place you know?" demanded Kelley.

"Looking for work?" countered Brown Beard.

"You've guessed it. Do you want to hire me?"

The Lank Man seemed on the edge of saying something vitally important. His eyes devoured Kelley as a critic studies a canvas. Kelley shoved the paper back into his pocket and turned away.

"Let me know when you're ready to talk," he said gruffly.

The Lank Man was at Kelley's side in an instant.

"Here, I'll show you the way." His hand rested on Kelley's arm as he pointed out directions. "You'll find it easily," he concluded. "It's on a main street. And pardon me for not answering; I went to thinking of something else. I'm very often absent-minded, you know. I'm glad we met. My name is Hamilton—Wall Hamilton. I hope we'll meet again."

"Same here!" Kelley was a welcomer of friendships. "My name's Kelley—plain Kelley."

"Good luck, Kelley!" The two shook hands. "Better look into that job thoroughly before you take it—don't set yourself up too high, and don't believe everything you see. Good-by!"

"He's a nut," mused Kelley as he went on his way. "I've seen 'em like that before. He's different though—that kind are mostly so wrapped up in themselves that they don't even see you. He's got eyes like a detective—" the big man chuckled. "Heck, wouldn't he surely make a right funny detective!"

CHAPTER II

The front door coolie at 600 Szechuen Road grinned understandingly at Kelley holding his morning paper, opened the door wide enough to admit the big American, pointed up the stairs.

"Topside," he said briefly.

Kelley climbed — one flight, two flights.

A door stood open before him; he looked. into a wide, low-ceilinged room. Soft coal smoked in the fireplace. A man—a white man with smooth black hair, heavy eyebrows, rich olive complexion—sat busy with documents at a square table. He glanced up inquiringly at Kelley in the doorway.

"I'm looking for a job," said Kelley, and pointed to his paper. The man at the table exhaled authority—gave Kelley the feeling that he ought to salute.

"Be seated!" From his voice the man was American. "I'll be through shortly."

There wasn't much in the room to attract Kelley's eye as he sat comfortably waiting. Sagging cracks in the white-washed ceiling … a map or two on the wall … a shelf of sheepskin books … a telephone … beyond the fireplace a rifle atop a wide mahogany chest. Kelley eyed the chest hopefully—here, he surmised, was an arsenal.

The man at the table was more interesting to look at than was the furniture of the room. Smooth skin, straight nose, strong chin, thoughtful mouth, glossy hair, all blended into insolent handsomeness. His air was capable, assured—the air that speaks of hundred-thousand-dollar positions. Kelley compared him to Brown Beard: the one a ragged roamer, dickering with a peddler on the street—the other a dependable man of affairs.

"I hope I land the job," wished Kelley, and smiled at Brown Beard's advice that he be wary of what he saw. "I guess I know the real thing when I see it," he argued inwardly. "I guess Hamilton's the one that needs a guardian—not me."

He waited for a long hour. The man of affairs worked steadily at his documents, occasionally consulted the map of China that hung on the wall, once made use of the telephone—to relay a cablegram in code to the Department of State at Washington. Kelley was more and more impressed; plainly this man stood high in Government service.

At length he swung around.

"Name?"

"Clay Kelley."

"Military service?"

"Three years in the Marines."

"Discharge?"

Kelley dug the treasured paper from an inner pocket and handed it over. The man at the table studied it closely, compared it with a typewritten docket which he drew from the table drawer, handed it back finally without comment.

"Last job?"

"On a tramp—the Mary Peter. I quit last week—here's a paper,"

Kelley proffered a "to-whom-it-may-concern" signed by the captain of the Mary Peter. The man gave it scarcely a glance.

"Have you been in China before?"

"Not before last Monday," admitted Kelley.

"Any friends here?"

"Not to speak of."

"Any money?"

Kelley grimaced. "Them sing-song girls are good gamblers," he said with apparent irrelevance.

The man bowed his head for a few seconds in thought.

"All right!" he said with decision. "You're hired."

"What for?" It was Kelley's turn to interrogate.

"Secret Service," the man at the table leaned forward confidentially. "I'll have to tell you a bit; I see you're the sort that can be trusted."

"You bet I am!" bragged Kelley. "You can just bank on me."

"My name is Leighton," went on the other.

"I'm working directly from Washington—even the consular officers here don't know that I'm on the field. That's to avoid any possibility of a leak. It's ticklish work—I'm cooperating with a like man from London. We're looking for exports of opium. A good deal is smuggled out from here. If we can stop it, it will be easier than trying to uncover and confiscate it at port of entry. Understand?"

"Sure!" approved Kelley. "That's a good idea. It's nothing to land opium in 'Frisco—I've seen it done enough times. Where do I come in?"

"So far I've been doing only preliminary investigating," continued Leighton. "I'm onto the gang now that's doing the smuggling—it's an organized ring, you understand. I have authority to conduct a raid whenever I have a chance to confiscate a sufficient amount to make it worth while. Raids will call for more or less force; I need a man who can give a blow or two when there's need, and who can be trustworthy and discreet. I'm giving you a chance at the job."

"When do I start? What do you pay?"

"You start today. I may arrange our first raid to-night. The salary is two hundred per month gold, and necessary expenses."

"I'm hired!" Kelley expanded his chest luxuriously. "Lead me to it."

"The car is ready," said Leighton in a low voice. "Let's go."

* * * *

It was eight o'clock—a dark rainy evening. Kelley had put in a lazy day, loafing most of the while in a room adjoining Leighton's office. He was tired of inactivity—hungry for action.

The two of them piled into the back seat of a touring car, atop two silent and impassive Chinamen. In the front seat sat two more—one of them driving.

"These boys are fairly trustworthy," whispered Leighton. "They've been with me for a year. They're Chinese—of course I don't dare trust them too far! They might be tempted to drop the loot in their pockets and make away. That's why I've hired you."

The car leaped away at reckless speed. They skidded through curving narrow streets, dodged rickshaw runners and foot-passengers, shot past a loaded tram, swung around sharp corners, passed saluting Sikh policemen, scraped the curb to avoid an aged woman with a teapot who was tottering on bound feet down the middle of the road. The driver honked incessantly. Through the rain gleamed the lights of tiny native shops. Once Kelley spied a painted woman leaning out into the night from an upstairs window.

"We're raiding a house where there's opium hidden," Leighton spoke with the sharp detail of a stage director. "It's a Chinese house — seven rooms, one behind the other, with open courtyards between. There's only the one entrance. I'll stay with the car so as to ensure you a safe retreat. Two of these boys will guard the door of the house. You and the other two will do the actual raiding. I hardly think you'll meet with any resistance. Show the badge that I pinned on your coat, wave your revolver, and shout 'Police'— that's a word they all know."

"That part's all easy," said Kelley. "You couldn't pack enough Chinks into a seven-room house to scare me. What I want to know is where to look for the opium."

"That's what I'm coming to," answered Leighton.

"One of these boys has been in the house and knows exactly where the loot is planted. In the third room back you'll find a mahogany chest with brass corners. It's a Chinese chest with a Chinese lock— easy to break open. Put this jimmy in your coat pocket."

The driver turned and spoke a word in Chinese to Leighton.

"We're almost there," said the chief. "Now listen: you'll find that chest full of clothes; throw them out. Clear at the bottom you'll come to a little box of carved ivory about two inches square. Don't stop to open it—drop it in your pocket quick and get away. We want to be gone before a crowd gathers; if we have to call for police help, it will make complications."

"Just that one little box?" asked Kelley incredulously.

"Just that," answered Leighton. "That's enough. There's enough opium packed in that little cube to pay ransom for a king."

It was too easy ... So reflected Kelley as he bent above the mahogany chest in the dimly lighted room and threw garments of tapestried silk out upon the tile floor. The aged door-tender had dropped from a tap of his fist; the two Chinese boys with waving revolvers and threatening shouts had herded the scared inmates of the house into an angle of the courtyard and were now standing guard while Kelley looted the chest. Nothing to do now but drop the little ivory box into his pocket and get away. Hardly a blow struck! It was too easy—it wasn't good sport.

The tiny box of carved ivory was in his pocket; he straightened up and turned, to leave.

Sudden uproar in the courtyard—fierce shouts of fighting men! Kelley, uncomprehending, started for the doorway.

The shouters broke in upon him—a posse of fierce Sikhs with clubs and guns— turbaned Sikhs of mighty stature, dressed, in policeman blue. Kelley had no thought for catastrophes. Were not these his allies? Was not he also on the side of the law? Leighton evidently had been driven to call them to his help.

The club of a Sikh lammed the side of Kelley's head. About him flamed spinning stars; he reeled. Sikhs grabbed his arms and kept him from falling—dragged him roughly through the door.

The courtyard whirled before his dizzy eyes— wavering torches—shouting policemen—his two Chinese confederates held captive—a lank white man in light summer suit with an outsticking beard of brown.

"What the hell?" whispered Kelley. His head sang; his thoughts were chaos. Wait till these dam' Hindoos find out their mistake— clubbing the very men they were sworn to aid. Just wait! The laugh will be on them all right then.

On they jerked him furiously—through room and court and room, out into the street. He looked hopefully for Leighton to set things right. In vain! Leighton and his car had disappeared.

Kelley's dizziness passed. He turned on his captors.

"See here!" he remonstrated. "You got things mixed; you—"

The police flourished their clubs; their grip tightened on his arms. Off into the rain they started. Kelley decided to be sensible. He shut up, and went along.

CHAPTER III

Things were happening too blamed fast; Kelley's slow mind couldn't keep up.

Only a minute ago there had been those fool policemen dragging him off to jail. And then through the darkness had loomed up the Lank Man with the Brown Beard. He had halted the Sikhs with a sharp word of command—had sent them about their business with a jabber of Hindustan— and now was leading Kelley off by the arm to God-knows-where—just the two of them footing it off alone through the rain.

"How come?" demanded Kelley.

"You're out on bail," explained Hamilton, "paroled to me. I know these Sikhs pretty well— I've been around Shanghai for some time. They know who I am and where I live. I convinced them that I knew you and that I'd be responsible for you; so they agreed to let me take you to my room and keep you till morning. I haven't much of a place, but it's better than jail."

Hamilton's explanation was labored and prolix. In a keener listener than Kelley it would have roused suspicion that he was handling only the fringe of the truth. But Kelley wasn't the suspicious sort.

"I saw you back there in the house," he said. "The way you stood there, I thought at first it was somebody bossing them policemen; and then I saw it was only you. How did you happen along just when you did?"

"Oh, I often roam around at night," evaded Brown Beard.

Kelley brushed cold drops of rain from his eyes. They were headed against the wind, and it was keen going.

"This is a hell of a night to roam around," said he.

"What made you do it?" countered Hamilton.

"We was out on official business," explained Kelley. "Them police will find they made a big mistake; they arrested the wrong men."

"Do you call it official business to break into a Chinese house and rob it?" asked Brown Beard quietly.

"Look here!" blustered Kelley. "I guess I know my business. You don't need, to think I'm a thief."

"It's what the judge will think," said Hamilton bluntly. "He's pretty short with Americans who break into Chinese houses. Only last month he sent two chaps to Bilibid. They forced their way into a Chinese residence under the pretext that they were international police searching for opium. When the Sikhs caught them, they were making off with five hundred dollars worth of jewelry. They're up for three years at hard labor."

Kelley had no answer. Here was something to worry about … Suppose Leighton shouldn't come forward to clear him.… But of course he would; he was the sort you could bank on. Kelley reassured himself thus again and again.

Hamilton was likewise silent, his head down against the rain. There was no further talk until they were snug in his warm room.

The room was a medley of Oriental curios— painted silks and crescent swords on the walls— vases and candlesticks on the mantel—choice bits of lacquer and brass and cloisonne on the round table.

"This is a swell room," said Kelley as he dropped into a chair before the open fire. "I sure appreciate what you're doing for me. I don't want you to think I'm a crook."

"I wouldn't let you loose in here with my curios if I thought that," said Hamilton. "All the same, you have to admit that the evidence is against you. Why don't you open up, Kelley, and tell me all about it? I happen to be a friend of the judge, and if I have the facts, maybe I can help you out."

"I'm going to tell you," said Kelley. "But I want you to keep it all confidential. Maybe you can keep it from coming out in Court. I'm employed in the Secret Service, you see, and that's why." He went on and told his tale through to the end.

"And I got the opium," he wound up triumphantly and pulled the little ivory box from his pocket. "Got it just before those fool police butted it. Good thing they didn't search me, or I wouldn't have it now."

Brown Beard gave the box no attention for the moment.

"What makes you so positive that your man Leighton is in Government Service?" he asked.

"I saw his papers," testified Kelley. "And I heard him sending a cablegram to the Secretary of State. And what's more, I'm a judge of men; I know an official when I see one. He's a big man; he ain't no ordinary sort like you and me."

"But supposing you're wrong." Brown Beard turned a plate of ancient porcelain, over and over in his slender hands as he argued. "Supposing he wanted that house robbed and put you up to do it—so that he wouldn't get caught at it himself. What then?"

Kelley looked about stubbornly for an answer—and found it between his fingers.

"Here's the box of opium," he retorted. "I guess that shows he was telling me the truth. There's enough dope in this here little box to pay a king's ransom."

"Must be going up in price," said Hamilton drily. He took the ivory box from Kelley's hand and glanced at it casually.

"By George!" he exclaimed, and sat up suddenly, straight and tense. His eyes devoured the carving on the little box with the rapt devotion of the connoisseur. He was again an artist, forgetful of all save the things of art.

"What's the idea?" asked Kelley, "That's just an ordinary little ivory box."

"Ordinary!" cried Hamilton. "Kelley, that's the most exquisite carving I've ever seen—the very soul of Canton done in ivory. And old!—see, it has the delicate yellow of antiquity!" He had taken a reading-glass from the table and was intent on the design carved on the box. "The imperial dragon," he went on, half to himself. "I understood there was only one box of this pattern in China. I wonder—" He broke off and sat looking for many minutes at the curio while Kelley watched with yawning indifference. "Did you look at the opium?—inside the box?" demanded Hamilton suddenly.

"Why, no," answered Kelley in bewilderment. "Leighton said it would spoil the evidence to open the box. But if you want to—"

"Oh, never mind," yawned Hamilton. He rose to his lank height and set the tiny box on the mantel. "It's tied with a peculiar silver cord that would take a while to undo—and I'd hate to cut it or break it. Kelley, you have one virtue: when you get an idea, you hang to it like a bulldog; but you have one Weakness: there's room in your skull for only one idea at a time—and therefore, you're a fool.... What say we go to bed?"

Kelley had slept through typhoons and hurricanes, and he was not the sort to keep awake over the logic that had dubbed him fool. He stretched out on his back beside Hamilton in the comfortable bed, and slept—and snored.

"Kelley!" said Hamilton sharply.

"Here!" Kelley had finished breakfast before the cheerful open fire in Hamilton's room, and was amiably picking his teeth.

"What's your honest opinion of Leighton this morning? Do you still believe he's on the square?"

"Why should I believe any different?" evaded Kelley; it was the most definite answer that he could make.

"In that case, you'd better go and see him this morning," ordered Hamilton. "You'll not be wanted in Court till afternoon. I'll look for you back here at one o'clock. Perhaps Leighton can help you get clear. Here, take him his little box of opium." He handed the ivory box to Kelley as he spoke. "Now trot along."

"I thought you wanted to open this first," Kelley sought to temporize.

"No, no," said Hamilton wearily. "I've seen opium before. Besides, I have a busy morning and want to be alone. One thing, though—" His voice had the ring of command. "Do not tell Leighton that you have been with me. Now good-by—and good luck!"

Kelley went. He had the feeeling that he was walking in the midst of mystery, but he lacked the brains to think through. Between forces that he could not understand, he obeyed their pulls and pushes — and trusted to. Kelley's luck.

It was a drab morning, but North Szechuen road was vivid with color. It was a little while before Kelley realized that the color was that of many turbans wound 'round the heads of black-bearded Sikhs.

"All the policemen in town is out this morning," he muttered. "I hope they don't start pitching on me again."

Onward he went with fear and trembling. The groups of armed Sikhs watched him, but offered no interference.

The front door coolie at Six Hundred peeped out cautiously.

"I want to see Leighton," announced Kelley.

"No can do." The coolie sought to close the door, but Kelley's foot was in the way. Kelley shouldered his way in, shoved the little coolie to one side, and made his way up the two flights of stairs.

Leighton had not heard him coming. He sat at his table in the cheerful room upstairs, his head buried in his hands. A revolver lay close to his elbow. The fire was cloyed with the light ash of many burned papers.

"Here I am," said Kelley.

"What do you want?" Leighton leaped warily to his feet; his hand reached for his revolver.

"Didn't you want me to come back?"

"What for?" Leighton's voice was suspicious and hard; the poise and self-possession of yesterday were gone; his mouth worked nervously.

"Why, to work, of course. I'm hired by the month, ain't I? The police butted in on me last night, but they let me go again. I'm out on bail."

"There'll be nothing for you to do for a few days," said Leighton, nobly pulling himself together. "Not till I get word from Washington. You may go where you please now. Tell me where you're staying, and I'll send for you when I want you."

"I have to appear in court this afternoon," related Kelley. "The judge is liable to send me to jail if he don't know I'm in the Secret Service."

"I'll telephone him," promised Leighton glibly. "He'll let you off all right."

"I got the opium O. K." Kelley pulled the little ivory box from his pocket.

"You did!" Leighton sprang forward and tore the box from Kelley's hand; his voice trembled with eagerness. "By Jove, that's it! Good for you! Did you open it?"

"No, of course not. You said not to. And I was lucky enough to keep it hid from the police."

Leighton made no reply. He turned his back and stood facing the window. He pulled a knife from his pocket; Kelley guessed that he was cutting the tiny silver cord that held shut the ivory box.

"All right?" Kelley took a step forward in his eagerness to see.

"You fool!" cried Leighton; he swung furiously on Kelley. "You ass! You crook! What the devil do you mean?"

"Mean?" Kelley in perplexity stooped and picked up the box that Leighton had dashed to the floor. A few waxy brown pellets were still clinging to its inside. He put them to his nose and sniffed. "That's opium, ain't it?"

"Of course it is," Leighton screamed with rage into Kelley's very face. "I suppose you call it a joke—you big thick-head! Do you think I'd go to all that trouble to get ten dollars' worth of dope!"

"Well—but—" Kelley grew angry in his turn. "Stop your cussing and talk sense. Look out—" His hands went up in self-defense.

He was a big man and strong, but he was slow—no match for a foaming wildcat like Leighton. He found himself thrown down two flights of stairs as neatly as if he had been a sack of rice. The front door coolie took hold handily and dumped him forth into the cosmopolitan publicity of North Szechuen Road. The door behind him banged shut.

"Well, heck!" Kelley got staggeringly to his feet; his hand still clutched instinctively the tiny ivory box carved with the imperial dragon. "Everybody says I'm a fool. I'd like to know what it all means."

The ring of turbaned policemen had gathered closer while he was inside. They gazed at Kelley after the manner of strong men, but let him pass without interference.

"Guess I'll go back and see Hamilton," muttered Kelley as he started off. "There's one thing I can tell him for sure; that man Leighton is nothing but a blamed crook."

Hamilton was sitting in his armchair before the open fire when the door opened and Kelley limped in.

"Back already?" he asked without rising.

"Didn't you find Leighton?"

"Sure I did! He's a crook! He threw me downstairs." Kelley flopped into a chair and gently massaged a bruise on his cheek.

"That's too bad. Sit still awhile and rest. I've been studying some of my curios."

Hamilton's occupation indeed was manifest. A brass bowl lay in his lap; a pair of porcelain vases and the Samurai dagger beside him on the table. His hand held a tiny object that glittered green.

"I wouldn't give a rap for all that stuff," said Kelley stiffly, "except that dagger—that's a real humdinger."

"You'll enjoy looking at this one." Hamilton handed across the tiny bit of green. "Handle it with care; it's valued at ten thousand dollars."

"Ten thousand dollars! Gee! What is it?" Kelley looked with awe at the treasure —a mite of cool green stone carved into a pendant an inch and a half long.

"That the finest specimen of carved jade in China. It was stolen last summer from the Imperial Museum in Pekin, and there's a reward of a thousand dollars for its safe return. You and I will start for Pekin tomorrow to collect the reward."

"Where did you get it?" Kelley failed to grasp the significance of the "you and I."

"Last night, while you were snoring," was the answer. "I took it out of your little ivory box and left some pills of opium in its place."

"Oh! Then that—" Kelley sat and thought with growing understanding— pleased at his own astuteness in being able now to see through the whole mystery. "Sure, I see it all now. Leighton and his gang must have found out some way about the jade and wanted to steal it. And they hired me to be the goat — the yellow bunch! Say, he pretty nearly fooled me at that. I could have sworn he was on the square."

"He's a good actor," said Hamilton. "And he's shrewd; it's mighty hard to get anything on him. Even now—"

"And he told me it was opium," chuckled Kelley. "It was sure a joke ori him when he opened the box and found it was opium. He's a crook all right He ought to be arrested."

"That's being attended to," said Hamilton patiently. "My men will pick him up this morning when he leaves the house. Perhaps you saw a few of them in the street."

"Your men?" asked Kelley. "I saw some policemen. Who the dickens are you?"

"I'm in the Secret Service," answered Hamilton. "I've been here in the East for some time — trying to round up a few birds like Leighton."

"You a detective?" said Kelley bluntly. "Well, there sure ain't nobody would guess it—not in fifty years."

"Thanks!" said Hamilton. "That's all to the good. But about this pendant—" He leaned forward and pointed with his pencil to the details of the Carving. "Observe here the cluster of pomegranates— and here the gnarled tree—and here the teahouse beside the one-arched bridge. The wisdom of a thousand generations graven on an inch-long gem."

"I can't see nothing to that," said Kelley. "Looks to me like it's all bunk. But, say, I want you to tell me one thing."

"Yes?"

"You called me a fool," owned Kelley. "And I am. But how did you guess it? And what made you believe I was honest?"

"Experience," answered Brown Beard drily. "Much experience—in the appraising of curios."

CHECKERED FLAG

Cliff Farrell

Doc Elton had never known fear, and he had felt none upon that day when his car left the course and headed for destruction. He had felt only bitter, unreasoning anger at young Stubby Burns.

It had happened during one of the last Vanderbilt Cup races at Santa Monica. It had been Doc's fault, and normally he would have blamed himself. But a man is not normal after nearly two hundred miles behind the wheel of one of those square-nosed, high-wheeled vehicles that were called racing cars in those days.

Doc had been nearly forty years old then, and forty is long past the deadline in the art of speed. But Doc had been an exception; still a top-notch driver. In second place, only five seconds behind the leader and with two circuits still to go, he had had his white car averaging ninety miles an hour, his heart set on winning.

He had made his mistake in attempting to pass young Stubby Burns on the Soldiers' Home curve in Sawtelle. Stubby, at that time a wild, reckless novice, was driving his first race against big league competition. Stubby did not dream that even Doc Elton would attempt to take him on that sharp curve. Not a driver in a thousand would have attempted such a thing, and so Stubby held the center of the road. Then he hit a soft spot just as Doc, confident in his ability, perhaps careless after nearly fifteen years of taking such chances, came alongside of him.

Doc's right wheels were in the loose dirt apron of the track when Stubby's car slipped into him. The shock was not enough to unbalance Stubby. He strong-armed his black car out of the curve and into the safety of the wide boulevard beyond. But Doc's white machine skittered off the road and burst through the bales of straw that had been piled there as a cushion for just such mishaps. It remained upright for a hundred feet.

Then it smashed through a picket fence fronting a little cottage. Its wheels caught and it flew up in the air, turning over and over like a toy.

Doc's mechanician was thrown out and landed on the lawn only slightly injured. But Doc stayed with the car until it crashed into the porch of the cottage. Tough and wiry, he was still alive, but he would never drive again. In addition to other injuries, an arm was done for. A surgeon at the hospital dubiously attempted to save the arm—and he did—but never again would it be flexible enough to nurse a speeding car around a fast curve.

Doc had raved considerably during the first two days in the hospital; and Stubby Burns' name had figured largely in his ravings. He never again mentioned Stubby after his head had cleared, but he was no longer the good-humored, smiling eyed Doc Elton that the speedways had always known. And it was not solely the fact that he was through as a driver that had changed Doc.

Perhaps it was a type of shock—crash-shock, something akin to shell-shock. But whatever the psychology of it, Doc Elton bore a grudge against Stubby Burns, unreasonable and far-fetched as that may seem.

Doc recovered, and in time was forgotten in the racing pits. It was generally understood by a few veterans who knew him that Doc was operating an automobile agency in Glendale, and that he was prospering. It was known that Doc was married and had a son about eleven years of age at the time of his Santa Monica crackup, But the name of Elton was no longer lettered on pit walls.

Motor racing evolved. Road racing was a thing of the past. The era of saucer tracks came and the pace grew faster. In Doc's day one hundred miles an hour was about the limit. But smaller and more efficient motors, slimmer bodies and better surfaces on which to ride, gradually pushed the average up. Cars were reduced to one-man capacity for the sake of speed. On the boards, men began to turn laps at upwards of one hundred and fifty miles an hour.

About ten years later, the name of Elton reappeared on a speedway entry list. It was at the Brookside dirt track in Los Angeles that Pinkie Elton, Doc's son, now grown to manhood, was introduced to the sport where men dared and too often died.

Pinkie bore little resemblance to his father. His mother, now dead, had given him dreamy gray eyes, a high forehead and thin, sensitive features. He had a trace of his father's bulldog chin; but all in all, he only faintly suggested the daredevil Doc Elton of the road racing days. He was more of the studious type, though his shoulders were square and his muscles sinewy, for he had been a track star in high school and college.

Pinkie appeared lost on that first day at the track with his father. Doc, however, was in a rhapsody of excitement. He had waited weary years for Pinkie to reach maturity, years during which he had bitterly watched, through the medium of the newspapers, the rise of Stubby Burns to international fame as a speedway star.

Stubby was a veteran now. He had been at the dangerous sport for so long that he was called the old master. At the peak of his career, twice national champion, winner of the recent Indianapolis five hundred mile race, Stubby's exploits behind the wheel were earning him a place along with Oldfield, DePalma, Milton, DePaolo and the other past and present greats of the motor world.

Once Doc had pointed to a newspaper picture of Stubby and had said to Pinkie, "There's the fellow who's going to eat the dust of an Elton again some day."

Doc was a hero to his son, and Pinkie had thrilled to the lore of the speedways. But he had always listened in an impersonal way. Not until that day at Brookside did he realize the full sacrifice that Doc was demanding of him. Pinkie preferred the law as a profession, but he could not brook his father's eager plans. And so, with a cheerful face and a leaden heart, he stood in the pits beside a new, tiny, four-cylinder racing car and listened.

"Take it easy today," Doc cautioned. "Don't try for speed. You know, this isn't like driving a boulevard. This is a slow track but a dangerous one. The curves are sharp, and you can hit a fence hard enough at sixty to muss things up. Get the feel of the car and the track. Take it easy."

"Right, dad," said Pinkie obediently. Only the vacant grandstands stared solemnly down at Pinkie as he drove out on the track, for this was early morning and the next event at Brookside was still two weeks away.

* * * *

Pinkie followed instructions. He learned how to handle the car. Each day he and Doc were at the track, and finally Pinkie was turning the circuit at respectable speed. But Doc felt that there was something missing. Perhaps he expected too much, but Pinkie's driving was listless, dead, mechanical. He did what he was told, and that was all. There was no fire, no spirit, in his work. Other drivers sometimes appeared for practice, and Doc noted that Pinkie avoided them when they were on the track with him. He never engaged in a friendly brush.

"How does it go, son?" Doc asked carelessly, ten days later. "Think you'd care to take a crack at real competition this week? We must sign an entry today if we're going to drive."

"Might as well start right away," Pinkie said indifferently.

"That's the spirit," said Doc heartily. "A year here at Brookside, and you'll be ripe for the high speed racket. Then you can take a fall out of this fellow Burns."

"Now listen dad," protested Pinkie. "I'm willing to drive my best in any race you want me to enter, but I'm not going to start a feud with Stubby Burns. It would be ridiculous. Burns is a great driver. He has nearly ten years' experience on me. Besides, Burns probably didn't intend to crack you up at Santa Monica. It was an accident."

"Accident!" shouted Doc. "Maybe he didn't intend to wreck me, but he crowded me! What right did a kid have crowding Doc Elton in a big race? I'll show him that an Elton can drive his wheels off."

That was it. Shell-shock or crash-shock or whatever one wanted to call it. On all other subjects Doc, now nearly fifty, was a normal, hard-headed business man. But he still saw red whenever the name of Stubby Burns came up.

Pinkie was a starter at Brookside the following Sunday afternoon. Now the Brookside track, while small, was not easy. It was a Class B circuit where the qualification rules and the car specifications were not as rigid as on the big time ovals. Youngsters who were anxious to graduate to the championship events were there at Brookside to prove their nerve and ability, and they always drove at peak speed. It was a testing ground for human endurance, and its examinations were too often written in blood.

"Don't try to win," Doc told his son as the field began to smoke up. "Just drive for experience."

Pinkie obeyed literally—too literally. There were fourteen entries in the fifty, mile event, and Pinkie finished tenth. Four of the original starters had dropped out during the course of the race because of motor trouble and a smashup or two, and so it took no figuring to discover that when it was all over Pinkie was last.

Pinkie's driving had been mechanically perfect. He sat the car easily and swept it around the curves calmly, his four wheels always smoothly in line. But Doc was disappointed. He had hoped that his son, in the stress of competition, would show some of the fighting spirit without which no man can become a champion in any line of endeavor.

Doc was persistent, however. For a year Pinkie drove at Brookside and other small dirt tracks in the southwest; a nerve-racking year which Pinkie endured stoically. He even began taking risks because he knew his father expected it. Finally, he began to win occasional small races, and the name of Elton seemed on its way again to ascendancy in the speed world.

Then, on Pinkie's birthday, Doc led him into a private workshop in the Elton motor establishment in Glendale. A new racing car sat resplendently on the floor, and even Pinkie was enthused by the sight of it. The machine was one of the latest products from the shop of Miller, in Los Angeles. Powered with a ninety-one inch motor, it was as compact as a bullet and as graceful as an arrow. Squatting close to the ground, its lines concealed its true bulk and sturdiness. That car had cost Doc nearly twenty thousand dollars.

"There she is, son," said Doc proudly. "A front drive straight eight. You can toss that four cylinder job on the scrap heap now. You're ready for a crack at real racing. I'm going to enter you at Ocean City in the three hundred mile roll next month."

"Whew," gasped Pinkie inwardly quailing at the thought, well knowing what speed they were making on the big mile and a half saucer track at Ocean City. "Do you think I can do it?"

"Think you can do it!" echoed Doc scornfully. "An Elton can drive on any track with the best of them. Stubby Burns will be riding against you.——Beat him, son! Beat him and show him what an Elton can do. You're ready. This car should be as fast as any in the world. It's equipped with everything to make it so. It's up to you."

Stubby Burns was at Ocean City on the first afternoon that Doc and Pinkie appeared there for practice. The race was two weeks away; but the score of drivers entered were wasting no time tuning for the event, for it was a championship race and it carried one of the biggest purses of the year. In addition, every man knew that it was to be a blistering speed test, for this bowl was so scientifically built with sweeping, steeply banked curves and sloping stretches that it was in reality a straightaway. The only limit to velocity was the ability of the motor and the nerve of the pilot.

Stubby did not recognize Doc at first, but he soon learned that the car was entered under the name of Elton and he realized then that Doc, in the person of his son, was back on the track. And so Stubby walked casually down to the pit that had been assigned the Elton car. Doc saw him coming and began glowering.

"Hello, Doc," said Stubby evenly, extending his hand. Both were thinking of that terrific moment at Santa Monica ten years before.

"You crowded me off the road and into a hospital once, Burns," Doc snapped, ignoring the hand. "You put me off the track for keeps. But another Elton is here to start in where I left off. You're going to eat splinters from now on."

"I wish you luck, kid," said Stubby, flushing and turning to Pinkie. And he said it sincerely. "If there's anything I can do to help you, let me know."

"The only thing we want you to do is to get out of this pit," yelled Doc, blind with years of pent up fury. "We'll do our talking on the track. And don't try to crowd us either."

Stubby retreated to his own pit. He waited until Pinkie was ready to drive out on the track, then squeezed into his own car, a marvelous red machine that had carried him to victory in half a dozen fiercely fought races. He drove to the backstretch and stopped on the apron. Pinkie appeared a moment later, driving slowly in low gear to warm the motor. Stubby waved an arm and Pinkie stopped alongside.

"What's it to be, kid," the veteran asked. "Peace or war?"

"I'd be a fool to declare war on you," Pinkie said honestly. "Don't take to heart what the Old Man says. He doesn't really mean it."

"I'm not afraid of anybody on the sidelines," Stubby smiled. "My worries are on the track."

"I'm only a greenhorn," said Pinkie. "The Old Man knows nothing about saucer track driving. If you can give me a few hints, I'll be grateful."

"Follow me," Stubby invited. "We'll turn about a dozen laps at slow speed. Then when I wave my elbows, be ready to give it the gun. Keep your arms in. Remember that the banked curves will help you negotiate them, so be careful and don't oversteer or you'll go into a spin."

Pinkie fell in behind the red car. Stubby drove at about ninety miles an hour, a snail-like pace for this track, until he felt sure that the novice had got the feel of his car. Then he gave the signal and gradually began to open up.

Pinkie was an expert at following instructions. He hung a dozen feet behind the pointed tail of Stubby's car, matching notch for notch the throttle increase. The speed reached two miles a minute, and Stubby looked back to study his pupil's work. Pinkie grinned, and Stubby turned back to his task. They turned the final lap at better than one hundred and thirty, and Pinkie handled his machine capably. It was a valuable session, for Stubby had taught the youngster the proper way to ride these sloping curves"

"You'll do," Stubby said as they drifted to the pits.

But Doc Elton was far from pleased, and Pinkie recognized the storm signals as he came to a stop.

"Why didn't you pass that skunk?" Doc growled.

"I didn't have the ability," Pinkie said truthfully.

"He hasn't the guts," Doc told himself later, voicing for the first time the fear that had been growing within him ever since that first day at Brookside when Pinkie had finished last. Doc was beginning to feel the fierce pangs of failure. He had produced a mechanically perfect racing driver, but one who was only a robot. Pinkie had no spirit, no will to win, and worse than that, he had accepted help from the very man upon whom Doc had sworn vengeance.

Pinkie practiced doggedly and faithfully, finally qualifying for the race by turning a lap at one hundred and thirty-six miles an hour. That placed him fifteenth in the list of twenty starters.

Stubby Burns had qualified at one hundred and forty-six miles and hour, but that was only good enough to give him the pole in the second row, as the cars lined up two by two. Pinkie, nervous and moody, and at the same time depressed and unmoved by the pre-race ceremonies and unresponsive to the crowd that packed the grandstands, sat pallid in his car, awaiting the final bomb.

Stubby grinned encouragingly back at him as the field smoked up and the pole car led the way slowly along the apron. It was to be a massed flying start, with three laps to get the race started.

Pinkie was dazed by the magnitude of the task. He flinched at the thought of what was to come, for he rode in the middle of a stream of thunderbolts that were picking up speed gradually in preparation for launching themselves into fierce competition.

On the second preliminary swing around the bowl, the pace reached one hundred miles an hour; and the cars, riding in pairs, were swinging higher up on the saucer. As they entered the third and final lap, the speed topped two miles a minute, and was still climbing steadily.

Pinkie faltered in the backstretch. Every other driver was tensed for the jump-off, but Pinkie lifted his foot. His white car lost momentum and fell back among the two pairs of machines following him. Those four pilots were forced to reach for brakes to avoid a general crackup, and the result was that the field was thrown into such confusion that the green starting flag did not fall.

It required two laps for the cars to realign themselves, and the drivers' taut nerves were twitching as a result of the false start. They thundered down on the green flag again. This time Pinkie did not falter. He had steeled himself. But Stubby Burns had fouled a spark plug during all the jockeying; and now he fell back, with one barrel missing, as the stream of cars poured across the starting line.

Pinkie swerved past Stubby, only vaguely realizing it; and before they had reached the backstretch, Stubby had fallen to the tail of the squirming mass of machines. But the plug was clearing now, and as the leaders completed the first lap, clipping along at one hundred and forty miles an hour, Stubby began to pick up his lost ground.

Pinkie was in fourteenth position, and content to remain there. But two laps later Stubby bore down on him, determined to work his way back to the head of the procession. Stubby rushed alongside Pinkie on the north turn, though Pinkie did not know that it was Stubby. He was too busy holding his humming bit of machinery between those two white fences that spun dizzily past. He merely sensed the shadow at his side.

Pinkie had been told by Doc to hold his position for the first hundred miles and then to begin to drive. He now attempted to follow instructions and he opened the throttle a fraction. His white car picked up more momentum. But Stubby was also moving faster with every turn of his wheels, and the red car and the white car sailed around the curve side by side.

Then Pinkie realized who was beside him. Furthermore, Stubby had the advantage of position, being in the top lane, where higher speed was feasible. In a panic over his temerity, Pinkie eased up. His car lost headway, and at that fateful moment the right front wheel struck the end of a board that had been loosened by the pounding of the cars.

The white car swerved out of line. Pinkie, accustomed to the dirt, wrenched the wheel viciously to the left to correct the skid. That finished what the loose board had started. Pinkie had oversteered, and the rear end whipped around.

The car began its spin as it entered the homestretch. Its momentum carried it, spinning end for end, down into the pits flanking the starting line and it struck the concrete retaining wall. Doc Elton, standing there a hundred feet away, gripping his black briar pipe between his teeth, felt cold and dizzy and too weak to move. The wall deflected the berserk car, and it shot back towards the board deck. But its wheel caught and it turned over. It rolled twice and then came to a stop, one wheel still intact and spinning feebly above the wreckage.

Pinkie had only a cracked rib. Doc Elton thought of nothing else but his son's welfare, until it was definitely established two hours later that he was unhurt. Then Doc gave way to his emotions in the field hospital.

"Burns wrecked you, son!" he swore solemnly. "He did it purposely. It may have been an accident at Santa Monica, but not here today.— He'll never do it again and live. And he'll never win another race in which you are a starter. I'll see to that."

"But dad," Pinkie exclaimed horrified by Doc's outburst. "It was an accident. My own fault. I oversteered."

"Listen," said Doc, ignoring Pinkie. The mechanical voice of a loud speaker on the public address system was just announcing the fact that Stubby Burns had taken the lead with only ten miles to go. He was a certain winner. "There's your answer. Burns knew you were a menace to him. So he eliminated you early in the race."

Pinkie gave up in despair. Crash-shock. That was the answer. Doc was still steering the blind side of the curve.

* * * *

During the next few weeks, Doc continued to rave and Pinkie to laugh it off. Doc's birthday was approaching, and Pinkie made a tobacco pipe from wrecked parts of the white car. He cut the bowl from the tough wood of the smashed steering wheel, and reamed out a stem from an aluminum conrod.

The pipe was a resplendent affair, its stem glistening from the polish Pinkie had given it. When he presented it to Doc, his father regarded the memento dubiously. But he went so far as actually to smoke it, laying away his seasoned briar with regrets. It was a sacrifice that he would have made only for Pinkie, for Doc and the briar had been inseparable companions for years.

* * * *

Six weeks later, Doc carried the aluminum pipe to Coltonia for the two hundred mile race. The white car had been repaired and rebuilt. It had lost none of its speed. And Pinkie seemed unaffected by his crash. He drove in the same old mechanical, efficient way at Coltonia, practicing faithfully and laboriously. He displayed neither brilliancy nor inaptitude. He was merely another driver who would clutter up the track while others scintillated and won the plaudits and the prizes. He was still a robot.

Doc began to abandon hope. To relieve his mind, he continued his bitter attacks on Stubby Burns. It was a habit with him now. He blamed the innocent Stubby for every mishap or minor irritation. Pinkie grew so accustomed to this quirk in his father's character that he no longer thought anything of it. Meanwhile, Stubby pursued his normal course of preparing to win the Coltonia.

On the evening before the race, Pinkie found something to worry about. He dropped into Doc's room at the hotel for their usual chat before retiring and found the old driver sitting at a table, busily greasing and cleaning a revolver. The weapon was a cheap, nickel-plated thirty-two of a popular make, and Doc had polished its barrel to a glistening sheen.

"I found it back of the radiator over there," Doc said carelessly in explanation. "Somebody hid or dropped it there. It was loaded but rusty. Thought I'd tune it up just to do something."

"Better give it to the management," Pinkie suggested.

"I may take it to the track tomorrow and potshoot the tires of any wild guys who try to pass you," Doc laughed. "A bullet can beat the fastest speed bug that ever lived."

Pinkie was thinking of some of the threats Doc had made against Stubby Burns. Crash-shock. Just how far could its evil work go? He did not sleep that night. He was still thinking of the gun as they towed the white car to the track at noon the next day. Doc seemed nervous, but Pinkie could detect no suspicious bulges in Doc's pockets and so his mind rested easier.

Pinkie had qualified far back in the list as usual; and as the twenty machines seared the stretch under the green flag, he settled down to his normal task of driving securely and conservatively. Stubby Burns, who had the pole, booted his red mount into the lead on the first curve, opened up a hundred yard gap over his nearest competitor in the first lap, and continued adding to his advantage as the race settled down to a fierce speed duel.

The Coltonia bowl was considerably slower than the Ocean City layout. Older, and built with less regard for drivers' comfort, its turns were pitched so steeply and the approaches were sharp and hazardous. Its mile and a quarter length was packed with perils.

Pinkie drove with his old mechanical perfection. He even found himself beginning to enjoy this race. The constant vigilance, the extreme delicacy necessary in handling the car on this treacherous surface, struck a responsive chord. Some of Doc Elton's old spirit glowed within him. Its flame was feeble at first, however, and Pinkie rode on, content to remain back in the field.

Stubby, at fifty miles, had rolled up an advantage of a mile over Pinkie, who was now eighth in place. The entire field was turning the bowl at an average above the old track record, because of Stubby's fierce leadership. Tommy Mandot, an experienced pilot as skillful and as daring as Stubby himself, was in second place only a hundred yards back of the leader. Mandot was riding Stubby fast into the turns, awaiting a chance to grab the lead should Stubby relax or be guilty of a driving error.

But Stubby did not relax and neither did he make a mistake. He had a heavy foot clamped on the throttle and he never eased off. He held Mandot grimly in second place. Notch by notch the average advanced, for the roaring motors seemed to wind up to greater power as they droned ever onward. Over the streaming oval gathered a pall of blue castor oil smoke, through which flickered darting tongues of flame from twenty screaming exhausts.

* * * *

Pinkie, to his father's amazement, was now more than holding his own. The leaders no longer gained on him. He clung determinedly to his position a mile behind Stubby. Now and then he mowed down an opposing car, sweeping past surely and expertly. At one hundred miles he was in fourth place. His driving was positive, almost brilliant.

Pinkie himself did not realize that he had pushed so far up in the list. He did not know why he was driving so swiftly. But somewhere back in his head something urged him to go on, to turn his wheels over ever faster. Perhaps he was subconsciously thinking of that gun he had seen in Doc's possession the evening before. Perhaps it was instinct. But anyway he was slamming his slim, white car over the boards faster than he had believed it possible for him to drive.

Jimmy Dance, in a red Comet Special was his next victim. Pinkie jockeyed past Dance on the treacherous south curve, thereby assuming third place. Only Stubby and Mandot were ahead of him now.

Pinkie's speed was beginning to cut into their advantage also, and the pit crews were awakening. Blackboards flashed signals to both Stubby and Mandot. White arrows, pointing to the number of Pinkie's car, informed the two veterans that a challenger was coming up. And Stubby and Mandot both bore down heavier on the gas.

Pinkie gained but little now. He was still half a mile behind, and the average was five miles an hour faster than was safe on this perilous course.

The velocity began to take its toll at one hundred and twenty miles. A green car, bearing an English pilot, came a cropper on the north turn, just as Pinkie was about to lap it. It swerved into the upper fence as its pilot momentarily swayed it off balance, ripping off a hundred feet of heavy steel guard railing as it did so. Then the remains of the machine tumbled down the track and onto the apron.

Pinkie dodged the wreckage by threading through it at one hundred and thirty miles an hour. He caught a glimpse of the Englishman's limp form lying down on the apron among the debris. Then he was past, his lips compressed, his eyes hard, and sorrow in his heart. He did not slow down. Neither did any of the others. It was part of the game, the sacrifice that any of them might be called upon to make at any time.

At one hundred and fifty miles, the field was thinned down by wrecks and motor trouble to an even dozen cars. Stubby still blistered the boards in the lead, with Mandot now half the length of the stretch behind him. Pinkie had moved up on Mandot and was desperately hanging to the tow from the veteran's car, trying to nurse enough speed from his humming four wheels to go past.

Pinkie could do no more. He believed he had reached the limit of his speed. On the turns now his car was almost out of control. He could hear the tortured tires squealing shrill protest above the song of the motor on each dizzy spin around a curve, He could feel the sickening sway of the machine as it leaned on its outside wheels, and he knew that the rubber was growing hot and thin under such punishment.

"But they're no better off," he told himself, revelling in this newfound thrill. He was being hypnotized by the lure of speed.

* * * *

Ten miles more were unreeled, and Stubby still held sway, using sheer, brutal speed to stave off every challenger. Pinkie had been so busy with his perilous task that he had ignored his pit throughout the race. He knew he was in third place, and vaguely he realized that the event was nearing its finish. But beyond that he had not glanced at a blackboard flash.

Now he looked down into his pit, a sudden thought coming to him. Doc Elton was standing there, leaning tensely on the front pit wall and there was something in his hand—something from which Pinkie caught the reflected, silvery gleam of the waning sun. It was a brief view as Pinkie flashed by, but it registered vividly on his mind. For Doc seemed to be holding that object so that none of the men in the pit with him could see it. He had his left arm carelessly draped around the right hand that held it.

'The gun! The gun!" Pinkie moaned. "He's gunning for Stubby."

Doc had sworn that Stubby would never defeat his son again in a race, and now he evidently was preparing to make good his threat.

Then Pinkie fought off the nausea that had momentarily gripped him and bent lower over the wheel. He began to drive as no man ever had driven that track before. He knew that he must beat Stubby Burns. It was the only way to save Stubby from the madness of Doc's plan—and the only way to save Doc, too.

Pinkie passed Mandot on the next lap, pushing by at the most dangerous apex of the rough south curve. It was fierce, reckless, death-defying velocity, a pace that seemed sure to carry the white car into the outside rail that it was grazing. But Pinkie held his wheels in line with superb control.

Stubby was nearly an eighth of a mile ahead. There were less than forty miles, less than twenty minutes of driving, to go. Stubby glanced back and recognized the oncoming menace. He still had a notch or two of both power and nerve, and he opened up with both. Pinkie now gained so slowly that it seemed hopeless.

Doc watched his son's epic battle for a few laps. Then he could stand it no more, for Pinkie's car was swinging wildly on the curves now, grazing the fence and threatening to go entirely out of control on every recovery in the stretches.

"Slow him down," he snarled to Bing Morgan, the pit captain. "He's going to break up at that speed. Slow him down, quick, before something awful happens!"

Bing had the blackboard ready, and now he held it aloft as Pinkie moaned by on his next lap. It carried only the easily read word 'SLOW' in big letters; but Doc groaned, for Pinkie had not even glanced into the pit. He did not see the command. So terrific was his velocity that he did not dare glance away from that dizzy, spinning track for even a fraction of a second.

Two more laps went by, and it was evident that Pinkie was beginning to eat into the gulf that separated him from the red-hot exhaust of Stubby's car.

Ten miles more, and Pinkie was only a hundred yards behind. Then Doc Elton suddenly screeched hoarsely as the white car darted past through the blue fog. A slapping sound accompanied the crescendo roar of the motor, and Doc caught a glimpse of a blurred object whirling around the right front wheel of Pinkie's car.

"He's throwing a tread," Doc shouted. "Watch out, son! Watch out! Slow down before that rubber blows." But Pinkie, of course, could not hear mere words, and so the blackboard with its frantic messages was again called into play. Still Pinkie did not see them!

Pinkie had felt the car lurch as the tread on the tire began to strip away from the casing. The tread had worn through in one section, and the heat from friction was melting it away from its seat. The revolving wheel completed the job on the back stretch. With a final slap and lurch of the car, the tread was stripped clear of the casing and hurled two hundred feet in the air.

* * * *

The tire was now down to the cords. Pinkie knew the peril in which he rode. That tire was ready to blow. It could not stand up long under the terrific punishment it was receiving, and nine times out of ten a flat front at one hundred and thirty miles an hour would turn a car somersaulting.

But Pinkie held his foot down. He was pale and shaken, but he ignored that thin, white streak that spun on the right wheel. He did not even dare look at it.

"I've gotta beat Stubby," he told himself over and over. "I've gotta.—Please don't blow now! Oh, God, how much longer? If I only knew. It must be almost over.—I've gotta beat Stubby!"

Doc Elton grew faint when he realized that Pinkie was continuing to drive on the weak tire.

"I drove him to it," he told himself, trembling as he followed the streaking course of the white bullet around and around the bowl, his tired old eyes dark with misery. He had stuffed the gleaming object into the pocket of his coat where it rested, forgotten.

Pinkie still gained slowly but surely. With two laps to go, he was only three lengths behind Stubby, and his face was being peppered with fine splinters thrown from the track like darts by the wheels of the leading car. They were knocking off the miles now with throttles to the floor. Neither eased off on the curves. They were riding wide open.

On the next to the last lap, Pinkie chopped another length from Stubby's advantage. Like phantoms, they bulleted down the homestretch in the late afternoon haze. Other cars were still on the track, battling for positions, but they were merely subsidiary characters to the two leading actors who were fighting in this dramatic duel for supremacy.

The blue flag denoting the last lap snapped before the two pilots' eyes, and then they were disappearing down the stretch on their final whirl around the bowl.

Pinkie knew that he could do no more in the way of speed. The motor on the white car was revving at top capacity, but top speed was not enough, so evenly were they matched.

Ordinarily, it is the unwritten custom to pass an overtaken car on the outside. But Stubby's speed was so great that he could not hold his car low, and Pinkie knew that his only chance was to cut down and pass beneath, as Stubby drifted high on the curves.

"Will that tire stand it?" Pinkie asked himself, even as he started the maneuver. He swung high on the takeoff from the stretch, and cut far down below the lower white guideline on the steeply banked south turn. At the same time Stubby drifted into the upper lane.

The tire did hold that time, and Pinkie emerged into the backstretch with Stubby only a wheel's width in the lead. They ate up that straightaway in a gulp, so beautiful in flight, side by side, that few in the grandstands realized the terrible peril in which they rode. Stubby, too, could now see the menace of that thin tire with its ever widening streak of white, for Pinkie's right front wheel hummed so close to Stubby's elbow that he could have reached out and touched it.

Then the last curve. Pinkie knew, now that he was on the inside, that he must stay there. The few feet advantage in distance that he would gain by the curvature of the track would win for him. The question was whether he could hold his machine there. It would attempt to drift high because of centrifugal force and because he did not have the advantage of entering this turn high and cutting low, as he had done before. If he wrestled with the wheel to hold the car down, it probably would scrape the last remaining protection from that thin tire.

But nevertheless he did hold it in the lower lane, manhandling the machine out of its tendency to slide up the track. He could hear his tires squealing and he smelt the pungent odor of burned rubber. But Pinkie's white car emerged into the last stretch half a length in the lead—and held it as the two machines flashed down upon the checkered flag. Pinkie held his foot down, but he was shrinking. He sensed what was coming. Intuition told him that the tortured front tire was finally going. Now! Now! Now! The checkered flag floated nearer, seeming to approach with the leaden slowness of a nightmare.

Then the white finish line gleamed beneath Pinkie's wheels a hundredth of a second ahead of Stubby's. He had won!

A pent up cheer rolled from the grandstand, but it ceased suddenly as though some titanic hand had closed the stops on a great pipe organ. For a pistol-like report sounded from the finish line just as Pinkie's victorious wheels crossed it. The white car continued its course for a hundred feet, then the right front could be seen spinning in a blur. It had blown.

Pinkie wrestled grimly with the wheel to hold it up. But no human hands could have prevented this crackup. Stubby swerved high out of the way as the white car whirled around and then shot down towards the pits, skidding backwards at more than a hundred miles an hour.

By a freak of chance, it shot directly at its own pit. Doc Elton stood there grimly awaiting it, hoping that it would take him with it when it struck; but Bing Morgan picked him up and tossed him out of its path in time to save his life.

The machine cut through the concrete wall as though the obstruction had been made of cheese. Then it reared up for a terrific moment on its crushed rear wheels, and sailed over the pit to land on the ambulance drive. For a few minutes dust and smoke obscured the scene as the wreckage caught fire. Then Doc Elton emerged from the fog, bearing Pinkie's limp form.

"He's dead and I did it!" Doc was crying. But Pinkie was not dead. The gas tank, nearly emptied, had acted as a cushion, and aside from bruises he was all right. To prove it he sat up.

"Hello, dad," he said weakly. "I beat Stubby after all."

Doc had learned his lesson. He wanted to get down on his knees and apologize to his son—and apologize to Stubby Burns, too. For thoughts of vengeance had forever been erased from his mind during those trying moments when he felt that he had sent Pinkie to his death. To cover his emotion, he mechanically reached in his pocket and produced his pipe. It was the one Pinkie had given him on his birthday. As Doc held it by its bowl, its gleaming aluminum stem jutted out like the barrel of a gun. Pinkie stared at it for a moment.

"Dad," he asked suddenly. "What did you do with that gun?"

"Why, I gave it to the clerk at the hotel like you suggested," said Doc in surprise, "But now let's go home to Los Angeles and quit this crazy racket. It's too dangerous."

"Nix," said Pinkie. "I really learned to drive today. It's great. I'm in this business to stay. I beat Stubby today, and I'll do it plenty times more."

"Crash-shock," said Doc sadly. But he was proud of his son now.

THE FIGHTING FOOL

Perley Poore Sheehan

CHAPTER I

The way Shattuck slid around that rock would have done credit to a fox. But, even as he did so, he knew that he was trapped. There was no other cover near. The rock had concealed him from the camp he'd been stalking. When he'd heard those voices from the rear his quick shift of position meant he'd be seen from below.

The people in these hills had eyes like hawks—eyes like those of their own hunting eagles.

In any case, he was out of rifle range from the camp. That lay about a mile below, in a hidden little valley. He'd been looking at it for the past two hours as he slowly approached it from above. In the high thin air of the mountains the camp lay microscopic—it had been like looking at it through the wrong end of a telescope, everything minutely clear, but too microscopic to be studied.

And he had to study his moves—did Shattuck.

All he knew was that he was somewhere in the midriff of Asia—Himalaya country— Pamirs—Hindu Kush; that one of those gossamer billows of blue and white off there to the north might be the Tien Shan—that is, the Heavenly Mountains, as the Chinese called them.

In a general way, he was headed for China.

China to Shattuck almost meant the United States. He'd passed his boyhood there—in Canton, Shanghai, Tientsin—where his father had lived and traded.

No other countries open to him at all! And perhaps not even China! A man without a country! He had no papers, no relatives. He could hardly think of a living soul who could link him up with his past—who could actually swear that he was Pel Shattuck—Pelham Rutledge Shattuck—and not some international tramp who'd merely appropriated that name.

Like a wild animal caught in his dangerous position he blended himself as best he could with the gravel and dead grass at the foot of his rock and there lay completely still.

For a time the voices he had heard were stilled. He might have been seen. Or the intruders might have spied some other game.

From where he lay, without other movement than that of his eyes, Shattuck could view the camp—or the better part of it—through a crotch of his sheepskin coat. No excitement yet!

Whatever happened, he'd have to go into some camp again pretty soon anyway.

He wondered where he was—wondered who these people were.

* * * *

These were some of the questions that had kept him on the scout ever since running away from Juma's camp. The trouble with Juma's camp was that Juma had a daughter, a girl named Mahree. And not even a man who has got himself in bad with governments will do certain things that a girl might propose.

"Khabadar!"—a voice near-by had spoken.

It was a word of warning. It hadn't been addressed to himself. But Shattuck knew that he'd been discovered.

His mind worked quickly. There was no friction even to thought in the thin air of these high altitudes. Down in the camp just now he'd seen a man staring up in his direction. He could guess the rest. The man had signaled to the hunters on the mountain....

It wouldn't do to let them take him for a wolf or a bear.

Shattuck began to whine a bit of song that he'd learned in Juma's camp—just a bar or two— then stopped short.

As if by accident he thrust his foxskin cap beyond the edge of the rock. No shot was fired.

He left the cap where it was and took a look from the other side. He saw four men—two of them elderly, with beards, and all of them slant-eyed. The quartet were fanned out and had their rifles ready, evidently in a maneuver to surround him.

"Let us drink tea," Shattuck offered, in one of the last phrases he'd picked up in Juma's camp.

It was an invitation to a parley, an offer to talk—they'd get the purport of it whether they understood his speech or not. He recovered his cap. He stepped from behind his rock with his own rifle ready.

"Who are you?" one of the bearded elders asked.

His language wasn't like the Kirghiz dialect of Juma's people, but it was close enough to it to be understood.

"Ameriki," Shattuck answered.

He smiled and raised his right hand in salutation. He'd dropped his rifle into the crook of his left arm but he'd be able to use it, he guessed, if he had to.

The four stared. They were a wild looking lot, dressed in sheepskin and felt. The two elders, those who were bearded, had their left ears pierced and ornamented with large turquoise earrings. None of them looked as if he'd been washed or had had his hair cut since the day of his birth.

As for that, Shattuck felt that neither had he himself.

The four converged closely as Shattuck approached. There was an air of tenseness about them that Shattuck didn't like. They were like strange dogs closing in on a dog they'd selected for a kill.

In an instant Shattuck had swung his rifle back to ready again and had them covered—ready to fire from the hip.

The movement was so swift that they were caught unprepared. He gave them a quick survey, then addressed the elder who carried the best weapon—that alone was enough to indicate he stood higher than these others.

"Let the guns fall," he ordered. "Quickly! Then, maybe, we shall talk like friends."

CHAPTER II

There is a sort of universal language, more of looks than of words or gestures—the sort of communication that had already thrown Shattuck on his guard. In the same way he could grasp the thought of these four now as they let their weapons fall.

"Here is a mad fool! We'll get him later!"

Shattuck pushed the four guns into a pile with his foot. One was a modern sporting rifle— English, he surmised. The others looked like copies of older models—clumsy imitations, but effective enough, such as might have been made in Lhassa or Kabul.

Even with his eyes down he surprised a movement from one of the younger men.

The emergency was so sharp that Shattuck spoke up in English. "Do you want to die?"

The young man had started to signal the camp in the valley. He'd done so already, perhaps. With their telescopic eyes most of these hill-men could flash signals or read them across amazing distances.

There was a lull, then the leader of the four spoke up.

"Huzoor—"

That was vernacular, an address of respect; but the rest of it was coming in English—as slowly, as creakingly, as a door forced open on rusty hinges, but English.

"Excellence, we mean you no harm; and I take it that you mean us no harm."

"Who are you?"

"Your servant, Tsarong!"

The humility was too great to be sincere. Shattuck looked the old man in the eye. The gaze that met his was veiled and shrewd.

"Who are your people?"

"Just a few poor Changpas."

Changpas! People from the Chan-tang!

As the meaning of this simple statement flashed into Shattuck's mind it was all that he could do to suppress a start. Even so he divined an answering start in the eyes of the old man.

The Changpas were Tibetans—the people of the tang, the desert plains of Tibet's Far West. It was an affair of Tibet and Russia that had got Shattuck into trouble with the Cheka, the Soviet Secret Service.

Shattuck smiled pleasantly.

"Sit down, Father Tsarong," he invited; "and tell your friends to sit down. Thus! You four sit down with your backs to the camp and I'll sit here in front of you. Like that, should you see any other of your people coming from behind me, you can signal them not to shoot—as they might miss and shoot you instead."

Old man Tsarong hesitated.

"We are unworthy of that honor," he said. "Only our lord, the general, is worthy such an honor."

"What you say is perfectly true," Shattuck replied. "Send for him."

"Send for him! He is the governor of the entire Chantang!"

"Father, do as I say. Tell him you've met an earth demon who knows everything. I know all about those Russian arms you've come to this valley to get. Dorje-Pamo, the pig-faced goddess, told me about them herself."

The old man was stricken.

He mumbled an order and the three others— including the other elder himself—were for setting off together. But Shattuck stopped the rush. Only one was to go, and he was to be the best runner among them.

As the runner started off down the mountainside, Shattuck could see that there was already some alarm in the camp. A string of yaks, horses, sheep and goats had begun to straggle in from behind a shoulder of the hill, driven by women and children.

"Are you not, then, English?" Tsarong asked.

"Ameriki," Shattuck replied.

He could see that the word meant nothing to the Tibetans. To them all white foreigners were English—that, or possibly Oross, Russian.

The three Tibetans sat in front of him and below him at a respectful distance, facing him, their backs to the camp. Shattuck also had folded his legs and seated himself on the ground, the four surrendered rifles piled in front of him and his own weapon across his knees.

The queer thought came to him that he was no longer an outcast and a man without a country, after all. He was now as a king seated on a throne.

The throne was a mountain. He had an arsenal. He had subjects who looked at him with awe, speculating, like other subjects, on the divinity of kings.

There was something about the vast panorama that surrounded him, that stimulated this thought—stimulated it to the point of sheer craziness. Yet, hereabouts, there were still legends of Alexander the Great, of Ghengis Khan and Kubla Khan and Tamerlane.

There was a persistent legend that from this part of the world would come the next great King of the World.

The three Tibetans were watching him. He was watching them.

"I am Pelham Rutledge Shattuck," he announced slowly.

He was making the announcement for himself as much as he was for them. It sounded strange to hear his own name spoken like that, even by his own voice, here in this Himalayan space. It was like some sort of a mantram—a spell. The name went vibrating off into the blue of Central Asia.

The Tibetans looked puzzled, even old Tsarong.

"Shattuck! Get that?"

There was a respectful murmur.

"Repeat it," Shattuck told them. "Shattuck!"

They tried it—first Tsarong, the linguist, then the others. They also seemed to think that it was some sort of a spell.

"Sha-dak!"

"Sha-dak!"

"Sha-dak!"

It might have been a spell, at that. As they pronounced it the name became a Chinese word meaning "trouble": Shadak.

They were repeating it with honorary titles added:

"Shadak-la!"

"Shadak-beg!"

"Shadak-khan!"

"My God," Shattuck muttered. "That's who I am, all right!"

In the silence of his thought it was as if an echo of silent thunder had come rolling back upon him out of space, calling him by a name to which he was fated:

"Captain Trouble!"

CHAPTER III

It may have been what some would have called just a coincidence, but as that new name of his vibrated in Shattuck's thought with a queer sensation of something magical about it, a din broke out in the camp below.

"Shadak!"

It sounded like trouble. It was a din of horns and gongs, drums, a shouting. The whole camp, it seemed, dogs included, had begun to turn out with its full capacity of noise.

Shattuck never winced. He'd become used to a lot of things since his escape from the Cheka in Samarkand. He'd become used to a lot of things before that.

He'd gone to Russia as a mining expert— especially as one who spoke Chinese—expecting to be sent to Manchuria. Instead of that, through some error, perhaps, he'd found himself switched to Bokhara. The error, it turned out, was that he'd been falsely accused of pro-Japanese activities. It was true that he'd lived in Japan for a while.

In Samarkand he'd broken open some boxes which should have contained some overdue mining machinery. The machinery turned out to be machine-guns instead, and destined for Chantang.

Suddenly, it had become desirable that he leave the country. He was on the Cheka's black list. He'd always wanted, anyway, to see Afghanistan; and the devil was there in the person of a former Afghan wazir, Michmander by name, to speed him on his way.

Michmander knew of certain lost mines in the Hindu-Kush. It was knowledge that had to be kept, of course, from the thieving government at Kabul, the Afghan capital.

Shattuck was willing.

* * * *

He stuck to Michmander in a trek that took them into mountains not marked—except vaguely and incorrectly—on any map. And they'd had a small army of cutthroats and all-round soldiers of fortune with them before they were through—Shattuck himself the only white man in the lot.

They'd penetrated to the depths of that great upheaval known as "the Purdah Lady"—"K-2"— a mountain as veiled and as hard to get to, that is, as a lady shut up in a harem.

And there they'd had a battle with wild natives who were armed with spears and long-handled hatchets.

It was a great battle.

Shattuck had seen almost all of it. And he must have done his share, for the last thing that Michmander—he who had led him into this mess—ever said to him was to call him a fighting fool.

Michmander—having been exiled from Afghanistan long ago—had passed enough time in America to have picked up some American slang.

He was laughing as he said it, in the thick of the fight, and trying to reload his automatic—a difficult job because he'd lost a couple of fingers; and Shattuck himself was swaying on his feet and covered with blood.

"You fighting fool!"

One of the few supreme compliments ever paid to any man; for, just as Michmander said it, a long handled hatchet came swishing down and split Michmander's head like a melon.

How the fight ended Shattuck didn't clearly know. Anyway, there were parts of it that he was willing to forget.

But he had a vague idea that he'd lived for a while in a cave where long ranks of stone gods a hundred feet high looked down on small brown men bearing saucerlike lamps.

After that, there followed months—it might have been years so far as he knew then—of wandering, always wandering and always amid mountains.

When he emerged from this daze or trance it was to find he'd been adopted by Juma, the Kirghiz chief, who was almost blind. He cured Juma's blindness by simple cleanliness and an application of boracic acid. He'd worked up the wash himself from borax he'd found in the bed of a dry lake.

In the meantime, he'd found out that he had been barred from India. The Government of India was taking no chances with tramps who'd messed things up in both Russia and Afghanistan. Yet he might have told those folks at Delhi about those boxed machine-guns had they let him in.

Or again he might have stayed on with Juma. He liked the old man and Juma had given him a rifle and ammunition, considerably more valuable than their weight in gold.

But the girl Mahree—fifteen, slender, full-breasted, with eyes like a fawn's—had broken an apricot in two and offered him half.

* * * *

The din from the camp had assumed something like order and processional movement, swelling louder, coming nearer— horns and gongs, clanging cymbals, that tumult of shouting. The voices of women and children split through all this now and then with a shrill like that of fifes.

There were, Shattuck judged, three or four hundred persons in the mob. Most of the noise seemed to come from a solid phalanx of men in the center. It wasn't long before he could see that these men were roughly uniformed in long red robes. At first he thought that these men were masked. But in a little while he could see that what he'd taken to be masks were simply their own blackened faces.

Somewhere he'd read about those blackened faces—the fighting monks of the Tibetan lamaseries. Even their name popped up. He repeated it:

"Dok-dokpa!"

He kept his air of unconcern. But he decided that, at the first show of battle, he'd seize old Father Tsarong over there, and hold him as both shield and hostage.

"They have heard," said Tsarong, "what your presence has said about Dorje-Pamo. They wish to honor the messenger of the Pig-Faced Goddess."

It was simply stated, but it sounded like irony to Shattuck. He had an idea that old Tsarong was not so simple as he would have it appear. Nor could Tsarong have been so unimportant, either. The other elder had placed himself slightly back of Tsarong. The beardless one was frankly remote.

"Stand up and face them, Tsarong La," said Shattuck.

"Your presence——"

"Stand up and face them! Signal them to remain where they are."

There was something besides blood that had begun to beat through Shattuck's arteries. It was always that way when a fight threatened— especially if it was apt to be a fight against overwhelming odds. It was a sort of lulling warmth. It was as sweet as a bugle call to a cavalry horse. It was a premonition.

As Tsarong still hesitated—pretending not to hear—pretending not to understand—Shattuck saw a glint of something in the old man's eyes that confirmed the premonition in his veins.

From where he sat, Shattuck jumped. It was a trick that Juma's young fighting bucks had taught him. They'd be sitting crosslegged on the ground—they might have been sitting like that for hours; and then—presto!— they could fling themselves to right or left, or forward or backward, as if their legs had been springs.

As Shattuck sprung, it was exactly as if a fragment of that swelling din from down the hillside had detached itself and had almost fallen upon him.

He came down crouching at the side of old Tsarong. As he did so he whirled and fired without taking aim. An instant afterward— and always afterward—it seemed to him that he must have seen what was coming up behind him with some sort of eyes different from those in the front of his head.

He'd as if seen that enemy sneaking upon him from behind.

Felt boots, red cloak, black face—it was a giant of a man, and he'd been on the point of cutting down on him with one of the biggest swords that Shattuck had ever seen.

The bullet from Shattuck's rifle had taken the giant through the shoulder. He was twisted back and around like a big tree hit near the top by lightning. The sword got a jerk that sent it spiraling like a boomerang for a good twenty yards.

"You next?" grunted Shattuck.

And even while this was happening he had caught an arm about the old man Tsarong's shoulders.

To Tsarong it must have been like an embrace from Death.

"Shadak—Shadak Khan!" Tsarong squeaked.

In the confusion of the moment the pronouncing of that name reached Shattuck like a happy portent—a sure enough mantram.

He was aware that Tsarong wasn't the only one who'd pronounced that name. So had that other elder—also perhaps the beardless boy. The fact that they had joined in the cry—some intonation of horror and pleading in their voices— gave Shattuck an idea.

"Ai-ya!" he laughed. "You thought to fool me, Old Man Tsarong. Why, you're the Governor yourself!"

CHAPTER IV

All this had taken place in full view of that mob of dokpas and civilians coming up from the camp. They'd been coming pretty fast. There'd been a crescendo to their racket culminating in a shriek and clang that was like the explosion of a high-powered shell.

The Goliath of the sword was staggering around in a narrowing circle like a dog looking for a place to lie down. Down he went—coiled, then straightened out. He was summoning all that vast strength of his to become a man again—become the hero he must have felt himself when he'd swung up that big sword of his to kill an earth demon, no less, and his whole tribe looking on.

It was a swift impression that Shattuck got— but detailed, one apt to be lasting. That big face of his, shining with grease and blacking, contorted with terror more than pain, was nothing human.

Then Shattuck saw that the big man had been merely the first of several. There must have been a dozen swordsmen headed in his direction.

In one respect, at any rate, his strategy had been correct. There wasn't a single gun in sight. Tsarong must have seen to that. Unwilling to take a chance on any dokpa marksmanship, he'd given his order accordingly when he'd sent his runner back to the camp.

Shattuck, still embracing Tsarong, gave an order:

"Tell your swordsmen to retire—" The old man panted, but did not speak.

"—else I'll kill you before their eyes!"

"The victory is God's!" Tsarong panted— slowly, fatalistically—in English. He raised his voice and shrilled something in Tibetan.

Just an affair of seconds all this was— seconds that galloped like horses in a race, but each horse of a second mounted by some watchful jockey that recorded every move.

"You haven't answered me, Tsarong La," said Shattuck softly.

"Wherefore, O Shadak Khan, when you know all things?"

"It's you, the Governor of Chan-tang."

"I am but half the Governor, as you see, O Shadak Khan. The other half is he who sat beside me. Each district has two governors."

Shattuck eyed the other bearded and earringed elder. He'd been sitting there in a white trance.

"And what's your name?" Shattuck asked.

The old man merely gasped like a carp out of water. He wanted to answer something. But he was afraid. He hadn't understood.

"Don't you understand even the language of heaven?" Shattuck asked in his best Chinese.

"Kuan-hua!"

The stricken elder recovered himself in a gulp of amazement that made him forget his fears.

"The Mandarin dialect," was what he meant.

"My lord speaks even the language of the Sons of Heaven!"

"I am, indeed, your lord, Old Uncle," Shattuck told him rapidly in Chinese. "And make no mistake. I have proved it. I am a spirit merely disguised as a Hairy Face. Which is the superior of you twain?"

"My brother, Tsarong, is the elder."

"Doesn't he speak the Kuan-hua?"

"Inadequately. While I went East, he went West."

"Tell Moon Face, here," said Shattuck, "to go get such help as is needed to carry away this crippled dokpa. He is to be cared for kindly."

Moon Face was sped on his way.

"And before he returns," Shattuck hurried on, "I'll tell you that both of you old men are deserving death. But see! Instead of that, here while all your people are looking on, I embrace you both. To him who went West I speak the language of the West. To him that went East I speak the language of the East. Who then, am I?"

"Verily, you are Shadak Khan!"

"I am Shadak Khan! I am Captain Trouble! V

Have you not heard—hasn't the Dalai Lama himself heard—that a new king is coming into the world? I am he! I've come to rule the world for a while! My name is—Shadak Khan! My name is— Captain Trouble!"

Something of this talk must have reached the crowd down the hill. It may have done this partly through that curious intuition of crowds— especially of crowds already incandescent and annealed by excitement. Moon Face, the messenger, may have spread something of it as he went down seeking help for the wounded man.

A dozen lamas not of the fighting sort but regular ge-longs—the superior sort who'd had brains enough to pass their examinations, and showing it in their faces—had responded to the call. The appearance of them gave Shattuck another idea.

"And is there not one among these," he asked, "who speaks either the language of the Chiling-ky-me?"—he'd put the question in English, but he'd used the only Tibetan word he knew. It made a pretty flourish.

Chiling-ky-me!

Old Juma had taught him that word. For Juma had conducted robber raids off and on into pretty nearly every section of the high country, even into Tibet. The word meant foreigners—that is, the English.

Before old Tsarong could pull himself together to answer Shattuck, it was another's voice who answered in English:

"Sir, my—father—"

Shattuck, just at the sound of that voice, felt a tingling thrill, he didn't know why. He didn't have time to ask. He'd raised his eyes and had seen the speaker—a lean face and a shaven head that might have belonged to some young Roman general. Even his tattered robe of a Tibetan lama might have been a toga.

The voice was forcing a calm that the brilliant eyes belied.

"Sir, my—father—was—American!"

CHAPTER V

It was Shattuck's turn to exert all his will at self-control. The other lamas were staring. So were the two old governors. Shattuck could feel that they were. But he kept his eyes on that soberly flashing face of the young lama who'd spoken.

"Brother," he said, "what is your name?"

"My Tibetan name is Champela."

"You have another?"

There was a long pause.

"John Day."

It had been his father's name, this young lama explained. His father had been a geologist who'd married his own Lalla Rookh in the Vale of Cashmere. They'd both been killed by an avalanche in that gorge called by the Tibetans "the Four Devil Pass."

It was also Champela himself who referred to his mother as Lalla Rookh. He'd read the poem as a boy.

"So did I," said Shattuck.

To Shattuck, after his months of exile, it was as if he'd stumbled onto a lamasery here in the heart of Asia floating the American flag.

While the other lamas carried the wounded black-face away, Shattuck deserted the two old governors and drew Champela aside.

"John Day," he said, "are you free?"

Champela reflected.

"As free as you are, Shadak Khan," he replied.

Shattuck let the title ride. There'd been no hint of mockery in it. If anything, there'd been something just the opposite. It was as if the title had been confirmed by a prophet.

"You're not held by any vows?"

"None but those I have made to myself."

"No chief lama is your master?"

"Not even the Dalai Lama himself, Shadak Khan."

"Why don't you call me by my right name, John Day?"

"I believe that I am calling you by your right name, Shadak Khan. Your coming has been predicted since a thousand years— since twice a thousand years—"

"You mean?"

"A scourge of God, perhaps—a Shadak Khan—a Captain Trouble. He has a thousand names. But so has the sun. So has Maitreya—He Who Will Come—"

They were standing there on the high slope of what has been called the Roof of the World. The sun was going down. And with one of those sudden transformations of light so common in mountain country the snow peaks had turned to flaming gold.

"You be my prime minister, John Day," said Shattuck.

He'd still intended his proposal, even then, to sound something like a joke. But it didn't sound like a joke at all. It was as if the very mountains were celebrating the event. This was something that had been predicted since, twice a thousand years.

"I'll be your prime minister," Champela told him.

"Shake!"

The young lama might not have caught the meaning of the word in that particular sense, but he was quick enough to understand the extended hand.

"Now I'm not free," he said.

"Neither am I."

"No man is free from his destiny—and this, our meeting, also was predestined—perhaps since the beginning of the world."

There was a barbecue in the little valley of the camp that night, though not in the American style. The Tibetans like to eat their meat boiled— or raw; washed down with gallons of tea and rancid butter, or *chang*, the beer of the country, and *arrak*, a whisky distilled from the beer.

The dung fires seethed and spit blue flames.

There was singing, dancing and fights, before it was fairly dark.

The people were celebrating the advent of Shadak Khan. They weren't quite sure yet just what this signified. But it had something to do with Dorje-Pamo, the Pig-Faced Goddess. They knew that much. And that was enough. The way to please old Dorje-Pamo was to gorge and souse, brawl and make love....

But John Day, prime minister of Shadak Khan, wouldn't let Shattuck partake of the feast— not even as a guest of the governors.

"They'll fill you with aconite," he said, "you'd be dead before dawn."

Most Tibetans were ardent poisoners in times of great emergency.

There was an early moon. In its ghostly light a cavalcade of ponies left the scene of the camp and wound its way further up the valley.

Shattuck was in the midst of it, in the place of greatest safety and honor. Those in front and those following, so far as he could see, were white lamas like Champela.

In the moonlight it was hard to think of Champela as John Day, American. For that matter, Shattuck found it hard to think of himself as himself. He was something else—something bigger than himself—something predestined since the beginning of the world.

Shadak Khan!

Captain Trouble!

CHAPTER VI

By the light of this same moon a caravan of more than three hundred camels came padding back into this same secret valley from the outlying desert. Unknown to Shattuck it was this caravan for which the warring Tibetans had been waiting.

The camel-bells made music in the night. It was a rhythmic music to which the swishing feet of the stock kept time like the feet of tireless dancers. It would have been hard to find a better equipped or a better conducted caravan anywhere.

Every man was armed. Even the camel-pullers were armed.

Any old caravan man would have spotted the sort of caravan this was without looking twice.

"T'u fang-tze!"

Opium-runners! Caravans like this brought the precious "white opium" of Persia through the Gobi to all points east. But even an old Gobi man might have been puzzled by the loads and the haste of this present caravan if not by the trails it followed.

No opium-train ever followed the regular roads anyway.

But these camels were carrying full loads— compact and strongly boxed. Arms! That would be sure. But the trail could lead nowhere except back into the wild and thinly populated Chantang country of Tibet's Far West.

Along a smooth bit of going the owner of the outfit, mounted on a nimble black pony, drew alongside of his caravan-master, who was riding half asleep and half awake on the pick of the camels. The relations of owner and master were about like those of owner and captain on a ship at sea.

They were speaking Mongolian, a language that had been largely developed in desert places. Their voices were no louder than the occasional bubbling of the camel the caravan-master rode.

"We'll soon arrive at the turn-off of the Thorny Well Trail, Big Man," the owner of the outfit said.

"What of it, Duke?"

"It is a short way and a safe way."

"To where we're going?"

"No, Big Man, to Kansu."

"We're not going to Kansu, Duke. We're going to the Lesser Valley of the Soaring Meditation."

"I can't help thinking about how much more money these arms would bring in China than they would in Tibet."

The caravan-master yawned and belched.

"Big Man, I mean it."

"Mean what?"

"The difference in price would enrich us both. General Hokwa is in Kansu with all the gold he collected during his last campaign."

"May it give him inflammation of the bowels!"

"But Kansu needs these machine-guns. Tibet doesn't."

"Search me!" groaned Big Man, or words to that effect.

He dropped his head on his chest and pretended to be sleeping again. The owner of the outfit still ambled on at his side.

"Big Man," he said, "when they've got you back there in the hills, how do you know that those louse-breeding Tibetans are going to pay you?"

"I don't know it."

"What then?"

"They'll pay first or they don't get the arms."

"They may take them anyway."

"From this bunch? Don't make me laugh? This bunch? I haven't got a man in my string who hasn't been slitting throats for the past ten years! We're a bunch of fighting wildcats."

CHAPTER VII

"We'll need a fighting-man like you," said the old abbot, as Shattuck stood before him.

John Day translated the Tibetan into perfect English.

"They are bringing fighting-machines into the Little Valley," the abbot went on in a whispering monotone, "and they that bring the machines are fighting men."

The abbot was very old. His eyes were so glazed that they appeared to be sightless. He seemed to be talking in his sleep about things that he saw in his sleep.

He sat cross-legged on a cushioned bench back of a carved teakwood table. On the table were a covered teacup and a bell. The table was like an altar. When the abbot was silent he sat so still it was easy to imagine that he was an image in a temple.

He was silent for a long time, then he spoke again.

"The spirit of revolution has entered Tibet. There are foolish men planning to put a king in the place of the Dalai Lama."

John Day translated. He saw that Shattuck was about to ask a question, but he raised a warning hand.

It was as if the movement had struck a spark of life from the image presented by the abbot. What he said was:

"I will answer your question, Captain Trouble."

And Shattuck knew then beyond all doubt— as he'd already been prepared to believe—that he was in the presence of an authentic Bogdo—a Living Buddha. Although the old seer continued to speak in Tibetan it was as if a skillful painter were now casting up a picture on some invisible canvas of the air.

"Along toward the next peak-shining time"— and Shattuck could see the light of the rising sun along a mountain-crest while it was still night in the valleys.

"—they will arrive at the narrow place of this valley of ours called the Jaws of the Wolf."

Shattuck would recognize that narrow gorge when he saw it— he would recognize it from what he was seeing now.

* * * *

Several times the Bogdo seemed to be on the point of speech again, and each time that he did so Shattuck caught some fleeting vision in which the movement and the figures were confused by a red mist. Each time when the red mist was shaping itself into something definite, the Bogdo made an erasing gesture in front of him with his slender hand and the unformed picture disappeared.

Finally he murmured two words, which John Day translated:

"Acquire merit!"

The Bogdo reached out and touched his teacup as if he were about to drink. It was a ceremonial gesture meaning that the audience was ended....

The Soaring Meditation Lamasery of the Lesser Valley—as the place was known—was like a series of setback houses against a steep mountain slope. As Shattuck and his new prime minister came out on an upper terrace they both could tell by the stars that the night was already far gone.

"It is time that I hit the road," said Shattuck.

"Pel—Captain—"

"Make it Pel."

"I'm going with you."

"You're not. I'm Captain Trouble. I'm even the Fighting Fool. I saw a blood-red mist when the Bogdo talked. You're not a man of blood."

"The camp is debauched and drunk. You'll have no one to help you."

"So much the better."

"You can't go alone. These are gun-runners—all fighting men."

"His holiness, the Bogdo, saw me fighting them there alone. So did I. That's why he mentioned that place where one man can turn them back. Is there a horse in the stables with a chestnut coat and a white mane?"

"Torang! The abbot's own! If he showed him to you in the vision he meant you to have him."

For an interval John Day closed his eyes. During that interval he had become Champela, the mystic desciple of Buddha again. He opened his eyes with a changed expression.

"I have just received a message myself from the Bogdo," he said.

"What about?"

"I'm not sure myself. Follow me."

They went down a dozen flights of steps as narrow and as steep, as ladders. Most of the time they were in almost complete darkness. Only here and there a butter-lamp burned.

They came into a dusky temple room and there, without hesitation, Champela, again the mystic, went over to where a monumental statue of Buddha reared its height and breadth into the shadows from a breast-high platform. The front of this platform Champela raised like the lid of a coffer. Into this receptacle he stood gazing for a few seconds with a rapt attention.

Then he drew out a long object swathed in fold after fold of silk.

"What is it?" Shattuck whispered.

The young lama also whispered, but his voice was thrilling.

"Something else the Bogdo is sending you— the sword of Kubla Khan!"

CHAPTER VIII

When Chief Juma awoke to the fact that his adopted son, Dak (the nearest he'd ever got to Shattuck) had put the wind between them he was very disconsolate.

Like many another hillman, nature had been generous to him in the matter of height. He was all of six feet seven in his well-worn chaplies, the sandals he stuck to in winter as in summer. And physically he was as tough as a bundle of rattan. But he was at an age when he was prone to go over and over the same story time and again.

And now that "Dak" was gone, he was worse than ever in this respect. Formerly he'd had a number of favorite stories—how he'd killed this or that blood enemy, how he'd robbed whole caravans single-handed.

But now he could think of only that one story.

He'd come on this crazy young sahib (Shattuck) back in the hills being more or less neglected by some roaming Kazaks. After all, even Kazaks may treat a crazy man no worse than a dog. And he was about to pass up the incident when, by mere chance, he learned from a renegade Afghan the sort of battle the lad had put up against great odds while trying to raid a government gold mine.

Thereupon, in the hope of merit in heaven and also, perhaps, a few honest rupees from the sahibs to whom this lad evidently belonged, he'd sought to turn "Dak" over to the English. But the cow-eaters wouldn't have him at any price.

He'd done something that had made him skip out of the country of the Oross, the English had said. Then he'd got into this battle in Kafiristan.

After that, Juma wouldn't have parted with the boy anyway—not at any price. He'd nurtured the lad like his own child; He'd spent a year's income on prayers and medicines for him. As a result, the boy came out of his dream. And having come out of his dream he'd put the healing touch on Juma's own eye-trouble.

* * * *

Juma couldn't understand it. They'd loved each other like father and son. Why had "Dak" put the wind between them?

And so it went on and on, day after day. Until the mother of the girl Mahree came and told Juma the tale she'd learned from Mahree herself.

"Now, by Allah and all the fiends of Gehenna," said Juma, "had Dak but whispered it to me I'd given him the girl as readily as I would have given him anything else I won. Didn't he restore my sight?"

After that, he kept his band on the move. He was looking for "Dak." Over high passes and into valleys he'd almost forgotten, into villages where there were unsettled blood-claims against him, into forbidden temples and lamaseries—there was no place where Juma wouldn't go in the pursuit of that strange search of his.

To make matters worse, Mahree was getting older. Also, she was gaining in beauty. He'd never gone in for purdah nonsense. He was able to take care of his women. But he'd have to wrap the girl up in a *burgua* at that, if he wanted to keep her for "Dak." He was getting higher and higher offers for her all he time.

Then, one day, Juma came on a fakir sitting naked on a glacier. And the devout neighbors assured Juma that the holy man had sat like that, unmoving since the last new moon. That meant the fakir had suffered killing frost for more than ten days. Yet he showed not the slightest ill affects from it. The man was holy.

When Juma went to see him, the holy man came out of his period of meditation and said:

"He whom you call your son is near death."

Juma said: "Sick?"

"No! In bloody battle!"

"Praise God, at least for that," said Juma. "Where?"

"I see—wait!—a lamasery in a little valley— a cleft between two hills—and there thy son is as one against a hundred——"

The sadhu stopped as if he'd never spoken at all.

"Where?" screamed Juma. "Or I'll tear you——"

The sadhu looked up at him unmoved. And Juma, for the first time in his life, began to quaver.

"Where, O holy one? See, I am getting old!"

The holy one looked at him with compassion. He made a forward movement with his hand to indicate a direction.

"That way—until the sun goes down!"

Juma turned and strode away as he stood. He didn't have his gun. He hadn't dared carry it into the presence of the holy one as he'd wanted to be sure of having his questions answered. But he had his knife. And the hills were rich in rocks of throwing and hammering size.

He'd covered a mile before he discovered that he was followed. It was that curse of a female, the cause of it all, the girl Mahree.

He tried to drive her back.

But to his amazement and her own, she defied him.

"Since when," she shrilled, "is a woman forbidden to fight for her man?"

CHAPTER IX

With Torang between his knees and the sword of Kubla Khan held close to his breast Shadak Khan, Captain Trouble, the Fighting Fool, was off to fight he didn't know exactly what.

Long ago he had known someone called Pelham—Rutledge— Shattuck. The name kept time to Torang's swift but easy lope. Pelham— Rutledge—Shattuck——

But it wasn't he—it wasn't he—who'd sat on a mountain throne and looked into the eyes of his subjects. It wasn't he who'd stood in the presence of a reincarnated Buddha and heard his fortune told. It wasn't he who rode an abbot's horse down a long dark valley with the sword of a great warlord against his breast.

No, those were pages from the life of Shadak Khan—Captain Trouble—Fighting Fool—

There came to the reincarnation who was himself the sharp pang of a realizing thought. The thought was this—that he might be riding to his death. He remembered the red mist—the half-seen astral pictures that the Bogdo had wiped away with his slender white hand, the old man's final words:

"Acquire merit!"

How? If death was the way, he'd take his chance!

He looked up just in time to see a meteor slide across the sky. It wouldn't be so bad to go like that.

He felt a sense of elation. It was as if the sword against his breast were coming to life— taking on a warmth of its own. It had no scabbard. The blade was a long strong scimitar, yet so exquisitely balanced to the hilt it could be handled like a wand.

He flashed it about his head. It sang.

To that faint note Torang let out a link or two of speed. In this light the gelding's dark body was invisible. His white mane and tail glinted along like a pair of detached specters.

It was this dash of white in the dark that had given the horse his name. Torang!—the first glint of daybreak; a high cloud shining white while the earth was dark.

There was a cloud like that hanging over the easterly summits when Shattuck passed the camp where, last night, the two old governors would have given him aconite. He spat in their direction.

It was a gesture as much for all their gorging, guzzling, lecherous herd of human swine as it was for them. And these were the men who'd barter for a revolution!

Before you could revolute a land you had to revolute yourself!

So said the heir to the blade of Kubla Khan.

The thought was still with him when the valley suddenly twisted and went into a corridor like that of some overwhelming ruin. He was at the very lips of the wolf's open jaws.

He didn't know how to pray but some instinct was telling him that the moment was solemn and that he ought to do something.

He reined in Torang, with a swift hand. He raised the sword of the great khan Kubla straight up above his head. His head went down. For a moment he was thinking of the strange John Day.

"I sure would be glad to be good enough," he whispered, "to have him not as a prime minister— you're crazy!—but merely as a friend."

A moment later he was stirred from his reverie by some faint spasm of nervous excitement that ran through Torang's lithe frame. It was like a faint current of electricity, a silent telephone call. Torang had arched his neck. His slender ears were focusing on a distant sound.

A moment later, Shattuck was hearing the sound himself—the faint, far-off clink and clank of camel bells.

CHAPTER X

The gorge of "The Wolf"—literally the throat—ran between towering cliffs for a twisted mile, and pretty bad going all the way. After the primordial earthquake had riven the mountains apart, a stream—or recurrent streams— had scoured out the bottom, leaving a debris of footless boulders, causing a cave-in here and a dike there and a pit like an elephant trap somewhere else.

The caravan-master knew all this. He had been through the gorge time and again before. It used to be part of the regular opium route until the old Bogdo of the Soaring Meditation Lamasery put an end to it.

The Bogdo was known to have great powers. Otherwise he would have "taken the aconite" a long time ago. There had often been talk among the caravan-master and his band that they could raid the lamasery and make their fortunes at it.

The place was isolated. There wasn't a drunken, brawling, dok-dokpa about the place— not a fighting man of any kind. And it was generally known that into the mountain back of every monastery the treasure caves were being dug deeper and deeper every year. That sort of thing had been going on for centuries. The treasure of even a rundown old lamasery like that of the Soaring Meditation would be enough to buy Japan.

But they'd never tried to make a raid. They didn't dare. The Bogdo had a reputation of being in league with certain ghosts.

It was that matter of ghosts as much as the uncertain footing of the gorge that had caused the caravan-master—a pastmaster in timing, like all good smugglers—to bring his weary train to the outer mouth of the gorge just at the "peak-shining" hour.

No more ghosts after peak-shining. And there would be light enough, although night got clogged in the narrow defile and stuck there like a fog until late morning.

He didn't dare halt now, even for a minute. Camels were peculiar creatures. You could keep them going and going—as he had this time—

"*Kwa-chi-cheng!*"

One forced march on top of another. But let up on them, after a race like that, and the beasts would flop down and die in their

tracks. Besides, inside the valley there were good grazing and water. Outside, there was none.

Still in the lead and only half awake the caravan-master pushed
on into the gorge. He'd scarcely entered it before there was a clattering of hoofs and he saw a lone horseman in the shadows ahead.

From the moment the caravan-master saw this man he felt the
approach of trouble—a dark horse with a white mane and tail.
Then, to a sharp increase of his trouble, he saw that the man in
front of him was unquestionably white.

The man came ambling toward him at a good swift track and
didn't stop or speak until the caravan-master's own camel stopped.

"I know you," said the man on the horse. His Chinese was that
of Pechili, with a good snap to it. "You're Wong Tajen." It was as
if to say, "Wong the Big Man."

Wong was beginning to simmer.

"This is no place to halt my caravan," he said.

He guessed the fellow might be a Russian. He'd heard about
big fights between opposing clans of the Oross beyond the Gobi.

"I'm halting it, Big Man."

"Who are you?"

"Don't talk to me from a camel. Dismount!"

Big Man's ears were picking up tell-tale sounds from back of
him as squad after squad of camels came to a halt.

"Dismount and send your camel ahead or all the camels will be
lying down on you. You know that, Fathead."

Wong did know it. He'd been handling camels for the better
part of thirty years. But not for twenty years had anyone dared call
him ta-tou, "fathead," except a fresh tax-collector whom later he'd
slowly killed.

With a curse and grunt he rolled himself from the riding camel
he was on. The beast was already smelling grass and water and
lurched ahead. The camel that followed also lurched. As it did so,
something amazing happened. It shed its load—one heavy box to
either side.

A sword had flashed across the pack rope—a mere swish, and
the rope had parted.

Even while Wong was rolling from his camel he'd found the
grip of the revolver he carried in the breast of his sheepskin coat.

He got that far when he stopped to think. This man might have an army back of him. Already two camels were past—his favorite of all the camels he'd ever slept on, leading the way.

The thought meant hesitation; the hesitation lost him his chance and two other camels. Two other loads had crashed down.

"Hands up and face the rock, you!"—this fellow spoke like no Russian.

There was a needle of steel against Wong's neck.

Wong's nerves were tuned to small things. In that needlepoint against his neck he could detect not the slightest quaver—no skipping, no torture.

His hands were up. His face was to the rock.

There were shocks of falling boxes, the grunt and scramble and heave of camels becoming frenzied by a prospect of camel heaven after a long, hard drag through camel hell.

And the fellow kept talking all the time— slanging the camel pullers and laughing at them; he was driving them back along the gorge as fast as he slit the lashings of the heavy freight. "Hey, you, Big Man! Why don't you ask me who I am?"

"Who?"—and Wong dared to turn.

"Hands still up, or I'll slit your throat as you did the widow's in the Traveling Sands!"

That was the most secret murder that Wong had ever done. His eyes were beginning to pop. The man leaned down from his horse— Torang wasn't very tall—and found with his left hand the pistol in Wong's breast. Wong felt a faint breath of courage when the white devil searched no further—else he'd found a second pistol lower down.

"Who are you, duke?" Wong asked placatingly.

"Not 'duke,' kahn!" He stopped to sever the ropes on two more camels and Wong had snatched his second pistol higher. "Shadak Kahn!—all same Captain Trouble. You savvy, Captain Trouble?"

Shadak Khan turned to yell at a camel puller who was trying to stop a camel by the nose-rope. The camel-puller was either stupid or deaf. He raised apologetic frightened eyes to the horse-riding duke and pulled harder than ever.

At that instant there was a crashing report—it sounded like a hand-grenade, there in the rocky confines of the gorge.

Shattuck felt a blaze of heat at his side as if his coat had caught on fire. But before he'd take note of this—more swiftly than Wong the Big Man could fire his Number Two gun a second time—Shattuck lunged. Like a thing alive and self-directed the sword of Kubla Khan slit the Big Man's throat.

CHAPTER XI

Tibetans are early risers. Their climate has made them so. Late night and morning hold about the only golden hours they ever know. Along about midday the horrible wind comes up—the buran, the hideous dry gale that blows stronger and stronger under a blanched and cloudless sky.

As often as not the people of Tibet will be up and about well before daylight even after a night of debauch.

It was so this morning in the little valley, in the camp of the two old governors, Tsarong and his brother. Then the black-faced fighting lamas where thirsty and on the prowl for fresh adventure so early—or so late—that there had practically, been no night for them at all. And the dokpas were the first to note that queer invasion of camels from the Throat of the Wolf. They were a superstitious lot, those dokpas—none more so, since to each of them had come, some time or other, manifestations of powers they could not understand.

These blubbering, crazed, and naked camels rocking into the valley like so many camel ghosts, and something really terrifying about them.

The governors were roused.

In an incredibly short time the whole camp was up and active. These were livestock people— more used to yaks than camels, but recognizing in this stampeded herd more value than a century of goats would ever bring.

* * * *

Old Tsarong wasn't long in putting two and two together. This was the munition train they'd come to meet. Something had happened to it. But what? Where were the men? Where was the freight?

Through the thin air of daybreak they heard that distant re-volver shot. After that, there were the muted staccato barkings of a small-arms battle.

While the governors were still shouting conflicting orders, a special shout went up and the people fell aside as if tossed by an in-visible plow and through this furrow—beautiful as a dream-horse and as elusive—they saw the horse of the Bogdo go trotting by.

"Torang!"

Torang they believed to be as holy as its master. They saw it saddled but riderless, unblemished, uncannily wise when it came to its keeping on its way. Wasn't it likely that it was ridden by a ghost?

It had come very close to that.

In less than a minute after Wong had fired— and died—Shattuck recognized that this was no place for an abbot's horse—or any horse. He had an overwhelming gust of pity for all horses, camels, dogs—and men! These men had fought the Gobi until they were as cruel as the Gobi itself! He'd sent Torang home.

This wasn't a chain of reasoning.

His reasoning all went into the fight—clear, precise, perceptive with a thousand eyes only opened in times like these.

Still with that revolver he'd taken from Wong in his left hand and the great scimitar in his right, he plunged on further into the pass.

Already the place of his first stand was being choked with cast boxes, and blue steel brought a flash of clairvoyant memory. He'd seen these self-same boxes, and at least a part of what was in them, back in Samarkand.

He cut more pack ropes and dodged. Camels slipped and straddled and disappeared. Horses were being kicked forward by hard-faced Mongols.

Shattuck would remember those faces. When the world needed fighters, these were fighters. But they'd have to be led, bled, cruci-fied, to be taught the things they'd known before when they con-quered half the world.

One was poking a gun in his face when Shattuck dodged under the horse's belly and cut the gunman down from the other side. An instant later he'd fired his first shot and had seen the horse jump from under its rider as if the fellow had been roped.

The confusion saved him a dozen, a score of times.

"Back!" he shouted. "Or you'll all be killed!"

"*Ya-ming!*"

That was shorter: "Sure death!"

Some of the riders were trying to turn back to regain the desert.

Camels were retching, moaning, grinding their teeth. Some thudded to a fall and squealed as panic wrenched them to their feet again.

A sudden weakness blew a breath over Shattuck. It was like the first whiff of the anaesthetic before an operation. But he felt no pain.

He gathered his nerves to a tighter pitch.

"*Ya-ming!*"

"And that means you," a calm voice echoed in his brain.

"Let me do this first," his thought replied.

He was drawing the great blade across another pack-tie when a Mongol struck down at him with the loaded butt of a whip.

At the same moment Shattuck fired.

Bullet and bludgeon both went home.

"I'm taking him with me," was the Fighting Fool's last thought.

CHAPTER XII

A bunch of the dokpas—faces black with grease and their dank hair making them look like devils on a frolic—were looting what they could find in the Throat of the Wolf.

They screeched and laughed. They stripped the dead and kicked the dying, leaving a number of naked and humiliated corpses in their wake.

Then they made the one gorgeous and outstanding discovery of the morning. They'd not only found the white devil of the preceding day— he who had called himself Shadak Khan—but leaning over him, trying to lift him, trying to recall him to life, one of the most beautiful female creatures they had ever seen.

They'd all heard legends about the Kashmiri maidens. They told filthy stories of their own invention about their affairs with such. They vaunted of local conquests that had Kashmiri conquests beaten a mile.

But here was the real thing. So they believed. Anyway, it was the first of her species any of them had ever seen. They crowded toward her and the white man like a pack of wolves at a spent doe.

Mahree was no spent doe, though, even if she had traveled for one full day and one full night over a terrain that would have strained a yak.

She turned to fire. Her eyes shone green. Her forehead seemed to flatten.

Before the boldest of the dokpas could carry out his plan of stepping on Shattuck's face and seizing her at the same time she'd literally brained him with a sliver of rock.

The unfortunate thing about this was that it gave an idea to the more cunning wits of the crowd. The dokpas also groped for rocks. At least two of them failed to do their groping fast enough.

Mahree threw a rock splinter with the free-shoulder grace and power of a professional ball-player—although she'd never seen one. She scored two perfect hits. Then a rock like the end of a sledge-hammer caught her shoulder and she staggered.

She was staggering, trying not to fall, when she saw another sort of lama coming through the gorge. He'd seen what was happening. His hands were up. He was shouting things that Mahree couldn't understand, but which the expression on his face told her were prayers on her own behalf and denunciation of the dokpas.

The black faces got his message. They turned on him with howls. One of them with a stone all ready let fly at him and scraped his head. The young lama covered his face with his hands and arms and kept on coming.

It was his only way of fighting back.

One of the black-face ruffians already had his hands on him when from behind and above the young lama a hand plunged down with a knife in it. That was one good knife that was apt to be lost forever. The dokpa went down with the blade out of sight in his shock of hair.

That was Juma's knife. It was Juma, looking more than his six-foot seven, who had followed John Day here—Champela, whom he'd found in the Lamasery of the Soaring Meditation. Champela himself was just setting out, having heard that Torang, the abbot's horse, had but then returned without the Shadak Khan.

Champela and Juma had then run the length of the valley. But Mahree, even so, had got there first—a long first, having followed some instinct of her own.

Juma cried to heaven as he tried to pull his precious knife from the dead man's skull. It wouldn't come. It was a tussel as short as it was fierce—Juma's struggle with the stubborn knife.

He was losing seconds, and in any sort of fight Juma never lost any time. He spat on the corpse and almost, without looking, had found the throat of another black face with his able hands.

The others were in full flight. Champela came to Shattuck's side. He lightly touched a temple; he thrust his fingers into Shattuck's shirt.

It was clear that he thought at first that Shattuck was dead—the end of a dream, the eclipse of a great adventure!

Mahree, with all that she had left of consciousness—after that wallop with a rock— centered in her eyes, let out the beginning of a wail.

"Ai-ya-yat I have killed him! He went away because of me! And I meant nothing! I loved him only as a sister!"

"Hush!" said the prime minister of Shadak Khan. "He's not dead!"

It was a message that went up to old Juma, too.

Juma, having just killed two men, one by stabbing and one by barehanded strangling, was leaning over with a great deep tenderness burning in the secret cavern back of his old-eagle eyes.

"Allah Akbar!" he said.

He gently pushed the prime minister aside. He stooped and picked up Captain Trouble, as if that famous Fighting Fool was the merest infant.

"Friend," he said, "if you know any effective magic, I'll see that you get a couple of those runaway camels."

"Get him quickly to the tent of the governors," John Day said. "You put them out and I'll do my best."

CHAPTER XIII

Shattuck was getting well. As soon as they were able to move him again they'd carried him up the valley to the Lamasery of the Soaring Meditation where there were some authentic records of Kubla Khan.

They'd found—by a well authenticated miracle, it was claimed—Kubla's sword where Shadak Khan had dropped it when he fell—as he thought—dead. And the sword was presented to the new khan by the old dogpo himself—the divine incarnation who had the power, it was generally believed, to look into the past lives of others.

Perhaps the good old man saw something in some past life of this modern Captain Trouble, something that linked him with the life of Kubla Khan.

It was, according to the secret books, about the time that an avatar should come about to purge the world before the coming of the Great New King.

The times were full of portent.

Tibet itself would have to be purged. There were mysteries in Tibet such as the world never dreamed of, John Day said. There were hollow mountains he knew about where the secret libraries of the ages had been stored away.

"Couldn't you and I find them?" Shattuck asked.

"We'd find them, all right; but how about the guardians?"

"What sort of guardians?"

"If I thought we had a right to get into those caves we'd get into them," said Captain Trouble.

"There you go! I thought you'd had enough of fighting for a time!"

"I'll never have enough of it so long as there is anything worth fighting for."

Unknown to Shattuck, there was a scribe in the monastery making a record of his stay. Some day, it was argued, such a record might be as valuable as such a one concerning Alexander the Great would be.

"And, according to the horoscope that three of the astrologers in three different lamaseries cast up, this man Shadak Khan, was going to have a number of stirring adventures...." He had one, in fact, before it was considered advisable for him to leave his bed.

He awoke one night to see a huge dokpa crawling into his room on all fours. It was this fact that discovered to Shattuck the identity of the man, because, walking on all fours like that, he revealed a limp in the shoulder where he'd been stopped by a bullet the day he tried to saber Shattuck from behind.

"Ah, go on and get out of here, you big bum!" said the Fighting Fool in English.

And that's what the big bum did—sneaked out and never showed himself again.

Juma had sent for his people, for Juma also would be lingering on in the valley indefinitely. He'd become as you might say the official steward of the loot—camels, horses, boxes of machine-guns, small arms, and ammunition.

Juma loved especially to sit in when Captain Trouble and his prime minister talked about cleaning up some robber band or other and starting an independent state where men could be free and women happy and everyone would get enough to eat—with a few punitive expeditions now and then, just to keep your hand in.

But, best of all, was when the two of them were alone on some upper terrace of the lamasery and the earth so uptilted about them that it almost seemed they were among the stars. Then it was no mere correction of some poor robber band that engrossed them. They talked greatly of great conquerors—men who had been sent into the world to boost men on—by struggle, pain, self-mastery.

There was the inevitable struggle between Asia and Europe—the never surveyed frontiers of China and Russia, for example; the necessary merging of nations that still hated and feared each other; there was the growing challenge of Africa—a riddle as ancient and profound as that of the Great Sphinx.

And when it was all over, when they had the world cleaned up, why, maybe then, they'd go back to America and settle down, like Cincinnatus, on some quiet farm.

GHOST LANTERNS

Alan B. LeMay

There were seven of us aboard the schooner *Terrapin* when she sailed north from Maranhão. There were still seven of us the third day up, when we were becalmed somewhere out of sight of the Brazil coast. But during the next three nights, four men disappeared.

We were lying in the flat calm of the doldrums when it happened. A flat, glistening sea, like hot, blue steel; a blazing sky, so glaring that it threatens to put out your eyes; hot, heavy air, that presses against you and bears you down; motionless sails, an idly drifting ship, a steamy smell of tar—that is the doldrums by day. By night the biggest thing is the silence.

Somehow, the doldrums seem worse on a little ship; and the two-masted schooner *Terrapin*, beating up and down in the catch-as-catch-can cocoa-trade, was little, very little. Perhaps it is the sense of confinement on a little, becalmed ship that makes a man want to get off and walk; or perhaps it is the dullness of a small crew. Nothing happens to break the stifling monotony. Or, if things do happen, as they did on the *Terrapin*, they are such that you never want to see them happen again.

Of the seven of us Cap Dorkin was the hardest boiled. He was a short, square-built man of indeterminate age, with the fishy kind of eyes that show the whites below the irises. Three of his four-man crew were similar—of the surly type of seamen. Jimmy, the cook, was of the other type, round-faced and merry. I was the fourth man of the crew, and was supposed to be mate, which meant that I slept in the cabin instead of the forecastle.

There was one other, a passenger named Harris; he was probably the only passenger the *Terrapin* ever had, a roughly dressed man with a fat, smooth face. And these were the seven of us that started the voyage from Maranhão to Santiago.

We were becalmed late in the afternoon of the third day up from Maranhão after two days of sluggish progress; sunset found us weltering under sails that caught not the slightest breath of air.

The night was heavy and still, and not until morning did anyone suspect the thing that happened in the dark.

Dorkin was the first to notice something wrong when we woke for breakfast.

"I don't smell no coffee," was the first thing he said. "Shake a hoof forward and see why that fat slob of a cook ain't cookin'."

There was no one in the galley, and the stove was cold. Nor was the cook in the forecastle, nor about the deck. Joe Bates and Sharky Steve were stretched out near the capstan, lounging drowsily.

"Where's Jimmy?" I sung out. "And why ain't he slinging the rat-killer?"

Joe and Sharky looked blank.

"Guess the old man must have him aft," Joe offered. "Don't we eat no more?"

"If Jimmy don't come forward a-hopping," Sharky added, "I figure to up with a mast and knock down that there cabin. I've eat every now and then for forty years, and I figure to keep right on."

"Well, he ain't aft," said I.

They sat up, at that. I turned to go aft, but paused with an afterthought.

"Where's Bill Grimes?" I asked.

"Ain't he aft neither?" asked Joe.

"There's somethin' pequiliar goin' on here," decided Sharky Steve, getting to his feet, "and I figure to know what it is. Bill ain't been forward all night."

"Naturally not," said I; "it was his watch."

"That don't account for it," said he, and I turned and went aft, the two seamen at my heels.

Cap Dorkin took the news of the disappearance without a word. He squirted tobacco over the rail and set about to search the ship, the rest of us following along, and Harris, the passenger, trailing after and looking blank. We found nothing. That is, nothing but one thing.

Hitched to the taffrail, and trailing in the water astern, was a half-inch line that had been coiled on the deck when last noticed. Cap Dorkin snatched at the line and hauled it in; but there was nothing on the end of it, and we knew less than we did before.

The men were gone.

"Maybe they gets in a fight and falls overboard," suggested Joe Bates. "And drowns, locked in each other's arms, as y' might say."

"All without makin' a sound, I suppose," sneered Sharky Steve.

"Maybe they falls down a hatch and busts a leg," Joe advanced. "An' can't yell, bein' knocked cold as a herring."

"Followin' which the rats eat 'em, leavin' no trace," Sharky supplied. "Can't you think up no more o' them good ideas?"

"Get forward," ordered the captain, and they went.

That day we lived miserably, sweltering under a melting sun, and eating little of the stuff that Sharky Steve scraped together in the galley. Forward and aft there had come over us that stolid uneasiness that falls upon men in the presence of circumstances unnatural and unexplained.

Cap Dorkin was especially silent and stubborn. Harris asked permission to search the ship again, and got it; but he found nothing more. After his own special search Harris was disposed to discuss the affair with Dorkin; but the captain was short of speech.

"Well," Harris would start up again, "what could have happened to them?"

"I dunno," Cap Dorkin would reply.

"Did you ever hear of anything like this before?"

"Like what?"

"Like these two men disappearing, this way?"

"I dunno." From the captain no further opinion was to be drawn.

Up forward there was a different sort of talk going on between Joe Bates and Sharky Steve.

"These here is bad waters at best," commented Joe. "I've heared of queer things goin' on in these seas before now."

"'Specially on sailin' vessels," said Sharky.

"Yeah," agreed Joe.

"Take that there brig, now, the *Rantoul*. She that was found aground on the Carragda Beach, with all sail set, an' not a hand aboard."

"What's the rest of it?" asked Joe.

"There ain't no more," said Sharky. "Her cargo was all there, just as it was stowed. But no hide nor hair of captain or crew heard of from that day to this. It's goin' on two years now."

"Real queer," admitted Joe, swearing, "but no queerer than the case o' Crazy Jim Clancy. Jim, he shipped on the *Pelican*, that there old brigantine. The *Pelican*, she sails out and don't never put into port again. Jim, they picks him up drifting in a longboat. When they asks him what happened he says nothin' didn't happen, only all hands disappeared off the ship, one by one—so he got scared and left in the boat. But the *Pelican*, she ain't been heard of since. Some say Jim's crazy," Joe added, "an' some say he ain't."

"There's queer things goes on in these seas," Sharky repeated.

"There's queer things goin' on on this vessel," said Joe.

And so it went. To these yarns I paid little attention, for I was familiar with their like; but Harris, when he wandered forward, drank them in silently.

As night closed down, a faint breeze fluttered the sails for a bit; but presently it died, and the night again became silent, clear, breathless. Cap Dorkin moved Joe and Sharky aft for the night. It was the first sign he had given of recognition that, aside from a peculiar accident, anything was wrong on the *Terrapin*.

No one slept before the dog-watch, which was Joe's.

* * * *

I was wakened by a sudden outcry from Sharky, and in an instant I was on deck, the captain at my heels. Through the starlit dimness of the tropic night I could see Sharky leaning over the taffrail, peering down into the black water astern.

"What's wrong—what's wrong?"

"Joe! Joe's gone!" Sharky answered.

Cap Dorkin shouldered past me. "Did you see what happened?" he demanded.

"I didn't see nothin'," Sharky whimpered. "I woke up feelin' somethin' was wrong. Too quiet like. I come on deck, and Joe was missin'!"

"Nothing?" Dorkin demanded again, thrusting his head forward with dog-like menace.

"Nothin', I swear! 'Ceptin' this here." He indicated the taffrail.

Tied to the taffrail with a couple of loose-thrown bights, as if bent by a man in great haste, was that same length of line, trailing in the sea as before. I hauled it in, waking phosphorescent sparks in the dark waters below; there was nothing on its end.

"Put up your hands—all of you!" came the captain's voice, low and hard. We turned to face a heavy automatic.

For the next few minutes I thought that Sharky, Harris and I were about to meet the mysterious end that had overtaken Joe and Bill Grimes and Jimmy the cook. I was convinced that a strange insanity had deranged the mind of Cap Dorkin, inciting him to uncanny and purposeless murder.

In single file, covered by the automatic, we were marched down the short ladder into the cabin. Once in the lantern-light Dorkin made us stand against the bunks while he minutely scrutinized the faces of each of us in turn. Then, after some moments of this, he stepped back. A baffled look was in the captain's face as he put away the gun.

"No," he said, "none of you done it. None of you done it. I'd know if you did. But you didn't."

There was no more sleep that night. We sat in the cabin smoking and speculating gravely. Sharky Steve spun a wild yarn about a giant octopus that once came up from unknown depths to fasten itself upon the bottom of a becalmed schooner. Three men, he said, were dragged over the side in two nights by the monster. So huge was this sea-horror that when it shifted its hold upon the bottom the ship listed. It was this slight listing of the ship in dead calm that led to the monster's discovery.

"Be still a minute!" said Harris. "Didn't the deck tilt a little bit just then?"

We sat silently looking at each other for a few moments, every nerve alert to discern a barely perceptible shifting of the hull. So greatly had my nerves been affected that for an instant I actually thought that the little *Terrapin* was listing, ever so slightly.

"There!" said Harris again. "Didn't she tip just a little then?"

"I—I dunno whether she did or not," Sharky Steve admitted.

"She did not list," said Dorkin decisively, and we accepted his judgment.

Sharky told other yarns, of strange unexplained disappearances, such as we just had seen; of weird sea-curses that followed ships to their dooms; of monsters unknown to men. He thought that some evil and mysterious fate was pursuing the *Terrapin*, taking her sailors one by one with the intention of at last taking her. Any other time, we would have laughed.

Dawn came at last, bringing another blazing day.

The next night was the third night of the calm. It was also the last night, had we but known. The four of us did not attempt to sleep, but sat upright in the lantern-light of the cabin. How I happened to doze at last I do not know; but I remember that Harris was dozing before me.

When I woke, at the sound of feet upon the deck, Sharky Steve was gone.

The circumstances were the same as before. The same line trailed from the taffrail, without other clue. As Harris and Cap Dorkin and I looked at each other, we both knew the other's thoughts. Who would be the next to go? We had given up asking how.

If only we could have wind! Just a capful of air—Sharky Steve was gone—

* * * *

It was morning. A breeze was coming up, very gently, and the *Terrapin* was beginning to forge ahead, very slowly and stodgily. Then Cap Dorkin sighted a sail.

It was evident to me that we had somehow got far out of our course, for in three days we had not sighted more than the distant smoke of a vessel of any sort. But now, plainly enough, a schooner had come into sight, a ship of about our own tonnage, headed our way.

Why Cap Dorkin wanted to take in all sail and put out the sea-anchor until the other vessel should come up I did not understand, but that is what we did. The breeze that early morning had promised did not increase, and all day long we lay waiting while the approaching vessel worked her way toward us. Slowly she drew nearer hour by hour; and at evening she answered our signal and lay to.

Captain Graves, of the Molly Bruce, wore a face totally without expression, but his gray eyes were keen. The two captains greeted each other coolly as we three from the *Terrapin* came aboard.

"I need men," explained Dorkin briefly when we were in the cabin of the Molly Bruce. "What can you spare?"

"Not a man," answered Graves. "I'm short-handed myself."

"All right," said Dorkin. "Will you take a passenger?"

"No," answered Graves. "I never take passengers."

"But I can pay!" Harris broke in. "I can pay well!"

"I'm not interested," said Graves again.

"Look here," cried Harris. "You don't understand me. I tell you, I can pay almost anything!"

Slowly Graves turned and surveyed the other man. The captain's face was still as a mask, but his eyes were hard as steel.

"I know you can," he said.

Harris appeared taken aback, and several moments of silence followed. "Then make me a proposition," he presently suggested.

"You know that I know who you are," said Graves, "and yet you want a proposition from me?"

Harris hesitated.

"Yes," he answered.

"Your name is Singleton," said Captain Graves. "You are probably under another name just now because you had to ship out of Maranhão on either the *Terrapin* or the Molly Bruce—or else lay over in Maranhão waiting for one of your own ships. You wouldn't dare ship under your own name because your business methods and the ships you inherited from your father have killed the little-vessel trade in the small ports. You went out to get us, and you've done well at it. Yet you want a proposition from me?"

"Yes," said Harris again, his voice cold.

Graves got out a pen and wrote for several moments, then handed the paper to the *Terrapin*'s passenger.

"Will you sign that?" he asked.

Harris' face flushed as he read the sheet.

"I'll see you in —— first!" he flashed.

Cap Dorkin had been staring gloomily through the porthole at the *Terrapin* lying deserted fifty yards away in the thick gloom.

"My sidelights are out," he remarked. "I've got to be getting back."

Then suddenly an oath burst from him.

"Step here," he said, his voice low, "and see do you see what I see!"

I peered out of the porthole and saw nothing, save the *Terrapin*, floating lightless under bare poles in the twilight.

"What was it?"

"Lanterns! They're gone now. No! There they are again! Look!"

He sprang up the ladder. Yes, I saw the lanterns, two of them, moving rapidly and with a peculiar smoothness along the little schooner's starboard rail. Then they disappeared, as quickly as if quenched in a bucket.

Cap Dorkin's hail roared from above. "Ahoy! The *Terrapin*, Ahoy! Answer, damn you!"

There was no answer; except that I saw the two lanterns appear again at the forward rail of the *Terrapin*, and slide aft with that same strangely smooth movement. It was enough to send the shivers along any man's spine. I thought, "Ghost lanterns, Sharky Steve would have called them."

"Kind of funny," commented Graves, "that there's no answer from your crew."

Harris was beside me, staring through the port. In the young light of the cabin-lantern his face was white as surf.

"The crew?" he said in a strange voice. "There—isn't any— crew."

Silence held while Harris and I stared across the still water at the *Terrapin*, lying lonely and deserted.

"Your captain wants to leave," said Graves. "You'd better stand by to go back to your ship."

"Go back? Go back to the *Terrapin*?"

Captain Graves' voice was like a saw on steel. "You are going back now," he stated, "unless—you like my proposition!"

"I can't go back there!" cried Harris.

"Then sign!" Graves shoved the paper toward him.

"It's unreasonable—impossible—"

"Sign!"

"I can't—"

"Then get back to your ship!"

Harris wavered, squinting through the port. "Ahoy! Ahoy, the *Terrapin*!" boomed Dorkin's voice above, in a long wailing hail.

But the ghost lanterns appeared no more. Unmanned and silent, the little ship looked even more hopeless than when those weird lights had slid along her rail.

"For the last time, sign or go!"

"I'll sign," said Harris, at last.

He signed, and sat down weakly upon a locker. I witnessed the signature, then followed the captain up the ladder. Then, as the two skippers met, once more a peculiar thing happened. The two men gripped each other's hands and shook heartily.

"All O.K., Bob?" asked Cap Dorkin.

"All set," answered Graves. "Good boy, Sam!"

I rowed Dorkin slowly back to the *Terrapin*.

"Eight years," said Cap, "eight years we've bucked that yellow-backed ship owner. Eight years of fighting upwind and losing. And now we've got him! That paper he signed turns the tables in the small-port trade! We've got him at last!"

"But what about—" I began.

"All that show? All for him! Why do you suppose I got clear off our course? Why do you suppose the Molly Bruce came up just at the right time? It was all planned out, you fool! I didn't tip you off because you're too young—you couldn't have faked it right. The boys had a terrible time stowed away in the hold, though. Hot and stuffy like. I'll sure have to make it up to them!"

Jimmy the cook, and Bill Grimes, and Sharky Steve were playing poker in the cabin when we boarded the *Terrapin* again. And Joe Bates was complaining that he had burned his thumb on a "ghost lantern."

"It was a phony idee anyway," he growled. "Why not stick a gun to the mucker's head in the first place and be done with it?"

But some of these old-timers do things in odd ways!

STORIES OF THE LEGION: CHOC

H. De Vere Stacpoole

*When France found herself faced with the problem of Algeria—
that is to say, with the problem of infinite wastes of sand inhabited
by a foe mobile and ungraspable as the desert wind—she formed
the Legion. She called to the wastrels, the criminals, the despairing, and the impoverished—and they came. Men of genius, street
sweepers, artists, doctors, engineers—it would be difficult to
touch a profession, a race or a grade of intellect not to be found in
the Legion. All the genius that Civilization has turned away from
her doors is here at command—for a cent a day.*

CHAPTER I

The first rays of the morning sun were stealing up the palm-
bordered roads toward Sidi-bel-Abbés, above whose ramparts the
minaret of the great mosque blazed white in the sky. Eighty miles
from Oran on the coast, set away in the vague, yellow, illimitable
wastes of the desert, the headquarters of the Foreign Legion, Sidi-
bel-Abbés is surely one of the strangest cities on earth.

It was built by the Foreign Legion; it is swept and garnished
by the Foreign Legion; it is held against the Arabs by the Foreign
Legion. At night the electric lights round the band stand of the
Foreign Legion on the Place Sadi Carnot blaze against the Algerian
stars, while the muezzins on the balconies of the minarets keep
watch over Islam, and their voices send north, south, east, and west
the cry that was old in the time of Sindbad the Sailor!

All' il Allah—God is great. But the marvel of Sidi-bel-Abbés is
not the fact that here Edison and Strauss face Mahommed in the
form of his priests, nor the flower gardens blooming on the face of
the desert, nor the roads along which the Arabs stalk and the auto-
mobiles dash. The marvel of the Sidi-bel-Abbés lies in the Legion.

When France found herself faced with the problem of Algeria—that is to say, the problem of infinite wastes of sand inhabited
by a foe mobile and ungraspable as the desert wind—she formed
the Legion.

She called to the wastrels, the criminals, the despairing, and the impoverished of every country and every city—and they came.

Men of genius, street sweepers, artists, doctors, engineers—it would be difficult to touch a profession, a race, or a grade of intellect not to be found in the Legion.

General de Négrier said that the Legion could do anything—from the building of a bridge, to the writing of an opera, to the painting of a picture— all the genius that civilization has turned away from its doors is here at command—for a halfpenny a day.

* * * *

The sun had touched the upper border of the huge, blank eastern wall of the Legion's barracks, and it was still a few minutes before reveille, when, in room No.6 of the tenth company, the garde chambre for the day slipped from his bed, stretched and yawned noiselessly, and glanced round him.

The room was like the ward of a hospital, and the likeness was made no less striking by the card above each of the twenty beds, a white card, setting out each man's name and number.

Radoub's number, as shown by the card on the bed he had just vacated, was 7083.

He was a small and wiry-looking individual, with the face of a gamin; that is to say, the face of a child who is a jester, who may be a cutthroat, and who is certainly, and above all things, a Parisian.

Radoub had, in fact, been an apache by profession, and Monsieur Lepine had given him the choice between a penitentiary and the Legion. He chose the Legion, because, as he said, he liked the name better.

He was quite aware that life in the Legion was worse than life in a penitentiary, and he did not care a button about the social difference; he liked the name better, that was all. He was an artist.

He stood now, for a second, gazing at the others, nineteen men stretched in all the attitudes of slumber. Germans, French, an Englishman, an American, a Greek, and a Russian. Then, shuffling on some clothes, he left the room silently as the shadow of a moving cat.

In a moment he was back with a huge jug of steaming coffee, and, as he entered, shouting to the others to wake up, the reveille came from the barrack yard. The reveille of the French army that sounds every morning across France, to find its echo in Algeria:

Ra tat tat ta. Rat tat tat ta,
Rat tat tat ta ta ta ta
Ra tat tat ta. Rat tat tat ta,
Rat tat tat ta ta ta ta

In a moment the room was astir. Between the reveille and the muster in the barrack yard there was only half an hour, yet in that half hour the coffee was drunk, the men dressed, the beds made, and the floor swept, Radoub yelling to the others to hurry up, hurry up, hurry up, as it was his duty to put the completing touch to the dusting and cleaning and fetch the water.

Then he came tearing down the stairs after the rest and out in the barrack yard, half cut in two by the blaze of the six-o'clock sun, and under a sky blue as a cornflower, the long, long lines of white-clad men fell in, while the echoes roused to the bugles.

Then, led by the bugles, the columns wheeled out of the barrack gates, making for the great drill ground, where the arms were piled and the men, in square formation now, were exercised at the double.

It was terrific; with the sun blaze now in their faces, with the sun beating now on their backs, and, now, with their sides to a furnace door, round and round and round the great parade ground they went, the dust rising and hanging about them in a haze.

Ten minutes, twenty minutes, thirty minutes, and then the thunder and movement ceased and the Legionnaires, released for a moment after their first exercise of the day, broke into groups, cigarettes were lit, and the dust-hazed air filled with the fumes of caporal.

Radoub, though sweating, showed little signs of stress; he had lungs of leather. Not so Casmir, a man in his company to whom he was talking.

Casmir was a bitter-looking individual who had once been a government clerk. His white uniform was clinging to him with perspiration, and he was just getting his wind back.

The two men were walking up and down rapidly, for it is impossible to stand still after half an hour of the double.

"Well," said Casmir, "this finishes me. This is the last time. I'm off." He had been threatening for the last week or so to make a bolt.

Radoub, a fountain of wisdom in most things practical, had always dissuaded him from this fatal course. The man who tries to escape from the grip of the Legion is, in ninety-nine out of a hundred cases, brought back, and, when he is brought back, Heaven help him.

"Take my advice," said Radoub, "and leave that alone. No good. Stick to it as I have done, and make the best of it. I have been at it four years and ten months to-morrow, and in another two months I walk out like a gentleman."

"Well," said Casmir, "I have been in it only six months, and in another twelve hours—well, you will see."

"Have your way," said Radoub; "you are a fool. Do you think a clever man like myself would not have cut and run years ago had there been a decent chance? I weighed it all ages ago. The chance is too small and the punishment too big. It's impossible to drill sense into a head like yours, else I'd say, 'Look at me. If running away is not good enough for me, it's not good enough for you.'"

"All the same, I'm going to do it," said Casmir.

"Then do it and be damned."

The bugle was sounding "Fall in," and the morning exercises went on. At eleven o'clock, sweating, dusty, fagged out, but cheerful, the vast regiment of Légionnaires, wheeling in column formation to the sound of drums as well as bugles, marched back to barracks.

As they passed through the gates, Radoub flung a word to a small and dusty figure that was hanging about by the gate. It was Choc.

He had picked up Choc one night, a year ago, in the town. A dog that seemed compounded of all the known breeds of dogs—with the exception of the noblest.

Choc was dust-colored, his hair stood in permanent bristle upon his shoulders, and he was terrific in battle; he had fought everything in Sidi-bel-Abbés and in the village that lies by the parade ground of the Foreign Legion, and, without any manner of doubt, his family tree, had it been worked back, would have disclosed an Irish terrier somewhere hi the not remote distance. But the fighting qualities of Choc made less appeal to Radoub than the fact that he was an out-and-out blackguard, an expert thief, an apache.

I have said that Choc was hanging about the gate. That was the impression he gave one. It was not the honest waiting of a dog for its master; it was the waiting of a confederate for his mate at a public-house door or the corner of a race course. There was no tail-wagging. As the column passed in, the dust-colored one sniffing about did not even cast an eye at Radoub. Then, when the last files had passed the gateway, he slunk in after them and hung about in the courtyard till Radoub, who was a friend of the cook, came out of the cookhouse with a bone for him.

This happened every day. Choc, who slept in some hole or corner of the town best known to himself, paid two daily visits to the barracks, at eleven and six.

At eleven o'clock he got a bone or, by chance, a bit of meat; at six o'clock he appeared to accompany his master into the town.

At six o'clock every day the work of the Legion is over, and you may see the Légionnaires, spick and span, streaming through the barrack gates to the town, there to amuse themselves as best they can. They have no money. Literally no money. The halfpenny a day paid them by government scarcely serves for tobacco; they have to buy their own soap, mostly, and washing is a big item in a regiment where white uniforms of washable material are worn, and must be worn speckless.

Radoub had taught Choc a lot of tricks. In the Place Sadi Carnot of an evening, with the band playing a march, you might have seen Choc, on his hind legs, marching up and down before his master. Visitors to Sidi-bel-Abbés, attracted by the animal's queer appearance and his tricks, would question Radoub about him, and the result was nearly always profitable to Radoub. It was said that Choc stole cigarettes for him in the native quarter of the town, sneaking packets from the Moslem traders' stalls while Radoub held the latter in light conversation, and not only cigarettes, but articles more bulky and more valuable.

To-day, Radoub, having given Choc his bone and dismissed him, was turning to enter the barracks, when he ran into the arms of Corporal Klein.

"Ah, there's that dog of yours again," said Klein. "I was looking for you to tell you. The colonel says he has had enough of him, and he's to be shot."

Radoub swore the great oath of the Legion—which is unprintable.

"Shot—and what for?"

"Biting the sentry. It was last night, after you had come back from the town. Seguer was on duty, and the beast stuck about the gate, and Seguer tried to make him go, and got bitten in the foot, right through his boot."

"He must have kicked him," said Radoub.

"Who knows. Not only that, but the colonel says he has been having reports about you and him and your doings in the town; says that the Legion has enough blackguards in it without enlisting four-footed ones, and there you are; the order is promulgated, the dog has to go."

"Catch him, then," said Radoub.

Klein, a big man, in spite of his name, came toward Choc, who was busy with his bone. Radoub whistled shrilly between his teeth, and the dog, picking up his treasure, started for the barrack gate. Flying pebbles and dust marked his path, and he was gone.

Klein laughed. He was a good-natured man, a friend of Radoub's, and he had no grudge against the dog.

"All the same," said he, "the dog has to go, you know what it is. The order has been given, and once the order has been given there is no staying it."

Radoub knew quite well what it was. He knew the colonel and he knew the Legion. Choc might evade capture, but caught he would be sooner or later.

He said nothing, however. The bugle call for soup rang through the yard, and, as he was orderly of his room, he had to rush off to the kitchen, from where, in a moment, he returned, bearing a steaming can for his men; then he had to return for bread.

No one noticed the least change in him, and if there had been a change in him, nobody would have bothered. The Legion never bothers about anything, and the most monstrous happenings pass with scarcely a comment from the hearers and beholders.

* * * *

All that afternoon Radoub was engaged on scout-patrol maneuvers, and, at six o'clock, spick and span, he left the barrack yard for the town.

Choc was waiting for him at the gate, but not close to it. The sentry having his orders, had tried to lure him in, but Choc, alarmed by this unaccustomed civility, had removed himself a full hundred yards away, where he was sitting, with his stump of a tail sticking out straight behind him.

He followed Radoub.

But Radoub did not make direct for town. He skirted the ramparts till he came to the western side, where the great, rough, yellow wall was blazing in the light of the sinking sun; then getting into the ditch, he followed the wall a certain distance, stopped, glanced up and down the ditch to make sure that no one was observing him, and then drew a stone from the wall, disclosing a hole, in which was seated, like a squat gnome, a little, fat linen bag.

This was his cache. The money he had collected by one means or another during the last four years and ten months. It was a fair sum, partly in gold, partly in silver, and he had intended it for that day, now only two months distant, when, to use his own words, he would walk out of the Legion like a gentleman. He was going to use it for a different purpose now, and placing the bag in his pocket, without troubling to close the cache, he turned and, followed by the dog, came back along the ditch.

Stars like the points of needles were piercing the pansy-colored sky when Radoub and his companions reacged the Place Sadi Carnot. The Place was crowded; Légionnaires, visitors, and townsfolk crowding around the band stand, some seated, others standing about in groups. The warm air was filled with the scents of jasmine and garlic, the African earth, cigarette and cigar smoke, all vague and blended to form the sell of Sidi-bel-Abbés *en fête*.

Then the electric lights blazed, and the band struck up. They were playing the "Sambre et Meuse," that splendid march of the French army, spirited enough almost to raise the slain, but Radoub did not beat time with his foot, nor, when Choc glanced at him, did he gve the dog the signal to start his tricks.

He walked about for a while, showing himself to his companions, then he disappeared from the Place, and, followed by the dog, sought the native streets.

Sidi-bel-Abbés is slashed across by two great boulevards running north and south, and east and west. Here you find plate-glass windows and Paris jewelry, motor cars, cocottes, American women in blue veils. Paris, Vienna, Berlin, London, and New York all represented by some fragment of their social life, just as in the Legion they are represented, each, by some of the universal diseases that prey on society.

Behind these gay boulevards you find the real Sidi-bel-Abbés.

You walk into the country of Islam. Passing through the narrow bazaars, the moon above your head becomes the moon that lit the three Calenders, and the lamps that light the gloom of the booths the lamps of Aladdin.

The Légionnaires swarm here, yet their blue-and-red dress uniform does not detract from the Oriental charm; they have about them some subtle touch of Africa that blends with the surroundings.

Radoub, followed by his companion, passed through several of the narrow streets till he reached an alley, where, at a door set in the wall, he knocked.

The door opened, and he went in, leaving Choc to wait for him outside, seated on the ground. Arab dogs came down the alley, saw the stranger, advanced, burbling and bristling, recognized him, and passed on; the rising moon laid a pale finger on the wall top, and from far away across the faint noises of the city came the cry of the priest from the balcony of the minaret calling the faithful to prayer; and now a window opened somewhere, and the laughter of a girl, the tinkle tankle of a guitar, and a snatch of song blew away on the night wind and then snapped off to the closing of the casement.

This was the Spanish quarter of the Moslem town, and perhaps the wickedest, outside the jurisdiction of the Bureau Arabe, and visited only by the shadiest characters among the European population of the place.

Twenty minutes passed, and then the door opened and a man came out. He was dressed in mufti, but the alteration did not deceive Choc. He knew his master at once, and, rising, followed him down the alley into the street.

Radoub had made up his mind to escape from the Legion. It was the maddest act of his life.

First of all, he was not an ordinary Légionnaire, but a criminal serving for rehabilitation. If he managed to escape, he would have to begin his life over again without papers. It would be impossible for him to find work in France; he must go to England or some other country where papers were not required Then, again, he had only to wait two short months and he would secure his rehabilitation and be able to leave the Legion and obtain work.

Though he had started in life as an apache, common sense had been talking to him for the last two years or so, pointing out that a franc made by robbery is not worth two sous made by work. The rate of exchange is always against the criminal; so appalling is it that one may wonder at any man with an ounce of brains doing business on such ruinous terms. Radoub had recognized this, and he had determined, on finding himself his own man again, to take to honest ways.

He was now ruining all the plans he had made for that future so nearly in his grasp. Throwing everything away —for a dog.

As a matter of fact, there was no struggle involved in the giving up of his plans. Cold plans for the future, dictated by common sense, did not stand for a moment before the warm desire to keep the dog and flout authority. Choc was his mate, and he was not going to lose him.

Passing a shop where viands were sold, he bought two sausages and put them in his pocket, then he walked on, striking toward the European quarter.

The band was still playing in the Place Sadi Carnot, and the faint sound of it came on the warm, perfumed wind.

To Radoub it seemed a month ago since he had left the Place, and it seemed extraordinary to hear the band at it still.

But he had little time to think of anything except his objective, and that was Oran, eighty miles away.

There is a railway between Sidi-bel-Abbes and Oran; that is to say, a trap for runaway Legionnaires. Radoub was not such a fool as to use the railway or even to walk along the embankments. Time was of no matter to him. The pursuit would be after him before he could reach Oran even by rail; he had to trust entirely to his disguise and to luck. He recognized that Choc would be his main difficulty; he could not disguise Choc.

He had lit a cigarette, and he passed along to the city gates without let or hindrance; a bourgeois taking an evening stroll with his dog excited no comment. At the gates it was the same, and, walking with a leisurely manner, with his hands in his pockets, he found the road to Oran and struck along it. It lay before him white in the moonlight, and, beyond the gardens of the town, on either side, stretched the sand wastes and rocks of the miserable desert that in daylight is yellow, parched, sun-bitten, and murderous in its desolation. A few stunted palms broke the sky line on the right, while on the left could be seen the lights of the railway and the furnace-lit smoke of a train just coming in from Oran. Radoub, noting these, looked up and down the road; to right, to left, not a soul was there to be seen. Then, calling to Choc, he struck into his stride.

Nearly five years of life in the Legion had rendered him almost impervious to weariness in marching. Four kilometers an hour is the regulation pace in full marching order and laden with rifle, ammunition, and equipment. Forty kilometers a day is the minimum on active service.

Five miles or so from Sidi-bel-Abbes, a mounted police patrol passed Radoub without halting and with scarcely a glance at him, but they were going toward the town, and would know nothing of his escape.

Then, thinking things over in his mind, he reflected that the fact of his escape would be still unknown even at the barracks, where it was just turning-in time. Legionnaires sometimes out-stopped their leave. The pursuit would not be on his heels till to-morrow morning, when, definitely declared absent, his description would be circulated, right to Oran.

But this did not incline him to slacken his pace. He kept on steadily, till he had reached a point some ten miles from the town, then he took his seat by the wayside, took the sausages, which were wrapped up in a sheet of the *Journal d'Oran,* from his pocket, and divided one with Choc. Then, noticing a prickly pear bush growing near by, he cut some of the fruit and carefully peeled it.

It was their first meal in the desert, and they had four, for it was not till the morning of the third day of his escape that Radoub entered Oran.

CHAPTER II

His adventures during that journey of eighty miles or less would fill a brilliant chapter of fiction. He was stopped and spoken to by a police patrol and escaped suspicion of being a deserter by assuming the role of a deaf mute. He joined a band of wandering Arabs, and, suspecting their good intentions, escaped from them. This little escape within an escape caused him more trouble than any other incident of the journey. Lastly, by means of a bribe of two francs, he managed to enter Oran in a cart loaded with esparto grass and drawn by two mules, thus avoiding the attentions of the gentleman at the gate of the town.

There was a rat in the cart, as well, and the maddening fumes of it surged through Choc's brain, but he did not lose his reason or his self-command, and held his place, crouching beside his master, though shivering in every muscle and thrilling in every nerve.

The driver managed to unload his passengers in a back yard, unobserved, and Radoub, with Choc at his heels, found himself in the streets of Oran with nothing but the sea between himself and freedom.

He had little fear of detection in these bustling streets, where every imaginable sort of business seemed going forward to the clatter of every European tongue.

Tall, white-clad Arabs stalked along, and barelegged Arab women, with faces veiled; negro porters, with glistening skins and red fez caps; Spaniards, Portuguese, Frenchmen, Italians, Spahis back from Senegal, sailors up from the warships in the harbor, and English travelers just arrived, formed the crowd through which Radoub made his way, with Choc at his heels, and not the faintest notion in his head as to what course he was going to pursue.

The obvious course was the mail boat that runs between Oran and Marseilles, but there were difficulties in the way. The boats were sure to be watched for deserters. Mail boats railway trains were simply roads to arrest. He had known and heard of numerous cases of escaped men caught either at the Oran railway station or on board the *General Chanzy,* or one of the other boats of the Algerian line.

He had an idea in his head of boarding some small trading vessel and either stowing himself away or making friends with the captain, and he was taking his way toward the harbor, with a view to this, when, at a street corner, he ran into the arms of Casmir. It was Casmir who recognized him, and not he Casmir. For Casmir had dyed his face with walnut juice, and, the suit of gray jean that he wore being too large for him, he had stuffed himself out at the waist with old newspapers, giving himself a corporation that was the very best disguise in the world. He looked like a disreputable old Spaniard.

"Mon Dieu!" said Radoub. "Casmir!"

Then he burst into a laugh. Only such a short time ago he had been warning Casmir, on the parade ground of the Legion, against running away!,

They walked along the. street to-gether, and Casmir explained matters.

He had run away, it seemed, on the same night that Radoub had made his evasion, had boldly taken the train for Oran, and, with the good luck that comes with daring, had found the matter perfectly easy.

"I was never stopped or questioned once," said he. "But here it is different. I cannot get across. It seems that they are watching the boats. I went down to the steamboat quay yesterday, and there was an official at the gangway of the boat for Marseilles, He was demanding the papers of all the passengers—the men. To leave this place one must be either a fish or a sea bird, it seems, and I am neither."

"Come into this cafe, and let us talk," said Radoub.

They entered a shabby cafe that was close by, and Radoub called for coffee and food for them both.

"How much money have you?" said he.

"A hundred francs," replied Casmir. "I had a hundred and forty to start with. I had received a money order from a relation for two hundred francs the morning I was talking to you. It cost me sixty francs to get this rig. It was that money order that fixed me in my idea of bolting, and I am beginning to wish now that I had never received it."

"Courage," said Radoub.

He said nothing for a few minutes, and then he began to disclose his plan. There were ships always leaving Oran for the French and Spanish ports. Ship captains of the lesser mercantile marine were venal folk; for eighty francs, say, the pair of them might be able to get a passage on some bark; a place in the hold, on top of the cargo, would do.

"Ah," said Casmir, brightening up, "now you are talking! If any man can do the trick, you can; you have the gift of the gab and a way with you that I have not."

"Well, then," said Radoub, "let's go down to the wharves now, right away, and try and fix up the business."

But Casmir demurred.

"There is no use in our going about the streets together," said he, "for, if one is caught, the other will be nabbed, too. I'll meet you here in an hour if you will go and try and do the business. The cafe won't run away, and you may be very sure that I won't, either."

Radoub saw at once the reason in this, and off he started, leaving Choc with Casmir.

Choc was fond of Casmir, who had often fed him with scraps; all the same, Radoub borrowed a piece of string from the dingy waiter and tied the end of it round the dog's neck.

"That will give you something to hold him by," said he, "in case he's up to any of his tricks."

Then he paid the bill and started off, leaving Casmir seated and holding the dog by the string.

* * * *

There are two harbors at Oran. An outer anchorage, not very good in rough weather, unless the wind is off the land, and a small, inner harbor, a little hole of a place, always full because of its small size.

Radoub came along the quay side, walking in a leisurely manner and smoking a cigarette. Beside the warships in the harbor there were two small, bark-rigged vessels, one discharging grain, the other with closed hatches and evidently a full cargo.

Radoub was walking toward the gangplank of the latter, when a hand fell on his arm, and, turning, he found himself face to face with Sergeant Pel-letier, of the military police of Sidi-bel-Abbes.

"That's all right," said the sergeant, releasing Radoub's arm and placing his hand on his shoulder in a fatherly way. "And you may be thankful your uniform was returned. Whoever sold you this rig sent it back, left it at the barrack gates, done up in a parcel. *Mon Dieu!* Radoub, but I would never have thought it of you, to play a fool's game like this! A smart Legionnaire like you, time nearly expired and all. What made you?"

Radoub laughed.

The game had gone against him, and there was no use in grumbling.

His mind was engaged less on the business of arrest than on the problem of what he should do about Casmir and Choc.

To regain possession of Choc, he would have to give Casmir away, and Choc being condemned to death, there was no use in regaining possession of him. So he did nothing.

He lit a cigarette, and, walking side by side with Pelletier, he went to the station, and twenty minutes later he was in the train returning to Sidi-bel-Abbes.

At the barracks, he was placed promptly under arrest, and he marched off to his cell with that terrible light-heartedness which is a legacy of the Legion, inherited from crime.

As no single item of his uniform was lost, he only received a month's imprisonment, and, at the end of the month, the Legion was marched off south, where the Arabs were kicking up a dust, and hard fighting helped him to work off the stiffness caused by imprisonment.

He seemed to have forgotten Casmir, who had not been recaptured, and the dog, which was never heard of again; yet, in the great battle that was fought that month near the Oasis of the Three Palms, an old Legionnaire—the same who told me this story—fighting beside Radoub, was amazed, even in the heat of battle, at the fury of the latter.

"He was working off the dog," said the old fellow. "It is always so with the Legion, and that is what makes the Legion so terrible in battle: They are not so much fighting with the enemy, monsieur; *they are bayoneting the past, and what the past has done to them.*"

THE WHISPERING CORPSE

Richard B. Sale

CHAPTER I

CHAMBER OF DEATH

It was a circular room with a smooth, marblelike glisten on the stony walls. The taciturnicy of death hung grimly over the place, enveloping it like turbid fog. There was only dim light. This did not dispel the unholy gloominess, but only served to increase the eerie ebony shadows which cavorted about grotesquely like tiny dervishes. On the marble walls were dull metallic handles which opened the huge drawers of the walls. These were arranged vertically in systematic columns like a steel filing cabinet.

Detective Bart Trevor, criminal nemesis at large, stepped soundlessly past the open door of the room and went in. He paused, screwing up his face wryly at the macabre aspect of the place. All around Trevor, cleverly concealed in slablike chambers, were bodies.

Trevor shivered.

He suddenly saw two men standing across the room from him, apparently straining to hear something. He walked over to them, his shoes slithering scrapily on the chilly cement floor. The two men jumped at the sound, momentarily startled.

"Hello, Bart," said Inspector Bill Brandt soberly. "You might've knocked when you came in. This place gives me the creeps. I never could go for the morgue much."

Trevor said, "Hello, inspector. Well, I got here."

Brandt nodded and turned to the man at his side. "Go ahead, Karl. Tell Trevor what you told me. Tell him why I phoned him to rush down here."

Karl Topeka, the grizzled old German attendant of the city morgue, shook his head sombrely at Trevor. His face was sallow beneath his white hair, and his eyes were wide in horror.

"What is it?" Trevor asked, puzzled.

"It iss one of the corpses," Topeka replied in a weird, sibilant whisper. "It wass talking tonight. It wass calling your name, Herr Trevor!"

Trevor stared at the German. "Calling my name?" he exclaimed. "You mean one of these dead stiffs sat up tonight and called for me?"

"Ja, ja!" averred Topeka. "That wass it! Gott, it wass terrible! Here I wass sitting, reading my newspaper. All of a sudden I heard some one whispering. I thought it wass my imagination. But no—it wass not! One of the corpses wass really whispering!"

Trevor scoffed, "Impossible!"

"That's what I said," Inspector Brandt cut in. "But damn my ears if I didn't hear it myself just a second or two before you came in!"

"You must both be crazy!" Trevor cried. "A dead man can't speak—not even in a whisper." He hesitated and eyed them carefully. "Which body is doing the ghost work?"

Inspector Brandt opened his mouth to explain. But he quickly closed it again with a snap! Another voice sliced out of the gloomy morgue walls. It was uncanny—a ghastly rasping slither like the hissing warning of an angry snake.

"Bart Trevor—Bart Trevor...."

Trevor gasped in astonishment and fright and whirled around to face the wall. The unearthly summons seemed to emanate right from the panel in front of them. It struck an icy dread into Trevor's pounding heart and left him panting hotly.

"That iss it!" Topeka groaned. "Listen!"

"Bart Trevor—Bart Trevor...."

It was like a banshee wail, the horrible plea of a damned lost soul searching among the grisly dead for a friend. Those were the only two words it said. None more.

"Try answering," snapped Inspector Brandt. "Try anything! Bart, for God's sake, I can't stand that sound!"

In a wary, tremulous voice, Trevor replied, "I'm here."

There was no further sound. Only the oppressive silence of the damp morgue.

"I'm here," Trevor repeated earnestly. "Bart Trevor is here. Who is it? What do you want?"

The answer came, slowly. Trevor went taut and listened. Karl Topeka reeled away, profoundly affected by the awesome paradox. Inspector Brandt gripped Trevor's arm crushingly.

"Go to Circle Drive—a, man lies in Circle Drive—he has been slain by the Murder Master...."

Bart Trevor's eyes narrowed instantly. Such pertinent information taxed his credulity to a breaking point. A corpse was dead. A corpse could not direct police to a murderer's lair. And while a moment before he had almost believed that a dead man was whispering, now he smiled crookedly and turned to the inspector.

Trevor said nothing. He jerked his head towards the door and walked towards it. Karl Topeka was standing there, shuddering. Trevor patted the old man's shoulder and took him upstairs away from the place. Inspector Brandt followed on his heels.

* * * *

Once away from the morgue, Trevor said, "It's a phony, inspector! I don't know how, but some one has rigged up something down there and is trying to make it look like spirit work." He turned to Topeka. "Any one been down there this last week or so?"

"Lots of people," said Topeka. "They always come to identify the bodies."

"Did any one try to identify the corpses in that particular panel we were in front of?" Trevor queried."

The German shook his head. "No."

Trevor scowled. "Who's in there? Room for three stiffs, isn't there?"

"Ja," Topeka said. "There iss three of them there. One iss a colored man. We don't know who he iss. The other iss a sailor. They found him in the East River."

"Know who he is?"

"No. But we know the third. It iss Robert Herrick, the racketeer who wass murdered yesterday."

"Herrick!" snapped Trevor. He thought rapidly. "Body is still there waiting for an autopsy, eh?"

Topeka nodded.

"I don't get it yet, inspector," Trevor said. "But I'd advise you to have your medico start sawing that corpse right away. I've got a hunch what this is all about. Herrick was up for investigation in this exposé of the Gruen Protective Association. Herrick was Gruen's right-hand man, you know. And the association is just a blind to bleed the sweating tailors of the city. Cleaners and dyers. Graft stuff, chief. Gruen was probably afraid that Herrick would squawk under pressure. So Gruen either bumped him—or had him bumped!"

"The Gruen graft ring!" Inspector Brandt exclaimed. "But isn't that the case you're working on, Bart?"

"I'll say it is," Trevor replied. "I've not only worked on it—I've finished it! I've got papers to prove that Walter Gruen and his gang of lecherous crooks have taken honest working men in this city for a ride of nearly five million dollars. Five million! And I've got the proof to back up the charge! It'll send all those crooks up the river for a long time."

Inspector Brandt frowned. "I'm beginning to see things," he said. "The idea of that whispering corpse is to get you off the case and onto something else. If my hunch is right, Gruen is behind it. He's trying to sidetrack you."

"Maybe," said Trevor, "and maybe not. I think that Walter Gruen is a little anxious. He's probably missed some very important documents which I had to steal from his own office. And he wants them back."

"God, Bart," Brandt cried, "you'd better be careful. He must be out to get you. He'll kill you!"

Trevor laughed harshly. "No," he said, "he won't kill me, inspector. He's had plenty of opportunity to do that. What he wants now are those papers. And while I'm alive they can follow me, hoping to find them. But if I were dead—Gruen could never recover them!"

"But why you?" Brandt questioned. "Hasn't the district attorney got them? He'll issue the warrants for the arrests."

"The D. A. only has copies. I and I alone know where those documents are. And in case I should die suddenly, they'll find their way swiftly to his office. I'm taking no chances on losing them while I'm alive. After that, it's some one else's worry."

Trevor's eyes gleamed. He felt in his rear pocket for the reassuring bulge of his revolver. Then he tightened his coat around his neck and said, "I'll be seeing you, Brandt."

The inspector asked, "Where're you going?"

"Out to Circle Drive," Trevor replied. "It ought to prove interesting. And if there is a dead man there, although I seriously doubt it, why perhaps I'll be able to work up a little charge of murder against Gruen and his gang, too."

"Don't be a fool, Bart!" protested Brandt "Your luck can't hold out forever. I tell you Gruen will have you bumped out there before you know it!"

"Not," said Trevor smilingly, "before he knows where those papers are."

* * * *

Trevor reached the sidewalks swiftly. The night was cold and a bitter wraithlike wind scorched his cheeks and blew his breath up into a gray opaque cloud. He hunched his shoulders to keep out the chill and scanned the curbing for a taxi. Circle Drive was a long distance from there.

A yellow hack sped up to the curbing at that instant, and the driver, anxious for a fare, called out, "Cab, sir?"

"Yeah," Trevor said, walking to it. "Circle Drive. And a dollar if you do it in twenty minutes!"

"Right!"

The driver climbed back into the front seat. There was the repellent whine and clash of grating gears, the thunder of the motor, and the taxi jumped forward into the night.

Ten minutes later, Bart Trevor became aware of the fact that the taxi was taking him nowhere near the vicinity of Circle Drive. The driver was guiding the machine dexterously in the opposite direction, avoiding red lights and brightly illumined highways, and backtracking down dark side streets. Trevor's lips tightened. He glanced out of the car. Then he leaned forward and knocked vigorously on the glass, panel which separated him from the driver. The driver turned.

"Where are you going?" Trevor demanded stridently.

The driver grinned and shook his head. Trevor looked grim. That glass panel prevented any sound issuing from the interior of the hack.

Trevor sat back and quickly tried to open one of the doors. It was locked. And so was the other one, too. It was a neat little trap. The handles which lowered the glass of the windows were dismounted. There was no way out of the interior. The only air Trevor got was that which whistled up through the mat-covered floorboards of the taxi.

Intentfully he drew his glinting blue-steel revolver from his hip pocket. He leaned forward, the gun steady in his right hand, and rapped against the glass panel with it. The driver turned, looked slightly surprised at the ugly yawning nozzle of the revolver, and then waved a contemptuous hand and laughed.

Trevor was puzzled. He could easily pot the fellow through the back of the skull at such point-blank range. But that would be suicide. He'd kill the driver, leave the hack without control, and perish in the ensuing crash himself!

He took careful aim at the thigh of the driver's right leg. That would only make a flesh wound, put the fellow's leg out of commission enough to make him stop the car.

Crack!

Trevor pulled the trigger steadily and felt the gun leap in his hand as a hot slug hurtled out of the barrel.

Outside the driver heard the explosion, despite the glass panel which muffled it. He whirled and took one wild glance at the glass.

Trevor himself was staring at it in amazement. For there, embedded in the panel, was the flattened lead pellet from his weapon, its flight abruptly halted. The glass was not even splintered. There were no jagged radiating lines from the vortex where the slug had struck. There was not even a hole through the glass.

The glass of the cab was bulletproof!

The driver turned and kicked the accelerator to the floor. The yellow taxi lanced ahead like a catapult!

At the same instant, a shrill piercing hiss flooded through the rear of the car. Trevor heard it, surveyed the car for the source fruitlessly. A queer fetid odor permeated through the tonneau, falling heavily upon Trevor's laboring lungs.

A nauseating dizziness encompassed him and the world swam before his eyes like a spinning gyroscope. He could not focus. Now he could not see. There was a cavernous roaring in his ears, and his body went numb. Down, down he sank to a fathomless abyss below. It was like years, that swaying and sinking. He hit with a soundless thud. Then oblivion....

CHAPTER II
TERROR TORTURE

When Bart Trevor regained consciousness, he could see nothing. He was an entity in a world of solid ebony pitch. He could not see his hand in front of his eyes. And the air was heavy, pungent with hostility.

Trevor groaned softly and rubbed his chest. It was terribly sore and each breath stung through him like myriad needles pricking his insides. He sat up dazedly. There was an odd odor on his clothes. Ether!

A flash of thought shot through him. He strove to recall what had happened. The slug in the panel. The bullet-proof glass. The queer hiss. Then—of course! In some clever manner, the cab had been constructed with an air-tight rear. When he had tried to make trouble, the driver had sent a stream of etherized gas coursing into the tonneau of the cab. It had knocked him out.

Trevor climbed to his feet silently and stood there in the obscurity cautiously. Where was he now? What had happened after the gas had deprived him of his senses? There was no sound about him. No light. Nothing. He walked straight ahead very slowly, holding his arms out before him. Presently they hit something. A wall.

He felt it. It was smooth, with a lustre like wax. He let his hands run along the wall, searching for a doorway. He made a complete circuit of the room. There was never a break in the regularity of the walls.

No door! He was trapped, Trevor was. And beautifully trapped. He was in a sealed chamber. There was no exit from it. Still, if there was no door anywhere, how had he gotten in here?

He glanced up through the darkness in the direction of the ceiling. That was it. He had been let down into this black chamber through an aperture in the ceiling—now invisible by the opacity of the dark.

Trevor felt in his pocket quickly. His gun was gone. Simultaneously, he heard voices. They were above him—hoarse virile voices of men. He strained to listen.

"He is unarmed?"

"Yeah. Louis had to use the gas on him in the cab. He tried to make trouble. Fired at Louis. Bullets couldn't go through, naturally, but Louis was afraid some one might hear the noise."

"Where is he?"

"Below. I put him in the water torture pool."

A momentary silence. Then, "Open it. I want to talk to him."

Trevor crouched quickly in a corner of the black room. He stared up above him. The ceiling appeared to lift up and away. A square patch of yellowish light filtered through the ceiling upon the floor of the chamber and shimmered there uncertainly. It was blotted out at the next instant by an ovular shadow as some one above leaned across the hole and called, "Trevor!"

Bert Trevor debated his situation rapidly. He did not answer.

"Trevor!" the man called sharply. "If you are awake, answer me. Stalling won't help you any!"

"I'm here," said Trevor evenly. "Who is it?"

The man above chuckled. "It is the Murder Master, my friend."

Trevor laughed stridently. "Murder Master, eh? You sound like an old pal of mine, Mr. Murder Master. You sound, in fact, like Walter Gruen. But you can't be he. He's too yellow a rat to even stick his head through a hole when an unarmed man is trapped beneath him!"

The Murder Master scowled. "Still the old bravado, eh, Trevor?" he snarled. "Well, you will lose it before I'm through with you. You can quit the bluffing. You haven't got a chance. And you know it—you're through!"

Trevor snapped "I've got every chance in the world, Gruen. You and your dirty murderers can't touch me!"

"So!" exclaimed the Murder Master. "I thought that was the cause of your insipid arrogance. You have some false idea that your life is a hostage, guaranteed safety until I can locate those very valuable papers which you so neatly stole from me."

"You bet!" said Trevor with acerbity. "And it's no false idea either. That's the prime reason I only gave the district attorney copies of those graft and bribe agreements! I'm safe, Gruen, as long as I and I alone know where that stuff is."

"You think so?"

"I'll say I do. And just in case you get a little rash and bump me off in a moment of recklessness, let me tell you this. The moment anything happens to me, those papers will find their way to the D. A.'s office and he'll put the screws right on you, and add a little charge of murder."

"And," finished the Murder Master, "there is not a man in this city more honest than John Walsh."

"The D. A.'s square all right," said Trevor. "You won't get those papers away from him no matter what you offer him."

"I dare say you are right," the Murder Master replied dulcetly. "Therefore I must try to get the papers in another manner. You agree there?"

Trevor did not answer. A sudden pang of dread cut him.

"So," said the Murder Master, "I will let you tell me just where you have put them."

Trevor replied caustically, "Go to hell!"

The Murder Master chuckled.

"Very well," he remarked blithely. "If you will not tell of your own accord and save yourself a lot of pain, I will have to make you tell." He made a surreptitious motion to the man at his side above the sealed chamber.

Instantly Trevor became aware of a new sound, a gurgling, rushing musical sound. He flattened himself against the wall, his keen eyes transfixed on the solitary spot of illumined floor where the shaft of light from above struck down. He could see something like sand creep steadily across the wood there and then pass on, omnivorously devouring the floor. The gurgle continued for a few seconds, then gulped like a drowning man and fell silent.

Trevor felt a cold clammy liquid wash his shoes. It crept up above the soles and then onward, slowly, tantalizingly, over his ankles. It was water! The man-devil above was flooding the chamber with water!

Trevor's jaw tightened grimly. He stiffened at the bite of the water against his knees. The shaft of light had disappeared without warning. Trevor glanced up swiftly. Gruen had replaced the panel of the ceiling over the aperture. There was no escape from the black pit.

The water surged hungrily up to his waist.

Still Trevor felt secure. This was only a minor form of torture. They were trying to frighten him into confessing the locality of the coveted graft disclosures. They wouldn't let him drown like a rat in a trap. They'd let the water rise up so far and then stop it.

But the rising seething eddies in the darkness did not hesitate at all. The water reached his chin. He could no longer stand. He lifted his legs up behind him and trod water calmly, saving his strength in case this ordeal should be prolonged. The water would stop soon now.

It didn't. It kept on rising, lifting him higher and higher. Trevor was coming closer and closer to the ceiling now. He could sense it. There was a dull thud as his skull cracked against the wood of the ceiling. The water persisted—up farther. Daunted now, Trevor floundered frenziedly in the rush of the torrent. He tried to swim. His head slapped the ceiling constantly. He flipped over onto his back and stuck his nostrils up as far as they would go. His nose rubbed the ceiling. He could feel the water careen over his ears and climb steadily past his jaw, up, up, to his mouth, over it.

It swam into his nose just as he took a deep breath and held it for life. The water smacked against the ceiling with a peculiar crumping sound. It covered him completely.

Midway in the jet maw of the water, Trevor floated on that one last breath. Clusters of strange scenes fled before his eyes. His lungs pounded harder than his pulsating heart. Trevor felt that they must soon split wide open from the pressure of the water and his failing wind. Sparks lanced in front of him. Bursting meteors detonated soundlessly in his ears. He let out that breath. Gigantic bubbles seemed to pass his eyes as the precious oxygen boiled upwards towards the ceiling.

Half-conscious, Trevor could still, however, distinguish the fact that heavy mauling hands had gripped him cruelly by the hair of his head and had yanked him. A burning light flared into his eyes and the sudden change from the delitescent chamber blinded him for several minutes. But the ghastly clutch of the water was gone. Clean fresh air washed his body and kissed his face.

Something stung him. He opened his eyes. Walter Gruen was standing in front of Trevor grinning like a devil. Even as Trevor discerned him. Gruen leaned forward again and slapped Trevor across the face with a resounding impact!

Weak, dazed, Trevor tried to rise. He found his arms and legs would not function. They were numb, paralyzed. He dimly heard men's voices guffaw mawkishly at his feeble antics. Gruen's open hand left another five-fingered welt on his cheek.

Trevor did not mind that so much. It didn't hurt. It helped to clear his fogged brain. So they had pulled him out at the last moment. That was something. They didn't actually plan to murder him yet, then. They really did want to know where those papers were.

He heard Walter Gruen speaking.

"You didn't like your little bath, did you?" Gruen gloated. "Not many do, Trevor. And you'll go back into it again for another try if you don't come across. Where are those papers?"

"The answer," Trevor gasped, "is the same as before. Only more so!"

Gruen slapped him.

"You filthy rat!" Trevor cried. "I'll kill you for that! You'll never even reach a jury!"

"Listen, Trevor," Gruen said in an even, ominous voice, "tell me where you stuck those papers and I'll set you free."

Trevor laughed weakly. "Set me free in hell," he said. "You'd knock me off in a second if you knew. I'm not telling, Gruen. You fiend! Now I know why the stoolies cower when your name is mentioned. Now I know why they call you the Murder Master! Go on—give me the water chamber again. I don't tell anything! Get it? And next time you'll pull a corpse out of there, and your goose'll be cooked!"

Gruen stared at Trevor, his face a knotted gnarl of fury. His pig-eyes swept across Bart Trevor's face furtively.

"All right, Trevor," he said at length. "We'll try something else. We'll give somebody else the works and let you watch. That'll be a little different. You'll have to tell to save somebody else!"

Trevor frowned. "I don't get you."

"No?" said Walter Gruen, grinning confidently. "Well, I'll show you what I mean. We have a friend of yours here. I think you'll know her. You've met her before."

"Her?" Trevor echoed, his eyes narrowing.

"Yes," said Gruen. "Her. I didn't want to have to do this. But I'll have to use her. I had her brought in just in case you acted up like this."

Trevor struggled to leap from the chair where he was sitting. His body responded, its strength returned. But something held him back. He glanced down. The Murder Master had shackled his two wrists to the arms of the chair. He tried to move his legs. They, too, were shackled. Trevor glanced cagily at the manacles. They were ordinary handcuffs. A crafty gleam pervaded the detective's eyes. He sat back quietly.

"Louis," ordered Gruen, "tell Droone to bring her in."

A man moved behind Trevor's chair. Trevor craned his neck and got a glimpse of the fellow. It was the driver of the taxicab. Bart also noticed another man behind him on the other side. He scrutinized him and recognized him as Bull Morgan, one of Gruen's right-hand men and a leader of Gruen's graft association.

"Whole family is here, eh. Gruen?" said Trevor sarcastically. "Hello, Bull. Won't this make a nice story when I break it to the tabs!"

Bull Morgan roared with laughter. "When you break it to the tabs," he leered. "Why, you thick-headed shamus, you'll never break it to the tabs! You oughta be wise to that now. No matter what happens. Gruen ain't gonna let you get outa here alive. You'll tell where you got them papers, and then well bump you."

"You're talking too much," snapped Gruen irascibly.

"Well, he's gotta know sometime."

"Still think you'll find the papers, eh, Gruen?" Trevor smiled. "Getting a little worried about them, too, aren't you? And you're going to bump me, anyhow? Well, listen, Gruen." Trevor's voice went taut. "I wouldn't tell where they are if you sliced me into a thousand little pieces. And as for this girl you're going to torment, I wouldn't tell you even if she were the D. A.'s own daughter!"

The door opened. Louis, the taxi driver, came in. He was followed by two men who carried an inert bundle between them in their arms.

"You're due for a shock, Trevor," smiled Gruen maliciously. "Because that's just who it is—the D. A.'s daughter. Ruth Walsh!"

Trevor snapped rigid in his chair at the words. He stared in stupefaction as the Murder Master crossed the room, yanked the bundle roughly up and stood it on its feet. There was a gray hood over the head of the bundle. Gruen tore it off. Trevor saw, dumbly, helplessly, that it was Ruth, the daughter of honest John Walsh, the district attorney.

"Gruen," Bart Trevor whispered eerily, "you're mad! You're insane! You'll never get away with this! This is a snatch! You're treading on Uncle Sam!"

Gruen smiled. "I'm treading on nobody," he said meaningly, "except you and this frill. Will you talk?"

"No!"

Gruen nodded to Louis. "Put her on that table," he said, "and strap her down. Okay, Harry and Joe. Clear out. Bull—go into the next room and bring in that red bottle on the shelf in there. The red one."

Bull Morgan nodded and strode out of the room. He reappeared presently carrying a quart bottle. Gruen accepted the bottle from Morgan. He strolled slowly over to Trevor and held the bottle directly in front of Trevor's face.

Trevor read on the inscription—Vitriol.

He blanched instantly and beads of sweat copiously exuded from his face. Lines furrowed his brow as he stared at that word. Fearfully Trevor raised his eyes up to meet Gruen's. Gruen looked like a gargoyle with an evil smirk flitting across his thick lips.

"Not—that...." rasped Trevor. "For God's sake, Gruen—"

Gruen's face was an inscrutable mask. "Will you tell?"

"Listen, Gruen," Trevor babbled, "leave her out of this. This is between you and me. Leave her out of it. She has nothing to do with it. She—"

"She has everything to do with it," said Gruen coldly. "I'm not stupid. I know I could pour this whole damned bottle down your throat and you'd kick in without telling. But it'll be different watching a girl struggle as this acid eats her flesh. It'll be different hearing her scream with pain. It'll be different watching her rot to death under the flaming teeth of vitriol because a stubborn shamus like you was too—"

Trevor gulped for air. He shook his head. "Gruen," he said, "if I tell you where those papers are, will you let her go?"

Gruen laughed harshly. "Let her go?" he cried. "Don't be a fool, Trevor! What do you take me for? She's seen me. She's seen my men. She'd squawk! No, Trevor, she's got to die—like you. But you can save her an unpleasant death for your story."

"And if I tell?"

"I'll be kind," sneered Gruen. "I'll let you both have a slug through the skull. Painless. Quick. Hell, what more could you ask?"

Trevor's face lifted up in repugnance. "Well, Gruen, you yellow skunk, my answer's the same as before—go to hell!"

Gruen recoiled in surprise. Then he hurtled forward and ploughed his pawlike fist into Trevor's chin. Bart took the crack without flinching. It sent his head spinning dizzily and left a livid patch of torn flesh on his cheek.

"You think this is a grandstand," bellowed Gruen, enraged. "Well, by God, I'll show you it isn't!"

He flew across the room to the table. Ruth Walsh lay on it just as they had left her there. She was unconscious as she had been when they carried her in. Gruen slapped her face vigorously a few times. Trevor gritted his teeth and watched Morgan move away from behind him to be near Gruen.

Ruth Walsh stirred under the smarting blows which Gruen dealt her. Her blue eyes suddenly fluttered open. She gaped up in horror at Gruen's bestial features. She cried out softly. Gruen pushed her head back and bumped it against the table. Ruth Walsh twisted and tried to turn on the table but the straps holding her down would not allow her body to move at all. Only her head. This she managed to jerk sideways.

Her frightened gaze fell upon the chair. She saw Trevor manacled there, grimly watching her.

Ruth cried, "Bart! Bart Trevor!"

Slap! Gruen let her have a vicious blow. She screamed in pain and let her head fall back.

"You dog," Trevor muttered. He was leaning forward now, concealedly doing his best to seem natural to Morgan, Louis and Gruen. Trevor's tie fell down towards his lap. The end of the cravat finally touched his legs. Then his manacled hands twisted tortuously around toward his legs and groped agonizingly for the end of the tie. His right hand reached it first. He bent forward, stooping, and his left hand reached the tie.

They grasped it tightly dexterous fingers ripped open the binding and searched feverishly through the inner lining.

Trevor's fingers found their treasure. Out of the lining of his tie came a key. It was a small key, dull and queerly shaped. A skeleton key. Trevor straightened up, the key in his right hand. He twisted his hand to try and insert the key in the lock of the handcuffs. He made it. The lock clicked, the cuff snapping open.

He transferred the key to the left lock quickly and snapped that open. He left the unlocked cuffs still on his hands. Bull Morgan turned and glanced leeringly at him. Then turned away. Trevor did not have any time to watch what they were doing to the Walsh girl. He stooped over and unlocked both of his leg cuffs.

At the same second, there was a gruesome, horrible screech of agony and terror as Ruth wriggled like a snake in her bindings.

Gruen laughed satanically and turned to Trevor. "Look at her," he grated. "That's acid there! We're starting with the cheeks. Then we'll go to the eyes and drop by drop we'll let it eat into her brain!"

"It burns! It burns!" screamed Ruth Walsh.

CHAPTER III

ESCAPE

Bart Trevor plunged headlong across that room like a shell fired from a cannon! Taken completely by surprise, Walter Gruen could only glare, petrified, in astonishment. Morgan never even saw Trevor's flashing frame until it was too late. But Louis had.

Louis leaped into Trevor's path, tugging at a gun. It flipped out in his hand, a stubby automatic. Crack! Crack! Twice it spit orange flame and belched lead in lightning stabs. The first slug zoomed into the opposite wall and ripped at the plaster there. The second tore at Trevor's coat as he dove and went on to knock the chair into a far corner by its impetus.

Then Trevor was on Louis! The two manacles were still on Trevor's hands, still around his fighting wrists. Trevor brought up his arms like the boom of a derrick and let them fall in a slashing, razorlike strike as swift and as deadly as that of a noxious diamondback!

The loose cuffs struck Louis full in the face as he yanked on his trigger for a third shot. But Louis' aim was shot to pieces. He jerked his gun. The jerk lifted the nozzle up high and sent the slug into the ceiling with a thudding sound.

The cuffs tore at Louis' face and continued on down through the flesh. Louis fell like a stone, his features a raw, gory pulp. Gruen was still standing there immobile, stunned and baffled by the sudden unwonted attack, at loss for its explanation and believing: it almost preternatural. But Bull Morgan was more practical.

Bull whirled to meet Trevor, his beastlike fists curled into miniature stones. He lashed out at Trevor's face, but Trevor ducked the wild swing and brought his own fist around in a haymaker. Bull weaved his head and Bart's fist ploughed through empty air.

But Bull had forgotten the dangling handcuffs on that fist. They swung out into space as Bart's fist missed its mark and the lock of the manacles caught Bull Morgan directly under the eye. Trevor saw it happen, but he never quite understood what really took place. The next thing he knew. Bull was standing there cursing and screaming in horrid agony, and Trevor felt sick when he saw that the cuff had sliced the flesh beneath the eye socket wide open and had popped the eye right out of Morgan's head.

Morgan continued to scream and shriek for several seconds. Then as the inhuman pain devoured him, he uttered a low groan and sagged down limply into welcome unconsciousness.

Trevor stepped back over the prostrate body of Louis, who was writhing around on the floor, moaning and clawing at his injured face. Gruen—the Murder Master—had moved to action. He fell against the table, his features contorted into animal rage, and hurled the bottle of vitriol right at Trevor's face.

Bart never even saw the vitriol flying towards him. He dove at that same split second for the ugly automatic which Louis had dropped to the floor when he fell. The vitriol scuttled through the air right over his stooped body and landed with a crash right next to Morgan, the acid bursting up into a fine spray as the bottle splintered into thousands of sharp pieces, and fell down on top of the unconscious Bull, splattering his face and burning into his unresisting flesh.

Bart Trevor fired at Gruen twice, but he did not seem affected by the slugs. He hurled himself forward! Bart cursed. Gruen was wearing a bullet-proof vest, of course! There was only one place for a slug then. Right between the eyes.

Trevor fired from the hip, jerking the pistol up. But there was only a metallic click. The gun was void of bullets. Louis had used some and the last two that Trevor had fired had depleted the supply. The gun was useless.

Frantically he flung the automatic in Gruen's face as the Murder Master grappled with him, catlike claws searching fiendishly for Trevor's throat. Trevor jabbed Gruen behind the ear and sent him whistling to the floor. Gruen tried to rise, shaking his head at the numbness which Bart's blow had caused.

Trevor dashed over to Ruth Walsh and unstrapped her just as the door opened and Droone and the man Gruen had called Joe rushed in.

"Ruth," snapped Trevor, "get into that next room. Use water on that vitriol. It'll dissipate ction of the acid!"

Ruth Walsh nodded fearfully and scurried through the open door into the room from which Bull Morgan had procured the vitriol previously.

Walter Gruen had risen to his feet. He was swaying unsteadily, his eyes red with pain and rage.

"Get him!" he roared furiously, "Get him!"

Harry Droone and Joe came on. Droone skirted the table and charged like a bull at Trevor, who lithely eluded the rush and sprang agilely around the other side of the table and ran to meet

Joe at the doorway. His fist hit Joe like an express train. The man fell. Trevor went through the door like a bolt of lightning.

Droone and Gruen went after him. Droone was in the lead, a grisly .45 revolver in his hand.

Trevor lit down the stairs three at a time. Crack! Droone fired the big blue-steel gun once. Trevor heard the slug buzz angrily past his ear. He reached the front door safely. For the moment, he was out of sight of the others in the delitescence of the hallway. He opened the door and slammed it.

But he did not leave the house. Instead, he cut back into the ebony shadows of the hallway and crouched there like a cornered panther while Droone reached the doorway, went through, looked around for a few seconds and came right back.

Droone said, "He's gone, chief! He got away!"

Trevor could hear Gruen cursing like a maniac at the top of the stairs.

"Want me to try and chase him?" Droone asked.

"No, you fool!" Gruen cried sharply. "He's miles from here now! He's gone to raise every cop within blocks for a raid on this place! We've got to clear out of here—leave no identification marks! It's Trevor's word against ours. He can't prove anything. Hurry up!"

"What about the dame?" Droone asked.

"We'll take her with us," said Gruen. "We're not through yet, Harry. If those papers ever get to John Walsh, the whole ring is sunk. Trevor can't turn them over. We have Ruth Walsh. I've got a fine plan. It just came to me. We'll hold the girl as hostage. Either Trevor gives himself up to us or we kill the girl!"

"But suppose Trevor don't, chief? Suppose he gets those papers to the D. A.?"

"Then we'll tell Walsh that unless he resigns at once, his daughter will be murdered. That'll put Jim Block into the D. A.'s chair."

Droone laughed happily. "I get it," he said. "Jim Block belongs to the Gruen organization! He'll get those papers and turn them back to you."

"Exactly," said Gruen. "Come on. Get that girl all wrapped up for delivery. We've got to travel tonight and right away. There's no telling where that fool Trevor has gone!"

Droone nodded and ran back up the stairs to the second floor. He did not know it, but almost in his shadow, another figure crept up the stairs after him. Trevor was afoot again. He paused in the dark hallway and watched Droone disappear after Gruen into another room. He heard a scream. Ruth's voice.

Trevor went taut. Then relaxed. They would not harm her here. They expected the police to come swooping down on the place. They were taking her with them. Trevor slithered up to the room where the chaotic mèlée had but recently transpired. He peered in cautiously. Louis was still there, rubbing his face dazedly. The man called Joe had disappeared. Bull Morgan lay on the floor. The vitriol had already left its macabre mark on the fellow. He was dead.

Trevor crept into the room. He had to take the risk. He frisked Morgan's pockets while Louis, his back turned to the shamus, rubbed his mauled features. Trevor felt the welcome grip of a pistol in Morgan's back pocket. He pulled it out, reversed and leaped onto Louis. One short blow, and Louis fell forward on his face unconscious.

Then Trevor went to the room into which Droone and the Murder Master had disappeared. He could not try the knob. He grabbed a rickety chair in the hall and placed it against the wall to one side of the door, the pistol in his hand. He looked into the room through the transom.

The transom was painted. It should have been opaque, but time had worn the paint and left a hazy transparency across the glass. Droone and Gruen were in the room all right. But what a room it was!

There were huge generators and electrical cabinets in the place with controls and volume dials replete across the face of the panels. A wired microphone was on a small table in front of these radio panels. Gruen was sitting down in front of the microphone. Droone went to the control board and switched on the juice.

"Want police calls?" Droone asked.

"No!" snapped Gruen. "Give me a short wave length of 211. That's the length I used on the receiving set I planted in Herrick's skull. The corpse may still be at the morgue. And there's just a bare chance that Trevor may go back to headquarters to that fool friend of his, Inspector Brandt. I'm going to try a message through the corpse again. It worked once."

At the open transom, Trevor was amazed at the whole layout. The mystery of the whispering corpse had bothered him greatly. He had not been able to see how any one could have fixed up the morgue with a receiving set. But he saw now. Gruen, the man-devil, had had Robert Herrick slain, fearful of Herrick's disclos-ing tongue. Then Herrick's skull had been trepanned and a small short-wave receiving set had been thrust into the brain cavity, the brain and other organs having been removed. The skull was then replaced and the body cast into the street where the police found it and took it to the morgue for autopsy. The Murder Master had called Trevor through the set in Herrick's dead head and was now trying to reestablish communication.

"Bart Trevor," whispered Gruen weirdly. "Bart Trevor...."

Through the loudspeaker across the room, Bart could hear some one gasp and then a voice cry, *"Gott in himmel!"*

He had to smile. Poor old Karl Topeka was being frightened out of his wits again in the morgue. This was all damned clever. They also picked up the sounds at the other end like a telephone.

Gruen frowned at Droone and said, "I don't think he's there. I'll leave the message for him anyway." He returned to the microphone and said. "Tell Bart Trevor that Ruth Walsh will be murdered un-less he returns to the spot where she is alone and gives himself up. Tell him that. Tell him to act immediately,"

Gruen cut the mike off.

"What now?" asked Droone.

"Quick!" said Gruen. "Switch me in on the police short-wave length—215 meters!"

Droone snapped a dial around and tuned in again.

"Calling Police Headquarters." said Gruen. "Calling Police Headquarters!" There was a short silence. "Tell John Walsh that these are the kidnapers of his daughter. If he has not resigned his office by midnight, his daughter will meet a horrible death. Relay that instantly."

Droone cut him off again. "What about the hideout, chief?" he said. "Hadn't you better let the boys over there know we're com-ing? You're going over to Long Island, aren't you?"

"Tune me in," snapped Gruen. "Wave length 200."

Droone worked the dials again. He turned on volume and waved to Gruen.

Gruen said. "Calling Hempstead Station. Calling Hempstead Station."

A metallic voice replied over the loudspeaker, "Okay, chief, we're listening."

"This is the Murder Master. We are coming out there directly by speed boat. Keep well under cover. Police may be wise. Signing off."

"That's got it!" exclaimed Droone. "But what about Trevor? He'll come here if he gets your message and we'll be gone!"

"I'm leaving Louis behind," said Gruen. "He'll wait for Trevor in case there's a police trap. Well leave the other launch for Louis and Trevor. Louis can handle it all right. Come on."

"How about all this?"

"Leave it!"

Bart Trevor, who had watched the whole thing, slunk back into the shadows of the hallway and watched Gruen and Droone leave the radio room and enter the room where Ruth had previously been tied. He followed them and peered in. The man called Joe had Ruth bound hand and foot. Louis had recovered and was wildly gesticulating and telling that some one had slugged him from behind.

"You're crazy!" snapped the Murder Master. "That crack Trevor gave you makes you see things. You're staying here, Louis, to wait for Trevor. He'll probably be back, but there won't be any fighting. He'll go along with you peacefully. Take him in the launch out to the Hempstead hideout up the Sound. Joe, Droone and myself are taking the girl in the speed boat."

Louis said, "Right, chief."

Joe and Droone packed up Ruth, whose mouth was covered with a piece of heavy white adhesive tape and carried her out, Walter Gruen following them.

Then Trevor, gripping the pistol he had taken from the corpse, followed the group silently down the stairs. They did not stop at the first floor, where the street entrance was, but continued on down into the cellar of the house. Trevor followed them cautiously, careful not to make any sound.

He descended the cellar stairs in their wake and heard the faint dull sound of slapping water. Where was this house? He didn't know. He had not been outside of it. And he had not seen how he had gotten there. Evidently it bordered a river—no doubt the East River since the men had spoken of riding up to Long Island across the Sound.

Suddenly, Trevor heard a guttering roar as a gasoline engine turned over, caught, and thundered staccato bursts in grinding cadence. There was a whine to the motor and a quick rush of power. Dreading the fact that he was too late, Trevor leaped down the stairs.

There was a flash of white boiling water, a swift vision of the stern of a motorboat, and Gruen and his killers were gone.

Trevor was too late! His quarry had flown!

CHAPTER IV

DEATH RENDEZVOUS

One thing that immediately impressed Bart Trevor as he stood there feeling beaten and helpless was the marvelous layout of this under-house mooring ground. It was the cellar of the place above. And this cellar was nothing but East River. The steps ended where a narrow pier began under the house. The river water came right in and washed the small pier. There were two mooring places. Trevor saw, swiftly, another launch, a bigger one. Yes, it was bigger, but it was also clumsier and it had only an outboard motor. Chase would be futile. A telephone on the wall caught Trevor's eye.

He leaped to it, lifted the receiver and listened for the voice of the operator.

"Number, please?"

Trevor snapped the number, got hold of Inspector Brandt and hastily told him what had happened. Brandt almost cried at the sound of Trevor's voice. He gasped out what had been happening. Police h.q. and the city in general were in an uproar over the abduction and threatened death of Ruth Walsh. Trevor told Brandt to warn the Long Island police that the hideout was on the waterfront at Hempstead.

"They've got a fast launch," Trevor breathed. "Or I'd go after them. You'll need some boat to catch them now. But the Long Island cops can nab the whole bunch when they land at Hempstead."

"Nuts," said Inspector Brandt. "The L. I. boys aren't going to take the credit for this case. Where are you!"

"Somewhere on the East River," said Bart. "About 20th Street, I think. I see a familiar sign over in Brooklyn there."

"My God!" Brandt cried. "You're right near the city police plane. Have you got a boat? They're at Seventeenth!"

"I have a boat."

"Then tear down to the police pier where they have the plane moored. Captain Kerry is in charge there. I'll phone ahead and fix it up for you. Good luck!"

"Thanks," said Trevor. He hung up.

Untying the hawser of the launch, he leaped into it and straddled to the stern, where the outboard motor was. He whirled the disc with a short piece of rope. The motor caught, and the launch under his guiding rudder nosed out of its pier into the river.

Trevor headed south. The launch went faster than he thought it would. In several minutes, a long amber finger shot out from one of the piers on the waterfront and lighted on him. A voice billowed out fantastically across the waves.

"Trevor?"

"Yes!" he yelled back.

"Turn in here. Police plane is waiting!"

Trevor stabbed at the rudder and shot the launch around vertically. The searchlight illumined his way and picked out a mooring place at the pier. He leaped out, shutting the motor off.

He heard a peculiar stuttering rhythm. He glanced over the side of the pier. Nestled there was a huge Sikorsky amphibian, riding the water easily, its twin engines turning over.

"Right here, Trevor," said a man next to him. "Hop in. Captain Kerry is waiting for you!"

Bart leaped down into the cabin of the Sikorsky. It was a spacious place with lounge seats along each side of the fuselage. Captain Kerry was up in the control cockpit, just forward of the cabin. Another man was with him at the controls. Kerry leaned out and called back. "Trevor?"

"Yes, captain."

"Good work. Trevor. I'm taking off. Hempstead, isn't it?"

"Yes, captain," replied Bart. "They're in a speed boat and they've quite a start!"

"We'll get 'em," said Kerry. "Sit tight."

In twenty minutes, Trevor could see the silvery stretches of the Sound beneath him. Off to his left was New Rochelle and the Westchester suburbs. Ahead loomed the dark coastline of Long Island. But he could see nothing of the speed boat in the semi-darkness.

Presently Kerry snapped, "Speed boat below us! I'm dropping a magnesium flare. Look sharp!"

Trevor clung to the window of the plane's cabin and stared down overside. He discerned the speed boat and its occupants swishing through the water in a nebula of flying spray.

"That's it!" he cried loudly. "There's Gruen at the helm. And there's Ruth Walsh in the stern with those other two rats! Go down on them, captain!"

A man next to Trevor in the cabin jammed something into Bart's hands. Trevor gazed at the object. It was a Thompson sub-machine gun.

"But we can't use an m. g. on them!" Bart protested. "Ruth Walsh is down in the boat with them!"

Captain Kerry sent the Sikorsky down in a shallow dive, nevertheless. Below him in the boat, Trevor could see a stuttering flame leap from the boat into the air. Then he heard a ripping sound and watched a line of holes bite into the doped linen of the wing.

Kerry banked the plane away. "They've got a machine gun on board!" he cried. "We've got to fire on them, regardless of the girl!"

"You can't!" protested Trevor. "It'll be murder. Ruth Walsh—" He was gazing down as he spoke. He gasped suddenly and went stiff as steel. "She's overside!" he roared. "Ruth Walsh just went overside. She jumped! My God, she's all tied! She'll drown."

"She knew we couldn't attack with her in the craft," said Kerry. "Great girl! She went over to let us pot the others!"

"But she'll drown!" Bart shrilled.

"No," said Kerry. "Look there!"

Behind them, where the faint white splash showed the spot where Ruth Walsh had hit the sea, a searchlight lit upon the place and the vague gray outline of a boat sliced through the sea towards her.

"Police boat!" snapped Kerry. "Brandt must've warned New Rochelle about the escape! They've sent out a police boat from Hudson Park. They'll pick her up."

"Then dive for the speed boat!" yelled Trevor excitedly. "Dive down, captain, and let's give her a raze of lead!"

The Sikorsky reared up like a living thing and then went over and down in a steep dive. Trevor forced the tommy-gun out of the cabin window of the ship.

Down the Sikorsky flew, the twin engines pounding out a terrific song of grinding power and zooming death!

The stuttering flame leaped upwards from the speed boat again. And again the slugs found a mark somewhere in the plane.

Tac-tac-tac-tac!

Trevor's finger tripped his Thompson trigger and his gun leaped up and down, barking like a savage dog and vomiting a stream of lethal gray lead down through the night!

Huge fountains of water shot high into the air around the speed boat as Trevor's bullets missed the craft and ploughed deep into the water like avenging hornets. The other cop in the cabin had a tommy-gun going now and the roar filled the plane.

The Sikorsky zipped right over the speed boat and went up into the air again to bank around steeply and come back in another dive. They were nearing Hempstead now, and Trevor could see myriad auto lights on the shore line. The Long Island police were on the job, raiding the hideout of the Murder Master's killers.

Kerry flung the amphibian down again. The ship went lower than before, so low that the cabin pontoon nearly scraped the waters of the Sound. Trevor had a flashing vision of the speed boat directly under him. He saw three white terrified faces as the big flying boat tore at the sea craft head on. It looked like a collision. The gun on the speed boat had stopped its vicious tongue.

Grimly Trevor drew a careful bead on the upraised staring face of Walter Gruen—the Murder Master. He tripped the trigger and sent an unerring line of lead slashing down through the sky. He saw the bullets plop into Gruen's face as the handful of lead splattered the boat. Gruen's face seemed to melt away into a ghastly black hole. The Murder Master flung up his arms and toppled limply over the side of the speed boat into the sea.

Kerry zoomed again to come back for another try. But it was no use. Trevor's bullets had taken their toll. The stern of the speed boat had exploded and orange flames licked the wood of the hull and sides hungrily, crackling like an enraged demon as the smoke and fire rose up from the ship.

"Sinking," said Kerry. "You potted it, Trevor. Must've hit the gas tank. Look at her!"

The speed boat was a flaming pyre of twisted metal and charred wood. The furnace reached up into the night in a ghostly flare, and in a few seconds the swift craft turned turtle and sank quickly from sight.

Trevor took his tommy-gun back out of the window and sighed. The case was over. The papers he had would never convict Walter Gruen of theft, fraud, graft and the other sundry crimes against him.

When the Sikorsky gently settled in the waters of the East River again and taxied up to its mooring place at Seventeenth Street. Bart Trevor, tired but happy, found Inspector Bill Brandt waiting there for him.

Brandt pounded him on the back and congratulated him for the good work.

"But Ruth Walsh," said Trevor. "Did they pick her up all right?"

"I'll say they did," Brandt exclaimed. "The New Rochelle police boat got her immediately after she jumped. She's a good swimmer, Trevor. She managed to stay afloat, bonds and all, until they reached her. She's some girl. She's home with her dad now, I guess. I think they took her in while you and Kerry were over at Hempstead."

"A clean sweep," said Trevor. "The Long Island police had found the hide-out just before we shot down Gruen, Droone and that other man in the launch. When we landed at Hempstead, the place was under arrest and they had taken every member of the gang there."

"Swell work, Bart," said Inspector Brandt. "And, by the way, did you find out the secret of that whispering corpse?"

Trevor laughed. "Corpses don't whisper, inspector. And I'll show you why when we go down to the morgue!"

THE MONKEY GOD,
by Jacland Marmur

CHAPTER I
Sudden Death

At the same instant, Kilimi, the giant Wambuba black, and the white man, Jeffrey Westman, in the lead of the safari, froze in their tracks. The ivory hunter was a veteran of the sinister Ituri forests. The Congo jungle was dangerous territory, full of lurking death. He knew it. Behind them, the porters crouched instinctively, tense and alert.

The two leaders looked at each other in silence. The same sound, harmless to the ordinary ear but unnatural to their keen senses, had startled them both—an approaching rustle of dank leaves, the crackling of tangled vines. The faithful black turned.

"Watu!" He breathed the word in Swahili and plucked his precious tarboosh from his head. Then he said again in a tense whisper: "*Watu, bwana*! People."

Westman nodded. Kilimi, sensing danger, tucked his red fez for safekeeping into his monkey-skin belt. In silence he snapped the heavy gun he carried from "safety" to "ready" and exchanged it for the light Winchester the ivory hunter carried.

"Quick, Kilimi! *Pesi-pesi*!"

Kilimi darted from the trail, swift as a flash of vanishing light. Westman gestured with his free hand to the frightened black porters of his safari. A moment after their ears had caught the first warning of danger, the elephant trail was completely deserted.

In the dense growth, Kilimi crouched by Westman's side. Two flaps of his cartridge belt were open now, ready in an instant to feed fresh shells to the gun Westman held in his hand. The rustling came closer, like the slithering progress of a snake. They could see nothing. Suddenly a piercing shriek shattered the stillness of the jungle.

Kilimi tensed. The white man clutched his ebony arm restrainingly. Behind them, the Wambuba porters grasped their spears more tightly, eyeballs rolling.

Again it sounded, a blood-curdling human shriek of terror that ended in a horrible gurgle. It mingled with the enraged chattering of monkeys—and then died to a dreadful silence.

Kilimi swayed. Westman peered through the mangroves. His lips were set in a hard bar.

"*Chui!*" the Wambuba whispered.

The ivory hunter shook his head. "The forest leopard does not hunt in daylight, Kilimi!"

He gestured with his hand. His heavy rifle in readiness, the pair crawled through the tangle of growth in silence, Kilimi's naked feet and Westman's mosquito boots making no sound as they circled to come upon the clear trail. Ahead, a shape lay motionless, with sightless eyes opened. Jeffrey Westman did not need to be told the man was dead. Yet he was armed—and they had heard no shot fired in his own defense. Only that shriek of horror; then silence and death.

A shudder swept Kilimi's giant frame. "*Wazungi!*" he whispered. A man does not let himself be killed with a loaded rifle in his hands unless tribal superstitions and dread of *dawa*—the jungle magic—was strong in his soul.

"*Wazungi!*" he whispered again in awe.

The ivory hunter nodded. There could be no question of it. The dead heap there was a white man. Death had pounced on him swiftly, silently, suddenly—and disappeared. The jungle swallowed all things.

In grim silence, Westman stepped into the open. The blazing Congo sun had yet an hour in the heavens. But in the depth of the great Ituri forest, the feverish African dusk was already deep on the ghastly festoons of interlacing creepers; and the age-old elephant trail was splashed with weird shadows. The throb of signal drums started, faint, distant, and invisible—the mysterious heartbeat of the land.

* * * *

Westman, tall and powerful and youthfully erect with his .475 elephant gun in the crook of his arm, had pressed through the jungle from Murumwa at a speed that showed plainly that this time he was not in search of that eternal dream of the ivory hunter, the father of all the elephants, whose tusks trail the ground. The summons of his friend, Scotty Macrae, of the Congo Concession Company, had been as imperative as it had been enigmatic.

Macrae was not a man to scare easily, yet he had sent a runner through the jungle to his friend in Murumwa. And now death met this friend as a sinister proof. Westman's sun-scorched face showed anxiety in his drawn jaw-muscles.

Staring down at that fellow in the middle of the trail, he saw a face lacerated horribly and twisted in the agony and the terror of death. They had heard his death shriek not more than a few moments before. His rifle was still in his hand. He had not fired so much as a single shot in his defense. Murder had leaped upon him mysteriously and swiftly.

The ivory hunter's trained eye passed quickly over the ground, then along the wall of the jungle for some sign, animal or human, to betray the cause of death. He saw nothing. What did it mean?

Westman dropped to one knee. The flesh of the dead man's face was torn, bleeding, the blood not yet coagulated. And as the ivory hunter bent closer, he cursed softly under his breath. He knew the fellow—George Craig, a Congo Concessions man sent out recently from Boma as Scotty Macrae's assistant.

Westman had met him once in Murumwa before the man went into the jungle to join the Scot on the back creeks of the Ituri River. There was no mistaking his identity. There was the strong, stubborn jaw and the shock of dust-colored hair. Westman hadn't thought himself so close to Macrae's compound.

What was the fellow traveling the jungle alone for? That in itself was suicidal. Was it a warning? If so, by whom? And for what reason? What had caused Craig's sudden swift death? Men don't just drop dead that way. And as sudden and violent as it had been, there hadn't been time for him to so much as fire a single shot in self-defense!

Westman's brow contracted in a frown. Very carefully he turned the body over. As the back came into full view, Westman's teeth ground together.

Between the shoulder blades were several slashes.

Native spears? He dismissed the thought instantly. There was no spear anywhere about, and native killers threw their weapons.

These slashes were clean stabs. One of them had penetrated to poor Craig's heart at the first thrust. No native weapon could have made them. Those thrusts could only have been made only by a razor-sharp blade of civilized steel.

But a white man's knife in the heart of the Ituri jungle must have a white man to wield it! Yet other than Scotty Macrae, there were no white men within twenty miles of the Congo Concession's gold and diamond workings on the crocodile-infested streams of the Ituri Valley.

Westman came quickly to his feet, barking an order in Swahili to his men to remain where they were without stirring. Carefully, with his eyes glued to the ground, he went over the terrain of the clearing, working slowly from one side to the other, back and forth. Meticulously he searched. He found—nothing. There was not so much as a single track of man or beast, other than a single trail made by Craig himself. Bordering the elephant trail, his trained eye spied broken vines and torn creepers. The dying man had clutched at these, no doubt, in his brief agony. But on the ground itself there was—nothing!

Baffled, Westman dropped again to one knee beside Craig's body. The shock of sand-colored hair seemed in spots to have been literally torn by the roots from the scalp. Jeffrey frowned. He recalled for a moment the gruesome tales he had eked out from the lips of Scotty Macrae's runner, the black who had brought to Murumwa his plea for Westman's help. Tales of mysterious, unaccountable deaths; of the dread superstitions that swept the natives like wildfire; of jungle magic.

And now, almost under his very eyes and not a mile from Macrae's compound, without any explanatory tracks or marks on the soft jungle floor, George Craig lay stabbed to death!

As he rose to his feet, Kilimi bent eagerly toward him. "You find marks, *bwana*?" he whispered softly in Swahili.

Westman shook his head. "No marks, Kilimi."

"*Dawa lutala. Watu lutala.* The magic of the accursed people!"

Jeffrey looked at him sharply, reclaiming his Winchester from the giant man's shaking hand.

"Nonsense, Kilimi!" he barked. "Kilimi no run away! Understand? We fight together before, no?" he went on levelly in guttural Swahili. "We fight together again."

For an instant Kilimi's eyes wavered to the body lying at their feet and darted swiftly to the walls of the jungle on all sides. Then he squared his shoulders. His free hand came up clenched, and he struck his bare chest a mighty thump.

"No," he growled, "Kilimi no run away. My master fight— Kilimi fight!"

"Good man," Westman replied. "Tell your Wambubas to make a litter for the dead *Wazungi*. We camp tonight with Scotty Macrae in the ancient village of death. You remember, Kilimi?"

Kilimi's face split in a savage grin of pleasure at the remembered battle in which he had partaken at that place Westman called the village of death.

"*Ndio, bwana,*" he growled. "I remember."

Westman took the lead again. With their grisly burden coming directly behind them, the little safari pressed onward through the jungle.

CHAPTER II
"The Accursed Magic Again!"

The westering sun dove abruptly beneath the jungle fronds in a bombshell of color and light. Several moments later, Westman heard the cries and noise of many men crashing toward them. Dominating the native clamor, he recognized the periodic bass hail of Scotty Macrae.

"Craig! Darn ye, where are ye? Craig!"

A bitter smile flitted across the ivory hunter's face at the Scot's naïve manner of search. In a moment Westman and his safari burst upon the rim of a large clearing.

To the right, the short, stocky form of the Scotsman could be seen, returning at the head of his search party of blacks.

The huge compound was entirely surrounded by a high stockade. Behind the pointed stakes and through the open gates the wattled native grass huts reared their cones. Ahead of Westman rose the administration building, a rough hut of thatch with a narrow step; and directly behind it a gigantic banyan tree sent drooping creepers weaving ghostily in the twilight.

Suddenly Scotty Macrae spied the newcomers and, mistaking the Wambubas for his own blacks and the white man for the man he was in search of, he let out an angry bellow:

"Craig! Ye bloody fool! Don't ye know better'n to run off at night into—"

"It's not Craig, Mac."

The Scot, coming forward on the run, stopped dead in his tracks. Then he let out a joyous shout.

"Jeff!" He sprang forward eagerly, rifle in hand. "Westman! God, and I'm glad you're here. Didn't even know whether my runner'd ever live to reach you in Murumwa."

"Your runner came in five days ago. I left at once."

"Knew you would, Jeff."

"He brought some pretty gruesome tales with him, Mac. Now what's all this magic nonsense?"

The stocky Scot sobered instantly, letting his huge hand come away from Westman's, which all the while he had been clasping in hearty welcome.

"It—it's a rotten mess, Jeff," he bit off between clenched teeth. "Talk it over later. Right now I'm worried about that kid they sent out from Boma. Went off by himself into the jungle an hour ago, and—"

"Craig?"

"Yes, he—"

"Don't hunt him any more, Scotty."

"You— What do you mean, Jeff?"

"He's dead."

"Dead!"

"My Wambubas have him on that litter. Stabbed through the back. Kilimi will bury him, Mac," the ivory hunter went on quietly, "like one of his own tribe. Standing upright with his rifle at his side like a warrior ought to be buried."

"My God! Another!" The Scot said this with savage bitterness.

For a moment the two friends stared at each other. Then in silence Macrae led the way to the administration building. Behind them, the door flap of *kasai* cloth fell back in place without a flutter. Outside, Westman's Wambubas mingled with Macrae's men, Kilimi growling orders, his brilliant Mussulman tarboosh the envy of all.

Scotty Macrae fell wearily to the rattan settee and turned up the grease lamp. In its light, his square face showed itself set in stony ridges. Westman dropped to a camp stool, his long legs before him. For a moment the pair listened intently to the faint, maddening beat of distant signal drums until suddenly the Scot's clenched fist came down with a thump on the narrow teakwood table. He swore savagely.

"I tell you, Jeff, it's enough to drive a man crazy out here. Blackness—the jungle— clammy heat and snarling blacks. Them drums going all night long. Death ready to jump on your back any minute!" He leaned forward.

"Westman," he barked fiercely, "I can stand the sight of blood drawn in a clean open fight as good as any man. I'm not squeamish, God knows. But this stinking back-sticking! It sends shivers up my spine. They don't know what a man's up against here, them company directors on the coast at Boma.

"Gold and diamonds, that's what they want! And they send a poor kid like Craig out here. Why, he didn't have a chance! I'm beginning to think I haven't, either. But I tell you this, Jeff!" His fist pounded the table again. "I'll get to the bottom of this if it—"

"Suppose you tell me about it," Westman said softly.

"You saw as much of what it's about as I know, Jeff," the Scot replied, more soberly, "when you found young Craig."

"Who—"

"I don't know."

"What was he doing in the jungle alone?"

"I've warned him a hundred times, Jeff. But he was a kid, full of fight. Only he didn't know how to fight out here. He was looking for a black who skipped out with a few raw diamonds from the diggings."

"Has that happened before?"

"The workmen making off with the stuff? Yes, before I sent for you, Jeff, half a dozen lit out." The Scot leaned forward, his eyes ablaze. "And every one of them was found murdered in the jungle! Every one!" he repeated. "Stabbed and lacerated and torn, those we were able to find, with handfuls of their hair yanked out by the roots as if—"

"What!" Westman barked fiercely, coming upright in his seat.

"The savages hide small stones in the kinks of their hair. You know that, Jeff. Someone's laying for them out there in the jungle. Whoever it is, after murdering 'em he hunts their scalps for the looted stuff. It's bestial, I tell you! Doesn't just pick the pebbles out of their hair. Blast him, he fairly rips the scalp off! Why, what's the matter, Jeff?"

Westman relaxed slowly. "Mac," he breathed, "that's exactly what I noticed about Craig's head when I found him."

"You—" Macrae stopped short. A moment of silence fell between the two friends.

"Are there any other whites around here beside yourself?" Westman asked at length.

"Not for twenty miles, Jeff." The Scot shook his head. "Not till Lulatala, an old slave-trading village far up the river. Trader called Joe Swango lives there. Comes down the trails once a month for me with supplies. Decent sort, only close-mouthed."

"These men of yours, Mac, who ran off and died. How'd you find 'em?"

"Riddled through the back with spear holes."

"And their own *assegai*? Were they flung? Was there ever signs of a fight?"

"Never, Jeff! Their spears were still in their hands. Too yellow to show fight."

"Would you call young Craig yellow, Mac?"

"Good Lord, no! He'd fight ten wildcats twice his size."

"Well, he never put up a fight, either."

"What—!"

"His rifle was still in his hand, without a shell fired. And the rottenest part of it is, Mac, that he was killed not more than five minutes before we got to him. And there wasn't even a bootmark or the track of a foot to show who did it!"

"Tommyrot! You must be wrong. What do you think killed him? Black jungle magic?"

"That's what Kilimi thinks, Mac," Westman said.

"Bah! You, too? Some savage leaped on his back and speared him for the diamonds he thought he had."

"Impossible! If couldn't have been a Wambute forest pygmy— their spears are always poisoned with datura lily extract. The wounds swell blue and they don't bleed. I tell you, it wasn't a spear at all. The holes are too clean, not like the wound from the broad paddle of a spear!"

"But for the love of God, Jeff, what was it then that—"

"A white man's long steel dagger. Nothing else makes wounds like that."

"But there isn't a white man between here and Lulatala!" Macrae gasped incredulously.

"Except this Joe Swango you tell me about," Westman reminded him.

"That's a wrong trail." The Scotsman shook his head. "Joe's no angel, but he hasn't the nerve for that. If you saw him, you'd know. Besides, he can't kill blacks and murder Craig a mile from my compound while he's in Lulatala twenty miles away. Half these blacks were murdered when runner boys of mine swear they were talking to him the same night in Lulatala. It's a band of savages, I tell you!"

Westman shook his head. He leaned back against the wattled wall of the hut, his hard, gray eyes half closed.

"Wrong, Mac," he mused. "Blacks don't work that way, and you know it. What chance would a black have of disposing of looted diamonds? Suppose he came to a post and offered raw diamonds to a trader? They'd jump him so quick he wouldn't know what struck him. No, there's something far more sinister and a blessed sight more dangerous about this than a band of stray savages or Wambute forest pygmies." The lean hunter straightened slowly in his chair. "You remember Abd el Hussan, Mac?" he asked quietly.

"I'll say I remember him! Didn't I have a time getting the Governor General to send the approval you wanted so that man of yours, Kilimi, could mummify the swine's head for his collection of post decorations!"

Westman grinned at this. Kilimi cherished those bizarre and ghastly relics of his hunts. But the smile vanished from his angular face almost at once.

"Well, Mac, I was wondering," he mused on. "You remember the Arab was digging here for raw diamonds before you and your company ever knew the deposit was here? I'll wager someone in Lulatala knew about his pretty game before we broke it up six months ago."

"But Abd el Hussan is dead, Jeff."

"Sure he's dead. But he's not the only crooked trader in the Congo."

"Well, I don't mind admitting I'm stumped, Jeff," Mac conceded. "Unless this killer flies through the night like a bat! All I know is there's murder stalking around this place till it's got me balmy. When I told Joe Swango about the way the blacks died, he grinned and said something was wrong with their face dye if it wouldn't keep off the jungle magic. They smear their faces with white *ngula* dye for night travel, you know. It's supposed to scare off the evil devils of the forest." Macrae shuddered. "I can't help thinking of poor Craig."

Westman nodded and seemed to be listening to the moan of the dank night breeze through the swaying creepers of the ancient banyan. At last he stood up.

"We'll both think clearer after a sleep, Mac."

"Aye, Jeff," the Scot murmured from his seat.

The ivory hunter turned away. But he never reached the curtained doorway of the sleeping room. At the instant his hand touched it, a piercing shriek stabbed the night outside. Westman whirled. Bellows of terror sounded outside now, hoarse native growls, the swift patter of naked feet racing for shelter.

Then that single blood-curdling shriek sounded once more, and it ended as if a savage hand had instantly clutched the throat.

Outside the door-flap, Kilimi's unmistakable bass sounded anxiously:

"*Bwana, bwana!*" he cried; and, waiting for no summons, he tore aside the curtain. "Come quick! The accursed magic again!"

Macrae leaped to his feet. Westman sprang forward, plucking up his Winchester as he went.

"Come along, Mac!"

One after the other, they plunged into the night.

CHAPTER III

White Man's Weapon

"Down, Mac! On the ground!" Westman warned the Scot.

At the foot of Macrae's hut, Kilimi had already fallen prone on his stomach, the ivory hunter at his side. For a moment, still blinded by their sudden dash into the dark clearing from the lamp-lit room, they could see nothing. Then gradually monstrous forms and waving shapes materialized amid the black tops of the jungle.

At the mouth of the native workers' stockade, the mob of Mac-rae's workers crowded, paralyzed with fright. In the center of the clearing, Westman's eight warrior porters crouched beyond the light of their dying campfire, all eyes glued to a single spot in the jungle's wall.

"Look, *bwana!*" Kilimi raised his hand, pointed.

A tall shape staggered into the dim light from the wall of forest. It swayed drunkenly from side to side: a stalwart savage, naked except for a loin clout. His face, streaked white with *ngula* dye, wobbled goblin-like above the jet torso.

"Tamwa," Macrae gasped. "The black who bolted with three stolen 'bort' stones—the one poor Craig was hunting."

He started up from his knees. Westman dragged him back to earth. And the black, reaching the edge of the clearing, let out again a single dreadful shriek of terror. At the same instant a dark shape leaped out of blackness, on to the terrified man's back. In the pale light something flashed three times in rising and descending arcs.

Westman came to one knee, the Winchester at his shoulder. Sighting carefully, he awaited an opportunity to fire. But the at-tacker, clinging to Tamwa's back, made a true fire impossible in that weird light. Only once his face was turned toward the clearing for an instant. It showed distorted, bestial, framed in shaggy hair, teeth gleaming between snarling lips.

"Batwa! Forest dwarf!" Kilimi growled.

"The swine!" Mac roared in helpless rage.

Tamwa collapsed, his attacker still clinging to his back.

Throwing caution to the winds, Westman pulled the trigger without any attempt at a hit, but more with the intention of scaring off the horrible shape. The flash of fire from his Winchester blinded them momentarily. When the smoke cleared, they caught sight of another short, dwarfed body darting out of the jungle. Once more Westman pumped his gun. It was like firing at dancing shadows.

"Kilimi!" he barked. "Throw wood on the fire. Quick!"

Macrae leaped to his feet. Westman followed. The Scot, enraged beyond all caution, started forward. The ivory hunter dragged him back.

"Don't be a fool, Scotty!" he snapped. "Get a brand from the fire. Kilimi! A torch!"

Kilimi came back with a smoking brand in one hand, his long *assegai* clutched in the other. Behind the stockade, a fierce pounding of tom-toms started as Macrae's savages took up the chant of their medicine man's desperate effort to scare away the evil spirits of the jungle devils.

"Come on," Westman bit off shortly. "Fire at the first moving thing you see, Mac!"

He led the way carefully toward the spot. On the rim of the jungle nothing stirred. It was as if everything they had seen had been a hallucination, a nightmare. Kilimi came closer with his rude torch. In the narrow circle of its light, Westman and Macrae inspected the torn terrain closely.

Tamwa's body had disappeared. Only a slight hollow betrayed where he had fallen. Macrae gasped, then caught the ivory hunter's arm.

"Jeff! Look here!"

He stooped quickly. When he straightened up, he held a long narrow-bladed dagger. It was red with blood.

"You were right, Jeff! It is a white man's knife that murdered poor Craig—and Tamwa."

Westman nodded. Taking the wicked looking poniard by the haft, he inspected it carefully. Its point was clean. There was no evidence of poison. Hair clung to the handle. When the ivory hunter handed the weapon back to Macrae and brought his fingers to his face, he caught the unmistakable animal odor of the jungle.

Westman turned to Kilimi. "Are you are sure you saw no white man?"

The Wambuba shook his head insistently. "No white man. *Batwa*—forest dwarf!"

"They've dragged his body off, Jeff," the Scot put in awed tones.

"Blast it, Mac!" the ivory hunter exploded in exasperation. "It doesn't make sense. Forest dwarfs don't use knives like this. Wouldn't know what to do with a thing like that if they had one. Spears and poisoned darts from blowguns are their weapons! And look at these tracks." He pointed to the torn earth revealed in the flickering light of their torch.

"One of them stabbed Tamwa. At least one more came to help him drag the body away. But, Mac, aside from the track your black left here, there's only one trail of naked savage feet! I don't believe in magic. Walking men leave footprints behind them on this jungle earth!"

Macrae shuddered. For an instant they stood stock still on the rim of the clearing. Kilimi watched his master. Then, as they stood there, irresolute, a distant drum beat a single reverberating thump. It echoed loudly on the fevered night air above the dolorous whine of the medicine man in the compound behind their backs. Then it sounded again in a slow characteristic rhythm that gradually filled the entire night of darkness with its monstrous throbbing.

Thump! Thump! Thump! Different from the cadence of signal drums. The ivory hunter knew that. Kilimi knew it, too, for he shrank back a pace.

"That's a sacramental drum, Mac," Westman explained with a strange softness to the Scot. "There'll be a moon soon. Somewhere in the heart of the jungle, they're calling the followers of Congo magic for the ceremony. That drum and the black we just saw murdered are bound together somehow, just as surely as Tamwa was killed by the same hand that murdered Craig. I feel it, Mac. I don't believe in jungle magic. Whoever is behind this business is playing for high stakes. He's using all he knows of white man's cunning and black man's superstitions. If we find the drum and the orgy it symbolizes, we'll find—something."

"You mean, Jeff, that—"

"I mean, Mac, that we can't sit here any longer waiting. Any one of us may be next! I mean to follow the sound of that drum and see where it leads to. The moon'll be up soon. We may find tracks—and we may not. But we can follow the sound, Kilimi and I."

"Let's go!" the Scot cut in harshly.

"Dangerous business, Mac," the ivory hunter warned. "If we come on a tribe of blacks in a ceremonial orgy and we're discovered, it's certain death."

"Better than sitting here waiting!"

Westman nodded and turned to Kilimi.

"We go to avenge the death of a black man and a white," he said quietly in Swahili, "We need Kilimi, the good hunter. You lead us into the jungle to the noise of the big drum?"

In the sputtering light of the torch, the black man's face was a study in emotion. Superstitious dreads, fear, and faithfulness struggled visibly on his jet countenance. Only for an instant he hesitated. Then he drew himself to his full height.

"*Bwana* go—Kilimi go," he growled.

"Good, Kilimi. Go pick four Wambuba men with strong hearts and long spears. They will come, too."

The black man turned toward the fire where his men stood anxiously waiting. Westman and Macrae followed soberly, intent on inspecting rifles and filling cartridge belts for their perilous venture. The Scot raised his face in undisguised admiration to the young ivory hunter.

"How in the world do you do it, Westman?" he asked softly. "That man of yours is scared to death, and he hasn't a thing to gain—yet he'd follow you into the jaws of hell if you told him to!"

"Pride, Mac," the ivory hunter muttered, almost to himself. "I've taught Kilimi to be proud."

CHAPTER IV

Worshipers of the Monkey God

As the little party moved along the trail, Kilimi and Westman, in the lead, guided their direction by the booming sound of the single drum. Macrae and the four blacks followed. For perhaps an hour, through tangles and festoons of jungle growth, they traveled the heart of the Ituri jungles, the deep, dull-throated boom of the drum beating ever closer and louder. Suddenly it ceased entirely.

The silence froze Kilimi in his tracks, his body tense as a tiger's set for the spring. For a full minute the drum remained silent. Then it started again on its repeated, single note like the beating of some gigantic heart. Kilimi's head came back on his shoulder.

"Karibu, *bwana*," he whispered. "Very close."

He dropped to his hands and knees now. Crawling forward, he parted the vines and peered through. Then he signaled with his free hand. With a silent gesture, Westman ordered the others to the ground. He led the crawling advance himself to the spot Kilimi commanded. At his side Macrae let out a low hissing of breath between his teeth.

Directly before them—in a slight depression of the land—the worshiping savages were revealed.

The narrow clearing lay bathed in moonlight. In its center stood a raised dais formed naturally by the rent trunk of a gigantic tree. Some of its dead limbs still reached weirdly upward from its sides. Upon it stood a naked dwarf savage before the great drum. With clenched fists, he pounded it in a maddening rhythm.

At the other end of the platform stood a huge cage of bamboo stakes. In it something black and fantastic, a shaggy creature, danced in a frenzy, chattering insanely with bared teeth. Besides the cage stood a man—giant by contrast with the Wambute pygmies—clothed in dirty white drill trousers and naked from the waist up. His face was covered entirely by a black cloth.

Below him and all about the riven tree trunk that served as their grisly sacrificial altar sat hunched on their heels the tribe of dwarfs. And these swayed backward and forward to the maddening beat of the drum.

In the light of the ascending moon their torsos looked brown and red rather than black, their faces imp-like and bestial. They were the savage forest dwarfs of the Ituri.

Macrae, crouching beside Westman, tensed angrily.

"That man!" he growled in a fierce whisper. "The tall one by that cage. He—Jeff, he's white. Look at his chest. What's he wearing that black mask for? Westman, he—"

"Quiet, Mac," the ivory hunter cautioned.

"*Shenzi nzombi!*" Kilimi's whisper was half dread and half a snort of rage. "Worshipers of the Monkey God!" And he spat to show his disgust—a frightened disgust, for he knew their terrible fanaticism.

Tense and anxious, they watched. Suddenly the white man below them dragged upward what appeared to be a human form. This he trussed by means of a rope creeper to one of the jutting limbs of the tree. There it dangled directly before him, a shapeless bundle with a grisly white-dyed face. From his thigh he whipped out a dagger and raised it on high. Above his head its steel blade caught all the light there was in a fierce and wicked gleam.

Macrae's rifle snapped to his shoulder. The next instant he would have fired. Westman grabbed the barrel and barked out a low command.

"Stop it. You want that whole mob at our throats?"

"Good God, Westman! You gonna sit here and let—"

"Don't be a fool, Mac. Look at the thing. It's a dummy. Sacking stuffed with grass and a white face painted on it. Look!"

Macrae gasped. His rifle came down from his shoulder. There was no mistaking it now.

The beat of the drum ceased. The swaying mob of pygmies leaned forward eagerly. In the silence, the brutal, senseless chattering of the thing in the bamboo cage rose with horrible clarity as it danced about in frenzy. The next moment the masked white man plunged his dagger downward into the grass-stuffed dummy. Again and again he buried the flashing steel blade.

At the sight, the watching savages beneath him let out a series of loud, whining wails. With a final savage thrust, the white man came upright, cut down the dummy, and flung the blade he had been using into the cage that stood close beside him. Instantly the beast behind the bamboo bars pounced upon it, bawling loudly and clawing the stakes of his cage with legs and arms, the steel blade clenched between his bared fangs.

"Great God, Jeff! It—it's—" Macrae broke off and clutched the ivory hunter's arm. "Look! The black they're dragging up there now! It— look at his face—dyed white with *ngula* dye. By God, it's Tamwa!"

Half a dozen of the hairy dwarfs were dragging the black man up on the dais. His limbs twitched occasionally. Life was still in him. The white man with the mask lifted both his arms toward the cage and started a weird, chanting wail. The surrounding worshipers took it up. The air filled with frightful sound. Inside the cage the beast snarled and raved, pulling in a fury at the bars.

Westman turned his head. There was loathing and grim bitterness on his face.

"No question of it," he growled in a low, husky bass. "That blasted renegade in the mask will pull the door open in a minute, Mac. That sacred ape in there—he's on a braided rope. He's been trained to make their sacrifices for them by watching the white swine knife dummies. When the cage opens—stand ready. Kilimi, do you hear? And your Wambuba men?"

"We hear, *bwana*," the Kilimi whispered softly.

Westman turned forward again. The white renegade had the door-trip of the cage in both hands. Suddenly he yanked it clear and leaped aside.

A wild shriek of savage joy sounded from the throats of the worshipers as the beast leaped out of its prison, stopped short only by the restraint of the rope that fastened it. Whipped to a frenzy, it crouched on all fours, snarling. Then, spying the supine body of Tamwa, it let out a throaty chortle and seized the dagger from its teeth by the haft.

The white-smeared face seemed to enrage it beyond all measure. And as it leaped upon the unstirring black, the crouching dwarfs shrieked their insane pleasure at the expected blood orgy, goading the beast on.

Westman snapped his gun from safety and brought it to his shoulder. Carefully he sighted down the sleek barrel. Only a moment he hesitated—and then he pulled the trigger.

The reverberating shot echoed like a clap of thunder through the fevered jungle night. Whether he had scored a hit or not, it was impossible to say, for the beast had leaped at the very instant of firing. It struggled ferociously now against its rope. The dwarf at the drum leaped in panic from the platform. Below them, the mob sprang to their feet, screaming and milling in terror.

On the raised dais, the white man with the masked face bellowed orders. Turning, he plucked a rifle from a corner. The dwarfs whirled about, blowguns at their mouths. A whizz of poisoned darts, like a flight of angry gnats, flew toward Westman and his hidden party.

"Let 'em have it, Scotty!" the ivory hunter cried, pumping his Winchester. "Careful of those darts."

The man on the dais emptied his weapon at the darting tongues of flame that leaped at him from the rim of the jungle. Kilimi and the Wambubas strained at their own enforced inaction like hounds on the leash. Suddenly the man on the dais, his gun empty, sprang side-wise toward the beast before its cage. It still chattered and snarled in bestial frenzy.

Feverishly he undid the animal's restraining rope and leaped clear. The freed beast let out a single inhuman snarl and sprang for the nearest tree, the gleaming knife-blade showing dazzlingly white between its teeth.

"Now, Kilimi!" Westman roared.

The black leaped to his feet, *assegai* in hand, an ancient Bantu war cry on his lips. Behind him, his Wambubas followed, roaring the battle cry of their native tongue. Macrae staggered upright, ramming fresh shells into his gun. Westman dragged him to earth.

"Leave be, mon!" the Scot bellowed angrily, the blaze of battle in his eyes. "Do ye think I'm sitting here while your blacks do my fighting for me? Leave be, mon!"

"Mud—dirt," the ivory hunter answered inexplicably. "Smear it on your face, Mac. Quick!"

His rifle momentarily at his side, Westman was clawing at the soft, wet earth at his feet. This he smeared thickly on his face, masking his sun-scorched countenance until its white texture was totally covered. The Scot looked at him in utter amazement.

"Are ye mad?" he shrieked.

"Mad or not, do as I tell you. Smear this mud on your face if you want to come out of this alive."

He fairly thrust Macrae's face into the soggy earth. Then, leaping to their feet, they followed the charge of Kilimi and his battle-crazed Wambubas. The blacks were far in the lead now. The air was filled with the blood-curdling bellow of their age-old war cry. Westman and Macrae fired as they raced forward.

The white renegade had vanished into the jungle. At his disappearance, the scattering Wambute dwarfs screamed in terror. On the edge of the clearing, they made their last stand. Arrows and darts from blowguns whirred through the air: But they had lost heart. Their magic gods had deserted them. Suddenly the last remnants of them turned tail and fled squealing from the shambles. Kilimi and his men took up the pursuit.

Westman bellowed after them. Hesitatingly the giant black man let off the chase. Panting and exulting, the party collected about the base of the tree platform. But the mystery of it still showed on Macrae's face, all smeared with blackening mud. There was little time then for explanations.

"Two of you make a litter for Tamwa here," the ivory hunter commanded. "Take him back to the diggings, Mac. Fast as we can make it. I've a hunch that's where we'll find the renegade—whoever he is. Quick! We've got to cauterize any wounds from those darts and arrows, or it means the finish."

In feverish haste, the blacks worked under Kilimi's direction. Not five minutes later, they were heading back for Macrae's compound at a trot. They flung all caution to the winds now. Speed was what was wanted.

CHAPTER V

Big Stakes

A fierce terrorized wailing greeted them as they crashed from the jungle to the edge of their own compound. The camp looked deserted. Every living soul had crammed into the space enclosed by the tall stockade. Then, from behind it, issued a few agonized shrieks from the superstition-ridden blacks. A few braver souls peered fearfully from the opening.

Smeared with the mud, as Westman had so inexplicably ordered, Macrae stopped in his tracks, panting. The Wambubas dropped their burden and flattened on the ground. Kilimi alone sprang to the ivory hunter's side.

"Look, *bwana*!" he cried "*Shenzi nzombi*! The Monkey God!"

Directly before them, behind Macrae's grass hut, in the towering branches of the banyan tree, a weird struggle was being enacted. A blood-curdling human scream sounded. It was answered by an angry chattering. The creepers of the banyan swayed and danced a grotesque dance.

"*Shenzi!*" Kilimi bellowed again.

A white shape leaped from the tree to the ground, bellowing in abject terror. It was the white renegade. But the black mask was gone from his face. His bare chest was gory and dripping blood. Following him from the branches of the banyan, another shape hurtled downward. It landed squarely on the renegade's back.

The man staggered, struggling vainly. Steel flashed before either Macrae or Westman could bring their rifles to their shoulders. Upward and downward it came in savage swinging arcs. The blade buried itself each time to the hilt between the man's shoulder blades.

Westman's gun spat flame. Three times he fired in rapid succession, his lips set. The two gruesome shapes collapsed to the ground.

"My God!" Macrae gasped in awe.

Westman led them forward in silence. The white man was on his back in a pool of dark blood, his glazed eyes staring sightlessly up at the purple velvet of the Congo sky. Beside him, the sacred monkey writhed in its last agonies, Westman's slugs in its heart, the glistening steel blade still clutched in its paw.

"What—what is it, Westman?" the Scot managed to gasp.

"The finest specimen of an Ituri Colobus ape I've ever seen," the ivory hunter replied. "That, Mac," he went on with grim quiet, "that was your murderer."

"It—it's uncanny, Jeff. It's almost as bad as jungle magic."

"The Congo is uncanny, Scotty," Westman agreed softly. "Who's the white man? Know him?"

The Scot nodded. "Joe Swango—the trader from Lulatala."

"White? He's a quarter-breed. See the kinky hair; the high, cheek-bones, and the thick lips? He—" Westman broke off. "God, what a game he played!"

"It don't make sense to me, Jeff," Macrae insisted, shaking his head. "Swango couldn't have done the killings. I tell you, he was in Lulatala on the night most of my blacks were murdered. And why—"

"Don't you see it, Mac?" the ivory hunter went on quietly. "He wanted to scare you off. The Colobus ape is highly intelligent. Swango trained it, the way we saw, to pounce on the back of every white-faced man it saw. Taught it how to use a white man's dagger. Swango himself could be in Lulatala—and the murders still be done miles away. That's why we never found tracks after the killings. The ape didn't walk. It swung along through the trees. Joe Swango knew that any black traveling at night from your compound would smear his face with white dye. I had you and myself smear our faces with mud in the temple of the Monkey God for that reason, to cover the white of our flesh."

Macrae nodded slow. "Aye."

"Then Swango, thinking his beast would attack us because our faces were white, came flying back here. He knew who we were the minute he heard our rifles back there. He traveled fast to get here first—and lost his black mask. When the ape didn't see any white faces back there, he followed his master. When he did see a white face—you saw what happened. The white face was Joe Swango's."

"But, Jeff. Why the orgy? Why did he turn king of a tribe of savage dwarf pygmies? Why want us out of the way at all? It don't make sense. Didn't he get what he was after when he trained the monkey to kill the escaping blacks and pluck out the diamonds they had hidden in their hair? He—"

"No, Mac, he was after bigger game. What he wanted was to get rid of you entirely—scare you away. As for his tribe of pygmies, he intended to use them as his final alibi. The Belgian government would have put the whole thing—if you and I had been murdered—to his pygmy tribe, while he went scot free with his loot."

"His—what?" the Scot burst out incredulously.

"Look—up in the tree. I spotted him trying to get it down." He climbed into the branches and heaved loose a lead-covered box still half hidden in a crook of the tree. It was heavy. He lowered it down, and the Scot took it and set it on the ground with a thump. It was a large oblong box of teakwood, covered with pounded lead as protection against decay and the ravages of the dread Congo ant.

Jeff said, "This must what he was after, Mac. Open it."

In silence, the Scot knocked off the padlock with the butt of his rifle. As the lid came off, he gasped aloud.

"Diamonds, Jeff! A rajah's ransom in raw diamonds! Look at that top one. Look at the size of—"

"Exactly, Mac," the ivory hunter cut in dryly. "Diamonds. Before Abd el Hussan died, he had already been working this diamond field for no one knows how long. It wasn't until after you and I got here some six months ago that we even knew there *was* blue diamond ground here."

Macra was nodding. "At that time, my company was simply prospecting."

"Abd el Hussan never shipped the stones away from here," Jeff continued. "It was too dangerous. Yet he must have mined them for a year or more before we broke up his little party. So they were still here. That was Joe Swango's logic. And somehow he discovered they were cached in that banyan tree. He meant to have them before you discovered them. Another week of his black magic, and he'd have scared every black of yours away. And you'd have followed. You couldn't have stayed on here alone. That was what he wanted."

Macrae looked at his friend, the ivory hunter, for a long time in silence. Then, still without a word, he turned and led the way to the stoep of his hut. The precious box was in his hand as he vanished behind the curtain of kasai cloth.

Inside, by the light of the fire, Westman and Macrae dressed carefully with antiseptic from their kits the wounds of the Wambubas. At length the two white men were alone. The tall, gaunt ivory hunter rose, a little wearily.

"I need sleep, Mac," he growled. "Been on the go ever since I got your message in Murumwa. Better turn in now."

"Jeff, you—I—" The Scot sputtered, then went on in a husky growl: "I'll have to hang on here until the company engineers come up from the coast, Jeff. Then I'm heading for Boma. I'll sure tell the directors about this—and about you. You deserve—"

"Yeah; all right, Mac. You always did have a touchy conscience. You think I need pay to come along when a friend like you—"

"Then what in blazes do you want, Jeff? You're a queer bird. Trekking the jungle. What for? What do you want?"

"Sleep right now." Jeffrey Westman grinned wistfully. "I saw some mighty fine elephant spoor out there, Mac. Tomorrow, Kilimi and I will have a try at finding the father of all the elephants an ivory hunter always dreams about. Some day I'll bring him down, Mac, the tusker whose ivory drags the ground."

He smiled again, his strong, lean face a deep red-brown against the grease-lamp light. "It gets into the blood, Scotty, elephants and the jungle."

ACKNOWLEDGMENTS

"The Black Adder," by Dorothy Quick, originally appeared in *Oriental Stories*, Summer 1932.

"Every Man a King, by E. Hoffmann Price, originally appeared in *Speed Adventure*, Nov. 1943.

"Son of the White Wolf," by Robert E. Howard, originally appeared in *Thrilling Adventure*, December 1936.

"Pearl Hunger," by Albert Richard Wetjen, originally appeared in *Action Novels*, April 1929.

"A Meal For the Devil," by K. Christopher Barr, originally appeared in *Action Novels*, October 1930.

"Jack Grey, Second Mate," by William Hope Hodgson, originally appeared in *Adventure*, July 1917.

"Said Afzel's Elephant," by Harold Lamb, originally appeared in *Adventure*, December 13, 1919.

"Adventure's Heart," by Albert Dorrington, originally appeared in *Top-Notch* magazine, May 1, 1922.

"Another Pawn of Fate," by F. St. Mars, originally appeared in *Adventure*, June 20, 1922.

"Mystery on Dead Man Reef," by George Armin Shaftel, originally appeared in *South Sea Stories*, October, 1940.

"Hag Gold," by James Francis Dwyer, originally appeared in *Blue Book*, May 1941.

"Maori Justice," by Bob Du Soe, originally appeared in *Far East Adventure Stories*, September 1931.

"Javelin of Death," by Captain A.E. Dingle, originally appeared in *High Seas Adventures*, February, 1935.

"The Screaming Skull," by J. Allan Dunn, originally appeared in *Frontier*, October 1924.

"Six Shells Left", by Allan R. Bosworth, originally appeared in *Submarine Stories*, March 1930.

"The Mindoon Maneater," by C. M. Cross, originally appeared in *All-Story Weekly*, March 10, 1917.

"The Spirit of France," by S. B. H. Hurst, originally appeared in *Ace-High Magazine*, First February Number, 1931.

"The Box of the Ivory Dragon," by James L. Aton, originally appeared in *Danger Trail*, June 1926.

"Checkered Flag," by Cliff Farrell, originally appeared in *Short Stories*, May 10, 1931.

"The Fighting Fool," by Perley Poore Sheehan, originally appeared in *Thrilling Adventures*, July, 1932.

"Ghost Lanterns," by Alan B. LeMay, originally appeared in *Adventure*, December 20, 1922.

"Stories of the Legion: Choc," by H. De Vere Stacpoole, originally appeared in *The Popular Magazine,* April 1916.

"The Whispering Corpse," by Richard B. Sale, originally appeared in *Secret Agent X*, August 1934.

"The Monkey God," by Jacland Marmur, originally appeared in *Thrilling Adventures*, November 1934.